SERAFINA
and the
SEVEN
STARS

SERAFINA and the SEVEN STARS

ROBERT BEATTY

DISNEY · HYPERION

LOS ANGELES   NEW YORK

First Edition, July 2019
10 9 8 7 6 5 4 3 2 1
FAC-020093-19200
Printed in the United States of America

This book is set in 12-pt Adobe Garamond Pro, Liam,
Qilin/Fontspring; Minister Std/Monotype
Designed by Phil Buchanan

Library of Congress Cataloging-in-Publication Data 2019011186
ISBN 978-1-368-00759-7

Reinforced binding

Visit www.DisneyBooks.com

Biltmore Estate
Asheville, North Carolina
1900

Serafina raced through the forest, her sharp panther claws ripping into the leafy autumn ground, propelling her long, black-furred body through the underbrush. She scrambled up moss-covered rocky slopes and dashed through shaded meadows of swaying ferns, making her way swiftly home.

The sound of rapid footfalls charged up behind her.

She burst forward with new speed, leaping over the trunk of a fallen tree, then tearing through an open field.

But now two of them were on her, snarling as they lunged at her sides.

The first mountain lion pounced on her back with a ferocious growl and tumbled her to the ground. The second slammed into her head.

She spun on them with a hissing bite, pushing them away with her legs and swatting them repeatedly with her claws retracted, then broke free and ran.

You silly cats need to get out of here, she thought as she leapt the stream that marked the back side of Diana Hill. *We're getting too close to the house. You've got to go back.*

She surged forward, trying to put enough distance between her and her young half sister and half brother that they would finally return to the depths of the forest. But seeing her attempts to outrun them, they became more invigorated than ever. Her sister bounded ahead of her, growling playfully as she looked back at Serafina over her shoulder, challenging Serafina to chase her.

Slow down, Serafina thought as they reached the top of the hill. *You need to be careful here.*

But in that instant, the air exploded with the loud, wrenching sound of twisting metal, bending wire, and a mountain lion yowling in pain. Her sister had been running so fast that she never saw the wire fence in her path—didn't even know what a fence was—and slammed right into it. The terrified lion kicked and clawed, trying desperately to fight this strange, coiling attacker.

The other mountain lion circled his sister's flailing, wire-entangled body in agitation, but was utterly unable to help her.

Serafina's heart lurched in panic. She quickly shifted into human form and moved toward her struggling sister.

The more the young mountain lion fought against the wire, the more entangled she became.

4

Serafina grabbed the rat's nest of metal with her bare hands and tried to tear it away. But the lion kept fighting, pulling against the wires, scratching and biting and growling.

"Just stay still, cat. I'm trying to help you!" Serafina told her sister in exasperation, but as the entwined lion stared up at her with her golden eyes, Serafina knew her sister couldn't understand her.

"I told you we were done playing for the day," she said as she pulled and pried at the wire. "You shouldn't try to follow me home. We're too close to the house."

As she worked to free her sister, she glanced around to get her bearings. A short distance away, surrounded by the vine-wrapped stone columns of a small gazebo, stood Biltmore's Roman statue of Diana, goddess of the hunt, with a bow in one hand, a quiver of arrows on her back, and a deer standing at her side.

We're far too close, Serafina thought again as she struggled with a length of wire that had ensnared her sister's legs. Her brother and sister might get themselves into all sorts of trouble if they passed into the grounds of the mansion; the last thing she needed was for someone to spot a mountain lion running across Biltmore's lawn.

From this high position atop Diana Hill, Serafina could see Biltmore House below her, with its pale-gray limestone walls and leaded-glass windows gleaming in the light of the setting sun, the steeply slanted slate-blue rooftops piercing the sky, and the misty ranges of the Blue Ridge Mountains rising in the distance.

The house was a beautiful sight, tranquil and serene. But she didn't trust pleasant feelings. Or beauty. And she definitely couldn't cotton to the nerve-racking peace and quiet that had been slithering around the estate for the last several months. This mishap with her sister aside, nothing sinister had happened at Biltmore in a long time, but she hadn't been able to shake the feeling that it soon would.

She finally managed to get her sister out of most of the wires, but there was still a bad one wrapped around her front leg. The lion kept yanking her paw away at the worst possible moment, anxious to get free, but hindering Serafina's efforts.

"Just hold on, girl," Serafina said, stroking the lion's head. "I'm almost done."

There were small cuts on her sister's shoulders and legs, but Serafina wasn't sure how she could help her. She didn't have any bandages, and even if she did, there wasn't any way to keep them in place.

I need Braeden, she thought in frustration. *He would calm the lion and heal her wounds.*

But Braeden was gone. And the shock of it still throbbed in Serafina's heart. After all their struggles, fighting to stay together and to stay alive, they had been undone by a few words on a wretched piece of paper in a city far away. She had wanted him to stand up, to fight, to slash at his uncle's words.

But he couldn't fight it. He knew he *shouldn't* fight it.

And now she was once again alone.

As she wrenched the last of the twisted wire from her sister's leg, the lion rose to her feet and rubbed her whiskered face appreciatively against Serafina's cheek. And their brother came over and rubbed his shoulders against them as well.

It seemed as if maybe they were a little sorry for their rambunctiousness, and she was sorry, too. She should have stopped running sooner than she did and warned them of the dangers of the man-made world. Biltmore's groundskeepers must have put up the wire fence to protect the stand of small maple trees they had planted at the top of Diana Hill. The cubs were full-grown now, but they were still young and inexperienced.

But as she was hugging her brother and sister, a shift in the breeze touched the bare skin on the back of her neck, and put a chill down her spine.

Startled, she turned and scanned the line of trees surrounding the distant house, looking for any sort of danger: a mysterious figure or encroaching enemy—anything that might signal that trouble was a-prowl.

She studied the balconies and towers of the house for unusual movement, and then the gate, the road, and the paths leading into the gardens.

Over the last few months, she had patrolled the grounds day and night, sleeping only when she had to, for her memories of her past battles never slept.

No, she told herself as she gazed down at the house and out across the mountains, she wasn't going to let any of this beauty and pleasantness fool her.

Something was wrong.

Something was *always* wrong at Biltmore.

Black cloaks and twisted staffs, shadowed sorcerers in the

murky night—she didn't know in what form it would come, but she was the Guardian of Biltmore Estate, and she knew she had to stay alert, or people were going to die.

When she heard a sound drifting through the forest from the north, goose bumps rose on her arms.

She tilted her head and listened.

The whispers of the wind moved through the boughs of the trees.

She didn't trust wind. Or trees.

In the months since her past battles, the slightest creak of a distant stick or the faint rustling of leaves had sent her into a twitch and a shifting glance. And now, as she stood on the hill and heard the sound of the whispering wind coming toward her, she wasn't sure whether it was truth or lie, but a crawling sensation crept up her sides.

Pulling a long breath in through her nose, she smelled something on the breeze, a trace of sulfur and charcoal that she hadn't smelled in a long time. It reminded her of death.

And then she began to hear the sound more clearly: the *clip-clop* of trotting hooves, a carriage coming up the Approach Road toward Biltmore.

The logical part of her human mind told her that not all carriages were filled with demons and murderers. But her lungs started sucking in air, as if they knew they would soon be needed.

This could be nothing, she tried to tell herself. *It could be a carriage full of kind and gracious gentlefolk coming for a pleasant visit.*

But her heart pounded in her chest.

The beauty. The forest. The wind.

She quickly turned to her brother and sister. "Now listen—get on out of here, right away! Run!"

For once, the two big cats did exactly what she told them, hightailing it into the cover of the forest.

Serafina ran to protect Biltmore even as a carriage and its team of horses came barreling through the main gate into the courtyard. Before she could even see who was inside, a second carriage came rolling in behind it, and then a third, until there were thirteen carriages in all, their drivers steering them straight toward the front doors of the house.

Serafina reached the front terrace and ducked behind the stone railing just as the carriages came to a stop.

Still trying to catch her breath from the sprint to the house, and staying well hidden, she peered out.

The carriages were disgorging a flood of passengers into the courtyard.

Some of the women wore long city coats with sweeping, upturned collars, but most of the new arrivals, both the ladies and the gentlemen, wore brown tweed jackets, autumn gloves, and leather lace-up boots for hiking and shooting.

A dozen of Biltmore's footmen and other manservants hurried out to attend to the new arrivals, unloading their strapped leather luggage, their riding gear, and their shotguns and hunting rifles protected in long oak cases.

The smiling Mr. and Mrs. Vanderbilt stood in the archway of Biltmore's open doors, shaking the hands of the new guests as they came in, embracing many of them—friends and family and acquaintances new and old—inviting them into their home.

Her eyes searched the new arrivals one by one. *How will the intruder cloak himself this time?* she wondered as she studied them. *How will he twist himself into our lives?*

The happy smiles and soothing charm of laughter didn't deceive her. There was an enemy among them, a killer, a kidnapper, an arsonist, she was sure of it, or maybe a doppelgänger, a haint, or a wraith-in-the-night come to drink their souls. She felt it twisting tightly around her mind, strangling her thoughts.

One of the new strangers was a distinguished, silver-haired, finely dressed man who gazed around at the surrounding forest and mountains as if he'd been dropped off in the middle of the wildest and most uncivilized place he had ever seen.

Another was a broad-shouldered, barrel-chested man in a khaki jacket and heavy boots wearing a stern hunter's gaze, as if he was just about ready to shoot anything that moved.

"Be careful of those rifles!" he shouted at one of the footmen unloading the stack of cases from his carriage.

As the very last figure stepped out of the thirteenth carriage, Serafina's senses seethed with anticipation. She was sure this was going to be the villain. But it was a young, dark-haired girl, maybe fourteen years old, in a plain, clean gray dress, a journeying satchel over her shoulder, and a pair of brass binoculars in her hand.

The girl looked around the surrounding forest, as if checking the trees for species of birds she had not yet seen, and then gazed at the lions, carved from Italian rose marble, sitting on guard on each side of the house's great oaken doors. Finally, she lifted her eyes up toward the immensity of the house.

The girl's face filled with an expression of awe as she took in not just the mansion's grand size, but all the details of its facade. Serafina watched her gaze up in wonder at the hundreds of ornate carvings of gargoyles and mythical creatures that adorned the walls, gutters, and steeples of the house. And then the girl's face bloomed into a smile of delight as she spotted the statue of Joan of Arc, a beautiful warrior in full plate armor carrying her banner into battle, and beside her, the statue of the chain mail–clad St. Louis holding his cross and longsword.

As Serafina saw the excitement in the new girl's face, the fierceness that she had been feeling moments before began to fade. None of these people looked like treacherous killers. And none of them looked like murderous demons. It had just been her old fears come a-boiling up again.

You're such a flinchy-clawed scaredy-cat, she scolded herself. *This ain't nothin' but thirteen bushels of everyday folk.*

She crumpled down onto the floor behind the railing, pulling her knees to her chest in discouragement and hugging them, her muscles twitching against enemies of the mind that she could not see and could not fight but that forever battled her.

Over the last few months, when guests in the house tried to strike up a conversation with her, she found herself watching the shadows at the edge of the room. She often startled at the clink of a teacup or the crackle of a warm fire. If someone touched her arm or brushed her shoulder, she flinched.

She was supposedly the Guardian of Biltmore, but she and Braeden had defeated all of the estate's enemies, and no new enemies had appeared. She had thought when this time of peace finally came, she would bask in the glow of trouble-free days. But nothing glowed. It *burned*.

What good was a Chief Rat Catcher once all the rats were caught?

What use was a warrior once the war was fought?

What worth was loyalty to a friend who had taken the train north to a different world?

I should have known, she thought as she glanced through the railing at the arriving guests. *The carriages weren't carrying enemies. They were just Mr. and Mrs. Vanderbilt's friends and family coming for the fall hunting season.*

They had come not just for the shooting, which was a long tradition among the ladies and gentlemen of wealthy society, but for the formal-dress dinners in the Banquet Hall, the elegant lantern-lit evening parties in the Italian Garden, and the late-night games in the Billiard Room. What better way to celebrate their own prosperity, and the arrival of a new century, than with the renowned company of the Vanderbilts?

And they had come for another reason, too. The night before, while sneaking through the rooms of a couple who had already arrived, she had overheard them whispering about getting their first glimpse of Biltmore's smallest and most beloved new resident.

Serafina had been waiting just outside the nursery with Braeden, Mr. Vanderbilt, and the other friends and family members when little Miss Cornelia Vanderbilt came into the world, a tiny bundle of wriggling coos in the arms of her loving mother. Serafina had heard Baby Nell's first cry, and she had played with her in the nursery many times since. During the night, Serafina had often lain on the balcony outside the nursery window, looking out across the grounds, swishing her long black tail back and forth in a guardian's contentment, while Baby Nell slept safely inside. She remembered thinking that Cornelia was the first Vanderbilt to be born in the mountains of North Carolina. Did that make her and Cornelia sisters of a kind? What would she be like? How would she speak? How would she see the world? Would the Vanderbilts of the future become people of the Southern mountains?

All through the summer and autumn days there had been an air of tranquility at Biltmore, a sense of new beginnings. She knew she should be happy. Just as everyone else seemed to be. She enjoyed her life in the workshop with her pa and her life around Biltmore, but when she was supposed to be sleeping, she tossed and turned. When she was walking the grounds, a mere squirrel dashing out in front of her would drench her limbs with fear. Several times while patrolling the forests around the house she had shifted rapidly into panther form, sure that an attack was a split second away, only to find nothing but a babbling brook or wind in the trees.

And now Braeden was gone as well.

"Sit down," Mr. Vanderbilt had said to her and Braeden as they came into his office that dreadful day. "Braeden, you know that in the time since your parents passed away, you have become like a son to me. I love you with all my heart."

Braeden sat quietly beside her, unmoving, as if he knew there was nothing he could do about what was about to happen.

"Your father specified in his will," Mr. Vanderbilt continued, "that his children should attend the school that he and the other members of the Vanderbilt family have attended for generations. It is incumbent upon both of us to put our personal feelings aside and do our duty to fulfill your father's last wishes. I'm afraid the time has come for you to leave Biltmore and return to New York City."

Braeden's brows furrowed, and he wiped his eye with trembling fingers. He looked more somber than she'd ever seen him. But he lowered his head, slowly nodded, and said very softly, "I understand, Uncle."

And now she found herself hiding, crumpled up behind a railing, without him.

School? Of all the godforsaken, no-good places on earth, why did he have to go to *school*? What kind of aunt and uncle would do that to a *child*? What good would school do for him?

He was already one of the smartest people she knew! And if he absolutely had to go to school, why did he have to go to school so far away?

She hated it. She hated everything about it.

When the day came that Braeden had to leave for New York, she went to the train station with him and Mr. Vanderbilt. She remembered standing on the platform in front of Braeden, not sure what to say to him. And she could see that he didn't know what to say to her, either.

For the last year, they'd been together almost constantly, but it had all come to this bitter end.

How do you say good-bye?

With all the various passengers shouldering past them and climbing hurriedly into the massive, steam-hissing black machine, she and Braeden looked at each other, their gazes locked. They had defeated their darkest foes, but they could not defeat this.

"I'm going to miss you, Serafina," Braeden said, very quietly.

"I'm going to miss you, too," she said in return, her voice shaking.

There were so many things she wanted to tell him, so many memories she wanted to recall together, but all the thoughts gathering in her head got stuck in her throat and she couldn't speak.

As the train whistle blew, he seemed like he was going say something to her as well, like he wanted to say good-bye, but he just kept looking at her as if he was struggling to find the words. When the conductor hurried by, shouting, "Last call!

All aboard!" Braeden muttered, "I've got to go," then climbed the steps into the train car and disappeared.

Standing at Mr. Vanderbilt's side, she watched the train pull away, the low rumble of its boiling engine and thumping wheels churning in her body.

She did not move.

She did not scream.

But she felt the pound of it in her chest even now as she remembered watching the train roll down the long, clicking steel tracks, and disappear.

I'm not just useless, she thought. *I'm lost.*

After the new guests had all gone inside, and the last two footmen closed the front doors behind them, Serafina picked herself up and made her way to the far side of the house.

How do you say good-bye? she wondered. *And how do you live after you have?*

She walked alone onto the South Terrace, near the windows of the Library, with the view of the mountains in front of her, and the thick vines of wisteria growing in the lattice above her head.

As the sun set and night fell, she remembered the time Braeden had sat alone on this bench in the darkness, wrapped in his woolen blanket, recovering from his wounds, and looking out at the stars. She had walked up behind him as pale as moonlight and put her wisp-of-a-spirit hand on his shoulder.

It seemed so long ago.

"Now *you're* the ghost," she whispered.

She gazed out across the forested valley at the view of the Blue Ridge Mountains as the sky darkened. There were not yet any stars, but the brilliant dot of Venus was setting over the silhouette of Mount Pisgah on the western horizon. The bright ball of Jupiter gleamed above, followed by the tiny pin-prick of Saturn, and then the reddish orb of Mars rising from the mountains in the east. It was a rare, blue glowing moment when she could see all four planets wheeling across the sky at once, as if spinning on a great invisible disk.

With Braeden gone, the planets had once again become her companions. And a few minutes later, thousands of stars began to fill the dark, moonless sky.

Once Venus had disappeared behind the mountain, it was Jupiter that burned the brightest and the longest, and she imag-ined that it was her long-lost friend. She tried to imagine his life in New York City. He had told her that there were so many electric lights there that it was hard to see the stars, but she imagined that he must be able to see Jupiter. *At least Jupiter,* she thought, looking up at the planet.

"Wherever you are, Braeden," she whispered, "stay bold!"

It was hard to imagine what her life at Biltmore was going to be like without him. He was not only her best friend, he was the only person in her life who knew who she truly was.

She still had her pa, who had found her in the forest when she was a baby, and who had loved her ever since, but even her beloved pa had never seen her in her true feline form like Braeden had. She'd been far too scared to tell her father anything about that.

Her pa was in charge of building and fixing the mechanical contraptions at Biltmore. He believed in tools and machines and iron things made by man, and in normal, everyday human beings, not strange and unnatural shape-shifting creatures of the night like her.

She loved to run with her feline brother and sister through the forest, but they were pure mountain lions, not catamount shape-shifters, so she couldn't strategize with them, sneak through the house with them, make secret plans, devise ingenious traps, kill demons, or do any of the things that normal friends did together.

After she and Braeden defeated their enemies months before, time had frayed, and the world gone slow. The days had become long, like feathery gray clouds with naught but murky shape stretched across the sky. And now that he was gone, it made it all the worse.

What worried her now was whether after all these months of peace at Biltmore she would still be able to distinguish a real threat from a startled jump. With her friend and ally gone, how would she gather and sort out the clues of a mystery? What would she be fighting for if there was no one at her side?

And on many nights, she missed her catamount mother, who had taught her so much of the forest and the mountains.

Her mother was a shape-shifter like her, but had been imprisoned in her feline form for so many years that even after Serafina had freed her, she was unable to fully rejoin the human world. She had gone off into the Black Mountains in search of new territory, more animal than human now.

Glancing through the windows into the Library, and down the long Tapestry Gallery, she saw the glow of the lamps and candles, and heard the mingling voices of the evening's revelry, with the women in their long, glittery dresses and the men in their black jackets and white ties, all smiles and grand hellos, sipping their champagne.

All this happiness here, she thought. *Is this my world now?*

But she knew there were other places out in the world that weren't as safe and protected as Biltmore. Earlier that summer she had gone to see her old friend Waysa, who lived in the Great Smoky Mountains, and she saw the plight of his Cherokee kindred, and many others as well, struggling through a violent attack on the forests there. Hordes of men with great steel saws and steam-powered winches were slashing down the ancient trees. She and Waysa had barely managed to escape. Was it right for her to stay here at Biltmore in this quiet, peaceful, empty place when she knew there were others who needed help?

Months before, there had been a frightening, soul-splintering time when she had shifted into mist and dust and other forms. But she had turned thirteen years old now, she had her feet on the ground, and all that was behind her.

But sometimes, late at night, when she was in her panther

form, it felt as if she might go out running through the forest and just keep going, like her mother had.

And sometimes, more and more when she was in her human form, it felt as if her senses and her brain, and even the core of her body, were changing in dark and primal ways, like she was becoming less human and more panther every day.

She knew it was the way of her solitary, feline kind to wander, to explore, but how could she just leave her home? How could she leave her pa? And what about her brother and sister living in the surrounding forest, and Mr. and Mrs. Vanderbilt, and little Baby Nell? She could never do it. Even if there was a way in her mind to say good-bye to the Vanderbilts, she knew in her heart she could never leave her pa. She had to stay in this lonely, empty place whether she belonged here or not.

As she was standing on the terrace, consumed in her thoughts, she heard the step of a foot in the gravel behind her. Startled, she spun around, her heart lurching as she raised her hands to defend herself.

She could see right away that there was indeed someone standing behind her.

But he wasn't attacking her.

He was just looking at her.

The hair on the back of her neck stood on end.

It wasn't a stranger.

She knew that what she thought she was seeing was impossible.

He seemed to be standing in front of her, his skin pale in the starlight, his tousle of brown hair more disheveled than usual, his brown eyes brighter than she remembered, and his face filled with tenderness. But there were dirty scuff marks on the shoulder of his jacket, the knees of his trousers were badly torn, and traces of crusted blood streaked his face.

Her heart shuddered in her chest as a terrible thought leapt into her mind.

Had there been a train wreck?

Was this his spirit coming back to say good-bye to her one last time before he left the living world for good?

Or had all her startled jumps and scaredy-cat fears finally shattered her mind?

She felt a slow aching dread filling her insides as she tried to open her mouth to speak. "Are . . ." she began to ask the apparition. "Are you real?"

Gazing at her with soft eyes, he gently asked, "Are you all right, Serafina?"

When she finally spoke, her words came out as a whisper. "Did something happen to the train?" she asked. "Are you actually here?"

"I'm here," Braeden said, nodding.

"But how? I saw you get on the train and it pulled away."

"I only made it as far as Tennessee," he said, shrugging a little, almost as if he was embarrassed.

"I don't under— What do you mean?"

"I was sitting on the train, thinking about everything, but I only made it as far as Tennessee, and then I couldn't take it anymore."

"What did you do?"

"I jumped off."

"*What?* How did you get back here?"

"My uncle gave me some money for my first semester at school, so I used it to buy a horse."

"You rode all the way home from Tennessee?"

"Fifty miles."

Serafina looked at him in shock, amazed by his story. He was filled with a rebellion she'd never seen in him. Mr. and Mrs. Vanderbilt, and all his aunts and uncles up in New York, were going to be so worried about what happened to him, and angry when they found out what he did. He had disobeyed them! And leave it to Braeden to solve his problems with a horse! He and his new horse must have been riding hard to get back home so quickly.

But as she stood in front of him, she became aware of the beat of her heart in her chest, and it began to drown out everything else. Her thoughts felt as if they were getting washed away in the warm new blood pumping through her body.

Braeden stepped toward her, his eyes looking down at the ground, then slowly rising up to look at her.

As he wrapped his arms around her and pulled her close, it felt as if he was pulling her into a warm blanket. They held each other, and the fretting anxiety and confusion she'd been feeling earlier began to melt away.

"Come on," he said, finally separating from her. "I want to show you something down by the lake."

"Aren't you going to get in trouble for coming back?" she asked as they went down the stone steps that led to the Pergola and into the gardens.

"Oh, yes, most definitely," he said with an odd cheerfulness.

"What are you going to do when they find out?"

"I don't know," he said. "Maybe they won't."

She couldn't help but glance at him in surprise that he didn't have some sort of plan worked out.

"I just wanted to see you one last time," he said.

As they followed the path past Biltmore's famous golden-rain tree, Braeden kept talking. "I know I was born in New York, and that's where my family comes from, but . . . I don't know . . ." He glanced at her and then cast his eyes sheepishly to the ground. "My life is here . . ." he said. "*You're* here."

She felt a pang of happiness when he said these words. It was as if she were becoming physically lighter.

"And you belong here, too," she said, suddenly realizing by the tremble in her voice why he'd struggled to say the words he'd said to her. Why were certain things—even things that were obviously and deeply true—often the most difficult things to say to someone?

"I'm glad you're home, Braeden," she managed to get out as they went down the steps into the Walled Garden, filled with its red and orange spray of autumn mums. "I've been moping around wonderin' what to do, and skittish as a long-tailed cat in a room full of rocking chairs."

"I know what you mean," he grumbled.

"When I'm in the house," she said, "I try to join in, I try to talk to people, I really do, but I feel like I'm just watching everyone else from a distance, like I'm disconnected from them."

"And from me, too?" he asked.

"Not you," she said, "but your aunt and uncle sometimes, and definitely the new guests. Especially the hunters."

"The way some of those hunters strut and brag and make bets on how many animals they're going to kill is disgusting," he said, scowling. "But that's not me and you, and it's not my aunt and uncle, either."

"Then why do they allow the hunters to come?" she asked, genuinely curious, but as soon as she said the words, she knew she shouldn't have. "I'm sorry. My pa would say I'm gettin' above my raising, and he'd be right. I know I don't have any right to tell your aunt and uncle who they should allow into their home. They allowed *me* into their home, and I'm decidedly suspect."

Braeden smiled as they walked. "Come on now, don't exaggerate. You're not *decidedly* suspect," he scolded her. "You're just plain old, regular suspect, a typical shape-changing, rat-catching, basement-dwelling, demon-killing mountain girl. Nothing wrong with that. We seem to need those around here."

She laughed at his description as he continued. "My aunt and uncle have hosted the hunting season every fall for years. It's a tradition in the old families, a way for family and friends to get together, but my aunt and uncle don't actually do any hunting themselves. They enjoy the riding, but not the rest of it."

"Not the killing, you mean," she said quietly.

After crossing through the Rose Garden, they took the brick pathway around the glass-roofed Conservatory. The trail that led down to the lake, which their old friend Mr. Olmsted, Biltmore's landscape architect, had called the Bass Pond, was covered in a carpet of pine needles, soft and quiet beneath their feet.

"I guess I just don't know what to do here anymore," she said.

"You don't need to *do* anything."

"That's just it. I feel useless, like I'm not any good to anybody."

"You're not useless," he said fiercely. And then he added with a smile, "At least not any more useless than I am these days, being a scofflaw fugitive from justice and all."

Serafina smiled with him, feeling better and better as they walked together down the path.

"Come on, I want to show you something," he said, quickening his pace as they approached the lake.

"What is it?" she asked, hurrying to keep up with him.

As they crossed through the last of the trees and approached the shore of the lake, she saw a clump of sticks on the ground, arranged into a small pile and surrounded by a circle of stones.

Braeden knelt down, struck a wooden match, and leaned in to light the dried leaves inside the stack of sticks. As he blew on the glowing embers, the smoke rose up around him.

"Oh yes, we were expecting you. We have your seat reserved for you right here, madam," he said to her with an exaggerated, elevated air and a sweeping gesture of his hand, as if he were inviting her into the most elegant of drawing rooms.

"What is all this?" she asked.

"It's a campfire."

"I know, but how did it get here?"

"I built it."

"When?"

"Just a little while ago."

"But how did you . . ."

Seeming pleased with her mystified reaction, he grinned, put his hands behind his head, and lay back on the ground, looking up at the stars.

It was hard for her to take it all in. He had apparently leapt off a moving train, then rode a horse like a mad boy through the mountain wilds to get here. He was in serious trouble. But he seemed so calm and relaxed, as if he finally had everything he wanted.

"Why did you build this campfire, Braeden?" Serafina asked as she sat on the ground beside him.

"I had a feeling you wouldn't like tonight's party too much."

"So you knew I'd be outside, on that particular terrace?"

"I thought you might be," he said, nodding.

"And you built this campfire for me?"

"Well, not exactly," he said. "*You* can see in the dark. So in a way it's more for me than you. But I thought you might like it."

"I love it," she said.

"Look at all those stars up there," he said, gazing up at the sky. "They're really putting on a show for us tonight."

She glanced up in the direction he was looking, but she'd seen plenty of stars in her life. What interested her now was *him*, the quiet, peaceful expression on his face and the way his eyes seemed to be taking in the sky above. She still couldn't believe he was home. It felt almost too good to be true, like it wasn't even real.

"Lean back," he said, "and take a look."

As she lay with her back on the ground beside him, her shoulder pushed up against his and she felt the warmth of it against the coolness of the night.

"Look at Orion the Hunter up there," he said, pointing toward the constellation. "Do you see how the three stars of his belt are pointing toward that one bright orange star over there?"

"I see it," she said, following his pointing finger.

"That's Aldebaran, the Leading Star. Now follow it a little farther in that same direction and there's a small bluish cluster of stars. Do you see it?"

"Yes, I see it," she said.

"My uncle told me that in Greek mythology those are the Seven Sisters of Pleiades," Braeden said. "But the Navajo called them *dilyéhé*, and the Persians called them *Parvin*. Everyone has a different name for the Seven Stars."

As she looked up at the small cluster of stars, she saw the seven he was talking about, but her feline eyes began to pick up the sparkling dots of light with more and more clarity. There were indeed six or seven particularly bright blue stars gathered together, but there were also hundreds of smaller, fainter stars sparkling in between them, all glowing in a hazy, bluish light, as if all the varied, dancing stars of the cluster were of one living spirit.

When she pulled in a long, steady breath, it felt as if a whole new kind of air were filling her lungs.

"A few days ago," Braeden said, "I was arguing with my uncle about why I had to go to New York. He could tell I was frustrated, so he told me a story he knew from the Bible. A guy named Job was mad at God because he couldn't understand why certain things happened the way they did. God said that the world was the world, beyond Job's comprehension and control. 'Can you bind the chains of the Pleiades or loose the belt of Orion?' God said to Job. 'Can you bring forth a constellation in its season and guide the Bear with her cubs?'"

She wasn't sure she agreed with or even fully understood what he was trying to say, but she liked the way Braeden's voice sounded when he recited the words.

"I think the part about the bear is talking about Arcturus," he continued, his shoulder brushing hers as he pointed to one of the other stars. "It's that really bright reddish one over there. Do you see it?"

"I see it," she said.

"But this is what amazes me," Braeden said. "My uncle said that the Book of Job was written two thousand five hundred years ago. That means that way back then those people were looking up at these same seven stars, just as we are now, giving them names, telling stories of their origin and their powers. And the Persians were doing the same thing, and the Vikings, and the Navajo out West, and the Cherokee here in these mountains, and people all over the world, for thousands of years."

"That *is* amazing," she said, taken with his spirit of

wonderment for the world. Where did it come from? Where did he get all the energy? By all rights, he should have been dead tired, and frantically worried, but he seemed to be brimming with the fullness of life.

As they huddled together in the crisp autumn night, the stars of Pleiades and a thousand others reflected on the smooth, mirrorlike surface of the lake, seeming to scatter it with glistening diamonds.

She wasn't sure why or how, but deep down into her living, breathing soul, she didn't feel nearly as anxious as she had earlier that day, or in the days and nights before. She wasn't scared. She wasn't jittery. She felt more content in this moment than she had in a long time.

Letting her mind wander, she imagined herself and Braeden leaping onto moving trains and fast-running horses, soaring up into rising planets and streaking down as falling stars. They swam through tepees of glowing embers and glided over lakes of mirrored glass, curled in clusters of sparkling light.

When the stars above her began to fall from the sky, she sucked in a sudden breath, not sure what she was seeing.

"Look!" Braeden gasped excitedly, clutching her arm as long, thin streaks of blazing light shot across the darkness. "It's a meteor storm!"

She'd spent so much of her life outside at night that she'd seen many falling stars flashing silently through the lonely heavens, but it had never looked or felt like this before, with Braeden beside her, the burst of meteors coming down one after another.

"Isn't it amazing?" Braeden asked breathlessly.

But the abrupt sound of men's voices coming from the top of a nearby hill interrupted her reply.

She quickly turned to look, then pivoted again to a much closer sound rushing toward her.

She saw it immediately: the startling sight of a pure white deer running through the woods.

She gripped Braeden's arm in surprise, so astonished by what she was seeing that she couldn't utter a sound.

In the light of the stars, the creature's white fur seemed to almost glow with incandescence as it ran through the darkness of the trees, leaping effortlessly over fallen branches and narrow gullies, and seeming to glide through the ferns.

Even as she was watching it, she knew it would be—for the rest of her life—one of the rarest and most beautiful things she would ever see.

And then a gunshot rang out.

The white deer stopped.

A single red spot stained her side.

Her head slumped.

Her knees buckled.

And her eyes closed as she crumpled slowly to the ground.

"No!" Braeden screamed, rushing toward her.

The wounded deer did not die immediately. She was trying desperately to get back up onto her shaking, weakened legs. She took three tentative, trembling steps, her head moving one way and then another, as if each step required vast effort, and then finally, she began to run, run in blind terror, away from the danger.

Another gunshot split the night air.

Erupting with powerful anger, Serafina sprang out her claws and snarled her fangs, her long panther body twisting as she whirled toward the sound of the hunters and sprinted toward them.

The frantic, running deer crashed into the water of the lake, shattering the smooth reflections of the stars, and tried to swim. But the deep water and her bone-shattering wound were too much for her. She thrashed in desperation, her head barely above the water as her front legs kicked and flailed around her, her eyes wild with fear, and her pink tongue protruding from her mouth in a bleating scream.

Braeden plowed into the water to reach her as another shot came ripping toward them.

Serafina raced up the hill, snarling and making as much noise as possible to draw the attention of the hunters as she charged straight toward them. There were at least three of them, all with rifles, but she didn't care. The anger boiled up inside her, filling her lungs, driving her muscled legs. She wanted to tear the men apart with her rage.

As one of the hunters spotted her black body and yellow eyes rushing through the darkness toward them, he stuttered in fear, "Wh-what is that?"

"Run!" said another.

The third shot at her, but was shaking so badly that the bullet struck a tree trunk behind her.

She lunged straight at him. The slash of her claws knocked the gun from his hands and scraped the skin of his neck.

Screaming, he tried to turn and run, but tripped and

SERAFINA and the SEVEN STARS

toppled to the ground. He scrambled back up onto his feet and fled with the others as they ran toward the house.

Serafina wanted to chase them. She wanted to *kill* them. She knew she could easily catch up with them and pull them down one by one with her teeth and claws. But a sudden dread flooded into her mind and she stopped.

She quickly turned and looked down the hill toward the last place she'd seen Braeden.

How many shots had been fired?

Where had all the bullets struck?

She burst into a run toward the lake.

As she reached the shore of the lake, she frantically looked around her, searching for Braeden. But he was nowhere to be seen. She scanned the grass and the shoreline, dreading the sight of a crumpled, bullet-wounded body lying on the ground. Then she gazed out across the surface of the water.

Braeden splashed up out of the lake and walked toward her, panting and dripping wet, the white deer cradled in his arms.

"I've got her," he gasped with a shaking voice. "But I think they've killed her," he said as he lowered the deer gently to the ground and knelt beside her.

Serafina shifted into human form as she came toward him, and then knelt down with him next to the small body of the deer.

It was only then that she realized how young the deer was. She was just a fawn. And her fur wasn't tan, but pure white over her entire body. She had black eyes and a black nose, so she wasn't an albino. Serafina had never seen anything like her. Whatever she was, and wherever she came from, it was clear that she was a rare and precious creature. But the fawn was bleeding from her side, gasping her last labored breaths, her head hanging limp and her long, spindly legs tangled up like broken sticks.

"I'm so sorry, Braeden," Serafina said gently, knowing that there was nothing more difficult for him than seeing an innocent animal suffer.

He placed his hands on the deer's side and neck.

Serafina had seen him restore the cracked bones of a badly wounded dog, mend the broken wing of a falcon, and help many woodland creatures. He had been blessed with the ability to commune with and heal animals, but with it came its own kind of suffering, too close to the life and death of the world.

"I can't let her die," he said.

Serafina watched as he closed his eyes and held the deer in that position, infusing her with his healing power. She'd seen him use his abilities before, but it always amazed her.

She glanced in the direction the hunters had run, wary of their return. She thought there was a chance they were local poachers who had been out hunting the Biltmore grounds at night, but the way they had immediately fled toward the house made her think that they probably weren't.

Her pa had told her that most deer hunters had a sort of

unwritten code that they followed. They didn't hunt at night or use electric light to mesmerize deer. They didn't shoot young deer. And they wouldn't shoot a deer that was trapped, too close to them, or special in some way. She was pretty sure they would never shoot a *white* deer. It was just too unusual, too easy to see. But these hunters had done exactly that. As if the trophy of a rare, all-white deer was just too much to pass up on.

As Braeden continued to work on the wounded deer, she knew there was little she could do to help, but she sat on the ground beside him and scanned the trees and the distant fields for danger, giving him the time and protection he needed.

They had been together long enough to know what they were both good at, and tonight, clawing was her job and healing was his.

Glancing up into the night sky, she saw that a thin veil of silvery clouds had floated in, very high, long, feathery strands obscuring most of the planets and the stars. Although it remained flat and calm, the water of the lake appeared gray in color now, and the reflection of the stars had disappeared.

When Braeden was finally done, he looked up at her. She was shocked to see how sickly and pale his face had become, filled with worry, and he was shivering from the cold.

"We need to get her warm," he said, struggling to get onto his feet with the deer in his arms.

"And you, too," she said, pulling him up until he was able to stand on his own.

As he carried the wounded deer toward the house, she stayed close to him, on guard all the way. They slipped in through the side door, and then crept up the darkened stairs to Braeden's bedroom on the second floor.

Braeden quickly lit a fire in his bedroom fireplace, then sat in the chair near the fire's warmth, gathered the deer in his arms, and wrapped her up in a warm woolen blanket.

"If I can get her through the night, then I think I can save her," he said, his voice weak, but a little hopeful.

"Who do you think that was out there?" Serafina asked.

"I couldn't see them," he said.

But as she looked at Braeden sitting in front of the fire, another worry came into her mind. "What are you going to tell your aunt and uncle in the morning when they discover you here?"

Braeden shook his head, clearly too tired and worried about the fawn to think about that.

"You need to sleep," she said. "You traveled hard to get here, and then you helped the deer. You look exhausted."

"Yeah," he said softly. He seemed almost sad that their evening together was finally coming to an end.

"Are you going to be all right here?" she asked as she wrapped another blanket around his shoulders.

"Yeah, I just need to sleep awhile," he said.

"Whatever happens tomorrow with your aunt and uncle, we'll get through it together, all right?" she said, hesitating near his door.

Braiden nodded, looking up at her. "Stay bold," he said gently.

"I'll see you in the morning. Stay bold," she said in return, and slipped out.

She made her way downstairs to the first floor, then down to the basement, through the vast network of corridors, kitchens, and storerooms, until she reached the workshop.

Over the last few months, her pa had been working on so many new mechanical projects that he had added two more workbenches, three more rows of storage shelves, and, thanks to Mr. Vanderbilt, a rack of brand-new tools: hammers, screwdrivers, pliers, saws, and metal cutters. Her pa was in seventh heaven.

And thanks to *Mrs.* Vanderbilt, the kitchen was now providing most of their meals, so they didn't have to cook them over the burning barrel as often as they used to. Biltmore had various types of kitchens, a prestigious chef from France, and many supporting cooks and staff, including her friend Mr. Cobere, the butcher and meat cook who worked in the Rotisserie Kitchen down the corridor. But even so, her pa was right determined to teach Biltmore's fancy cooks how to smoke up a good old-fashioned Carolina barbecue pulled-pork sandwich.

Her pa was a big man, strong of arm and thick of chest. He lay sleeping in his cot now, snoring away like he did every night. His snoring probably would have bothered most folk who weren't his kin, but she was so used to it that she probably couldn't fall asleep if the timbers weren't shaking at least a little bit.

Her pa's face looked placid, as if he was dreaming of equipment that never failed and machines that always did what they were supposed to. But then she realized that wasn't quite right. If the electrical generator, dumbwaiters, leather-strap-driven clothes washers, and all the other newfangled contraptions in the house always functioned properly, then her pa wouldn't have a job to do and he'd be miserable, just as she had been earlier that day. *Useless.*

She was dead tired and worried about Braeden now, but she felt so much better than she had.

She thought it was interesting. If all the horses in the stable behaved perfectly on their own, was there still a need for the horse trainer? If all the souls in the church were already angels, what would the pastor do? If a mother's baby cared for itself, would she love the baby as much? It seemed as if human beings longed for everything to be easy, she thought, but deep down, we didn't want it. It seemed as if everyone had a job to do, a role to play, to fix the always breaking world.

She crawled into her little cot behind the equipment and curled up beneath the soft sheets and warm blankets that Mrs. Vanderbilt had given her.

Her two young cats, Smoke and Ember, came trotting across the workshop floor and hopped effortlessly into her bed. They curled up with her in their usual spots and started purring, one of her favorite sounds and feelings in the whole world. She couldn't help but purr back to them in return.

Smoke was a large dark gray cat, strong and quiet, with watchful green eyes. Ember was a skinny little orange tabby, talkative and opinionated, fast and lean, and she loved to run and pounce. She was small, but there was a wild, bushy-tailed fierceness to her that Serafina loved.

She had found them as tiny kittens in the ashes of the crumbling chimney of an abandoned building, their eyes still closed, mewing for their momma. But their momma had passed away. Serafina took them home that night, and with her pa's permission, began to take care of them. As they learned the darkened air shafts and shadowed passageways of the basement, and figured out how to sheathe and unsheathe their claws, it seemed only natural that she give them a job as her rat-catching apprentices.

Most of the night was over, but she was grateful to sleep for a few hours before her pa woke for the day, and more than anything, she was grateful to have seen Braeden again. There was something about his voice, his smile, and the way he looked at the world that always made Biltmore feel like home.

Within seconds after resting her head on her pillow, she felt so comfortable and nuzzled-in that it was as if she'd never moved from there, as if she'd been sleeping there all night, just dreaming away.

"Wake up, Sera."

Several seconds went by.

"Serafina," the voice came again.

She swam slowly up through the thick black molasses void of deep sleep, unsure where she was.

And as she came awake she felt the slow shock of entering a world different from the one she'd been in moments before.

"Wake up, Sera," her pa said as he shook her shoulder. "You've got to get up."

As she rubbed her sleep-crusted eyes and looked up, her pa was standing over her, his face filled with a frightful scowl.

"What's wrong, Pa? What time is it?" she asked as she

sat up and hurriedly looked around the workshop. "What's happened?"

"The master is comin' down."

"Mr. Vanderbilt down here? Now?"

"What sort of trouble did you get into last night?" her pa asked.

Her stomach dropped at the question, but there was no place to hide. His voice wasn't angry or accusing, but it was clear he was trying to figure out what was about to happen.

"Serafina," Mr. Vanderbilt said as he strode through the door and into the workshop.

Startled, Serafina jumped out of bed and quickly straightened her wrinkled dress.

"Don't worry about that," Mr. Vanderbilt said. "I'm sorry to come down here, but I need to talk to you."

They caught Braeden, she thought. *They caught him bad, and he's in big trouble for sneaking back to Biltmore. And they know I helped him.*

"What's wrong, sir?" she asked, struggling to keep her voice steady.

Mr. Vanderbilt shook his head, his hand held to his tightly pressed lips, as if he himself was still trying to comprehend what was happening and how to describe it. She had never seen him this upset.

Seeing the master's distress, her pa grabbed him a workbench stool to sit on and steady himself, and her pa did the same. It was a right peculiar situation to have Mr. Vanderbilt—the great gentleman of Biltmore Estate—sitting with her and her pa in the basement workshop, but that was the situation she suddenly found herself in.

Mr. Vanderbilt was normally well rested and relaxed, reading his books and enjoying the company of his guests, but today he had a worn, haggard look to him and was filled with the tight breaths and nervous glances of an anxious man.

"I know that you have—" he began.

"Sir, let me explain," she tried to interrupt, thinking there must be a way to help Braeden through this.

But Mr. Vanderbilt plowed ahead. "I know that you have helped this house in the past," he said. "When the children went missing a year ago, and the other times as well . . ."

"Yes . . ." she said slowly, trying to understand where he was going with all this.

"I think of you as one of Biltmore's friends, Serafina, one of its protectors," he said. "You have been especially adept when it comes to . . ." He paused there, as if he didn't quite know how to say it, and then he finally said, "Certain kinds of forces."

Serafina stared at him in shock.

"I need your help," he said.

"Did something happen, sir?" she asked. "Did you see something?"

"I don't know what I saw," he said, wiping his mouth as he glanced over at her pa, then looked back at her.

Serafina's temples started pulsing. This wasn't about Braeden. And Mr. Vanderbilt wasn't angry. He was *scared*.

"If it's all right with your father," Mr. Vanderbilt said, "I would like you to move up onto the second floor. Today. Before nightfall."

"The second floor?" her pa said in surprise. The second floor was reserved for the Vanderbilt family members.

"The Louis XVI Room," Mr. Vanderbilt said.

"The room next to the Grand Staircase . . ." Serafina said slowly, understanding his thinking.

"Yes," Mr. Vanderbilt said.

"Where I can observe the comings and goings of the house . . ."

"That's right."

"And where I can watch over Mrs. Vanderbilt and Baby Nell . . ."

"Exactly," Mr. Vanderbilt said, lifting his dark eyes and gazing at her. "I think it would be best if you were closer to Cornelia's room than you are now."

Serafina nodded. If there was danger afoot, then it made perfect sense for her to be up there.

Mr. Vanderbilt turned and looked at her pa. "But we will only do this if we have your father's permission."

Her pa looked startled. She suspected that he knew she was different from other people, but he didn't know exactly what powers she had developed in the last year, or exactly how she had used them. And here was the master of the house asking for her help in matters too dark to say out loud. But if there was one thing her pa understood—if there was one thing he'd taught her—it was loyalty to the ones she loved. If Mr. Vanderbilt needed her, then she had to help.

Her pa looked at her, his dark brown eyes serious and unblinking. "It sounds like there's a job that needs doing," he said.

Serafina nodded, understanding, then turned back to Mr. Vanderbilt. "I'll move upstairs today, sir."

"And if you're willing," Mr. Vanderbilt said, "there's one more thing I need you to do."

"Just name it, sir."

"Starting tonight, I want you to come to dinner in the Banquet Hall each evening."

"You mean, with all the guests?" she asked in surprise.

"I want you to get a clear view of the people here and their interaction with one another."

She had no idea how a country cat like her was going to fare in a room chock-full of fancy folk like that, but she said, "I will do it."

"I know that formal dinners aren't something you're used to," Mr. Vanderbilt said. "But I will provide you with the funds to acquire the dresses and shoes and whatever else you need. And I'll ask Mrs. King to assign a lady's maid to help you."

"Begging your pardon, sir, but if it's possible, I would love for Essie Walker to help me. She's a good friend of mine and she's helped me before."

"I'll talk to Mrs. King about it right away," he said as he rose to his feet. "Mr. Doddman, the new security manager, and I have business in town to attend to, but I will see you at dinner tonight."

She wanted to ask Mr. Vanderbilt more questions, to get a

better understanding of what had occurred that would cause him to take these actions, but he rose to his feet, quickly thanked her and her pa, and left the room as swiftly as he'd come.

In the wake of his departure, there was an awkward, unsettled air in the room.

"Well," her pa said finally. "That's a slug of a thing to wake up to on a Monday morn."

"It sure is," Serafina agreed. "The master seemed so scared."

"Something must have spooked him pretty bad."

She turned slowly toward her father. "Are you truly all right with me doin' all this, Pa? I'll just be upstairs, but I won't go if you don't want me to."

"I think you better lend a hand where a hand's needed," he said. "For Mr. Vanderbilt's sake, and for yours, too."

"Pa?"

"Look, Sera," he said gently. "I know you've been frettin' away, feelin' a bit worse for wear, worrying about this and that, jumpin' at the slightest sound. I can't say I won't be down here worrying about ya, but I know ya wanna help up there, and I want ya to."

"I'll come down every morning and we'll eat breakfast together just like we always do."

Her pa nodded, agreeing, but she could see by the misty squint in his eye that he didn't want her talking like that anymore.

"You're a good, girl, Sera," he said softly. "And I suspect that most of the people up there are decent folk, but stay on your guard. Some of them might not take to you right away—for the wrinkle in your dress, or the keen look in your eye, or for whatever reason—for you being a girl of these mountains instead of wherever they come from. And it's clear the master's seen somethin' unsettling, so keep your wits about ya, ya hear?"

"I hear ya, Pa," she said. "I hear ya well and good. I'll be real careful."

After they ate their breakfast, and her pa slung his tool bag over his shoulder and went off to work, Serafina knew that she had to tell Braeden right away what was happening.

She ran down the basement corridor and up the narrow stairs to the first floor. In the Main Hall, a party of men and women dressed in hunting jackets and leather boots was just going out through the front doors. She continued on up the wide, curving expanse of the Grand Staircase, the sunlight pouring in through the spiral of slanted windows. As she reached the second floor, she tried to glance into the Louis XVI Room that Mr. Vanderbilt had asked her to move into, but the door was closed and she didn't have time to linger.

On the way down the second-floor corridor, she passed two uniformed maids coming in the other direction. She had been walking openly in the house for months, but it still felt peculiar to allow herself to be seen. With her long jet-black hair and her unusual amber eyes, they knew who she was, and that she worked for the Vanderbilts, but they did not truly know her, not deep down, and they did not know her purpose. But they knew enough not to bother her.

When she came to the T at the end of the corridor, she

paused. To the left, the door to the nursery was ajar, and she could hear Mrs. Vanderbilt singing to Baby Nell. But Serafina slipped down the corridor on the right, past several doors, and finally reached Braeden's room.

She rapped on the oak door, then turned the knob, saying, "Braeden, you won't believe what's happened," as she entered the room.

But there she stopped cold.

The room was empty.

It was a large corner suite with fine walnut furniture, a carved marble fireplace, maroon damask wallpaper, and windows facing the mountains to the west on one side and the South Terrace on the other. The sunlight pouring into the room made it seem so different than it had been the night before.

Serafina frowned.

The bed was made. None of Braeden's clothes or shoes or other belongings were lying about. There was no sign at all that he'd been there.

She checked through the small door that led to the bathroom and the water closet, and the other door that led to the clothes closet. Nothing.

She walked over to the bed, checked the nightstand and the dresser, and looked out the window to the terrace below.

The blanket that he had wrapped the deer in the night before was folded neatly, resting on a small table near the window, as if it had never moved.

Perplexed, she got down on the floor and felt the Persian rug with her fingers. Braeden had gone into the lake, so he must have tracked water into the room. But the rug wasn't wet. Could it have dried so quickly?

She tried to stay calm, but her lips pursed and she began to breathe through her nose as she gazed around in bewilderment at the empty room.

She looked under the bed and into the brass grate that covered the heating shaft that they had once used to escape the room.

She checked all the places she and Braeden had hidden before.

But there was no sign of him.

There was no Braeden at all.

He wasn't just gone.

It was like he'd never been there.

She rushed headlong out the side door of the house, her mind swirling with confusion as she ran. *Was Braeden hiding from his aunt and uncle or did he already go back to New York?*

She raced through the garden, hurrying past the finely dressed ladies and gentlemen strolling casually along the flowered paths, and dashed toward the lake.

In the muted light of the cloudy day, the rippled surface of the water looked moody and dull of color, much different from the shining black mirror that had reflected the stars the night before.

When she arrived at the edge of the lake, panting from the run, she went straight to the spot where the campfire had been.

But the campfire wasn't there.

She stopped and looked around her.

This can't be. . . .

She studied the ground, but there was no sign that she and Braeden had been there, no ashes or kindling where their campfire had burned, no impressions of their bodies where they had lain on the grass.

Nothing.

She searched up and down the shoreline, but there were no footprints where he had entered the water or come back out after saving the white deer. She looked out across the water and then up toward the hill where the hunters had been.

Could I have imagined it all? Could I have dreamt it?

She growled in frustration. It had felt so real! Had she just *wanted* Braeden to come home to see her? Had she just *wanted* to fight an enemy? Was all this just another trick of her mind?

But if Braeden hadn't actually come home—and if there was truly nothing wrong at Biltmore—then what had Mr. Vanderbilt seen that had frightened him so badly?

Her stomach sank.

What if *that* hadn't happened, either?

She thought about Braeden's ghostlike arrival on the terrace the night before, and the master of Biltmore coming down to the workshop and asking her to move upstairs. . . .

She stared glumly down at the ground.

It all seemed so unlikely now.

At what point did she wake up? Where did the dream end and the reality begin?

As she pulled in a long, ragged breath, a deep and aching loneliness settled into her chest.

She looked out toward the mountains to the north. Was Braeden back on a train to New York? Or had he been up there all along and she had just imagined his return? Or was he here on the property someplace, too frightened to face his aunt and uncle?

And then a darker thought crept into her mind.

What if he had come home last night but then something had happened to him after she left him? Had some sinister new adversary found its way into his bedroom? Should she tell Mr. Vanderbilt everything that had happened during the night and that they should start looking for Braeden?

But was she even certain that he was missing? She'd seen no signs from Mr. and Mrs. Vanderbilt or any of the servants that there was any kind of worrisome telegram from New York. And there was no way for her to reach Braeden directly without raising too many alarms.

It felt as if her thoughts were fraying in a hundred different directions at once.

Still trying to think it through, she started making her way back toward the house.

It had been an easy, downhill run through the gardens to the lake, but the walk back up was steep, dragging at her legs.

She decided that she would find her pa and ask for his help. If Mr. Vanderbilt's visit to the workshop had been a figment of her imagination, then he would dispel that notion soon enough.

You've been makin' up stories in your head again, girl, he'd say. *Better keep your feet on the ground.*

She ascended the stone steps and entered the long promenade of the Pergola, with its profusion of wisteria hanging down from the lattice above and its line of vine-entangled columns that overlooked the flowers and trees of the garden. The other side of the Pergola ran along a stone wall adorned with fanciful statues and exotic plants. Gentle spouts of water poured from the mouths of scaly stone fish and mythical creatures, splashing into small bubbling fountains. A clutch of children was leaning into the basin of the nearest fountain, giggling and squealing in excitement as they grasped frantically at what looked like a large frog in the water. But it was perplexing because she had never seen any frogs there before, and it seemed far too late in the year.

She walked past several couples and small groups quietly enjoying the coolness of the Pergola's leafy shade, but then she noticed someone coming down the path at a hurried tilt. It appeared to be the girl who had arrived with the carriages the day before, walking fast, her long dark brown hair shifting wildly as she glanced behind her. The girl seemed so agitated by whatever was driving her forward, Serafina wasn't sure she would even notice her, but as they passed each other on the path, the girl looked up and gazed at her with the most striking sapphire-blue eyes Serafina had ever seen.

Serafina reflexively tried to nod politely as they passed, as she had seen the gentle ladies do, but the girl immediately lunged toward her.

"You live here, don't you?" the girl said, reaching out her hand.

Serafina was surprised by the speed at which the girl had surmised that she was a resident of Biltmore rather than another guest. "I work for the Vanderbilts," she said. "My name is Serafina."

"I'm Jess," the girl said quickly, her attention flitting from Serafina's eyes to her hair to her clothing, as if rapidly cataloging everything about her. It reminded Serafina of how the girl had studied the details of the house the day before.

Jess wore a well-made slate-blue dress, and it was clear she was educated. As far as Serafina knew, all the new guests were American, mostly Northerners, and Jess certainly seemed American in her appearance and clothing, but it almost sounded as if she spoke with the trace of a foreign accent.

Where are you from? Serafina was about to ask her, but as quickly as the girl had arrived at the Pergola, she was gone again, moving swiftly down the path.

"Be careful, Serafina," she whispered as she turned the corner around the hedge and disappeared. "And warn the others!"

"Warn the others?" Serafina said to herself as she continued up the stone steps toward the house. What did the girl mean? Warn *who* about *what*?

Jess had only arrived the day before. What could she possibly have involved herself in so quickly that she was giving warnings?

Crossing the terrace in front of the house, Serafina passed behind the row of stone columns, each one carved with a different elaborate pattern and topped with griffins, gargoyles, and other fantastical creatures. She entered the house through the small side door that led beneath the sweeping arc of the Grand Staircase, and then went down the narrow servants' stairs that led to the basement. For every awe-inspiring room in the mansion, there was a smaller, hidden path behind it—like the darkened passageways behind a magnificent theater stage—and she knew them all.

When she arrived in the workshop and saw that her pa wasn't there, she hurried down the corridor, past the clattering din of the busy kitchens and workrooms, all bustling with servants, and went down the brick stairs into the subbasement.

She found her pa on his knees at the base of one of the huge coal-fired, steam heating boilers, his metal-and-wood tools scattered around him.

"This one's giving me fits again," he grumbled as he wrenched on one of the valves.

She had once heard Mr. Vanderbilt say with pride that Biltmore was one of the first homes in America with a central boiler to provide heat to all its rooms. She had no idea how her pa could make heads or tails of the contraption, with all its twisted tubes and steaming pipes, but that's what he liked to do, and Mr. V depended on him for it.

"Pa, I hate to bother you, but I need to ask you somethin' about this morning," she said.

Her pa set down his wrench and looked at her. "What's on your mind, Sera?"

She narrowed her eyes, not quite able to read his initial reaction.

"Did the master . . ." she began. She wasn't sure if it was embarrassment or just plain cowardliness, but her words faltered.

"I can't hardly believe it none, either," he said. "It doesn't seem real, the idea of you actually moving out of the work-shop, goin' on upstairs with the Vanderbilts—doesn't seem like it could be happening. Is that what you're battlin'?"

A wave of relief passed through her.

"But that's what Mr. V asked me to do, right?" she asked, just to be sure.

"White as a haint he was, and wants you up there lickety-split," her pa said.

She nodded, satisfied. At least she hadn't conjured up *that* part of all this.

"But we'll be all right, Sera," her pa said, his voice getting a smidge grave. "It's just a flight or two of stairs. . . ." But even as he said the words, his normally strong, gruff voice cracked a little.

"Aw, Pa," she said as she moved into his chest and wrapped her arms around his bearlike body.

"Just a flight of stairs," he mumbled again, sounding like he was trying to reassure himself as much as her. "You know that I'm real proud of you, Sera, real proud, and I love ya somethin' fierce."

"I love you, too, Pa," she said, holding him tight.

After she had reluctantly said good-bye to her pa and walked glumly away, tears wetted her cheeks, but she didn't let herself sniffle until she was out of his earshot.

When she stepped into the workshop to gather her belong-ings and begin her move upstairs, she felt a heaviness in her arms and her legs. She had grown up in this place, slept here, played here, eaten her meals with her pa here. This was where she had started her hunts each night and returned each morning. This workshop was her home.

As if to make the point, her cat Smoke sat on one of the timber frame beams, staring at her. Ember walked with jaunty steps along the stone ledge above the benches, chirping complaints and looking down at her with her round, feline eyes.

"What are y'all looking at me like that for?" she asked. "It's just a flight of stairs!"

But she could tell by the looks on their faces that they weren't impressed with her argument.

"I'm sorry," she said, "but I've got to. Mr. V needs my help."

But even saying these words out loud made her feel like a naive little child. How ridiculous it was to think that Mr. Vanderbilt actually needed her. He was the richest, most powerful person she had ever met. Why would a man such as that need her help? With all her eye-flitting, scaredy-cat flinchiness and her strange dreams in the night, could she even be trusted to identify the dangerous visitors among the harmless ones? Was Mr. Vanderbilt asking for her to do this because he genuinely thought she could help protect his family? Or was there something else going on with him that she didn't understand?

She walked over to her little bed and picked up the piece of shredded red cloth she'd saved from the gown Braeden had given her more than a year before. It had been torn to pieces during her battle with the Man in the Black Cloak that fateful night in the Angel's Glade, but she'd always loved that gown.

And thinking about the gown made her think of Braeden. "*You're* here," he had said to her by the lake, so quietly, but so fiercely, as if that simple fact explained everything. Remembering the sensation of his breath touching her ear when they embraced, a chill ran up her spine.

Flustered, and seeing Smoke and Ember still looking at her, she said, "Don't y'all have mice to catch or something? Go make yourselves useful!"

Pretending to be annoyed by her tone, they dropped down from their perches with soft thumps of their furred feet on the floor, trotted out of the workshop with mildly perturbed meows, and went out to start their day.

They'll probably go to sleep on a windowsill someplace, not a care in the world, Serafina thought.

Dragging her mind back to the reason she was here, she gathered up the blanket, sheets, and pillow that Mrs. Vanderbilt had given her and prepared to go. She didn't have much in the way of belongings. She meant to just walk out of the room in a quick-like fashion, and not look back. But the moment caught her. She stood in the middle of the workshop and looked around. It was the place of almost every happy memory she had shared with her pa.

Finally, she took one last look, pulled in a long, deep breath, and left the room.

As she made her way up the servants' stairway carrying the bundle of her bedding and belongings in her arms, she noticed a streak of motion out of the corner of her eye. Startled, she turned quickly to see what it was, but the animal dashed away and was gone before she could get a good look at it.

Was that a rat? she wondered, but it had moved more like a small cat or woodland critter. It couldn't have been Smoke or Ember, so maybe it was a little mink or something that had gotten into the house.

A black-and-white-uniformed maid passed her on the stairway, her arms too full with laundry to say hello. But it jostled Serafina back to attention, and she continued up the stairs.

In the Main Hall, she noticed Cedric, Mr. Vanderbilt's Saint Bernard, along with Gidean, Braeden's Doberman, lying on the floor.

"At least I'll have some good company up here with the fancy folk," she said to the dogs. Creatures of her ilk didn't usually take too kindly to the canine type, but she had come to know and trust these dogs as good old friends, true of heart and fierce in a fight.

Her nose itched nervously as she walked through the Main Hall of the house in plain view—right past the butler and maids and all kinds of guests—holding her bundle of belongings in her arms.

Although she kept her chin low and her gaze lower, so that no one could accuse her of putting on airs, it still felt like she was striding up the wide, sweeping curve of the Grand Staircase to the second floor like she suddenly owned the place.

The ivory-colored limestone steps of the Grand Staircase blazed in the morning light, with the elegant, deeply filigreed wrought-iron railing on one side and the curving cascade of windows on the other. The staircase spiraled up through all the floors of the house, with a great, multistory wrought-iron chandelier hanging down through the center of the spiral.

When she reached the second floor, the stairway opened up to a living hall with plush Persian rugs, comfortable places to read and talk near the fireplaces, and fine English tables adorned with many of the small bronze animal sculptures that Mr. Vanderbilt had collected on his trips to Europe. A small alcove led to Mr. Vanderbilt's bedroom, and then down a short corridor to Mrs. Vanderbilt's rooms, while the hallway on the left led to baby Cornelia's nursery, Braeden's room, and several others.

It made her feel a bit queasy in the stomach to think she was going to live *here*, this close to the family, but she had drawn her lot in life, and this was it. She was now an official inhabitant of the second floor.

She turned and faced the closed white door of the Louis XVI Room.

Stoking her courage, she drew in a breath, pushed opened the door, and stepped into what was now her new bedroom.

The first thing she heard was a purr.

And the first thing she saw was the cats. *Her* cats! The soft, gray-furred Smoke, who was keeping watch from the window-sill, gave her a quiet, thoughtful meow, as if he wasn't quite ready to accept that this was their new home. He had seemed even more guarded and wary of his surroundings than usual for the last couple of days, and she knew the room change wasn't going to make it any easier for him.

The not so reserved Ember was stretched out on the large, queen-size bed, happily luxuriating, purring and meowing loudly, as if she were saying, *This bed is so much nicer than the old one!*

"How did you two get in here?" Serafina asked in surprise. She had assumed she'd go down to visit them in the basement every once in a while, but here they already were, all moved in. "Well, just because we're up here now, don't think you can shirk your duties in the basement," she told them firmly. "I saw a big old rat or something down there, so keep your eyes peeled for varmints. If you see something, it's your job to get it."

Smoke just stared at her, almost apprehensively. But Serafina knew he was well capable of catching even the largest rat.

Ember, on the other paw, closed her eyes and flexed her claws in and out, piercing the fine silk fabric of the bedspread, as if she was more than happy to pounce on some scurrying little thing.

"And there'll be none of that on the silk, Miss Ember," Serafina scolded. "Keep your claws in your paws or Mrs. V will kick us out for sure."

When Ember complained with raspy, chirping meows, Serafina said, "Hush up now. I don't wanna hear no sass."

But regardless of her firm tone with little Ember, she was secretly relieved that they had found their way up here and that she wasn't going to be alone.

Finally, she turned away from her feline companions and took a good long look at her new room.

She'd been in this room several times before, but the morning sunlight pouring in through the open windows basked the Louis XVI with a grace that made her sigh. It was a lavishly appointed, oval-shaped bedchamber with a gently domed cream ceiling and elegantly curved walls—the wallpaper, draperies, pillows, and even the upholstery on the gold-leafed, French-style furniture, all done in a fine silk fabric of red peony flowers.

There was a cushioned chaise lounge for relaxing and a sitting area with a low table for morning breakfast and afternoon tea. *If Braeden was here, that's where we'd sit and have our meals,* she thought wistfully, but then the bad thoughts started creeping into her head again. She still didn't know if he'd returned to New York, or was in trouble and needed her help, or had never come back to begin with.

She felt so helpless. She wanted to spring out her claws and tear something. She wanted to find an enemy and fight it. But she had looked all over for Braeden and he had just disappeared. When the heating register in her new room ticked, she flinched wildly and spun toward it before she could stop herself.

Just get hold of yourself, she thought. *One way or another, you'll figure this out.*

Trying to calm down, she turned and looked at the other side of the room.

There was a canopied bed with a red silk bedspread and a makeup table with delicately curved legs and a gold-leafed mirror. She could smell the scent of silk and freshly laundered linens, but it was the red roses in the vase on the mantel of the white marble fireplace that filled the room.

It seemed to her that Mr. Vanderbilt couldn't possibly have picked a room more different than her dark little corner down in the workshop with its rough-hewn stone walls, its greasy tools, and its smell of oil. Up here on the second floor, she would have probably felt more at home curled up in the back of a dark closet or maybe inside a cabinet rather than this luxurious bedchamber. But here she was, a denizen of the basement and a devout creature of the night, swimming in a world of silk and gold and blazing light.

But just as she began to doubt Mr. Vanderbilt's judgment, she stepped over to the window and saw the view it provided her of the front courtyard. Even now, at this very moment, she spotted Mr. Kettering, one of the gentlemen guests, walking up the Esplanade toward the stables. Dressed in his tan-colored hunting coat and carrying a rifle over his shoulder, he looked tired, but satisfied. Another hunter walked with him, and their servants followed with the carcasses of two antlered bucks. Their early morning hunt had been successful.

The room Mr. V had picked for her didn't just provide the perfect position to guard the stair's entry point onto the second floor; it was also an ideal spot from which to observe the front courtyard, and all the comings and goings of the house. It was a stark and welcome reminder that she wasn't on the second floor because she was a cherished member of the family or an honored guest. She was a *guardian*. And that suited her just fine. It was a job she understood, a job she wanted. She just hoped she could do it. What use would she be if she couldn't tell the difference between what was real and what wasn't? What use would she be if she flinched at every sound?

As she looked around at the opulence of the room, it was still hard to believe she was here. Even this felt like a dream. How was it possible that a little rat-catching girl from the basement was suddenly living in a beautiful bedroom on the second floor?

"But this is real," she told herself firmly. "And you have a job to do."

A rap on the open door behind her startled her out of her thoughts.

"Y'all look like three kittens in a basket up here," Essie said as she entered the room, looking at Serafina, Smoke, and Ember with a warm and happy smile. Essie was wearing her usual black-and-white maid's uniform, her cheeks beaming, her dark hair stuffed under her white cap. By training, a maid was supposed to remain formal, quiet, and restrained, but Essie was just a couple of years older than Serafina, and they knew each other far too well for all that nonsense.

"Tickled fine to see you, Miss Serafina!" Essie said, her Southern mountain accent sounding warm and familiar.

"Good to see you, too, Essie!" Serafina said, walking straight toward her and abruptly hugging her.

"Oh my," Essie said in surprise, flustered at her show of emotion. "Thank you, miss, thank you."

And this is real, Serafina thought as she tightened her arms around Essie.

"You reckon you're all right, miss? Has somethin' hard-gone happened?" Essie asked.

"I'm fine, Essie," Serafina said quietly, "just happy to see you is all."

"Well, I danced my own little jig when I heard the kitchen all a-gossiping about y'all movin' upstairs," Essie said.

"It came as quite a jolt to me as well," Serafina admitted.

"And now we gotta get workin' like it's harvest day, right?" Serafina nodded. "Mr. V wants me ready by dinner tonight."

"Oh Lordy, these men with all their ideas! They have no conception of what goes on to put a lady in a dress and a proper pair of shoes!"

Over the next few hours, Serafina got out of her old clothes, took a bath, and worked through the process of getting ready. Essie helped her wash her long black hair and brush it smooth, and then sat her down at the little table and applied various kinds of makeup to her face in what she called "the style of the day," which Serafina didn't quite understand, since dinner began at eight o'clock.

Just as they were finishing up with all their preparations, there was a knock at the door. Mr. Pratt, a tall, handsome footman in formal black-and-white livery, entered the room with a dark green dinner gown held gently in his white-gloved hands.

"Thank you, Mr. Pratt," Serafina said, happy to see her old colleague. He was a lean but not quite gangly bachelor in his mid-twenties, with a sharp-looking face and slicked-back dark hair. It amused her how he was the quintessence of formal reserve and stately decorum when he was upstairs in view of the Vanderbilts and their guests, but quite the boisterous rogue when he was downstairs in the kitchens.

"You're most welcome, Miss Serafina," he said, gave her a hidden smile, and bowed out of the room.

Once he had gone, Essie helped her climb her way into the new dress and buttoned up the back for her. After applying a few more flourishes to her shoes, her ears, her neck, and her hair, Essie stepped back and looked at her. For several long seconds, she just stared at her and did not say a word, but then she finally spoke.

"I sure do wish the young master could come a-jumpin' back home and see how beautiful you look."

"You're being very kind," Serafina said.

"No, I am not. If I could wish upon a star, I'd bring him right back from that school up there. He doesn't need all that Northern bunk. I reckon he's a proper Southern gent now, don't you?"

"You got that right," Serafina said, smiling, but then turned more serious. "You haven't heard any news about Master Braeden, have you?"

"Aw, you really miss him somethin' awful, don't you?" Essie said. "I'm sure he's fine up there, otherwise we would've heard about it."

Serafina nodded, hoping Essie was right. "I'm afraid my company tonight is going to be far less agreeable than Master Braeden."

"Oh, yessin," Essie agreed. "And have ya heard about the thief in the house?"

"The thief? What are you talking about?"

"Things goin' missin'," Essie said, "Everybody's on about it."

"What kind of things?"

"I don't know what all, but I heard that some of Mr. V's expensive bronze animal sculptures have disappeared, for one."

"That *is* peculiar," Serafina said, wondering. But over the last few months of peace and quiet, the convolutions of her mind had snagged on so many wicked snares, and she had startled at so many empty shadows, that she didn't know what to trust anymore, whether it was backstairs gossip or the odd comment of a newly arrived guest. All she knew for sure was that the master of the house wanted his rat catcher at dinner tonight.

When she finished fastening up the gown and straightening out the fall of its skirt, Essie touched Serafina's shoulders and gently rotated her toward the full-length mirror.

"Whoo-eee! Take a look at that, why don't ya," Essie said, seeming at least as proud of her own handiwork as she was of Serafina.

Serafina stood in front of the mirror and gazed at herself in amazement. She had worn a fancy dress a few months before, but she had never looked quite like this. She had certainly filled out here and there. And her face . . . What did she see? Was that confidence? Fear? Determination?

But she couldn't help but take a hard swallow. She'd never stepped into a room full of high-society ladies and gentlemen without Braeden by her side. But this time she was going to walk right into a snake nest full of them all on her own.

With her long, shiny black hair falling down onto her shoulders instead of bound up in a traditional bun, her large amber eyes, and her sharp, feline cheekbones, she knew she wasn't going to blend in with the other high-society girls. Essie had colored her cheeks, shadowed her eyes, and done her best to mask the traces of long, jagged scars on her neck and face, but the wounds were still visible. She was pretty sure the gentle folk at dinner were going to take one look at her and grimace a nasty scowl. But even so, standing before the mirror at that moment, it was the first time in a long time that she looked at herself with a strong and steady gaze and thought: *This is me. The Guardian of Biltmore Estate.*

"Thank you so much, Essie," she said softly.

"Don't let none of them fancy folk give you any guff, Miss Serafina."

"I sure won't," she said, nodding with a smile.

11

She had come down the Grand Staircase hundreds of times, under all sorts of circumstances, but never like this, all washed and polished, her hair brushed and shaped, wearing her beautiful new forest-green gown for all to see. But more than all that, there was something else that had changed. This time she had come with a mission. Mr. Vanderbilt hadn't said the words out loud, but she knew her purpose: *Find the rat.*

She wasn't sure what the fancy folk were going to make of her when she entered the room, but as she crossed through the candlelit Main Hall on her way to dinner, Mr. Pratt and another footman, standing at attention near the house's front doors, smiled.

"You look good, Miss Serafina," Mr. Pratt said encouragingly, and her chest filled with a little hope.

The servants of the house didn't know exactly what her purpose was—rumors had run rampant over the past few months—but more and more, they were getting to know her and see her as one of them.

But as she walked along the wide, formal corridor, past the tropical plants of the Winter Garden, and approached the Banquet Hall, her heart began to thump in her chest, and she could feel the perspiration rising beneath her dress. The footmen, the laundresses, and maids—whether they were brought over from England, or Northerners, or Southern mountain folk—these were her people. But the well-heeled ladies and gentlemen at dinner were some of the richest high hats in all of America—ambassadors to foreign countries, famous writers and painters, lords and ladies from Europe, owners of railroads and steamship companies, wealth and privilege of every ilk and strain. And she knew from experience that she couldn't trust a single one of them until she caught the devious rat she suspected to be hiding among them.

As she passed the bronze sculpture of Mr. Vanderbilt in the corridor, she whispered, "Wish me luck in there, Mr. V."

And then she pulled in a deep breath and stepped into the radiant light of the Banquet Hall.

The grand room's barrel-vaulted ceiling was so high that a flock of Braeden's crows could have an aerial battle in its heights, and its massive carved stone fireplaces were blazing with great fires, but it was the silk-wearing denizens of this magnificent cave who held her attention.

She seemed to have arrived just at the moment when dinner was about to begin. More than fifty ladies and gentlemen in formal dinner attire were already sitting at the enormously long table. The grand event was set in lavish Vanderbilt style, with silver serving trays, crystal goblets, and fine Biltmore china among vast sprays of flowers, and a silver candelabra rising above, casting it all in a glowing light.

She carefully scanned the dinner guests, one after the other, looking for any signs of danger. And she listened intently as they talked quietly among themselves, many of them whispering in anticipation that their host would soon announce the beginning of the evening's festivities.

Mr. Kettering, the hunter she'd seen from her window earlier that day, came into the room behind her, looking flustered that he was late. He smiled at her in a friendly, almost nervous manner, and she nodded to him in return.

"Oh, Serafina," Mrs. Vanderbilt said as she bustled toward her and guided her gently forward into the room. "Come in, come in. Mr. Vanderbilt told me that you would be joining us. Your seat is just here, my dear." The mistress of the house gestured toward an empty chair at the table, and then hurried back to help Mr. Kettering find his place.

The embodiment of the perfect hostess, Mrs. Vanderbilt seemed to know all the guests personally, why they were there, and where they should sit.

As Serafina took her seat, she was careful not to pull the

tablecloth with her legs or disturb the beautiful place setting in any way. She noticed that a few of the ladies and gentlemen sitting near her were staring at her. They did not appear alarmed or indignant to see her among them, but they seemed keenly interested in her, as if wondering just what sort of exotic creature she was.

Once she took her place at the table, she realized she was sitting in the exact seat in which Braeden normally sat. It felt so wrong, like Braeden had died and now everyone—including *her*—was just fine with it and going on with their lives. *He should be here,* she thought fiercely as a pang of lonesomeness swept through her. Somehow, she'd managed to lose track of her best friend, and now she had taken his chair!

"Hello, young lady," a woman said in a kindly, aristocratic voice tinged with a New York accent.

"Hello," Serafina said, a little surprised that the woman next to her had turned to speak with her.

She was an elderly, stately woman, in an expensive gown and wearing an elaborate diamond necklace. "My name is Mrs. Ascott. What's yours?"

"I'm Serafina," she said, sitting up.

"That's a very nice name. And from where do you hail?"

Serafina thought it might be a bit melodramatic to say "The basement," so she said, "Around these parts."

"Ah!" the woman said, seemingly delighted. "So you're a local girl."

"Yes, very local," Serafina agreed.

In between her comments about the loveliness of the

table settings and the particularly breathtaking hue of the Vanderbilts' candlelight, Mrs. Ascott took a sip from her water glass. Serafina tried to drink from her own glass, but ended up taking too big a gulp, and the water dribbled unceremoniously down her chin as she quickly growled and wiped it away. She despised drinking water that had been sitting still in a glass. She was far more used to drinking straight from the faucet in the utility sink in the basement.

As Serafina tried to focus on the job she'd come for, Mrs. Ascott spoke with her in a polite and pleasant fashion. But Serafina couldn't help glancing down the length of the long table full of glittering guests. Her ears were keen enough that she could hear almost all of their conversations. The flurry of words came to her in a crisscrossing jumble of traveling stories, hunting tales, and comparisons of the latest clothing styles. But none of them seemed like evil conspiracies or treacherous plots. Despite what she had been imagining in her twitchy mind, everyone here seemed harmless.

Was this where she belonged now? Were these her new people? If she was wearing an extravagant gown, and hobnobbing with the most fashionable members of society, did that make her a civilized person?

At the very end of the table, several gentlemen were talking to Mr. Vanderbilt. Dressed for dinner in an immaculate black tailcoat and white tie, and freshly shaven and prepared for the evening, he looked so different than the bristled, haggard man she'd seen earlier that morning. And she knew she must look so very different to him as well. When he noticed her looking at him, she saw the recognition in his dark eyes, but he did not nod or draw attention to her in any way. *This was business. Find the rat.*

But then an irksome doubt flitted into her mind like an annoying little bird. What if he hadn't actually needed her help, but had given her a job and invited her upstairs because he felt sorry for her? Maybe Braeden had asked him to do it, or her pa. Maybe she was just imagining all these dangers and dramas and adventures-in-the-night, just remnants of a past that her troubled mind was having difficulty letting go of. *The nerve-racking peace and quiet,* she had called it. What if the people who cared for her were even more aware of her problems than she was herself, and they had conspired to help her?

But before she could dwell on it too long, she spotted the furry, dark gray shape of Smoke slinking slowly under the table, right between the feet of an unknowing Mrs. Ascott. And there was Ember madly clawing her way up the rare sixteenth-century Flemish tapestry on the wall. Serafina hissed in exasperation, just loud enough for Ember to hear, letting the little scoundrel know that she better make herself scarce and quick.

"Oh, are you all right?" Mrs. Ascott asked her, seeming to think that she had choked on her drink again.

"I'm all right, thank you," Serafina muttered, trying to avoid sounding and looking like a wild, snarling, yellow-eyed beast.

But glancing quickly at the people around her, she was

relieved to see that most of them were far too occupied with chatting with their neighbors and drinking their wine to notice anything else.

All except one.

The dark-haired girl named Jess was sitting right across from her, and the girl's sapphire-blue eyes were staring straight at her.

12

$\mathcal{S}$erafina wanted to confront Jess right then and there, to ask her what she'd been talking about earlier, and why she was always watching her so intently. But just as Serafina opened her mouth to speak, Mrs. Vanderbilt rose to her feet.

Gathering everyone's attention, the lady of the house stood beside her husband and began to address all of her guests.

"If everyone would please stand," Mrs. Vanderbilt said. "George will be saying grace for us."

Murmurs of quiet approval and respect ran through the crowd as Mr. Vanderbilt nodded. "Thank you, Edith," he said, "And thank you for arranging this wonderful gathering here for all of us tonight."

Enthusiastic cheers of agreement exploded from the crowd,

everyone thanking Mrs. Vanderbilt, who beamed in modest gratitude.

Serafina could see from his soft smile that it pleased Mr. Vanderbilt that everyone loved his wife. But then he turned more serious, and a contemplative expression came over his face as he folded his hands in front of him and bowed his head in prayer.

When all the guests around the table bowed their heads, Serafina lowered her head with them as Mr. Vanderbilt said grace.

"Amen," everyone said in unison when he finished.

A handsome young man wearing the dark blue-and-gold dress uniform of a United States cavalry officer rose to his feet and held up his glass.

"If I may have everyone's attention," he said, his voice as soothing as a cup of warm autumn cider. "There's one more thing to do before we begin our dinner."

"Oh, it's Lieutenant Kinsley," Mrs. Ascott said excitedly as she leaned toward Serafina. "Such a lovely boy."

He looked surprisingly young to be an officer, fresh-faced and neatly kept, with wavy blond hair swept to the side, soft gray eyes, a cleft chin, and a well-trimmed blond mustache. He stood with the erect posture of a fencer, and wore a cavalry saber belted at his side. And it was clear from his sly but good-natured smile that he knew he was standing among welcoming company.

"If you would please raise your glasses," he said as he lifted his crystal wine goblet, and everyone around the table followed his request. His smile and his eyes were almost sparkling when he turned toward Mr. and Mrs. Vanderbilt with obvious affection. "I would like to propose a toast to our grand and admirable hosts, George and Edith. May Biltmore always reign!"

"Hear, hear!" everyone cheered. "Hear, hear!"

They all raised their glasses, smiling and nodding, as they looked upon Mr. and Mrs. Vanderbilt, who smiled back in return. And then, together, everyone drank from their glasses.

"You are too kind," Mrs. Vanderbilt said graciously.

"And one last toast," Lieutenant Kinsley said, raising his glass once again as he looked at the people gathered around the table. "We have come down to these Southern mountains to be with our good friends, both new and old, in this year of 1900, the start of a bold new century. As you all know, it is tradition in our families to come together at this time of year to spend the hunting season with one another. And I, too, look forward to our 'time in the woods,' for the challenge and the camaraderie it brings. I would ask that we hunt with honor and respect, not just for the beautiful hunting grounds that our generous hosts have provided us, but for the natural world we are about to enter. For it is in the mystery of these forests that we begin to find our true selves. So, finally, I would like to propose a toast to everyone here tonight. May all of our hunts be bountiful, all of our card games be exciting, and all of our teatimes be . . ." Here he seemed to be unable to find a suitable elegant phrase. "Full of tea!" he said finally, laughing, and everyone laughed with him. "And most importantly," he said, turning more heartfelt now, "may our time with our beloved friends and family be fulfilling to our souls."

"Bravo!" many of the guests shouted, nodding warmly.

"Hear! Hear!" others called as they raised their glasses and drank.

She wasn't sure if she belonged among these ladies and gentlemen or not, but watching what Mrs. Ascott, Mr. Kettering, and the others did with their glasses, Serafina raised her water glass and participated in the toasts with everyone else. There was something that she liked about this simple gesture of honoring the people around her, sharing in that moment with them. It made her feel as if she was one of them, part of their family. And she marveled at the bold young lieutenant, the way he was so relaxed and charming in front of everyone. She had been so nervous to even attend the dinner. She couldn't even imagine standing up in front of all these people and speaking to them. And she had to admit that, despite what else was going on, the lieutenant's toast had made her feel at home, as if things were going to be all right after all.

And as Lieutenant Kinsley sat down, his gray eyes looked across the table at her and he smiled kindly.

Serafina thought for a moment that he might try to speak with her, but as the footmen around the table began to serve the first course, a loud, overbearing voice at the other end of the table broke in.

"Well, I will tell you this," the man bellowed to those

around him. "It's not the gun, but the hunter pulling the trigger that makes the difference in the kill."

The man reminded her of an old, musclebound bull, with a swollen chest and bulging shoulders. He had a square jaw, a blockish head, and deeply tanned, weathered skin, like he'd spent years of his life outdoors.

"But since you're asking the question," the man continued, his booming voice filled with self-importance, "I do my hunting with the most effective weapon that has ever existed, the venerable 1873 Winchester Henry Repeating Rifle." As he talked, he sat with his chest stuck out like a rooster showing off for hens, which in this case were the men and women gathered around him at the table, listening excitedly to his stories. "You see, the Henry Repeating Rifle is known as the Gun that Won the West. I fought with it in the Indian Wars and I've hunted with it all through North America, South America, and Africa."

Many of the people around the loudmouthed hunter seemed enthralled with him, but Serafina noticed that Lieutenant Kinsley, who was trying to eat his soup, glanced at the man with a flicker of distaste. The lieutenant didn't seem to like the man any more than she did.

"And what do you make of Africa, Colonel Braddick?" one of the ladies asked, filled with starry-eyed admiration for a man who had traveled to such distant places.

"Oh, the hunting there is marvelous," the colonel said. "I'm proud to say that I bagged all of the Big Five: Cape buffalo, black rhinoceros, African lion, elephant, and leopard—the five game animals renowned for being the most difficult and dangerous to hunt on foot. But I wasn't done there. I went on to kill every species the safari continent has to offer: Thomson's gazelle, hippopotamus, warthog, greater kudu, springbok, impala, eland, zebra, serval cat, caracal cat, cheetah— You name it, I shot it."

Serafina felt her gut tightening as she listened to this man bragging about his trophies. She had taken pride in doing her job as Chief Rat Catcher, so she understood the thrill of the chase, but it seemed so wrong to go around hunting all those beautiful animals. They weren't harming anyone, and he didn't need them for food. He just wanted to kill them for killing's sake.

She couldn't understand why Mr. Vanderbilt had invited people like this into his home to go out into the forest and kill its animals. It seemed so wrong. Why was he allowing this?

"With all your honors and success, Colonel, what keeps you going at it?" a wealthy gentleman named Mr. Suttleston asked. "I mean, it can't be easy trekking through the wilds of Africa."

"It's the challenge of it all, really," the colonel replied philosophically. "I love the idea of using my abilities to track down an animal. Perhaps it's the most powerful, or it has the largest rack of antlers, or it's the rarest and most beautiful of animals— doesn't really matter—it's the challenge I love. The trophy head on the wall isn't just a record of a killing; it's a badge of honor, a remembrance of personal skill and experience coming together into a single striking moment."

"With all you have done, you must find the hunting in

North Carolina to be rather tame by comparison," said a rotund, bearded Southern gentleman as he thirstily drank his wine.

"Oh, you're right," Colonel Braddick said. "The hunting here is only a mild diversion for me, and it won't be anything I'll be boasting to my friends about, but I do have certain interests here."

"What are you after, Colonel?" Mr. Kettering, the deer hunter, asked.

"In these grand United States of ours," the colonel began to answer, "I've killed mule deer, white-tailed deer, mountain elk, moose, gray wolf, buffalo, pronghorn antelope, grizzly bear, black bear, bobcat, coyote, boar, and all the rest."

"Speaking of bores, maybe you could just shut up for a little while so we can enjoy our meal," Lieutenant Kinsley said beneath his breath as he sipped his soup.

Serafina gasped in surprise that he would say such a thing, but then realized that he had said the words so softly that only she and Jess had heard them. Jess didn't seem to react to the comment. She remained strangely motionless. But Serafina couldn't help cracking a little smile of appreciation.

"There is only one American beast that has managed to elude me," Colonel Braddick continued loudly. "Let's just say I've got a score to settle with this particular breed of varmint."

The colonel pulled up his sleeve for all to see the thick white lines of old scars on his arm. "This was done by none other than America's largest and fiercest feline predator, the cunning and dangerous creature known as the North American mountain lion. Some folks call it a cougar, a puma, or around these parts, a panther or catamount."

Most everyone was listening to the colonel with rapt attention, but Serafina noticed that Mr. Vanderbilt seemed far more alarmed by this loudmouthed guest than impressed by him. The master of the house looked over at Lieutenant Kinsley, who looked back at him with serious, knowing eyes, as if they were both in agreement that something needed to be done about this man. It was at that moment that she realized just how close a personal friend the young Lieutenant Kinsley was to Mr. Vanderbilt.

"What about the other wound you have there, Colonel Braddick?" one of the younger gentlemen asked, pointing to what looked like a fresh cut on his neck.

"Oh, that's just a little scratch I got last night," the colonel said, pulling back the collar of his shirt and showing off four jagged lacerations.

Many of the guests around him recoiled from the gruesome sight of it, while others stared in wide-eyed fascination.

But Serafina's pulse quickened as she looked down at her own fingernails. *Could it have been?*

"What in the world did that?" one of the women asked, clearly impressed.

"Well, the boys and I were out scouting for signs of game last night, just minding our own business, and one of the local varmints attacked our group totally unprovoked, just pounced on us out of nowhere for no reason. That's the mettle of these wild creatures. They'd sooner kill ya than look at ya."

"Tell us what happened, Colonel," one of the admiring young men said breathlessly.

"Well, I was fearful for the safety of the other men, so when the beast attacked, I charged straight at it. I fought the big cat, my bare fists against its razor-sharp claws. We tumbled head over heels down the side of a mountain. First I was winning, then he was winning. There was no telling which way it was going to go. But finally, I got my Bowie knife out and stabbed him just as he sunk his teeth into me. And at that point, the cowardly beast ran away."

It was startling to hear the colonel tell so many lies in so few sentences.

"That's amazing!" one of the guests gasped, and even the footmen had stopped to hear the hair-raising tale.

"You say it sank its teeth into you . . ." Lieutenant Kinsley said quietly. "And yet—mysteriously—there are no puncture wounds in your chest. . . ."

"So, you see," Colonel Braddick continued, nearly shouting, "ever since that first run-in that mangled my arm years ago, and now this encounter last night, the mountain lion is the only game animal—on any continent, mind you—that's gotten away from me. And I take that as a personal affront. When my friend Turner here said he was coming to visit George Vanderbilt's little cottage in the mountains, I was obliged to invite myself along for another try. And after last night's battle, I think I've come to the right spot to bag the trophy I'm looking for."

When Serafina glanced over at the colonel's friend, Mr.

Turner, the poor man looked positively sick to his stomach that he'd made the mistake of bringing this rude and vulgar man into the private dining room of George and Edith Vanderbilt.

Mr. Turner looked at Mr. Vanderbilt with a profoundly apologetic expression on his face, but the master of the house wasn't looking at him. Mr. Vanderbilt's dark and penetrating eyes were locked steady onto Colonel Braddick now, as if he were studying every minute detail of a monster that he was going to slay.

As the colonel carried on with harrowing tales of his "astounding skill" with a rifle, and people encouraged him with questions, Serafina's blood boiled. She was sitting here at the dinner table, with her pretty hair and her pretty dress, pretending to be one of these people. But she wasn't one of them. These humans wanted to hunt and kill the animals of the forest. They wanted to hunt and kill her own kind, her own brother and sister. Why would she want to be one of them? Why would she want to *protect* them? Why would she want to be a protector of Biltmore if *this* was Biltmore?

She imagined seeing this great white hunter, this famous Colonel Braddick, alone out in the forest, up on his horse with his rifle in his hands. She would stalk him from behind, moving slowly at first, her long slinking black body crouched low to the ground, then charging so swiftly and so silently that he would never even see her coming. She would launch herself at him, rip him from his screaming horse, slam him to the ground, and tear him to pieces with her teeth and claws. Then he would truly know what a "Southern varmint" could do.

As she sat there at the table with a pretty bow in her hair, she could feel her nostrils flaring, the sweat oozing from her pores. She wanted to do it so bad that she could taste it like blood between her fangs.

Regardless of how she had been feeling a few moments before, she knew now that she didn't belong here in this so-called civilized place. She didn't fit in among these people laughing and smiling at the colonel's stories. She was a creature of the night. A slinking, clawing animal with the soul of a panther.

She squeezed her eyes shut, trying to block out the violence of her thoughts.

The house, the forest, the wind, the trees, the people, the beauty, the peace, she didn't trust any of it. But most of all, at this moment, she didn't trust *herself.*

"I once shot and killed a running cheetah at a distance of five hundred yards," Colonel Braddick was saying cheerfully to his admirers. "So the next time I see a mountain lion in these hills, you can believe me when I say that it's going to come to a quick end."

In one last bid to maintain her quiet and civilized composure, Serafina glanced over at Lieutenant Kinsley. It was clear that, like her, he had been struggling to sit passively through this braggart's boasting. And now, finally, the lieutenant raised his eyes, looked at the colonel, and spoke loud enough for all to hear.

"But if mountain lions are as cunning and elusive as you say, Colonel," he asked, "how do you plan to find one to shoot?"

Lieutenant Kinsley had phrased his question such that it seemed as if he was genuinely interested, but it was evident to Serafina that the young officer was baiting him. The fight was afoot now, sides were being taken, and she knew hers.

"Well, it's true that mountain lions are the most cowardly and treacherous of wild beasts," the colonel said. "But I am a man of great experience and tracking ability. If I work long and hard enough, I'll find my quarry and kill it. You can be sure of that, Lieutenant."

13

As the evening proceeded through the seven courses of the meal, Colonel Braddick continued with what were meant to be enthralling stories of his bravery and grit.

All the while, Serafina watched as the dark-haired girl named Jess sat quietly across from her. The girl ate her food. She drank her water. She never looked at Colonel Braddick, and she didn't seemed to be listening to him. But she glanced at the other guests and the details of the room, one after another in rapid succession, her eyes glistening in the candlelight as she took in her surroundings.

When Jess's eyes finally fell upon Serafina, the girl studied her for just a moment before her eyes flicked away again. But

Serafina had the impression that Jess took in more information in that split second than another person might do in an hour.

After dinner, as everyone was getting up from the table, Mrs. Ascott said, "Well, it was very nice to meet you, young lady."

It took Serafina a beat to realize that the woman was speaking to her. Flustered, she said, "And it was very nice to meet you as well, Mrs. Ascott." She bowed slightly, as she had seen the other girls do. "I hope you enjoy your stay at Biltmore."

"Oh, yes, of course. How could I not enjoy myself in such a peaceful and lovely place as this?" Mrs. Ascott said warmly, gesturing to the grand scale of the room.

Serafina turned and looked across the table to say good-bye to Jess, but was disappointed to see that she had already left.

When someone close beside her touched Serafina's arm, she jumped, startled, and turned quickly.

"I didn't mean to—" Jess began to say apologetically.

"No, it's fine, it's just me," Serafina said, trying to explain. "I'm just—"

"I liked seeing your friends earlier," Jess interrupted. "I wished they had stayed a little longer."

"My friends?" Serafina said in surprise, then realized who she must be talking about. She didn't think anyone had noticed her little rat catchers slinking around in the shadows of the huge room. "How did you know they were mine?" Serafina asked, not trying to deny it, but mighty curious.

"I saw them listening to you," Jess said.

"They're usually decidedly bad at that," Serafina said with a smile.

Jess smiled in return. "What are their names?"

"The dark, quiet one is Smoke and the little orange ball of clawed fur is Ember," Serafina said.

Jess was about to say something in reply, but visibly winced when Colonel Braddick's voice clanged like a broken bell across the Banquet Hall.

"Come on, gents, it's finally time to get this party started," he bellowed, putting his arm roughly around the squeamish Mr. Turner and dragging him from the room. "I didn't think that meal would ever end! Seven courses? My God, who on this planet ever needs more than five?"

As Colonel Braddick, Mr. Turner, Mr. Suttleston, and some of the other hunters left the room, Jess said calmly, "They're going to go play poker now."

Three seconds later, Colonel Braddick's voice rose above the others. "Let's play some poker in Vanderbilt's Billiard Room!"

Colonel Braddick and his group pulled their cigars out of their breast pockets as they headed to their card games. Many of the other guests wandered over to the Salon to enjoy an after-dinner coffee or stepped outside onto the Loggia to partake of the late night air. Another group availed themselves of a tour of the Winter Garden with Mrs. Vanderbilt. But Serafina noticed that Mr. Vanderbilt and Lieutenant Kinsley remained in the Banquet Hall, standing near the fireplace at the far end of the room, talking privately in hushed voices, sometimes looking toward the Billiard Room, as if they were hatching some sort of plan.

The bellowing voice of Colonel Braddick could still be heard ringing through the corridors of the great house.

"Listen," Jess said, leaning toward Serafina with a conspiratorial whisper. "Don't let him fool you. He'll drink and gamble most of the night, but that won't stop him from getting up early in the morning to go hunting. You need to leave here and warn whoever you need to warn."

Serafina looked at her in surprise. This girl was getting downright spooky now. "What do you mean?" she asked. "Warn who?"

"I saw your reaction earlier," she said. "You weren't just put off by his story about mountain lions, you were angry and you were *scared*, and not for yourself. I could see it."

Serafina just gazed at her, unsure of what to make of this peculiar girl with the eyes of a hawk. Should she pretend she didn't know what she was talking about? Should she deny it? Was there even any point in denying it? The girl seemed to already know.

"You have to understand," Jess said. "He's not just an aggravating braggart. He's a liar and a cheater as well. He said that in the days ahead he's going to use his skills and experience to track a mountain lion, but the truth is he's already hired a local man with a pack of hunting dogs to do the work for him. As soon as the tracker finds a mountain lion, the colonel will go to its den and shoot it. Then he'll tell everyone grand and exciting stories about what a great hunter he is."

ROBERT BEATTY

Serafina tried to stay calm, but a jolt of new fear ran through her. Her brother and sister were out there. And Colonel Braddick was going to hunt them down.

"How do you know all this?" Serafina asked in amazement.

But before she could answer, Colonel Braddick's voice rose up above the voices of the other men in the Billiard Room. "Oh yes, I'm sure she'll be tagging along," he replied to a question that someone had asked him. "She's a good, obedient girl, tougher than you might think out on the trail, but I gotta tell ya, gents, she's a god-awful terrible shot with a rifle. She couldn't hit the side of a barn if her life depended on it. And sometimes she's unbelievably loud with her feet when we're trying to stalk up on a good kill. She sounds like a herd of tramping elephants in those girly boots of hers!"

As the entire room of men erupted into laughter, Serafina looked at Jess. Her face was quiet of expression, almost emotionless, as if she had heard that same joke so many times it didn't affect her anymore.

"You're Colonel Braddick's daughter," Serafina said softly.

"He makes me go out on his hunts with him," Jess said. "But I'm a liar, too."

"What do you mean?"

"My bullet always hits a tree," Jess said.

Serafina smiled, liking that answer and the girl who had said it.

"She's like any girl, I guess," Colonel Braddick was telling his friends, "totally worthless at the practical things in life. But I gotta bring her along or she'd have no place else to go, poor

97

little soul. Her mother's been gone all these years now, left us to fend for ourselves nearly from day one. Tuberculosis, God rest her soul."

As Colonel Braddick droned on in the distance, Jess stepped closer to her.

"We lived and traveled in Africa for years," Jess said. "When I was very young, I remember my father asking me all kinds of questions when we were out hunting, day after day, year after year."

"What kind of questions?" Serafina asked.

"He'd ask things like 'Which of these game paths do you think looks more trodden than the other?' and 'What kind of animal makes this kind of track in the dirt?' For a long time, I thought he was asking me because he was trying to teach me, and maybe he was, I don't know. . . ."

"But what happened?" Serafina urged her, fascinated by her story.

"I had heard that the African leopard was one of the most elusive and beautiful animals in all the world. I had always wanted to see one. I learned where they lived, what kind of tracks they made, and how they behaved. Finally, I spotted a gorgeous leopardess sleeping high up in an acacia tree, nearly impossible to see."

"Was she amazing?" Serafina whispered, envious of seeing such an animal.

"My father shot her," Jess said bitterly. "It was at that moment that I realized the true purpose of my father's questions. For the last few years, he wasn't teaching me. He had no idea that leopards frequented this particular part of the savannah or that they preferred acacia trees. And he had no idea of the particular way in which they draped their sleeping bodies over a branch so that their spots camouflaged them just right. And his eyes weren't that good."

As Serafina listened to Jess's story, she began to understand the level of trust that Jess was putting in her. She must have seen something in her, not just that she *could* share this story, but that she *should* share it.

"My father had used my skills to track the leopardess and kill her," Jess said. "And I realized that he had been doing that for years. I swore in that moment that I would never show my true self to my father again."

"I'm so sorry, Jess," Serafina said, touching her shoulder.

"But truth is, I thank my father every day," Jess said.

"What do you mean?"

"A daughter grows up watching her father, seeing everything he does. Whether he realizes it or not, he is teaching her. From *my* father, I learned what I most don't want to be."

Serafina looked at Jess, and Jess looked back at her. This time Jess's sapphire eyes did not flit away. She held Serafina's gaze. It felt as if it was in this moment that the two of them were truly meeting each other.

"I understand," Serafina said, touching her arm in the way Jess had tried to touch hers earlier. "Thank you for warning me about your father. I mean it. I truly appreciate it."

"You'd do the same for me, right?" Jess said, a tinge of hope in her voice as she looked up at her.

Serafina nodded. "Yes, I would," she said, but she couldn't help but wonder exactly how Jess had determined that about her so quickly. "Do you *know* me somehow?"

"No," Jess said, a little surprised by the question. "I just got here yesterday. You saw me arrive."

"Wait," Serafina said, startled. "Did *you* see *me* when you arrived?"

"You were on the terrace, behind the stone railing," Jess said.

This girl truly does see everything, Serafina thought. And as they were talking, Jess's eyes flicked over to the main corridor.

A messenger had come in and was now walking toward Colonel Braddick.

A moment later, Colonel Braddick and several of his men hurried out of the Billiard Room.

"He never leaves a card game that quickly," Jess said, her voice tight with worry.

"What's it mean?" Serafina asked, feeling herself already relying on this girl's startling powers of observation.

"The local tracker he hired must have found something—"

"Jess!" the colonel barked. Jess jumped at the shout. "Get out of that gown and into your hunting clothes! We're going out right now!"

"You'd better get going," Jess whispered to Serafina.

"I will, right away, but please tell me: Why are you helping me like this?"

Jess looked her in the eye. "Because I've seen too many dead cats."

Serafina ran through the forest, her four furred feet tearing rapidly across the ground, propelling her forward, her body nothing but a black streak through the murky darkness of the trees. The colonel's pack of hunting dogs chased close behind her, running, barking, howling after their prey. She knew from experience that hounds only bayed like that when they were close on the scent. But they weren't on *her* scent. She had come up behind them and gone far around them. She scanned the forest ahead of her, looking frantically for a flash of tan. Her sister and brother were out here someplace, running for their lives. They must know the baying hounds were coming for them. And there was no escape. A mountain lion could easily kill a single dog, but a pack of twenty mindless, biting hounds—all willing to die to get in a single bleeding bite—was more than most mountain lions could handle.

Finally, she heard the whisking sound of two mountain lions sprinting through the thicket in the distance. Looking across a rocky, mist-filled valley, she saw them scurrying up the slope across from her, instinctively heading for high ground.

Not up there, Serafina thought, recognizing the ridge they were headed for. *Not up there.*

The pack of dogs came out of the forest close behind them, loud now, howling with new fervor. The hounds had been chasing the two mountain lions for miles, all through the night, relentless in their pursuit, and they knew they had finally gotten close to their prey.

With nowhere else to go, the two young mountain lions bounded from rock to rock up the ridge, then scrambled their way up an old, dead tree snagged at the top of it. Their shoulder muscles bulged and their claws ripped into the loose bark as they scaled the trunk and reached the upper branches.

The two wildcats were now stuck at the top. They turned, panting, and looked down at the barking, snarling, howling dogs surrounding the base of the tree.

The cats pulled back their ears and wrinkled their whiskered faces in nasty snarls as they hissed at the dogs.

Serafina ran across the valley to help, but then she heard the sound of the hunters crashing through the underbrush on their horses.

"The dogs've got 'em trapped!" the dog handler shouted in

his mountain twang as the hunters came into view through the swirling fog rolling across the slope of the mountain.

The hunters quickly dismounted and forced their way through the thicket on foot, pushing their rifles out in front of them.

"They've treed two of the varmints!" one of the hunters shouted as he climbed up the rocks to get a better look.

The helpless cats stared down at the barking dogs and shouting humans. The dogs were out of their mind with bloodthirsty excitement, their mouths dripping with spit, their tails wagging feverishly as they paced and circled. Many of the hounds were trying repeatedly to run up the trunk of the tree, one after another, some of them getting up to the lower branches before falling down to the ground, picking themselves up, and trying again, howling all the while.

Even lion-hunting dogs couldn't climb trees, but the dogs didn't seem to care about the illogic of it or their own well-being. They just kept trying over and over again, desperate to sink their snapping jaws into the hides of the big cats.

Colonel Braddick came crashing through the thicket on his horse, the last to arrive. "Get back!" he shouted to his men as he dismounted, handing his reins off to Jess, who was there on her dark bay horse, her rifle in her hands. "Nobody shoot!" the colonel shouted. "This is my shot! My shot!"

Still gasping for breath from the exertion of the chase, the colonel lifted his rifle and aimed at the closest mountain lion.

The crack of the colonel's rifle rang through the night air, echoing off the surrounding mountains. A piece of bark flew up next to the lion as the cat leapt to a different branch of the tree.

Swearing in anger that he had missed the shot, the colonel took several steps closer, levered his rifle, and fired again. Once more, the lion leaped away just in time, slinking from branch to branch as her brother hissed and snarled to keep the frenzied, stupid tree-climbing dogs at bay.

Serafina ran toward her brother and sister as fast as she could, her claws out and ready to fight.

The colonel fired again, and then again, twigs breaking, bark exploding, the lions hissing and snarling, the sound of the repeated shots echoing across the mist-filled valley.

Discouraged by the colonel's poor accuracy, the other hunters began to position themselves to shoot the mountain lions themselves and get it over with.

"My shot!" he screamed again as he moved closer.

Serafina ran straight toward them, her powerful chest expanding with raging power. She was almost there.

But on the colonel's next shot, she heard the bullet thwack into her sister's body.

Serafina watched helplessly as her sister fell from the branch of the tree and tumbled through midair, her limbs flailing as she plummeted toward the rocks below.

15

Her sister's body hit a branch as she fell, then hit another and another, until the cat finally flipped upright and landed on her feet, claws out, right on top of the pack of dogs. Two of the dogs yelped in pain and surprise as the wildcat came down on top of them. But the other hounds turned on the lion, lunging at her with their biting, snapping attacks.

Serafina leapt into the battle, knocking the largest of the dogs away with a powerful swipe of her claws, then clamped her jaws onto another and pulled it to the ground. She swiped another dog as the two behind her latched onto her back with their teeth. Spinning with a ferocious, angry snarl, she grabbed one of the dogs in her fangs and hurled it down the slope of the mountain.

As Serafina fought, her brother came down the tree head-first and then leapt onto the backs of the dogs that were biting his wounded sister, sending them into wild, screeching yelps. His sister managed to get to her feet, and the two of them dashed away, disappearing into the mist-cloaked underbrush.

Serafina felt a quick burst of relief that her sister and brother had escaped, but then one of the attacking dogs lunged teeth-first at her throat. Reacting on pure reflex, she cocked her head and snapped the dog's neck in her jaws. As a second and third dog lunged in at her, she swiped at them with her claws.

A dense fog had rolled across the ridge like the breath of ghouls, making it difficult to see more than a few feet around her, but through a narrow opening in the white swirling mist she caught a glimpse of the colonel and the other men scrambling hurriedly through the brush and back up onto their horses in panic.

She charged toward them. She could see Colonel Braddick up on his horse with his rifle in his hands. She moved so rapidly through the underbrush that she was invisible, her long slinking black body crouched for the kill. Her chest filled with a growling anger. Her fangs were dripping with blood. Her claws sprang out. She launched herself straight at the colonel in a ferocious, snarling attack, determined to make sure the vile human never shot another animal again.

As she leapt toward Colonel Braddick and the other hunters she found herself plunging into a wall of fog so thick that she couldn't see anything in front of her. Something large brushed past her. She heard the blowing snort of a startled horse, the crack of steel-shod hooves on the rocky ground. Men shouted warnings to each other as they tried to control their frightened beasts. The horses lunged and turned and lunged again, one rider crashing into another, shouting as their mounts scraped so close that the riders' knees struck and nearly ripped each other out of the saddle. A frightened hunting dog darted past her. She caught a glimpse of a horse's haunch, its dark brown hide glistening with sweat and slashed with bloody gashes.

"There it is!" one of the hunters shouted, sounding as frightened and confused as she was.

"Watch out!" shouted another.

Three dogs tore past her, yelping and crying, glancing over their shoulders as they ran. Her heart hammered in her chest as she tried to understand what was happening. She looked up to see a rider frantically yanking his reins as his horse jostled him one way and then the other.

A burst of light lit up the fog like a flash of lightning and a gunshot cracked the night. And then another gunshot, and another.

"Jess!" Colonel Braddick shouted, his voice ripped with fear.

Serafina hissed as something shoved past her. But then it pivoted and charged straight at her. She dodged the attack and swiped at it with her paw. Her claws raked across something so hard that it didn't feel like skin or muscle, but a mesh of steel, and then it was gone. She heard the collision of something striking a horse's side, the great grunt of the beast, a man shouting, gunfire. One of the bullets grazed Serafina's shoulder, slicing her with a blaze of pain. She struck out with her paw against whatever it was, blind in the fog.

A quick movement dashed behind her. She spun to defend herself, opening her fanged mouth in a hissing snarl. A whimpering dog went limping by, its bloody leg hanging loose from its body.

A sound came rushing in. She sprang to the side. A girl's shouting scream rose up ahead of her, and then the high-pitched neighing of a frightened horse. Serafina leapt forward.

She saw Jess up on her horse as it treaded backward in terror, Jess lifting her rifle and firing at something in front of her, the muzzle flashing, the cracks of the shots splitting the air one after another.

Serafina lunged forward to help Jess, but Jess's horse spooked at the sight of her coming in from the side, its eyes white with fear as it rose up onto its hind legs, rearing and striking. Jess fought valiantly to stay in the saddle, but the horse was out of its mind with panic. It neighed and kicked, rising higher and higher, until it finally toppled, throwing Jess to the ground.

A massive, charging weight slammed into Serafina. It knocked her tumbling across the rocky ground and right over the edge of a drop-off. Her body fell, then struck rock, then rolled and fell again as she plunged down the steep slope of the mountain. She flung out her paws, clawing at trees and rocks, anything to hold on to, trying desperately to stop her fall.

Serafina slowly opened her eyes and stared into the darkness.

She did not know how long she'd been unconscious. Her body lay splayed across the ground, racked with pain. It hurt to breathe. It hurt to move. But she knew she had to. Gritting her long panther teeth, she slowly pushed herself up onto her four feet.

There were no more gunshots. No more people screaming. No more horses neighing. All she could hear was the dripping of the moisture from the surrounding branches. Nothing was moving except for the swirls of gray fog drifting between the trunks of the trees like writhing ghosts.

Shaking off the wet dirt and debris that had stuck to her fur, she scrambled back up the slope. She didn't understand what had happened, but she knew she had to get up there to help Jess.

When she reached the top of the ridge, the fog was so thick that she couldn't see anything. Crouching down, she waited and listened for the movement of enemies. She sniffed the air, smelling humans, horses, dogs, trees, wet earth, gunpowder, and ferns.

She let several more seconds pass, just waiting. The chaos of the battle had ended.

Staying low to the ground, she crept blindly forward several feet into the fog.

She found a dead dog lying on the ground, an open wound at its neck.

A few yards beyond the dog she found one of the hunters. She could tell by his simple mountain clothing and the raggedness of his beard that it wasn't one of the gentlemen guests. It was the local man named Isariah Mayfield, whom the colonel had paid to track down the mountain lions with his hounds. Isariah lay crumpled in the leaves, bleeding from a kind of wound she'd never seen before, a single straight slash to the chest.

She shifted into human form. Still staying low to the ground, she crawled forward to help the man, but when she saw Isariah's face, and his open eyes, she knew immediately that he was already dead.

Pulling in rapid, frightened breaths, she scurried along the ground through the fog more quickly now.

She came to Mr. Turner, his eyes wide and his dead hands

still clenching his rifle in terror, and then to Mr. Suttleston, his body facedown.

And then she came to the colonel.

His broken leg bone was sticking out of his thigh where his toppling horse had smashed him against a rock, and there was a large, deep wound to his chest and belly, the blood oozing from it every time he tried to take in a breath.

"Colonel," she said as she rushed toward him. "What attacked you?"

"It's you . . ." he said. "What are you doing here, girl? Where's Jess? Forget about me. You've got to help my Jess, please . . ." he said, his voice ragged and weak.

"I'll find her, Colonel, but tell me what attacked you."

"It was a black panther and—" He gasped violently for a gulp of air, his chest heaving and blood coming out of his mouth.

"Colonel," she said, watching helplessly as his eyes fell closed, his head slowly dropped down, and the last, long, rattling breath of his life came out of him.

She had despised this man. She had hated him with all her heart. But she still couldn't help but feel a pang of remorse to see him die like this.

She looked around her, trying to gaze out into the fog-filled forest. Who or what had done this? Was it still out there?

She slowly leaned toward the colonel and studied the wound to his body. It wasn't a straight cut like the other. And it wasn't the punctures of an animal's fangs. And it wasn't bullet wounds. His chest and belly had been sliced open with four long slashes, like a large cat's claws. Like *her* claws.

A sickening feeling sank into her. She had seen her brother and sister run off, so she knew it hadn't been them. And she knew her mother wasn't in the area.

She looked at the dead body of the colonel, and all around at the bodies of the other hunters and the dogs lying on the forest floor.

She tried to remember the exact sequence of events, everything she had seen and heard. In all the fighting and confusion, was it possible that *she* had done this? Had she, in her panther form, been the one who had frightened the horses? Had she lost her mind in some kind of revenge-fueled rage? She had hated these hunters for what they were doing. But had she actually *killed* them? Had her dark, black panther soul taken her over?

Gasping for breath, she got to her feet and backed away from the colonel's dead body.

Her ankle hit a lump on the ground behind her. Another body. Another victim. She turned to see a girl with long, dark hair crumpled among the roots of an old tree.

"Jess . . ." she cried, filling with anguish as she dropped to her knees beside her friend.

Serafina grabbed Jess's shoulder and turned her over.

She was expecting Jess to be cold and stiff like the others. But she wasn't. She was warm and breathing. Her eyes were closed, but she was very much alive.

"Jess," Serafina said excitedly, her heart leaping with hope.

Serafina looked for a wound, thinking that Jess must have been struck down the same way her father and the other men had been, but she couldn't find any such injuries. Jess's torso, arms, and legs appeared unhurt. But then Serafina found blood in Jess's hair. Serafina remembered seeing Jess shooting her rifle at something in the fog. And then . . . What had caused her horse to rear up in panic?

It was me, Serafina thought. *I sprang to help her, but all Jess's horse saw was a panther charging at it out of the fog.*

She tried to piece everything together in her mind, what she saw, what she heard, but it had happened so fast.

All she knew now was that she had to get Jess back to Biltmore, to a doctor.

But then a small stick broke on the forest floor in the distance behind her.

For days she had been second-guessing herself. For months. But this time she was sure.

There was something out there moving through the underbrush.

She rose to her feet and scanned the trees.

Then she heard a much closer noise: the dragging of heavy footsteps coming toward her through the woods, the movement of metal mesh, and the clanking of one piece of metal against the other.

The muscles in her legs tightened, telling her to run, to flee for her life. Her heart felt like it was somersaulting in her chest. Her breaths were getting shorter, more frantic.

She knew she shouldn't leave Jess lying here alone and wounded on the ground, but she felt a powerful, overwhelming need to follow that sound.

One way or another she had to know! Had she lost her mind and killed these men? Or was there something out there?

She shifted into panther form and charged into the darkness, straight toward the sound.

19

She dove headlong through the forest, plowing through the swirling fog, the underbrush catching on her whiskered face.

When the fog became so thick she couldn't even see a few feet in front of her she had to slow down, but she kept moving, listening ahead.

She heard another dull, clanking thud and the heavy, dragging footsteps.

She rushed forward in a fast, slinking prowl, claws at the ready.

But the farther she went, the fainter the sound became.

She stopped and listened into the murkiness of the midnight fog, but the noise had faded.

She waited and listened.

Growling, she doubled back and tried to pick up the sound where she'd heard it last.

Come on, she thought in frustration. *It's got to be here. I'm so close.*

She turned, and then turned again.

As she crept through a thick stand of trees and bushes with low, twisting branches, she used her whiskers to find her way.

The pulsing, rhythmic buzz of the forest's night insects surrounded her now. She could hear dew dripping from the trees, and the whistle of a whip-poor-will in the distance. And then she heard something much softer just ahead, the touch of small feet moving *tap-tap-tap* across the autumn leaves.

She crept forward, ready to pounce.

The fog began to clear in front of her. The clouds overhead were thinning. And the silver light of the crescent moon shone down into a small meadow.

The fur on the back of her neck tingled.

And then she finally saw it.

The creature was standing there, perfectly still, in the center of the moonlit meadow, its head turned toward her. It was staring at her with its black, otherworldly eyes.

It was a small white deer.

She gazed at the deer in awe.

At first she was too startled, too shocked by the sight of it, to understand what it meant. But then it slowly began to sink in.

That night with Braeden had been real.

She hadn't dreamed it.

She hadn't imagined it.

An immense sense of relief, almost euphoria, poured through her body.

It had all been real.

The white deer stood in the middle of the meadow and stared at her. Serafina was surprised that it wasn't frightened of a panther watching it from the edge of the forest. Did it somehow recognize her? Did it know she and Braeden had helped it?

For a long time it did not move. But finally, it walked into the cover of the trees on the other side of the meadow and disappeared.

Serafina felt her heart sink.

Why was it here, on this ridge, in this part of the forest, at this moment?

She knew now that Braeden had definitely come home, but where did he go?

I just wanted to see you one last time, he had said that night. She remembered the tremor in his voice when he said it, the loyalty, the fierceness, but there had been a twinge of sadness and resignation as well.

Did he know all along that he was going to leave again the next morning? Is that what he had been trying to tell her?

But what did the white deer have to do with it all?

With all the peculiar things that were going on, why would Braeden leave without saying good-bye? She couldn't help feeling a hole in her heart, like something that should have happened didn't happen. *Stay bold,* he had said the night before. Had that been his good-bye?

She realized that he hadn't seen many of the peculiar things that she had. It was possible that he had returned to New York without realizing what was happening here. Life at Biltmore had been safe and peaceful for months, so maybe he thought everything was still all right.

But it isn't all right, she thought, feeling an ache in her chest, *it isn't right at all.*

As she turned to go back to Jess, she looked around at the trees and vegetation and realized that she didn't know which way it was.

Her sense of direction was normally very strong in the forest. But now she was confused, uncertain of the path back.

She took a few steps to see if she recognized one of the trees or a jagged rock, or if she could get her bearings in some other way. But nothing looked familiar.

A bout of panic and irritation rippled through her. *What's going on? This never happens to me. What if I can't find Jess?*

As she went deeper into the forest, she looked for any sort of sign or detail that might help her find her way back to her friend.

She felt a slight itching on the back of her neck. The cringing sensation of being followed crept into her shoulders.

She stopped and listened behind her.

For a moment she thought she heard the faint sound of rustling leaves, but whatever was following her stopped the instant she did. When she resumed, it resumed as well, the leaves rustling in the distance.

She couldn't shake the feeling that something wasn't just following her but *hunting* her.

She moved more quickly now, slinking quietly and rapidly through the underbrush.

Whatever was behind her moved just as fast she did, staying right with her, closing the distance between them.

The air rushing in and out of her panther lungs got louder as her breathing became heavier.

She went one way through the forest, and then the other, desperately trying to throw off her pursuer. But at the same time she had to find her way back to Jess.

Finally, she spotted a rock she recognized. She ran in that direction, and then saw a familiar tree.

But as she returned to the area in the forest where the hunters had been killed, her gut tightened with the memory of what happened there, the white-eyed fear of the horses and the bullets flying past her. She remembered the screams of the men and the barking of the dogs all around her.

In the cloud of anger that had boiled up inside her during the battle, and all the confusion of what was happening, had her darkest and most vicious instincts driven her to claw and bite and kill?

Was she transforming more and more into the panther part of herself, just like her mother had, more wildcat than human?

She didn't want to see their faces and the blood, so she skirted carefully around the dead bodies of Colonel Braddick, Mr. Turner, Mr. Suttleston, and Isariah Mayfield.

When she finally reached the spot where she had left Jess, Serafina stared at the empty patch of ground.

Serafina's chest tightened. She looked all around. She circled the area looking for her, but found no sign of her, not even footprints.

She sniffed the ground, searching for Jess's scent, but couldn't find it among the dead humans and trampled earth.

She went farther out into the forest. She searched for hours. But Jess was gone.

Serafina felt an almost overwhelming sense of hopelessness, like the more she tried to help, the worse things got. The more she tried to understand, the more incomprehensible things became.

Growling with frustration, she flexed her claws and began to run, just to get away from the place where the men had died. She ran and she kept running.

Driven on by the anguish roiling in her heart, she made her way toward the abandoned cemetery where so many events of her and Braeden's lives had occurred. She didn't even know why she was going there, except to find some sort of refuge, some sort of protection and understanding.

She crossed through the swampy marsh, then entered the old graveyard, which had been overgrown by the creeping, dripping-wet forest decades before. Black strands of vines strangled the crooked trunks of the gnarled trees. And thick carpets of choking leaves toppled the gray, weathered gravestones to the ground. Over the course of withering years, the roots of the trees had taken grip on the coffins beneath the earth, twisting them and breaking them and wrenching them to the surface, while long beards of grayish-green moss hung down from the branches above.

She shifted into human form as she walked into what she and Braeden had named the Angel's Glade.

Deep in the forest of the graveyard, the glade consisted of a small, open area of perfect, bright green grass encircled by a ring of graceful living trees with leaves that never fell. Surrounded by the death and decay of a long-abandoned world, this was a place of everlasting life.

In the center of the glade stood a magnificent statue of a winged angel holding a sword. She was dark green with age, and spots of lichen and moss covered many of her surfaces. She had long, flowing hair and a beautiful face, but the stain of weeping tears dripped down her cheeks like rain.

Standing in the glade, in front of the stone angel, Serafina lifted her eyes and looked up at her.

"I don't know what to do," she said, her voice pleading, but the angel did not reply.

As Serafina gazed around at the Angel's Glade, it didn't seem as if its grass was as bright green as it normally was. And the trees around the glade weren't as alive. This had once been a place of such awe-inspiring power and glittering magic, but not now. It felt cold and lifeless and alone, as if it too was gone from her world.

There were just so many questions swirling in her mind.

She crumpled to the ground.

In the center of the glade, she lay on her back, with her shoulder pressed up against the stone pedestal of the angel, and looked up into the night. The mist had gone and the air was clear, but very high up in the sky, a thin layer of silver-gray clouds shrouded the stars. She couldn't see the belt of Orion, the blue glow of Pleiades, or any of the stars that she had seen with Braeden. She missed them, her brothers and sisters of the night.

But as she kept looking, she saw a single persistent dot of light directly above her. Not a star, but a planet—the small, glowing orb of Jupiter, shining through the thin layer of clouds, like a valiant friend.

That's my Braeden, she thought, and suddenly her heart felt as if it was drowning.

"I'm in trouble here, Braeden," she cried out, her voice trembling. "I need your help. I don't know what's going on. I don't know what to do. I might have done something real bad. Come home now, just come home, as soon as you can. Please, I need you here. Just come home."

She knew it was impossible, but as she said the words, it almost felt as if he could hear them, as if at that moment, he woke from his bed, looked out into the nighttime sky, and imagined the sound of her voice.

She had to believe that he was safe, that he was up in New York like he was supposed to be, that their bond had not been broken, and that somehow, someday, he would return to her.

As she lay there alone with no idea where she could go or what she could do, it was only the glowing light of Jupiter that kept her from despair.

More tired than she had been in a long time, she wanted to sleep here in the faint but steady light of distant Jupiter, lying on the ground at the base of the stone angel, just as he had done for her in this very spot so long ago, calling her name into the darkness.

But she knew she had to go. She hadn't known the four men well, and she despised what they were doing out here, but the truth was that four human beings had been killed. And Jess was still missing. She had failed Jess! She had lost her! For all she knew, she had actually *killed* her with her own claws, or at least spooked her horse and caused it to throw her. One way or another, her friend was gone!

She didn't know the how or the why or the who. But the rock-hard truth was that she had failed to protect Jess and the hunters from evil—whether it came from her or from somewhere else. She didn't understand this evil. Or how to fight it. Was it inside her? But one way or another, with or without Braeden, she had to do it. She had to go back to Biltmore. And she had to face whatever was to come.

She pulled herself up onto her feet, wiped her eyes, and began the journey home.

As she walked across the courtyard toward Biltmore's front doors, her mind was consumed with what was going to happen when she stepped inside. But she spotted her little orange cat, Ember, running between two of the large terra-cotta planters and then darting out of sight. It was unusual to see Ember outside. And even more unusual that Ember didn't come running to greet her. It was as if she was chasing something. *Or being chased.*

Serafina went over to the planter, uncertain.

"Ember?" she said, but the cat did not come.

When Serafina took a few more steps forward and looked behind the planters, she found a small hole that Ember must have slipped down into.

"It appears that you've found a rat," Serafina said, thinking that maybe Ember had finally begun to take her job seriously.

But as she went inside and crossed through the Vestibule, she looked over and noticed scratches on the wall.

She stopped. She didn't remember seeing scratches there before. Had they been there all along and she'd never noticed them?

She took a step closer to them.

The striations almost looked like something Smoke and Ember would do, but they were far too thick, and the limestone walls of the Vestibule were far too hard for their little claws.

Serafina wondered, but she knew she couldn't linger here or follow this path. She had to go inside.

As she opened the doors and entered the Main Hall, the house was in turmoil, servants running, guests crying, dozens of men on the move, many with knives at their sides and hunting rifles in their hands.

"Serafina," a stern voice called.

She turned to see Mr. Vanderbilt stepping away from the group of men he had been talking to and striding toward her.

"I need to talk to you right away," he said. "Some sort of wild animal attacked the hunting party last night."

Serafina stood before him, and tried to keep breathing, but she could barely look at him. She hated the grim tone of his voice, and the desperate look in his eyes, like the world was coming apart at the seams and he had no idea how to stop it.

"From what we've pieced together," Mr. Vanderbilt said,

"Colonel Braddick and several others were tracking a mountain lion, and there was some kind of . . . apparently it . . . the mountain lion turned on them and attacked. Some of the men are saying there were actually two mountain lions."

As he spoke, Serafina felt her lips tightening and her eyes watering. She could hear in his voice all the sadness and confusion churning inside him.

But underneath all of it, she could hear something far worse: the creeping edge of doubt.

Doubt in *her*. And why not? She doubted herself.

Finally, she took a hard swallow and began to speak. "You're right that the hunters and their dogs chased two mountain lions," she said. "They treed them out on the North Ridge."

Mr. Vanderbilt looked at her with his eyes wide, clearly startled that she'd been so close to what had happened that she could actually confirm it.

"Did . . ." he began to ask her. "Did you have something to do with this, Serafina?"

She didn't even know where to begin to answer his question. She had *everything* to do with it!

She wanted to run away, to hide, to get away from it, but she knew she couldn't. Mr. Vanderbilt needed her help. That was the only thing she could cling to. Even as she was, he needed her.

"I helped the mountain lions to escape," she admitted.

"And the mountain lions came back and killed all those men?" he said in amazement and dismay.

"No, sir, that's not what happened," she said emphatically. "The mountain lions did not come back. I know that much for certain."

"Then what was it? What killed those men?"

"There was a dense fog," she said, shaking her head, "so much confusion, fighting and gunshots, all the horses panicking, the dogs running around. I was there. But I do not know what happened. I truly don't."

"Did something attack the hunters?"

"Yes, but I do not know what it was."

"And did you see Colonel Braddick's daughter?"

The question hit Serafina hard. "I . . ." she began, but then faltered.

"Tell me what happened," Mr. Vanderbilt urged her. "We must work together if we're going to deal with this."

She nodded, knowing he was right, and appreciating the way he said *we*, as if at least a little part of him still believed in a little part of her.

"I saw the bodies of the dead hunters in the forest," she said. "When I found Jess, she was injured, thrown from her horse, but she was still alive."

"Then what happened? Did you try to help her?"

When Mr. Vanderbilt asked her this simple question it was as if he were stabbing her in the heart. She knew that it was what she *should* have done. She should have helped her friend. But the anger had been boiling inside her, and then she got so lost and confused when she tried to return to her.

"I heard a noise that I thought was the attacker," she said. "I tried to follow it, but I lost track of whatever or whoever it was. And then, by the time I got back to Jess, she was gone."

"What do you mean she was gone?" Mr. Vanderbilt said.

"I thought she must have woken up and stumbled away. I looked for her for a long time in the surrounding forest, but I couldn't find her. She's a very observant and capable girl, and she's used to being outdoors, so all I could do was hope that she made it home."

"She did not," Mr. Vanderbilt said, his hand pressed in worry to his mouth.

And then, for a long time, he just stood there thinking, absorbing all that she had told him.

"It's a terrible thing," he said as he stared at the floor, and then he lifted his eyes and looked at her. "But whatever happened out there, Serafina, we need to protect the occupants of this house. Mr. Doddman and Lieutenant Kinsley are organizing the men. They're going to find and kill whatever animal did this. And they'll be searching for Miss Braddick as well. But for now, you need to rest. You look exhausted. And then you'll rejoin us."

Serafina's heart lurched. She knew what *find and kill whatever animal did this* meant to the men out there. They were going to ride out into the forest and shoot whatever animal they saw—most especially her brother and sister.

"I can't rest," she was about to say to Mr. Vanderbilt, but at that moment, Lieutenant Kinsley strode abruptly into the house and walked up to them, his manner brusque and filled with purpose.

He was no longer in his dress uniform, but wearing rugged outdoor clothing for riding, and he had exchanged his long officer's dress sword for a sheathed knife and a holstered sidearm. He glanced at her, and his eyes seem to flicker with something—relief, concern, irritation, she wasn't sure what it was—but then he spoke directly to Mr. Vanderbilt.

"I took care of that first matter, sir," he said.

"Very good," Mr. Vanderbilt said.

"And the men are ready to go out. I will be leading one of the groups myself, sir."

"And the security manager?"

"Mr. Doddman will be leading the other group."

"You both have the same mission: kill whatever beast did this and find the Braddick girl."

"We will, sir. You can count on us." Lieutenant Kinsley nodded curtly, glanced at Serafina, and then exited as if he had just been given orders by his commanding officer.

After the lieutenant had gone and she left Mr. Vanderbilt, she headed quickly down to the basement to see her pa. She knew she didn't have much time—she had to make sure her brother and sister had fled the area—but she also knew her pa was going to be fretting about her.

"Come on over here," her pa said gently as he wrapped his arms around her. And she held him in return, just resting there in his arms for a few moments. After everything that had happened the night before, it was good to see her pa. It felt like she'd been gone for days. And she knew he must have been worried sick about her when he heard about the attack during the night. As he held her, there were no suspicions from her pa, no doubts, no uncertainty, no complications, not even any words for a long time. Just love.

"Come on," he said finally, "you're gonna need some breakfast in your belly."

"I can't, Pa, I gotta go back out."

"Understood," he said, nodding. "Go do what you need to do and get back safe."

She liked the way he didn't grill her with questions or demand that she stay clear of what was happening. Her rats had gotten bigger, and a whole lot nastier, but he knew she had a job to do.

After leaving her pa, she went straight upstairs to the second floor, knocked on the nursery door, and poked her head into the room.

"Come in, my dear," Mrs. Vanderbilt whispered as she set the blanketed bundle of baby Cornelia carefully into the rocking crib, which was stuffed with down pillows and white bedding.

"Is Cornelia all right?" Serafina asked as she came in.

"We had a difficult night, but she just fell asleep," Mrs. Vanderbilt replied.

The nursery was a newly finished room, with gold-and-maroon cut silk velvet wallpaper, and the delicate curves of fine French furniture.

"Did you see or hear anything strange in the night?" Serafina asked.

"There were a few creaks and bumps here and there, and then all the commotion of the men downstairs, but that was all," Mrs. Vanderbilt said.

"Good," Serafina said. "Does Baby Nell like her new crib?"

"Oh, yes, I think so," Mrs. Vanderbilt said. "But what about you? The maids said that when they went to make your bed this morning that it hadn't been slept in. Is it not to your liking?"

"I'm sorry, ma'am, I haven't had a chance to sleep," she replied, suddenly feeling terribly ungrateful for the kindness that Mrs. Vanderbilt had shown her.

"There's no need to apologize, my dear," Mrs. Vanderbilt said. "I understand that you must have been very busy with the shocking news about the hunting party, but I just want you to promise me that you'll rest as soon as you can. I'll make sure none of the servants disturb you."

"Thank you, ma'am, I will, as soon as I can," Serafina promised, but a moment later she headed outside.

As she stepped out into the cobblestoned courtyard at the front of the house, she saw that it was filled with the men preparing their horses and weapons. Lieutenant Kinsley stood nearby, loading the leather saddlebag on the side of his horse, a beautiful dappled gray mare.

"Bring plenty of ammunition!" the lieutenant was saying to the other men. "And make sure your girth straps are tight. We're going into some very steep terrain."

She marveled at how much he had changed in mood and action since she'd seen him at dinner.

The news of what had happened had brought the whole house up in arms. Country strolls and afternoon tea had given way to hunts for rabid beasts and searches for a lost child. Everyone was helping, servants and guests alike.

When Lieutenant Kinsley saw her standing there alone, he turned toward her in surprise. "Miss Serafina . . ."

"Hello, Lieutenant," she said.

"Have you come to join us?" he asked hopefully. "I'll have a horse brought up right away."

She hadn't expected the invitation. His gray eyes seemed to

flicker as he gazed at her, his face filled with not only the grim seriousness that it had possessed a few moments before, but a kind of encouragement as well. It was as if they were comrades-in-arms now, working together toward a common goal, the darkest of circumstances pushing them together.

"I wish I could," she said sincerely, "but I think it would be better if I went out on my own."

He gazed at her in surprise, as if trying to figure out exactly what kind of person she was.

"On your own?" he asked, his tone steady and respectful.

She didn't know how to tell him that she had never ridden a horse. Nor did she know how to tell him that while he and his men were hunting her feline kin, she'd be making sure they got away. She knew it must confuse him why a lone thirteen-year-old, seemingly with no weapon or steed, would venture out when a vicious animal was stalking the forest.

"In what direction will you be going?" she asked.

"Up to the North Ridge first," he said. "Where the attack took place and Jess was last seen."

"That sounds like a good idea," she said. "But stay on the lookout. It's very rocky and there are many gullies and cliffs. And if you end up going east, down into the low ground, stay well clear of the swamp. It would be treacherous terrain for your horses."

He nodded as he glanced toward his horse, seeming to take the advice to heart. "Arabella here is my pride and joy," he said, patting his horse's shoulder. "We've been together since I was a boy. We went through officer training together." And then he lifted his eyes and looked at Serafina. "And in which direction will you be going?"

"West to the river, then upstream. The last time I got lost up in those mountains, I used the river to find my way home. Jess may try the same thing."

"And you'll be careful, too . . ." he said, not with the forcefulness of a demand, or even a question, but with the softness of a request.

It amazed her how a man who was about to go out and shoot whatever moved could be so thoughtful, so gentle of heart toward her. She wondered, if Lieutenant Kinsley saw her out in the forest in her true form, how fast would he pull the trigger? Was there truly even a difference between a panther and a girl?

"I will be careful," she promised. "And don't worry. I'm a fast runner." And then, realizing she should change the subject, she asked, "So, you know Jess Braddick well, then?" She couldn't help but notice how seriously he was taking the responsibility of finding her.

"No," he said. "I met her at dinner, but that is all. But if she's still lost out there, we've got to help her. George Vanderbilt has been a friend and mentor to me since I was very young. He put me through school, and arranged my commission as an officer. I owe him a great debt. I just hope that when the moment comes, I can prove myself worthy of his trust in me."

Hearing the gravity in his voice, it was clear that he was expecting to come face-to-face with the man-killing beast they were all talking about. And for all she knew, it was out there, some sort of horrible creature she hadn't yet seen.

"Everybody mount up!" Lieutenant Kinsley shouted as he turned, and all the riders began to move in earnest, hurriedly tightening their saddle straps and making last-minute adjustments.

In the single, smooth motion of a well-trained young cavalry officer, the lieutenant vaulted deftly into his saddle. As he took up Arabella's reins, the horse shifted her hooves and tilted her head, raring to go.

"Please be careful out there, Lieutenant Kinsley," she said, looking up at him on his horse. "No one knows what we're dealing with."

"Whatever it is, we're going to find it, and we'll bring Miss Braddick home," he said, clearly trying to be brave and confident just as his training had taught him.

"But please keep yourself safe in the meantime," she said. "Dinners in the Banquet Hall wouldn't be the same without you."

He smiled, seeming pleased with her comment. "And you as well, Miss Serafina," he said. "I will see you at dinner."

And then he tipped his hat, turned forward, and spurred his horse away.

As the hunting party rode out, she watched him canter toward the front of the group.

"We need to cover as much ground as we can," he shouted to the other men. "And keep your rifles ready!"

She waited three beats of her heart and then ran for the line of trees, thankful that cats' paws were faster than horses' hooves.

The moment she was out of sight of the house, she shifted and ran, her panther legs taking her miles through the forest.

Nose to the ground, it didn't take her long to find her brother and sister. The two mountain lions were already wild-eyed and on the run. They had smelled the coming horses and heard the shouts of the men.

She had worried that because they had seen her in human form so many times, they had become too careless around humans. But it was clear that just as Kinsley only saw her as human, her brother and sister only saw her as cat, no matter what form she was in. It had been that way since she met them as spotted cubs just outside their mother's den more than a year before. She was relieved to see that their instinct to flee humans was still strong.

She got their attention with a rub of her shoulder, and signaled them to follow her, leading them deep into the very swamp she had warned Kinsley to avoid. They would need to stay there until the danger passed.

From there she traveled alone, upstream along the river for several hours, looking for any sign of Jess or the man-killing beast. She wasn't even sure it existed. But *something* had killed the hunters. Was it possible it was out here? It must have been large enough to shove a horse and deadly enough to slash a man right down the center of his chest. What could do such a thing? A hunger-crazed bear? A wolf? A man with a weapon? Could it truly have been her own claws? Or was there some sort of demon prowling through the forest?

The night before, she had already scoured the North Ridge where the hunting party was going, but she still hoped they might somehow find Jess. And she prayed that Lieutenant Kinsley and the other members of the hunting party would stay safe. There was no doubt in her mind that they'd try to kill any large animal they encountered, but they didn't deserve to die.

After searching all day and into the night to no avail, she finally turned and headed back toward Biltmore, totally exhausted. She'd been up for far too long.

As she traveled through the forest, she heard the sound of horses. Still in panther form, she climbed a tree and watched from a safe distance as the hunting party moved past her.

Their enthusiasm for the kill had waned, their heads and their rifles hanging down. Wet and tired, they were heading home, just as she was. It was clear that they hadn't found what they were looking for. But then she realized that one of the men was missing. Lieutenant Kinsley was no longer with them.

Her heart tightened. Had he been killed? Lost? Or had he decided to continue the search for Jess even after sending his exhausted men back home?

When she finally got back to Biltmore, she checked in on her sleeping pa in the workshop, then headed upstairs to the second floor. Both of the hunting parties had returned hours before. The house was dark and still, everyone asleep after a long and difficult day.

As she went into her room, Smoke and Ember both purred gently, as if pleased to see that she'd made it home. And she was pleased to see them as well, especially little Ember, whom she'd been worried about after seeing her outside.

Ember seemed content to sleep, but Smoke studied her with watchful eyes.

"Are you all right?" she asked him gently as she petted his neck. With his gray eyes watching her, he seemed more worried than usual.

She lit a small fire in the bedroom fireplace, casting the room in a soft flickering light and filling it with a gentle warmth, then took off her dress and crawled between the silky sheets to get some much-needed rest. The down padding of the bed and the comforting weight of the blanket over her body made her feel warm and protected.

Her two apprentices joined her on the bed, snuggling up with her, Ember actively purring and kneading her chest with her little paws, and Smoke sitting quietly behind her calves, looking out into the rest of the room, ever on guard. There was nothing in the world quite as comforting as taking a long nap on a soft bed with two cats.

Exhausted, she quickly slipped into a deep sleep.

Her plan had been to sleep for just a little while, but when she woke, the fire had died out and the room had gone cold and black.

Ember was upside down asleep beside her, her paws up in the air as if she were still kneading her chest.

Smoke's eyes were open and watchful, and she could swear the dark gray fur on his body was more puffed out than usual.

Glancing out the window as she rose from the bed, she could see that Jupiter had set, which meant it was probably well after two in the morning, and the moon was rising. The upper sky was clear, but isolated banks of fog were rolling down the sides of the mountains, enveloping the trees.

Remembering where she was, she glanced at the clock on the mantel, which confirmed that it was twenty past three in the morning.

She wasn't sure what had awoken her.

She looked out the window again and then crossed to the other side of her bedroom.

Everything appeared to be as it should be.

Then she heard the sound of running footsteps outside her door, the sharp scrape of furniture.

143

Her heart began to hammer in her chest.

Something crashed to the floor and shattered.

A man screamed in horror.

Serafina ran for the door.

She burst out of her bedroom and looked frantically around, expecting to come headlong into an attack. But there was nothing there.

She was sure that the scream she'd heard had come from the living hall right outside her door, but the large, open room was quiet and still.

Had she heard the scream in a nightmare and woken up suddenly, thinking that it was real?

A wash of moonlight was pouring through the windows, casting the room in ghostly light and holding it all perfectly still as if it were an image in a dream.

She scanned the room again, looking across the empty, ghost-lit chairs, and the dark shapes of Mr. Vanderbilt's animalier sculptures on the tables. The tall, wrought-iron floor lamps stood like wraiths in the night, casting long black shadows across the pale moon floor.

She could not see anything out of the ordinary, but she felt a crawling sensation on the back of her neck.

Standing very still, she moved her gaze from one empty chair to the next, into one dark corner and then the other, to the small black cave of the dead fireplace, to the murky voids beneath the tables, scanning every nook and cranny for any sort of danger lurking in the shadows.

Smoke and Ember padded slowly forward on either side of her, fanning out across the living hall floor.

"Go flush it out," she whispered as she searched the shadows.

She made her way carefully over to the Grand Staircase. Leaning over the railing, she peered up to the third and fourth floors above her, thinking that maybe the scream had come from up there, but she saw nothing out of place.

She gazed down the steps that flowed in a sweeping arc to the first floor. *Nothing.*

But when she looked straight down over the railing, through the spiral of the staircase, to the area of floor directly below her, she saw it.

A chill ran up her spine.

There was a dark shape lying on the floor.

She reflexively glanced behind her, filled with a sudden feeling that someone was creeping up on her.

She scanned the moonlit living hall once more, still sensing the presence of something. Smoke and Ember had disappeared, so she was alone.

Her instincts were telling her to go right back into her bedroom, shut the door, lock it, and hide. But she knew she couldn't do that.

We all have a job to do, she thought. *And this is mine.*

When she looked over the railing again, the dark shape was still there on the floor, exactly where it had been. No tricks of the mind this time.

Slowly pulling in a long, steady breath, she crept down the stairway, watching the slide of the shadows as she went. The moon shone through the windows of the Grand Staircase, casting everything in a bright silver light.

When she finally reached the bottom of the stairs, she saw the shape more clearly. It was lying on the floor. Very still. The body of a man.

Goose bumps rose up on her arms and her temples began to pound.

She glanced across the Main Hall toward the Winter Garden and down the corridor toward the Billiard Room.

There was no movement, no people, just the moonlight and the shadows, and the ticking of the grandfather clock in the Main Hall.

She made her way slowly toward the body.

The man was wearing a simple white cotton nightshift and she could see his bare feet. It was as if he had come running out of his room.

Carefully avoiding the pool of dark liquid that was seeping across the stone floor from his head, she moved closer and looked at his face.

It was Mr. Kettering, the gentleman who had come in late to the dinner, just as she had. She had not known him, but he had seemed like a kind and good man. And now he was dead.

She slowly tilted her head and looked up at the third floor some fifty feet above.

Had he come out of his guest room and fallen over the railing by accident?

And then she remembered the sound of commotion and the horrified scream, and the intense fear that she had felt when she stepped outside her room.

Had he seen something so frightening that he'd flung himself over the railing to get away from it?

Not wanting to look down at the gruesome sight of the dead Mr. Kettering again, she traced her eyes along the arc of the stairs. It had always disturbed her how on some nights the Grand Staircase looked so lovely and benevolent in spirit, but other nights, when the moonlight poured in, it seemed haunted with a pale, cold menace.

Tap-tap-tap . . .

She quickly tilted her head toward a sound in the distance.

Tap-tap-tap . . .

Coming closer. Tiny cloven hooves on the stone floor.

Tap-tap-tap . . .

Fear flooded into her limbs. Her body froze, unable to move. Suddenly, she felt as if she was being hunted again, like she was being tracked down. She was going to be killed. Was this the terror that had driven Mr. Kettering over the railing? Should she try to spin and fight? Should she try to flee?

Tap-tap-tap . . .

Whatever it was, it was right behind her now. Just a few feet away. But she was too frightened to turn and look.

A loud crashing noise exploded on the second floor above her, then the wailing caterwaul of a terrified cat. It was Ember!

As Serafina leapt to her feet, she glanced behind her, bracing herself for a startling fright. But to her surprise, there was nothing there.

What she thought had been there just a moment before was gone now.

She didn't have time to think about it. She sprinted up the stairway to help her cat.

She could hear the snarling, hissing little tabby fighting something, lamps getting knocked over, vases smashing onto the floor, like she was in a fierce, knock-down, drag-out battle to the death.

That ain't no rat, Serafina thought as she ran. And as she came up to the top of the stairway, she saw it. At first her brain couldn't comprehend what she was seeing. It appeared to be a hunched, lizardlike creature, about the size of a dog, but it had scaly skin, clawed feet, a long, writhing tail, leathery bat-like wings, and ugly bulging eyes. The sight of the unnatural beast jolted her with such intense fear that it almost paralyzed her. But she was desperate to save Ember. She charged forward.

The bizarre beast scurried away from her, running beneath a chair and then a sofa. Then it scuttled down into a ventilation shaft and disappeared, leaving her with nothing but a shudder down her spine.

Serafina ran back to help her wounded cat. "Poor little kitten," she whispered as she picked Ember up and held her. "I've got ya. We're all right now."

But Ember's body went limp in her hands.

"Are you all right, little one?" she cried.

But as Serafina held her, she could tell that Ember wasn't all right.

Her little legs hung loose, her eyes were closed, and her head was tilted down at an odd angle.

Her body was still warm, but Ember was dead.

Serafina's stomach churned.

Whatever that terrifying creature was, it had killed her cat.

Serafina held her in her hands.

"Good-bye, little one," she whispered as she looked down at her, stroking the fur on her cat's head and ears. She wanted Ember to open her eyes, to look at her, to purr like she used to.

Tap-tap-tap . . .

Serafina heard the sound coming up behind her, little hooves on the hardwood floor.

Tap-tap-tap . . .

She slowly set Ember's body back down, and then turned and looked behind her.

Her eyes widened.

Here, on the second floor of Biltmore, down at the end of the darkened corridor that led to the nursery and to Braeden's bedroom, stood the white deer.

And it was staring straight at her.

The white deer looked at her with the blackest eyes she had ever seen, filled not just with the darkness of the midnight sky, but the unsettling moonlike shimmer of *knowing*.

Serafina did not turn, but she knew that the moon was visible in the window behind her. And as she studied the deer, she could swear that she saw the reflection of herself and the moon in the deer's eyes.

She thought it must be the same white deer she had seen before. But now it was larger in size and it had a full set of antlers sticking up from its head like clusters of branches. She knew that normally only male deer had antlers, but this was a doe. It seemed to be changing every time she saw it, as if it wasn't just growing at a startling rate, but morphing its shape from one thing to another.

As she gazed at it, she kept thinking it was going to *do* something, run away or attack her, or even speak, but it just stared at her with those beady black eyes.

"What do you want?" Serafina asked the deer. "Why are you here?"

The deer made some sort of noise, but she could not tell what it meant.

When Serafina took a small step to the left to get a bit closer to the escape of the staircase, the deer took a small step to the right.

Feeling a creeping shiver run up the back of her neck, Serafina glanced into the shadows behind her, half expecting some horrible beast to lunge out at her, but there was nothing there.

When she turned back to the deer, it was gone.

She was left standing there in confusion.

What in the world? she wondered in exasperation. *What is going on in this place?*

And then she remembered Ember. She turned and saw Ember's body lying on the floor.

Her heart filled with aching pain as she slowly crumpled onto her knees next to her dead little cat. Her hands rose to her face and pressed against the bridge of her nose, and she breathed long, ragged breaths, pulling air in through her fingers. Ember's head was tucked in the way she used to when she was a little kitten, and her paws were curled tight.

Serafina remembered finding Smoke and Ember when they were just bundles of fuzz a few weeks old, and bringing them into the house, and feeding them, and letting them sleep curled up with her in bed, purring. She remembered teaching them how to hunt for mice and rats, and telling them that they had to make sure there were no vermin in the house.

No vermin in the house, Serafina thought now, her heart breaking. *That's exactly what Ember had been trying to do.*

"Poor Ember, you must have fought so hard," she said, crying. "This was a kind of vermin that you were too little to fight."

She just hoped that Smoke had somehow managed to escape.

Tears welling up in her eyes, Serafina lifted Ember's limp body in her cupped hands. The little cat's head hung down on one side of her hands and her long tail hung down on the other. Her fur was still so soft and her body still warm.

Serafina slowly carried her back into their bedroom and gently set her on the windowsill. She would bury her out in the garden by the azaleas. But right now, there were other things she knew she must do.

When she was younger, hunting rats down in the basement, she had crept through the shadows alone night after night, but over the last year she had learned many things, and one of them was that sometimes she needed to get help.

She crossed the living hall, went into the alcove, and knocked on the oak door of Mr. Vanderbilt's bedroom.

"It's me, sir. It's Serafina," she called through the door. "Something has happened. You need to get up."

Knowing that it would be difficult to rouse Mr. Vanderbilt from sleep in the middle of the night, she was just about to call out again, but the door suddenly opened and he stood before her. It startled her to see that he was not only wide-awake at this hour, but fully dressed.

"What is it? What's happened?" he asked.

"There's been an attack," she said. "Mr. Kettering is . . ." She had trouble saying the words. She knew he had been Mr. Vanderbilt's friend. But she had to tell him. "Mr. Kettering is dead, sir."

"*What?*" Mr. Vanderbilt said in dismay. "How?"

"There was some sort of creature . . ." she said. "Mr. Kettering fell over the railing of the stairs."

"Tell me what it looked like," he demanded.

It startled her that he didn't seem surprised by the news that there was a murderous creature in the house. He just wanted the specifics. As she did her best to describe it, she glanced into Mr. Vanderbilt's private bedchamber behind him, looking for some clue as to why he was up in the middle of the night.

She could make out the deep maroon curtains blocking out the night's moonlight, and the matching upholstery on the dark walnut furniture. With all the ancient Greek frescoes, oil paintings, and bronze sculptures in his room, it was like an art museum all in itself, so different from the sunlit velvet airiness of Mrs. Vanderbilt's suite, which was connected to his by the formal Oak Sitting Room where they shared their breakfast each morning.

When she was finished describing the creature to him, Mr.

Vanderbilt nodded. "I think that's what I saw the other night. It frightened me so badly that I couldn't even utter words to describe it. I didn't think it could be real. I prayed I had imagined it. For days now, I have been doubting my own sanity."

"I understand," she said, and she truly did. "But now we both know that it's very real. And I'm so sorry about Mr. Kettering. I know he was your friend."

Mr. Vanderbilt nodded appreciatively, and said, "You had better take me to him."

Serafina led him along the corridor, through the smashed-up living hall where Ember had died, and then down the Grand Staircase.

But when they got to the bottom of the stairs, she stopped abruptly in astonishment.

The floor was empty.

Mr. Kettering's body was gone.

"I don't understand," Mr. Vanderbilt said, looking at her.

"I heard him scream, I know I did," Serafina said, her voice shaking with uncertainty. "And I saw Mr. Kettering's body lying right here. I swear it. Right here."

But even as she said the words, the doubt began to creep into her mind.

Serafina watched Mr. Vanderbilt carefully as he stared down at the empty space on the floor.

She still didn't understand how it was possible that Mr. Kettering's body wasn't there. There wasn't even any blood. But she had heard the struggle from her bedroom and she had seen his body lying on the floor. Had that all been a bad dream?

She knew that Mr. Vanderbilt had already wondered how and why she'd been so close to the hunting party when it was attacked. Now what would he think of her? She'd gotten him up in the middle of the night with outlandish stories of dead bodies lying in the Main Hall.

When she saw the strained, uncertain expression on his face she was sure he was regretting his decision to move her up to the second floor. It was obvious now that she couldn't protect him and his family. She had no idea what was going on. She couldn't even tell the difference between real and unreal!

"This is indeed inexplicable," Mr. Vanderbilt said in confusion, his eyes still staring at the empty spot on the floor. "But I know you wouldn't make something like this up."

"I honestly don't understand where the body went . . ." she said in exasperation.

"It's possible that someone, or some*thing*, moved it," he said. "I will go and speak with the security manager. There has to be some kind of explanation."

It surprised her that he seemed so calm and logical about it all—she wasn't quite sure how he managed it—but there was something even more startling.

He believes me, she thought in wonder. *He actually believes me.*

It felt as if up to this moment she'd been buried in heavy stones, and now someone was lifting the stones away one by one. Finally, she had an ally, someone who truly trusted her, someone she could fight alongside. Maybe she wasn't losing her mind. It didn't seem possible that she had killed the hunters in the forest. And she was pretty sure she hadn't imagined Mr. Kettering's body lying on the floor. If someone as smart and honorable as Mr. Vanderbilt believed in her, then she should believe in herself.

She nodded in agreement with his plan, but Ember's death, and then Mr. Kettering's death, had shaken her badly, and her mind kept going back to the reason Mr. Vanderbilt had brought her up to the second floor. "I'm sure Baby Nell is fine, but I'm going to go back upstairs and make sure she's all right."

She quickly parted from him and hurried to the second floor. As she slipped into the darkened nursery and closed the door, she saw Baby Nell sleeping safely in her crib. A nursemaid usually attended to her, but Serafina was surprised to see that tonight Mrs. Vanderbilt was there, sound asleep in the moonlight, curled up on the settee beside the crib, her hair tumbling loosely around her shoulder. It was as if her mother's instinct had told her that something in the house was amiss.

Serafina could hear, beyond the closed nursery door, that the house had gone still and quiet again, and that suited her just fine. *We need some peace and quiet,* she thought.

She stepped over to the window and scanned the moonlit courtyard in front of the house, looking for any signs of trouble.

Pulling back from the window, she draped a blanket over her sleeping mistress, and stoked the embers in the fireplace to warm the room.

As she tiptoed back to the crib, she was expecting the baby to still be asleep, but little Nell looked up at her with her big beautiful eyes. The baby gazed at her for several seconds, then broke into a huge smile when she recognized her. Baby Nell began making little purring noises, imitating the sounds that Serafina had often made to her.

"Shh, shh," Serafina whispered gently, patting Nell before she woke up her mother.

Thonk-thonk.

Serafina jumped in surprise. Something had thudded against the nursery door. But then she realized what it was. When she opened the door a few inches, Smoke ran into the room.

"I'm glad to see you, my friend," she whispered, as she scooped him up into her arms and hugged him tight. But he was in no mood for cuddling. He jumped down from her arms and darted down the corridor, meowing. It wasn't like him to meow.

"What is it?" she asked as she closed the nursery door and went after him. "Show me."

She followed him around the corner, through the living hall, and down the Grand Staircase. She didn't want to leave Mrs. Vanderbilt and the baby, but it was clear that Smoke was on the trail of something.

"Where are you taking me?" she whispered, but Smoke just kept going, quiet and serious now.

As soon as he reached the first floor, he darted down the narrow servants' stairs into the basement and ran toward the kitchens.

"This better not be about getting a bowl of milk," she whispered.

Tap-tap-tap.

She stopped in the basement corridor and froze. It wasn't about a bowl of milk.

Tap-tap-tap.

The muscles in her back tightened.

Tap-tap-tap.

Her teeth clenched. *Not this again,* she thought.

Tap-tap-tap.

Fear pulsed through her veins, but she was sick of this! She wanted answers! She spun around, determined to confront her enemy once and for all.

In the split second it took her to turn, the corridor was already empty. She heard the *tap-tap-tap* of her enemy's feet trotting around the corner.

She dashed down the corridor and made the turn, only to catch a fleeting glimpse of something turning the next one.

She burst after it, rounding the next corner, but there was nothing there.

She paused and listened for any sort of sound coming from ahead of her. But then she heard the *tap-tap-tap* of the creature's footsteps immediately *behind* her.

That thing's wicked fast, she thought, but before she could even turn to see it, a clattering racket rose up from the kitchens, glass breaking, pots and pans crashing to the floor. A man screamed in horror. She charged toward the sound.

Her cat Smoke shot out of the Rotisserie Kitchen like a gray streak, his tail huge, his claws skittering across the tile floor in panic.

"Run, Smoke!" she shouted as they passed each other.

The moment she reached the doorway of the kitchen, she lurched back in confusion. Mr. Vanderbilt was there! And he was charging straight at Mr. Cobere, Biltmore's butcher and rotisserie cook.

Mr. Cobere tripped backward, trying desperately to escape him. "Stop! Please! No!" he begged as he threw up his shaking hands to defend himself. But Mr. Vanderbilt attacked, filled with a violence she had never seen in him.

Mr. Vanderbilt grabbed Mr. Cobere and shoved him back until the poor man crashed against the butcher block. He lost his balance and fell against the large black iron rotisserie spit where he had been roasting a haunch of venison on the cook fire.

As the two men grappled, Serafina froze in shock. Who was she supposed to fight, the attacker or the attacked?

"No! Please!" Mr. Cobere begged as Mr. Vanderbilt struck him repeatedly with his fist. Mr. Cobere tried to struggle away, tried to fight back, but he was a small man and there was little he could do. And then Mr. Vanderbilt grabbed one of the wrought-iron fire pokers and slammed it hard against his head. Poor Mr. Cobere toppled to the tiled floor.

Serafina gasped in horror.

Mr. Vanderbilt turned and saw her for the first time. His face looked bronze-colored in the dim, flickering glow of the rotisserie fire, and his eyes were filled with terrifying wildness. He dropped the iron poker to the floor with a ringing clatter and ran from the room, fleeing down the corridor.

She knew she should go after him, fight him, capture him, *something*, but she was too stunned by what she had just seen to even move.

A bout of black-haze dizziness swept through her like a sickening wave. She pressed her hand to the wall to steady herself. *How could it be?*

Her mind swirled in anguish and confusion, her temples pounding. It felt like everything she had ever counted on in the world was crashing down around her head. But she knew she had to stay focused, she had to stay sane.

Just get your wits, girl, she told herself fiercely.

She grabbed a rag from the counter, fell to her knees, and tried to stanch the blood oozing from Mr. Cobere's head.

His eyes were open, and he gazed up at her in utter shock of what had happened to him. "Why, Serafina?" he asked in a weak, raspy voice. "Why did he do that?"

"Just hold on, Mr. Cobere, hold on . . ." she cried, but even as he looked at her, his body went limp and his eyes went glassy.

Mr. Cobere was dead.

And Mr. Vanderbilt was the murderer.

29

She stumbled down the corridor away from the scene of the crime, every step she took pounding in her head, the walls of the passageway undulating with darkened colors. The floor felt slanted beneath her feet.

All she could see in her clouded mind was the sight of Mr. Cobere raising his arms to cover his head as Mr. Vanderbilt struck him down.

In all her dealings with him over the last year, Mr. Vanderbilt had always seemed like a fair and gentle man. She just couldn't understand how he could possibly have murdered Mr. Cobere. But she had seen it with her own eyes!

And she knew Mr. Cobere was a good man. He wasn't

some kind of criminal or demon or a treacherous fiend that Mr. Vanderbilt had to defend himself against.

As she made her way down the basement corridor, she could still hear the echo of Mr. Cobere's screams in her mind.

What was she going to do now? She had no place to go. No place was safe. If the master of Biltmore was a murderer, what was he going to do next? He had *seen* her watching him. He knew she had witnessed him killing Mr. Cobere.

She didn't want it to be true. She didn't want it to be real. But she knew it was.

There must be some dark, violent part of Mr. Vanderbilt that I didn't know about, she thought. *Did everyone have some sort of black panther living inside them?*

If she couldn't trust Mr. Vanderbilt, then who could she trust? The pain of it seeped through her brain.

When she finally made it to the workshop, she stumbled to her sleeping pa and crawled into his cot with him, desperate for any kind of refuge.

She knew she had to keep moving, she had to figure out what to do, but her legs had stopped working and her mind couldn't think. How do you respond to something that's impossible? How do you move?

Her pa stirred and muttered as he pulled her close. "What's wrong, Sera?"

She buried her face in his arms.

"What's wrong?" he asked her again.

"Everything," she cried in despair, her voice wet and raspy.

"I want to help you, Sera. What I can do?"

"Nothing," she said miserably.

How could she tell him that the man he admired most in the world was a murderer? How could she tell him that heinous, winged beasts were slithering into Biltmore? How could she tell him that his daughter was a strange, shape-shifting creature of the night? It was just too much.

"All these bad things keep happening, all jumbled together, but I don't know how to stop them!" she cried.

"Listen, Sera," he said, holding her tight, "when you're down in the muck of the swamp and your feet are stuck in the mud and the weeds are so thick you can't see in front of you, then you *know* what you gotta do."

"I don't!" she cried.

"You do, Sera! You *know*."

"I don't!"

"Are ya gonna say that the swamp is too big and you can't get across it? Are ya gonna sink down into the water of the swamp and give up? Will that get you home?"

"No," she said.

"No, it won't," he said emphatically. "If you're stuck in the swamp and you give up, it's gonna get darker, you're gonna get hungrier, colder, more and more tired. There's an old saying: *The only way out is through.* Do you understand? When it feels like you're stuck in a swamp, you gotta keep goin', Sera, that's what ya gotta do. You might be tired, you might be runnin' blind, but you gotta keep pushing. You go on faith."

"Faith?" she said doubtfully. It felt like the whole world had broken, every part of it shattering. "Faith in what?"

"Faith in what you know is true," he said forcefully. "It might be hard to see, but you find it. Faith in yourself. Faith that there must be an end to the swamp, that it has another side. *The only way out is through.* Do you understand what I'm saying?"

"I understand," she said, opening her eyes and wiping her nose. "But I gotta tell ya, Pa, I'm right in the middle of a big ol' swamp, and it's a bad one."

"You'll find your way, Sera," he said. "Just keep pushing through."

As she felt the black darkness in her heart beginning to fill with something else, she wanted to tell him everything right then and there. She wanted to tell him who she truly was, not just a girl, not just his daughter, but a catamount, a panther, half human, half cat, a being with two halves to her soul, and she had fought battles against the darkest of enemies. But she knew she couldn't tell him. Deep down, she was just too scared. If he knew the truth, what would he think of her? How would he react? She wanted to tell him that the whole world was a lie and it was crumbling down around them. But she lay there, just holding him, too scared to tell him any of it.

She dreamed of Braeden coming to her on the terrace beneath the stars and saying her name. She dreamed of a white deer with a red stain. But she awoke to the sound of a woman screaming.

"Get up, Sera," her pa said, shaking her. "Something has happened."

She followed her father down the corridor toward the kitchens. It appeared that the servants had come in to begin their day. Twenty cooks, scullery maids, and other servants were gathered outside the Rotisserie Kitchen, gasping and whispering and asking questions no one had answers to.

"What's this all about?" her pa asked as he approached them.

But Serafina's stomach twisted. She already knew.

"Is someone hurt?" her pa asked them, trying to get through the crowd. Her father had known Mr. Cobere. They had been friends. And he was just about to see him dead.

But then the crowd of servants suddenly parted as someone else approached from the other direction.

Serafina's heart lurched when she saw Mr. Vanderbilt coming down the corridor.

"What is going on here?" the master of the house demanded in a firm voice.

"Mr. Cobere is dead!" one of the washerwomen cried out, sobbing.

Mr. Vanderbilt's face went grim and he shoved his way through the bystanders.

There he is, Serafina thought. *The murderer. Right there!*

Her pa pulled her back from the crowd of servants and the gruesome sight of what was lying on the kitchen floor, saying, "You don't need to see this."

She didn't have the heart to tell him that she'd already seen it, she'd seen it bad, the murder and the blood, and the great Mr. Vanderbilt, his friend and employer, was the one who had done it!

As her father led her away from the commotion, Serafina could hear many of the people in the crowd whispering about what might have happened to Mr. Cobere. And then, just as she and her pa turned the corner of the far corridor, Mr. Vanderbilt's voice rang out. "Has anyone seen Serafina? I need Serafina!"

Serafina ducked down, her heart accelerating in panic. Was he going to drag her away someplace and kill her? Imprison her?

Accuse her of something? She had no idea how she could face Mr. Vanderbilt after what she saw him do.

There was a part of her that wanted to point at him in front of everyone and scream out, *He's the murderer! He's the murderer!* But there was another part of her that remembered the horrific way he had killed Mr. Cobere. She imagined Mr. Vanderbilt charging toward her, striking her with the iron fire poker. She had seen everything he did, and now he was going to kill her!

"I'm sorry, Pa," she said, hurrying forward without him. "I'll come back later, but I've got to go."

She scampered up the servants' stairs to the main floor and fled the house through the side door, headlong into the pouring rain.

Her running legs took her across the courtyard through the storm, the blustering wind buffeting her body as thunder and lightning crashed overhead.

When she reached the cover of the trees, she lunged forward and landed on four clawed feet.

Snarling with frustration, she raced through the forest, the wind and the rain whipping her face.

She had such power with these muscles, such sharpness in her teeth and claws. She could fight any enemy. But how could she fight Mr. Vanderbilt, a man she admired and looked up to? And if not Mr. Vanderbilt, then who? Who could she fight?

She kept running, not even thinking about where she was going. She followed rocky, narrow ridges and crossed through thick stands of rain-dripping pines.

When she noticed fresh claw marks and scratches on the trunks of several trees, she brought herself to a stop. She had seen scratches like this before.

Even through the rain, she smelled the strong odor of blood, and saw its dark stains on the pine-needles. Then she saw the body.

A small black bear cub was lying dead on the ground.

At first she thought that the search party, the men hunting for the beast, had shot the cub. But it was clear that something had attacked and killed it in the most vicious manner.

It seemed like death was everywhere, coming faster and faster. And she had no idea what was causing it or how to stop it.

She continued on, running beyond the pines, through a deep forest of oak and hemlock, and then down into a thick, watery marsh.

It wasn't until she saw the gravestones that she knew where she was going.

Why here? she thought. *Why do I keep getting drawn back here?*

Longing for Braeden, for a friend, for anyone who would understand, she made her way through the graveyard to the Angel's Glade.

When she shifted back into human form, she wiped the rain from her face and squinted up at the stone angel. The angel stood tall above her, her wings aloft and her sword held strong.

Serafina read the familiar inscription on the pedestal.

OUR CHARACTER ISN'T DEFINED

BY THE BATTLES WE WIN OR LOSE,

BUT BY THE BATTLES WE DARE TO FIGHT.

Serafina thought about holding Ember in her hands as she died, and Mr. Kettering lying dead on the floor, and the sight of Mr. Vanderbilt murdering Mr. Cobere. And she thought about all the other things she had seen.

"How?" she screamed up at the angel's unmoving, tear-stained face. "How do I fight this?"

Serafina lifted her hands and shook them at the angel. "What good are these claws when there's nothing I can attack? What good are these teeth when there's nothing I can bite? Do you want me to kill Mr. Vanderbilt? This isn't a battle! It's chaos!"

But no matter how loud she screamed, the angel did not reply. Her face remained as stone and stoic as it always did.

In the past, Serafina had always imagined that the angel was on her side, speaking to her and guiding her, deep in her heart. The angel had seemed to possess a wondrous inner magic—her glade always green, her sword always sharp, and her presence filled with the power to hold life and death at bay. But now the Angel's Glade seemed dead and lifeless, and she felt a pang of doubt whether the spirit of the angel was even real.

And the more she sank into her thoughts, the angrier she became. What exactly was she fighting for? For Biltmore, the place that hosted the hunters who had come to kill her kin? Was she fighting for Mr. Vanderbilt, a devious, two-faced rat of a man who had murdered Mr. Cobere? What was this ideal called Biltmore Estate?

"It's nothing!" she snarled. *"It's nothing!"*

As she gritted her teeth and turned from the statue, the torrent of the rain finally began to slow.

The rushing sound of the storm gradually fell away and all that remained was the rain dripping quietly from the bare branches of the trees and the mist rising from the ground.

As her mind cleared, and she began to calm, she thought about what her pa had told her.

The only way out is through.

But how?

There was no doubt she was stuck in the swamp just like he said—tired, lost, and losing hope.

How could she get through?

Over the last year, she'd come up out of the basement, found her claws, and learned to fight. She had defeated all her enemies in battle. But she couldn't claw her way out of this. She wasn't even sure what the *this* was. She wasn't even sure if she could trust what she had seen with her own eyes, what she had heard with her own ears, or even what she herself had done. How could any of it be true? She knew it couldn't be, but it was.

And what if what she was fighting for wasn't even worth fighting for? What if Biltmore itself was evil? What if Biltmore and the man who built it needed to be destroyed?

The more she thought about it, the more she realized that what scared her the most was that this time, she wasn't the hunter. She was the hunted. There was something a-prowl, killing them off one by one. She wasn't thinking—she was reacting. She was running. She'd been desperate to catch someone, to fight someone, but she was flailing. She was blind.

She had to figure out what her enemy was doing, what was driving him, what he wanted, and then maybe she could anticipate his next move. It was no good finding poor Mr. Kettering lying dead on the stone floor at the bottom of the Grand Staircase. He had already fallen. It was no good watching Mr. Vanderbilt kill Mr. Cobere. Before she could figure out what to do, the killing blow was already struck.

One of the things her pa had taught her from a young age was that when it seemed like everything was coming at her, when life was just too confusing and overwhelming to bear, then she should stop, sit down, and ask herself one question: What is the most important thing? What is the one thing that I *must* do? And then focus on doing it.

What is the one thing? she wondered. *What must I make sure I do no matter what?*

It did not take long for the answer to form clearly in her mind.

I must protect the good and innocent people of Biltmore.

That meant her pa, and Essie, and Mrs. Vanderbilt, and poor Jess, who she'd abandoned in the forest, and so many others. And most of all, it meant little Baby Nell.

She couldn't just sit here in the graveyard feeling sorry for herself, scared and shaking, a little mouse among other mice, all getting hunted one by one.

No matter how frightening it was, no matter how confusing, she had to do her job the best she could.

She had to protect them.

As she finally made her way back to Biltmore, the sun was setting and she found herself slipping through the foggy cover of a coming night, the clouds hanging so low that it was impossible to tell if she was below them or inside them.

She approached the house quietly and unseen, trusting no one.

Avoiding the front doors and the Main Hall of the house, where she feared there could be footmen, guests, or even Mr. Vanderbilt himself, she circled through the woods, down into the valley, and snuck along the back side, where the mansion's massive stone foundation rose up out of the steep slope like the wall of a castle.

She followed closely along the wall until she came to a small rectangular pit at its base, then wriggled her body down through its iron cover-grate. When she reached the bottom of the pit, she shinnied up a brick-lined vertical shaft some thirty feet, her back pressed against one side of the shaft and her feet pressed against the other, inching her way up like a little crevice-dwelling caterpillar.

She had used this method to enter Biltmore many times when her life in the basement had been unknown to the fancy folk above, and that was the secrecy she needed once again.

Thanks to the house's architect, Mr. Richard Morris Hunt, this well-hidden shaft fed fresh air to the giant boilers in the subbasement, like the windpipes of a gargantuan stone-and-steel beast, and established the central spine of the mansion's vast ventilation system.

When she reached the top of the shaft, she pushed up the metal grate, crawled out, and arrived in one of the subbasement storage rooms. Making her way through the piles of long, criss-crossing, storm-damaged copper gutters, she felt like she was crawling through the weathered bones of an ancient dinosaur in a dark, primordial cave.

She climbed up the narrow brick stairway to reach the basement level of the house. Then she darted from one shadow to the next, making sure that no one walking through the basement corridors late at night would see her, especially Mr. Vanderbilt or one of his men. Then she dashed up the back stairs to the second floor.

When she arrived in the back corridor near Mrs. Vanderbilt's suite of rooms, she crouched in a shadow, waiting and listening. The passageways of the second floor were dark and quiet. Everyone seemed asleep in their rooms.

She scurried forward and around the corner, slipping as quickly and quietly as she could past Mr. Vanderbilt's bedroom. He was the last person in the world she wanted to encounter in a dark, empty hallway.

As she passed the windows in the corridor, the arched glass roof of the Winter Garden was visible below. The white fog that she had traveled through to get home floated in the moonlight just outside the windows, like ghosts waiting to get inside.

But as she walked through the second floor living hall to get to the other side of the house, her pace faltered. She knew it wasn't possible, but when she looked across, she could swear the fog was now actually *inside* the room, floating over all the empty chairs and sofas, and around the cross-armed wrought-iron lamps standing like scarecrows in the pale, cold moonlight.

It felt as if she had been in this moment before.

But it's just a trick of the light, she told herself. *It's impossible for the fog to be inside the house.*

She ducked past the railing of the Grand Staircase and the doors of several bedrooms, and then paused uncertainly when she reached the T at the end of the corridor, everything so still and empty in the darkness. The right led down a dark hallway to Braeden's bedroom, closed and unused. The left led to the nursery.

She had walked down this corridor and turned this corner to the nursery a hundred times, but now her skin was crawling and she stopped cold, shrinking into the shadow along the wall.

There's something there, she thought as she stared at the corner and tried to keep her breathing steady.

It's right there.

She jumped violently when her cat Smoke burst toward her, his tail as thick as a feather duster. He ran straight to her and circled his body around her legs.

Crouching down, she held the frightened cat in her hands, and tried to listen to what was ahead.

Just around the corner, she heard a slithering, scratching noise.

Her lips went dry and her temples began to pound. There was definitely something there.

It sounded like the tips of sharp claws digging into wood, like something scratching incessantly at the nursery door.

She leaned down and whispered to Smoke, "Get downstairs and out of the house. Hide in the stables!"

As the cat scurried away behind her, she heard his feet pattering rapidly across the floor and down the back stairs. *Keep going, Smoke.*

When she was sure he was safely away, she turned back toward the corner.

She crept slowly forward, her heart pounding in her chest.

The scratching, scratching, scratching at the nursery door

continued incessantly. Something was trying to dig its way into Baby Nell's room.

She came to the edge of the wall and slowly, ever so quietly, peeked her head around the corner to see what it was.

What she saw scratching at the bottom of the nursery door was a sinewy, four-legged creature with a long, twisting body, almost like a large lizard, but squatting on all fours like a mammal, and it had bare, dark gray, leathery skin, bulging muscles, and visible protrusions of vertebrae along the length of its spine. Its neck was two or three times longer than any natural animal she had ever beheld. And its almost doglike, hairless head had long, sharply pointed ears, bulbous eyes, and a prodigious snout with rows of sharp, protruding teeth. In movement, it was fast, continuously scratching and sniffing as if it knew exactly what was on the other side of the door it was working desperately to dig through. In mind, it seemed obsessed, like a starved animal digging for a succulent piece of food.

She pulled back from the corner, her muscles pulsing, readying her for the fight.

This wasn't the exact beast that attacked Ember and Mr. Kettering. The other one had wings and its head was a different shape. But it was similar. She remembered the scratches in the Vestibule, and Ember running behind the planter and down into the hole. Then the sight of the dead bear cub in the forest flashed into her mind. Whatever these terrifying things were, they had a penchant for killing small animals. She didn't know exactly how she was going to fight this one, but she knew she couldn't let it get anywhere near Baby Nell.

She had always been very careful about showing people who she was. No one currently at Biltmore had ever seen her as a panther. But she wasn't sure she could kill this beast in her human form. It looked exceedingly dangerous.

She decided she had to risk being seen.

So right then and there, in the darkened corridor on the second floor, just outside the nursery, she shifted into her feline form.

Suddenly, the corridor felt so small and narrow. Her large, muscled panther body seemed as if it could barely fit. And the smells of the wood flooring and Persian rugs were so foreign to her panther nose.

But she knew she had no time to linger. Lowering her long, black-furred body nearly to the floor, she inched forward, and then slunk like a shadow around the corner.

She crept down the corridor toward the exposed, hunched back of the creature as it dug at the base of the door. She stalked so slowly, so quietly, that the creature did not detect her.

She crept closer and closer, sometimes stopping completely, so still that she was invisible in the darkness, just waiting, and then she continued slowly onward, inch by inch, foot by foot, until she was just a few steps away.

The instant the creature noticed her sneaking up behind it, it jerked back and hissed in alarm.

She lunged forward, striking at it with her claws. But the screeching thing scampered straight up the side of the wall, tearing into the wallpaper and clanging against one of the brass sconces. She pounced at it, heaving her body against the wall with a thump, but it scuttled upside down along the ceiling like a spider or a crab. She leapt at it again, swinging her paw at it, desperate to catch it or kill it, but it scurried out of reach, slipped into an air vent, and disappeared.

Gone, she thought angrily, panting through her fangs.

She quickly shifted back into human form before anyone spotted her, then pressed her back against the nursery door and looked down the darkened corridor, guarding the only way into the baby's room.

As she caught her breath, she tried to make sense of what she had just seen.

Was the master of Biltmore some kind of sorcerer who was controlling these creatures, or were they wild beasts crawling in from the forests hunting their prey? And what about the four men who had been killed on the North Ridge? Had that been Mr. Vanderbilt as well? Or did he have help to do all of this?

She knew Mr. Vanderbilt had many loyal employees at Biltmore, but would they murder Mr. Kettering on the Grand Staircase and then hide the body? Maybe it was more likely that one of these weird creatures had dragged the body away and then lapped up the blood from the floor.

But still, Mr. Vanderbilt must have had some sort of accomplice, maybe more than one.

Her first thought was Mr. Doddman, the security manager Mr. Vanderbilt had hired a few weeks before. She wasn't sure if the brutish man had been a police commander, an army sergeant, or a wretched crook before he came to Biltmore, but he seemed more than capable of violence.

And there was Mr. Pratt and the other footmen, and the head butler, and Mr. Vanderbilt's new valet, and the stablemen, and so many others. She didn't even know where to begin.

And then she remembered Lieutenant Kinsley. She thought about how he always said "sir" when he spoke to Mr. Vanderbilt, and the way he took orders from him like he was his commanding officer. *I owe him a great debt,* Kinsley had said.

Kinsley had seemed like such a good man. But could she trust what *seemed*?

As she gazed down the length of the corridor, watching and listening, she had to keep her flinchy mind from imagining that she could see traces of fog drifting in the shadows. She didn't trust shadows anymore, and especially didn't trust fog.

When she was out in the forest, she had seen that Kinsley hadn't returned to the house with the rest of the search party. That meant he was still out there someplace. But why? Had

something happened to him or was he up to no good? Maybe he was the one who was controlling these strange creatures.

The truth was, she didn't know if Mr. Vanderbilt was working with accomplices or not. All she knew for sure was that he was a murderer and she had to do something about it. But what could she do? Who could she tell?

Good morning, Mrs. V, she imagined saying. *I hope Baby Nell is doing well today, and oh by the way, your husband is a murderer!*

The other thing she couldn't figure out was why Mr. Vanderbilt had asked her to move upstairs to the Louis XVI Room. Was it to get her out of the basement, away from the kitchens, so that he was free to murder Mr. Cobere?

Or did he ask her to move upstairs to protect his family? Did he know he was dangerous? A bizarre and startling thought sprang into her mind: What if he *wanted* her to kill him?

But what does the white deer have to do with this? she thought suddenly.

The more she wrangled with it all, the less any of it made sense.

It was like the entire Biltmore property was cursed in some way, like the house itself was murdering people.

But why? What was the rhyme and reason of it? Was there a pattern she wasn't seeing?

The first attack had been against the colonel, his daughter Jess, his friend Mr. Turner, the other hunter Mr. Suttleston, and the dog handler Isariah Mayfield.

And then she had found Mr. Kettering dead at the bottom of the stairs.

And then she had seen Mr. Vanderbilt murder Mr. Cobere in the kitchen.

She tried to think it through.

What did all of these victims have in common?

What was the pattern?

There is none, she thought in frustration as she pressed her back against the nursery door. *They're just random people who don't have anything in common at all. It's just death all around.*

How could she fight this? How could she defend against it?

Every day, every night, someone was dying. And it was getting worse.

At the far end of the corridor, she heard the sound of a claw scraping the wood wall.

She crouched, ready to spring.

The scratching noises moved toward her.

She peered into the darkness, looking for the source of the sound.

As the scratching came closer, she tried to figure out exactly where it was coming from, but then she realized it was actually coming from several different angles now, all moving toward her.

She readied herself for battle. Her heart pounded in her chest.

It sounded as if there were multiple creatures clawing their way toward her and the nursery door behind her.

They were surrounding her, *hunting* her.

Her eyes flitted from one shadow to the next, searching desperately for them, but she still couldn't see them.

It was impossible. How could she not see them?

The noises came even closer.

The creatures had to be just a few feet away from her now, but it was like they were invisible.

And then a thin stream of dust drifted down from above, the fine particles reflecting in the moonlight.

She snapped her eyes to the ceiling.

The creatures were above her!

They were in the air shafts!

While she was guarding the corridor, they had been crawling their way over her head. They were going to drop like clawed, leathery spiders into the nursery, right into the baby's crib.

Serafina charged into the room.

The moonlight was falling through the sheer white curtains of the bay window, casting the room in a haze of glowing fog.

She scanned the ceiling, looking for signs of the dangling creatures.

Mrs. Vanderbilt was asleep on the settee beside the crib, just as she had been the night before. Baby Nell was lying asleep in her crib, wearing her little sleeping outfit and a tiny cap on her head, all cuddled up, not too much bigger than Ember, and far smaller than a bear cub.

You have one job, Serafina, she thought fiercely as she scanned the ceiling again. *You've got to protect that baby! That's the one thing you absolutely must do.*

Bile rose in her throat as a desperate thought forced its way into her mind. She tried to swallow the bile down, but it burned.

Then she heard the scratching noises in the ceiling above her head. Fine lines of dust streamed down into the room.

The creatures were coming.

She didn't want to do what she was thinking. It was too horrible. But the more she thought about it, the more she knew she *had* to do it.

She glanced at the sleeping Mrs. Vanderbilt, and then leaned into the crib and lifted the baby into her arms.

She had to protect her.

She had to take her away from this place.

And she had to do it now, before it was too late.

Serafina clutched the whimpering baby to her chest and crept out of the room with her.

She scurried down the corridor, glancing this way and that as she ran, terrified that someone or some*thing* was going to catch them.

The thought that she was actually stealing Baby Nell from her mother made her sick to her stomach, and her vision blurred around the edges like she was running through a gray tunnel. But she had to protect the baby no matter what and she kept on running.

Every instinct in her body was telling her that the creatures were *hunting* the baby, that they'd follow her. The only consolation was that maybe they'd leave poor Mrs. Vanderbilt alone back in the nursery.

By the time Serafina made it to the second turn in the corridor, her chest hurt so bad she could barely breathe. She stopped at the corner, gasping and leaning her shoulder against the wall, Baby Nell cradled in her arms.

Just as she was about to continue and dash quickly past Mr. Vanderbilt's bedroom door, the door swung wide open.

Mr. Vanderbilt walked out of the room.

A burst of terror jolted through her body.

He seemed to be searching for something in the area outside his bedroom door.

She quickly stepped back from the corner and held the baby tight, praying she wouldn't squeal or cry.

Finally, she heard the sound of Mr. Vanderbilt's footsteps walking away from them, and then down the Grand Staircase.

As she began to breathe again, her skin prickled with the vestiges of fear still pulsating through her limbs.

Knowing it might be her only chance, she darted out and ran for the back stairs. She bounded up the steps two at a time until she reached the fourth floor, surprised by how much the baby in her arms slowed her down.

Running through the darkened corridor that led to the bedrooms of the sleeping maids and other female servants, she ducked through the tight passage beneath the North Tower, scuttled along the narrow arched hallway, and came to the third door on the right.

"Essie, I'm coming in," she whispered as she entered the

room and found the warm bundle of her friend covered in blankets in her bed. "Wake up, Essie," she said, touching her shoulder. "Please, I'm sorry, you've got to get up."

"What's goin' on?" Essie mumbled groggily, rubbing her face. "Am I late for my shift? Oh, miss, it's you! What are you doing up here? Is the house on fire?"

"I need your help," Serafina said.

"I'm ready," Essie said as she lurched out of bed and nearly tumbled to the floor. "Oh Lord, it's a baby!" Essie cried out when she saw Cornelia in Serafina's arms. "What are you doing with a baby? Is that—that's not—that's not Baby Nell, is it? What are you doing?"

"Something is wrong with Biltmore, Essie," she said. "We've got to get the baby out of here."

"Oh, Lord in heaven!" Essie said, her voice quaking.

"I need you to run down to the stables and get a carriage."

"Now, miss?" Essie said as she pulled on her cap. "Is it morning?"

"No, but we need it right away. The stable boy's name is Nolan. He sleeps by the horses. Tell him the carriage is for me and he'll do anything you say. I'll meet you in the Porte Cochere with the baby."

"I'm on my way, miss," Essie said as she pulled her coat over her nightgown and hurried out the door. Serafina heard her running down the corridor.

Once Essie was gone, and the darkened room went quiet and still again, Serafina looked down at Baby Nell in her arms and saw that her eyes were open and she was staring at her. It was then that she realized the true magnitude of what she was doing, how irreversible it was. Once she did this, that would be it. She could not take it back. The people of Biltmore weren't going to understand. They weren't going to forgive her. They were going to hate her. They'd kill her if they had to.

She wished she could somehow reach her pa and tell him what she doing and why, but she knew there was no time for that. It was far too dangerous. She had to get out.

As she snuck down the back stairs with the baby, now gurgling away in her arms, she began to hear the noises that she had prayed she wouldn't hear. A rushing wave of hissing and scratching was coming down the stairway behind them.

She hurried more quickly down the stairs, glancing over her shoulder into the blackness of the shadows above her.

She couldn't fight the creatures here, not like this, with the baby in her arms. And she knew there were at least two of the creatures pursuing them.

Then she heard the sounds of claws scrabbling through the walls around her.

There were more of them.

When she finally reached the first floor, she ran through the shadows toward the Porte Cochere, where she prayed the carriage would be waiting.

She desperately wished she could stop all this. She wished she could go back upstairs and convince Mrs. Vanderbilt to flee in the middle of the night with her and the baby. But the creatures were everywhere and there was death all around. If she couldn't trust Mr. Vanderbilt, then who could she trust? And she knew that she'd never be able to convince the mistress that her husband was the killer. Serafina barely believed it herself and she had seen him do it!

Just as she was about to reach the Porte Cochere, Baby Nell began to wriggle and squawk, as if she suddenly realized that some vile creature of the night had filched her from her mother's crib and was thieving her out into the cold.

At the same moment, Serafina heard a man's footsteps coming down the corridor toward her. She peered past the black shadows to where faint rays of moonlight were slicing in through the narrow windows. The bars of light and darkness flickered as the silhouette of the man moved through them. The murky shape of Mr. Vanderbilt came into view, walking straight at her, his expression grim, his eyes cast toward her, and a long iron fire poker clenched in his fist.

Serafina gasped and ran, gripping the squirming baby tighter to her chest. Nothing but the wind of movement now, pulling her hair, pressing against her cheeks, the baby's little fingers reaching up and grasping her face as she raced toward the door. Shifting the bawling baby to her left arm, she slammed her right shoulder against the door, working frantically at the lever until it flew open and she stumbled out.

"Go, Nolan, go!" she screamed to the skinny ten-year-old stable boy sitting atop the carriage as she sprinted toward it with the screeching bundle in her arms.

The startled Nolan snapped the reins of the four black horses, jolting them to attention, and his hollering shout drove them into a bolting gallop that lurched the carriage away.

"Here!" Essie called as she threw open the carriage door from the inside, and Serafina leapt in, tumbling onto the carriage floor with her arms still wrapped around the crying baby.

"Fly, Nolan, fly!" she shouted as she clambered to her feet in the swaying carriage, the baby in her arms.

Nolan drove the running horses with wild shouts and snapping reins, their steel-shod hooves clattering on the cobblestones of the courtyard, rising up into the night and filling the house with ominous, echoing sound.

As the galloping horses charged out through the main gate, Serafina peered through the small window at the back of the carriage. The last thing she saw was the lights on Biltmore's second floor coming on. And the last thing she heard was a terrifying sound rising up into the night, a shriek that could only be one thing: a mother screaming for her missing child.

The carriage swayed back and forth as the horses traveled down the road at a fast, steady clip. The baby was quiet now, but looking up at her with uncertain, worried eyes.

"I've got you, Nell," Serafina whispered to her reassuringly, and the baby replied to her with soft cooing, babbling noises.

"What are we doing, miss?" Essie asked, her voice strained and anxious as she stared wide-eyed at her from the opposite seat.

"We're keeping the baby safe," Serafina said.

They were traveling down the Approach Road, which wound its way through the forest for three miles toward Biltmore Village, where there was a collection of small houses, shops, and a train station. She thought that if they could just get through Biltmore's outer gate and reach the village, then they'd somehow be safe.

"I don't know my way around the village, Essie," she said. "I'm going to need your help when we get there."

"But why isn't the mistress with us?" Essie asked. "Did she tell you to do this?"

"The truth is, she didn't, but it needed to be done to protect the baby."

"Who was that man coming out of the house behind you with that stick? It looked like Mr. Vanderbilt."

"Yes, it was him," Serafina said soberly, knowing that it wasn't going to settle well with her companion.

Essie swallowed hard as she gazed at her, and then said, "Are you sure we're doin' the right thing, miss?"

"I don't understand it all, either," she admitted. "But there was no time to talk to anyone. We just needed to get out of there."

"But we're goin' back, right?" Essie asked. "I mean, we ain't really leavin'."

It was hard to imagine, but once they reached the village, she might have to keep going, as far away from Biltmore as she could get, all the way to Asheville and beyond if she had to.

As she and Essie were talking, Serafina saw something through the back window of the carriage. She leaned forward and peered through the glass. In the distance, a group of dark shapes were coming up behind them on the road.

It took her several seconds to make out that ten or twenty

men on horseback were following them, whipping their running horses mercilessly.

Serafina threw open the side window and screamed up at Nolan, "Riders behind us! We can't let them catch us!"

"Got it, miss!" Nolan called back to her.

He snapped the reins and shouted "Yee-haa!" to his team of horses. The carriage lurched forward as the horses accelerated into a canter, pulling the carriage at great speed, thundering down the road, Nolan's wild shouts driving them on.

But when Serafina looked back behind them, she saw that the riders were still coming.

Their carriage crossed stone bridges over rushing creeks, and rounded tight curves that snaked through the hilly terrain, but their pursuers did not relent. The men behind them were closing the distance between them, spurring their horses on, striking them with their crops, coming closer and closer.

"We need to go faster, Nolan!" Serafina shouted again.

"I'm trying, Miss!" Nolan cried out. With the next snap of the reins the four black horses bent their necks and broke into a full-out gallop, yanking the carriage forward at startling speed. Serafina held Baby Nell tight as the carriage was buffeted back and forth, the baby's bright, wide eyes gazing up at her in bewilderment.

"Oh Lord, please don't let us die!" Essie screamed.

"Faster, Nolan!" Serafina screamed. Hearing the turmoil in her voice, Baby Nell began to wail for her mother.

"There's another carriage!" Nolan shouted.

Had she misheard him? How could another carriage have caught up with them so quickly? And then she realized that it wasn't *behind* them.

She peered out ahead of them. A black coach was barreling down the road toward them. Nolan pulled the reins, steering their carriage around a sharp bend in the narrow road, the whole carriage careening wildly. Essie screamed and pressed her outstretched hands to the inner walls as the carriage tilted dangerously to the side.

"Hang on, everybody!" Nolan shouted.

Serafina tucked her knees, wrapped her arms around the baby, and held on tight.

The wheels of the carriage skittered off the edge of the road, biting into the gravel, throwing dirt and rocks in all directions until the wheels collapsed into the ditch and the whole carriage toppled over with a terrific crash, and then scraped along its side, tearing itself apart as the horses neighed and battled against their twisting harnesses.

The crashing carriage heaved her and banged her body, one blow after another as she tumbled against the walls and the roof, holding Baby Nell tight in her arms.

When they finally came to a stop, she found herself upside down, crumpled on top of herself, cradling the baby to her chest. She quickly hugged the baby close and cuddled her reassuringly. "Don't worry," she whispered to the little one. "We're gonna make it out of here just fine. You watch."

But the truth was that the roof of the carriage had come

down on top of them, and the walls had collapsed like an accordion with them inside.

She heard the movements and gasping breaths of someone digging them out of the wreckage, frantically pulling the debris away.

"Come on, we've got to get them out!" the voice shouted, and a second person joined in the effort.

But who was it? It couldn't be Nolan or Essie. They were undoubtedly just as buried as she and Nell were.

"Are you hurt?" the voice asked in a shaking, worried tone. "Take my hand."

Serafina reached up to the boy's outstretched hand and grasped it in astonishment. The moment they touched she knew exactly who it was.

It felt like it was impossible, but her eyes were telling her that Braeden was right in front of her.

"Are you hurt?" he asked again as he helped her to her feet. "Is Cornelia all right?" He examined the baby, running his hands over the little one's head and body with the anxious concern of an older cousin.

"I think she's all right," Serafina said, cradling the baby.

As Serafina glanced at the wreckage of the pulverized carriage, a coachman in a long greatcoat and tall hat was helping Nolan scramble out of a tangle of horse reins and busted-up boards. And closer to her, a second pile of the wreckage began to move.

"Are we all dead and gone?" Essie asked loudly as she pushed aside the debris and crawled out.

"Oh, Essie, are you hurt?" Serafina gasped, hurrying toward her.

"My head took a wallop," Essie said, as she rubbed her temple and squinted her eye, "but I ain't no worse for it."

Braeden looked around at all of them, and then brought his gaze back to Serafina. "What were you all doing out here at this time of night with the baby?"

"And why were you going so fast around that turn?" the coachman challenged.

As if in reply, the thundering sound of running horses came barreling around the bend in the road.

"Stop right there!" one of the riders shouted as a dozen grim-faced men surrounded them and aimed their rifles at Serafina.

She sucked in a sudden breath and froze. With the baby in her arms, and Braeden and the others around her, she could not fight them or run.

The riders dismounted and surrounded her, pointing their rifles directly at her head.

"What are you doing?" Braeden shouted at them, shocked by their behavior.

"Do not try to move!" Mr. Doddman ordered Serafina, ignoring Braeden.

The security manager was a heavyset, thick-necked man with massive hands and callused knuckles, aiming the long black barrel of his rifle straight at her, just inches from her face, as if he was trying to make sure that when he pulled the trigger he wouldn't hit the baby in her arms.

Knowing she was a single finger-twitch from death, Serafina remained perfectly still. In all her life, she had never had the muzzle of a gun pointed at her. Now there were twelve. If any one of these men decided to pull the trigger, or even sneezed, she was dead.

"Stop this!" Braeden shouted at them.

"Step away, Master Braeden," Mr. Doddman ordered him.

"What do you think you're doing?" Braeden asked angrily.

In the distance, beyond the men who surrounded her, Serafina saw two more riders approaching.

Mr. and Mrs. Vanderbilt rode up on their cantering horses and came to a sudden stop. Serafina's stomach knotted at the sight of them.

The master and mistress of Biltmore quickly dismounted, handed their reins to one of the men, and hurried toward her and the baby.

"Serafina, what are you doing?" Mrs. Vanderbilt demanded, her voice roiling with dismay.

"I was trying to help—" Serafina cried, the anguish ripping through her body.

"But why did you take Cornelia?" Mrs. Vanderbilt shouted at her.

Braeden watched all of this in confusion.

"I swear I would never do anything to hurt the baby," Serafina pleaded with Mrs. Vanderbilt. "I was trying to protect her!"

Mr. Vanderbilt strode straight at her, pulling off his leather riding gloves as he came, his dark eyes glaring with fury. Surrounded by his men, she was defenseless against him.

"Get the baby," Mr. Vanderbilt ordered, the tenor of his voice vibrating with harshness.

Mr. Doddman immediately shouldered his rifle and stomped forward. He ripped Cornelia from her arms and thrust the now crying baby at her mother.

Serafina didn't try to resist him as his giant hand shoved her brutally to the ground. "Down! Now!" he shouted at her, his spittle hitting her in the face.

"Stop this!" Braeden screamed, charging forward and trying to hold Mr. Doddman back from hurting her.

But Serafina didn't cry out or fight back. She knew she couldn't, not here, not like this.

She lay on the ground where Mr. Doddman pushed her. As she looked up at Braeden, and Mr. and Mrs. Vanderbilt, and all the surrounding men, she knew she couldn't explain everything she'd seen and she couldn't accuse Mr. Vanderbilt of murder. No one would believe anything she said.

The physical pain of the carriage crash and being shoved down to the rocky ground at the side of the road began to radiate through her body, the aches and bruises, but worse than that was the sickening feeling of what she had done to poor Mrs. Vanderbilt and how it must look to all of them.

"Aunt Edith, why are you treating Serafina like this?" Braeden beseeched Mrs. Vanderbilt.

"She kidnapped Cornelia, Braeden!" Mrs. Vanderbilt screamed at him.

"If she took the baby from the house," Braeden said firmly, "then Cornelia's life must have been in danger. Don't you see that?"

As Serafina gazed up at Braeden, her heart began to swell.

He *believed* in her.

He had seen for himself that she had been fleeing the house with the baby in the middle of the night. And now they were all shouting at her and pointing their guns at her, accusing her of a most heinous crime. All the evidence in front of Braeden's eyes was clearly and obviously against her. But it didn't seem to matter to him. He *believed* in her, without doubt, without question.

"Uncle," Braeden said, moving toward him. "You *know* Serafina is the Guardian of Biltmore, the protector of our family. Why would you ever doubt this? Why?"

"You don't understand what's been happening here, Braeden," Mr. Vanderbilt told him.

"Look at her," Braeden said, gesturing toward her on the ground. "You don't think she could just flee from you right now and disappear into the darkness if she wanted to? You don't think she could fight all of you? She was obviously trying to protect the baby, and she still is!"

"But where were you taking her?" Mrs. Vanderbilt cried out at Serafina.

Away from your husband, the murderer! Serafina wanted to scream in reply, but she knew she couldn't.

"If Serafina thought Cornelia was in danger, then she was in danger," Braeden said bluntly, the force rising in his voice.

"How many times does she have to save all of your lives for you to know this?"

"But she snatched Cornelia out of her crib and skulked away with her in the middle of the night!" Mrs. Vanderbilt said, straining with shaking emotion as she spoke. "She should have spoken to me!"

"She obviously had to act quickly. So now you chase her down and aim guns at her?" Braeden said, boiling with frustration.

Mr. Doddman, provoked by Braeden's insolent tone, pushed toward him and shouted at him in his gruff, commanding voice, "Tell us, boy, just how did you get here anyway?"

Braeden turned toward him and faced him head-on. "How did I get here?" he replied, his voice edged with sharpness.

"The trains do not arrive at the station in the middle of the night," Mr. Doddman challenged him.

"They do if your family owns the railroad and all the trains on it, Mr. Doddman," Braeden said fiercely as he stepped toward Serafina and pulled her up onto her feet. "Now put down your guns. This is foolish."

It was at that moment that she realized that it wasn't just luck that Braeden was here. He didn't just happen to be traveling down the road for no reason. He had come from New York with great speed and purpose. And she could see that Braeden's confidence in her was wearing down the resolve of her accusers.

"But what happened to you, Serafina?" Mrs. Vanderbilt asked, looking at her. "What did you see that made you do this? Why did you not speak to me first?"

Serafina stared back at her, trying not to glance over at Mr. Vanderbilt standing a few feet away.

"Tell us what you saw, girl," Mr. Doddman demanded, shoving her with his hand.

She felt an overwhelming urge to bite him with her long panther fangs. But she had to get out of this. She had to get these men away from her so that she could talk to Braeden alone and tell him what was really going on.

As she looked around at Mr. Doddman and all of the other men surrounding her, an idea came into her mind. It wasn't the whole truth, but it might be just the right amount of it.

"I saw two wickedly unnatural creatures," she said, purposefully putting a tremor of fear into her voice. "They were lizardlike, but with sharp teeth and long, nasty claws. One killed a bear in the forest. Another killed my cat. Then I saw the creatures trying to scratch their way into Baby Nell's bedroom."

Everyone around her stared at her in shock. Several of the men couldn't help but glance into the darkness of the forest behind them.

She lowered her voice to a barely audible whisper. "Mr. Vanderbilt saw the creatures, too."

"What did you say, girl?" Mr. Doddman said, shaking her by the shoulder.

"I said that Mr. Vanderbilt saw the creatures."

Everyone turned and looked at Mr. Vanderbilt.

The master of Biltmore studied her for several seconds. It was clear he didn't want to talk about strange creatures crawling through the house. But now he had no choice. He looked around at the others. "It is true," he admitted finally. "I did see some sort of unnatural beast."

"One of the creatures attacked and killed Mr. Kettering," Serafina said, hoping to stir a little more fear among her accusers, and sure enough, they all began looking out into the surrounding forest.

"And Mr. Cobere was killed as well," Mr. Vanderbilt said.

Serafina gasped, shocked by the deviousness of his lie. *He* had killed Mr. Cobere, not the creatures!

She didn't even know how to respond to what he had said, but she continued with her plan, turning to look at Mrs. Vanderbilt. "When I saw the creatures crawling into Baby Nell's room, I had to get her out of there as fast as I could. I'm so, so sorry I took her like that, but I had to!"

Mrs. Vanderbilt stared back at her, speechless.

Serafina could see in her mistress's eyes that maybe her anger and suspicion were finally beginning to subside.

Seeing the opportunity, Braeden stepped forward and spoke to everyone. "If there are nasty creatures prowling around, then we better all get to safety," he said, and many of the men immediately agreed with the young master.

"Let's mount up and get home," Mr. Vanderbilt ordered the men. "I want four guards around my wife and daughter on the way back."

"Yes, sir," several of the men said in unison.

"Mr. Doddman," Mr. Vanderbilt said as he turned toward the security manager. "When we get back to Biltmore, my family will be spending the rest of the night in my chambers instead of the nursery. Post additional guards around the room and throughout the second floor."

"Yes, sir. I'll see to it," Mr. Doddman said.

As she heard Mr. Vanderbilt's orders, Serafina's mind raced with suspicion. It made sense for all of them to get out of the forest, but the creatures were in the house as well. No place was safe. And Mr. Vanderbilt knew that. But Mr. Vanderbilt and the others were all so used to Biltmore being a place of refuge that their minds couldn't think in any other way.

Or maybe that wasn't it at all. Maybe Mr. Vanderbilt had a more sinister, hidden plan. Maybe it wasn't about safety, but entrapment. How could she convince them all that Biltmore itself was the danger, that the man in charge was the one they should be most frightened of?

All she knew for sure was that she still had to do her job, still had to protect little Cornelia and the other innocent people of Biltmore.

She watched as Mrs. Vanderbilt handed Cornelia to Essie, mounted her horse, and then took Cornelia back into her arms. There was only one way Mrs. V was returning to Biltmore, and that was with her baby. One of the men helped Essie up onto his horse, and they all began the journey home.

"Braeden," Mr. Vanderbilt said, looking at his nephew with harsh, troubled eyes. "I don't know what you're doing back here at Biltmore when you should be in New York, but you need to come with me now and explain yourself."

"I will, sir, I'll come right away, I'll explain everything," Braeden said quickly. "But I need to attend to the horses that may have been injured by the crash." He gestured toward Nolan and the coachman trying to disentangle the four black thoroughbreds from the wreckage of the carriage.

"Get yourself and the horses home as quickly as you can," Mr. Vanderbilt said as he climbed up into his saddle.

"I will, sir," Braeden said, nodding.

"And *you*," Mr. Vanderbilt said sternly as he turned toward Serafina and locked his black searing eyes on to hers. "I will see you at Biltmore as well."

Serafina stared at him, her heart pounding, but she did not reply and she did not look away.

Finally, Mr. Vanderbilt turned his horse and followed the other riders back up the road to Biltmore.

She knew there would come a time very soon that she would meet that man alone, face-to-face, and there would be no place for either of them to go.

36

The moment his uncle was gone, Braeden looked over at Serafina in relief, and then hurried on to help the entangled horses.

Nolan and the coachman used knives to cut the horses out of the hopelessly twisted harnesses as Braeden steadied the horses' heads.

"We're all right," Braeden whispered to the horses in quiet, reassuring tones. "We're all together."

She knew that years before, these four fine thoroughbreds had carried the caskets of Braeden's mother, father, brothers, and sisters during the funeral in New York City after a cata-strophic fire burned down the family home. Braeden and these four horses had been companions ever since. When he moved to Biltmore to live with his uncle, he came with no possessions other than his black dog Gidean, who had saved him from the fire, and these four black horses, who had saved him from the devastating sorrow that followed.

As Nolan and the coachman finally got the harnesses cut away, they led the horses out of the ditch and up onto the road.

"I'll take them on up to Biltmore, master," Nolan said, jumping onto the bare back of one of the horses.

"We'll be right behind you," Braeden said. "Be careful on the road."

As she and Braeden watched Nolan ride off with the horses, she said, "I'm very sorry I put them in danger."

"I know. Come on, let's get home," he said, gesturing toward the carriage he had arrived in.

"Do you think you can get us around all this wreckage, John?" he asked as the coachman climbed up into the driver's seat.

"I can manage it," the coachman said with a quick nod.

Serafina thought it was kind of Braeden to open the carriage's door for her and hold her hand as she stepped up into it. He was always a gentleman, even to a girl who was more often a prowling cat than a fancy young lady.

It wasn't until Braeden climbed into the closed space of the carriage, sat in the seat across from her, and let out a long sigh that she realized how nervous he'd been about standing up to his uncle and all those other men. He had seemed so brave, so resolute, but she realized now that his heart had probably been pounding just as hard as hers.

"Thank you for believing in me back there," she said, her voice quavering.

"You would have done the same for me," he said, nodding. Again, there was no doubt in him.

Sitting alone with him in the carriage as it traveled down the road reminded her of the first carriage they had ever been in together, a year before, traveling through a dark forest, not that different from this one.

"I'm very glad to see you," she said, and then, in as soft a voice as she could, she asked him the question that she couldn't help from asking. "After the night by the lake . . . what happened to you?"

Braeden dropped his eyes to the floor and slowly shook his head. "I'm so sorry, Serafina," he said, his voice rife with shame. "I left for New York early the next morning. I couldn't face you to say good-bye. After everything I said by the campfire, I didn't know how to tell you that I still had to go . . . I still had to leave. . . . The whole thing made me sick."

As she listened to his words, and heard the remorse in his voice, she could feel her heart opening up to him. She nodded, trying to show him that she understood. "I thought that you must have gone back, but I didn't know for sure," she said, more disappointed in her own confused, frightened, flinchy mind than in him, but he still took her words hard.

"I shouldn't have done it," he said, shaking his head. "I should have faced you. I should have come to you and said good-bye. I'm a total coward sometimes."

She looked at him and tilted her head in surprise. "You're

not a *total* coward," she said. "You're just a plain old, regular coward, a typical horseback-riding, train-jumping, animal-healing mountain boy. Nothing wrong with that. We seem to need those around here."

He smiled a little bit. "Thank you, but I *am* a coward, at least about some things."

"Maybe *some* things," she said. "But not where it counts. You stood up to those people. You were the only one who believed me."

"But tell me what's wrong," he said. "What happened to you after I left?"

"First, tell me about the white deer," she said.

He frowned in confusion. "Do you mean the little fawn?"

"Yes. What happened to it?"

"When I woke up, she looked like she was going to survive, so I released her back into the forest. I hope she's all right. Did you see her or something?"

She didn't even know where to begin. He had no idea what he had done or what had happened since.

"Tell me what you did after releasing the white deer."

"I cleaned up our camp so that no one would know that I snuck back home, and then I headed to the village to catch the next train to New York."

She nodded. All that made sense. She had been trying to tell herself that was definitely one of the possibilities. "But why are you here, Braeden?" she asked. "Your school must still be in session. Why did you come back now?"

He gazed at her without speaking; his eyes and face held

an expression that she could not fathom. Had her questions startled him? Was it embarrassment? Fear? It was a species of emotion she had never seen in him.

"Why did you come home, Braeden?" she asked him again.

He looked out the window of the moving carriage, and then down at the floor. "It was last night, or two nights ago, I don't even know anymore, I've been traveling so long," he said. "I was in my dorm room, and I was sleeping. It wasn't a dream and it wasn't a vision. It was more like a feeling. Like someone was calling out to me." Finally, he lifted his eyes and looked at her. "Like *you* were calling out to me, Serafina. I woke up. I listened for you. I didn't hear you again. But I could still *feel* you. And it was frightening. I didn't understand. But my heart was pounding. I could swear you were in trouble and you needed my help."

She listened to his story in amazement, remembering how she had lain in the Angel's Glade, her shoulder up against the pedestal of the statue as she cried out into the midnight sky.

"I *am* in trouble," she said finally. "And I *do* need your help."

"I came home as fast as I could," he said gently.

"You commandeered a train to do it," she said, smiling as she gazed at him.

"Well," he said, blushing. "One of the perks of being a Vanderbilt, I guess." And then he became far more serious. "But what's this all about? My uncle was so angry. And I've never seen my aunt so scared."

"She has good reason to be," Serafina said, glancing out the window into the darkness they were traveling through, then back at Braeden. "People have been dying ever since you left. I've been trying to figure out who the killer is and how I can stop him."

Braeden looked at her in surprise. "Why do you say 'him'? I thought you saw some sort of weird, unnatural creatures."

"There *are* creatures," she said. "But there is also a murderer, a man. I saw him."

"Did you get a good look at him?" Braeden asked, leaning toward her. "Who is it? We'll tell my uncle."

"This is going to be difficult for you to hear, Braeden. . . ."

"What do you mean? Why'd you say my name like that?" Braeden replied, his voice edged with a trace of fear. "What is it?"

"It's your uncle," she said, watching him carefully, trying to figure out how she could help him through this.

His brow furrowed. "I don't understand. What are you saying?"

"Your uncle killed Mr. Cobere."

"No, that can't be," Braeden said, shaking his head. "That's not possible."

"I saw him do it with my own eyes."

"My uncle would never kill someone. Or if he did, he must have been defending himself from an attack."

"No, he wasn't," she said firmly. "Mr. Cobere was begging him to stop. Your uncle struck him in the head with an iron fire poker and killed him."

Braeden stopped talking. His expression clouded as he tried to digest what she had told him. "But if that's true," he said finally, "then what does it all have to do with the white fawn and the strange creatures?"

"I don't know," she said. "That's exactly what we need to figure out."

As she and Braeden were talking, the carriage trundled along down the road, rocking gently back and forth. Despite everything that had happened and all there was yet to do, there was something invigorating about trying to solve a mystery with her old friend at her side.

She wasn't sure how much farther they had to go, but it looked as if they had left the forest and were now traveling past some of Biltmore's farm fields, which were bare for the coming winter.

Braeden's eyes narrowed as he looked out the window.

"What is that?" he asked.

She turned and looked.

"Stop the carriage!" she shouted to the driver.

The moon hung low and hazy in the night sky, casting the empty field in silver light as swirls of gray mist and fog drifted across it. Out in the distance, there was a man walking in the middle of the field. He looked like a young man, his blond hair almost white in the moonlight. He was carrying a rifle and something large draped over his shoulder. The man's face and arms were cut and bleeding. And by the way he was limping through the field, it was clear that he had been walking for a long time.

At first she thought he must be a hunter carrying the carcass of a deer he had shot. But as the man continued to trudge toward them, she realized that the body he was carrying was not a deer.

"Is that a person walking out there? Who is that?" Braeden asked.

"It's Lieutenant Kinsley . . ." Serafina said as she exited the carriage. "Come on, we've got to help him!"

As she ran across the field, the soft, tilled autumn earth pulled at her feet.

Lieutenant Kinsley's jacket was ripped and stained. One of his gloves was gone and the other torn and bloody. He looked like he barely had the strength to keep standing, let alone walking.

As he lifted his head and saw her coming toward him, his face filled with relief and he collapsed to his knees in exhaustion, gently laying the body he was carrying onto the ground.

"Kinsley," Serafina gasped as she held his shoulders to keep him upright.

"I found her," he muttered, nearly out of his mind with fatigue.

Lying on the ground beside him there was the body of a girl, her neck smudged with mud, her hair tangled with sticks, and her fingers so curled from the cold that she looked dead. But she was tucked in on herself, her arms crossed over her chest, and she was visibly shivering. When the girl finally lifted her head, the first thing Serafina saw were her bright sapphire-blue eyes.

"Jess!" Serafina gasped, and threw her arms around her.

"Serafina . . ." Jess muttered.

It was only when Serafina heard the exhausted raggedness of her friend's voice that she truly began to realize what Jess and Kinsley had been through.

Braeden knelt down and gave them water from a leather skin he had retrieved from the carriage, and fed them pieces of leftover biscuits that he had stashed in his satchel during his long journey home.

"What happened to you out there, Jess?" Serafina asked.

"The dogs treed two mountain lions, and my father started shooting . . ." Jess said, her words so faltering that she almost seemed delirious. "But over the years my father taught me many things. . . ."

"What did he teach you?" Serafina asked, grasping her arm.

"How to adjust the sights of a rifle," Jess replied, looking up at her. "Before we went out that night, I set his sights three clicks to the right, and five clicks down. He got so angry and confused when his shots kept missing, but there was no way he was going to hit those cats. . . ."

Serafina's heart swelled. It had been Jess all along!

"But then the fog rolled in," Jess continued. "There were gunshots and flashes of . . . I don't know what it was. . . . I saw something metal . . . and then something black. . . ." Jess looked straight at her now, her eyes wide. "I shouldn't have tampered with my father's gun, Serafina. He was shooting, but he kept missing. He couldn't defend himself! My father died because of me!"

Serafina held Jess as she cried.

"But what attacked you, Jess?" Braeden asked, his voice shaking.

"Something black came at me from the side. My horse reared up. I was thrown. When I woke up, my head was bleeding, my leg twisted. I could see my father and the other men were dead. I knew I needed to get back to Biltmore, but my horse was long gone. I could kind of limp along on foot, and I thought I remembered the way home. But as I was going, I saw a white deer in the underbrush. It began to follow me. I saw it behind me, then tracking alongside, getting closer and closer, like it was hunting me. I thought for sure I remembered how to get back to Biltmore, but I got hopelessly lost. I was so cold. I was sure I was going to die. But Lieutenant Kinsley found me. He gave me all his food and water, and he wrapped me in his coat. We rode together on his horse, but then we started seeing the white deer again. . . ."

"We need to stop talking," Kinsley said forcefully as he got himself up onto his feet. "There's no time for this." He scanned the line of trees in the distance. "We need to get out of here."

"You're safe now," Serafina said, putting her hand on his shoulder to reassure him. "We're almost home. We'll take you the rest of the way."

"I can help you to the carriage," Braeden said to the lieutenant, trying to hold Kinsley's arm to help him walk.

"You don't understand!" Kinsley snapped, pulling away from him. "It's still out there!"

He peered out across the field toward the forest, his trembling white fingers gripping his rifle. "It's not going to give up! It's coming for us!"

As she gazed at the panicking lieutenant, Serafina recognized the same fear and confusion she had felt, a sense that the world wasn't just coming apart at the seams in some random way, but that she was actually being tracked down. And she remembered seeing it in Mr. Vanderbilt's eyes the morning he arrived unexpectedly in the workshop.

"We've got to go!" Lieutenant Kinsley said, glancing frantically all around.

"You're right, let's go, right away," Serafina said, and pulled Jess to her feet.

The four of them trekked as quickly as they could across the field toward the carriage.

"How did you get back to Biltmore?" Serafina asked as she helped Jess along.

"We were crossing through a swamp, and the white deer came again," Jess said.

"I took a shot at it to scare it off, but it just kept coming," Kinsley said, looking over his shoulder. "Every time we shifted direction, it reflected our movements."

"Our horse panicked and ran," Jess said, gasping for breath as they moved quickly across the field. They were nearly to the carriage now. "One of its hooves went down into some kind of hole and it broke its leg. Kinsley had to put the poor animal out of its misery."

"My sweet Arabella is dead," Kinsley said, "and I was the one who killed her!"

"I'm so sorry, Kinsley," Serafina said as they finally arrived at the carriage.

"It's going to be all right now," Braeden assured them as he opened the carriage door and helped Jess inside. "We'll get you in front of a warm fire, with a hot cup of tea, and—"

Braeden stopped midsentence.

He froze right where he was standing, his eyes locked on something in the distance.

"She's back . . ." he said.

38

Serafina turned and saw the white deer standing at the top of the nearest hill, its antlers sticking up around its head.

"There it is!" Kinsley shouted. "Everybody go! I'll hold it off!"

Standing suddenly strong and fierce, he swung his rifle and aimed at the deer.

"No," Braeden said, lurching forward and pushing the rifle down, a reflex to protect any animal from harm. "Don't shoot her."

Kinsley pushed him away. "You don't understand, Braeden. It's been hunting us!"

And then he retook his aim at the deer and pulled the trigger. His rifle flashed in the night with a startling *crack*. But even more startling, Serafina heard the bullet whiz past her ear and smash through the window of the carriage behind her.

"We can't let it get any closer!" Kinsley screamed as he levered his rifle and shot again. The bullet hit the dirt at their feet.

The bullets are being deflected, Serafina thought suddenly, *like reflected light splintering from a diamond.*

Kinsley levered another cartridge and fired again.

"No, Kinsley, stop shooting!" she screamed as she lunged toward him, but it was too late. He pulled the trigger.

"Aaagh!" Kinsley shouted out in pain and surprise as the bullet ripped through his arm. He dropped his rifle and clasped his hand against the bloody wound, stumbling back against the wheel of the carriage, and then collapsing to the ground.

"What in tarnation is going on?" the coachman asked as he hurried down from the driver's seat in a panic and pulled a knife from his belt. "What is that thing out there?"

The white deer began walking toward them.

Serafina's heart hammered in her chest. The moment she began to move, she could feel the deep, soft soil clinging to her feet.

And then she caught something out of the corner of her eye and turned.

"Braeden, what is that coming toward us?"

A cold, moonlit fog had risen from the moist soil of the farm field, and there were three shapes rushing toward them out of the trees from the direction of the house.

"It . . . I . . ." Braeden stammered.

"Run!" Kinsley shouted as he struggled back up onto his feet despite his bleeding wound.

Serafina gazed in astonishment at the three shapes coming toward them, unable to believe what she was seeing.

A living, flesh-and-blood medieval warrior—a young woman clad in full plate armor and brandishing a long, steel-tipped spear—was charging toward them. And there were two huge male African lions charging with her.

"All of you, run!" Kinsley shouted again.

But Serafina did not run.

She didn't understand what she was seeing. But she knew she couldn't let herself and her friends die.

"Into the carriage, now!" she shouted at Braeden and Jess as she pushed them inside and closed the door behind them.

Then she turned toward the oncoming attackers and shifted into a black panther.

The knife-wielding coachman standing nearby screamed at the sight of her. A medieval warrior, a pair of African lions, and now a strange, black-haired thirteen-year-old girl changing into a black panther right before his eyes was all too much for him. He dropped his knife and bolted across the field in panic. She wanted to go after him, to show him that she didn't mean him any harm, but she knew she couldn't. She had to face the attackers charging toward her and Kinsley. Sticking together was their only hope.

As she turned to join the lieutenant, she bared her panther

fangs with a snarl of readiness and took her place at his side. Kinsley's eyes went wide in startled surprise as he said, "Well, that explains a lot!"

Then he pivoted his rifle and pointed it at the warrior and the lions bounding toward them.

He stood without fear or hesitation, and he aimed with perfect steadiness. But when he pulled the trigger, he shouted at the pain of the rifle's stock jamming into his wounded shoulder.

His first shot hit the warrior in the chest, but the bullet thudded against the slope of her fluted-steel breastplate. He immediately levered his rifle and shot again.

As their enemies charged toward them across the field, Serafina crouched, readying herself for the incoming attack.

Kinsley's second bullet hit the curve of the warrior's shoulder plate, but sparked away without doing her any harm. Despite the bullets striking her, the warrior kept coming, completely unafraid, thrusting her spear ahead of her.

And then one of the running lions spotted the coachman fleeing across the field in the distance and sped toward him. Serafina's heart lurched. She wanted to run to him, to protect him, but she knew it was too late.

The coachman screeched in horror as the great maned beast pounced onto his back and slammed him to the ground. The bleeding, screaming man scrambled away on all fours and got to his feet. But the lion lunged forward with incredible speed and struck him with its claws, knocking him down again.

Serafina couldn't believe the impossibility of what she was witnessing before her eyes. How could all this be happening?

How could a medieval warrior and two African lions even be here?

Kinsley fired again, their enemies seconds away now.

The wounded coachman punched and kicked, rolled through the dirt, and broke free, then sprang up and limped away, determined to stay alive. The lion hurled itself forward and tackled him, clamping its front paws around him, the full weight of its body dragging him down as it sank its massive fangs into his neck. When the screaming stopped, there was no doubt in Serafina's mind that the poor man was dead.

And then the lion was up and running again, sprinting to rejoin the other two attackers racing toward her and Kinsley. The sight of it startled her. A normal predator didn't immediately abandon its kill to join another fight, but here it came, straight at them.

Her powerful panther heart pounded in her chest. Her muscles tightened. At the last second, as the two big cats burst ahead of the armored warrior, Serafina leapt forward, her long black body speeding across the ground to meet them head-on.

39

Knowing she couldn't fight both lions at the same time, she attacked the closest one with everything she had. Her plan was to kill it quickly and move on to the next before they could gang up on her.

But the first of the five-hundred-pound beasts reared up on its hind legs and slammed into her, chest-to-chest. The lion wrapped its front legs around her in a violent, bearlike embrace, then dug its claws deep into her back and threw her to the ground. The heavy blow immediately stunned and knocked the wind out of her. And then the lion held her down by the neck, its massive jaws clenched tight, pinning her on her back, her legs flailing helplessly in the air.

Any thought that the attackers were figments of her jittery

imagination or ghosts in the autumn mist was instantly gone now. She was seconds from suffocation.

Pinned upside down by the lion's colossal weight, she twisted her long, feline spine, bent herself in half, and snagged all four of her clawed paws onto the lion's face. Then she pushed. The lion roared with the pain of her claws tearing through its skin and muscles, scratching against the bone, as it tried to wrench itself free.

She burst upward, spinning in midair, and landed on top of it, clawing into its sides. But with a deafening, guttural growl, the lion twisted away, ripping into her and trying to clamp on to her head with its long fangs.

Serafina spun again, clawing the lion's back. Then the lion twisted and turned and threw her off, lunging at her with a fierce triple swipe of its claws as it charged. Serafina sprang back, and back again, dodging the swipes, then threw herself into the lion with a snarling, biting counterattack.

The second lion lunged at her at the same time, sending spasms of pain through her legs as it ripped four streaks of blood across her haunch. And she caught a glimpse of Kinsley striking at the armored warrior with a mighty swing of his rifle. It would have been a killing blow, but the warrior blocked the strike with the steel vambrace of her raised arm, then used her other hand to thrust the tip of her spear into Kinsley's stomach. Kinsley cried out in pain as he clutched at the shaft of the spear.

Outnumbered and outmatched, speed and agility were Serafina's only weapons against the two lions, her only means of survival. She clawed at one lion, then sprang at the other.

She bit the head of an incoming attacker, then dodged to the side, spun, and swatted the face of another. Back and forth, bite and claw, lunging and leaping, twisting and darting, she was everywhere, all the time.

But these lions would not give up. She had scratched them, pierced them, torn at their faces, but they would not retreat like normal cats would. They weren't *lions*, they were mindless killing machines.

She dashed away, ran twenty strides, and then pivoted. The two lions charged toward her. She lunged at the closest one just as she had done before. And just as before, it reared up onto its hind legs and wrapped its front legs around her, trying to throw her to the ground with the weight of its shoulders.

But this time, she didn't try to fight against its weight and strength. She didn't try to overpower it. She could not battle a male African lion in the way male African lions fought. Instead, she folded her body straight to the ground, dragging her claws down the entire length of the lion's exposed underside.

She felt her claws tearing into it, the blood coming down.

Just as the first lion collapsed and died, the second lion slammed into her. The two of them tumbled across the ground in a ball of snarling teeth and ripping claws.

Instead of trying to fight against it, she twisted herself upside down, turned underside-out, and sprang free. She leapt upward, spinning in midair, and came down hard on its back.

As her fangs clamped onto its spine, its body jolted and went still.

The moment the second lion was dead, Serafina pivoted

toward the armored warrior, who was thrusting her spear into the wounded Kinsley for the third time.

Snarling with anger, Serafina sprang toward her, flying through the air.

She pounced onto the warrior's back and tore her clanking, metal-clad body tumbling to the ground.

Leaping on top of her, Serafina clawed her and bit her, but she couldn't get through the warrior's armor plates. She scraped and scratched to no avail as the warrior pummeled her sides with her gauntleted fists.

Realizing that brute force wasn't going to work, Serafina extended the claws of her right paw, hooked them on to the warrior's uppermost shoulder plate, and pulled it back to expose the warrior's neck. Then she slammed her fangs into the warrior's throat and clenched her panther jaws.

With her full weight holding the warrior down, and her teeth clamping the warrior's throat, she sensed her enemy's death was near. Even as the warrior began to die, she kept fighting Serafina, kept trying to do as much damage as she could. But the truly disturbing thing was that she wasn't fighting to *live*. She wasn't fighting to *breathe*. There was no last-second burst of strength to escape, no all-consuming instinct to survive. Just as with the lions, it was as if killing was primary, and living was secondary.

As Serafina held the warrior's windpipe clamped shut, she felt the warrior's lungs begin to deflate, her heart stop beating, and her blood stop flowing.

Finally, the warrior was dead.

But it was as if, in some ways, she had never been truly alive.

Serafina crouched low over Kinsley's fallen body, growling as she protected him, her claws still out as she scanned the field for the next attack. When she looked over her shoulder to make sure Braeden and Jess were still safely inside the carriage, she saw their blanched faces peering out of the window at her and Kinsley. And then she searched the top of the distant hill and the forest beyond. But there were no more attackers, and the white deer was gone.

She shifted into human form and dropped to her knees beside Kinsley, staring at him in dismay.

He was lying on the ground flat on his back, sunk deep into the soil of the field, gasping desperately for breath. The skin of his face was white with deathly pallor as he gazed up at her in shock. It seemed so *wrong*! They had fought hard, they had stuck together, they had done everything right, but he was still down, still wounded, and there was nothing she could do!

"Just hold on, Kinsley," she cried. "We're gonna get you through this!"

But the truth was, she didn't know how to help him. She didn't know how to save him.

And as she pressed her hands against his wounds to stanch the bleeding, a lake of warm blood welled up between her fingers.

She tried to stop the bleeding, to hold him, to talk to him and give him hope. But Kinsley looked up at her one last time, and then his eyes drifted shut. A long, ragged breath escaped from his struggling body, and he went still.

She wasn't sure if he was dead or alive, but her chest filled with aching pain. All Kinsley wanted was to be a brave and worthy friend to Mr. Vanderbilt. All he wanted to do was lend a hand to the people around him. *I'll see you at dinner,* he had said to her the last time they parted.

"Braeden, Jess, come quickly!" she shouted toward the carriage.

Braeden came running out, Jess stumbling behind him.

"Kinsley's been stabbed," Serafina said, her eyes tearing up, as Braeden knelt down and put two of his fingers to the lieutenant's neck. She knew Braeden couldn't heal humans the way he could animals, but she desperately hoped he could help in some way.

"I can't feel a pulse," Braeden said, shaking his head.

Serafina's heart sank at the discouraged sound of his voice.

"He's not dead," Jess said from behind them.

They both turned in surprise.

"Look carefully at the bullet wound at his shoulder," she said. "The blood is welling up in the hole. If he were dead, his heart would be stopped, and the blood would sink to the lower part of his body."

Serafina felt a surge of relief and nodded to Jess: her eagle-eyed friend was back.

"We've got to get him to a doctor right away," Braeden said as they got to their feet and worked together to drag Kinsley's unconscious body.

As they pulled him toward the carriage, Serafina gazed sadly out across the field at the body of the coachman in the distance. They would need to return for him later.

"Get back to Biltmore as fast as you can," Serafina said as Braeden climbed up into the driver's seat of the carriage and took up the reins of the horses.

"What about you?" Braeden asked, clearly startled that she wasn't coming.

"I'll catch up," she said.

As Braeden snapped the reins and the team of horses sped

the carriage away, Serafina ran back to where Kinsley had been wounded.

She gazed at the dead body of the medieval warrior lying on the ground. The girl looked about seventeen or eighteen years old, tall and strong, and she had a handsome face with white alabaster skin. The triangular white-and-gold battle standard attached to her spear lay crumpled around her, unusually long, as if it was designed to be seen across the murky chaos of a battlefield filled with the peasants, knights, and kings of old. There was nothing about her that seemed fake or conjured. There was even what looked like a gold cross hanging around her neck. And beneath the plates of her armor, she wore a tunic of chain mail.

And there Serafina paused.

Chain mail, she thought.

She slowly crouched down.

She reached out her hand, and touched her trembling fingers to the skin of the dead girl's cheek.

Her face felt cold.

But also *hard.*

Moments before, this girl's face had been flush with life. But now her cheek didn't feel warm. It didn't even feel like *skin.* More and more, it felt disturbingly like *stone.*

And not just stone, Serafina thought. *Limestone.* She knew limestone very well. Biltmore was constructed out of it.

A notion so strange that it could barely be believed crept into her mind.

She ran over to the two dead lions and reached out her hand.

Their bodies weren't limestone. But they weren't lion, either. They were cold and hard, smooth to the touch, and reddish in color.

"Italian rose marble," Serafina whispered in amazement.

As she said the words it felt as if a dam was breaking and a rushing flow of thoughts poured through her mind.

She shifted into panther form and ran for the carriage.

41

A thirteen-year-old human girl could not run as fast as cantering horses. But a panther could.

She streaked down the Approach Road and came up behind the moving carriage. The horses must not have had blinders on their harness that night, because they soon spotted her with their rear vision. Panicking, they broke into a full-on gallop to escape the vicious black predator charging up behind them.

It was just the burst of speed she wanted from them. The faster they got Kinsley home, the better.

She accelerated toward them and leapt onto the roof of the hurtling carriage. Then she shifted into human form and sat down in the driver's seat next to Braeden.

"Glad you made it," he said, glancing at her as he steered the carriage at barreling speed through Biltmore's main gate and into the courtyard.

"Mr. Pratt!" he called as he brought the carriage to a fast stop at the main doors. "Lieutenant Kinsley is badly hurt. Get him into the house right away and get the doctor."

"Yes, sir," Mr. Pratt replied, shouting for the assistance of several other footmen as he opened the carriage door to retrieve the lieutenant.

"Miss Serafina," Mr. Pratt said as she climbed down from the carriage roof. "Mr. Vanderbilt wants to see both you and the young master in his office immediately."

"I understand," she said as she helped Jess out of the carriage. "Please make sure you take care of Miss Braddick as well, Mr. Pratt. She needs food and water, and she needs to get warm."

"Yes, miss, right away," Mr. Pratt said as several of the footmen took Jess's arms and helped her into the house. "Don't worry, we'll attend to her."

It felt good to have their help, to be working together with the other servants of Biltmore, to be able to depend on them.

The moment she saw that Jess and Kinsley were in good hands, she looked at Braeden.

"Come on, we have things to do," she said and walked across the front terrace.

"But what about my uncle?" Braeden asked, the strain in his voice making it clear that he didn't want to see Mr. Vanderbilt any more than she did.

"We've got to figure this out," she said, pulling him along, and then she stopped him with her hand and pointed to the empty area of the terrace just to the side of Biltmore's front steps. "Look! Do you see? They're gone. The lion statues. They're actually gone!"

It felt as if all the planets were finally coming into alignment. The two lion statues that normally sat on either side of Biltmore's front doors were no longer there.

Braeden looked back toward the fields where the battle had just taken place. "But they're not just gone . . ." he said in amazement. "They're dead."

Serafina felt a wave of recognition crashing through her as the connections came together in her mind. Finally, things were beginning to make sense.

"Come on," she said, and they headed farther along the front terrace.

She gazed up toward the external wall of the Grand Staircase, where the spiral of slanted windows and intricate carvings rose up with each floor of the house.

Biltmore's front facade was so vast, and so ornate with statues, gargoyles, and châteauesque decoration, that few people even noticed the details of it, but what she saw now astounded her.

"That's it!" she said triumphantly, pointing up toward the corner of the tower.

Braeden gazed up in the direction she was pointing.

High above, between the second and third floor of the Grand Staircase's external wall, the carved limestone statue of Joan of Arc was gone.

The statue had been a grand and romantic representation of the French heroine, dressed in full battle armor.

"I just killed Joan of Arc," Serafina said in disbelief.

"Saint Louis is gone as well!" Braeden said, pointing to the adjacent alcove where the statue of the ancient French king was supposed to be standing.

She remembered that Saint Louis had been depicted with a helmet, full chain mail armor, and his famous longsword.

"A longsword," she said, remembering the battle on the North Ridge and the sight of Mr. Turner lying dead on the ground in the forest, a long, straight slash across his chest. And she remembered the clanking metal sounds that she had heard in the fog that night.

"It's the *house*," she said in astonishment. *"It's coming alive. . . ."*

Braeden's eyes widened as he gazed up at the two empty alcoves where the statues had been, and his mouth opened as he tried to gather words. "How can . . ." he stammered, and then he paused and looked at her. "Is it just the lions and these two statues, or are there more?"

She stepped back and looked up toward the front walls of Biltmore looming above them. Her lips went dry with nervousness as she slowly scanned the details of the facade. There were many graven ogres, griffons, harpies, minotaurs, satyrs, and other mythical creatures covering the wall.

And then she saw it.

High above.

An empty spot where there had once been a stone gargoyle.

It had been a nasty-looking, grotesque creature, with a hunched back, four reptilian legs, large bat-like wings, bulging eyes, and snarling teeth.

And then she turned and looked out across the Esplanade, up toward the top of Diana Hill, which rose directly in front of the house.

"Come on," she said.

"What's up there?" Braeden asked as he followed.

"If I'm right," she said, "it's more a question of what's *not* up there."

As they reached the top of the hill, she and Braeden gazed at the white statue of Diana, goddess of the hunt.

"She's still here," Braeden said, confused. "I thought she was going to be gone."

"Look more closely," Serafina said, "at the base of the statue."

"There's a part missing," Braeden said as he examined it.

"Diana was standing next to a deer," Serafina said.

"The *white* deer," Braeden said in amazement.

"Exactly," Serafina said.

"But what does this mean?" Braeden asked.

"Everything," Serafina said, a tremendous wave of relief surging through her body. It felt as if she was waking up from

a dark and awful nightmare and realizing that it wasn't true. "Let's go," she said excitedly. "There's one more place to check. The most important of all."

The two of them ran back down the hill and down the length of the Esplanade. By the time they reached the front door, they were gasping for breath.

"Miss Serafina," Mr. Pratt said as he came out to meet them. "Mr. Vanderbilt is demanding your presence immediately."

"Thank you, I'll be there as soon as I can," she told him.

She went in through the Vestibule, entered the Main Hall, and turned to the right. Following the corridor that ran along the Winter Garden, she passed the door to the Billiard Room, and walked toward the Banquet Hall.

And there, in the corner, she saw the spot where it had always been.

The bronze statue of Mr. George Washington Vanderbilt, the grandson of the famous Commodore Cornelius Vanderbilt, and the master of Biltmore Estate.

Mr. V.

And just as she had hoped, it was gone.

Serafina couldn't help but smile. Now she knew for sure that Mr. Vanderbilt hadn't killed anyone. She wanted to cheer. She wanted to hug him. She wanted to shout to the heavens that something finally made sense in the world.

Have faith in what you know, her pa had told her, and she should have, but her faith had been mightily shaken. She kept thinking about poor, wounded Kinsley and all the people who had died. But despite how strange and almost inconceivable it was that the statues were doing all this, she felt a swell of excitement that she was finally starting to put some of the pieces of the puzzle together.

"I don't get it," Braeden said bluntly. "Why are the statues coming to life now after all this time? What's the cause of it all?"

"It might be a sorcerer or a spell," Serafina said, "some sort of evil intruder."

"But why? Why would a sorcerer want to kill all these random innocent people?"

"There must be some connection between them, some kind of pattern," Serafina said.

"It all started on the night Colonel Braddick died, didn't it?" Braeden asked. "He was the first one attacked."

"Along with Mr. Turner, Mr. Suttleston, Isariah Mayfield, and Jess," she said.

"Who was next?" Braeden asked.

"Mr. Kettering at the bottom of the stairs," she said. "And then Mr. Cobere in the kitchen."

She thought about the people on their list. What was the pattern, the motivation?

And then she asked the same question she had asked herself before and not been able to answer. "What do all these victims have in common?"

"Maybe the key is that they don't have anything in common," Braeden said.

"What do you mean?"

"Maybe there's an important difference between them, and we're not seeing it."

"Colonel Braddick, Mr. Turner, Mr. Suttleston, Isariah Mayfield, Jess Braddick, Mr. Kettering, Mr. Cobere . . ." Serafina listed off.

"Rich and poor . . ."

"Male and female . . ."

"Northerner and Southerner . . ."

"Biltmore resident and Biltmore guest . . ."

"How they died . . ."

And then she paused.

"Dead," Serafina said.

"They aren't all dead!" Braeden said.

"That's right," Serafina said. "Jess wasn't killed that first night."

"Was she just lucky?" Braeden asked.

"There's a pattern," Serafina said, feeling the surge of realization in her chest. "At least at the beginning of it all, there was definitely a pattern. . . ."

Keen on the trail, she and Braeden hurried down the corridor.

"In those first few nights, what did all the *dead* victims have in common with each other, and how were they different from the one victim who wasn't killed?"

As they crossed through the Banquet Hall and into the back corridor known as the Bachelors' Wing, she went through the list of questions in her mind. Rich or poor. Male or female. Northerner or Southerner. Resident or guest . . .

"The victims were all so different from one another," Braeden said.

"But something connected them," Serafina said.

Pausing in the corridor, she thought about Colonel Braddick at dinner bragging about his gun. And she heard the baying of the hounds as they chased down the mountain lions. And she remembered looking out the window of her new bedroom and seeing Mr. Kettering returning from a hunt.

A shiver ran down her spine. She remembered searching through the fog and darkness for Jess after the battle on the North Ridge, the feeling of being hunted. And she remembered how Kinsley had been in such a panic right before the battle with the lions in the field. He, too, had said it felt as if something were hunting him.

When she looked up, she realized that they were standing in front of the Gun Room.

As she and Braeden stepped into the room, she gazed at the glass-fronted cabinets that encased the long rows of rifles and shotguns. And then she looked up at the hunting trophies lining the walls—the heads and antlers of many deer.

She knew that Mr. Vanderbilt was not a hunter. When he built the house he purchased these mounted animal heads as decor to create what was supposed to look like the gun room of a proper country gentleman.

She thought again about the people who had died. "The pattern is right here. . . ."

"But what about Mr. Cobere?" Braeden said, clearly following her train of thought. "Mr. Cobere wasn't a hunter. He had no connection to the hunters at all."

"He was the butcher and meat cook . . ." she said, remembering the sight of him lying on the tiled floor of the Rotisserie Kitchen. "He was in charge of preparing and cooking the fish and game brought in by the hunters and fishermen. The trout, the wild turkey, the rabbit—"

"And the deer," Braeden finished.

"Exactly," Serafina said. "In those first few nights, the

difference between the ones who were killed, and the one who wasn't, was simple."

"Hunting," Braeden said.

"That's right," Serafina said, feeling the excitement of the discovery scintillating in her mind. "Jess had tried to work against the hunters. It wasn't a coincidence that she was the only one who survived that night. The connection to hunting was right in front of my eyes all along, but I didn't see it."

"But if someone is murdering people connected with hunting, then that's all of us," Braeden said. "We all live here!"

Serafina's brow furrowed as she wiped her mouth. Did the acceptance of an act mean you were guilty of the act? She wasn't sure. But it was clear that they were still missing pieces of the puzzle. The pattern seemed to be breaking down, the violence getting worse and worse, more random, like it was spiraling out of control now. Baby Nell's nursery had been attacked. And the bear cub and the coachman had been killed. . . .

"When did all the trouble begin?" she asked.

"The night Colonel Braddick and the other mountain lion hunters were attacked."

Serafina paused, wondering. "Or did the violence truly begin the night before that, the night the white deer was shot?"

"Are you saying . . ." he began uncertainly, "the white deer is the *cause* of all this, or she's trying to help us?"

And then a thought that she'd had earlier came back into her mind. "It's the *house*," she said. "The house itself is bringing its statues to life. The white deer was just the first one."

"But why now?" he asked. "My uncle has been hosting the hunting season here for years."

"Did it begin the day the thirteen carriages arrived?" Serafina asked. "Could one of those guests be the cause of all this?"

As they were talking, a series of images began to flow through her mind. She remembered standing on the terrace the night Braeden came to her like a ghost. And she remembered them lying on the shore of the lake with all the stars above them. That was the first time they saw the white deer. It had seemed as if it was a beautiful young fawn, running through the forest, glowing in the light of the stars, almost magical in its appearance. It had brought her such a sense of peace and joy to see it.

But Colonel Braddick and his hunting companions saw this same magnificent, rare, magical creature and they shot it. They tried to kill it so that they could add the unusual specimen to their collection of trophies. Or maybe it was just boredom, or a bit of sport to see who could hit such a small, moving target. But in the end, whatever the reason, they shot it.

As she thought again about lying beside the lake with Braeden, she began to feel something tingling in her mind. *That's it*, she thought. *That was the moment it all began.*

She sensed she was getting closer and closer to the answer.

But then she heard the rushing sound of many footsteps coming down the corridor. Mr. Doddman and six other armed men stormed into the Gun Room and surrounded her and Braeden.

र्म्य

Mr. Vanderbilt walked into the Gun Room immediately behind Mr. Doddman and the other men.

When Serafina saw him, she felt a rush of glorious emotion. It was startling how dramatically one's opinion of someone improved when you realized they weren't actually the heinous murderer you thought they were.

She walked straight up to the master of Biltmore and embraced him.

Mr. Vanderbilt was clearly taken aback, but he did not reject her embrace.

"I'm very sorry about taking Cornelia. I was so confused about what we were fighting," she explained as they separated and faced each other. "But not anymore."

"What are you talking about?" Mr. Vanderbilt asked.

"If there is anyone still out hunting for the beast or searching for Jess, we need to bring them back immediately," Serafina said. "And if anyone sees a white deer, they should run."

She knew what she was telling Mr. Vanderbilt and his men sounded ridiculous, but she said it firmly and with confidence.

"A white deer . . ." Mr. Doddman repeated suspiciously.

Serafina looked at the security manager and the other men. "If anyone sees an animal or someone they don't know, they should immediately get away from it."

The master of Biltmore studied her for a moment, and then looked at Mr. Doddman. "Send out word that no more search parties should go out, and all hunting must stop immediately. And everyone should stay clear of this white deer creature. Get everyone safely into the house."

"Sir, if I may," Serafina interrupted. "Please don't bring everyone into the house. Get everyone *out*. Load the carriages and send them away, the guests, the servants, your family. A great danger is upon us and only those who have skills to fight should remain."

All the men stared at her in utter shock.

"There is absolutely no cause for such drastic action," Mr. Doddman said forcefully.

But Mr. Vanderbilt said, "You want to actually abandon Biltmore?"

"Yes, sir. We must."

"She's right, Uncle," Braeden said. "Everyone is in danger here."

"If this so-called white deer is so dangerous," Mr. Doddman said, "then we should hunt it down and kill it."

"No," Serafina said, shaking her head. "That's going to make it worse. This whole thing started small, but now it's getting much, much larger. Do you see? The violence is bringing violence. Bullets aren't going to hurt the white deer anymore. Its magic has grown too strong. Your guns will be effective against the newer creatures at first, but not the white deer. That's how Kinsley was hurt. In his attempts to protect Jess, he tried to fight it."

The men listened to her with blanched faces, as if they weren't quite able to believe or comprehend what she was saying.

She had gone many days and nights without knowing what was going on, without knowing what to do, but now she did know, at least some of it, and she had to tell them as plainly and bluntly as she could.

Mr. Vanderbilt had listened intently to everything she said, but she could still see the hesitation in his eyes.

"It's the statues, sir," she said finally.

"I don't understand what you're saying," he said. "What's the statues?"

"They're coming to life and they're killing us," she said, her voice as steady and serious as she could hold it, her eyes locked on his.

His expression tightened and his brow furrowed. She knew that what she had just told him was so foolishly impossible that it barely warranted serious thought. And yet . . . And yet there was *something* she was telling him that caught him. She could see him thinking it through.

"It was a gargoyle . . ." he said in amazement.

"That's right," she said.

"And there's a statue of me in the house . . ." he said, his voice so low and uncertain that it was barely audible. "That's what scared you so badly . . . why you didn't come to me . . . why you took Cornelia. . . ."

Serafina let out a long breath, relieved that Mr. Vanderbilt was beginning to realize why she acted the way she did. "I saw a person who looked like you kill Mr. Cobere," she told him. "I couldn't understand it. It seemed impossible! But there have been many others, and there's going to be more."

At that moment, the pressure in the room seemed to immediately change. Mr. Vanderbilt turned to his dumbfounded men, who had been listening to all of this, and gave them new orders.

"Now listen carefully," he told them in a strong, firm voice. "We're going to do exactly what Serafina says. Get everyone into the carriages, women and children first, including my wife and daughter, and send two armed men with each and every carriage to make sure everyone gets out safely."

"Yes, sir," Mr. Doddman and the other men said together, and immediately moved into action.

"We're doing what needs to be done, sir," Serafina said. "I'm sure of it."

"I've been so frustrated that there was nothing I could do

about all these terrible things that were happening," he said. "I'm no marksman or soldier, but this is one way I can lend a hand."

Lend a hand, she thought, the same expression that her pa had used. And it surprised her to hear the same dismay in Mr. Vanderbilt's voice that she had felt in herself just days before. This man of power and experience had been caught in the same roiling sense of worthlessness that she had suffered.

As Mr. Vanderbilt hurried away to organize the evacuation of Biltmore, Serafina grabbed Braeden's arm.

"We need to figure out specifically what's causing all this," she said.

"What's your plan?"

"Down by the lake, when everything started," she said, "do you remember how we could see all those stars that night? You were telling me what they meant. And then we saw the white deer running through the forest—"

"You think it was a constellation . . ." Braeden said in amazement. "You want to use Biltmore's Library. . . ."

"Unless you already know what we're looking for, I think it's our only hope."

Seconds later, as they ran through the Main Hall, dozens of guests were hurrying toward their rooms to grab what belongings they could. Others had abandoned their belongings entirely and were now fleeing directly for the carriages that were lining up at the front door.

As she and Braeden dashed down the length of the Tapestry Gallery, maids and footmen rushed to and fro around them, battening down the window shutters and closing up the piano, others trying to protect the gallery's fine furniture and its three hand-woven twenty-foot-wide silk and wool Flemish tapestries.

Serafina could hear Mr. Vanderbilt's voice in the distance behind her. "There's no time for all that," he ordered his staff. "Leave it and go!"

The whole house was erupting with activity. It would be the first time in her entire life that they would attempt to actually empty this vast house of nearly all of its inhabitants.

As she and Braeden entered the Library, the brass floor lamps glowed with amber light, reflecting on the gold-leaf titles of the books lining the shelves, and a gentle fire crackled in the marble fireplace. It was a peaceful sight, but the sounds of chaos filled the house behind them. She didn't know how much time they had, but she knew it wasn't much. And as she looked up at all the books, it just seemed so daunting. There were over ten thousand books on these shelves, and another twelve thousand scattered throughout the house. How could she find any answers in a place like this?

"Astronomy . . ." Braeden said as he quickly went over to one of the shelves near the wrought-iron spiral staircase that

ROBERT BEATTY

led up to the Library's second level. He tilted his head as he scanned the titles and then pulled out a dark leather-bound book.

As they leafed through the pages, Serafina caught glimpses of Greek gods and goddesses, great Titans and epic heroes.

"There are all kinds of myths and legends about the constellations," he said, "but I don't remember any stories about a white deer."

"What about the stars you were telling me about that night?"

"We saw Orion . . . and the star of Aldebaran . . . and Pleiades . . . and—"

"You were telling me about Pleiades," she said. "The Seven Stars. Do you remember? They were very bright."

"My uncle said that the Seven Sisters were the daughters of Pleione, some sort of nymph or something."

Serafina listened to what he was saying, but it didn't seem to have anything to do with what was happening at Biltmore. "You told me a story from the Bible where God says, 'Can you bind the chains of the Pleiades or loose the belt of Orion?' Do you remember that? You said that nearly every culture in the world had old stories about the Seven Stars."

Outside the Library, at the far end of the house, something glass smashed onto the floor. They both jumped at the sound of it, but Serafina was determined to stay focused on what they were doing.

Braeden hurried over to one of the shelves near the fireplace and pulled out a second book. "This one talks about how a

Māori god named Tāne collected seven stars and then threw them up into the heavens to adorn the god of the sky."

"I don't think that's it, either," Serafina said.

"Then let's try this one," Braeden said as he pulled out a much thicker black tome and began flipping through the paintings of constellations, Cygnus the Swan, Taurus the Bull, Orion the Hunter, page after page.

When she spotted a cluster of stars in a haze of glowing blue light, she stopped him. "That's the Seven Stars."

They leaned in and began reading the text, descriptions of Celtic myths and druid priests, of witchcraft and long-forgotten lore.

Now she could hear people shouting to one another in the distance. She wanted to go to them, to help them. *We don't have time for reading,* she thought frantically, but then she came to this:

There were seasons for all things, but autumn in particular was known as a time of change and calamitous events. Every fall, when the Seven Stars first rose high in the midnight sky, it was believed that the veil between the physical world and the magical world was at its thinnest. It was said that during this time if the Seven Stars were caught in a reflection, then they would reflect their magic into our world, while at the same time reflecting our world into their magic, like a mirror into a mirror. Whatever was occurring at the moment of the reflection—the good, the evil, the wondrous, and the vile—would become manifest in our world.

As she read the words, it felt as if her thoughts were glowing with heat in her mind.

"The reflection on the lake . . ." she whispered in astonishment.

"And the meteor storm . . ." Braeden gasped.

"It must have all started that night."

"But there's still nothing here about a white deer," Braeden said.

They quickly continued to the next paragraph.

It was generally believed, among the druid priests and the common people alike, that in some years the Seven Stars had the power to bring the dead into the realm of the living. This has long been thought by historians to be the origin of what we now observe as Halloween. It was also believed that in other years the Seven Stars had the power to bring spirit to that which did not have spirit. The exact stories varied from year to year, and from region to region, but they all had one aspect in common: Once the reflection of the Seven Stars faded, their magic faded with them, and the daylight world returned to normal.

"But this can't be right," Braeden said. "There's still nothing about a white deer. And if we were dealing with the magic of the Seven Stars, then it should have only lasted for a few minutes on that one night."

Gunshots split the air and echoed through the cavernous halls of Biltmore. She knew that people were in trouble, but she had to stay strong.

What Braeden had just said seemed to eliminate the Seven Stars as a possibility for what they were facing, but she remembered the ethereal sight of the white fawn running through the forest that first night, and Joan of Arc charging toward them a few nights later, and all the other creatures that had come alive.

"*'The power to bring spirit to that which did not have spirit . . .'*" she whispered, trying to think it through. "It's like the magic of the Seven Stars has been entwined with Biltmore."

Braeden looked up at her. "But do you realize what that means? It's a reflection of ourselves at the moment when it occurred. The hunters shot the white fawn!"

"It bespelled the entire house, the grounds, *everything*!" she said. "And it's getting worse every night, twisting the stone of Biltmore with its own evil."

"No," Braeden said. "With *our* evil, you mean. *Our* evil! Don't you see? Like a mirror into a mirror. It's a reflection of *us*, all turned against us! It's the violence, the cruelty of that moment, turned against the hunters. It's the killing of small, defenseless animals. It's the terrifying feeling of being hunted. It's all of it!"

A bank of windows shattered in a nearby room.

"And it's reflecting into itself, spiraling out of control," she said.

"Especially when we try to fight against it, like Kinsley did."

"But it said that the magic would only last as long as the reflection."

"So why is it still here? Why is it still happening?" Braeden asked, his voice strained.

A sickening, sinking weight filled Serafina's stomach, and her face must have shown it, for Braeden's darkened immediately.

"What?" he said. "What's wrong?"

"The white fawn was meant to die," she said.

"What do you mean, *meant to die*?" he said, aghast.

"Not that the deer was meant to be shot by the hunters or that it *deserved* to die. But when the reflection of the stars in the lake faded, then the magic in the white fawn should have faded with it. The deer should have passed away or become stone again."

"Then why did she stay alive?" Braeden asked, but even as he said the words, she heard the hitch in his voice. "She stayed alive because I healed her," he said, his words laced with the realization of what he'd done. "I used my healing powers to help her, to infuse her with life. . . . I'm the cause of all this!"

"Braeden, you didn't know," she said. "It's not your fault. You didn't shoot the deer."

But what shocked her the most as she gazed up at the shelves of the vast library was that the answer to the puzzle had been here in these books all along. She'd been so close to it.

She had admired the beauty of the star-filled sky a thousand times, but until Braeden had told her about it, she had never heard of Pleiades, or the Seven Stars, or known much about the glistening objects sweeping through the darkness of space above her.

What if Colonel Braddick had known not to shoot the white deer? What if Braeden had known not to save it? What if Kinsley had known not to fight it during his heroic efforts to defend Jess?

Serafina stopped.

What if *she* had known *any* of it? She could have prevented this.

But they were all just doing what they always did. Killing and saving and defending and clawing.

A wave of screams rose up from the Main Hall, people running in panic. Serafina knew that they only had seconds left. But an idea sprang into her mind. "Braeden, did the Joan of Arc statue have any history behind it, any kind of dark past?"

"No, my uncle had it made for the house," Braeden said. "It was just a plain old stone statue."

"Was the real Joan of Arc a vicious fighter?"

"My uncle said that she wore armor and carried a sword into battle, but she was more of a spiritual leader, to boost the morale of the French troops. I think mainly she wanted peace."

"She sure didn't seem too peaceful when she was trying to kill us," Serafina said. "And the lions didn't act like real lions. They're all being brought into motion by the power of the reflection. . . . But how do we fight them?" As she tried to think it through, she knew that whatever they came up with, they had to act quickly. "We just saw that we can kill at least some of them with weapons and claws, but we've also seen what happens when the power of our world mixes with theirs."

Braeden nodded. "The white deer is darn near indestructible thanks to me."

The smell of smoke filled the air, the acrid stench of woolen tapestries on fire.

"I think we need to talk to her," Braeden said, his eyes solemn. "We need to somehow communicate with her, get her to stop doing this. I healed her, so she knows me. She knows I wouldn't hurt her. She'll trust me. If she's reflecting violence, then let's not give her any violence to reflect."

"I don't think that's going to work," Serafina said. "I already tried talking to it the night the hunters were killed and it didn't respond to me. And it's not just the white deer, it's statues all over the entire estate, the house, the gardens, the lake—"

A large vase just outside the Library smashed onto the floor. Whatever it was, it was coming and would soon be here.

"How do we fight the entire house?" Braeden asked in exasperation.

"We can't," Serafina said. "We've got to think of some other way to stop it."

"We just need more time," Braeden said, looking up at all the books. "The answer's got to be here somewhere!"

Tap-tap-tap.

The rap of cloven hooves moving across the hardwood floor drifted down the Tapestry Gallery toward the Library.

The hair on the back of Serafina's neck stood on end.

"What's that?" Braeden asked.

Experience was a peculiar thing. And reading books and asking questions and talking to one another . . . There were *many* teachers. But she feared that up to this moment, she had not been listening.

She turned to the door, knowing that the killing creature would soon be there, and she said, "We're out of time."

ap-tap-tap.

The sound of the tiny hooves grew louder.

"Get back," Serafina whispered to Braeden as she moved quickly forward to peek out through the archway of the Library's open double doors.

She looked down the length of the Tapestry Gallery, dark and full of shadows, the glow of the moon seeping through the sheer curtains on the tall, narrow windows.

The white deer stood at the far end of the long room, the creature's beady black eyes fixed on her. Its antlers rose above its head like a hovering crown of sharpened, deadly sticks.

Serafina stared straight into the eyes of the white deer, locking on to its gaze, and breathed as steadily as she could.

"Braeden . . ." she whispered without turning her head. "I want you to go out through the French doors behind us that lead to the South Terrace. I'll hold off the deer as long as I can."

"I'm going to try to talk to her," Braeden said, walking forward.

"Braeden, no!" Serafina screamed, but it was too late. He had already stepped into view of the white deer and was now walking down the Tapestry Gallery toward it.

Serafina wasn't sure if it was the bravest or stupidest thing she had ever seen him do, but Braeden was determined. He walked right toward the white deer, raising his open hands in a conciliatory manner as he went.

"There's nothing to fear from us," he said softly, his voice as smooth and soothing as when he talked to a spooked horse. "We welcome you here."

The deer pivoted its head and stared at Braeden. It made no sound. And its expression was utterly incomprehensible.

"It's not listening, Braeden," Serafina whispered. "It's not a true animal. You can't talk to it. Please come back now, don't frighten it, don't anger it, just come back. . . ."

But Braeden took another step forward.

"We mean you no harm," he said gently. "We can help you adjust to this world. Whatever we have done, we can make amends. We can live in peace together."

The deer gazed at Braeden and took a step closer to him.

"Yes, come . . ." Braeden whispered encouragingly.

The deer took another step forward, just staring at him.

It looks like it's actually working, Serafina thought in amazement.

But as she watched Braeden move slowly toward the white deer, it felt as if a snake were wrapping around her neck and tightening against her throat. She couldn't speak. She couldn't breathe.

It's a trick! she thought as she watched Braeden helplessly. *Don't go, Braeden. Come back!* She gritted her teeth in fury and frustration, trying to break free of the deer's gaze.

Suddenly, the deer's nostrils flared in anger. The deer raised one of its front hooves and slammed it down, sending a jagged ten-foot crack splintering through the hardwood floor.

Serafina wanted to charge at the deer, but she was frozen, like helpless prey, by the deer's spell.

"Braeden, it's not working!" she managed to hiss through the constriction of her throat, but Braeden took another step toward the deer.

"Don't worry, no one is going to hurt you . . ." Braeden said.

From the Main Hall, far behind the white deer, the sounds of shouting people rose up into the air.

Still staring at Braeden, the deer tilted its antlers down and shook its head once, then twice, and when its head came back up again the deer snorted loudly and stepped aggressively forward, a warning, a threat.

"It's going to be all right," Braeden said in his soothing tone, seemingly impervious to fear. "I won't let anyone hurt you. . . ."

A woman's bloodcurdling scream rose up from the Main Hall. The men, women, and children of Biltmore were rushing out through gaping front doors, fleeing for their lives. Something that sounded like a large wooden crate full of brass springs but was probably Biltmore's massive grandfather clock crashed down and shattered into pieces on the floor. Men were shouting to each other, as if coordinating some sort of counterattack. Others were running with shrieks of terror. The bellowing snarl of some sort of unearthly mythical creature echoed off the limestone walls of the house. The smell of singed furniture and acrid smoke filled the air. Baby Nell wailed. Her mother cried out. The clatter of horses' hooves stormed into the front hall.

Serafina wanted desperately to charge toward the chaos on the other side of the white deer and help those poor souls escape, but she knew she couldn't.

As the deer stared steadily at Braeden with its wicked eyes, Serafina saw something emerging from the shadows behind it. She heard the sound of coming footsteps, a gentleman's dress shoes, and then there he was, walking past the white deer and right toward her and Braeden. The walking man had black hair and mustache. It was Mr. Vanderbilt!

And then she saw the deadness in his eyes, and a surge of white-cold fear shot through her body, breaking the deer's spell.

The footman Mr. Pratt came running from the Main Hall to get Mr. Vanderbilt's attention.

"Watch out, Mr. Pratt, that's not him!" Serafina shouted, but it was too late.

As Mr. Pratt came up behind him and reached out to touch

his arm, the doppelgänger of Mr. Vanderbilt whirled around with a forceful, striking blow and slammed Mr. Pratt in the head with the iron fire poker clenched in its fist.

The stunned Mr. Pratt stumbled backward on his heels, his arms flailing as if trying to catch himself, blood streaming from his eyes. When the backs of his calves struck a coffee table, he crashed down into the splintering pieces of it and fell to the floor, blood pooling beneath his head.

Serafina desperately wanted to help Mr. Pratt, but even if she could find a way to break the spell and move, she couldn't abandon Braeden. As Braeden stood there face-to-face with the white deer, she kept thinking that maybe his idea would somehow work, that it *had* to work, that he'd find a way to communicate with it. But the deer stared at Braeden with its black, incomprehensible eyes, and Braeden stared back, frozen, as the doppelgänger pivoted and rushed toward him.

"Run, Braeden!" she screamed as the doppelgänger charged forward and raised its iron weapon.

But Braeden did not run. He stood completely immobile, caught in the white deer's bewildering, hypnotic power. He did not turn away. He did not raise his arms to block the blow from striking his head.

Instead, he took one last step forward, straight into his death.

Something ripped through the air past her ear and struck the doppelgänger in the forehead with a thud. It collapsed to the floor like a puppet with its strings cut.

"Will you two please get moving!" a young female voice shouted at her and Braeden, as if she was angry that they had just been standing there like a couple of deer caught in lantern light.

Serafina shook herself out of the mesmerized stupor, feeling the focus of her dilated eyes coming back to her.

She immediately grabbed Braeden by the arm and yanked him back into the Library, nearly pulling him off his feet but finally breaking the confounding power of the deer's stare.

Serafina was surprised to see that it was Jess who was

helping them. A jagged cut of dark crusted blood traced her forehead, but it looked like she had changed into a fresh dress, grabbed one of her rifles, and was ready to go.

"You're a sight for sore eyes, Jess," Serafina said as they took cover behind a set of bookcases. "I was afraid we lost you for good."

"Mr. Vanderbilt sent Kinsley and the other wounded to the hospital in Asheville, but I thought I should come and lend a hand."

"We're glad to have you," Braeden said, looking mighty relieved to be out of the deer's spell.

But there was no time to linger. The screaming chaos of the people trying to escape through the Main Hall's front doors, and the snarling viciousness of whatever creatures were attacking them, came roiling down the length of the gallery.

The priceless Flemish tapestries that covered the walls of the gallery were on fire, the flames licking up toward the exquisitely painted wood beams on the ceiling, its gold leaf flickering in the light of the flames.

Amid all the violence and destruction, Serafina looked up to see a large white swan flying down the length of the Tapestry Gallery toward her, flapping in deep, graceful pulls that curled the plumes of smoke at the tips of its outstretched wings. The swan was so white that its feathers seemed to scintillate with the incandescence of the brightest stars.

Serafina couldn't do anything but gasp at the sight of it. As it flew over her head, the rushing air of its wings brushed her cheeks and lifted her hair.

But in the same instant, a snarling griffin with the back legs and body of an African lion and the front legs, head, and wings of an eagle came charging into the Library and straight toward her. The mythical beast knocked her off her feet, took flight with a mighty heave of its wings, and slammed into Braeden, dragging him brutally to the floor with its savage talons.

Jess swung her rifle and fired, the sharp report of the shot buffeting the ceiling.

Forgetting about the boy it had pinned to the floor, the beast lunged viciously at Jess, screeching and hissing. She retreated rapidly, but never stopped firing, *bang, bang, bang* at point-blank range, until the griffin finally went down.

"Two more!" Serafina shouted, ducking as a pair of griffins came diving into the Library with great sweeps of their wings, books and papers whirling in all directions.

She pulled Braeden to his feet and dragged him toward the French doors that led out to the South Terrace. But even as they reached the doors, she saw through the panes of glass that dozens of large, lizardlike gargoyles from the rooftop were crawling and scraping there, looking for a way in.

She and her companions were trapped on both sides.

48

As the gargoyles smashed through the glass doors and slithered their way into the Library, Braeden wiped the blood from his face and shouted, "We're not getting out that way!"

Jess shot another griffin dead, levered her rifle, and shot again, trying to keep the snapping beasts at bay.

Braeden went deeper into the Library, shouting, "Everyone, this way!"

As they quickly followed him, Serafina could hear the screaming and crashing noises in the distance; she and her friends weren't the only ones fighting for their lives.

Another griffin stormed into the Library, its clenching claws shredding the Persian carpets and gouging the walnut woodwork as its slashing beak knocked the brass lamps to the floor, shattering their glass globes. The barrel-size, blue-and-white Ming vases rolled off their stands and smashed to pieces. A dozen writhing, black-skinned gargoyles broke through the French doors and poured into the room.

When she and her companions reached the far side of the fireplace, Braeden led them up the spiral staircase to the railed walkway that provided access to the books above.

"Through here," he said as he pushed open a hidden door behind the upper section of the massive fireplace.

It was a good way to reach Biltmore's upper floors, but as soon as she saw that Jess had a way to escape, Serafina knew what she had to do.

"Go and help the others," she told Jess. "I'm going to try to draw the creatures away from the house."

"Got it," Jess said, darting through the door.

"I'll go with *you*, Serafina," Braeden said.

"You're gonna need to hang on tight," Serafina said, nodding.

An instant later, she transformed into a massive black panther. Braeden leapt onto her back, and she dove claws-first, with a roaring growl, into the mass of gargoyles below her.

"Yee-haa!" Braeden shouted as they flew through the air and landed on the floor below. She knew he'd ridden plenty of horses, so he had the skill and balance to stay on, but judging by his whoop, he'd never experienced anything quite like riding a leaping panther.

She hit the ground and sprang through the gargoyles, across the Library, barreling straight into the griffin blocking the door. She slammed into it, exploding into a black ball of snapping teeth and slashing claws, battling with the eagle head and the talons, finally striking the beast down.

Spotting the white deer in the Tapestry Gallery, she ran straight at it, like a huge black bullet. She knew she probably couldn't truly hurt it, but she had to get its attention. As she leapt toward it, she lifted her paw and took a mighty swipe, striking it right across its flank. It was a strong, killing blow. But the tips of her claws scraped across the deer's side like she was striking glass, and a priceless painting on the wall behind her tore open and went spinning across the floor. The startled, snorting deer skittered aside, nearly toppling, then turning with a crack of its cloven hooves against the floor as if it expected another swipe. But instead of striking the deer, Serafina ran right past it.

Violence brings violence, so come and get me!

She sprinted down the length of the gallery, leaping over its damaged sofas and broken tables, darting around the splintered grand piano with its black and white keys spilled across the floor, and flying past the burning lamps and shattered windows.

When she reached the scorched walls and demolished remnants of the Main Hall, furniture and suitcases were strewn across the limestone floor.

Every sculpture and relief inside and outside the house was coming to terrifying life. Mr. Vanderbilt's visions of exquisite ancient art, grand operas, heroic journeys, beautiful ballets, and classic stories of literature had become a living nightmare.

Maids and footmen with lanterns were scurrying in all directions. Guests in nightshirts were calling to one another, trying to stay together in the smoke and darkness.

As Serafina ran toward the archway of the open front doors, she glanced over and was startled to see her pa and Essie hurrying down the Grand Staircase.

In all the turmoil and violence that had befallen the house, her pa must have stayed behind and run upstairs to the Louis XVI Room to find her. But he had found Essie instead, and they had become allies in the chaos, working together, helping each other, fighting to stay alive.

"It's not much farther, we're almost out," her pa was assuring Essie as they rushed down the stairs together. Their clothes were torn, their arms and bodies scratched and bruised. It was clear that they were fleeing some horrifying beast from the floor above.

When they reached the bottom of the stairs and looked up to see a massive, yellow-eyed black panther directly in front of them, both of their faces fell white with dread. It was as if they had been fighting and fighting to survive, but knew now, at this moment, that this was a fight they could not win.

They didn't seem to see or comprehend at first that there was actually a boy clinging to the panther's back. They were transfixed by the panther's black body, the massive head, the fangs, and the yellow eyes staring at them.

But Braeden rose from her shoulders and screamed, "Get down!"

Her pa pulled Essie to the ground just as Serafina sprang straight over their heads at the hellish winged lion charging down the stairway directly behind them. She and Braeden and the fighting lion went tumbling down the stairs, knocking her pa and Essie off their feet. The roaring growls of the two big cats exploded into violence as they battled with claws and teeth.

Braeden was flung from her back, but immediately sprang

to his feet and ran to help her pa and Essie scramble out of the way.

Her pa turned toward her, gazing in awe at the astounding sight of a black panther battling a winged lion. But high above them, Serafina heard the dome of the Grand Staircase crack under the weight of what sounded like a massive flying beast landing on the rooftop. As the bolt that held the four-story-tall wrought-iron chandelier was ripped from the dome, she suddenly remembered her pa's elaborate descriptions of how he had helped install the huge, seventeen-hundred-pound chandelier years before. Now it was falling, collapsing down through the center of the spiral staircase, *smash, smash, smash,* one level crashing into the next, with him standing right below it. She yanked herself away from the snarling battle with the winged lion and sprang toward her pa.

50

The full weight of her panther body slammed into her father, and they went tumbling across the floor as the wrought-iron chandelier crashed onto the charging winged lion and exploded into hundreds of clanging pieces.

Lying on the floor a few steps away, Serafina and her pa disentangled themselves and looked at each other face-to-face, the oak-brown eyes of a human being and the bright yellow eyes of a black panther.

She was expecting fear, horror, shock. But the first thing she saw in her father's expression at that moment was *recognition*.

He knew he was looking at his daughter.

Whenever she had thought of this moment, she had imagined her pa roiling with dismay, turning away from her in revulsion at the unnatural creature she was, and angry at how dishonest she had been to hide it from him all this time. But what she saw in her father's eyes was amazement, heartfelt pride and awe at what his little girl had become. She had gone for so long without him knowing who she was; she had felt so alone, so adrift. And now, in the midst of all this chaos and violence, a tremendous sense of relief poured into her body, a tremendous sense of love, to finally be seen by her father in her fullest and truest form.

"Come on, Serafina, the white deer's coming!" Braeden shouted as he ran toward her and leapt onto her back.

Serafina took one last look at her father and dashed out the front door of the house.

Several carriages had been split open at their doors by some great force. The wooden spokes and metal rims of their wheels had been smashed. The horses, still trapped in their harnesses, were dragging the broken carriages across the cobblestones, the bare axles throwing rooster-tails of sparks in all directions.

Mr. Doddman, the security manager, was cramming the elderly Mrs. Ascott and a half dozen other guests into one of the carriages that was still intact. But as he was shutting the carriage door and shouting instructions up to the terrified coachman, an arrow whizzed through the air and sank into Mr. Doddman's chest, stifling his shout.

He clutched at the shaft of the arrow desperately as his entire prodigious body crumpled downward and then fell dead to the ground.

Serafina looked out to see Diana, goddess of the hunt, charging toward them, firing arrows as she came.

Mr. Vanderbilt, bleeding from a wound to his neck and head, was frantically helping his wife and child into the next carriage.

Mrs. Vanderbilt held the crying baby Cornelia wrapped tightly to her chest as the barking, snapping Gidean and Cedric fought off a pack of gargoyles surrounding them.

The goddess Diana drew her second arrow, aimed straight at Mrs. Vanderbilt, and let the arrow fly.

Serafina threw herself at Mrs. Vanderbilt and slammed her against the side of a horse as the arrow whizzed by.

Then she charged straight at Diana, praying she could sprint faster than the goddess could nock another arrow.

Just as she made her final lunge at the goddess, the arrow shot past. Braeden screamed as it tore a gash out of his arm and struck a footman in the head behind them.

Mrs. Vanderbilt—stunned from being slammed against a horse by a huge cat, but still holding on to her baby—staggered forward, away from the wildly spooked horse, as her husband pulled her and their daughter into the carriage.

Nolan, the stable boy, scrambled up into the driver's seat

and grabbed the reins of Braeden's horses, harnessed at the front of the carriage.

"Go! Go!" Braeden shouted directly to the horses, and the horses charged forward, pulling the carriage away.

Two gargoyles leapt onto the carriage before it escaped and were now crawling across its roof toward Nolan's back as he concentrated on steering the galloping horses.

The remaining gargoyles turned on Gidean and Cedric with new viciousness. Serafina ran straight at the pack of them, swiping at the nasty beasts with her claws to give Gidean and Cedric enough time to break away and dash after the carriage. Nolan and the Vanderbilts were going to need all the protection they could get.

There were more carriages, more people trying to escape, but Braeden shouted, "We've got to keep running, Serafina!"

She turned to look behind her. The white deer was emerging through the front doors, its eyes scanning the chaos of the fleeing humans without emotion. It was looking for *her*, the panther that had charged toward it and clawed its side. And as soon as it saw her, it locked its powerful black eyes onto her.

"I think we've got her attention!" Braeden shouted.

Serafina wanted desperately to lunge at the deer, to claw it, to bite it. But fighting it was no use. Violence and attack made it stronger. It was as impervious to her claws as it was to Kinsley's bullets, and growing more and more powerful by the second.

Knowing what she had to do, Serafina pivoted and ran.

She didn't hide. She didn't go for cover. She ran *away*. Away from Biltmore. Away from her pa and Essie, and Mr. and Mrs. Vanderbilt and little Cornelia, away from all of them.

When she reached the flat, open area of the Esplanade she pushed herself harder, driving the force into her legs and blazing across the grass.

Come on, deer, she thought as she sped away. *Let's go for a little run!*

When she was sure she had put a good strong distance between her and the house, she glanced behind her, hoping to see the white deer following after her.

But what she saw struck cold, hard fear into her panther heart.

The white deer stood at the very front of Biltmore House, staring toward her and Braeden up on the hill. It was just standing there—with its all-white body, and its white antlers protruding from its head. For a moment, Serafina thought the bizarre creature had given up, that it had chosen to finally stop pursuing them. But then hundreds of gargoyles, chimeras, and other monstrous creatures poured from the facade of the house in an all-enveloping black wave. Thick channels of beasts streamed out of the front door and out through all the broken windows, like black swarms of hornets vomiting from an ungodly nest.

There were hissing, viper-headed fiends with burning eyes, grotesque humanlike ogres, hook-beaked hyenas, muscled wine gods with curved ram horns protruding from their chiseled heads, and hundreds of snarling, hunchbacked, razor-clawed gargoyles.

And they were all coming straight for her and Braeden.

"We better get out of here!" Braeden shouted.

Serafina turned and ran, sprinting as fast as she could up toward the top of Diana Hill. Her powerful panther heart pounded in her chest. Her great lungs pumped like bellows. Her feet drove against the ground, pushing her and Braeden forward.

She could run fast, *very fast*, but she couldn't run as fast as those wicked creatures could fly.

Halfway up the hill, two of the giant, bat-winged gargoyles bore down on her and Braeden. Braeden clung to her back with one hand and tried to fight them off with the other, swiping and punching at them as they came in for their attacks.

One of the gargoyles seized her back leg with its talons, dragging her to the ground, pulling her down the steep slope of the hill. Another gargoyle grabbed her front leg.

She roared with pain as a third gargoyle landed on her back, piercing her spine with its claws and snapping at Braeden with its teeth. Braeden kicked it in the snout and pushed the snarling, snapping creature back, but it lunged forward and closed its jaws around his shoulder, Braeden screaming in agony.

Serafina swiped her claws at one of the gargoyles, tearing it away with a powerful, roaring blow, but two more came in its place, biting her leg. She struggled to keep going, fought to keep pushing her way up the hill, but there were too many of them. She crashed to the ground under their weight. She tried to stumble forward, to press on, to keep running, but more and more of the winged beasts landed upon her.

A gunshot rang out. A splash of blood splattered across Serafina's shoulders and head. She sucked in a startled breath and craned her neck to look behind her, thinking Braeden had been struck, but he was still clinging to her back, his eyes white with astonishment as he wiped the blood from his face. The gargoyle that had been clutching his shoulder fell dead.

Another shot rang out. The creature holding Serafina's front leg slumped to the ground. She looked back toward the house and saw the flash of a third shot coming from the roof.

Someone was shooting at them.

But this third shot hit the gargoyle that was clamped on to her back leg.

Whoever was shooting wasn't shooting *at* them, but at the creatures all *around* them.

"It's Jess!" Braeden shouted in excitement.

The girl whose father thought she always missed wasn't missing anymore. She was hitting exactly what she wanted to hit.

Jess had taken a position high atop the front tower, looking out across the open grass of the Esplanade. And now she was firing shot after shot, bringing down gargoyle after gargoyle.

Another shot ripped past Serafina and thudded into the gargoyle charging toward her, toppling it to the ground.

Realizing that Jess was doing everything she could to give her and Braeden the chance they needed to escape, Serafina growled with new determination. She sloughed the dead gargoyle from her back, shook the dead gargoyles from her legs, and dragged herself to her feet.

"We can do it, Serafina!" Braeden shouted as he hunkered down on her back to prepare for her leap.

She took one last look at the horde of gargoyles coming behind them, and then, with all her power, ran forward and lunged into the woods.

As she hit the speed of her stride, she heard the shots behind her, knocking down one attacker after another. A running gargoyle charged up beside her. But just as it opened its fanged maw to bite her and drag her down, a bullet sent it rolling across the ground, falling dead in her wake.

As she ran deeper into the forest, the gargoyles, and the

sound of Jess's shots, fell long behind her. But she kept running.

When she finally slowed down enough to listen, she heard the sound of the white deer's hooves treading across the ground in the distance.

Perfect, Serafina thought.

But there were other sounds behind her, too, the footfalls of large cats, but with a pounding forcefulness rather than the soft grace of real cats.

What vile creatures have come to life now? she wondered.

She traveled down into a low river valley, then scrambled under the trunks of wind-toppled trees and through a bog of chokeberry and fetterbush.

She soon found herself wading through the green, swirling water of a swamp. Moss hung down from the craggy limbs of the tupelo trees, and thick coats of lichen grew on the ragged trunks of the old cedars. As she waded through a lagoon that was open to the glistening blackness of the night sky above them, thousands of stars were reflecting on the flat surface of the water.

Glancing back over her shoulder, she saw that Braeden's face and body were scratched, bruised, and bleeding, his clothes stained and torn. He was as wet and bedraggled as a storm-drenched dog, droplets of gargoyle blood and swamp water scattered across his forehead. His arms and legs were shaking with fatigue. And she felt it, too. After the long stretch of running and fighting, her lungs ached and her muscles were giving out.

The only way out is through, she thought.

And as she pushed onward, it seemed as if the ground was finally sloping up toward the high ground. They crossed through an area of dense thicket and undergrowth. And then saw what she had come for.

Hundreds of weathered gravestones reached into the distance, their cracked, gray shapes overgrown with vines, many of them tilting or sunken down into the earth.

"Why here?" Braeden asked, his voice filled with trepidation as he climbed from her back. "Why the cemetery?"

She shifted into human form and stood beside him.

"We need to get to the Angel's Glade," she said. "It's not much farther."

She turned and looked behind them, back toward the swamp they'd just come through. They had traveled miles from Biltmore.

As she tilted her head, closed her eyes, and listened out into the darkness, Kinsley's eerie words drifted through her mind. *It started following us. It's not going to give up!*

And sure enough, she heard the faint sounds of four spindly little legs slowly swishing through the water toward them.

"It's still behind us," Serafina whispered to Braeden.

"Then we've got to get out of here," he said, peering through the vegetation for an escape, but she grabbed his arm.

"No, we've got to go deeper into the graveyard," she said, remembering her pa's words to have faith in herself and what she knew to be true. "We've got to get to the Angel's Glade."

But at that moment, the white deer emerged from the foliage.

She was expecting some sort of mythical, cat-footed animal to be with the white deer, maybe even two of them. But something else entirely arrived.

As she looked up at it, her first, split-second thought was, *So that's what landed on the rooftop and crashed the chandelier.*

And then she grabbed Braeden by the shoulders and threw him to the ground as the large, flying, dragon-like creature burst out of the upper trees and bore down on them with daggerlike claws.

The scaly beast had a long, chomping snout, two powerful hind legs, and large bat wings.

The corrupted magic of the Seven Stars had brought to life a *wyvern.*

53

The talons of the wyvern crashed down through the cover of the brush above them, tearing through the vegetation and knocking her and Braeden to the ground.

They scrambled frantically out of reach of the talons, the beast's claws ripping through the ground like plows and pulling up the roots of the trees.

"Run, Braeden!" she screamed as she rose to her feet and pulled him with her. "Into the graveyard!"

With a leap into the sky, and great, billowing flaps of its wings, the wyvern went airborne again, screeching as it pivoted in midair and came sweeping in low to the ground in pursuit of them. It was a fast and agile flyer, but the thickness of the forest helped them. Serafina leapt behind a large tree just as the wyvern's talons came slashing through the branches above. She thought she had escaped the attack, but the wyvern wheeled around with a mighty burst of its wings, and then its claws clenched right into her shoulder with a lightning bolt of piercing pain. The force of the blow lifted her off the ground. Screaming, she reached out and grabbed at the branch of a tree, yanked herself out of the wyvern's talons, and tumbled hard to the ground.

Her ribs reverberated with splintering pain as she crawled rapidly across the ground. *Stay low, stay low,* she thought as she scurried beneath a thicket of underbrush like a little weasel escaping the talons of a great horned owl. But where was Braeden?

As the wyvern circled overhead, Serafina hunkered down against the trunk of a gnarled old tree, caught her breath, and scanned the forest for him.

"I'm here!" Braeden said as he came crawling on his belly through the wet leaves toward her. Her heart surged with hope.

She thought they'd get a few seconds to figure out what to do, but then she heard something coming toward them through the underbrush. It was the sound of cat paws, moving fast and strong.

Two vile beasts emerged from the brush. They had the lower bodies of lions, but the upper bodies and heads of human women. They were the sphinxes that had adorned Biltmore's gate. These once beautiful feline sculptures had been transformed into vicious creatures with clawing feet and gnashing teeth.

The sphinxes crouched low and sinister, looking more like rabid hyenas than either lions or humans, growling and snapping, saliva dripping from their mouths.

The sphinxes lunged toward her and Braeden. She dodged the attack and sprang behind the trunk of a tree, but one of them got hold of Braeden and pulled him to the ground, biting at his throat as he grappled against it. Serafina leapt at the sphinx and knocked it away from him, but it immediately turned on her. Braeden picked up a large branch and slammed it into the sphinx.

And at that moment, the wyvern came crashing through the canopy of the forest and landed immediately in front of them, its great maw roaring as it drove toward them.

"I've got an idea," Braeden shouted as they scrambled away from the massive beast. He tilted up his head and made the strangest sound she'd ever heard a human make, a loud, croaking call up into the night sky. "Now go!" he shouted at her. "Run for it! Get to the Angel's Glade!" And then he sprang to his feet and charged straight at the wyvern.

"What are you doing? Braeden, no!" she screamed.

Suddenly thousands of flying black shapes came out of nowhere, seeming as if they were exploding from the trees themselves.

It looked like Braeden was intending to somehow battle the wyvern head-on. Surrounded by the black shapes that he'd called from the forest, he ran straight at it.

But with a great swoop of its wings, the flying beast leapt upward, and clutched him in its talons.

He screamed as the massive claws clenched around his body.

In a desperate panic, Serafina rushed forward to help him, but the wyvern flew upward and pulled him out of her reach.

"Braeden!" she screamed, her whole body filling with anguish.

The creature had grasped him in its claws and there was nothing she could do. It lifted his bleeding body up into the sky, Braeden screaming in pain, his arms and legs flailing.

The last she saw of him he was rising higher and higher away from her, dangling in the talons of the wyvern, until he disappeared into the darkness above the canopy of the forest.

"Braeden!" she screamed again, her throat straining with lacerating pain.

She tried to hold on to hope that he had somehow survived the attack of the wyvern and would call out to her.

But there was no reply.

Braeden was gone.

Her entire body throbbed with the ache of it. Her heart was shuddering in her chest.

How could she let this happen? Why did he run at the wyvern like that?

She could feel the sobs welling up inside her, ready to burst out. But there was no time to think or feel. The two growling sphinxes were moving toward her, forcing their way through the underbrush, and a thick horde of running, crawling, flying gargoyles were pouring through the forest straight at her.

She had to fight them. But she couldn't fight them.

She had to go after Braeden. But she couldn't go after him.

Her pa's advice came into her mind: What was the most important thing? What was the one thing she *must* do? She had to *run*, run for the Angel's Glade, and there she would confront the white deer in the only way she had left.

She turned and sprinted up the hill. She ran past grave after grave, darting between the broken headstones and tilting crosses.

When she finally looked behind her, the white deer was there, right with her, coming toward the Angel's Glade.

I hope this is gonna work, she thought as she scurried behind the pedestal of the stone angel.

The white deer moved toward her with unnerving speed, scuttling more like a scorpion than a deer. Every sphinx and gargoyle attacked. And every gravestone ripped out of the earth and flew at her.

A great, swirling maelstrom of wind and debris and flying gravestones rose up from the ground.

Serafina hunkered behind the pedestal, bracing herself for the barrage. But the first gargoyle flew past her. The second—a six-legged beast with no wings—ran straight at her, but then broke off to the side. The gravestones hurtling through the air tumbled to the ground behind her.

Not a blade of the perfect green grass was disturbed in the circle of the Angel's Glade.

All the sphinxes, gargoyles, and monstrous beasts converged

on her and attacked her. Hundreds of gravestones plunged through the air at her in a storm of violence. But she clung to the pedestal of the angel, unharmed by the attacks.

And yet she knew she could not stay in the glade for long. She was surrounded and there was no way out. She could not fight. She could not defeat her enemy.

The white deer, the sphinxes, and the gargoyles stood just outside the perimeter of the Angel's Glade staring straight at her. She knew they had probably already killed Braeden. And now they were going to kill her. They would not stop until they did.

"Come on!" Serafina screamed at the white deer and the other beasts. "You killed the hunters! You attacked Kinsley! Come on! Do it! Do it now!"

The white deer just stared at her with those malevolent black eyes.

You need to kill me, Serafina thought. *And I've left you only one way to do it.*

"Come on!" she screamed, spitting out the words. Then she picked up a fist-size rock and threw it at the deer, striking it in the side. *Violence brings violence.* "Come on!"

Finally, the white deer turned to the statue of the angel standing on the pedestal in the center of the glade.

That's it, do it, Serafina thought. *Do it!*

The stone angel began to move, coming alive just as the others had.

The white deer pivoted its head and looked directly at Serafina.

Despite all that Serafina had done to get to this exact moment, her chest seized in fear and her breathing stopped.

But the angel did not immediately attack. She gazed around her at the forest-choked graveyard and the storm of violence surrounding the glade. She gazed at the white deer, and the maelstrom of flying gravestones and attacking gargoyles. And then, finally, the angel tilted her head down and gazed at Serafina crouched at the base of the pedestal.

Serafina had looked up at this angel of stone so many times, had spoken to her, cried to her, and never once had the angel moved or made a sound. But now the living, flesh-and-blood angel was looking right at her, her eyes as alive as any human's eyes, as green as the moss that had once grown on her shoulders, and as powerful as any woman who had ever lived.

And Serafina saw in those eyes one thing: *understanding.* No one had ever looked at her and comprehended her more fully than in that moment. Everything she was now, everything she had ever been, and everything she wanted to be. The angel understood.

And then the angel looked at the white deer standing at the edge of the glade.

Unlike the inert, lifeless stone of Biltmore's statues, the angel in the glade was filled with a deep and powerful spirit all her own.

The white deer stared at the angel with those terrible, mesmerizing black eyes, as if trying to drive the angel with its will, trying to force her to attack.

But the angel did not bend to its will.

And the angel did not look away.

The angel raised the fullness of her great gray feathered wings up above her shoulders and her head, and she held them there, trembling, on the cusp of unimaginable transformation.

Serafina cowered behind the pedestal and covered her face with her arm as she peered out.

And then the angel brought her wings down.

The angel's wings came together in one blazing, swooping motion that sounded like a thunderstorm tearing the length of the sky. Her wings threw a hurricane of wind that snapped the trunks of the surrounding trees. Dirt and rocks flew from the earth. The gargoyles and sphinxes were thrown tumbling away, and the white deer was buffeted back.

The angel rose up, hovering above her pedestal, roaring with fury, her power engulfing everything around them.

Serafina clung to the base of the pedestal. She tried to suck in a breath, but there was no air to breathe, just wilding wind and clamorous noise.

As the white deer struggled to keep its footing against the terrific forces bashing against it, it used its powers to hurl massive rocks and gravestones at the angel, but the angel deflected them with gestures of her hand. And in her other hand, she held her long, straight, sharply pointed sword.

Still hovering, the angel glided forward through the air, then came slowly down to the grass of the glade and walked toward the white deer.

The white deer hurled rock after rock at her, and then entire gravestones and monuments, but it meant nothing to the angel.

The angel lifted her wings above her head once more, and stepped closer to the white deer.

With a deafening shout, the angel swung her sword, low to the ground and then upward toward the sky, in a great sweeping motion.

Serafina watched in amazement. The sword didn't cut through the white deer. Its tip sliced open the earth and sky, as if rending a seam in the fabric of the universe. The blade tore through space and time, creating a gaping split of blackness filled with nothing but stars.

For a fleeting moment, as if all time had come together in a great, swirling torrent, Serafina glimpsed the white deer as it had been the first time she saw it, a luminous magical creature springing through the forest.

And then the white deer and all the creatures around it exploded into bursts of blazing pieces. The painful blast of heat singed Serafina's skin, and the bright light burned her eyes.

With a great thunder crack of sound, the blinding rush of a meteor storm flew up into the sky, hundreds of fragments searing the air around her, ripping and smoking as they hurtled upward toward the Seven Stars.

55

The white deer was gone.

The fury of wind had stopped and the world had become still.

The snarling sphinxes and gargoyles had turned to stone where they stood.

And the screeching wyvern had gone silent and fallen from the sky.

All that remained of the battle in the Angel's Glade was the drifting, acrid smell of what Serafina thought must be the remnants of burning stars.

Her skin was still tingling, and her body still shaking, as she peeked slowly out from behind the pedestal.

The angel was walking toward her, calm and peaceful now.

She was tall, with long striding legs that moved in a fluid, graceful motion, and flowing silvery hair that seemed to be filled with light. Her gray feathered wings rose up from her shoulders like the wings of a swan. She was the most beautiful being Serafina had ever beheld.

When the angel stopped in front of her, Serafina could barely breathe.

The angel smiled, took Serafina's head gently into her hands, and kissed her forehead with a long, tender kiss that felt like the touch of a warm breeze against her skin. In this touch, in this moment, she felt a sense of acceptance more powerful than she had ever felt before, as if everything she had ever done right, everything she had ever done wrong, everything *she was*, was *perfect*. In this moment, she felt all that it meant to be loved.

For several seconds, Serafina was so overwhelmed by everything that had happened, and so stunned that the angel had actually looked at her and touched her, she could not move.

Finally, she gathered up her courage and, still trembling, rose to her feet and turned toward the angel. *Who are you?* she was about to ask. *What is your name? Why have you helped me?*

But the pedestal was empty.

The angel was gone.

I need to find Braeden . . .

She turned in the direction she'd seen the wyvern go down.

Was it possible that he had survived?

She headed out into the forest to look for him, but immediately ran headlong into an obstacle. The ancient willow tree at the edge of the glade, which had once been the den of her mother, brother, and sister, had toppled to the ground, its trunk and branches a crisscross of broken destruction. She pushed into the fallen tree and clambered through its branches.

When she reached the other side, she got back onto her feet and tried to run, darting between the scattered, broken gravestones and the statues of gargoyles, but her feet sloshed through the inches of swamp water seeping out of the ground all around her. The gravestones and the trees and the fallen statues were sinking into the earth, the swamp engulfing everything, as if it had been only the Angel's Glade that had prevented it from doing so long before.

She climbed up and over the massive root ball of a fallen oak tree, and came down into two feet of green water.

Pushing through the swamp, she passed the stone bodies of the two sphinxes, with only their heads above the water now.

Her chest tightened as she gazed out at the dark and murky devastation of the flooding graveyard.

"Braeden!" she shouted desperately. "Braeden, can you hear me?"

She sloshed through the water in one direction and then the next, frantically looking for him. She could feel the heat of despair rising in her face. She had no idea which way to go. But she had to find him!

Frustrated, she stood in the waist-deep water and scanned in all directions, looking out across the drowning forest, trying to figure out what to do.

In the distance, she saw a single black shape circling above the canopy of the trees.

At first she thought it was the wyvern, flying way up in the sky, but then she realized that the wyvern had turned to stone and fallen.

Is it some kind of bird?

Still not sure, she moved toward it, her feet dragging and tripping on the rocks and branches beneath the water's surface.

Then she saw another dark shape similar to the first, and she began to make out the flapping of wings.

They definitely looked like birds, and they were circling.

It's the crows! she thought, pushing harder in that direction. *Braeden's crows!*

As she came closer to the spot over which the crows were circling, several other crows rose up from a branch and started flying around her. Soon there were dozens of crows, and then hundreds. The crows were everywhere, cawing raucously.

At first it seemed as if they were attacking her, but then she realized they were urging her on, guiding her where they wanted her to go.

She gasped in dismay when she spotted a pale white shriveled hand sticking up out of the swamp water.

Serafina shoved herself through the muck of the swamp. She could see the white limbs of Braeden's body down in the murky water, trapped under the large stone pieces of the broken wyvern. But one of his arms was sticking straight up out of the swamp, like he was raising his hand in class, as if he'd been trying to make sure she saw him there. It was as if he knew she would be coming for him. His other arm was under the surface, clinging desperately to a half-submerged toppled tree. And there, pressed against the trunk, was his head, his mouth just inches above the water.

"Braeden!" she shouted, lurching toward him and grasping his upraised hand.

His eyes opened suddenly. "You found me!" he said in relief. "I'm stuck, I can't get out!"

She reached under the water, grabbed on to him, and tried to pull him forcefully to his feet, but it was no use. A part of one of the wyvern's stone talons still gripped his leg, holding his lower body down into the water.

"The water level's rising fast," he said.

"Hold on," she said, as she looked hurriedly around for ideas. She needed some sort of leverage.

Then she spotted something gray sticking up out of the water nearby. She thought at first it was a gravestone. But it was actually a piece of the wyvern's stone wing. It wouldn't work as a pry bar, but she had another idea.

She gripped it in both hands and tried to lift it, but it was far heavier than she expected and it nearly pulled her off her feet.

Filled with anger now, she grabbed it again. With a heavy grunt, she raised it above her head. Her whole body tilted under the weight of it, leaning one way and then the other as she stumbled and splashed through the waist-deep water.

"Watch out, Braeden!" she yelled as she came barreling toward him.

"But I can't get out of the way!" he shouted up in panic as the stone came slamming down from above her head and smashed into the wyvern's talon, cracking it to pieces.

"You did it!" Braeden said, yanking his leg free.

Mighty relieved that she hadn't killed him, she pulled him to his feet. "Come on, we've got to get out of here."

SERAFINA and the SEVEN STARS

"I couldn't agree with you more," he said, and they set off at a steady push. They waded through the swamp together, Braeden sometimes reaching out a hand to help her over the trunk of a fallen tree, other times Serafina leading the way through a particularly nasty thicket of bramble.

As they put the swamp behind them, Serafina glanced back over her shoulder. It was hard to believe, after all the time that she and Braeden and her feline kin had spent there, but the Angel's Glade and the old, abandoned graveyard that surrounded it had been destroyed.

"That was a good idea to use your crows to signal me," she said. "I would have never found you in time on my own."

"Some people send up rescue flares, I send up crows," he said, smiling. "They don't normally fly at night, but it was kind of them to help us."

Once they found their way out of the swamp, they traveled for several miles through the forest, back toward Biltmore.

When it was clear that they had left the battle well behind them, they rested for a few moments, climbing together into the shadowed hollow of an old tree that had been struck by lightning years before.

The space inside the tree was cramped, and the night air cold, so they huddled together, wrapping their arms around each other without saying a word.

They had meant to rest for just a moment to catch their breath, but once they were in the warmth of each other's arms, they stayed in the hollow of the tree for a long time, just holding each other.

Her heart stopped pounding so hard in her chest. Her body stopped shaking from the cold.

Braeden's panting breaths slowly quieted and his head tilted down, gently touching hers.

They had finally escaped.

Huddled there in the darkness, they did not move. They did not speak.

She could feel the pulse of her blood moving gently through her veins, her chest slowly pulling air into her lungs.

For a few moments, she simply *existed*, grateful to be alive.

Finally, Serafina said, "We'd better get on home."

"Yeah," Braeden said softly, and they reluctantly disentangled themselves from each other and crawled out of the tree.

As they headed home, she could sense that, like hers, Braeden's thoughts were turning to what lay ahead.

"What do you think happened at Biltmore after we left?" he asked.

"I don't know," she said, thinking about her pa and everyone else back at home.

As she and Braeden continued on their way through the forest, she asked, "Why did you run toward the wyvern like that?"

"The wyvern was preventing you from getting to the Angel's Glade."

"So you threw yourself into its talons?"

"I didn't throw myself!" he protested with a laugh. "I charged at the wyvern and tried to fight it, but it grabbed me! I didn't do it on purpose."

"What happened after it got you?"

"As it was flying, I kept fighting and kicking, trying to grab branches in the trees to hold myself closer to the ground. I knew I couldn't let it take me up too high or I was done for, so I called the crows. There wasn't much they could do against the wyvern, but they mobbed it and harassed it like it was a giant hawk in their territory. Crows don't like hawks. We weren't winning the fight, that's for sure, but at least we were distracting it and keeping it close to the ground."

"You were *distracting* it?" she said incredulously, remembering how her heart had lurched when she saw him dangling from its talons fifty feet in the air. "That was your plan, to throw yourself at the wyvern and distract it?"

"You make it sound like I tried to sacrifice myself in some sort of heroic, last-stand suicide attack or something."

"It looked an awful lot like a heroic, last-stand suicide attack to me," she said with a smile.

"Well, I think it was more of a flailing, screaming, hanging-upside-down sort of thing," he argued.

"But what were you thinking, doing something like that?"

"I told you, I wanted to give you time to get to the Angel's Glade."

"But you didn't even know why I wanted to get there," she said.

He walked on through the forest without saying anything for a few moments, as if her questions had stumped him a little bit, and then he said, "I knew you must have had some sort of plan."

"You *knew*," she repeated as she walked beside him, wondering about that word.

"I was right, wasn't I?" he said.

"Yeah," she said with a smile. "You were right."

"So what about you? How did you know the statue of the angel would do what it did?"

She wasn't sure she could give him an adequate answer, but she tried to explain it the best she could.

"From the books in the Library, we learned that people long ago thought that the magic of the Seven Stars had the ability to slip through the veil between the physical and the magical world, and that it had the power to bring spirit to that which did not have spirit."

"Like the statues at Biltmore," Braeden said.

"And that's the key. Unlike the statues at Biltmore, the angel in the glade already had a spirit."

Braeden took a few more steps, and then said, "So when the magic of the Seven Stars awoke the angel, it couldn't control her. . . ."

"That's right. The angel was far more powerful."

"But I don't understand. How did you know the angel had a spirit? How did you know she wasn't just plain old stone like all the other statues? Was that from a book, too?"

Serafina just kept walking.

59

Serafina and Braeden crept slowly out of the woods at the top of Diana Hill, near where the goddess of the hunt statue had been, the very place Serafina had been standing days before when the thirteen carriages arrived. She remembered she had been looking desperately for an evil intruder among those new arrivals. It never even occurred to her that the passengers of the carriages would be the *victims*.

She didn't know why the deer standing beside Diana had been the first of the statues to come to life. She had learned so much about what had happened, but there were so many things about the magic of the Seven Stars that she still didn't understand, and probably never would. She had come to realize that there would always be more mysteries. And there would always be more to learn.

"Was the white deer . . ." Braeden began to ask as he stared at the empty spot where the statue had been. "What would have happened if the hunters had never shot it that first night? Or if we hadn't tried to fight it? Was the white deer good or evil?"

She thought about it for several seconds.

Obviously, the white deer was evil: It had been killing people. So it had to be stopped.

She and the people of Biltmore were good. So *it* was evil. Right?

But the more she thought about it, the more she realized it wasn't that simple.

"I don't know," she admitted finally.

"I think maybe it was like the stories said, some kind of reflection of our world in the moment it came. And it splintered and bounced in all different directions, like light in a jewel."

"Or light on the water of a lake," she said.

"Right," he said.

"And there was something else, too," Serafina said. "The way it attacked mainly the hunters at first. That made sense to me. And even the spiraling out of control when we started trying to defend ourselves, when Kinsley was attacked and the others. But it took me a little longer to understand the rest of it."

"What do you mean?" he asked. "What rest of it?"

"When we confronted the deer in the Tapestry Gallery, did

316

you see the way it snorted at us and shook its antlers? It seemed so angry, so fierce, like it wanted to kill us."

"Yeah, I saw that all too close."

"But why did it do that? On that first night when we were down by the lake, the hunters didn't shoot the white deer out of anger. They shot it for sport, for the trophy of killing an unusual animal. Not out of rage or hatred. So, if it was reflection, where did the anger and fierceness come from, that drive for vengeance?"

"You're right," he said. "I never thought about it like that."

Serafina remembered that night by the lake, seeing the beautiful fawn and then hearing the gunshots. She remembered the way she had turned on those hunters, charging at them, her fangs snarling, her claws slashing.

"I think . . . I think maybe it came from me," she said, trying to absorb the meaning of what she was saying even as she was saying it. "A reflection of our world in that moment."

Braeden looked like he was about to open his mouth to argue with her. But then he paused and looked away, maybe beginning to realize that it was possible she was right.

"I don't know if that's what it was," he said finally.

"I don't, either," she admitted, and it was the truth, but it made her wonder.

It *all* made her wonder.

As she and Braeden stood near the empty pedestal, she turned and gazed out across the expanse of the Esplanade toward the house. But instead of being a wide, flat open area of grass, the Esplanade was strewn with hundreds of stone statues—fallen gargoyles, slain ogres, and savage beasts of all descriptions.

The walls of Biltmore Estate looked as if they had been decayed by time, as if bits had fallen off and parts were missing—all the empty spots where the carven ornamentation had been.

It gave the house a gray, weathered look, and she imagined it was dead.

She had hoped to see people gathered outside, or perhaps in the windows or on the terraces, but there was no one there.

Her eyes darted from one area to the next, but she didn't see a single person.

Serafina knew that she and Braeden had been gone from Biltmore for far too long. They had to get home.

"Let's go down," Braeden said gravely, both of them sensing what awaited wasn't going to be good.

He led the way through the field of statues toward the house. She and Braeden moved quickly but warily, half expecting one of the statues to come back to life.

When they reached the front of the house, the doors were hanging wide open, broken off their hinges and tilting to the side. She was expecting to see a footman or someone else guarding the entrance, but no one was there. The house was eerily quiet and still.

"Let's go inside," Braeden said, sounding as nervous and uncertain as she was.

The stained-glass windows had been crushed in. The tall wrought-iron lamps had toppled and their glass globes broken. The magnificent grandfather clock had been knocked to the floor, its oak sides split, its springs sprung, and its gears in pieces. Vases that once held whimsical arrangements of flowers had crashed down and shattered across the floor. The carcass of the winged lion, now solid stone, lay among many other stone creatures.

Serafina swallowed hard and kept walking, Braeden quiet at her side.

As they made their way through the Tapestry Gallery, she could see that much of the furniture had been shredded by the claws of the gargoyles. Many of the Flemish tapestries had been burned or torn down and lay crumpled on the floor. But worst of all, the dead body of her friend, the footman Mr. Pratt, lay on the ground where he had been killed.

Serafina tried to keep breathing, tried to keep standing, but the sight of it was almost too much to bear.

As Braeden reached out and held her arm, he said, "We need to find my aunt and uncle. . . ."

"And my pa . . ." she said, her voice trembling.

As they went into the Library, they saw that it, too, had been severely damaged, but like the other rooms, it was empty of living souls.

"Where is everyone?" Braeden asked. "Did they all get away?"

"If they did, they should have been back by now."

"Let's try the other end of the house," he said unsteadily.

Staying close to each other, they walked back toward the Main Hall. They checked the Winter Garden, the Billiard Room, the Banquet Hall, the Gun Room, the Salon, the Breakfast Room, the Butler's Pantry, and all the other rooms on the first floor.

Normally filled with bustling maids, hurrying footmen, relaxing guests, and countless other people going about their business, it was so eerily peculiar to find it so quiet.

"In all the time I've been at Biltmore, I've never seen it empty before," Braeden said in a daze.

"Come on, let's check upstairs," she said. "There's got to be someone."

They moved quickly now, checking room after room, and they started calling out. "Hello, is anyone here?"

"Mr. Vanderbilt, are you here?" Serafina shouted, but her voice just echoed across the hard marble floors and limestone walls.

"What about the dogs?" Braeden said. "Gidean!" he shouted. "Come on, boy! Gidean!"

"Cedric!" Serafina shouted.

But no dogs came to their call.

"What about the stables?" Braeden asked.

They ran upstairs, out through the Porte Cochere, through the stable courtyard, and into the stable itself. The normally perfectly pristine brick floors were cracked in multiple places and scattered with hay, horse dung, and hurriedly discarded equipment. The cream porcelain-tile walls were scuffed with marks.

"It looks like there was a battle here, too," Braeden said gravely.

But what truly shocked her was that the sounds of their movement and their words echoed in the emptiness of the place.

Every coach, carriage, and cart was gone, and all the horse stalls were empty. Every last harness horse, sport horse, trail horse, draft horse, and pony had been taken.

Serafina heard a sound just ahead, a faint shuffling noise.

"Wait," Serafina said, touching Braeden's arm to keep him still. "Listen. . . ."

When she heard the shuffling again, she moved toward it.

"Be careful," Braeden whispered.

She stepped into the dark stall that it was coming from.

But as she moved through the darkness, she heard a single plaintive, desperate *meow*.

She found Smoke curled up in the hay in the back corner of the stall.

"It's all right, Smoke, I've got ya now," she said as she lifted the frightened gray cat into her arms.

"At least somebody's here," Braeden said in relief, and then a thought seemed to occur to him, and he said, "I'm going to check out back."

Serafina set Smoke down and followed Braeden to the rear of the stable, and then into the dry lot behind it.

There was a paddock there, with a single powerful black thoroughbred inside it.

The horse neighed when it saw them.

"It's good to see you, my friend," Braeden said happily as he walked toward his old companion.

Someone had left them a horse.

Braeden walked toward the horse and, in one quick, graceful motion, swung up onto its back.

"Come on," he said, extending his hand to her.

Serafina's eyes widened in surprise. Braeden knew full well that she had never ridden one of the great hoof-stompers, and he knew full well that she had always been frightened of them, but here he was offering his hand to her.

She hesitated a little, but then, feeling a rush of excitement, she grasped his hand and leapt up behind him. As she wrapped

her arms around his torso, the horse lunged forward with startling speed.

"My uncle would never leave us behind, and neither would
your pa," he shouted over the clattering of the horse's hooves as
they crossed through the courtyard. "Now hang on!"

With the slightest nudge of Braeden's legs, the horse seemed
to know exactly what he wanted and burst into a gallop. Serafina
felt the push of the movement against her body, and the undu-
lation of the horse's gait as it ran. She clung to Braeden, her
hair whipping behind her, the wind brushing her cheeks as they
sped across the fields.

The clear Southern sky glowed blue over the mountains as
they rode, and the orange blaze of the rising sun began to come
into view. More and more, she could feel the warmth of its rays
on her cheeks.

She remembered the previous year, before she had become
known to the Vanderbilts, watching the young master running
across these fields on his horse. She remembered longing for a
friend, someone to talk to, someone she could count on. And
here she was, running across the very same fields with him.

"There!" Braeden shouted and pointed.

Way across the open land, on a distant hilltop, Serafina saw
a mounted search party. It was a group of men on horseback,
with the lean black shape of Gidean and the brown-and-white
Cedric running with them. She could make out Mr. Vanderbilt
and several other men. She even spotted Nolan, the young stable
boy. And there, in the brightness of the sun, was Jess Braddick

on a new horse, with her rifle in her hand. It brought Serafina such relief to see them all, to see them safe and fighting strong.

Then she spotted the figure of one more man, riding one of the estate's large, sorrel-coated Belgian draft horses. He was a stout and heavy man, more used to stomping through the machine rooms of the basement in his thick boots than sitting in a saddle atop a horse in the sunlight, but there he was.

Tears welled up in her eyes. After all that had happened, after all she had done, and after all he had seen, she was still his daughter. And he had come out in search of her.

In the days that followed, there were solemn funerals for Mr. Pratt, who had been killed by the doppelgänger, Mr. Doddman, who had been struck by one of Diana's deadly arrows, and for all the others who had passed away.

She had heard that Lieutenant Kinsley was recovering well at the hospital in Asheville, and she was looking forward to his return to Biltmore.

I'll see you at dinner, he had said, and she was going to make sure he kept that promise.

Over time, most of the servants who had escaped the attack returned to Biltmore, and the effort to clean up and restore the estate began, everyone working in their own way to bring life back to normal again.

Mrs. Vanderbilt returned with Baby Nell, and several additional members of her and her husband's family came down from New York for an extended visit. The autumn shooting had passed, but a few new guests began to arrive—a famous painter who hoped to capture the beauty of the Southern mountains, a naturalist who was studying species of trees, and a writer who needed a quiet place to work on his novel.

Colonel Braddick, Jess's father and her last living relative, had been killed at the estate, so with Mr. Vanderbilt's permission, Jess remained at Biltmore while the authorities determined what should become of her. There was talk of sending her to the orphanage in Asheville, or to an institution in the North. There was even talk that she might return to Africa, where she had spent much of her life. No one was quite sure where she should go. Serafina, for her part, just wanted her new friend to find a home.

Almost immediately after the patterns of life began to return to normal, Mr. Vanderbilt organized the destruction of the statues littering the Esplanade, and commissioned new sculptors, stonemasons, and craftsmen to come to Biltmore and restore the estate to its previous artistic glory. He replaced the Joan of Arc statue, the Saint Louis statue, the lions near the front doors, and many of his other favorites. But he did not replace the wyvern, the winged lion, the bronze statue of himself, or the nastiest of the gargoyles, saying, "I'm drawn to a friendlier sort of company these days."

But now, for reasons that Mr. Vanderbilt never spoke of, he had the new Diana statue made with a trusty dog at her side instead of a white deer. And although the new Diana did have a quiver of arrows on her back, she no longer held a bow in her hand with which to shoot them.

Serafina, for her part, began to settle in to her new life at Biltmore, enjoying the gentle routine of both the day and the night. She often ran through the forest with her brother and sister like she had before, leaping mountain streams and racing through the meadows. And she enjoyed her time in the house as well.

She had always loved her pa, and her pa had always loved her, but her pa knew her now in ways that he had never known her before—in all her forms—and it brought a great joy to her heart.

Jess, her comrade-in-arms during the battle against the Seven Stars, knew of her abilities as well. But Essie, Mr. and Mrs. Vanderbilt, and the other residents of the house thought of her as just a girl, and that was fine by her.

Late at night, she would often lie in her panther form on the balcony outside the nursery, her black silhouette nearly invisible in the darkness and her yellow eyes watching over the grounds. Sometimes, when no one else was around, she would play with little Baby Nell. She never told anyone, but Serafina was pretty sure that Cornelia's first word was *kitty*.

One afternoon, Serafina began pacing in her bedroom on the second floor, jumpy as an anxious cat. Essie had helped her wash her hair and laced her into the new dress that Mrs. Vanderbilt had given her. But Serafina still didn't feel ready.

"Don't fret, he'll be here soon," Essie said encouragingly, but Serafina wasn't so sure. She just kept pacing. Even Smoke meowed to her from his spot on the windowsill, wondering what had gotten into her.

Finally, there was a light rapping at the door.

"I told you, didn't I," Essie said happily. "Now you stay right there like a proper lady, and I'll get the door for you."

Essie opened the door, quickly bowed, and invited Braeden into the room. He was smartly dressed in one of his light brown jackets, with a high white collar and matching kerchief in his pocket.

"I hope I'm not too early," he said cheerfully.

"You're right on time, Master Braeden," Essie said, leading him into the center of the room, where a number of soft, comfortable chairs encircled a low table. Essie had set up a formal English-style tea, complete with a white tablecloth, fine porcelain cups, white cloth napkins, silver spoons, and a pyramid of scones and tea cakes with clotted cream and an assortment of jams alongside.

"This looks good," Braeden said, and then, glancing at Essie playfully, he added, "Eh, the battle in the house was pretty frightening, wasn't it?"

Essie narrowed her eyes at him, as if she was pretty sure he was up to some kind of mischief.

"Did you see that big black panther? Amazing, wasn't it?"

"Braeden Vanderbilt!" Essie scolded him, quite happily, using his name to his face for the first time in her life. "You stop that right now!"

"Why, what are you talking about?" Braeden said with exaggerated innocence, but laughing all the while.

"I've brushed that lovely black hair enough times that I would recognize it just about anywhere, so don't think you're foolin' anyone with this silly talk, pretending that I don't know! I didn't just fall off the turnip truck!"

When Essie glanced at Serafina, she winked and smiled, and Serafina smiled in return, happy that her friend had surmised the truth.

"Believe me, Essie," Braeden said, holding up his hands in a gesture of abject surrender. "I know I'm not fooling anyone."

Finally, Braeden turned to Serafina.

"Hello, Braeden," Serafina said quietly, stepping forward, and feeling oddly flushed at the sight of him. She'd seen this boy battling black cloaks and white deer, climbing into the attics of Biltmore's highest towers, crawling through the mud of the vilest swamps, digging graves in the pouring rain, riding his horse through forest fires, dangling from the talons of wyverns, and all manner of other activities. But for some reason, *this* moment made her heart thump in her chest.

She and Braeden slowly, almost awkwardly, took their seats at the table and tried not to look at each other for too long as Essie poured the tea into their cups, serving them in the manner of a proper English-style afternoon tea, just as she would for Biltmore's finest of guests.

As Serafina sipped her tea, she could feel Smoke lying on her feet beneath the table. And Gidean, Braeden's dog, sat at his side.

A boy and his dog, and a girl and her cat, she thought, and smiled a little.

"What's so funny?" Braeden asked as he slipped several of his tea cakes to Gidean, who gobbled them down appreciatively.

Noticing this, Smoke gave a little chirp of a purr and gazed up at her, making it clear he wouldn't mind a dab of the clotted cream.

Slowly, as she and Braeden began to relax, she came to realize that they were actually enjoying a lovely and delightful afternoon—the so-called "peace and quiet" that she had once scorned. It was unlike any they had ever spent together.

But near the end of it, when Essie stepped out of the room for a moment, Braeden brought up a subject that immediately darkened the mood.

"My uncle said he wants to talk to me tonight about New York," he said glumly.

"He's going to send you back," she said, feeling her heart sink as she said it.

"Yeah," he said. "I think you're right."

She raised her eyes and looked at him across the tea table. "But if you have to go," she said, trying to stay strong and positive for her own sake as much as his, "please know that I understand. I know it's important. I know it more than ever now."

"What do you mean?" he asked.

"I am a fighter, a warrior, a catamount, a black panther . . . but the truth is, I didn't defeat this enemy with my teeth and claws. And when I think about it, I didn't defeat the Man in the Black Cloak that way, either."

"I don't follow what you're saying."

"Last year, we only figured out who the Man in the Black Cloak was because of the Russian words we learned in the Library, do you remember? We only managed to survive against the sorcerer Uriah because of what we learned of Biltmore's past. And we only figured out how to defeat the magic of the Seven Stars by what we read in your uncle's books. It took *knowledge* to solve these mysteries and defeat these enemies.

Not just bravery and determination, not just sharp claws and muscled limbs, but *knowledge*. That's what made the difference. If we're going to succeed in whatever we set out to do with our lives, we need to *learn*, Braeden, we need to learn everything we can. For me, as the Guardian of Biltmore, it will literally be the difference between life and death. And the same is true for you. You've got to learn all you can."

Braeden nodded solemnly, as if he knew what she was saying was right, but he didn't like what it meant for the two of them. And then he looked up at her. "Do you remember that story from the Bible where God asks Job if he can bind the chains of Pleiades or loose the cords of Orion?"

"I guess it means that sometimes there are just things outside our control," Serafina said.

"Right," he said, "sometimes there are. But in this case, I keep thinking that maybe we *can* bind the chains of Pleiades and loose the cords of Orion."

Serafina smiled, not sure what he was talking about, but liking the sound of it.

"I think I might have an idea," he said.

The following morning, Mr. Vanderbilt asked Serafina and Braeden to join him in the Observatory at the top of the house's front tower, which he sometimes used as his private office.

"Have a seat," he said in a serious tone to Braeden, gesturing toward the leather chairs in front of his desk. "We need to talk about your schooling."

Serafina glanced at Braeden, encouraging him to say what he had come to say.

"I don't wish to be disrespectful, Uncle," Braeden said, "but I would like to present an idea to you."

"And what is it about?" Mr. Vanderbilt said, clearly unwilling to be derailed from the matter at hand.

"Three years ago, when my family passed away in the fire . . . I became my father's only living descendant."

"Yes, that's true," Mr. Vanderbilt said.

"So that means that I may have certain resources. . . ."

"You have *significant* resources," Mr. Vanderbilt said. "I am the executor of your father's estate, and you are its sole living beneficiary. It's being held in a trust for you until you reach the age of majority."

"Until I'm eighteen."

"That's right. It's my job as executor to make sure that you are safe and taken care of until that time. And I have been doing my best to do that. Although, sometimes, it feels suspiciously like you and your young companion here are taking care of me rather than the other way around."

"When I was on the train going up to New York, I had an idea."

"From what I've heard, it was to leap off the train and buy a horse with the money I gave you for school," Mr. Vanderbilt said, rather sternly.

"Yes, that's true," Braeden admitted, stuttering a little. "But first, I was thinking about Baby Nell."

"What about her?" Mr. Vanderbilt said.

"I was wondering where she will go to school."

"She's six months old," Mr. Vanderbilt said bluntly, as if he sensed that a challenge was being laid out before him.

"I mean when she's six or seven years old, and it's time for her to go to school," Braeden said. "Are you going to send her to New York?"

Serafina felt her throat go dry. She could only imagine how Braeden must feel at this moment, confronting his uncle in this way.

"Aunt Edith started a school here in Asheville for the local girls to learn weaving and sewing skills so that they can get jobs and earn their own money," Braeden said. "And at the church you built in Biltmore Village, you started a school for all of the local children to attend."

Mr. Vanderbilt listened intently to Braeden's words, but did not speak.

"Your library is one of the largest collections of books in the country," Braeden continued. "And you yourself are considered one of the best-read men in all of America."

"What is your point exactly?" Mr. Vanderbilt said, cutting him short.

"I was just wondering if maybe we could start a school here," Braeden said.

"You mean a school for you," Mr. Vanderbilt said flatly, "so that you can stay at Biltmore. Is that what this is all about?"

"A school for me, yes. But also for Cornelia in a few years. And for Serafina. And for Jess Braddick as well. We need to ask Jess to stay at Biltmore, Uncle. We can't just send her away. She saved our lives. Doesn't she deserve the best schooling we can give her? And what about the children of the servants? We'll call the school Carolina School, or Asheville School, or Biltmore School, or whatever you want to call it. We'll spend the money in my trust to do it. You've been assigning me books to read from your library, and I like that. We could keep doing more of that. And you could teach us about art and ballet and opera. The men at the Biltmore Forestry School that you set up could teach us about the trees and the mountains. Serafina's pa could teach us about electricity and machines. And we could bring in tutors and teachers from all over the country. We could build a very good school, something we could be proud of."

When Braeden finally stopped talking, his uncle did not speak. He just looked at him. And then, after a long time, he asked, "When exactly did you come up with all of this?"

"When I crossed the border into Tennessee."

"Why did Tennessee make you think of creating a school?"

"Because Vanderbilt University is in Tennessee," Braeden said.

Mr. Vanderbilt smiled, as if he was beginning to realize the extent to which his nephew had thought this through.

"Vanderbilt University is one of the most respected universities in the country," Mr. Vanderbilt said.

"And your grandfather founded it," Braeden said.

Mr. Vanderbilt nodded and smiled again, like a man who knows he's being checkmated, but isn't quite sure if he minds or not.

"I know that traditions are good, Uncle," Braeden continued. "It's how we pass down the good parts of our lives from one generation to the next. And I truly respect that my father wanted me to attend school in New York as he did. But sometimes, old traditions need to be changed and new traditions need to be made."

"I'm sensing this isn't the only tradition you're talking about," Mr. Vanderbilt said.

"There is one other," Braeden admitted. "It has been a tradition in our family for a long time to host the hunting season. And in the Blue Ridge Mountains it has been a tradition to hunt mountain lions, to kill off all the predators that live in these forests. But I think, in our family at least, we all agree now that, tradition or not, we're not going to do it anymore, we're not going to allow that kind of hunting on our land. We're going to protect our forests and our wildlife as much as we can."

Mr. Vanderbilt stared at Braeden in silence. At first Serafina thought that he must be angry. But then she realized that wasn't it at all. She could see in his eyes at that moment that Mr. Vanderbilt was immensely proud of his nephew.

"I couldn't agree more," Mr. Vanderbilt said. "I've been thinking the same thing."

"I think that some traditions need to be valued," Braeden said, "but others need to change. We shouldn't just follow the ways of the past. We should lead the way to a better future."

"If we move forward with this school idea of yours, it will require a considerable amount of work and commitment," Mr. Vanderbilt said as he studied Braeden. "It's obviously far more difficult to build an entirely new school than it is to go to an established school. Are you sure you want to do this?"

"Yes, I'm sure, Uncle," Braeden said, glancing over at Serafina. "I'm very sure."

"Once we start, you'll have to follow it through."

"I understand," Braeden said. "I'm ready."

And then the master of Biltmore turned and looked at her. "And what do you say about this idea?"

Serafina smiled excitedly. "When can we get started?"

That night, she sat with Braeden on the grass of a small hill nestled in the Biltmore gardens.

"Do you see that planet up there?" Braeden asked, pointing up into the star-filled sky.

Jupiter, Serafina thought wistfully. She had seen it nearly every night while he was gone, even on some of the cloudiest nights when no other planets or stars were visible. She could almost always see Jupiter shining through.

"When I was up in New York," he said, "I couldn't see most of the stars because of the lights of the city. But I could see Jupiter. And I always imagined it was you."

For a long time, she did not move or speak. She just let the moment flow around them and through them, his words, his tone of voice, his presence sitting beside her. She had never felt so deeply calm in all her life. And she wondered what could ever disturb that calm.

"It seems like we keep having to fight these battles to stay together," she said.

"And we'll keep fighting them," he said. A few more seconds passed, and then he added, "You *know* why I came back to Biltmore that night by the lake, right? And you know why I couldn't find the words I wanted to say before I left in the morning."

Serafina's heart began to pound in her chest.

"I think I do," she said, feeling as if her lips were suddenly going dry.

"I jumped off that train because I wanted to be with you, Serafina," he said. "I didn't care about anything else."

She smiled, letting the words soak down into her soul. And then she said, "Maybe next time wait until the train comes to a stop."

"Aw, that's no fun," he said, laughing softly. "Where's your sense of adventure?"

"Yeah, that's me," she said, "no sense of adventure," as she put her arm around him and rested her head gently against his chest.

And she knew, in that simple gesture of affection, that the great river of their lives had shifted course, and was pouring now across new ground, new worlds, places they had never seen or felt before.

"I love you, Braeden," she whispered.

"I love you, too, Serafina," he whispered in return.

About the Author

Robert Beatty is the #1 *New York Times* best-selling author of *Willa of the Wood* and the Serafina series. He lives in the mountains of Asheville, North Carolina, with his wife and three daughters. He writes full-time now, but in his past lives he was one of the pioneers of cloud computing, the founder/CEO of Plex Systems, the cofounder of Beatty Robotics, and the CTO and chairman of *Narrative* magazine.

Visit him online at www.robertbeattybooks.com.

SERAFINA
and the
SPLINTERED HEART

SERAFINA and the SPLINTERED HEART

ROBERT BEATTY

DISNEY · HYPERION

LOS ANGELES   NEW YORK

First Edition, July 2017
10 9 8 7 6 5 4 3 2 1
FAC-020093-19200
Printed in the United States of America

This book is set in 12-pt Adobe Garamond Pro, Liam,
Qilin/Fontspring; Minister Std/Monotype
Designed by Maria Elias

Library of Congress Cataloging in Publication Control Number: 2017001301
ISBN 978-1-4847-7504-2

Reinforced binding

Visit www.DisneyBooks.com

Biltmore Estate
Asheville, North Carolina

Serafina opened her eyes and saw nothing but black. It was as if she hadn't opened her eyes at all.

She had been deep in the darkened void of a swirling, half-dreaming world when she awoke to the sound of a muffled voice, but now there was no voice, no sound, no movement of any kind.

With her feline eyes she had always been able to see, even in the dimmest, most shadowed places, but here she was blind. She searched for the faintest glint of light in the gloom, but there was no moonlight coming in through a window, no faint flicker of a distant lantern down a corridor.

Just black.

She closed her eyes and reopened them. But it made no difference. It was still pitch-dark.

Have I actually gone blind? she wondered.

Confused, she tried to listen out into the darkness as she had done when she hunted rats deep in the corridors of Biltmore's sprawling basement. But there was no creak of the house, no servants working in distant rooms, no father snoring in a nearby cot, no machinery whirring, no clocks ticking or footsteps. It was cold, still, and quiet in a way she had never known. She was no longer at Biltmore.

Remembering the voice that had woken her, she listened for it again, but whether it had been real or part of a dream, it was gone now.

Where am I? she thought in bewilderment. *How did I get here?*

Then a sound finally came, as if in answer to her question.

Thump-thump.

For a moment that was all there was.

Thump-thump, thump-thump.

The beat of her heart and the pulse of her blood.

Thump-thump, thump-thump, thump-thump.

As she slowly moved her tongue to moisten her cracked, dry lips, she sensed the faint taste of metal in her mouth.

But it wasn't metal.

It was blood—her own blood flowing through her veins into her tongue and her lips.

She tried to clear her throat, but then all at once she took in a sudden, violent, jerking breath and sucked in a great gasp of

2

air, as if it were the very first breath she had ever taken. As her blood flowed, a tingling feeling flooded into her arms and legs and all through her body.

What is going on? she thought. *What happened to me? Why am I waking up like this?*

Thinking back through her life, she remembered living with her pa in the workshop, and battling the Black Cloak and the Twisted Staff with her best friend, Braeden. She'd finally come out into the grand rooms and daylight world of the fancy folk. But when she tried to remember what happened next, it was like trying to recall the fleeting details of a powerful dream that drifts away the moment you wake. It left her disoriented and confused, as if she were grasping for the tattered remnants of a previous life.

She had not yet moved her body, but she felt herself lying on her back on a long, flat surface. Her legs were straight, her hands neatly lying one over the other on her chest, like someone had laid her there with respect and care.

She slowly separated her hands and moved them down on either side of her body to feel the surface beneath her.

It felt hard, like rough wooden boards, but the boards felt strangely *cold. The boards shouldn't be cold,* she thought. *Not like this. Not cold.*

Her heart began to pound in her chest. A wild panic rose inside her.

She tried to sit up, but immediately slammed her forehead into a hard surface a few inches above her, and she crashed down again, wincing in pain.

She pressed her hands against the boards above her. Her probing fingers were her only eyes. There were no breaks or openings in the boards. Her palms began to sweat. Her breaths got shorter. A desperate surge of fear poured through her as she craned her body and pushed to the side, but there were boards there, too, just inches away. She kicked her feet. She pounded her fists. But the boards surrounded her, closing her in on all sides.

Serafina growled in frustration, fear, and anger. She scratched and she scurried, she twisted and she pried, but she could not escape. She had been enclosed in a long, flat wooden box.

She pressed her face frantically into the corner of the box and sniffed, like a trapped little animal, hoping to catch a scent from the outside world through the thin cracks between the boards. She tried one corner, and then the next, but the smell was the same all around her.

Dirt, she thought. *I'm surrounded by damp, rotting dirt. I've been buried alive!*

Serafina lay in the cold black space of the coffin buried underground. Her mind flooded with terror.

I need to get out of here, she kept thinking. *I need to breathe. I'm not dead!*

But she could not see. She could not move. She could not hear anything other than the sound of her own ragged breathing. How much air would she have down here? She felt a tight constriction in her lungs. Her chest gripped her. She wanted her pa! She wanted her mother to come and dig her out. Someone had to save her! She frantically pressed her hands against the coffin lid above her head and pushed with all her strength, but she couldn't lift it. The sound of her screeching voice hurt her ears in this terrible, closed-in, black place.

Then she thought about what her pa would say if he was here. "Get your wits about ya, girl. Figure out what ya need to do and get on with doin' it."

She sucked in another long breath, and then steadied herself and tried to think it through. She couldn't see with her eyes, but she traced her fingers along the skirt and sleeves of her dress. They were badly torn. It seemed like if she had died and there had been a funeral, then they would have put her in a nice dress. Whoever had buried her had been in a hurry. Had they thought she was dead? Or did they want her to suffer the most horrible of deaths?

At that moment, she heard the faint, muffled sound of movement above her. Her heart filled with hope. *Footsteps!*

"Help!" she screamed as loud as she possibly could. "Help me! Please help me!"

She screamed and screamed. She pounded the wood above her head. She flailed her legs. But the sound of the footsteps drifted away, then disappeared and left a silence so complete that she wasn't sure she'd heard the sound at all.

Had it been the person who buried her? Had he heaved the last shovel of dirt onto her grave and left her here? Or was it a passerby who had no idea she was here? She slammed her fists against the boards and screamed, "Please! I need your help! I'm down here!"

But it was no use.

She was alone.

She felt a dark wave of hopelessness pour through her soul.

She could not escape.

She could not survive this . . .

No, she thought, gritting her teeth. *I'm not gonna let myself die down here. I'm not gonna give up. I'm going to stay bold! I'm going to find a way out . . .*

She slid herself down toward the end of the coffin and kicked. The coffin's rough boards felt thin and crudely made, not like a proper solid casket, but like a ramshackle box nailed together from discarded apple crates. But the earth behind the rickety wood braced the boards so firmly that it was impossible for her to break them.

Then she had an idea.

"Six feet under." That was what her had pa told her years ago when she asked him what they did with dead people. " 'Round here they bury folk six feet under," he'd said.

She squirmed inside the dark, cramped space, bending her body up like a little kitten in a lady's shoe box, and positioned herself so that she could put her hands on the top center of the coffin's lid. She figured that six feet of dirt must weigh an awful lot. And her pa had taught her that the center of a board was its weakest point.

Remembering something else he'd taught her, she knocked on the board above her and listened. *Tap-tap-tap.* Then she moved down a few inches and knocked again. *Tap-tap-tap.* She kept knocking until she found a place with a slightly deeper, more hollow sound where the dirt was packed a little less firmly behind it. "That's the spot."

But now what? Even if she managed to crack the board, the dirt above would come crashing down on her. Her mouth and nose would fill with dirt and she'd suffocate. "That's not gonna work . . ."

Suddenly an idea sprang into her mind. She buttoned her dress tight up to her neck and then pulled the lower part of the dress up over her head, inside out, so that the fabric covered her face, especially her mouth and nose. It was cramped in the coffin and difficult to move, but she managed to get the dress bundled around her head and then wriggled her arms out of the sleeves so that her hands were free. If she was lucky, the fabric over her face would give her the seconds she needed.

Knowing that her hands alone weren't strong enough to break the boards, she rolled onto her stomach and positioned her shoulder at the top center of the coffin.

Bracing herself, she pushed upward with her arms and legs and the strength of her whole body. There wasn't enough space inside the coffin to get herself all the way up onto her hands and knees. But she bent herself into a coil and pushed the best she could, slamming her shoulder against the coffin's lid over and over again. She knew that one strong blow wasn't going to do it. And slow pressure wasn't, either. She needed to get a good, hard, forceful rhythm going. *Bang, bang, bang.* She could feel the long boards of the coffin's lid flexing. "That's it, that's what we need," she said. *Bang, bang, bang* she slammed. "Come on!" she growled. Then she heard the center board cracking beneath the weight of the earth above. "Come on!" She kept pushing. *Bang, bang, bang.* The board began to split. Then she felt something cold hit her bare shoulders. She should have been filled with joy that her plan was actually working, but her mind filled with fear. The lid had cracked! The coffin was caving in! Cold, clammy, heavy dirt dumped all over her, pushing her down to the coffin floor. If she hadn't tied her dress over her head, her mouth and nose would have filled with dirt at that very moment and she would have been dead.

Working blind, with nothing but her grasping hands to guide her, she grabbed great handfuls of the incoming dirt and chucked them into the corners of the coffin, packing the dirt away as fast as it poured down through the hole, but it just kept coming, coming, coming. The terrible weight of the dirt surrounded her legs and shoulders and head. It was getting more and more difficult to move. She sucked in breaths through the fabric of her dress as fast and hard as she could. Her chest heaved in panic. She couldn't get enough air!

Finally, when there was no more space in the coffin to push the dirt, she tried to make her escape. She jammed her head straight up through the hole, pushed with her legs, and started digging toward the surface. But the dirt came down so fast, and pushed in so hard, she never had a chance. Even as she dug, the dirt began to suffocate her. Its crushing weight pushed against her chest, driving one last scream from her lungs.

Loose earth poured down around her head and shoulders, collapsing onto her faster than she could dig it away. She felt the pressing weight of it all around her, closing in on her, trapping her legs, but she kept clawing, kicking, squirming her way blindly up through the darkness, desperately trying to pull gasps of air through the fabric covering her face. She felt the material pushing deeper and deeper into her mouth as the dirt pressed in, gagging her, shutting off the flow of air to her aching lungs.

Then she heard a fast scratching sound above her, like the frenzied digging of an animal. She hoped that Gidean, Braeden's dog, was trying to rescue her, but a terrible, low growling sound told her it wasn't her canine friend. Whatever kind of creature it was, the beast's claws tore at the earth, ripping it away with terrific power. Was it a bear digging up its supper? It didn't matter. She had to keep climbing. She had to breathe!

Sharp claws raked across her upstretched hands. Serafina shrieked in pain, but she grabbed hold of the beast's paw. *Gotcha!* She held on for dear life. The force of the paw yanked her body up through the ground.

The snarling beast jerked its paw again, trying to free itself of her, yanking and pulling, but Serafina held on tight.

When her head finally broke the surface of the ground, she sucked in a mighty gasp of air, flooding her lungs with new life. Air! She finally had air!

She lost her grip on the beast's paw and it pulled away, but she clambered out of the dirt until her shoulders and arms were free.

Hope filled her heart. She'd made it! She'd escaped! But as she reached up and pulled the fabric from her head, she heard a loud roaring snarl, and the claws came down at her again, raking across her scalp just as she tried to duck away. Clutching wildly at the earth with her hands, she quickly scrambled out of the grave and got up onto her hands and knees to defend herself.

She had crawled out of the ground into a moonlit graveyard, overgrown by a dense forest of trees and vines. A large stone angel, with her wings raised up around her, stood on a pedestal in the center of the small clearing. Serafina had no idea how she'd gotten here, but she knew this place. It was the angel's glade. But before she could take it all in, she heard something behind her and spun around.

A black panther was coming straight toward her, crouched low for the lunge, its ears pinned back, its face quivering with fierceness as it opened its mouth and hissed with its long fangs bared and gleaming, ready to bite.

$\mathcal{S}$erafina stared into the face of the angry panther. Its bright yellow eyes were as savage as she'd ever seen in a wild animal, filled with a looming and ferocious power. She crouched down low, ready to defend herself. When the panther showed its long white fangs and snarled at her again, Serafina bared her teeth and hissed right back, fierce and fiery, challenging it with everything she had. But to her astonishment, the black panther turned its head away, then slunk into the forest and disappeared.

Overwhelmed with exhaustion, Serafina collapsed to the ground. She sucked in long and heavy breaths, just relieved to be alive. *That big cat had me as good as dead,* she thought. *Why in the world did it slink off like a socked possum?*

As she lay there recovering, she tried to comprehend what had happened. Someone had buried her. But they hadn't just buried her, they had buried her in the old, abandoned graveyard that had been overgrown by the forest decades before.

And the more she thought about it, the more she couldn't believe what she had just seen. *How could there be a black panther?*

Her mother had been a catamount, a shape-shifter with the ability to turn into a mountain lion at will, but when Serafina finally learned to shift, she was a black panther like her father had been, a rare variant of the race. According to mountain lore, there was only one black panther at a time.

She kept thinking that the panther must have been her father, but her father had died in battle twelve years before, the night she was born. Her pa, the man who had found her in the forest that night and taken care of her ever since, was the only father she had ever known. And the more she thought about it, the more she was convinced that the panther she'd just seen hadn't been a full-grown male, but a young cat, lean and uncertain. It might have been her half sister or half brother, but they were just spotted little cubs. When her catamount friend Waysa was in lion form, his fur was dark brown. Maybe the light had been playing tricks on her eyes, but if it had been Waysa, why would he run away from her?

Questions reeled through her mind, but the sensations of her body began to overwhelm her. Her head hurt from the swipe of the panther's claws, which had left a bleeding wound, but it wasn't too bad. After what she'd experienced in the coffin, it felt so good to just have air moving in and out of her lungs. She could feel the warm breeze on her bare skin, and smell the clover and ferns growing nearby, and see the glorious stars above. Her senses seemed more acute than ever before.

As her strength returned to her arms and legs, she brushed the remaining dirt from her body and straightened out the plain beige dress she was wearing. That was when she noticed the large, dark stains around the rips in the material. Frightened, she quickly looked herself over and found dried blood all over her bare torso, shoulders, and arms. But there were no recent wounds. Just scars.

At that moment, memories of her life began to flow slowly through her like a quiet river. She saw herself eating supper with her pa in the workshop, and lying on Biltmore's highest rooftop with Braeden as they counted stars in the midnight sky, and running happily through the forest in panther form with her mother and Waysa. She saw herself sitting in front of the fireplace in Mr. Vanderbilt's library as he told her stories from his books and travels, and sitting quietly at morning tea with Mrs. Vanderbilt, who had recently announced that she was with child.

Then she remembered her friend Essie, one of Biltmore's maids, helping her lace up the beautiful golden-cream gown that Braeden had given her for the Christmas party. She remembered looking at herself in Essie's mirror, seeing a twelve-year-old girl with sharp, feline angles to her cheekbones, amber-yellow eyes, and long, shiny black hair, and thinking, for the first time, she was going to fit in just fine.

The memory of the Christmas party swirled around in her mind. She could so vividly remember the softness of the candlelight, the scent of the wood on the fire, the smile on her pa's face, and the warmth of Braeden's hand on her back as they entered the room together. It was a moment of peace and triumph, not just because she and Braeden had defeated their enemies, but because she felt like she truly belonged.

The last night she remembered at Biltmore, she had been making her rounds through the house on a winter evening. The memory came to her in snatches. She was the Guardian, the protector against intruding spirits and other dangers. Everyone else had gone to bed, and she had the darkened corridors of the house to herself, just like she liked it. She stepped out onto the formal back patio, which the Vanderbilts called the Loggia. The sheer white curtains in the doorway glowed in the moonlight as they fluttered in the cold winter breeze. She looked out across the grounds of the estate toward the forest and the mountains in the distance. The full moon was rising over the peaks.

All was still in the house, but then she felt an unusual movement of air around her and a disturbing chill ran up her spine. The hairs on the back of her neck went up. Suddenly she sensed something behind her. She spun around, ready to fight, but all she could see was a black and roiling darkness where the walls and windows of the house should have been.

Something struck her chest with piercing pain. A storm of wind swept around her. Her mind filled with confusion. She fought with tooth and claw, growling and hissing and biting. Blood was everywhere.

But then it all went black, and the memory faded.

She stood now beside her own grave in the pale light of the moon in the center of the angel's glade and looked around her. She was miles from home. What a strange and haunted place to find herself crawling from the ground! The loose dirt was tracked with human footprints and what looked like shovel marks. There was no gravestone, just a mound of dirt. She reckoned that whoever buried her didn't want her found. Had someone attempted to murder her and then hide the body?

She looked up at the stone angel. "What did you see that night?"

But the angel didn't answer. She stood on her pedestal of stone as mute and immutable as she always did. The angel was old and weathered, mottled with dark moss and green patina. She had long, curling hair and a beautiful face, with tears of dark sap streaming down her cheeks. To Serafina her face seemed to be filled with the silent wisdom of knowingness, as if the angel held inside her the fate and fortune of those she loved, and it was all too much to bear. The angel held her mighty, finely feathered wings above her, and she gripped a long, sharp steel sword in her hand. It was the very sword that Serafina had used to cut and destroy the Black Cloak.

The angel stood in the center of a small clearing of bright green grass. The leaves on the trees and bushes around the angel's glade stayed green all year round, never drying in the summer's sun, or changing color in autumn, or falling to the ground in winter. The angel's glade was a place of eternal spring.

The north side of the glade led deep into the rest of the old graveyard, which had been taken back by the encroaching forest long ago, with vines covering many of the headstones and stringy moss hanging down from the black limbs of crooked trees. The graveyard stretched on for as far as Serafina could see, endless rows of tilting, toppled, half-buried monuments marking the graves of hundreds of dead, rotting bodies and lost souls. A gray whispery mist floated listlessly through the graveyard, as if searching for a place to linger. As Serafina peered across the graveyard looking for signs of movement, she hoped that she was the only body that had crawled forth from the grave tonight.

Finally, she said to her buried companions, "Sorry to be gettin' on my way so soon, but it turns out that I was just a-visiting for a while."

She walked to the other side of the angel's glade, which led into the natural part of the forest that she knew so well. Looking into the trees made her think about her catamount mother. She had learned so much from her mother. They'd run through the forest together and hunted together. She'd learned the sounds of the night birds and the movement of the woodland creatures. She wondered why her mother hadn't sensed her and come to her like she had so many times before.

It began to sink in that her pa hadn't come for her, either, and neither had Braeden.

No one had come.

She was alone.

Fear began to well up in her mind. As she thought about what might have happened to the people she loved, her heart felt heavy in her chest. She didn't know what had attacked her or how long she'd been gone. She wondered what the people of Biltmore would think when she walked into the mansion covered in graveyard dirt, but her true fear, deep down, was that they wouldn't be there at all, that she'd find the house empty, full of nothing but shadows.

Anxious to get moving, she headed into the forest, following the path that would take her to Biltmore. She had to get home.

Serafina followed the path through the darkened forest at a quick pace, down into a ravine dense with ancient maple and hemlock trees. Her legs felt strong and steady beneath her as she weaved between the great trunks of the forest's oldest inhabitants.

A chorus of tree frogs, peepers, and insects filled her ears, and the scents of primrose and moonflower wafted past her nose. The evening flowers stayed closed during the day, but opened with their sweet smells at night.

Everything seemed unusually vibrant to her tonight, like her body and her senses were alive with new sensations.

The forest grew thick with rosebay rhododendron bushes glimmering in the silver moonlight. Hummingbird moths hovered over the white and pinkish blooms, dipping into the recesses of the flowers and sipping out the nectar within. It almost felt as if she could hear the beat of the moths' wings against the night air.

Fireflies floated in the darkness above the shiny green leaves of the laurel. Soft flashes of lightning danced on the silver-clouded sky behind them, and a gentle thunder rolled through the darkness, moving on the rising heat of what felt like a summer breeze.

"This is all so strange . . ." she said to herself, looking around her in confusion as she traveled. The last night she remembered, it had been winter, but the air felt strangely warm now. And these plants and insects didn't come out in winter. Had the magic of the angel's glade somehow extended out into the rest of the forest?

When she glanced up at the moon, what she saw stopped her dead in her tracks. The moon was not all the way full, but large and bright, with the light on the right and the shadow on the left.

"That's not right," she said, frowning. That night she was on the Loggia the moon had been full, which meant what she was seeing now was impossible.

She knew that the moon was only full one night a month, then it would wane for fourteen nights, with the light on the left side, getting smaller and smaller until it was dark for a single evening. Then it would wax for fourteen nights, with the light on the right, until it was full once more. Then it would start all over again.

The moon was the great calendar in the sky by which she had marked the nights of her life, wandering through the grounds of Biltmore Estate by herself. The steady phases of her pale companion, the slow sweep of the glistening stars, and the curving transit of the five brightest planets had been her silent but loyal confidants for as long as she could remember. They were her midnight brothers and her dark-morning sisters. She had spoken to them, learned from them, watched them as a girl sees the members of her family moving around her.

But tonight she looked at her sister the moon in confusion, a thumping urgency in her temples as she tried to figure out the meaning of what she was seeing. The moon was lit on the *right* side. That meant it was *waxing*, getting larger each night. But if the moon had been full the last time she saw it, how could it be waxing now?

It was as if she'd fallen backward a night in time. Either that or something equally unimaginable: She'd been underground for more than an entire cycle of the moon.

"That means twenty-eight nights have passed, maybe more . . ." she said to herself in astonishment.

The breeze whispered through the tops of the trees as if the hidden spirits of the forest were nervously discussing that she had discovered the universe's ruse. Time flew forward. Time flew back. Nothing was as it seemed. People were buried underground and people came back. She was in a world of many in-betweens.

Another set of flashes lit up the sky and danced silently

among the clouds, then the thunder rolled on, echoing across the mountainsides.

She had always been able to see things other people could not, especially in the dark of night, but tonight there seemed to be a special magic in the forest. It felt as if she could actually see the evening flowers slowly opening their petals to the moon and the glint of starlight on the iridescent wings of the insects. She felt the caress of the air as it slipped through the branches of the trees, around her body, and against her skin. She sensed the stony firmness of the earth and rock on which she stood. The tiny droplets of dew on the clover leaves around her suddenly glistened, and a moment later, the white light of the distant lightning shone in her eyes. Water and earth and light and sky . . . It was as if she had become intermingled with the faintest elements of the world, as if she were in tune with the slip and sway of the nocturnal realm in a way that she had never been before.

She continued walking, but as she gazed through the trees she spotted what appeared to be a crease of blackness in the distance. She tilted her head in confusion. Was it a shadow? She couldn't make it out. But as she narrowed her eyes to look at it, she realized that whatever it was, it was *moving*, not toward her or away, but hovering in the air, like a rippling black wave.

The skin on her arms rose up with goose bumps. She couldn't help but wonder if what she was seeing was related to the black shape that had attacked her at Biltmore.

She knew she should leave it alone, but she was too curious

to turn away. She slowly moved closer until she was maybe a dozen steps from it, then she stopped and studied the black shape. It appeared to be about five feet long, floating of its own accord a few feet off the ground, like a long banner held in the breeze. And it was utterly black, blacker than anything she had ever seen.

Suddenly, a wind swept through the trees. A gust kicked up from the forest floor, swirling small tornados of leaves around her. The branches hanging above her began to creak and bend, like the swaying limbs of old, twisted men, their long, twiggy hands dangling down onto her head and shoulders. When the cold mist of a coming rain touched her face, she realized that a storm was near. And then she spotted a dark figure making its way toward her through the trees.

Serafina sucked in a breath in surprise and dropped to the ground to hide. She scrambled beneath the base of a half-toppled tree where the spidering roots had pulled up from the earth and created a small cave. Pressing herself in as deep as she could go, she peered out through the small holes between the roots.

The man, or creature, or whatever it was, moved toward her through the forest with a slow and deliberate pace, like a predator hunting for prey. It stalked on two long, gangly legs, its back hunched over and its head hanging down, its shoulders swaying one way and then the other as it gazed from side to side. Even as hunched as it was, the creature was very tall, with long, crooked arms dangling in front of it like a praying mantis, and the elongated fingers of its spindling hands like white, scaly talons, tipped with sharp, curving, clawlike fingernails. It moved with steady purpose, scraping its feet through the leaves of the forest floor, the movement of its bones sounding like cracking branches.

What kind of godforsaken thing is that? she thought, cowering in her hole. *Is it some kind of vile creech that crawled from the grave the same way I did?*

The creature came closer and closer. As it stepped within a few feet of her, Serafina couldn't keep her body from trembling. Her only hope was that the creature wouldn't see her hiding beneath the roots at its feet.

She could hear its breathing now, the slow wheezing, ragged, hissing breath, like a wounded animal, and she could see it more closely than she had before. A white haze lingered about its body like the smoke around a dying campfire, and straggly gray strands hung around its head like the stringy hair of a rotting corpse. When the creature turned and she saw its face, she gasped. The creature's face had been slashed with a savage wound that oozed with the blackish, festering blood of an injury that never healed. She couldn't tell whether the creature was a mortal man or a hellish fiend, or some combination of the two, but its sharp, pointy teeth chattered with anticipation as it scanned the forest, swaying its head back and forth as it crept forward with its dangling claws.

At first it seemed as if the creature was going to pass her by, but then the thing stopped, standing right over her.

Its talon-like hand grasped one of the roots of the toppled tree beneath which she was hiding. Serafina sucked in a startled breath and held it, too frightened to exhale. The creature looked one way into the forest and then the other. It seemed like it knew she was there, that it sensed her presence, maybe smelled her, but it had not yet detected exactly where she was. She held her breath like a trembling rabbit in her little den.

The creature opened its mouth and a low, vibrating, guttural sound emerged. Then Serafina began to actually see the white air rushing from its lungs. It wasn't just an exhalation or a long scream, but a *storm*. The air around her began to twist and turn, the leaves swirling up, the branches on the trees bending and cracking. The air exploded with blowing rain. The terrible noise coming from the creature's mouth was getting louder and louder as the storm rose up all around.

The storm-creech peered down into the mound of roots where she was hiding. Its silver-glowing eyes looked straight at her, shocking her with a blast of fear. The creature's talons closed into a fist, crushing the roots that it had been holding. Then it began tearing the roots away with both hands, its teeth chattering as it ripped its way toward her.

As the creature attacked, Serafina reflexively tried to shift into panther form to defend herself, but it didn't work. For some clumsy reason, she couldn't change. She tried again, concentrating on envisioning herself as a panther, but she couldn't do it. She remained in her human form.

Not knowing what else to do, she cowered down. She tried to stay out of the creature's reach as it ripped the roots away. She thought about leaping up at the thing and fighting it with her bare hands, but it seemed far too powerful. At the last second, just as its claws touched her, she scrambled out of the roots on her belly and darted out the other side.

A storm raged through the forest. The pelting rain roared around her. The wind blew so hard that her hair and clothes pressed against her face and body. It felt like it wasn't going to just blow her away, but tear her into little pieces.

But she couldn't let the storm slow her down. The creature was right behind her. She had to get out of there. She ran headlong into the swirling rain and just kept running.

When she looked over her shoulder, she expected to see the creature charging up behind her, grabbing for her, but it wasn't. It was in the distance, still ripping at the roots where she'd been hiding.

Confused, but relieved that she'd managed to escape the wretched thing, she quickly turned to keep moving, but she nearly ran straight into an eerie black shape similar to what she'd seen before. She stopped abruptly, recoiling from it like it was a venomous snake.

It floated right in front of her now, so sharply black that it seemed like an impossibility. The light of the moon and stars disappeared into it, and she could see nothing on the other side of it. Rain fell in, but did not come out. It was like a tear in the fabric of the world.

The sight of it tightened her chest. Her skin buzzed. She backed away and ducked into a thicket of bushes to hide.

When the black shape drifted in her direction, she caught her breath in surprise. She couldn't tell if it was drifting on the winds of the storm or was actually drawn to her in some way.

The roiling black shape floated slowly closer. She thought that the thick foliage would protect her, but the leaves and branches snapped and hissed as the black shape touched them, bursting them one by one, as it moved toward her.

She frantically squirmed away, but the edge of the black shape touched her shoulder. The searing pain felt like she was being slashed with a burning, white-hot blade. She screamed in agony and wrenched herself away.

Driven by blind fear, she clambered out of the thicket and ran. She spotted a rocky area and sprinted for it. When she saw the drop-off of a steep mountain slope, she jumped.

She hit the ground hard and rolled down the earthen slope, her shoulders and legs thudding against the rocks and trees as she fell, then sprang to her feet and fled.

She tore through the forest, gasping for breath, but pushed herself on, looking over her shoulder for signs of the storm-creech and the black shapes.

As the rain and wind slowly died down, and the storm faded behind her, she kept going at a hurried pace.

Finally, she was relieved to see the glow of the moon peeking through the clouds. Day folk knew that the sun rose in the east and set in the west, but many didn't realize that the moon did as well. Its black shadows among the trees were like arrows pointing the way home. As soon as she got her wits about her, she figured out what direction she needed to go, and went as fast as she could. She had to warn the people of Biltmore about what she had seen.

But just as she began to make progress, she came to the edge of a river blocking her path. She scanned the surrounding area in confusion.

"Don't tell me you've gone and gotten yourself lost," she scolded herself.

She had thought she was close to home. She remembered a creek near here, small and shallow, just a quick leap across. But what blocked her path now was a powerful river, turbulent and strong, ripping through the trees. Its shores weren't the rocky edge of a normal river, but the flooded forest.

It was strange how so much had changed. If the little creek she remembered was now this churning river, then there must have been many other storms like the one she'd just fought her way through. A knot of worry bunched in her stomach. There were few things in the mountains more powerful and damaging than the rushing waters that had formed them.

Knowing she had to get home, she stepped into the dark water of the river to cross it. The current felt like tiny shards tearing at her bare skin. She'd waded across plenty of rivers, but this was a strange and alarming sensation that she'd never felt before. When she took another step, it became very clear that the river was far too deep and turbulent for her to cross. It seemed like it wanted to suck her in and pull her under.

Looking out across the river, she was amazed to see an entire tree—branches, trunk, and roots and all—floating downstream, tumbling through the current, like a great, leafy leviathan. Many of the largest and oldest trees at the edge of the river had toppled into the current, the earth beneath their roots ripped away by the powerful pull of the rushing water.

She stepped back out of the flooded river and away from the edge, convinced that the dark, malevolent water wanted to consume her. She couldn't cross here. But if she was anywhere near where she thought she was, there were no roads or bridges for quite a while.

"We're in a real pickle now, girl," she said, talking to herself the way her pa did. "What we gonna do about it? That's the question."

Then she had an idea.

She made her way upstream along the shore until she found one of the tallest trees hanging over the river, its great, spreading boughs almost reaching across and touching the trees on the other side. She knew the relentless current tearing at its roots would soon bring the tree crashing down into the river, but for now it was her path.

She climbed up the trunk and then outward on the limbs, high up over the river's tumbling flow, moving from branch to branch, her goal to cross over the river the way she'd seen squirrels do it, using the canopy of the trees as her bridge.

But as she crawled farther out, the tree's branches became slender green saplings bending and whipping in the wind. It felt like the wind was going to sweep her away. Every muscle in her body clenched as she bobbed and swayed in the upper branches. She could see the closest tree on the other side, a great pine with sturdy branches thick with needles, but she couldn't leap across such a great distance. It was just too far.

Looking down, all she could see a hundred feet below her was the swirling black water of the river. If she lost her grip here, or tried to jump to the tree on the other side, then she'd go plummeting down. She'd either die when she hit the water or get swept away in the current and drown. One way or another the river would have her, just like it wanted.

As she was trying to figure out what to do, she heard a stick break on the forest floor down below her, back in the direction from which she had come. She swiveled, scanning the forest for danger. Had the storm-creech followed her scent and tracked her here? But then she spotted a robed figure moving slowly through the trees.

What kind of devil-spawn is comin' now? she thought in exasperation. *I just want to get on home!*

She squinted her eyes and peered down through the branches of the trees, trying to make out who or what was down there.

It was a man wearing long robes, and a hood of some sort covered his head, like one of the old Celtic druids from ancient Britain that she'd seen depicted in Mr. Vanderbilt's books.

As he made his way through the forest, the robed man opened a pale and delicate hand in front of him. Suddenly, a glowing, hissing torch of blue light, like a tiny ball of lightning, rose up from his palm and hovered over his shoulder, lighting his way through the darkness.

Some kind of sorcerer, Serafina thought as she crouched lower. Her heart began to pound in her chest. *The storm-creech, the floating black shapes, the storms . . . They were all his doing.* Everything she had seen must have been the sorcerer's conjurations. Had it been the sorcerer who attacked her on the Loggia? Had he already taken over Biltmore? She had to get home.

But how? She was stuck up in a tree a hundred feet above a raging river.

When the dark-robed sorcerer stopped walking, the hair on the back of Serafina's neck stood on end. Her whole body began to shake. Every sense inside her was telling her to fight or flee. *Flee*, her mind kept telling her. *Flee before it's too late!*

The sorcerer slowly lifted his head and looked up into the trees in her direction.

Serafina scurried for cover, pushing herself farther out onto the thinner branches of the tree even as they bent and twisted in the wind, lifting her and dropping her in sudden movements that made her stomach feel like it was floating.

She scanned the branches on the opposite side of the river. A moment before, it had been too far to jump, but her muscles were bursting now, her whole body filled with panic.

She focused her eyes on the branch she had to jump to, tilted her head to study the angle, then leapt for it with a mighty grunt.

As she flew through the air she envisioned herself as the black panther deep inside her soul and tried to shift her shape.

She could see her panther form clearly in her mind. This was the moment. She was in midair. She *had* to do it now!

But the shift didn't come.

She reached out desperately with her thin, human arms as she sailed through the air, trying to grab hold of the branches of the pine tree on the other side. When she felt her hands touch the branches, she grabbed hold. She had made the distance! But her body swung too hard, and she immediately lost her grip and continued to fall.

Her arms flailed, reaching out in all directions as she tried to catch hold of something, *anything*, on the way down.

She slammed into a thick branch. It knocked the wind out of her with a painful crack. She twisted around and frantically tried to hold on to the branch, but couldn't.

She fell again, hit the branch below her, reached out, fell, grabbed, fell, slipped again, reached out, slipped, then grabbed hold with an infuriated snarl and finally held fast.

She found herself clinging to the bough of a pine tree some fifty feet lower than where she'd started. Her arms and legs were scratched and bleeding. The long, curving spine of her back, usually so supple and strong, hurt something fierce. Grabbing at the hard branches on the way down had jammed her measly human fingernails painfully into her fingers.

Frightened to make any more racket than she already had, and still wincing from the pain of the crashing fall, she gritted her teeth and quickly crawled into the cover of the pine tree's inner branches and hid.

She peered out from her hiding spot, sure that the sorcerer must have heard her. She expected to see him staring up at her, or casting a spell, or summoning one of the black shapes to finish her off.

Instead, the smoking, hissing blue ball of burning light came toward her, floating up into the trees, illuminating everything around it in a bright halo as the sorcerer looked on from below. Serafina cowered into her hiding spot in the thick cluster of pine needles as the eerie blue light came closer.

The buzzing, burning light smelled like a lightning storm, and made her hair float up around her head. But she stayed hidden where she was, her skin tingling.

Finally, the light floated on, and the sorcerer continued his journey through the forest.

Serafina let out a deep sigh of relief and started breathing again.

She watched as the sorcerer made his way through the ferns that grew along the edge of the river. He leaned down and pulled some sort of plant from the ground, then moved on.

Suddenly, Serafina noticed something out of the corner of her eye, something moving much closer to her. Snapping her head toward it, she saw a large, silvery spiderweb glistening in the starlight, its eight-legged spinner lurking on the outer edge with its many eyes watching her. As the spider moved, tiny droplets of dew on the web shimmered in the light, some jostling loose and falling to the forest floor below, others moving like quicksilver along the strands. Serafina knew it was impossible, but she swore she could not just see, but *hear* the droplets sliding along the strands of the web. She could actually *feel* them skittering along, like a shudder down her spine.

Startled, she climbed away from the spider's web and looked back down into the forest. The druid-sorcerer, or whatever he was, had gone down onto his knees now. The burning blue orb hovered over him like a lantern, giving him light to work. He dug through the boggy area at the edge of the river, gathering the tall, pitcher-shaped carnivorous plants that grew there.

Just as she was about to creep away, the sorcerer spoke. He did not stop his work or look around him. He didn't speak in a deep and frightening man's voice like she expected, but a surprisingly soft, calm, steady tone. It was as if Serafina wasn't hidden in a tree a hundred feet away but concealed in the bushes beside the hooded figure.

"I can't see you, but I know you're there," the voice said.

Serafina burst out of her hiding spot and fled. She leapt from branch to branch down through the tree. As soon as she hit the ground, she ran, her bare feet thrashing quickly across the forest floor. When she looked over her shoulder, she didn't see any sign of the sorcerer, but she kept running.

Putting the dark river behind her, she fled way up into the rocks and trees of a high ridge, then through a wide, forested valley. When she finally slowed down, she could tell by the type and age of the trees that she was getting closer. She could see a soft glow of light in the distance, and it drew her home like a beacon.

As she made her way along the edge of Biltmore's bass pond, she noticed that the little stream that normally trickled into it was swollen with rain, filling the pond with more water than usual. *The storms are coming,* Serafina thought.

The calm, flat water of the pond reflected the light of the stars and the moon, but she didn't linger to admire it. She was anxious to get home, to make sure Braeden and her pa were all right, and to warn them about what she'd seen in the forest.

She followed the garden path up through the pink and orange azaleas, which were blooming as bright as the moon itself. When she saw a faint green glow up the hill toward the rest of the gardens, she paused, uncertain. She knew Biltmore's gardens well, but had never seen a greenish light like this before.

Her first thought was that the sorcerer was already here, had already taken over and made Biltmore his domain. Then she heard the murmur of many voices.

As she approached more closely, she saw that the green glow wasn't a sorcerer's spell, but the Conservatory all lit up for an evening party, the light shining through the leaves of thousands of orchids, bromeliads, and palms, and out through the greenhouse's many panes of glass.

She crept along the edge of the building and looked into the Walled Garden, where she saw hundreds of ladies in formal summer dresses and gentlemen in black tailcoats gathered for the party. The windows of Biltmore House blazed above, the south walls and towers of the mansion rising like an enchanted castle into the night.

The Walled Garden had been strung with the kind of softly glowing Edison bulbs that her pa used. And smaller lights hung along the wooden arbor that covered the central path of the garden, the lights tucked among the leafy vines and flowering blooms like little faeries taking refuge among the leaves. She had never seen so many beautiful lights in her life.

Hiding in the bushes near the rose keeper's stone shed, she scanned the crowd for Braeden, but she didn't see him. He was a reserved boy, not always the center of attention, but his aunt and uncle usually encouraged him to attend the estate's social events. She and Braeden had shared so many adventures. And they had been through so much together. He was her closest and most trusted friend. She couldn't wait to see him.

The fancy folk were mingling about on the perfectly manicured paths of the garden, holding champagne flutes in their elegant, flawless hands, chatting and sipping lightly as they promenaded among the roses, dahlias, and zinnias. Bathed in the Conservatory's glow, a string quartet played a beautiful song. Footmen in their formal black-and-white livery strolled among the crowd serving custard tarts, cheeses, and freshly baked cream puffs from their trays. Serafina suddenly felt pangs of hunger.

But everything about this party flummoxed her. It must have taken weeks of planning to arrange all this, and yet she hadn't heard anything about it. And why wasn't Braeden here? There were so many strangers. Where were Mr. and Mrs. Vanderbilt?

A few of the more adventurous adult guests and a coterie of their fancifully attired children huddled together and lit candles inside small paper lanterns, then held them aloft. As if by magic, the rising heat of the candles lifted the lanterns upward out of their hands into the nighttime sky. Serafina watched with the other children as the lanterns floated slowly up into the heavens. She couldn't help but smile at the sight of it, but then a sadness swept through her. She knew it was foolish after everything she'd been through, but she felt so sad that she hadn't been invited to this wonderful party. It was an *evening* party. And she was a creature of the night! If anyone should have been part of it, she should have been! It felt like so much had changed, like the whole world had been slipping by without her.

After destroying the Black Cloak and freeing the estate's lost children from its dark imprisonment, she had entered the daylight world upstairs. The Vanderbilts had welcomed her into their home. She had become part of Biltmore now. Hadn't she? So why wasn't she at this party? It made her qualmish in her stomach thinking about it. What had happened? What had she missed? Hadn't anyone noticed that she wasn't there?

It was hard to understand how all these fancy-dressed people could gather for this lovely party, when just a few miles away a storm had raged through the forest. A short distance down the hill the inlet stream was quietly flooding the pond. A dark force was coming, but they seemed to have no idea.

When she heard Mrs. Vanderbilt's gentle laugh in the distance, Serafina turned hopefully toward the sound. She saw right away that Braeden wasn't there, but Mr. Vanderbilt and Mrs. Vanderbilt were standing together with several of their guests near one of the rose trellises.

Mr. Vanderbilt was easily recognizable with his black hair

and mustache, and his lean, shrewd face with dark, inquisitive eyes. He was dressed in a handsome black tux with tails and white tie. Many of the men she'd spied on over the years were loud of voice and boisterous of manner, but Mr. Vanderbilt was a quieter, more refined, thinking kind of gentleman. Usually, if he wasn't reading in his library, he was watching and learning from those around him. He was always kind and welcoming in spirit when he spoke to people, whether they were guests or servants or workers on the estate, but he also seemed to enjoy watching people from a distance at parties, taking everything in.

Mrs. Vanderbilt was more outgoing, more talkative and social with the guests. She had dark hair like her husband, and a similar spark of intelligence, but she had an easy charm and a gracious smile. She wore a lovely, loosely flowing mauve dress, but what truly stunned Serafina was that Mrs. Vanderbilt's belly was large with her baby. The last time Serafina had seen her, she couldn't even tell that she was with child.

It hasn't just been twenty-eight days, Serafina thought. She felt as if she were being lowered into a deep, dark well. *I've been gone for months . . . They've all forgotten about me . . .*

"And where is that dear nephew of yours tonight?" one of the lady guests asked Mrs. Vanderbilt.

"Yes, indeed," said the lady's husband. "Where is Young Master Braeden?"

"Oh, he's around," Mrs. Vanderbilt said lightly, but Serafina noticed that the mistress of the house didn't actually look around her when she said these words. It was as if she already knew her nephew wasn't nearby. She was acting cheerful in front of her guests, but Serafina could hear the twinge of concern in her voice.

As Mrs. Vanderbilt and her friends continued their conversation, Mr. Vanderbilt stepped back from them and looked up toward the Library Terrace. Serafina could see the wrinkles of worry around his eyes and mouth.

"So, how has Braeden been doing?" one of the guests asked Mrs. Vanderbilt.

"Oh, he's fine," Mrs. Vanderbilt said. "He's fine. He's doing well."

One *he's fine* was enough, Serafina thought, but two was too many. There was definitely something wrong.

"If you'll excuse me for a moment," Mr. Vanderbilt said. He touched his wife's arm, and then left them.

As Mr. Vanderbilt walked quickly through the crowd, several people tried to talk to him, for he was host of the grand party, but he kindly gave his regrets and kept moving.

Ducking through the hedges, Serafina followed him. After being away for months, the sight of her was no doubt going to startle him, but as soon as he was alone, she was going to tell him about the dangers she'd seen in the forest. She could show him the rising water of the pond as evidence of it all. But she sensed the urgency in his movement.

Mr. Vanderbilt ascended the steps through the Walled Garden's arched stone entrance and up the next set of steps to the path through the shrub garden. Serafina darted through the roses and then weaved behind the fruit trees to follow him, careful to avoid the detection of the guests. She had lost her ability to shift shape, but she certainly hadn't lost her knack for sneaking unseen or unheard. She was as fast and light on her feet as she had always been.

She followed Mr. Vanderbilt up past the purple-leafed beech and then the elm tree with its low, splaying branches, until he went up the steps and reached the Pergola.

"Wine, sir?" a footman said as he hurried down from the house toward the party with his tray restocked.

"No, thank you, John," Mr. Vanderbilt said. "Do you happen to have a sweet tea on your tray?"

"Oh, yes, sir, I do," the footman said in surprise, for iced tea was not his master's normal drink. *Braeden,* Serafina thought.

"Thank you very much, John," Mr. Vanderbilt said as he took the tea and kept moving. "Take good care of everyone."

"I will, sir," John said, a worried twinge in his voice as he watched his master rush up the steps toward the terrace.

Finally the footman turned and continued on his way toward the party.

As Serafina slipped behind a tree trunk to avoid the passing footman's notice, she couldn't help but wonder about how little people noticed the things around them. She knew that theoretically she could walk openly among the guests of the house, and she had felt left out about not being there, but the truth was, she still felt far more comfortable spying on a party than attending it. And the soaking wet, grave-dirtied, dress-torn, bloodstained look of her would have shocked them all.

Right now, she had her eyes fixed on one person, and that was Mr. Vanderbilt.

Serafina went right after him. She ran across the gravel path, making barely a rustling step of noise, then bounded up the stone steps at the southeast corner of the house to reach the Library Terrace. It was a flat area just outside the glass doors of the Library with a view to the forest and the Blue Ridge Mountains. The terrace was covered by an arbor heavily laden with long, hanging purple wisteria. The vines grew thick and twisty around the arbor's stout posts and up into its latticework above. The warm amber light of the Library fell through the open doors onto the terrace.

A boy was sitting on a bench, facing out toward the forest. When she first saw him, she didn't recognize him. But as she crept closer and saw his face, she knew.

It was Braeden.

But what she saw—the way he was sitting and the look of his face—struck her such a blow that she couldn't help but suck in a gasp of air. She was too startled to move immediately toward him like she normally would have. She watched from the shadows and tried to understand what she was seeing.

The first thing she noticed was that Gidean, Braeden's once-beloved black Doberman, wasn't lying at his young master's feet like he normally did. The poor dog was lying twenty feet away, his head down, his ears drooped, a sad, dejected expression on his face, as if Braeden had sent him away, scorned and unwanted.

Braeden sat on the bench alone. There was a plaid blanket around his legs despite the fact that it wasn't cold outside. He was twelve years old, but he looked smaller, frailer than she had ever seen him before. His brown hair was longer, his skin different, paler, like he hadn't been outside as much as he usually was. But what caught her most of all was that there were long, jagged scars on the side of his face, and his right leg had been strapped into some sort of leather-and-metal brace, with hinges at the knee.

Her heart swelled with grief. She wanted to reach out to him. What had happened to Braeden? Had the dark forces she'd seen in the forest already attacked him?

"It's just me," Mr. Vanderbilt said softly as he approached his nephew. "Are you all right?"

"Yes," Braeden said, his voice somber, "I'm all right," but his words were laced with tones that tugged at her heart.

Braeden seemed so sad. His mouth hung grim. His eyes were dull of spirit. And as she crept closer to him, an even darker, more despairing expression clouded his face, as if something was suddenly causing him even more anguish than moments before.

But she could see him trying to steady himself the best he could, at least for his uncle's sake. "Did you come all the way up here for me?" he asked.

"There wasn't anything to do down there," Mr. Vanderbilt said, smiling a little, and Braeden gave him a wan, knowing smile in return.

Mr. Vanderbilt offered him the glass of sweet tea. It had

46

always been Braeden's favorite. But as he reached out with his left hand to take the glass from him, his hand was shaking so badly that it was clear that he wouldn't be able to hold the tea without spilling it.

"I don't want that!" Braeden snapped at his uncle, knocking the tea away.

Mr. Vanderbilt stepped back and took a long breath. The master of Biltmore wasn't at all used to someone treating him like that, but after a moment, he stepped closer once more.

"Try it again," he said gently, handing the glass to Braeden. "Your right hand works better, I think."

Braeden looked at him sharply, but slowly reached over with his right hand and took the glass. His right hand was trembling, too, but not nearly as badly as the left.

Steadying the glass of tea in two hands now, Braeden took a long drink in silence. When he was done, he nodded. It was as if he had forgotten how much he liked the drink. "Thank you," he said to his uncle, almost sounding like his old cheerful self again for a moment, but then he pressed his lips together and shook his head, barely holding back tears.

Mr. Vanderbilt sat on the bench beside him. "Is it bad tonight?"

Braeden nodded. "For the last few weeks it finally felt like I was getting a little better, but all of a sudden, I feel so awful."

"Is it the party?" Mr. Vanderbilt asked regretfully.

"I don't think so," Braeden said shaking his head, "I don't know . . . maybe . . . maybe it's the beautiful night, the moonlight, the stars. She loved nights like this."

"I'm sorry," Mr. Vanderbilt said.

"Sometimes, I almost feel like I'm going to get back to normal again, but other times I feel a terrible aching inside, like she's standing right beside me."

I am, Braeden, Serafina thought. *I'm here!* But she was so transfixed by what she was seeing and hearing that she couldn't speak or move. It was like she was locked in a dream that she could only watch.

"Sometimes," Mr. Vanderbilt said gently, "you have to push on through your life even when you don't feel too well. She might have left Biltmore for any number of reasons. But if the worst has happened, then we need to keep her in our hearts. She'll live on in your memories of her. And she'll live in my heart as well. She was a good, brave girl, and I know she was a very special friend to you."

Braeden nodded, agreeing with everything his uncle was saying, but Serafina noticed a peculiar expression on Braeden's face, a hesitation in his movement. Serafina knew him well enough to know that there was something he wasn't telling his uncle.

Mr. Vanderbilt put his arm gently around his nephew. "No matter what's happened, we'll get through this."

It was strangely fascinating to watch and listen, to imagine a world where she had disappeared, but Serafina couldn't stand it anymore. She had to tell them that she was alive and well, that she was finally home. And more than anything, she had to warn them. The talon-clawed creature, the black shapes, the storms, the dark river, the sorcerer . . . they were coming.

Taking in a deep breath, she stepped out from behind the column and showed herself to both of them.

"Braeden, it's me. I'm back."

Braeden and Mr. Vanderbilt didn't turn toward Serafina or react to her in any way. They seemed not to hear her or see her even though she was right in front of them.

"Braeden, it's me!" Serafina said again more loudly as she stepped even closer to them. "Mr. Vanderbilt, it's Serafina! Can you hear me?"

But neither of them responded. She couldn't believe it. This was impossible.

"Braeden!" she shouted frantically. She was standing right in front of them and they couldn't see her! What in the world was going on? Her body began to tremble with fear.

Preparing to return to his guests, Mr. Vanderbilt patted

Braeden's shoulder. "Stay here as long as you like," he said gently. "But when you're feeling up to it, think about coming back down to the party."

"I will," Braeden said. "It *is* beautiful. I can see the lights from here."

"I think maybe Serafina's pa was trying to light Biltmore up so brightly that she could find her way home," Mr. Vanderbilt said, his voice filled with a warm and gentle melancholy.

Gidean, still lying twenty feet away, watched Mr. Vanderbilt walk back down toward the party, then looked glumly back at Braeden.

"Gidean, can you hear me, boy?" Serafina said to her old friend, but he didn't look in her direction, and his long, pointed ears didn't perk up. He just gazed at Braeden with sadness in his eyes.

How was all this possible? She was right in front of them, as plain as night.

Serafina studied Braeden, and then looked at herself. The rays of moonlight coming down through the vine-covered lattice above her shone onto her body, casting her in an eerie, dappled-white light.

Am I truly here? she wondered.

Or am I still buried underground in the coffin and just imagining that I crawled out?

Have I been cursed by a spell?

Or am I some sort of whispery ghost or haint or spirit?

She thought about how quickly she'd been able to dart away

from the talon-clawed creature in the forest, how skillfully she'd escaped the sorcerer, how quietly she had slipped past all the guests at the party.

She brushed back tears as the emotion welled up inside her. What had happened to her?

Determined to make it stop, she stepped closer to Braeden.

"It's me, Braeden. I'm back. It's me," she said again, her voice cracking.

But Braeden did not respond. He looked out across the moonlit forest and fields. His heart seemed forlorn, his mood dark. There was a tension in his face that she'd never seen before.

She lifted her hand and looked at it. She slowly turned it one way and then the other in the moonlight. It seemed normal in every way to her, and yet he could not see her. She had felt hungry earlier, but maybe it was because she had seen the food at the party. She had felt pain when she fell from the tree, but maybe that was what she *thought* she should be feeling. Was she just *remembering* how things felt?

Braeden breathed a long, heavy sigh, then began to move. He gripped the side of the bench, and with much effort, his arms shaking, he managed to get himself up onto his crooked legs. He stood lopsided, tilted over like his body had been broken. Clearly exhausted by the exertion of getting onto his feet, he rested there, leaning his shoulder against the column for a moment.

When he tried to take a few steps forward, it seemed at first as if he was going to be all right, but then he winced and his leg buckled beneath him. The metal brace tripped him up and he lurched off-balance. Serafina reflexively darted forward to catch him so that he didn't fall, but he hit the ground anyway, grunting in pain as he crashed into the gravel.

Serafina stepped back in confusion. She was certain she had reached him in time, but she hadn't been able to hold him up.

As Braeden struggled to get to his feet, she stepped forward again and grabbed his arm to lift him. At first she thought she was touching him. She *had* to be touching him, because she could see her hands were on him. But then she slowly realized that she could not actually feel him the way she should, the true warmth of his living body. She knew she *should* feel it. She could *imagine* feeling it. But this was more like a *memory* of feeling.

Her spirit was remembering the physical world the way an amputee lying in a hospital bed remembers his missing leg, feels the movement of it, suffers the pain of it, even though it's gone.

She slowly reached out and tried to touch his shoulder, and then his bare hand. There was something there, something like a physical object, but she couldn't feel the living warmth of it, and it was clear that he couldn't feel her at all.

Up to this moment, she'd been interacting with the world based on her memory of her past life. But now she was like the amputee who sees with his own eyes that his leg is actually gone. It was becoming clear to her that she could no longer affect the physical world around her. It was as if the more she realized what was happening to her, the more she faded away.

Gritting her teeth, she tried to hold herself together, but it was no use. She pressed her hands to her face and squeezed her eyes shut, trying just to breathe. She began to cry in confusion and fear. A dizzying nausea swept through her stomach. It felt like she was going to pass out, but she had to hold on.

Braeden slowly dragged himself and his bad leg over to the terrace's stone railing. He clung to the top of the railing for support as he looked out into the night. He seemed lost in thought, like he was remembering something. At first she thought he was gazing out at the trees and the bank of clouds rolling in across the night sky, but then she realized that he was looking in the direction from which she had come. He was looking specifically toward the graveyard and the angel's glade.

"No, she's not *missing*," Braeden said as if his uncle was still there. "She's dead and buried."

Serafina stepped back in horror. *She's dead and buried,*
Braeden said.

Was Braeden the one who buried me?

Is it possible that I'm actually dead?

She knew she'd been buried, there was no denying that, but
dead?

She didn't *feel* dead.

And even in Braeden's discouraged hopelessness she sensed
something else, some other uncertainty in his eyes and tone
of voice. He seemed to be waiting, frustrated, biding his time.
Despite everything, despite the anguish and pain, there seemed
to be a faint trace of *hope* in him.

After Mr. Vanderbilt went back down to the gardens to

rejoin his wife and the guests at the evening party, Serafina wanted to stay with Braeden, just to keep him company if nothing else, but the longer she stayed there, the more upset he seemed to become. She could see it in the shaking restlessness of his hands and legs, in the pained expression of his face, and even the unsettled way he was breathing. The mere closeness of her presence seemed to sadden and disquiet him.

After Braeden went to bed and the partygoers went up to their rooms in the mansion, Serafina went down into the basement to see her pa. She passed maids and manservants she knew by name. She saw footmen and assistants. But none of them saw her.

When she finally came to the workshop, she found it empty. There was no sign of her pa. She waited a few moments, thinking he would soon return, but he did not.

Her heart began to fill with a terrible dread. Had this, too, changed?

She searched the basement room by room, the kitchens and pantries, the workrooms and the storerooms. Biltmore was just too large! She finally found her pa repairing the small, wheeled electric motor that powered the house's dumbwaiter. She sighed with relief.

Her pa was on his knees, pulling a wrench. The muscles on his bare, sweating forearm bulged. He was a large, gruff man with a barrel chest and thick limbs. He wore simple work clothes, a leather apron, and a heavy leather belt laden with tools. She had seen him working a thousand times, had handed him screwdrivers and hammers when he needed them, had run to retrieve parts and materials for him. But she'd never seen him like this. There was no joy in his work tonight, no sense of purpose. He moved slowly, doggedly, his eyes mournful. He was going through the motions of his life, but his spirit was gone.

"Pa . . ." she said, standing before him. "Can you see me?"

To her surprise, her pa stopped his work. He slowly turned as if gazing at the empty air around him. It was clear that he couldn't see her, but he stared at the emptiness for a long time as if he was sure something was there.

After a few moments, he pulled out a rag and wiped his brow. Then he lowered his head and wiped his eyes, a wave of emotion racking through his shoulders. She could see the flicker of memories in his face, the sadness in his eyes. She didn't know what Braeden knew of her demise, but one thing was certain: her pa thought she was dead.

She could see it in his face and in the way he moved. His dream of having a daughter had been the joy of his life for these twelve years. But now she was gone. He was alone, true and certain.

Seeing him there by himself, her heart broke.

Finally, he gave up on fixing the machine and sighed as if it was all pointless anyway. She'd never seen him break from a job before the job was done. The idea of leaving a machine unmended was inconceivable.

As he hoisted his leather tool satchel over his shoulder and trudged back toward the workshop, Serafina followed him. He walked slowly, without spirit or purpose, like a wanderer who has nothing to go home to.

She stayed close to him as he moved back and forth in the shop, putting his tools away and preparing his late-night meal.

As he cooked his supper of chicken and grits over his little cook stove and then ate alone, she sat across from him in her old chair. It was here that she used to listen to his stories and share her own, telling him about the rats she had caught or the falling stars she'd seen streaking through the sky. But now her plate and her spoon sat on the bench, unused for months.

"I'll eat my grits, Pa, I swear I will," she said out loud as tears welled in her eyes.

A little while later, when he lay in his bed and fell asleep, she crawled onto her own empty cot behind the boiler and lay down. She didn't know what else to do.

When you're dreaming, what happens if you fall asleep in your dream? Do you dream? And is your dream real life?

If she was dead and buried, how could she be tired?

She didn't know, but maybe sleep wasn't about the body, but about rest for the mind and the spirit.

All she knew was that she was exhausted. Trembling and forlorn, she curled up in a ball.

As she fell asleep, she slipped into a dream where she was biting and clawing, fighting in a black, swirling world, and then it all fell away and all she could feel was the earth and the river and the wind, a vast world without form, and she felt herself being swept through it like she was nothing but a particle of dust, and then a tiny droplet of water, and then a wisp of air, until she finally dissolved into nothingness.

She started awake with a violent jerk.

When she looked around the workshop she didn't know whether she was awake or asleep. Did she just dream of her death? Or was her death the reality and what she was experiencing now the dream?

She remembered the frightening sensation of her feet being torn into little pieces by the current of the river, and the feeling of the wind high in the trees almost sweeping her away. *I only have so much more time left here,* she thought, *and then I'm going to fade away completely.*

She looked at her surroundings, trying to understand. It was dark, the witching hour between 3:00 and 4:00 a.m.

Still shaking from the dream, she rose from her bed and stood in the workshop, not sure what to do. She just stood there and breathed and tried to figure out whether she was truly breathing or dreaming of breathing or remembering breathing.

Finally, she went over to her pa sleeping on his cot.

She tried to touch his side to make sure he was truly there. She felt a vague shape, but no warmth, no response to her touch. It was just as it had been with Braeden.

Even though she couldn't feel her father's warmth, and he couldn't feel hers, she curled up beside her pa like a little kitten so small and light that it wasn't even felt against its master's chest. And she tried not to sleep.

In the morning, when her pa woke and began his day, she tried to touch him, tried to speak with him, tried to tell him what was happening to her, tried to warn him about what she'd seen in the forest, tried to tell him to check the stream flowing into the pond, but the more she tried, the more sadness it seemed to cause him. Her presence wasn't a comfort to him, but a sorrow. She was *haunting* him.

Finally, when he gathered his tool bag and went off to work, she let him go, not because she wanted to let him go, but for mercy's sake.

Serafina sat alone at the bottom of the basement steps, her head on her hands. She had to figure out a way to get back into the world and warn everyone that they were in danger. She'd been attacked, and clearly Braeden had been attacked, and she was sure that there were more attacks to come.

"But what can I do?" she asked herself. How could she talk to the people she loved? How could she warn them?

She had found Mr. and Mrs. Vanderbilt, Braeden, Gidean, and her pa, but there was one more person at Biltmore who might be able to help her. She went up the back stairway to the fourth floor and down the corridor into the maids' quarters.

When she came to the particular maid's room she was looking for, the door was ajar.

As Serafina paused, a bad feeling crept into her.

"Essie?" she asked quietly. "Essie, are you there?"

Finally, Serafina slipped slowly into the room.

Her friend Essie's room was empty and lifeless. Essie's books and newspapers weren't on the nightstand by the bed. Essie's drawings of flowers and plants weren't on the wall. Essie's clothes weren't strewn across the floor and chair. The bed had no sheets or pillows.

Serafina's heart sank.

No one was living in this room anymore.

Essie was gone.

Remembering her friend's old mountain stories of haints and nightspirits and other strange occurrences, Serafina had hoped that maybe Essie could help her, that maybe she could even talk with her in some way, but it was all for naught.

It just seemed so unfair, so wrong. She was home, but she felt homesick. Why couldn't everything just stay the way it had been? She'd made friends and found new family. She'd worn beautiful dresses and had English tea with lots and lots of cream! She'd met her mother and run at her side. She'd nuzzled her head and felt her purr. But what had happened to her mother and the cubs? Were they gone like Essie? Serafina couldn't bear the thought that something bad had happened to any of them.

As she stood in the room, she noticed the mirror on the wall.

As soon as she saw it, she froze where she was and her heart began to pound.

"Oh, no, I'm not doin' that . . ." she said firmly.

She didn't want to move toward it. She was too frightened to put herself in front of it and look at it.

What would she see?

Her old self? A whispery haint? A grave-walking ghoul bloodied with the wounds she could see on her torn, blood-stained dress? She was a ghoul. Suddenly she was sure of it. The last thing she wanted to see was the bloody, corpsy sight of her walking death.

Get hold of yourself, you frightened little fool, she scolded herself. *You've got to figure this out! You've got to look!*

She pulled in a long, deep breath.

Then she took a step toward the mirror.

Then another.

Finally, she slowly moved a little bit in front of it and looked at herself.

All she could see in the mirror was a glint of light, a faint blur of motion when she moved, as if she was nothing but air itself.

She had no reflection. She was nobody and nothing.

She remembered back to the time she'd looked into this mirror and noticed her amber eyes starting to change, and her black hair starting to come in, and how proud she'd felt of the beautiful dress she'd been wearing. Now she had no eyes, no hair, nothing.

So much of what she had come to know and love had just slipped away. Was this the work of the sorcerer, or was it simply how time passed?

It felt like it was more than that. It felt as if her world had been shattered into a thousand pieces like a Ming vase on a tiled floor. She kept wondering if she could pick up the pieces and put them back together again.

"Stay bold," she told herself sternly. *Stop this nonsense, feelin' all sorry for yourself. Dream or real, dead or alive, you don't give up, you don't give in to hopelessness. You keep fighting!*

Then, even as she was thinking these thoughts, she saw something very faint in the movement of light and air in the reflection of the mirror. There was something behind her. When she turned to look at what it was, she noticed the tiny particles of dust floating in random motion in the rays of morning light coming through the window.

She stepped toward the floating dust.

She marveled at how she could see the shape of each particle, the way it turned and caught the light as it tumbled through the air. The dust reminded her of the words spoken at funeral rites when a loved one was buried.

"And we commit her body to the ground," the pastor would say. "We all go to the same place. All come from dust and all return to dust. Earth to earth, ashes to ashes, dust to dust."

As she studied the slow swirling motion of the dust in the sunlight, she whispered, "That's what I am now." *Specks of dust floating in the air.*

She lifted her hand and passed it slowly through the rays of light. Her hand caused no shadow, but she could swear that the motes of dust whirled up in little clouds around the movement of her hand.

"I'm here," she said. "Just a little bit . . . I'm still here."

Even if I'm just a minuscule speck of dust or a gust of air, then I still exist. There's still hope.

She looked around at Essie's empty room. The past was behind her. The future unknown. But what now?

She looked out the window toward the mountains. Great banks of dark clouds were rolling across the peaks, vast sheets of rain drinking up the rays of the sun. The water of the French Broad River had risen so high in the last few nights that the ancient river had burst its banks and flooded the lagoon. The lagoon had been drowned in the water of the rains and completely swept away.

The storms are coming, she thought.

And I've got to stop them.

n her way down to the first floor, Serafina descended the long, gentle curve of the Grand Staircase, walking in broad daylight past the guests on the stairs. She jumped up and down in front of them and tried to touch them. She swiped her hands across the long skirts of the ladies' dresses, trying to make the material fly. But it made no difference. She'd spent her whole life hiding, but now she just wanted one person, *any person*, to know she was there.

"Hello, there!" she said loudly to one of the many new lady guests who had arrived for the upcoming summer ball. "Beautiful dress you're wearing today!" she shouted to another. "Your hat is on crooked, sir," she said to one of the gentlemen.

Reaching the main floor, she went into the Winter Garden, where a number of young ladies in beautiful powder-blue and yellow dresses were chatting over English tea. She tried to steal their sugar cubes and knock over their teacups, but she couldn't affect a thing. Then she noticed the faint trace of steam coming off the tea in one of the cups and she had an idea. She bent down and blew gently into the hot vapor, and to her surprise, it actually swirled in a new direction and disappeared into the air. Serafina smiled. She was making progress.

Encouraged, she crossed over to the back corridor and slipped into the Smoking Room with its rich blue damask wallpaper, elegant velvet chairs, and gold-leafed books on the shelves. When she had come here with Braeden on Christmas Eve, they had been dressed in their finest clothes for the first Christmas party she had ever attended. *I just hope it wasn't my last,* she thought glumly.

But she wasn't going to stand around feeling sorry for herself just because she was dead.

She walked over to the room's fireplace, with its finely carved white marble mantel, and was relieved to see that the barn owl was still mounted there.

Her old enemies, the powerful conjurer Uriah and his treacherous daughter-apprentice Rowena, had been shapeshifters, able to change into the white-faced owl at will.

Long ago, Uriah had stolen this land from its rightful owners and formed his dark dominion in the hidden forests of these mountains. He had killed many of the forest animals, as well as

Serafina's panther father. But the arrival of Mr. Vanderbilt and the construction of Biltmore Estate freed the mountain folk and the forest animals from the conjurer's spells and brought new light into the area. Uriah had been obsessed with destroying Biltmore ever since.

Filled with a hateful vengeance, he had created the Black Cloak, which allowed its wearer to steal the souls of its victims. And he had used the Twisted Staff to enslave the animals of the forest and attack Biltmore.

As Uriah was flying in owl form, she had raked him from the sky with her panther claws, sending the bloodied bird tumbling toward the ground. She and her allies had struck down Rowena that same night.

Serafina had hoped that she had destroyed both of them, but the truth was, she didn't truly know. Waysa had told her, *It is the way of his kind that even when he seems to be dead, he is not. His spirit lives on. He hides in a darkness the rest of us cannot see.*

The morning after the battle, Biltmore's groundskeepers had found a dead owl in the forest, and they had it mounted over this fireplace. She remembered that it had looked so lifelike, but now it seemed dead and worn, its feathers graying and tattered, the living spirit gone. It reminded her of the dried, white, desiccated shell of a rattlesnake after it had shed its skin and become anew.

She couldn't help but wonder now if the robed sorcerer she'd seen by the river might have been Uriah in some new form.

Had Uriah been the one who attacked her on the Loggia

the night of the full moon? Was he the sorcerer causing the storms in the forest?

Had he returned to destroy Biltmore once and for all? Or was it some new enemy that she'd never seen before?

Whatever the answer was, she had to stay watchful.

For the rest of the afternoon, she practiced moving particles of dust, shaping tendrils of steam, and causing candles to flicker as she studied the comings and goings of Biltmore. She followed people through their daily lives, watching them from the shadows, a shadow herself, looking for signs of suspicious behavior and clues to where something was amiss.

It wasn't until later that evening that something caught her eye.

The formal dinner in the Banquet Hall started promptly at eight, with many of the guests and staff talking about the heavy rains, the muddy condition of the roads, and the water collecting in the fields where vast acres of crops were being lost to the flooding. Braeden was sitting near his aunt and uncle. Her friend seemed to be in somewhat better spirits than the night before, well enough to at least come to dinner, but there was still a dark and unsmiling gloominess to him.

A mustachioed gentleman at the table tried to speak with him. "It's good to see you, Master Braeden. I was terribly sorry to hear that you've given up your riding. I know you have always enjoyed your time with your horses."

It seemed as if the gentleman was trying to be kind, but Braeden's face hardened at his words.

Serafina wondered if she could get Braeden's attention by swirling the water in his water glass or something. There had to be some way to signal him, to let him know she was there with him. But as soon as she approached him, Braeden became even more upset, muttered that he was tired, and quickly excused himself from the table.

"Good night, Braeden," Mrs. Vanderbilt said, concerned that he was leaving so soon.

"Sleep well," Mr. Vanderbilt said to his nephew, but then touched Braeden's arm, drew him closer in, and spoke to him in a soft and quiet tone. "Remember, the servants will be double-locking all the doors tonight and guards will be posted."

Braeden clenched his jaw and walked away from his uncle without saying a word.

Serafina was taken aback by the rudeness of Braeden's behavior. And she thought that if Mr. Vanderbilt had some inkling of the dangers surrounding Biltmore, then locking the doors and posting guards made perfect sense. But it almost seemed as if Mr. Vanderbilt was telling Braeden that the doors would be double-locked not to keep something out, but to make sure Braeden didn't try to leave the house. And Braeden was none too happy about it.

She followed her friend as he trudged up the stairs to his room, dragging his metal-braced leg behind him. In months past, she had seen him heal a fox, a falcon, and other animals—it was part of his connection to them, part of his love for them—but he couldn't heal humans, not even himself. And it was clear that something had gone terribly wrong with him.

His dog, his horses . . . It was so sad that his grief had kept him from his only friends.

When Braeden arrived at his bedroom door, Gidean was waiting quietly for him outside his room.

"I don't want you following me," Braeden said harshly to Gidean. "Just stay away from me!"

The look on the dog's face was so miserable that Serafina wished she could kneel down beside him and pet him like she used to. "I'm sure he doesn't mean it," she said to Gidean, even though the dog couldn't hear her, and the truth was, she wasn't sure of anything anymore. Maybe Braeden did mean it.

As Serafina followed Braeden into his bedroom, she was surprised by the state of it. The last time she'd seen his room, it had been warm and tidy, but now it was messy and disheveled, with days-old food trays piled on the dresser and dirty clothes all over the floor. The four-poster bed was unmade. The drapes were covered with dust. It looked like he hadn't cleaned his room in months, and hadn't let the servants in, either.

He exhaled a long, tired breath as he collapsed into the leather chair by the small, unlit fireplace. He rubbed his bad leg with his shaking hand. His other leg moved in constant restlessness. And he kept pulling his hand through his hair, then wiping the side of his face. He wasn't just exhausted, but anxious and frustrated.

Serafina remembered visiting him here one night and curling up on the rug in front of the warm fire with Gidean as Braeden slept quietly in his bed. But now he just stared blankly into the dead ashes of the empty black hearth.

Suddenly, Braeden got up. His metal brace thumped the wooden floor as he paced, pressing his trembling fingers to his skull as if there were voices in his head.

More agitated than even before, he changed out of his black dinner jacket and trousers, and put on the rugged clothes he used for hiking. Then he got down onto his hands and knees and pulled a coil of rope out from under his bed.

"What in tarnation are you gonna do with that?" Serafina asked out loud.

As the rest of the house retired for the evening, Braeden opened one of his windows and hurled the rope out into the darkness. It had been raining hard all night, and now the wet spray of it blew into the room.

"Just what's goin' on in that head of yours, Braeden?" she asked him, feeling a terrible tightness in her chest.

She could see that his hands were trembling something awful as he struggled to tie the end of the rope to the bed. The shaking was so bad that he could barely manage it. Then he went over to the window.

"Braeden, whatever you're thinking about doing, don't do it!" she told him.

But he climbed onto the windowsill, his hands and knees slipping on the rain-slick surface, and started to crawl out. He couldn't maneuver his braced leg well enough by its own power, so he lifted it with his hands, then dragged himself over, and began climbing down the rope on the outside of the building.

This was an insanely dangerous thing to do for even an able-bodied person in dry weather, but the sickly, crooked-legged boy was climbing out the window in the middle of a rainstorm. There was a forty-foot drop to the stone terrace below. The fall was going to kill him.

"Be careful, Braeden!" Serafina shouted at him angrily, the storm whipping her hair as she leaned out. All of a sudden, a gust of wind lifted her off her feet, trying to sweep her away with the blowing rain. She felt herself rising upward, pieces of her spirit, her soul, whatever it was, tearing away and disappearing into the gale. All she could do was cling for dear life to the window jamb and try to stay whole.

As Braeden climbed down the outside of the building, she watched helplessly. If he lost his grip, she couldn't save him! He'd fall and die.

Lightning flashed through the sky, then a roar of thunder cracked overhead.

$\mathcal{S}$erafina clung to the window feeling like the universe itself was trying to pull apart what little was left of her, but she finally managed to climb down the side of the building and put her feet on the solid ground. Spirit or ghost or whatever she was, she squatted down and put her hands on the stone tile of the terrace, grateful for the plenum of the earth.

It was becoming clear that the universe was taking her back, that her spirit only had so much more time to roam the earth before it faded into the elements from whence all things came.

When Braeden made it safely to the ground on the Library Terrace beside her, he took a moment to catch his breath and wipe the rain out of his eyes.

"Where are you off to in the middle of the night?" she asked in the rain, still angry with him for endangering himself like that.

As if in reply, he gathered himself and headed into the storm. Tonight there was no party or music, just darkness and rain.

She followed him down the steps and through the garden. He couldn't move quickly with his braced leg. He dragged it behind him, the metal scraping along the stone with each step, but he moved with determination and made pretty good time. It was clear that he knew where he wanted to go.

He followed the winding path of the shrub garden, past the golden-rain tree, then down the steps, through the archway and into the Walled Garden.

She didn't know where he was going, but it felt good to be with him and a part of his adventure into the night, whatever it was. Despite her narrow escape on the windowsill, she was still clinging to the hope that she could figure out what had happened to Braeden since she'd been gone, how she could communicate with him, and somehow get back to him. But she felt a wrenching loneliness, too, a separation from him that tore at her gut. She couldn't speak to him or help him. She couldn't ask him what he was thinking. When she looked at his stark, grim face, it was filled with such desperation that it frightened her.

She followed him down the length of the central arbor and into the rose garden. He ducked into the small stone shed used by the master rosarian, Mr. Fetlan. The shed was filled with rakes, hoes, and other garden tools along with pots, trays, and wired wooden apple crates.

Braeden grabbed a lantern and a shovel and headed back out into the rain again. The boy was soaked to the bone, and she could see him trembling, but he pressed on regardless.

Through the garden he went, then down the path that led toward the pond. After passing the boathouse, it appeared he was going to cross the large redbrick bridge that arched over the eastern spur of the pond, but at the last moment, he diverted to the left and went into the woods.

"This is getting stranger and stranger," she said. "Where are you going now?"

He followed the edge of the pond beneath the overhang of the trees until she heard the sound of rushing water. They had come to the stream that fed into the pond. But the water didn't go straight in. A low brick structure had been built across the stream to block and control its flow. The structure was over-grown with several seasons of bushes, moss, and vines. It took her a moment to remember what it was.

Years before, when Biltmore House was built, her old friend Mr. Olmsted, the estate's landscape architect, had decided that no estate was complete without a tranquil garden pond. He had told her that he had designed a similar pond in Central Park. She'd never been to New York City or anyplace outside the mountains. She couldn't even imagine what flat ground looked like, how strange and disorienting it must be. But she remembered enjoying Mr. Olmsted's stories of the great city's park. There were no natural lakes on the Biltmore property, or anywhere else in these mountains, but years before, an old farmer had dammed the creek to make a mill pond, so Mr. Olmsted expanded it, redesigned it, and made it part of Mr. Vanderbilt's garden.

Serafina remembered that her pa had brought her out to this very spot and showed her the inlet to the pond.

"It's a gentle little creek," her pa had explained, "but every time a storm comes in, it swells up bad and wants to dump muddy water, sticks, and debris into the pond. A farmer and a bunch of cows don't pay no never mind about a muck-filled pond, but it would never do for an elegant gentleman like Mr. Vanderbilt, so Mr. Olmsted had an idea."

As Serafina remembered her pa's words, she couldn't help but think about how happy and filled with life he'd been when he told her these stories.

"Mr. Olmsted had his workers build this brickwork structure across the creek to gather in the water and control how it flowed. You see, the water slips real smooth-like right into that big hole there. If the water's clean, then it runs on toward the pond. But look down in the hole real close, Sera. You see that metal contraption in there? Mr. Olmsted asked me to rig up a steel basket and a sluice gate so that if there's a big storm, and the creek water is all muddy and full of debris, then it won't flow into the pond."

"But I don't understand," Serafina had asked in confusion. "Where's the storm water go? It's gotta go somewhere, doesn't it?"

"Ah, you see! There's the trick of it. When we built this

thing, Mr. Olmsted instructed his work crews to construct a long, winding brick tunnel called a flume under the pond. The tunnel goes from the inlet here, all the way underneath the pond to the far end, nigh on a thousand feet away. So, now, when it rains hard and the creek overflows with muddy storm water, the metal basket fills with sticks and debris, the weight of it tilts the mechanism, the sluice gate opens the entrance to the tunnel, and the whole mess of it pours in. The storm water and debris flows through the tunnel underneath the pond and gushes out at the far end without ever having a chance to muck up the clean water in the pond. From there, the storm water continues on its natural course down the creek, eventually ending up in the big river the way God intended."

As her pa finished his story, Serafina could hear the reverence in his voice. "You see, Sera, you can accept things the way they are. Or you can make them better." And Serafina knew that both her pa and Mr. Olmsted were the kind of the people who made them better.

As Serafina remembered her pa's story, Braeden leaned down into the brick structure and used his lantern to look around inside. The stream was running strong and smooth with a large volume of rainwater pouring down into the main intake hole, but the water was clear of debris, so the metal sluice gate had not yet opened, allowing the water to flow directly into the pond.

Braeden began chucking sticks and branches into the metal basket.

"What in the world are you doing that for?" Serafina asked.

As he filled the basket with the weight of the branches, the sluice gate scraped slowly open. Braeden grabbed his equipment and climbed into the flume tunnel.

"Braeden!" she said in astonishment.

Down in a tunnel that ran beneath the pond was the last place on earth she wanted to go tonight. She'd already been buried once. She definitely didn't want to do it again—especially if it involved getting drowned at the same time.

But as Braeden disappeared, she had no choice. She had no idea where his new recklessness was coming from, but she couldn't let her friend go into that awful place on his own.

Pulling in a frightened breath, she climbed into the tunnel behind him.

Following the light of Braeden's lantern ahead of her, Serafina made her way through the flume. It was a narrow brick passage with a low arched ceiling. An inch of water was running along the floor. At first the tunnel was high enough that they could both walk normally, but the farther they went, the lower and narrower the tunnel became.

She didn't like this place one bit, but what she truly hated was the water dripping down from the ceiling onto the back of her neck, sending tingles down her shivering spine. And she hated the dark runnels of water sliding down the black, slimy, algae-coated walls like spidery tentacles. The heavy, putrid smell of the water hung in the air. She and Braeden were actually walking *under* the water of the pond.

As they went deeper, Serafina felt the cool temperature of the damp air, the clamminess of the walls, and the rising storm water at their feet. She wasn't sure if the sensations she was experiencing were real or shadow, but they felt as sharp as if she herself was part of the water, part of the stone, part of the bits and pieces from which the world was made.

The water in the tunnel was soon flowing around their ankles. Braeden had forced the sluice gate open, so the stream was pouring in. She had no idea why he was going through the flume, but it was even more mystifying why he would do it now, tonight, in the middle of a rainstorm with the water gushing in. What in the world could be so important?

Crack!

Startled by the sound, Serafina hit the floor with a splash, accidentally taking in a gulp of the water.

Crack!

It was steel against brick. Then she heard a prying sound.

She got back up onto her feet and sloshed through the rising water toward Braeden. He had set the lantern on a small ledge to give himself light to work by as he dug into the tunnel floor.

Using the tip of the shovel, he pried up one of the bricks. He pulled it up out of the water, set it aside, then picked up the shovel again and started working on the next one. Working in what was now six inches of rushing water, he was digging out the floor brick by brick!

Braeden's movement was hampered by the metal brace on his leg, but he worked with a steady deliberateness. Soon he had removed a dozen bricks. Then he reached down into the dark water, deep into a hole, and pulled out a dripping metal box.

"You've hidden something here," Serafina said.

With the storm water rising by the second, Braeden seemed to understand the danger he was in. Now that he'd gotten what he'd come for, she expected he'd turn around and go back up toward the opening of the tunnel. But he didn't. Leaving the shovel and lantern behind, he grabbed the box and continued forward into the darkness, down into the narrowest part of the flume.

"Now, where are you going, you crazy boy?" she shouted at him over the sound of the rushing water. "We've got to go back up!"

But he paid her no mind. As they proceeded down the tunnel, the ceiling became so low that she and Braeden could no longer walk upright. They hunched themselves down to fit, then they had to crouch. Finally they had to crawl on their hands and knees, the hinges of Braeden's brace creaking and twisting under the strain of his bending leg. At the same time, the level of the storm water gushing through the tunnel continued to rise. The flood of water pushed hard against her, now inches from her chin, almost to the ceiling, splashing and swirling with great force around her neck and shoulders, making it more and more difficult to breathe.

As she crawled, it felt like the water wasn't just rising around her, but dragging at her, wearing at her, pulling her skin away, tugging at her bones. Soon she'd become nothing more than tiny droplets scattered in the stream. *Just hold on,* she thought, gritting her teeth. *I'm not done yet!*

Braeden crawled faster and faster into the darkness, pushing himself through the water, pressing his mouth up toward the ceiling for air, but still dragging the metal box along with him.

Suddenly, a huge swell with a tumbling raft of branches came gushing down through the flume and crashed into them, filling the entire tunnel with water. She closed her mouth and held her breath, for whatever good that would do, and refused to die. She braced herself against the slimy brick walls so that the water couldn't take her. She had to hold on! But it was no use. The powerful current slammed into her, tore her fingers from the walls, and pulled her somersaulting upside down through the rushing water.

The storm water swept her away, tumbling her down through the narrow chute of the flume. Her arms and legs twisted and crashed with the turbulence of the rushing water. It didn't feel like she was going to drown, but like the last pieces of her soul were going to wash away.

Finally, she shot out of the flume's gushing outlet pipe and splashed into a swollen creek. She came up quickly, gasping for air and struggling to get to her feet. She grabbed frantically at her arms and legs, incredibly relieved that they were still there. She hadn't dissolved into the elements just yet. She'd fought it off one more time.

Braeden lay at the edge of the creek in the torrential rain, exhausted and pulling in great lungfuls of air, but still gripping the metal box as if his very life depended upon it.

Serafina climbed up onto the creek's rocky shore and looked around her in bewilderment, trying to figure out where she was. It took her several seconds to realize that she and Braeden were in the narrow ravine at the base of the pond's dam.

When the water had started coming down the flume in force, Braeden had made the decision that it was better to escape through the outlet rather than trying to fight upstream. That decision had saved his life. And maybe hers too—if the thing she was clinging to was indeed a life.

Serafina couldn't help but smile, relieved that they'd both made it. She gazed up through the pouring rain at the stone face of the dam. The water of the overflowing pond was pouring over the spillway high above her, coming down in a great waterfall into the creek.

As she turned back toward Braeden, a flash of lightning struck the sky with a piercing crack of thunder. Braeden tightened his jaw, wiped his wet hair out of his eyes, and got up onto his feet. Whatever he was doing, it was clear he wasn't done.

He knelt down on the rocks at the edge of the storm-swollen creek and opened the metal box.

Serafina had no idea what was inside it, but the moment he opened it, she could see something extremely black inside.

She stepped back in uncertainty.

Braeden pulled out a long black garment—fine black wool on the outside, and an inner lining of black satin.

A sickening feeling gripped Serafina's stomach and twisted hard.

She could see that the garment had been badly torn. Many parts were nearly shredded, as if by the claws of a wild beast.

A blinding glare of white light glinted on the garment's small silver clasp as a lightning bolt burned up the sky.

Her palms started sweating. Her lips tightened. The rain poured down her face.

As Braeden gathered the garment in his hands, it began to writhe and rattle like a living snake. A smoky cloud began to hiss out from it, as if it was annoyed that it had been closed in the box so long.

Then, with the rain pouring down all around him, and the lightning flashing in the sky behind him, Braeden stood, and with a great sweep of fabric roiling around his shoulders, he pulled on the Black Cloak.

16

*S*erafina watched in dread.

She could see that the cloak had been badly torn, but it was still the Black Cloak she feared and hated. Its dark, slithering folds hung down from Braeden's shoulders, writhing with power. But in the tears of the cloak was not simply the absence of cloth, but an impenetrable darkness blacker than she had ever seen. *No!* That was wrong. She *had* seen it! It was the same black as the black shapes she'd seen floating in the forest.

Whenever Braeden moved, the cloak's fabric moved with him and the terrible black shapes came wheeling outward into the world around him, tearing through time and space. The cloak threw these torn fragments of roiling, inky black shadow in all directions, blotting out the ground and the leaves of the trees and the stars above.

You've done well, boy . . . the cloak hissed in its raspy voice.

As soon as she heard it, Serafina wanted to pounce on the cloak and kill it. But she had no claws, no fangs, nothing but fear and confusion filling her heart.

I'm not going to hurt you, child . . . the cloak hissed.

Months before, she and Braeden had seen the cloak's evil with their own eyes. It had many powers, but the most sinister was that it allowed the wearer to absorb people, body and soul, deep into the black void of its inner folds. Her mother had been imprisoned in the cloak for twelve years until Serafina cut it to pieces on the angel's sword in the graveyard and freed her back into the world. Destroying the cloak that night had also freed Clara Brahms, Anastasia Rostonova, and the other children who had gone missing.

But the point was that she had slashed the cloak! She had destroyed it! How could it be here again? The last time she remembered seeing any sign of it, there had been nothing left of it but the silver clasp. Detective Grathan had found the clasp in the graveyard and died with it in his hand the night he was killed by the rattlesnakes. Had Braeden somehow retrieved the clasp and reconstituted the black fabric of the cloak? But if so, for what terrible purpose would he bring such an evil thing back into the world? And if it had been remade, why was it so badly torn?

Still wearing the cloak, Braeden stared at the ground, his face clouded with what looked like hatred, violence, and bitter despair all at once, his mind consumed with thoughts he could not bear. "Please forgive me, Serafina," he whispered to himself.

"Forgive you?" she said even though he couldn't hear her. "What did you do?"

She still couldn't believe what she was seeing. Braeden was actually wearing the Black Cloak.

"Tell me what you did, Braeden!" she shouted at him. She didn't understand what was happening. Had he turned evil?

Then, as if in reply, Braeden reached back around his shoulders and gathered the material of the Black Cloak's hood into his fingers.

"Don't you do it!" she shouted at him. "Don't put on the hood!"

But then he slowly pulled the hood up onto his head. His face flashed with terror and revulsion. A storm of torment wrenched through him. As he turned toward her, the hanging pieces of the cloak's shredded fabric went wheeling outward, ripping the air with splintering black shadow, tearing through everything around her.

She knew the black tears were at least as much in her world as they were in his, the connection, the uncrossable bridge between the two planes. She didn't know if he could see her now, or if he even had any idea she was there, but the twisting tears of blackness riving through the air struck her like a physical blow, slicing her with a blaze of searing-hot pain, and knocked her to the rocky ground.

Filled with nothing but blind panic, she belly-crawled frantically over to a tree for cover. But when another black shadow tore through the space around her, the tree made no difference. The blackness cut right through it, bursting a section of the trunk to pieces and bringing the top of the tree crashing down.

Seeing another black shadow coming toward her, she ducked down and tried to scramble away, but she tripped hard and tumbled head over heels. She splashed into the cold depths of the swollen river. And in that moment, she came to understand that sometimes the key to survival wasn't *resisting*, but *giving in*.

"*Water*," she commanded herself, and she disintegrated instantaneously into millions of droplets of water and flowed away downstream.

In that moment of pain, confusion, and fear when she fled Braeden and fell into the river, Serafina grasped one thing: she was a shape-shifter. Whether in body or spirit, a living whole or a wisp of elements, she was a shape-shifter.

She flowed down the river for a long time, knowing only movement, a constant, sweeping, pulling force that carried her along through the current.

She tried to pull herself back together again into spiritual form, but she couldn't do it. She had shifted into the water, but now the water didn't want to give her back. She could feel her droplets spreading apart, blending with the rest of the water, slipping into eddies, swirling behind rocks, seeping back into the universe.

"Spirit!" she commanded forcefully, using the word to focus her mind, and finally pulled her spirit back together again. She crawled from the river several miles downstream from where she began.

She didn't know exactly what she had done when she splashed into the river, or how she'd done it, except to let herself fade into the water, to will herself into it, to envision herself becoming one with it, but now she clambered up onto the rocky ground and looked around her at the river and the forest. It was still dark and raining. She checked her arms and her legs. She flexed her hands, turned herself around, and moved her head back and forth. She was whole again. Maybe *whole* wasn't the right word. She definitely wasn't *whole*, she knew that, but she was the spirit she had been before.

An idea leapt into her mind. "Body!" she said excitedly.

But nothing happened. She did not change. Some part of her was broken. Her body was gone. Was this what death was, to be pulled back into the elements that made up the world? But if that was true, and she was dead, then why wasn't she already gone? Why hadn't she already disintegrated back into the world? What was her spirit clinging to?

Finally, her mind turned back to Braeden and what she'd seen that night. Picking a direction, she headed into the forest, her only thought to put as much distance between her and the darkness-spewing Black Cloak as she could.

When she was miles away and the rain finally stopped, she slowed down and caught her breath, but she kept moving.

Every few steps, she checked the forest behind her, terrified that Braeden and the Black Cloak would be there.

When dawn came with the dull glow of gray light slowly filling the southern sky, she came into a shaded dell of ferns in a secluded spot she had used before, and there the weight of all that she'd been through finally caught up with her. She collapsed to her knees in exhaustion, grief coiling through her in trembling sobs, then she curled up in a little ball on the forest floor and wept. Her heart ached so bad that it felt like it was going to break apart.

She couldn't believe what had happened. How was it possible that Braeden had the Black Cloak, and why had he put it on? Had he been *using* it to capture people's souls?

Still crying, she tossed and turned in her bed of ferns, her heart filled with anguish. She wasn't sure if Braeden had actually seen her and had been *trying* to attack her with the cloak's searing black shapes. Was it possible that Braeden had truly turned on her?

She ran the back of her hand across her runny nose, wiped her eyes, and sniffled. She was a spirit, but she couldn't separate herself from the memories and sensations of the physical world, the longing and the pain of it. Her chest and legs hurt from running. Her face hurt from crying. But more than anything, the pain was in her heart. Was heartbreak any less painful because it wasn't physically real?

She pressed her eyes shut, curled into a tighter ball, and covered herself with her trembling hands.

After she crawled from the grave, she had rushed back to Biltmore to warn everyone about the evils she'd seen in the forest, to help them fight the coming storms and darkness, but it was hopeless. It was already all over. The darkness had already come. Her enemy had already attacked her and defeated her and pulled Braeden into his evil realm. Or maybe Braeden *was* the evil realm.

What was she going to do now?

She was nothing but a spirit, bodiless, powerless, dead and buried. The storms and the floods were coming to Biltmore. The water was rising. That clawed creature she'd seen in the forest was on its way. The sorcerer had already cast his spells, and she had already lost. She had lost everything. Her world was ending, and there was nothing she could do.

Her only relief was when she fell into an exhausted sleep. She dreamed she was a droplet of water tumbling in the flow of a turbulent river, then drifting into the still waters of a placid lake, then lifting on the heat of the midday sun and sailing on a tumult of moisture-laden clouds, until she was rain, falling back down through the sky again, landing on a leaf, and then dripping down to the earth, and then running along the ground until she slipped into the flow of the river where she began. The water, the sun, the earth and sky . . . It felt as if she could see all the inner workings of the universe.

She knew her time in the living world was coming to an end. She didn't know how many more nights she had left before she faded, or how many times she could shift before she couldn't shift back, but her body and her spirit were being absorbed back into the elements. Soon, she'd become so intermingled with the world, she would cease to be any semblance of what she had been before.

When she woke, the forest was fresh and cool with morning air, but she felt so disoriented that she had to remind herself where she was and how she got there. It took her several seconds to piece together everything that had happened the night before.

And as she lay there on the forest floor trying to understand, she gradually realized that she was not alone. A large animal lay in the grass a few feet away from her. It was a mountain lion, long of body and dark of fur.

Serafina smiled and pulled in a long, deep, pleasurable breath. Seeing the cat lying there filled her heart with joy. It was a catamount she knew well.

18

Not sure if the mountain lion knew she was there, and worried that she might scare him away, she did not move. She watched him for a long time, the gentle rise and fall of the cat's chest, the slow curling of his tail and the small flicking of his huge paws. It was her friend Waysa. And he was dreaming.

As she lay in the ferns beside him, she closed her eyes and tried once again to change into her feline form. But it didn't come. Tears rose in her eyes, and she pressed her eyes shut and gritted her teeth.

She would have loved to have lain in this beautiful shaded place with Waysa in her panther form, to find just a little bit of peace, just a little bit of gentleness at this moment. That was all she wanted right now, to have her thick black fur, and her whiskers, and her claws, and her muscles, and her long tail, and her four padded feet, and her twitching ears. She just wanted to be a cat. She just wanted to be herself.

The breathing of the lion beside her changed. Waysa slowly opened his beautiful brown-and-amber catamount eyes and scanned the forest for friend or foe. As his gaze turned toward her, she lifted herself up and looked at him, hoping beyond hope that he'd somehow see her there, lying in the ferns beside him, but he looked right through her. Waysa could see her no better than the others could.

With Waysa near, she wondered where her mother and the cubs were. A pang of worry rippled deep through her belly. Had the sorcerer killed them like he had killed so many others?

She looked around her and realized that she recognized this tranquil dell of ferns beneath the shade of the trees where she had taken refuge. In all her running and her panic during the night, she hadn't come here by chance. This was a place that she and Waysa had spent time before.

"Waysa, can you hear me?" she asked, her voice quivering with both hope and hopelessness. She missed her friend more than she could bear.

Waysa's ear twitched, but he didn't look at her. He looked in the opposite direction. Then he rose to his four feet.

Serafina heard a faint rustle of leaves, something coming slowly and quietly through the forest toward them.

Waysa crouched down low onto his haunches as the sound approached. She wasn't sure if he was frightened, uncertain, or excited about what was coming.

Then Serafina saw it.

The black head came through the brush first, then the impossibly bright yellow eyes, and the muscled black shoulders, the long black body, and the sweeping black tail. Serafina caught her breath. It was the young black panther she'd seen before.

There can only be one black panther, Serafina thought. *And there she is. It's not me anymore. It's her.*

Serafina felt like she should know who this panther was, but she didn't.

The panther scanned the meadow of ferns and spotted Waysa.

Waysa hunched down his body even further. Serafina wasn't sure if he was getting ready to pounce on her or if he was trying to make himself less threatening—for a cat, sometimes it was both at the same time.

But whatever kind of movement it was, it was enough to spook the young panther. The panther turned away and bounded into the forest the way she came.

Waysa sprang after her. At first Serafina thought he must be defending his territory against her, but then she realized that he wasn't attacking her, he was trying to catch up with her, trying to run with her.

"Good-bye," Serafina said wistfully, as Waysa and the black panther disappeared into the forest together.

Serafina found herself once again alone. Every friend she had made, everything she had gained in her life, was gone now. A deep and overwhelming pain filled her chest. She had to find out what had caused all this. The storm-creech she'd seen in the forest was still out there, and the black shapes were coming, destroying everything in their path. It felt like Biltmore and the people she loved were in more danger now than they had ever been.

But she was powerless. In the physical world, she had no body, no claws, no teeth, no hands, not even a voice. *But what is power?* she wondered. Was it the weapons and tools to act, or the ability to think? Was it talking to someone, or doing something? If you have only a small amount of power, and you're able to do only the tiniest, most insignificant things, does that mean you're *powerless*? Or with that tiny power, do you have all the power in the world?

She dropped down to her hands and knees and pushed at the dirt with her fingers. Nothing happened. Just as before, the world affected her, but she couldn't affect the world. She tried again and again, and then gave up.

The night before, she had shifted into the water of the stream, but she didn't want to *become* the dirt. The grave, the dirt, the dust, that was the last thing she wanted to become. She'd never be able to get back. She wanted to *move* the dirt. To *affect* it. To change *it*, not *her*.

A bumblebee buzzed by her, its dangling legs laden with clusters of yellow pollen. Getting an idea, she followed the bee. She came to a bush blooming with pale red flowers—bees, wasps, and other flying insects hovering around the bush, battling each other for position as they dipped in and sipped the nectar. Tiny yellow grains of pollen floated in the light of the sun. When she raised her hand and moved it slowly through the light, the bees and the pollen seemed to move away from her hand.

Hopeful, she pulled in a lungful of air and blew out at the floating pollen, but nothing happened. She remembered a famous musician, a flute player, who once visited Biltmore. One of the children at dinner asked if she could play his flute. But no matter how hard the girl blew into the instrument, she could not get it to make a flutelike sound. "It takes a lot of practice," the musician said kindly. "You have to do it just right."

And now here Serafina was trying to play the flute of the world. She blew the pollen from different angles and in different ways, slowly but surely figuring out how it worked. If she blew too hard or too soft or at the wrong angle, nothing happened. But if she blew just right, she could get the pollen to float in the way she wanted.

I can't do much, but I can do something, she thought, *and if I can do even the smallest thing, then I am a powerful being.*

As she practiced, trying to figure out what she could do and how she could do it better, she remembered something her pa told her when she was younger.

"Sometimes I reckon the universe we live in is one of God's great machines," her pa had said. "Its gears are nigh on invisible, and its spinning wheels are often silent, but it's a machine all the same-like, with patterns and rules and mechanisms. And if you look real close, you can *understand* it, and for just a spell, in just the smallest way, you may be able to get it to do what you want."

When her pa told her that, he was talking about the mechanical devices he dealt with every day. He definitely wasn't imagining his daughter as a whispery little haint blowing primordial dust, but she reckoned the principle was the same.

By practicing over and over again, she found that she could move dust and pollen floating in the air where she wanted it. She could rustle the edge of a leaf and change the flight path of a bee. And it all made her laugh. The mere act of having an effect on something, *anything*, caused her immeasurable joy. It meant that, at least for a little while longer, she was *real*.

She went over to the bank of the stream and tried to see if she could use her hands to channel the water in a certain way, creating little turbulent eddies near the stream's shore. She found that she couldn't block the water with her fingers or lift it in the cup of her hands. But sometimes, if she focused on the flowing water in just the right way, she could shape its movement.

She slowly realized that one of the most important things was that she had to let go of this idea that she was a human being or a catamount with a physical body in the living world. She had to accept the idea that she was a different kind of thing now, a spirit, just thought, and soul, a tiny wave of energy and elements—dust and wind and water. And when she began to accept this, to let herself slip away with the flow of the world, she began to see the fabric that held everything together, and she could give it a little tug.

Through all this practice, she kept thinking about the terrible evil spreading across the land. Somehow, she had to fight it. But the loneliness of it all was nearly unbearable. She wanted to talk to Waysa and run at his side. She wanted to warn Mr. Vanderbilt about the coming dangers. More than anything, she wanted to ask her pa for advice about what she could do.

But of course, there was no point now. Waysa and Mr. Vanderbilt and her pa and the others couldn't hear her words. There was *no one*, absolutely *no one* in the world, who even knew she was there.

And then she looked in the direction of the dark river she'd seen a few nights before, and she paused.

Or was there?

The sorcerer by the river, Serafina thought.

"I can't see you, but I know you're there," the sorcerer had said. He'd actually *spoken* to her.

But it had frightened her, and she ran away like a startled deer.

If I had only known, Serafina thought.

When she tried to remember the details of that first strange night, she could still feel the fear in her heart. The sorcerer had been walking slowly through the forest by himself in the dead of night, working close to the ground. He had possessed some sort of dark power.

Serafina didn't want to return to where she had seen him by

the river. The thought of it put a twisting knot in the pit of her stomach. But the truth was, she had run out of other paths to take. Her pa had told her once that true courage wasn't because you didn't feel fear. True courage was when you were scared of something, but you did it anyway because it needed to be done. If she was going to get back to the land of the living, she had to stay bold.

She started walking in the direction of the river. As the sun rose toward noon, she thought she still had one more ridge and valley to go. But she heard the sound of rushing water ahead of her and soon came to a deeply flooded area. She realized this was the new shore of the river.

This river in the forest had swollen far past where it had been before, flooding the trees for as far as she could see, the roots and trunks drowning in moving water. The flooding was so deep and wide that she couldn't even make out the main course of the river, let alone the other side of it. The dark brown current rushed by, tearing at the vegetation and carrying it along, swirling in large, twisting whirlpools, and crashing up into whitewater torrents where the water passed through the upper branches of the trees. Her mind was slow to comprehend the unimaginable: the river had filled the valley. The water was tearing away everything in its path, trees and rocks—and now mountains—everything getting swept away.

As she walked along the flooded bank, she realized that the place where she had seen the sorcerer a few nights before was long gone. She could feel the muddy earth she was standing on slipping away beneath her feet, the inexorable pull into the all-consuming current. The thought of it would have frightened her even in the best of times, but in her current state, she was terrified by the thought of getting sucked into a mudslide. She turned tail and headed for high ground.

In the afternoon, she curled up beneath the overhang of a rock to rest. A few hours later, she started awake with a sudden jerk. But when she woke up, she couldn't move her arms or legs. She couldn't raise her body from the ground. She tried to pull air into her lungs, but she felt the solidness of the earth against her, all around her, holding her in and pressing her down. Clenching her teeth, she clawed and snarled, twisted and bent, cracking the brittle stone around her. "Not yet!" she told the earth as she climbed out and brushed herself off.

It's getting worse, she thought, stumbling away from the crevice of stone that had nearly caught her. *I've got to keep moving.*

As she continued her search for the sorcerer and the sun began to set, she came to a steep slope and followed it down into a wet area of bulrushes and cattails. She found her way into a mountain bog where the ground was nothing but thick layers of spongy sphagnum moss and peat, the ancient fiber of a hundred forests that had come before. The bog exuded the dense, vaporous aroma of year upon year of amassed plants and thick black soil. The moss felt damp and strangely buoyant beneath her bare feet as she walked.

Cinnamon fern and swamp laurel with dark pink flowers grew out of the wet, mushy trunks of long-fallen trees. Tiny red cranberries grew all over the leafy ground. And delicate purple and violet dragon-mouthed orchids hung spiraling down.

As she delved deeper into the bog, she stayed alert for any signs of the sorcerer.

In the puddles on the ground, yellow-spotted salamanders scurried this way and that, and small bog turtles with orange necks crawled around. Southern irises, trout lilies, and arrowhead plants were growing everywhere, along with pitchers, sundews, and other carnivorous plants.

Just ahead, she heard a faint, buzzy *peeeent.*

Curious, she moved toward the sound and came to a small meadow in the bog. The sun had set behind the trees just a few minutes before and a soft, dusky orange light filled the western sky.

Peeeent!

She finally saw it: a small, pudgy, well-camouflaged brownish bird with an extremely long bill sat on the ground in the center of the meadow.

It was a timberdoodle.

Hunters who came to visit the estate called the birds woodcocks. Mountain folk called them bogsuckers or brush snipes. She thought it was interesting how different people had different names for the same thing. Mountain lion, puma, panther, painter, cougar, catamount . . . there were many names for her kin. Waysa had taught her that the Cherokee word was *tsv-da-si.*

She wondered what kind of name people had for what she had become. A haint, a haunt, a shade, a phantom, a spirit, a specter, an ethereal being . . .

Suddenly the shy little timberdoodle burst up into the air

in a crazy, spiraling flight, its wings whistling and all a-twitter, flying great sweeping circles up into the twilit sky. When it reached the very top of its spiral, the woodcock hovered for a moment, as if held in the air, then sang out a liquid song. From there it began to fall, tumbling back down toward the earth, folding and fluttering like it had been shot with a gun, but all the while singing through its vainglorious display.

Serafina smiled. She'd never seen the sky dance of the timberdoodle before, but her pa had told her the stories. In this place, in this moment, for just a few minutes during sunset, this normally shy, lonely little bird called out to the world, *I'm here! I'm here!*

He's just looking for a friend, she thought. *I wonder if something like that would work for me . . .* The thought of standing out in the middle of the meadow and leaping in great circles, tilting and twittering, and yelling, *I'm here! I'm here!* brought a cheer to her heart.

Finally, the timberdoodle landed exactly where he'd started.

It was then that Serafina lifted her eyes and saw the silhouette of a person standing and watching from the other side of the meadow.

It was the dark-robed sorcerer she'd seen by the river. Serafina ducked down to conceal herself, not sure if the sorcerer could see her.

When the hooded man finally turned and walked away, Serafina stayed low, gave him a few minutes to put some distance between them, then skirted the meadow and followed him. Serafina moved as quietly as she could through the wet forest bog, but she was determined not to let the sorcerer slip away.

Then the sorcerer stopped and stood very still.

Serafina hunkered down and hid behind the trunk of a large tree.

The sorcerer turned his head and looked in the direction she was hiding.

She thought that after a moment the sorcerer would turn back around and resume walking toward his destination, but he did not.

He lifted his head, then raised his thin, delicate hands and gently pulled his hood down until the dark cloth gathered around his shoulders.

That was when Serafina saw the sorcerer's face for the first time. It was not a man, but a girl! About fourteen years old, she had a pale complexion, dark red lips, and long red hair. The girl's green eyes scanned the forest, looking right where Serafina was hiding. Serafina crouched down even farther, but she couldn't help peeking through the vegetation back at the girl.

Her expression was filled with a grave and somber stillness, as if she had suffered a great loss. She had about her the feeling of someone who was hiding, diminished, but stoically unwilling to relinquish life, like a broken owl who no longer has the heart to fly.

The girl was nearly unrecognizable in manner and form, but Serafina knew exactly who it was.

Fear shot through Serafina. She hunched down low and peered through the bushes. It was *Rowena*! Too close now to flee, Serafina wanted to pounce fast and fight her old enemy. A growling, seething anger rose up inside her for all the terrible things Rowena had done. But the more she watched the wretched girl, the more curious Serafina became.

Rowena had changed. The angles of her face, the movement of her body, and especially her spirit and mannerisms, were all different. Her hair was still red, but it wasn't dressed up into fancy curls like before. It was long and thick around her neck and shoulders. Her face was still pale, but she wasn't wearing any lady's makeup to brighten her lips or shadow her eyes. And she wasn't wearing a stylish dress like she always had.

She wore simple, dark robes, like a hermit who had withdrawn from the world. She did not appear to have a horse or carriage anymore. She walked through the forest alone.

Rowena peered in Serafina's direction for several long seconds, studying the bushes where she was hiding as if she knew she was there. Serafina remained very still, unsure what Rowena could and couldn't sense.

Finally, Rowena pulled the hood back up around her head and continued walking through the misty lowlands of the bog.

Serafina released a long, steady breath, relieved that she'd avoided Rowena's detection. There was a part of Serafina that wanted to turn around and go home, go the other way, let wounded owls lie. But there was another part of her, the bolder, fiercer, more determined part, that was saying, *Don't let her get away*.

Serafina decided to follow her.

Pretty sure that she was invisible to even Rowena, Serafina tracked through the bog behind her, but kept a safe distance, just in case. Sometimes she lost the girl in the gray mountain mist, but then she would catch up again.

Soon they came to a faint path that wound even deeper into the wetlands, through a dark and shadowed grove of old, ragged cedar trees, with leafy ferns all around and moss-covered trunks.

Finally, Serafina watched as Rowena came to a small habitation.

At first it seemed like nothing more than a large clump of tree branches. Thin, twisty twigs had grown downward from the larger limbs of the trees, and the spidery roots had grown upward, creating tight, interwoven walls of sticks with a stick-woven roof overhead. The embers of a small cook fire glowed in front of the shelter's entryway. Various collections of plants lay here and there on logs, as if drying in what little sun might filter down through the trees during the day.

Serafina watched as Rowena tended to a row of carnivorous plants growing near her lair, mumbling strange and unrecognizable words as she pinched small, struggling flies and hornets in her fingers and dropped them into the awaiting mouths of the plants.

A few inches from where Serafina was crouched, and in various other areas of the forest around the shelter, hazes of white spiderwebs stretched between the trees. Feeling a crawling sensation on her spine, she looked more closely into the mass of web and saw thousands of black spiders with crooked legs and red hourglasses on their backs. Sucking in a gasp, she quickly moved away and found a new tree to hide behind. Her pa had taught her that the black widows were the most dangerous spiders around, but she'd never seen them bunched into large nests like this before.

She watched as Rowena worked. Pitcher plants, butterworts, and other carnivorous plants grew all around the shelter, up the walls and the rooftop. Rowena took several small plants out of her satchel, positioned them nearby, and moved her hand over them, mumbling something Serafina didn't understand. When Rowena lifted her hand, the plants had taken root in their new position.

When Rowena was done planting what she had gathered, she went over to the small stream that ran nearby, its water tinted light brown with the tannin of the swamp, where she slowly washed her hands. Serafina couldn't help but notice that it was the only small, gentle stream she'd seen in a long time. She wondered if the storm-creech did not know about this hidden place.

Serafina crept deeper into Rowena's lair, more and more curious about what she was seeing.

Several chickens and gray spotted fowl roamed nearby, along with a tribe of goats with long, shaggy black hair, thick, curving horns, and strange, square pupils in their eyes.

Serafina peered into the shelter of woven sticks. Other than the simple bed and a place for food, it seemed to be filled with glass flasks and orbs containing green, yellow, and milky-white liquids.

As she watched Rowena slowly and calmly gather leaves from some of the plants outside the shelter, Serafina frowned. Rowena had been deceitful and dangerous, but she had been alert and full of life. Now she seemed so grave in spirit. It was as if a great loneliness had grown within her, and now had nearly taken her over, like a thick carpet of moss overtaking a tree that had fallen onto the forest floor.

"I can feel you watching me," Rowena said.

Serafina froze right where she was, her heart pounding.

"I told you to leave me alone," Rowena said harshly. "I'm through with you!"

Serafina moved back a little and crouched down in the bushes.

Rowena pulled back her hood and shouted angrily out into the woods in the other direction, "Just get out of here! I don't want you here!"

It seemed that Rowena couldn't see her after all. But who was she talking to?

Curious to see what would happen, Serafina stepped a little closer.

"No! I told you to go away," Rowena said as if she knew exactly what she was doing. "I can hear you breathing down my neck. I'm not going to do your bidding anymore. I'm through with you, so stop bothering me!"

As Rowena stood up in anger, the air around her compressed and expanded violently, buffeting Serafina back. Frightened, Serafina quickly retreated into the forest.

Serafina knew she should turn and slink away from Rowena's wet, boggy lair. It was obvious that her old enemy had become far more powerful. But in other ways, the girl seemed so diminished.

Serafina thought about abandoning this idea of approaching Rowena and just skulking back to Biltmore and trying to make the best of her situation, but she hated the thought of it. She couldn't talk to them, she couldn't warn them, she couldn't help them in any way. In the nights to come, when the storms finally hit Biltmore and the rivers burst, what was she going to do? And what about Braeden? Had he started sucking up the souls of lost children like the Man in the Black Cloak, greedy for more power and more life, his skin slowly rotting from his body? Was he the root of all this evil or a victim of it? And no matter what he was, could she abandon him? When she thought about Waysa, she remembered him looking straight through her like she didn't even exist anymore. The world was wrecked. It broke her heart to think about enduring another night of this. She pulled in a breath, plucked up her courage, and spoke.

"I haven't been bothering you," she whispered. "I just got here."

Rowena immediately froze, obviously surprised by the sound of her voice.

For several seconds, Rowena did not move or say a word. Her dark red eyebrows furrowed.

"Who are you?" she asked.

21

Serafina couldn't believe it: Rowena had heard her! She was actually talking to her!

"I'm warning you," Rowena said sternly, looking up into the air. "I'll summon you out by force if I have to."

As Rowena lifted her open hand, the trees above Serafina began to shake and rattle with a threatening violence. Serafina could feel the air around her pulsating.

"I know you're there," Rowena said, "so don't just lurk out there. Tell me who you are!"

Serafina was too frightened to answer, fearing that Rowena would destroy her the moment she said her name. She wanted to run while she still had the chance. But Rowena was the only person she'd encountered since she'd crawled from the grave who could hear her.

"Are you living or are you dead?" Rowena demanded.

Serafina froze. She didn't know what to do.

"I asked you a question," Rowena said. "Are you living or are you dead?"

Finally, feeling like she had no other choice, Serafina decided to speak again. "I . . . I don't rightly know," she admitted.

Rowena seemed to understand that answer in ways that Serafina did not.

"But who are you?" Rowena asked again. "Where do you come from?" Her voice was gentler now, almost kind, as if she'd enticed reluctant spirits from the shadows before.

"I . . ." Serafina began, but then stopped, too uncertain to continue.

"Don't be frightened," Rowena said, her voice filled with a compassion that Serafina had never heard from her before. "Just tell me your name. No harm can come from that."

"I'm . . ." Serafina stopped again.

"Yes?"

Serafina ducked down behind a tree. "I'm . . . Serafina," she said finally.

"The cat!" Rowena hissed, her face blanching as she spun around and peered out into the forest. She crouched down and looked all around her like she thought a catamount was going to pounce on her at any moment. And Serafina knew that she probably would have attacked the sorceress if everything had been the way it was before, but in her current form how could she fight Rowena? How could she do *anything*?

"Something's happened to me," Serafina told her.

"But you're still here in this world," Rowena said, her voice filled with uneasiness as she looked warily around her for signs of attack.

"Part of me, at least," Serafina said.

Rowena paused, taking in these words. "But why have you come here?" she asked suspiciously.

"You're the only person I've found who can hear me," Serafina said.

Rowena pressed her lips together and nodded. "I can speak to both sides now."

"You mean the living and the dead . . . Were you the one who woke me from the grave? Were you talking to me?"

Rowena ignored her question.

"Was it you?" Serafina pressed her. "What did you say to me?"

Rowena shook her head. "It doesn't matter now, just the ramblings of a troubled soul, nothing of consequence. I have to be careful when I go to a cemetery, but especially that one." Then Rowena's tone took on a harder edge, like she wanted to change the subject. "Did you come here to my home to kill me, is that it, to seek your revenge?"

Serafina knew it was a fair question. But as she had been talking to Rowena, she felt more and more relieved that she was finally able to interact with someone. Whether she wanted it to or not, her hatred for Rowena was slowly fading behind her into a past that seemed so long ago.

"No," she said to Rowena. "I didn't follow you here to kill you. To be honest, after the battle for the Twisted Staff, I thought you and your father were already dead."

"We're not easy to kill," Rowena said.

"But I don't understand what's happening. Is Braeden on your side now?"

"No," Rowena said.

"But I saw him with the Black Cloak . . ."

"Where did you see him?" Rowena asked quickly, her voice filled with so much interest that it made Serafina reluctant to answer.

"I don't understand," Serafina said. "Where did the Black Cloak come from? I destroyed it on the angel's sword the night we defeated Mr. Thorne."

"We remade it," Rowena said. "The silver clasp is the core of its power, not the fabric."

Serafina frowned in aggravation, regretting she hadn't found the clasp and melted it down when she'd had the chance. Rowena seemed to have so much more knowledge than she did, so much more capability, and yet there was something about her . . . a hopelessness in her, a feeling of resignation, of giving up. And there had been fear in her, too. She'd been frightened of something, telling it to go away. Who or what was she hiding from deep in this forest bog?

"The truth is," Serafina said finally, "I have no wish to harm you, Rowena. With the way I am now . . . I'm just right glad to know that I'm not just a gust of wind."

"A lot has happened since I fought against you," Rowena said, her voice somber and weary. It was clear to Serafina that she, too, had suffered.

"What do you mean?" Serafina asked, moving toward her. "You've corrupted Braeden, haven't you? You've pulled him to your side."

"*No,*" Rowena said again, her voice edged with fierceness. "I haven't."

"But he's not who he was before," Serafina said.

"None of us are," Rowena said.

"He no longer cares about his animals, he's lying to his aunt and uncle, and I told you, I saw him wearing the Black Cloak! You've taken him!"

Suddenly, Rowena turned, looking around her toward an accuser she couldn't see. "You think you know him?" she snarled. "You think you can see what's inside his heart, whether he's good or bad, strong or weak? You don't know anything about any of us, cat. You're such a little fool!"

"But I don't understand!" Serafina screamed at her in reply.

"You think you've lost your friend? Is that it?" Rowena scoffed. "You don't even know what friendship is!"

"And you do?" Serafina snarled.

"I've seen it!" Rowena hissed.

"What are you talking about?" Serafina cried in confusion.

"Sometimes you're blind, cat, with more teeth and claws

than sense," Rowena shouted as she grabbed a flask from her cache. "I will show what I've seen!"

Rowena hurled the glass flask toward the sound of Serafina's voice. It crashed against the trunk of a tree and exploded with a great blast of whirling smoke and a bright, blinding haze. Then Rowena threw another flask and it shattered against the ground, its darkened blue contents rising up in a great swirl. Then she threw another, and the whole world felt as if it were shifting beneath Serafina's feet. Serafina felt cold air all around her, and then the world disappeared.

$\mathcal{S}$uddenly, Serafina found herself standing inside Biltmore, the air strangely cold. The French doors to the Loggia were open, the sheer white curtains glowing with the light of the full moon and fluttering in the cold winter breeze.

It's the night I was attacked, Serafina thought.

She stepped slowly out onto the Loggia, the long, beautiful outdoor room with its carved columns and sweeping archways looking out onto the forest and the mountains and the radiance of the stars above.

These aren't just my memories . . . It's like I'm here, living through it all again.

This was her home, her place in the world. She was

Biltmore's Guardian, watching over the people she'd sworn to protect.

She ran her eye along the Loggia's stone railing looking for any sort of creature that might be hiding there. She checked the vaulted ceiling sweeping over her head, looking for shadows that didn't belong. And then she gazed out across the canopy of the forest, her eyes scanning for danger in the distance.

But then she sensed a presence with her on the Loggia. The hairs on the back of her neck rose up as a dark shape emerged from the shadows behind her. She heard a *tick-tick-ticking* sound followed by a long, raspy hiss. She turned just in time to see something coming toward her.

She ducked and leapt aside, then shifted into panther form. Her lungs filled with air and her muscles bulged with power. Her claws sprang out. She roared into an attack even as the hissing folds of the Black Cloak swept over her head and plunged her into darkness.

She twisted her spine around and bit into the attacker's shoulder with her long fangs. Her panther heart hammered in her chest, driving her with dire strength. She clawed viciously at the attacker's side. She couldn't see his face, but she could feel him fighting to capture her in the cloak, pulling it over and around her. An ice-cold darkness soaked into her bones. The awful stench choked her. She fought through the dark rippling void as the Black Cloak engulfed her. She could feel her sharp panther claws slashing through the fabric, shredding it. The sound of the ripping cloth filled her ears. She kept twisting and swiping and striking, swatting wildly with her paws, fighting for her life, like she was drowning in cold black water. The slithering cloak wrapped itself around her, tightening like a coiling snake, even as it wrenched her soul away from her body and sucked her into its dark folds.

She saw inside the cloak a black, swirling, horrible world, but then it all began to change. Her claws had slashed through the cloak's fabric. It could no longer hold what it had captured. The ruptured cloak hurled the inner reaches of its dark void out into the world, and her soul with it.

A boy came running on two strong legs out onto the Loggia and charged toward the attacker. As the attacker turned, the hood fell away and Serafina saw the face. The attacker wasn't Braeden. And it wasn't Uriah. It was Rowena.

Barking a vicious snarl, Gidean leapt upon Rowena, knocked her to the ground and tore into her neck. Braeden, fighting strong, grabbed her and tried to hold her down.

Serafina had already wounded Rowena, but she was still far too strong. The sorceress threw wicked spells, one barrage after another, that gashed Braeden's face, tore at his legs, and threw him against a column.

Gidean lunged for another attack, biting into Rowena's side. She struggled frantically and escaped the dog, then turned to flee. Braeden clutched the shredded Black Cloak and pulled it from her just as she dropped over the railing's edge and disappeared into the dark of night.

Serafina lay wounded in human form on the stone floor of the Loggia, unable to move. Rowena's spells had torn her chest and stomach with gaping wounds. When she tried to take in a breath, a lightning bolt of pain shot through her ribs. She tried to move her bloody arms and legs, but they lay uselessly around her. All she could do was watch the dark red pool of her own blood spread slowly across the floor. She knew she was going to die.

The black fragments, the inner darkness of the Black Cloak that had been riven by her claws, floated all around her in the Loggia and began to drift with the wind.

She tried to tilt her head to see if Braeden had survived the battle, but her neck moved in a painful jerking motion. When she finally managed to look over, she saw a terrifying sight: it wasn't Braeden, but the body of a black panther—*her*—lying wounded on the floor beside her, the panther's flesh torn in the same way hers was, her sides bleeding and her bones shattered.

Both she and the panther were moments from death.

She knew it was the end.

She tried to look for Braeden, but she could not see him.

"Braeden . . ." she gasped, blood gurgling in her throat.

Finally, he came into her view. Her heart leapt when she saw that he was still alive. But his head dripped with long, jagged cuts, and he dragged his leg behind him. She watched as he knelt beside the panther and put his hands on her sides, closing his eyes as he infused the cat with his healing power. He caressed the cat's head and spoke to her in words that Serafina couldn't hear, running his hands down the length of her long, furred body.

When he was done with the panther, Braeden moved quickly over to her.

"Braeden . . ." she tried to say again, but her voice was so weak she knew he couldn't hear her.

As he frantically examined her wounds, she could see how badly she was hurt reflected in the grimace of his face.

"I don't know what to do, Serafina . . ." he said as he ripped his shirt apart and tried to stanch her bleeding with it. He couldn't heal humans the way he could animals.

"I'm sorry," she whispered. "I don't want to go . . . Please say good-bye to my pa . . ."

But with a heavy grunt of pain, he gathered her up into his arms. "Hold on, Serafina . . ." he told her, a fierce determination in his voice.

She wrapped her arms around his neck and tried to hold on to him the best she could, but she could feel her strength waning, her consciousness drifting into a swirling black void.

Braeden carried her outside into the darkness, struggling on his bloodied leg, but unwilling to give up.

"Stay with me, Serafina . . ." he said as he carried her, and she clung to the sound of his voice.

As blood dripped down onto her shoulder and neck, she didn't know whether it was his or hers. They were both shaking, bleeding, and terribly wounded, holding on to each other with their last hope. But Braeden kept moving, carrying her through the darkness.

He took her down into the gardens and set her on the ground outside the master rosarian's shed. Then he shouldered open the door, stormed in, and came out with supplies—old wooden apple crates, a hammer and nails, and other tools. He quickly made a crude stretcher-like box with shallow sides, and dragged her body into it. Then he fastened the end with a rope, called Gidean over, and the two of them began dragging her across the ground toward the trees.

She drifted in and out of consciousness as Braeden and the dog pulled her through the forest, Braeden dragging his bloody leg behind him.

When Braeden finally reached the graveyard, he dragged her to the foot of the statue in the angel's glade and begged for the angel's help. "Take care of her!" he shouted, his voice cracking. "You have to save her!"

As Braeden pulled away from her, Serafina reached out with her last strength and grasped his arm. "Don't leave me here," she whispered hoarsely. "Don't leave me . . ."

"I'm not going to leave you, Serafina," he told her. "I promise you, I will never leave you!"

As she lay dying, with the blood seeping from her body, she looked up at the stars above her head and thought it was the last time she would ever see them. Her body was getting cold now. Her limbs were numb. The pain was receding. She could feel her life slipping away from her, her eyes closing for the last time.

Then she heard the sound of digging. She saw the blurry image of Braeden frantically digging a hole in the ground in the middle of the angel's glade.

The last thing she saw was Braeden dragging the crude coffin that contained her lifeless body into the bottom of the grave he had dug. His only hope was to bury her in the place of eternal spring.

"Take care of her," Braeden begged the angel. "I will find a way to put her back together again!"

And then Serafina saw no more.

The darkness that followed was so black and so long that she did not stir.

Finally, a girl's voice came into the darkness. "You must return now."

When Serafina opened her eyes, she found herself standing in the forest bog by Rowena's lair just where she had been. A warm summer breeze drifted through the trees. The vision was over.

Rowena was standing there alone. Her voice was filled with emotion when she said, "*Now* you know what friendship is."

Serafina, realizing that Rowena, too, had seen what Braeden did on the night of the full moon, looked at her old enemy in amazement. "And so do you . . ."

"And so do I," Rowena said.

Serafina sat down on a log and gazed absently at the things around her. All she could think about, all she could feel, was the vision. She knew now that the Loggia was where she had died. *Died* . . . Was that what happened? She'd been buried, that much was certain. But she wasn't truly dead, was she?

Had Braeden saved her?

She thought about what he must have gone through. He could never let anyone know what truly happened or the horrible thing he'd done. He had dragged the bloody body of his best friend through the forest and buried her. And he hoped that she was still alive when he did it.

In the days that followed, he must have been filled not just with the sadness of losing her but with a terrible guilt. As he lied and covered things up, deceit must have mixed with anguish. His body had been hurt and his heart torn as cruelly as hers.

After months of sorrow and healing, he must have just been finally finding his way back into the world when she crawled from the grave and began to haunt him. She remembered how her presence had upset him. He had seemed so frustrated and hopeless.

Her vision of the night of the full moon was over, and she finally knew what had happened to her.

She thought about her body lying in the grave in the angel's glade all those nights.

She thought about the young black panther she'd seen running wild in the forest.

And then she thought about her whisper of a spirit crawling from the grave and creeping through the gardens back to Biltmore.

Three, she thought. *Three pieces. My human body, my panther body, and my spirit. My trinity was split.*

And as horrible as that was to imagine, and as difficult as it was to accept, everything finally began to make sense in her mind.

She knew from the stories of the mountain folk that there could only be one black panther in the forest at a time.

And it's me, she thought. *It's still me. I'm the black panther running through the forest.*

And I'm the dead girl lying in the grave.

And I'm this lost spirit finding her way through the living world.

On the night of the full moon, she and Braeden had fought an epic battle against Rowena. And they had lost.

She had lost.

The damaged Black Cloak had torn her asunder and flung her pieces out into the world. Time and space, body and spirit, dream and waking, were all a-jumble now.

She was not exactly dead. She was not exactly alive. She was not spirit or body. She was all these things and none, thrown to the winds of chaos, like the black shapes still floating in the forest and destroying everything they touched. They were the torn inner remnants of the Black Cloak.

Still stunned, she looked over at Rowena. "How did you show me this vision? It felt so real. I remember walking onto the Loggia that night and standing at the rail, but once the cloak went over my head, I was torn apart. I couldn't have seen all those things you showed me. Those couldn't have been my memories alone."

"No," Rowena said softly, lowering her head. "Your memories, my memories, the light of the moon, the slip of the stars . . . it's everything that happened that night, the print of our movement on the thread of time."

Serafina began to reply, but she was unable to find the right words, and she was still trembling from the experience of it. "It was startling," she said finally.

"What I did is called scrying," Rowena said. "It provides a vision of past events, a glimpse into the thread."

"And you have seen it before?"

"Yes," Rowena said, and Serafina could see that it had affected Rowena as powerfully as it had affected her.

"You attacked me on the Loggia," Serafina said, trying to connect everything together in her mind. "You tried to kill me with the Black Cloak."

"And I almost succeeded," Rowena said.

"You probably thought you had me as good as dead."

"I did, indeed," Rowena admitted, obviously annoyed. "There was no way you should have been able to survive that."

"I reckon I'm not quite as easy to kill as you figured, either."

"Apparently not," Rowena said with a ghost of a smile.

Serafina frowned in confusion and looked up at her. "But . . . you still showed me the vision . . ."

Rowena turned away, hiding her expression.

"But why?" Serafina asked. "Why did you show me that?"

"Because you were starting to annoy me with all your mewling-weepy-crying about Braeden."

"But I have always been your enemy, and yet you showed this to me . . . You helped me."

Rowena shook her head. "Don't flatter yourself, cat. I'm not trying to be your friend. I just showed you what happened. The truth is the truth. The past is the past. It cannot be changed. But things have changed now."

"What do you mean, things have changed?" Serafina asked, sensing that there was far more on Rowena's mind than she was saying. But Serafina's thoughts kept going back to what happened on the Loggia. "The cloak was torn . . ." she said, trying to grasp what she had learned.

"You've been *splintered* . . ." Rowena said.

Serafina had seen it, experienced it, but when she heard the word *splintered* spoken out loud, her mind recoiled from the sound of it. It seemed too awful to comprehend, that her heart, her soul, had been splintered from her body, and now she was in three pieces.

"How do I fix this?" Serafina asked. "How do I get back?"

Rowena shook her head. "You don't. You're just a spirit now, harmless as a fly, and soon you'll begin to fade, if you haven't already. You can't last in this world, and then you'll be gone. *We all go to the same place; all come from dust, and to dust all return.*"

Serafina looked at her in surprise. It was the passage she'd thought about when she saw the dust in Essie's room.

"So that's why you thought you could show me the vision . . ." Serafina said.

"I'm not stupid, cat," Rowena said. "I know your claws too well."

As Serafina made her way through the forest back toward Biltmore, one thought dwelled on her mind: before she faded away, she had to help Braeden. She didn't know to what extent the Black Cloak had drawn him into its power, but she had to save him, even if she couldn't save herself. She had seen the violent storms in the forest, the claw-handed storm-creech, and the floating black shapes. Something was driving these evils toward Biltmore, something so powerful that even Rowena hid from it. Was it some dark force in the forest? Or someone inside Biltmore itself? Or was it Braeden using the Black Cloak?

When she arrived at the estate, strong winds were blowing through the trees. She felt light on her feet, like if she lifted her arms she would actually float away and become a flurry of drifting air. She was tempted to try it, to keep learning her new skills, but she dared not test the power of the gale, lest she never return.

Crawling through a small shaft in the back of Biltmore's foundation, Serafina found her way back into the house.

Her pa was working on some sort of electrical accoutrements with many copper coils, wires, and bulbs for the summer ball. She wanted to watch him, just *be* with him for a while, but she knew she shouldn't.

As evening came, Mr. and Mrs. Vanderbilt and their many guests gathered in the Banquet Hall for dinner. More newcomers were arriving every day for the ball, and now some sixty people sat around the long oak dining room table, displayed in sparkling fashion with its fine Biltmore-monogrammed porcelain settings and silver candelabras.

She scanned the room. There was an empty chair next to Mr. Vanderbilt, but she didn't see Braeden. She wondered what had become of him after he put on the cloak.

Finally, just before dinner began, Braeden came into the room. He was still limping with the metal brace on his leg, but he appeared fresh and clean, and he was wearing a fine dinner jacket.

She studied him carefully, trying to understand what he was thinking and feeling at that moment, but she couldn't read his face. What had been going on in that head of his? Had the despair of losing her driven him to the Black Cloak?

His dog, Gidean, followed several yards behind him, not at his side. When Braeden took his seat at the table next to his uncle, the dog went over to a distant corner out of Braeden's line of sight and lay down, his head on his paws.

Serafina thought Braeden must have hidden the Black Cloak away somewhere in the house or back in the flume under the pond, but she wasn't sure.

As she watched him talking with the others at the table, it reminded her of watching Mr. Thorne months before in this very room as he lingered among the guests and their children. There was something in the look behind Braeden's eyes that she could not quite fathom, not just the sadness and detachment that she'd seen, but as if he was going through the motions of his life, biding his time, waiting to get to what was important. But that was the question. What was important to him now? Was it using the cloak each night? Is that what he longed for, the dark embrace of its power?

She watched him all through the evening, looking for signs. Was his skin flaking off his hands as it had with Mr. Thorne? Did he watch the children in the room with particular interest? *You have to resist it, Braeden,* she kept thinking.

She looked for signs of good and evil in her friend, of truth and deceit, wondering which side was winning. She could see him doing the things he was expected to do, but was it truly him? Or was he like one of those weird horned beetles that wears the shell of another beetle on its back to hide itself?

But then something happened.

When he thought no one was looking, Braeden slid his hand under the table, and he tapped his fingers lightly on the wooden edge of his chair.

In the corner across the room, Gidean sat up and tilted his head in curiosity.

Braeden tapped again.

Gidean rose to his feet and moved quickly toward Braeden. The dog slipped under the table and put his nose against Braeden's hand to let him know he was there.

Without anyone noticing, Braeden slid the food from his plate and gave it to Gidean beneath the table. The surprised Doberman gobbled the food down in an instant and looked up appreciatively for more.

Serafina smiled. This was new. Something was changing in Braeden. She didn't know if using the cloak had turned him evil or not, or to what degree he could control his use of it, but for the first time in a long time, this was the Braeden she knew, the one who fed his dog from his plate, the one who would fight for his friends no matter what. This wasn't the cloak's doing. This was something else. Somehow, someway, he was still in there, deep down inside, at least a little bit. And this was the Braeden she held on to in her heart.

When the final course was done, Braeden politely excused himself from the table and said good night to everyone. They all wished him a pleasant good night in return.

As Serafina followed him out of the Banquet Hall and around the Winter Garden, she was glad to see Gidean walking with him. But then Braeden took Gidean over to a side door, let him outside, and continued on through the house without him.

"That's strange," Serafina said, and followed Braeden up the Grand Staircase to the second floor.

As Braeden entered his bedroom, she thought he was going to go to sleep, but then he got down on his hands and knees and dragged a heap of outdoor clothes from under the bed. They were dry, so they weren't the clothes he'd worn in the flume, but the shirt, trousers, and boots were stained with dirt. They'd been used before without being washed. He quickly pulled the clothes on and then grabbed the rope out from under his bed.

"Here we go again," she said as he went out the window.

Serafina climbed down the rope to the terrace below and then followed him through the gardens. "Back to the Black Cloak again?" she asked him.

But then Gidean came running toward him out of the darkness. Instead of going toward the pond, Braeden and Gidean followed a path into the forest. It was a path she knew well. And clearly so did Braeden.

He was heading for the graveyard where she was buried.

erafina followed Braeden through the forest at a distance, uncertain how her presence might affect him. That first night she came to him, he had suffered such anguish. She wasn't keen on driving him afoul again, so she let him get a fair piece in front of her.

She made her way through the darkened cemetery on her own, following the path that she thought Braeden was on. But she could no longer hear him and Gidean walking ahead of her. Either she'd let them get too far up the path or something else had happened. Suddenly, she felt very much alone.

As she crept past the weathered headstones marking the graves, the graveyard's swampy moist air clung to her skin like leeches. A low chorus of crickets, cicadas, and other buzzing insects pulsed around her. Long, wispy trails of mist oozed across the ground at her feet. The twisting roots of the old trees weaved through the damp earth beneath her bare feet, and vines hung down from the trees' crooked, dangling limbs.

She had already read many of the epitaphs chiseled in block letters on these gravestones, and she had no desire to do it again tonight, but as she moved among them, the voices of the dead came alive.

Here lies blood, and let it lie, speechless still, and never cry, one said, but she tried not to look or listen.

Our bed is lovely, dark, and sweet. Come join us now and we shall meet, said the two sisters lying in the ground side by side. It felt as if they were talking to her, inviting her back to where she belonged.

She hurried past the cloven man and through the six-sixty crosses of the buried Confederate soldiers. When she finally made it through the graveyard, she came to the small open area of the angel's glade.

She found Braeden lying stretched out facedown on the dirt mound of her grave. His body was flat to the ground. His left leg was straight, but his right leg was bent beside him, clenched in the metal brace. His arms were up around his head, the fingers of his hands splayed, as if he had been holding the earth. Gidean lay flat on the ground a few feet away, just as still as he.

Serafina's heart filled with fear, for it looked like they were both dead. She couldn't breathe.

But then Braeden's head moved and Serafina exhaled in relief.

Braeden's eyes were closed and his face filled with sadness, but he was alive. He had come to visit her, to sleep there on the ground, stretched out on her grave.

She noticed the dried stains on his trousers and the old dirt on his boots. He'd been here before. Many times. He hadn't been sneaking out of the house every night to use the Black Cloak. He'd been coming here.

She imagined him coming out here night after night, sleeping on her grave when his family thought he was home in his bed.

Had Mr. Vanderbilt come during the night with a search party and looked upon his nephew in dread? Was that why Mr. Vanderbilt had been so concerned about him? Was that why he'd told Braeden that he had double-locked Biltmore's doors?

As Braeden lay on her grave, his shoulders moved with a slow and troubled breathing.

She gazed upon him in sadness, pursing her lips as she felt a thickness catching in her throat.

For a long time, he did not speak or move from the grave. He just lay there in the dirt. It was as if his thoughts had overwhelmed him and he'd collapsed there.

She moved closer to him, her chest rising and falling, slow and steady, with every breath she took, and she knelt down beside him.

She could see that his hands were trembling.

She studied his face, and his closed eyes. When he squeezed his eyes shut even tighter, she watched a tear roll down his cheek, fall, and drop into the dirt. Tiny specks of dust floated into the air around where it fell.

She pulled in a sudden, heaving breath of emotion, and tried to let it out with a measured calm, but her sigh was ragged.

When he finally lifted his face, he looked up at the stone angel. "I gave her to you," he said, his voice shaking. "But what have you done?"

Serafina felt a storm of dizziness passing through her. Tears welled up in her eyes.

As she looked around the gravesite, she noticed that the mound of dirt he was lying on seemed strangely undisturbed. She was surprised that the broken boards of the coffin weren't sticking up out of the ground where she had crawled out.

"What do you want me to do?" Braeden shouted desperately at the angel. "Tell me what to do!"

She wished she could reach out to him, somehow touch him, somehow talk to him. "I'm here, Braeden," she said. "I'm here!"

She put her hand on his. She could not truly feel the living warmth of his hand, and it was clear that he could not feel her, but the closeness of her spirit seemed to rack him with new grief. His face contorted with a dark and terrible sorrow.

Horrified by what she was doing to him, she quickly rose to her feet and stepped back. "I'm sorry," she said, her voice weak.

"I'm not going to leave you, Serafina," he said, getting himself up onto his feet. "I'm not going to abandon you!"

He hadn't heard her words, he was still speaking to her in the grave, but it pulled at her heart. She desperately wanted to show him a sign that she had heard him. No matter what had happened, they were still friends, they were still together. Her death wasn't going to be the end of them. It couldn't be.

She looked around her, determined to find a way to communicate with him.

Dust to dust, she thought. *Of earth they were made, and into earth they return.* That was what was happening to her. She was *returning.* But for the moment, there was still a little trace of her that lingered in the world.

Harmless as a fly, Serafina thought. But even a fly can do things. And now she had an idea.

Wanting to make as big a movement as possible, she stepped onto the mound of the grave and spun around in a circle, shouting and kicking, jumping up and down, trying to make every kind of wild commotion she possibly could.

But nothing happened. The dirt didn't move.

She was useless.

But then she remembered. *Play the flute . . .*

She got down onto her hands and knees, leaned down, pulled some air into her lungs, and blew out a gentle, perfect breath just like she'd practiced.

Suddenly, a tiny flurry of dust swirled up into the moonlight in front of Braeden.

She cheered with a great shout. She'd done it just the way she'd practiced, and at just the right moment!

But Braeden did not see it.

She had accomplished nothing.

More discouraged than ever, she flopped to the ground. The whole thing was hopeless.

But then she noticed that Gidean had sat up and was looking in her direction. His ears were perked and his eyes alert. He wasn't looking at *her*, but at the dust she had stirred.

He was staring straight at it.

He tilted his head quizzically.

"It's me, Gidean!" she shouted.

She blew into the dirt again, and another little cloud of dust curled up.

Gidean rose slowly to his four feet. He tilted his head, trying to understand what he was seeing.

"I'm alive, Gidean!" she shouted.

Finally, Gidean barked in recognition. And then he started digging.

Serafina pulled back in surprise, startled. She wasn't sure what she had been expecting, but she definitely didn't think the silly dog would dig! But she didn't know how to stop him.

Gidean dug furiously with his front paws, throwing a rooster tail of dirt behind him.

Startled, and spitting out the flying dirt hitting his face, Braeden scrambled out of the way.

"What's going on?" he asked in confusion. "What are you doing, boy?"

But Gidean just kept digging straight down into Serafina's grave, throwing dirt like he was a steam-powered digging machine.

"Stop, Gidean. Don't!" Braeden commanded him. He grabbed the dog by the shoulders and tried to hold him back, but the boy was no match for the dog's strength.

"What are you doing?" Braeden demanded, his voice filled with worry and fear. "Don't do this! We can't do this!"

Serafina knew he was scared of what anyone would be scared of digging up a grave, that he'd find her grotesque, putrefied body.

But Gidean didn't stop. He just kept digging.

Braeden stepped back, obviously unsure what to do. He watched as his dog dug a deeper and deeper hole.

Serafina could tell by the horrified look on Braeden's face that he didn't think he was prepared to see what he was about to see. And yet, at the same time, there was something tearing at him, some macabre curiosity, some overwhelming desire for Gidean to keep going. They had to change the dark and terrible world they'd been living in, they had to do *something*, and now Gidean was doing it!

Braeden dropped down to his knees and started digging at Gidean's side. He clawed rapidly at the earth with his bare hands, throwing the dirt behind him.

Serafina didn't know what they were going to find in the grave. Would there be an actual body? But she'd crawled out! She'd been walking through the world. There *couldn't* be a body in the grave! *But was there?* Were they going to find her corpse rotting in the dirt? She could imagine her gray, decaying skin hanging from the broken white bones of her earthly remains.

When Braeden and Gidean finally reached the coffin, Serafina was surprised to see that the lid was unbroken and still in place. Brushing aside the last of the dirt, Braeden pried the coffin's lid away.

Serafina gasped in astonishment at what she saw.

26

Her body was lying in the coffin. She knew she should have expected it, but there was no way to prepare for it. She closed her eyes and shrunk away from the sight of it, bending at her waist and grabbing on to a tree to keep from falling over or collapsing to her knees. She covered her face and eyes with her other hand and struggled to pull in steady breaths of air—but with what lungs, what air? It felt as if her whole world was collapsing in on her. How could this be? How could she be in the grave?

She didn't want to look at the body, but she knew she must.

She slowly turned and looked again, her nose and mouth wrinkling as she expected to see her body's rotten skin peeling back from her bones.

But her body wasn't rotten. Her body was facing upward, with her eyes closed, her hands neatly lying one over the other on her chest, like someone had laid her there with respect and care. As she looked closer, she could see that some dirt had spilled into the grave onto her, but her face and body were not rotted. She was not a grotesque corpse. She appeared to be in some form of suspended animation, as if she lay in eternal spring. Braeden had brought her here to the angel's glade, where decay and seasons and the cycles of the universe had no sway.

Serafina stood over her own grave and stared down into the coffin at her body in disbelief. Braeden and Gidean stood beside her.

Her body was clearly dead in that there was no life in her, no breathing or movement, and yet, her body was not blue or grayish of skin or decayed in any way. It seemed perfectly protected there, as if nothing would ever harm it.

Serafina studied Braeden's expression. He did not seem surprised that her body was in the coffin. He seemed to expect that. He had put it there. But his eyes were wide and his face filled with shock about something else.

"All the wounds are healed," Braeden said in amazement. Her dress was badly torn and stained with old blood, but her body was in perfect condition.

He turned and looked up at the angel.

"You *healed* her," he said, almost apologetically after the accusations he'd slung at her earlier that night. "You've been *protecting* her," he said, as he wiped tears of relief from his eyes.

Serafina gazed all around at the angel's glade, with its beautiful, peaceful willow trees and its lovely green grass. It had always been this way, winter, spring, summer, and fall.

Braeden looked up at the angel again and spoke to her as if she was not only a living, sentient being but a true friend. "But what do I do now? How do I help her?"

He looked at the angel expectantly, but after a long time, his excitement faded, and some of his old sadness returned.

"Don't give up hope," Serafina whispered.

Finally, he laid himself down on the dirt next to her open grave like he himself was dead.

"I'm not going to lose hope, Serafina," he said. "Somehow, I'm going to get you out of here."

She knew he hadn't truly heard her. They had been feeling the same thing at the same time.

Serafina gazed down at Braeden lying beside the grave and she tried to understand it all. Her human body lay in the coffin. Her panther body was out in the forest, a wild animal. Her restless spirit had crawled out of the grave, carrying with it all the trappings and constraints she remembered of the physical world—the steadiness of the earth, the challenges of physical obstructions, the essence of sight and sound and feeling, pain and hunger and sleep. But it had left her body behind, like a cicada crawling out of its dried shell. Her spirit had made it all the way to Biltmore and haunted those within. And now she was back again. Her spirit was here once more.

For a long time, she just tried to understand the difference between thought and action, between dream and waking, between the physical world and the spiritual, between perception and reality.

She tried to figure out what Braeden meant when he said he was going to get her out of here. Out of the grave? Out of her dead body? She didn't understand, but at least she knew now, without any doubt, that even after all this time, after all that had happened, he was still her friend, he was still fighting for her, and he still had hope. He had tremendous hope, brighter than the darkest night.

He was lying on his back now beside the grave and his eyes were open. Gidean crept forward and curled up close beside him, and Braeden put his arm around him. For months, Braeden had been pushing his dog away, ashamed of the boy he had become, but now the rift between them seemed as if it was beginning to heal. Serafina was glad to see them together, but why was it happening here and now? What had changed?

As Braeden stared up through the opening in the trees, she wondered what he was looking at, what he was thinking about in that moment.

She went over to him. She did not go near her dead body lying in the grave. She was scared of what might happen if she did that. But she went to his other side.

As she moved, she noticed a pair of yellow eyes staring from the shadows. The cat's black fur was nearly invisible in the darkness, but Serafina could see the panther's face and the outline of her ears. The panther had crept up close and was lying down now, still and quiet, gazing into the glade toward them.

Serafina slowly made her way over to Braeden and lay down in the dirt next to him.

Lying on her back beside him, she gazed up through the opening of the angel's glade into the nighttime sky. She and Braeden were looking up into the stars just like they had when they used to lie on Biltmore's rooftop together. Those nights seemed so long ago now, like they had been a dream. But it had all been real, and somehow, this was, too.

Lying side by side, they gazed up at the crystalline black ceiling of the midnight sky. It was a beautifully clear night. They could see thousands of points of light splayed above them, clusters of many stars, Saturn and Mars and Jupiter glowing in all their glory, and the bright swath of the Milky Way galaxy splashed across the glistening heavens.

They watched the stars and the planets sliding slowly over their heads, marking time so precisely that it was barely perceptible, like a great, steady celestial clock, keeping the time of their inner lives, showing them that out there in the world everything was always changing, but here in the center of the world, where they were lying side by side, everything would always remain the same.

For the first time, Braeden did not seem upset by her spirit's presence. With her spirit on one side, her human body on the other, and the panther nearby, all was well again. It had been the terrible separation of the three that had caused him such tearing grief. But now, he lay quietly.

As Braeden fell asleep beside her, and she fell asleep beside him, she began to slip away, not into a nightmare like before, but into a lovely dream. She dreamed she was a tendril of moving air, flowing from place to place, without weight or body, only movement, constant movement, from forest to home, from mountain to field, she swept and rolled and turned, like the music of a gentle symphony gliding on the breeze.

For once in a long time, she and Braeden were together, and they were finally at peace.

When Serafina woke, she found herself lying in the angel's glade with Braeden and Gidean standing nearby. She quickly got herself up onto her feet to see what was happening.

"What do you think you're doing?" a male voice asked in a forceful tone.

Serafina looked around the forest.

"I wasn't going to hurt anyone," Braeden replied. "I swear. Nothing happened."

"Something always happens with that thing," Waysa said as he stepped out of the forest. His long dark hair hung down around his shoulders and his brown skin glistened in the morning light. His chest was bare and he wore simple trousers. The pattern of his tribe's ancestral tattoos marked his face and arms.

"What's wrong with you? Why did you put on the cloak?"

"I'm sorry," Braeden said to him, shaking his head. "I . . ."

"What was it?" Waysa demanded. "What happened?"

"My aunt and uncle were having a party in the rose garden with all the guests—"

"Oh, yes, that's a good reason. Lots of excellent victims to choose from," Waysa said sarcastically.

"No!" Braeden said. "I was sitting on the bench up on the Library Terrace away from everybody else. And then a strange feeling came over me."

"What do you mean, a strange feeling?" Waysa said, narrowing his eyes.

"I don't know what it was," Braeden said. "Terrible sadness and pain . . . like I was going through it all over again, like she was actually there and she needed my help, but I couldn't help her. It felt like I could almost reach out and touch her, but I couldn't. I just felt so hopeless, like all this was never going to end. I thought maybe if I put on the cloak I could find her, reach her somehow, and help her . . . I had to do *something*."

"But not that!" Waysa said. "Never put it on. It's too dangerous. Especially now."

"I won't be doing it again, believe me," Braeden said. "It was awful. I need to find my own way through all this."

Waysa nodded, seeming to understand. "You frightened me, my friend," he said as he walked toward him. The two boys shook hands warmly, with the ease of familiarity, then embraced briefly and separated.

Serafina was happy to see Waysa here, but it surprised her

to see them greet each other so warmly. They had first met during the battle against Uriah and Rowena, but they had not been close. It was a peculiar feeling to have her two friends become friends without her.

She thought it was interesting how different they looked from each other. Waysa was taller than Braeden, and much physically stronger, with muscled arms and legs. He was a boy of action, taut and fierce. Braeden had lighter hair and a younger, softer face. He was a quiet, polite, smartly dressed boy of the house, with his dog at his side.

Waysa turned and looked at her body lying the grave. She could see from the moody look in his eyes that he wasn't in agreement with what Braeden and Gidean had done. "First you put on the cloak, and then you do this . . ."

"I don't understand what comes next, Waysa," Braeden said. "What are we waiting for? What's going to happen?"

But Waysa didn't reply.

"That's all that's left of her," Braeden said despondently, pointing at the body in the grave.

"You know that isn't true," Waysa said, setting his jaw.

"But she's been buried here since the Loggia. How can this go on?"

"This is just her human body," Waysa said. "As long as the angel protects this part of her, then there is hope."

"But hope for what? Where's the rest of her? Where'd she go?"

"I'm right here!" Serafina said.

"I've seen her," Waysa said.

"*What?*" Serafina said, looking at him in surprise. "You've *seen* me? What are you talking about? You haven't seen me!"

"Sometimes she lingers here, near the grave . . ." Waysa said.

"Yes, I'm here! I'm here now!"

"Does she recognize you?" Braeden asked, keenly interested in what Waysa was saying.

"I don't honestly know," Waysa said sadly. "She seems as wild as the forest itself. The last time I saw her, I tried to follow her, but she attacked me."

Serafina frowned. They weren't talking about her spirit. They were talking about the panther.

Braeden shook his head in sadness. "I've seen her from a distance, but she doesn't come to me . . ."

"Her *tso-i* is split," Waysa said.

"I don't understand what that means," Braeden said.

"Her three, her trinity, has been torn apart," Waysa said, trying to explain it the best he could. "Her *a-da-nv-do* is gone."

"What does that mean?"

"It's her heart, her spirit," Waysa said.

Braeden shook his head as he looked down at her body. "I wish I could have done more for her."

"You did all you could do," Waysa told him.

"But I didn't save her . . ." Braeden said.

"We don't know that yet," Waysa said. "There are still many feet traveling many paths."

Braeden looked up at him. "What do you mean? Is something happening? Have you spoken with Serafina's mother?"

"No, it's not that," Waysa said, shaking his head sadly.

"Her mother was devastated by what happened. After Serafina's death, she lost all hope."

"But where is she?" Braeden asked.

"Everything in these forests reminded her more and more of Serafina: the trees, the rivers, the rocks and sky, even you and me. It was breaking her heart to stay here. She went west with the cubs to the Smoky Mountains to find more of our kind."

"I understand," Braeden said, nodding.

Serafina listened to Waysa's story of her mother with fascination. It made her so sad to think that her mother had gone, but she was relieved to hear that she and the cubs were all right.

Then she thought, *Serafina's death.* That was what Waysa had said. That was what they were calling it. Her *death.*

Braeden looked at Waysa. "But *you* didn't go to the Smoky Mountains with them."

"No."

"But why?"

Waysa lifted his eyes and looked at him, almost angry that he would ask him that question. "The same reason you didn't go to the hospital in New York when your aunt and uncle told you to. The doctors might have been able to fix your leg."

"You're right," Braeden said. "But what did you mean that there are still many feet traveling many paths?"

"Something is coming this way," Waysa said. "I've seen a clawed creature with terrible powers. Dark storms have been ripping through the forest each night. The rivers are swelling, destroying everything in their path. And the black folds are increasing. The people of Biltmore are in grave danger."

"Is it *her*?" Braeden asked, a sudden fierceness in his voice.

"I do not know."

"But you've seen her again, haven't you?"

"No, not since the night she left."

Serafina didn't know who or what they were talking about, but when Waysa said these words his voice was edged with emotion, almost as if he felt guilty about what had happened.

"Not since you helped her, you mean," Braeden said, his voice filled with bitterness. "I still don't understand why you did it."

"When I found her in the forest she was bleeding so badly. She couldn't move or speak. She was going to die, Braeden."

"Yes, I know. You should have finished her off!"

"You don't understand," Waysa said. "She wasn't just suffering from the wounds from the battle on the Loggia. I know what wounds from dog bites and panther claws look like. Something else had gotten her. I found her curled up under a fallen tree, shaking in misery. Something had beaten her savagely, broken her bones, tore into her flesh, even burned her. I've never seen anything like it."

"I don't understand," Braeden said, fear gathering in his eyes. "You mean, like some sort of animal? Or a wicked curse? What do you mean something else had *gotten* her?"

"I don't know what attacked her, but it was the most disturbing thing I have ever seen," Waysa said.

"But she was our enemy, Waysa. Why didn't you destroy her right then when you had the chance?"

Waysa looked down at the ground. He didn't know how to

answer Braeden's question. "You're right that I may have made a terrible mistake," he admitted. "But when I saw her there lying on the ground, suffering so badly, I just kept remembering the night Uriah killed my sister. I could not save my sister from death. No matter how hard I fought, I did not have the strength and speed and fierceness I needed to protect her. But as I was looking at this helpless, wounded girl on the ground, I realized that I could save *this* girl. I have been fighting for a long time now, but that is not what I was before. It's not all I wish to be. My mother and my grandmother taught me that sometimes you win the battle not by fighting, but by helping and healing. Sometimes there is more than one path to follow. It is not always clear which way to go, but I wanted to follow the *du-yu-go-dv-i*, the right path, at least the best I could. When I saw Rowena lying there like that, something stayed my claws. Do you understand?"

For a long time, Braeden did not look at his friend, could not look at him, for he did not want to forgive him, but finally he looked up at him and he nodded. "All right. Tell me what happened next."

"I picked her up and carried her to a safe and hidden place. I bound her wounds and I helped her through the days and nights that followed. I gave her water and food and a place to sleep and heal."

"Then what happened?"

"On the night of the quarter moon, I came back and she was gone. She just disappeared."

"Disappeared?"

"She slipped away. I looked for her for several nights, but she had become nothing but mist in the swamp."

"The creature you spoke of, the storms and the swelling rivers . . ."

"I don't know if she's causing all that," Waysa said. "Or if that creature is the thing that attacked her and caused those terrible wounds."

Serafina couldn't help scanning the forest around them. Waysa had seen the storm-creech. And he knew something was coming.

Braeden looked down again at her body lying in the grave.

"But is this how it's all going to end, Waysa?" Braeden asked. "With Serafina in the ground?"

"We stay bold, my friend, that's what we do," Waysa said. "We fight."

"Even if we've already lost the battle?" Braeden asked in dismay.

"Especially then," Waysa said. "This war isn't over. We stay strong and we stay smart. You still have the cloak, right?"

"I still have it."

"Keep it well hidden. Keep it safe. The cloak is our only hope. And whatever's coming, we'll fight it together."

Braeden nodded his agreement. "And you keep the panther safe."

"I'll do my best," Waysa said solemnly. "Stay bold!"

With this, Waysa leapt into the forest, changed form in midair, and bounded away on four legs.

Braeden watched Waysa go. He and Gidean remained at

the side of the grave alone. He seemed to be thinking about Waysa's words, trying to understand what he should do next.

Then he slowly turned back to the coffin and looked at her body in the grave.

"Come back to me," he said to her.

"Believe me, I'm trying," she said as a pang of sadness moved through her.

Braeden replaced the lid on the coffin and slowly, almost reluctantly, pushed the dirt back into the grave and reburied her.

When the work was done and he was about to leave, he looked up at the angel.

"Take care of her," he told her, and then he turned and headed back toward Biltmore.

Serafina wanted to follow him, but she let him go. There was nothing she could do to help him in that direction. She had to join them in their fight against the coming darkness, and she could see only one path to follow.

28

That night, Serafina made her way through the bog and crept up on Rowena's lair. The sorceress had just returned from one of her hunts with a satchel full of herbs she'd collected. She had also captured a flask full of cicadas and flies, which she dutifully fed to her growing clutch of hungry plants. Her hood was down, her long red hair hanging around her shoulders. Her face was solemn like before, filled with thoughts that Serafina could not fathom.

"I can feel you," Rowena said as she fed a fly to a carnivorous plant. "There's no sense lurking out there."

"What did you mean when you said much has changed?" Serafina said, staying where she was.

"Much is always changing," Rowena said.

"But what specifically were talking about when you said it?"

"I meant that you had no idea what had happened since you took your little catnap in the grave."

"Then tell me," Serafina demanded.

"From the tone of your voice, it sounds like you already know," Rowena said, seeming to realize that Serafina had seen Braeden and Waysa.

"No. Not all of it."

"You've seen all the pieces. You just have to put them together," Rowena replied. "You just don't want to accept it."

Serafina thought about what she was saying. "You mean that I'm dead."

"Of course you are. Or as good as. You're on your way."

"And a dark force is attacking Biltmore . . ."

"You already know that. It always has been. Nothing's changed at all, and yet everything has. The world is circles, and the circles are broken."

"You're not making any sense," Serafina said.

"There can be no sense in the world to someone who doesn't want to understand it. You look at me, but you don't see me. That's what I meant."

"What do you mean I don't see you?"

"You see your enemy."

"You tried to kill me!"

"Yes, I did," she said, almost nonchalantly. "And you me."

"Waysa found you and he saved you."

"Yes, he did," Rowena said quietly, her tone guarded, like she didn't want to talk about it, or her feelings about it, but maybe what Waysa did was the exact point. "There are many paths . . ."

"Are you the cause of all these storms in the forest? Are you going to attack us? Are you trying to destroy Biltmore? What are you doing here?"

"I'm trying to survive."

"But you're speaking in riddles," Serafina said.

"Only to a person who thinks the world is a broken thing that she can put back together again," Rowena said. "Sometimes you can't fix it. Sometimes you have to hunker down and hold on the best you can."

"Or just go ahead and die . . ." Serafina said bitterly.

She wanted to get down to the bottom of what Rowena was hiding, but she began to hear a deep pounding sound all around.

She looked up to see a dark cloud passing over the top of the forest. The stars disappeared. Her legs flushed with a cold surge of sudden fear.

The sound was low in volume at first, but it got louder and louder as it came closer. The earth and trees began to shake, a heavy heartbeat pounding the air. *Boom . . . boom . . . boom . . .*

A swirling wind rose up, and the leaves on the trees began to vibrate. The sticks on the forest floor lifted up and rose slowly into the air, levitating around her. She tried to be brave, but her arms and legs began to tremble, and she couldn't catch her breath. Rowena's goats bleated as they scurried around the lair in terror.

Rowena ran inside and came back out clenching a potion-filled flask. Ducking down in panic, she looked up into the blackened sky and all around her, ready to fight, holding the flask up in her shaking hand like she was going to throw it at the attacker.

"He's found us!" Rowena whispered over to Serafina. "You need to go!"

"But who is it? What's happening?" Serafina asked as she took cover behind a large tree.

"Don't be a fool, cat," Rowena shouted at her. "Get out of here!"

Serafina ran through the forest to escape the storm. The trees twisted and thrashed as branches cracked overhead and came crashing down around her. A gust of wind buffeted her so hard that it knocked her off her feet and threw her tumbling across the ground. She scrambled back up and kept running, but then heard Rowena scream behind her.

Gasping for breath, Serafina turned and looked back.

Serafina could see Rowena cowering by her lair. A great blow of force came crashing through, breaking the limbs of the trees all around. The strength of it pushed Serafina back like a giant wave, lifting her off her feet and dragging her along. She grabbed the swampy earth to stop herself and held firm. Then she began fighting her way back toward Rowena, who was consumed in battle against the unseen attacker.

With the dark, swirling wind and flying branches, Serafina couldn't see everything that was happening, but she saw the figure of Rowena running into her partially destroyed lair, grabbing a potion, and threatening to throw it. "Don't hurt me!" she screamed, her voice shaking in both fear and anger. "I swear I'll fight you!"

Serafina looked all around, searching the trees for a glimpse of the attacker, but she couldn't see him.

Serafina felt her feet getting wet and sticky. She looked down. The mossy ground welled with a dark blood. Insects and worms oozed out of the ground around her.

"Stop it!" Rowena shouted. "Leave me alone!"

A blast of force sent a large, broken tree limb sailing through the air at Rowena. The branch slammed into the girl, knocking her to the ground with a brutal blow. The branches attacked her like tearing fingers, ripping terrible, jagged cuts across her back.

Serafina gasped when she saw not just the fresh bleeding wounds on Rowena's bare back, but the scars of the past all across her back and sides. This wasn't the first time she'd suffered this attacker's wrath. For all her ability to cast spells and change shape, it appeared there were some scars that even a creature of her ilk could not heal.

But Rowena didn't stay down for long. She quickly got back up onto her feet, wiped the blood from her swollen mouth, and looked out into the forest in fierce defiance. Before the next attack came, she scrambled to her cache of potions. She grabbed a flask and hurled it into the forest, filling the bog with a dense mountain mist.

As if in angry reply, a blazing ball of fire came hurtling out of the forest straight at Rowena.

She threw up her arms with an explosive flurry of ice and snow, extinguishing the fireball in a burst of steam.

Through all this, Serafina looked for the attacker, but she couldn't see him.

"Tonight!" a voice blared. "Get the cloak tonight or I'll kill the boy myself!"

"If you kill him, you'll never find the cloak!" Rowena screamed angrily.

But as if to make the final point, another massive fireball came barreling out of the darkness straight at her, this one coming twice as fast as the one before. She leapt out of the way just in time, but the fireball struck the tree behind her and exploded, throwing burning sap in all directions.

Rowena screamed in pain as the searing liquid scalded her bare skin and lit everything around her on fire.

Serafina rushed forward to help her, dodging between the flames. She dropped to her knees beside Rowena as the girl twisted in pain from the burning sap. Knowing that she had to help her, Serafina closed her eyes and let a part of herself fade down into the porous ground, sinking down to where the water lay. Then she focused her mind and swept up her arms and with the force of sheer will began to pull the water up through the spongy moss of the bog, flooding everything around them. The rising water doused the lingering flames and flowed over Rowena's body, sweeping the burning sap away, before receding back into the bog beneath them.

Stunned by what she'd done, Serafina collapsed to the ground in exhaustion next to Rowena.

She and Rowena lay in a heap of scorched, soaking-wet, shredded trunks and branches. The attacker was gone and the fire was out.

The two of them lay there for several seconds, just recovering.

Then Rowena opened her eyes. She slowly crawled out of the wreckage, gathered herself, and struggled to her feet. She seemed barely able to move. Her robes had been torn from her bleeding, dirt-stained body, and she had suffered many bruises and burns. But she was alive.

She gazed desolately around at the destruction, then she took a long breath and seemed to steel herself.

Going into the part of her lair that was still intact, she opened a vial and started rubbing a viscous gray mud onto her burned arms and legs, wincing and gritting her teeth against the pain.

Rowena didn't say anything to Serafina, but the sorceress seemed to understand that Serafina had saved her life, or at least the agony of immeasurable more pain than she had already suffered.

In the next moment, Rowena grabbed her satchel and began to quickly gather some of her crystal flasks and other accoutrements of her dark arts.

Serafina watched in fascination. Rowena did not wallow in fear and misery. She did not cry. She seemed filled with new urgency, a new, angry determination to fight and survive.

Just when Serafina thought she had seen everything strange under the moon, Rowena pressed her hands flat to the top of her head and ran her palms slowly down the length of her hair, changing her hair color from red to black. Then she touched two fingers on each hand to her face just below her eyes. She pressed her fingers onto her cheeks, wiping in a hard, steady motion, changing the contour of her face as she went. Next, she reached down to her feet, pulled off her shoes, and pushed the little toe into each foot until it disappeared. Finally, she touched the center of each of her eyeballs with the pad of her index finger, tinging her eyes with a golden-amber color.

Serafina stared in mystified disbelief. Step by step, Rowena had transformed herself into someone else. Someone who looked disturbingly like *her*!

It was as if Serafina was looking into a mirror, but the girl who was looking back at her was far more beautiful and alluring than she was.

"Wait, Rowena," Serafina said. "I don't understand. What are you doing?"

"You heard him," Rowena said. "I want this over."

"But who was that?" Serafina asked. "Who was attacking you?"

Rowena pulled her torn robes around her and started walking fast through the forest, following the same path Serafina had used to come here.

"Hold on, just stop, where are you going?" Serafina asked desperately. "Please, tell me what you're going to do."

"Stop pestering me, cat, I have a summer ball to go to," Rowena said.

Serafina followed Rowena through the forest, knowing that Braeden was in grave danger. But in the early-morning hours a thick cloud of mist lingered in the mountain valleys and floated along the ridges, drifting slowly, white and eerie, through the trees, obscuring Rowena's path. Serafina wasn't sure if it was a natural fog or one of the sorceress's concealing potions, but one way or another, Serafina finally lost track of her.

As she looked for Rowena's trail, Serafina felt the coolness of the mist on her skin, and sensed that if she stood still a little too long, she'd slip into the vapor, whether she wanted to or not. *Dust to dust, and now mist to mist.*

She had learned to enliven some of the elements in tiny ways, and she had shifted into the water in the stream, but the more she interacted with the elements, the more she sensed herself slipping into them.

It broke her heart to think about leaving the people she loved behind, but she knew there probably wasn't anything she could do about dying now. As Rowena had said, she was already on her way. It felt like she had one more night, maybe two, before she was gone.

Everyone dies, she told herself, trying to stay brave, *but I need to protect the people I love.*

But how? That was the question now.

She'd seen the violent force terrorizing Rowena, bringing in storms, casting fireballs, and burning her as it demanded she retrieve the Black Cloak. Braeden and Waysa were playing a dangerous game by hiding it, but maybe it was the only thing keeping them alive.

All through the afternoon, she searched for Rowena, looking for tracks and other signs, but the sorceress had disappeared.

Finally, she headed back to Biltmore, dreading what was going to happen. It was the night of the summer ball.

She emerged from the forest trees near the statue of Diana, goddess of the hunt, atop the hill that provided the most dramatic view of Biltmore's front facade.

From there, a long stretch of green grass ran down a steep hill to the Esplanade, the flat expanse of manicured grass with its carriageways on each side leading up to the entrance of the house. Biltmore House rose up with its intricately carved limestone walls, its fine statues and strange gargoyles, its steep peaks and slanted rooftops, and the rolling layers of the mountains in the distance. She had once stood here in this spot in a beautiful red-and-black gown, with Braeden and Gidean standing at her side, the three of them gazing down at the house together. But not tonight.

Tonight, she was alone, standing in the moonlight, still wearing the torn, dirty, bloodstained dress that Braeden had buried her in.

Flickering torches lined the grand carriageway that led up to the main door of the mansion, and all the windows of the house were aglow. The slanted, spiraling windows of the Grand Staircase were ablaze with glittering brilliance. But it was the intricate glass panes of the domed Winter Garden—the center of the ball—that shone the brightest of all. It was difficult to imagine, but it seemed as if it would be there that Rowena would try to weave her web around Braeden.

Serafina watched a steady chain of horse-drawn carriages ride through the mansion's gates. The main road to the estate had been muddy and partially flooded, but the bridges were holding, and the carriages had managed to get through. They proceeded in a long line, one after the other, up to the front doors of the house, where two tall, perfectly matched footmen in their formal black-and-white livery uniforms welcomed the arriving guests.

Quiet and watchful, Serafina walked down the hill toward the incoming carriages.

"Oh, it's positively breathtaking!" one fine lady said to her gentleman husband as she opened the carriage window to see the house more clearly.

"Look at it, Mama, it's like a fairy tale!" a young girl in the next carriage said to her mother.

"More like a horror story these days," Serafina grumbled quietly to herself.

Most of the carriages were pulled by two horses, while the wealthiest members of society had carriages that were pulled by four. But then Serafina spotted something she had never seen before.

One of the carriages didn't have any horses at all. It *looked* like a carriage, with four spoked wheels, lacquered wood sides, and four passengers sitting on tufted leather seats, but it appeared to be moving by its own magical power. Serafina's eyes darted around as she looked for the sorceress, thinking that she must have cast some sort of spell, but Rowena was nowhere to be seen.

The carriage with no horses made an odd puttering sound, and the man in the front seat wore a funny hat and goggles. It took Serafina several seconds to realize that it wasn't her enemy's dark magic, but some sort of newfangled machine.

All her life, her pa had been telling her that times were changing, that all over the country men and women were inventing things that were going to change the world. She never knew exactly what he was talking about. But maybe this strange, horseless carriage was the beginning of it. She wished her pa was there to see it and tell her what it was.

Still on the lookout for Rowena, Serafina slipped through the line of carriages, up through the congestion of four-legged hoof stompers, top-hatted coachmen, and glittering ladies.

She skulked up the steps and hid behind the Guardians, the marble lion statues that she had always imagined protected Biltmore from evil spirits. But tonight *she* was the spirit; she was the strange ghost of the night creeping into the house.

As each carriage pulled up to the house, the footman flipped down the carriage's steps and opened the carriage door. The gentleman inside exited first, then offered his hand to help the lady as she alighted in her voluminous gown, carefully navigating the tiny carriage steps in her sparkling shoes. Once she was safely to the ground, she took the gentleman's arm, and they walked through the grand arched doors together into the Vestibule and up the red-carpeted steps into the house.

The light and heat and sound of the ball, with hundreds of guests already inside, poured out of the mansion's broad doorway, and hundreds more were still arriving. As Serafina slipped into the house, it felt as if she were being absorbed into a hot, glowing, gigantic organism.

The only thought on her mind was whether she could find the sorceress in time to stop her from hurting Braeden.

As Serafina entered Biltmore's main hall, it was thick with the aroma of burning candles, fine clean wool, and women's perfumes, all mixed together with the scent of the thousands of roses and lilies that had been strung along the archways and beams of the house. The genteel murmur of the guests' voices mixed with the sounds of rustling satin, pouring wine, and tinkling glasses. There were so many people in the room from wall to wall that the arms of strangers touched each other where they stood, and friends leaned to one another to say a private word, but all the guests seemed happy and respectful, honored to be a part of the grand festivities. Serafina scanned the crowd but did not see Rowena or Braeden.

The gentlemen at the ball wore formal evening attire, dark

tailcoats and trousers, neatly pressed white shirts with wing collars, dark waistcoats, and white bow ties or cravats. Some of the men were lean, others heavy, some with long handlebar mustachios or neatly trimmed beards, others clean-shaven. They all wore white gloves on their hands, and many had watches in their pockets, with long dangling gold or silver chains. A few even had silver-topped canes or formal walking staffs, but none were twisted.

What struck Serafina most was just how pleased the men were to see each other, to be talking and drinking, laughing and carrying on, like a great, gregarious flock of black-and-white jays cawing to each other, with no idea that a young boy of their ranks had buried a body nearby and that the fading, lost spirit of a dead girl walked among them.

The ladies wore long, full, shimmering dancing gowns made from satin, taffeta, and many other fine and luxurious materials, in dark purples, strawberry creams, peach chiffon, lilac, and blue—an endless variety of colors that reminded Serafina of the summer's blooms.

She peered suspiciously at each of the women and girls in the crowd, searching for a girl that looked like her. She had a hunch that the sorceress would be hiding in there someplace among the others, for deceit was her specialty.

Serafina watched the sometimes slow, sometimes flighty interactions between the young ladies and the young gentlemen. Many of the ladies and older girls held embroidered fans, opening or fluttering them to signal interest to a possible suitor, closing or snapping them shut to signal disdain.

As she studied the young ladies and gentlemen maneuvering and interacting with one another, it reminded her of the sandhill cranes that sometimes stopped on their migration to practice their mating dance in the spring fields, hopping and raising their wings, dipping their heads and tossing sticks to one another, spinning and chortling with abandon.

She didn't know exactly why the cranes and the young ladies went through all that or what it all meant, but she sensed that it was a hidden language all its own.

The younger children who weren't yet cranes gathered in small groups together, whispering and watching all the various proceedings in the room. Gaggles of giggling girls pulled each other excitedly through the crowds toward unseen adventures. Clutches of young boys gathered near the food tables.

Among the adults, the room was full of society types and fashion plates, industrialists and politicians, authors and artists, ambassadors and dignitaries of a nature that Serafina did not understand. She missed her old friend, the smiling, storytelling Mr. Olmsted, who had returned to his home far away.

As Serafina made her way into the room, the soft, lovely sound of harps and violins began to fill the hall, and then the deep sound of cellos and other instruments joined in. Row upon row of musicians, each one in black coat and tie, were arranged in the center of the main hall playing the most beautiful, sweeping, romantic music she had ever heard. Mr. Vanderbilt hadn't just arranged for a soloist or a string quartet. He had brought an entire orchestra into his home!

Serafina remembered years before when she was but a little child, sneaking around the house late at night. Mr. Vanderbilt's friend, Thomas Edison, had given him a music-playing phonograph with a crank handle and a large brass horn. She had often watched the master of the house sitting alone in his library listening to his opera music. Mr. Vanderbilt loved *Tannhäuser* so much that he commissioned the famous sculptor Mr. Karl Bitter to depict an epic scene from the opera in the frieze above the Banquet Hall's gigantic triple fireplace.

She remembered that Edison's music machine had produced a scratchy, tinny sound that she hadn't liked, but *this*, this live orchestra, was something else entirely. Mr. Vanderbilt had traveled all over Europe collecting art and furniture for Biltmore, but also attending concerts and operas, and now she understood why. She could finally see and hear what he loved so much.

All the musicians were playing together in such perfect harmony, with all the violins and cellos and other instruments sweeping into gorgeous waves of sound, like nothing she had ever heard before. She overheard a gentleman say to one of the other guests that the music was from a new ballet called *Swan Lake*, which Mr. Vanderbilt had heard in Europe and fallen in love with, so he'd arranged for the orchestra to play it tonight.

The rising music carried through Biltmore's soaring archways to all the grand rooms of the house, to all the elegant ladies in their glimmering dresses and the handsome gentlemen in their evening coats. There were flutes that made the sound of thrushes in the morning, and reedy oboes that sounded like the little grebes that landed in the lagoon in the fall, and majestic French horns like coming kings—instruments of so many kinds that she couldn't name them all.

That was when she finally spotted Braeden. She felt a flush of happiness that her friend was all right. Rowena was nowhere to be seen, and Braeden was safe. Perhaps the night was going to turn out better than she'd feared.

Braeden made his way through the crowd up to his aunt and uncle. He was wearing black tails, a white tie, and white gloves, and he looked every bit the well-to-do young gentleman.

"You look very handsome, young man," Mrs. Vanderbilt said cheerfully.

"Thank you," Braeden said, blushing a little.

"You seem more chipper today," Mr. Vanderbilt remarked.

"I'm feeling a little better," Braeden agreed.

"Well," Mrs. Vanderbilt said. "I know several little ladies who are reserving a spot on their dance cards for you."

Braeden's mood darkened. "I would rather not."

"I know your heart's not in it, Braeden," Mrs. Vanderbilt said gently. "But when the dancing begins, it would be ungentlemanly if you didn't ask some of the girls to dance with you. Many of them have come a long way to be here with us."

"I understand," Braeden said glumly.

"Does your leg feel all right?" Mrs. Vanderbilt asked compassionately. "Do you feel well enough to dance?"

"It's not that. I just . . ." Braeden began, but then faltered.

Serafina could see that he didn't want to lie to his aunt, but he didn't want to tell her what she didn't want to hear, either.

"I know she was a good friend," his aunt said. "But eventually, for your own sake, you're going to have to accept that she's gone."

"I know," Braeden said sadly.

"I'm not gone yet, Braeden!" Serafina cried out despite herself, forgetting her mature and somber acceptance of her death just a few minutes before. "Don't let me go! Hold on to me!" But of course no one could hear her.

In the next moment, the conductor of the orchestra brought the evening's musical prelude to an end, everyone clapped politely, and then he tapped three times on his stand and lifted his white baton.

An excited murmur ran through the crowd. They knew what was coming.

The sound of the orchestra rose up into a lively and sweeping waltz perfect for dancing.

Little bouts of enthused clapping rose up among the guests, everyone happy that the time had finally come. Gentlemen young and old throughout the ball walked over to the ladies of their choice, bowed deeply, took their hands, and asked them to dance.

The palm trees, furniture, and works of art that normally filled the Winter Garden had been cleared away to make room for the dancing. And while many of the mansion's rooms and corridors were lit with candles, the finely carved beams above the dance floor were strung with thousands of tiny electric lights, like fireflies in a magic garden, so that the ladies' dresses glowed and shimmered in the light.

So that's what Pa had been working on, Serafina thought, and at that moment, she caught her breath, for her pa was standing across the room from her in a handsome dark suit, leaning against one of the black marble columns of the Winter Garden.

He was not in the formal, white-tie evening wear of Biltmore's guests, but he was washed and shaved, and he looked more handsome and dignified than she had ever seen him before. He was gazing at the lights that he'd put up for the ball and listening to the pleased reactions of the delighted couples as they walked out onto the dance floor. There was a proud and satisfied look on his face. And all the emotion that she'd been feeling moments before welled up inside her.

She wanted to go over to him and hug him and tell him how proud she was of him and how much she loved him. Her pa had never been to school and knew no magic spells, but tonight he was the wizard of light.

As the elegant couples began filling the dance floor, Serafina noticed a girl standing across the room. She was dressed in a long, beautiful, dark green, iridescent gown. The girl had severely angled cheekbones, long black hair, and large amber eyes. The hackles on the back of Serafina's neck went straight up.

There she is, Serafina thought.

Rowena's face possessed a disturbing resemblance to her own, but it was different from her, too, like a more alluring, better version of herself. It appeared that Rowena wasn't pretending to be her, but an older sister or a cousin. She must have stolen or used some sort of spell to create the dress. And she had fixed her long black hair up into an elaborate arrangement. To Serafina, she looked magnificent and beautiful and evil all at once.

Rowena was almost perfect in her appearance, but when Serafina looked more closely, she saw at the edge of her high collar the trace of the terrible scar on Rowena's pale white skin. Determined to stop the sorceress before she started, Serafina walked straight toward her.

But even as Serafina charged forward, what she heard behind her made her heart sink.

"All right," Braeden said softly to his aunt as he noticed the mysterious but strangely familiar black-haired girl in the green gown. "I'll ask *her* to dance."

"That's excellent, thank you, Braeden," Mrs. Vanderbilt said, barely noticing the girl, but immensely encouraged by her nephew's sudden willingness to do his gentlemanly duty for at least one of the young ladies in the room.

"Do we know that girl?" Mr. Vanderbilt asked, eyeing Rowena with concern.

"I'm sure she's from a good family," Mrs. Vanderbilt said, obviously pleased that Braeden was finally beginning to socialize.

As Braeden moved toward the girl to ask her to dance, Serafina moved toward her as well.

"You shouldn't be here!" Serafina hissed at her.

"Skedaddle, kitty cat, I've got work to do," Rowena whispered beneath her breath, and then lifted her face and smiled a gracious smile as Braeden presented himself to her, bowed, and offered his white-gloved hand.

To those around them who happened to be watching, none of this seemed out of the ordinary. Serafina knew ballroom etiquette enough to know that it was the duty of every young gentleman to ask the young ladies of the ball to dance, and it was in fact rude for a gentleman to allow a young lady to stand for long without a partner. And for her part, if a young lady was properly and respectfully asked, she should not refuse to dance with a gentleman unless her dance card was already full.

"My name is Braeden Vanderbilt," he said in a kind but formal way as he put out his hand to her. "Will you do me the honor of dancing with me?"

"With pleasure, sir," the girl replied in the sweetest, most exquisite Charleston accent that had ever been spoken by a Southern belle, and placed her delicate hand in his.

Serafina watched helplessly as Braeden and Rowena walked slowly and formally out onto the dance floor among the other dancers. It was clear that he didn't recognize who she was, but he seemed strangely drawn to her.

"Not her, Braeden!" Serafina shouted. "Anybody but her!"

Serafina tried to figure out what she could do to stop them. Could she create a blast of air to send all the musicians' sheet music flying from their stands and halt the orchestra? Could she splash the water in the fountain onto all the dancers and send them running?

Rowena leaned toward Braeden and spoke to him in her lovely high-society Southern accent. "I was so positively petrified by the thought that no one would ask me to dance this evening," she said, meeting his eyes with hers. "You are a fine gentleman for rescuing me."

Rowena was acting so sickeningly sweet that it made Serafina want to scream her throat out.

She knew that Rowena was trying to trick him, but she didn't understand her plan. And what was Braeden thinking? Why was he doing this? He had no idea who this girl was! Was he going to dance hand in hand with every creature that slithered in out of the forest in a nice dress and fancy hair? And with the brace on his leg, his dancing was going to be a painful, clumsy affair at best.

But before Serafina knew it, the two of them faced each other in a ceremonial fashion. As was the custom, Braeden put his white-gloved hands behind him and bowed deeply to his dance partner. When it was her turn, his lady did a slow, deep curtsy to him, with one leg out in front of her, her head bowed, and her arms elevated beside her like the wings of a graceful swan. *What on earth!* Serafina thought.

And then the two dance partners came together, holding each other in a formal and decorous fashion. Their dancing started out slow and easy, synchronized with the gentle overture of the orchestra's music and the movement of the other dancers, but when the waltz rose up to its full tempo, they began to move more swiftly, turn and turn and turn and dip, sweeping across the dance floor with astounding grace and beauty.

It made Serafina's heart sink to watch it.

She had no idea Braeden knew how to dance like that. What amazed her even more was that he could move so smoothly and effortlessly with the brace on his leg. He normally dragged it along behind him, barely able to walk, but here he was gliding with the music of the waltz, like his feet were barely touching the floor.

Then Serafina looked down at his feet.

It was difficult to detect, even for her narrowed, suspicious eyes, but when she looked very carefully, she could see an unnatural glint beneath his feet. He wasn't dancing. The sorceress was pulling him along, literally sweeping him off his feet with her power and deceit. But poor Braeden had no idea. He was smiling, euphoric, happy to be dancing, moving with such strength and athleticism on legs that had been weak and pathetic for so long.

Serafina looked around at the other dancers and the people watching to see if any of them could see the sorceress's work.

Mrs. Vanderbilt looked onto the dancing couple with a smile on her face.

Others, too, seemed to be pleased to see the two young dancers enjoying themselves. It was only Mr. Vanderbilt who appeared to be studying his nephew and his dancing partner with a careful eye. There was neither happiness nor rejection in his expression, but a steady evaluation of what he was seeing, as if he sensed that something wasn't quite right.

"It's because she's a sorceress!" Serafina screamed.

"*Shush, kitty!*" Rowena whispered as she and Braeden danced, knowing that only Serafina would hear her through the sound of the music.

A few moments later, when the music died down and the

dance was over, Braeden and his lady partner stood apart and faced each other once more. Braeden bowed and his lady curtsied, just as they had done before. Then Braeden presented his right arm, his lady took it, and they walked off the floor.

"Did you enjoy the dance?" Braeden asked her.

"Oh, yes, very much so. And you?"

"Yes, my leg is feeling much better than it has in a long time," Braeden said, his voice light and happy.

Serafina followed them up the steps to the promenade that encircled the Winter Garden. The whole area was crowded with mingling guests.

It was customary for the gentleman to escort his dancing partner back to her family or friends, but Braeden did not appear to know where to take her.

"I am here alone," his lady partner said softly.

"She doesn't have any friends," Serafina interjected, "and you definitely don't want to meet her family!"

"I see," Braeden said uncertainly. "Would you like to partake of refreshment in the Banquet Hall?"

"Yes, that would be delightful," she said, and they began walking in that direction.

"Pardon me for asking," Braeden said, "but have you been to the house on a previous occasion? Have I met you before?"

"Yes, I believe we have met," she said mysteriously.

Braeden's expression changed. He leaned toward her and whispered, "Are you a catamount? Are you a friend of Waysa's?"

When the girl did not immediately reply, Braeden asked, "Are you related to Serafina?"

Then he looked down at her feet, knowing that some catamounts had four toes on each foot even when they were in human form. Rowena's feet were covered by her glittering shoes, but at that moment, Serafina began to realize just how carefully Rowena had planned this out. *From head to toe, she's all a trap. She's luring him right in.*

"I came to the ball tonight to speak with you, Braeden," she said, her voice gentle and calm, but filled with just enough urgency to give it an edge.

"With me?" Braeden asked in surprise.

"Perhaps we could go someplace more private," Rowena said.

"Don't fall for her tricks, Braeden!" Serafina shouted at him, wondering if she could swirl her arms and start up a great wind inside the house to send Rowena's hair a-flying and knock her tumbling down the stairs to the basement.

"All right," Braeden said calmly. "Come this way . . ."

Rowena betrayed a crooked smile as she followed Braeden through the Banquet Hall. The room was full of guests, many of them eating and drinking as they enjoyed the lively festivities of the ball.

Serafina looked back through the archway toward the Winter Garden hoping to catch a glimpse of Mr. Vanderbilt watching Braeden and Rowena from a distance, but she couldn't see him.

"What are you doing, Braeden?" Serafina asked. He seemed determined to slip away from the ball and get her alone. It was very unlike him.

Serafina followed the two of them into the Bachelor's Wing and down the dark and empty passage.

"Perhaps we could go in here," Braeden suggested, gesturing toward the Gun Room, with its cabinets full of shotguns, hunting rifles, and other weapons. As was customary for a gentleman, Braeden entered the dark room first to find and turn on the light.

"Rowena, I'm warning you, whatever you're doing, don't do it," Serafina said fiercely. "I mean it. Stop it."

But Rowena ignored her.

"When you were attacked, I helped you!" Serafina reminded her.

"Oh, don't fool yourself," Rowena whispered. "We both know that you're not all cotton balls and kitten paws. You helped me because it was the smart thing to do."

"But what are you doing here?" Serafina demanded. "Leave Braeden alone!"

"My plan should be clear to you now," Rowena said impatiently.

"Pardon me?" Braeden said, looking back at Rowena in confusion.

"I was just saying that Biltmore must be a wonderful place to live," Rowena said more loudly, slipping back into her Southern accent as she stepped into the room with Braeden. Serafina followed her into the room.

"The electric lamp isn't working for some reason, so I lit some of the candles," Braeden explained.

Serafina was surprised when Braeden closed the door. It was highly improper for a young gentleman to lead a girl away from a formal ball into a dark, private room and actually shut the door.

The sights and sounds of the grand ball disappeared. The Gun Room was a small and quiet place, the candlelight flickering on the dark woodwork all around and the glass cases filled with guns. Serafina noticed a table with a display of finely crafted hunting knives. She thought it was odd that one of the knives was missing. Mounted animal heads hung on the hunter-green walls, and there was a small, rustic fireplace in the corner, glowing soft and warm with embers.

"We can talk here," Braeden said.

As Rowena turned to him, it seemed as if she had lured Braeden exactly to where she wanted him. She gazed into his eyes and moved closer to him.

"The truth is," she said in a soft and vulnerable voice, "I need your help."

She spoke the words with the most gentle, sweetest tone, and Serafina thought, *That's it, we're done for! We're lost! She's tricked him, we're all dead for sure!*

Braeden looked at Rowena and said, "I'm not going to help you," as he pressed the point of a wickedly long, sharp hunting knife against the satin brocade of her dress, just where he could push it straight into her side. "I know who you are."

"Oh dear, you have a knife . . ." Rowena said in her sweet Charleston accent, raising her hands, feigning dismay and confusion as she slowly backed up. "I don't understand. What's happening?"

"I know who you are, Rowena," Braeden said, holding the knife out in front of him, his hand trembling and his eyes wide with the fear of facing down a sorceress who could throw a spell at him at any moment.

"Braeden, listen to me," Rowena said in her normal voice.

"You can wear as many masks as you want, Rowena, but you're always a monster underneath."

"I'm not going to hurt you . . ." Rowena said, trying to calm him.

"That's just what the cloak says!" Braeden shouted at her, pressing toward her with the knife in sudden panic, filled with more fear and agitation than Serafina had ever seen in him.

"Don't kill her, Braeden, we need her!" Serafina shouted, but he couldn't hear her.

"Please let me explain," Rowena said, moving away from him as he pushed forward.

"Then spit it out," he said, shaking the knife at her. "What are you doing here? What do you want?"

"Tell him the truth or he's going to stab you!" Serafina shouted frantically.

"I came to tell you that my father is back and he's going to kill you and your family," Rowena said.

Serafina sucked in a breath of surprise. That definitely wasn't the calm and reassuring explanation she was expecting.

But then Rowena's words begin to sink into Serafina's mind. She'd had her suspicions, but now she knew for sure: Uriah had come back. The storm-creech she'd seen in the forest had been him, his talons and scaly skin the remnants of his old owl form. The unhealed wounds across his face had been inflicted by her own panther claws. Uriah was the one bringing the storms, flooding the rivers, and tearing away the trees. He had come to wreak his vengeance on Biltmore.

"This is how you're trying to win my trust?" Braeden said. "By telling me that you and your father are going to kill me?"

"I'm not going to wage my father's war anymore," Rowena said, her voice sharp. "I'm tired of the fighting and the blood, the endless cycle of hate and retribution."

"Another lie," Braeden said.

"I know that I tricked you, I attacked you, I harmed you in so many ways, but I'm through with all that."

As Serafina listened to Rowena's words, everything began to make so much more sense. Uriah had been the one who had inflicted the terrible wounds on Rowena the night Waysa found her and helped her. Uriah had punished Rowena for failing to kill her on the Loggia and for losing the Black Cloak to their enemies. He was the one Rowena was hiding from in the bog, who had been threatening her, attacking her, the one she'd been screaming at the first time Serafina came to her in spirit form. Serafina couldn't even imagine what Rowena had been going through all this time. The girl had become a powerful sorceress in her own right, but it was clear that her father had been twisting her heart and her body for many years. He had a terrible grip on her, and probably always had. Serafina couldn't even imagine her own pa doing that. It was threat, it was hurt, it was a thousand things, but it was not love.

"Then why have you come?" Braeden demanded.

"I need the Black Cloak," Rowena said.

"I don't have it," Braeden spat back.

What surprised Serafina wasn't Rowena's trickery or Braeden's fierceness, but the fact that Rowena hadn't thrown a potion, cast a spell, or tried to outright kill him. So far, she had not only refrained from attacking him, she had told him the truth. This was the weariness, the loneliness, that Serafina had seen in her before. *Much has changed,* Rowena had said. Serafina realized now that she'd been talking about herself.

"You said that you don't want to hurt anyone," Braeden said. "But you want the Black Cloak. That doesn't make sense."

"I'm trying to help you, Braeden," Rowena said, and even to Serafina's suspicious ear it sounded strangely sincere. Rowena seemed to truly care for him.

"Help me?" Braeden snapped at her in disgust. "You killed Serafina!"

Braeden screamed the words with such powerful emotion that it broke Serafina's heart. All the fighting and deception between them, but *this* was the offense that he could not forgive. *You killed Serafina.* The words were so final, so devastating to him. She realized now how deeply his heart had been damaged.

For as long as she had known him, he had always been the trusting one. He had defended his friend Mr. Thorne. He had trusted Lady Rowena when she first came to Biltmore. He had always been the person to open his arms to someone new.

And Serafina knew that she had always been the suspicious one, the one who *didn't* trust people. She had suspected Mr. Vanderbilt was the Man in the Black Cloak because of the type of shoes he wore. She had suspected the footman Mr. Pratt, and the coachman Mr. Crankshod, and the detective Mr. Grathan, and all the others. She was always hunting for the rat.

But now she realized that she had changed, too, maybe just as much as Braeden had, but in the opposite direction. She could feel herself starting to listen to Rowena, wanting to believe what she was saying. She had seen Rowena that first night in the forest walking alone by the river, her spirit so changed. And she had heard the fear in the girl's voice when she shouted out into the darkened forest. And she had seen Rowena fighting off her father's attacks, screaming at him in savage defiance.

Could all of this have been an elaborate trick designed to gain her trust? Serafina knew it could be, but it felt like Rowena was telling the truth.

But more than all that, Serafina knew that it didn't matter how scared she was, how uncertain or suspicious: she needed Rowena. If Rowena didn't succeed tonight, Uriah was going to kill Braeden. That much was certain.

But here was Braeden on the opposite side of it. He *hated* Rowena. Rowena had harmed him, scarred him, and *killed* his friend.

Serafina tried to think. What could she do? How could she talk to Braeden? How could she show him that she was here?

She looked around the softly lit room, the guns in the glass cases, the sizzling embers and gray ashes in the fireplace, the upholstered chairs and the wooden table, and the Persian rug on the floor. She could see Braeden and Rowena's reflection in the cases, but she couldn't see her own. She was just a glint of light in the glass.

Then she looked at the fireplace again.

Ashes to ashes, she thought as an idea sprang into her mind.

"Rowena, listen to me," she said, "we need to get Braeden's attention. Get him over to the fireplace."

Rowena didn't seem to understand and didn't respond.

"Do what I say," Serafina demanded. "He's never going to listen to you alone, not like this. You need my help."

As she watched Rowena pause and think it through, she

realized that even the sorceress had to be careful about whom she trusted.

"Braeden," Rowena said finally. "I need to show you something by the fireplace."

"Good, that's perfect . . ." Serafina encouraged her. "Just get him over there and I'll do the rest."

"No!" Braeden said, pointing the knife at her.

"It's about Serafina," Rowena said.

"What about her?"

"Come over to the fireplace and I'll show you."

"I'm not going to do what you say," Braeden said.

"You've got to convince him," Serafina told her.

"He's not going to do it," Rowena said.

"Who are you talking to?" Braeden asked her.

"Find a way," Serafina said. "Act harmless. Lay on the floor!"

"I'm not stupid," Rowena said. "I'm not doing that!"

"You're not doing what?" Braeden demanded.

"Get on the floor!" Serafina said again. "If I'm going to trust you, you need to trust me."

"Fine!" Rowena snapped resentfully, but then she spoke to Braeden in a softer, gentler tone. "Braeden, I understand that you're frightened of me. I would be, too, if I were you. So let me do this. I will not resist you. Hold your knife to me so that I cannot harm you."

Watching the sorceress carefully, Braeden moved the knife toward her. Rowena slowly lowered herself and lay flat on her back in front of the fireplace. Braeden followed her down, kneeling beside her, and pressed the blade against her throat.

"Your move, cat," Rowena said.

"What are you saying?" Braeden asked.

"Now, ask him to blow into the ashes," Serafina said.

"Braeden," Rowena said, "I need to show you something that I know is important to you. I will not move in any way. I want you to blow into the ashes of the fireplace as hard as you can."

"Who are you talking to?" Braeden asked.

"I'll show you," Rowena said.

Braeden stared at her malevolently, then finally sucked in a deep breath, and blew into the ashes. The ashes and the glowing embers went flying up in a great, swirling cloud into the room.

"That's perfect!" Serafina cheered.

As the embers and ashes floated down, she moved her hands back and forth through the air, guiding the way they fell. Filling her lungs, she blew here and she blew there, bringing new life to the glow of the embers and pushing the ashes up into curling, floating motion, until they all began to fall into tiny lines onto the hardwood floor.

"What's happening?" Braeden asked, his voice trembling with the mystery of what he was seeing.

Serafina guided the ashes and embers down until they fell together into small, scratchy, glowing lines:

I T S M E

"What is that?" Braeden asked in fascination. "Does it spell something?"

He leaned toward the glowing ashes and tried to make out

the rough letters in the faint, flickering light of the candles.

"*I . . . T . . . S . . . M . . . E . . .*" Braeden said as he deciphered the letters one by one. "It says . . . *It's me* . . . But who is it? Who's *me*?"

"Well, you definitely have his attention now," Rowena said as she sat up.

"Who are you talking to?" Braeden asked again.

"The answer to all your questions is the same, Braeden."

"What?" Braeden asked in frustration.

"It's Serafina," Rowena said.

"What do you mean it's Serafina?"

"Serafina is here."

"Here?"

"She's here now, in this room with us."

"You're lying!" Braeden said. "You're a nasty liar!" Angry and disgusted, Braeden blew the ashes away contemptuously, as if to say, *I don't believe a word of this!*

The ashes and the flaring embers swirled up into the air and floated around the room. Over the next few moments they should have gone dark and fallen randomly onto the floor and furniture, but Serafina moved her hands and blew with her lungs and brought them down right back on the floor where they had been before, glowing with new life.

TRUST HER

Braeden gazed in wonderment at the letters, but then he caught himself.

"Oh, stop it!" he said. "This is just more of your tricks!"

"It's the cat," Rowena said flatly.

"No, it isn't. Serafina's dead. I buried her myself."

"I thought she was, too, but we were both wrong. She's not totally dead. Serafina's spirit is in this very room."

"Just stop this!" Braeden screamed at her, his voice shaking with indignation as the two of them got to their feet and faced each other. "You're always lying!"

"But she's here . . ." Rowena said.

"How do I know that you're not lying to me like you have so many times before? If she's truly here, then prove it to me."

"Rowena," Serafina said. "Tell him to ask you something that only Serafina would know."

When Rowena said these words, Braeden's expression changed. He thought for several seconds, then narrowed his eyes suspiciously at her.

"What were the first words I ever spoke to Serafina?"

Serafina thought back. What were the first words he'd ever said to her? She tried to think. It was the morning after she'd seen the Black Cloak for the first time. She had just crept upstairs into the daylight . . .

" 'Are you lost?' " Serafina said. "That's what he said."

" 'Are you lost?' " Rowena said.

Braeden's eyes widened in surprise; for a moment he almost believed her. But then he remembered who he was dealing with and became distrustful and angry again.

"It's a trick," he said. "I'll do another. The second time I saw Serafina, I came upon Mr. Crankshod shaking the living daylights out of her. What did we pretend she was?"

Serafina smiled. This one was easy. "A shoeshine girl."

"We pretended I was the shoeshine girl," Rowena said, not just repeating Serafina's words, but taking on the exact sound of her voice, allowing Serafina's spirit to speak through her.

Hearing Serafina's voice, Braeden gazed around the room in shocked amazement.

"Serafina is in this room at this very moment," Rowena said to him softly in her own voice. "She arranged those letters in the ash. She's asking you to trust me."

"But how are you able to do this?" Braeden asked.

"A wise man once said, *That which does not destroy us makes us stronger.*"

"I don't understand," Braeden said.

"After you and the two cats struck me down during the battle for the Twisted Staff, it took time, but I came back, and I was stronger than ever. I'm not just a sorceress now, I'm a *necromancer.*"

"What is that?"

"I can sometimes speak to the spirits of the dead and the in-between."

Braeden stared at her in dread, clearly not sure if he should believe her. "I want to do another test," he said. This time he spoke to the room, like people do when they speak to ghosts at a séance. "Serafina . . . If you're here . . . I once gave you a gift, long and red . . ."

Serafina thought back.

A gift, long and red . . .

What had he given her?

"The red dress!" Serafina said excitedly, and Rowena repeated it in her voice.

"This is amazing . . ." Braeden said, spellbound by the sound of Serafina's voice. "And when was the first time you wore it?"

"I used it to trap the Man in the Black Cloak," Serafina said, and Rowena repeated the words with haunting emotion. "The morning I brought the children back home, I was standing at the forest's edge, with Gidean on one side and my mother in lion form on the other. I saw you up on your horse as you gathered a search party to look for me."

"And you looked so fierce and beautiful standing there at the edge of the forest in your torn dress . . ." Braeden remembered.

Hearing her friend's words, and feeling the ache of his heart in her own, Serafina began to cry.

"Oh, please. You're not beautiful, you're a cat!" Rowena snapped. "He likes cats. That's all it is! Now do get hold of yourself or this whole thing isn't going to work!"

Serafina wiped her eyes and toughened herself, knowing that Rowena was right.

"Look," Serafina said to Rowena sharply. "If I ask Braeden to give you the Black Cloak, what are you going to do with it? What is your plan?"

"You may be fast with your claws, but you sure are slow with the rest of it," Rowena said in a scathing tone. "Have you been following along at all?"

34

"Braeden, it is truly me," Serafina said, her voice as steady and serious as she could make it, and Rowena repeated the words in the exact same way.

"But where are you, Serafina?" Braeden asked.

"My body is in the grave where you buried me, but my spirit is here with you. I've been with you for these past few nights."

"I thought I could feel you," Braeden said, his voice quivering with recognition.

"You were sitting on the bench on the Library Terrace."

"That's right!" he said, nodding. "That's when it started."

"But I have to tell you, my time is short, a night or two at most, so we have to hurry."

"A night or two before what?" Braeden asked.

Serafina didn't want to answer or even think about his question, so she pressed on the best she could. "Uriah is alive and he wants to kill you. That much is true and certain, but Rowena says she's going to help us."

"But how?" Braeden asked.

"We need the cloak," Serafina said.

"But, Serafina . . ." Braeden begged her. "It's a horrible thing. It's too dangerous! We can't—"

"I know," Serafina said, remembering not just the cloak's sinister powers, but the terrifying fragments of darkness that shot from the folds of the torn fabric.

"What is Rowena going to do with the cloak?" Braeden asked.

Serafina shifted her attention back to Rowena.

"Your move, sorceress," she said. "Before we give you the cloak, tell us what you're going to do with it."

"There are no words to describe what I plan to do, and if I tried to explain it, it would only frighten you," Rowena said.

"Frighten us?" Braeden and Serafina said in alarm at the same time.

"Which of us?" Serafina asked.

"Both," Rowena said. "I cannot explain it in words. I will show you in person. I give you my word that I will not hurt either of you." Here she looked at Braeden. "If you wish, the cloak will never be out of your sight or possession. And I will show you what I'm doing for as long as you wish to watch. But I warn you: you'll not want to watch."

"You're speaking in riddles," Braeden said, staring at her in suspicion and confusion.

"No, I'm speaking as clearly as I can, but the only way for you to understand is to see it."

As she fixed her eyes on Rowena, Serafina tried to think it through. What was the sorceress up to? If she wanted to attack Braeden, she could have already done it. Serafina wished she had some other path she could follow, but she couldn't see it.

"We're going to have to trust her, Braeden," Serafina said, and Rowena repeated the words in Serafina's voice.

"So if we do this," Braeden said, "when are we going to do it?"

"We can't do it here, not right now," Serafina said, and Rowena repeated it. "We've been in this room too long. Your aunt and uncle are going to be wondering where you are and come looking for you. You need to get back to the ball, at least for a little while."

Braeden nodded, knowing she was right. "But when will we be back together again?" he asked, clearly alarmed at the idea of separating from her.

"We'll meet tonight, very soon," Serafina said. "Did you put the cloak back where it was?"

"No," Braeden said. "I moved it to a different spot."

"Good," she said. "To be safe, don't tell Rowena or me where it is. After the ball tonight, when the clock chimes half past one, go collect it and bring it to the place where the three friends once stood beside the stone hunter. Do you know the place I mean?"

"I know it," Braeden said, nodding his head. "Are you sure about this, Serafina?"

"No I am not, but it seems like it's our only path. Be careful."

"And you be careful, too," he said.

With this, Braeden slipped through the concealed door that led into the Smoking Room, and then on through the next concealed door into the Billiard Room. Serafina followed him just long enough to see him walk out into the main corridor and rejoin his aunt and uncle at the ball.

When she returned to Rowena in the Gun Room, she said, "Well, we did it. We convinced him."

"It seems we did," Rowena agreed with satisfaction.

"Now, there's just one more person we need to convince, and he's not going to be so easy."

"Oh, no, we don't need him!"

"He saved your life!"

"He's still a cat! There's no getting around that!" Rowena shot back, feigning annoyance, but her voice betrayed the nervous uncertainty of meeting someone she owed a debt that she knew she could not repay.

"We include him or it's off," Serafina said fiercely.

"You're turning into quite a stubborn little grimalkin," Rowena said.

"Better stubborn than dead," Serafina retorted.

"You're already dead."

"I thought we agreed I wasn't totally dead quite yet."

"My characterization of you being dead was less a comment on your current state than on your future prospects."

"Enough of that," Serafina said in annoyance. "Let's go find him."

A short time later that same night, after Rowena had shifted back to her normal appearance, Serafina guided her to the dell of ferns where she and Waysa sometimes rested. He wasn't there, or in the next place they checked, but they kept looking.

She finally spotted her friend standing in human form gazing at a rocky gully in the forest where a powerful gush of water had rushed through, ripping at the earth and trees, tearing away everything in its path. The flooding was getting worse each night.

Serafina led Rowena to an area of open, rocky ground out of sight from Waysa.

"I don't know how he's going to respond when I approach

him," Rowena said. "He may be angry or violent. He helped me when I was wounded, but he's not going to trust me now."

"You can't approach him. He's a catamount. You have to get him to approach you," Serafina said. "Let him know you're here, from this distance, but don't scare him off."

"How do I do that?" Rowena asked.

Serafina knew that Waysa's reflexes were incredibly strong, that if they approached or surprised him in any way, his first instinct would be to fight or flee. That was how he'd survived so long. She needed to get his attention in a way to get him to think before he reacted.

"Make the sound of a blackbird and then wait," Serafina said.

"But your blackbirds here don't come out at night."

"Exactly. When Waysa and I are in human form in the day-time forest, the blackbird's click is one of the secret calls we use, so if he hears it at night, he'll not know what to make of it."

Rowena nodded, then made the clicking sound of a blackbird.

Within a few seconds, Waysa began moving toward them through the forest. He stopped at the edge of the trees when he saw Rowena standing alone out in the middle of the open area.

"Good. Now stay perfectly still," Serafina whispered to Rowena. "No threatening movements."

Doing exactly what Serafina said, Rowena did not move.

Waysa studied her from a distance, and Rowena studied

him, the two of them gauging whether they could trust the other. It was as if the two of them were looking for the marks of their shared past, the battles they had fought against each other, and the care he had shown her.

"You've come back," he said warily to her from his position in the trees.

"Talk to him, convince him," Serafina said.

Rowena slowly nodded to Waysa. "Yes," she said quietly. "I came to thank you for what you did."

Waysa did not move or speak. He just watched her.

"No one has ever helped me like that before," Rowena said, and then paused.

After a long time, Waysa finally emerged from the trees. He walked slowly toward her until he stood some twenty feet away.

"Why did you save me, Waysa?" Rowena asked gently, her voice soft and uncertain.

Waysa frowned at the question, looked at the ground to collect his thoughts, and then looked back at her. "I do not wish to get lost," he said.

"What do you mean?" she asked him.

"I will destroy the conjurer and make sure those I love are safe, but then I will cleanse myself of blood and fight no more. My heart is on a journey from where it lives. But I must remember my way home."

Rowena stared at Waysa, seeming to understand what he was saying. "I've come here tonight to help you," she said finally. "And to ask for your help once more."

"I've already helped you," Waysa said, as if, despite what

he had just said, there was still a part of him that regretted the foolishness of giving aid to his sworn enemy.

"I know you helped me," Rowena said, "and you have no reason to trust me, but I have a plan to help your friends."

"What are you talking about?" Waysa said, his eyes narrowing.

"Tell him what I told you," Serafina said to Rowena.

"If you need me, winter, spring, or fall, come where what you climbed is floor, and rain is wall," Rowena said. It was the riddle that Waysa had written to Serafina so that she could find him.

"Where did you get those words?" Waysa asked, stepping toward her.

"This is good," Serafina said.

Waysa stared at Rowena, his brown eyes blazing with intensity. He was ready to fight her if he had to, but there was curiosity in his expression as well.

"I want you to tell me. Where did you get those words?" Waysa pressed her again. "And the clicking sound you made . . ."

"I will explain why I've come, and how I know these things," Rowena said. "But first, I want to tell you what I have seen in the past of your people."

"What are you talking about?" Waysa asked again.

"Long ago, many members of your tribe were driven by force away from their homes to the barren lands in the west, but a few stayed behind in these mountains, unwilling to leave their homeland. And you came into this world from them."

"You speak my grandmother's truth," Waysa said, "but how do you know this?"

"When you were taking care of me, I used my powers to look into your heart, to see your past and the past of your people. I know that my father killed your mother, your father, your brothers—"

"And my sister," Waysa said bitterly.

"And your sister," Rowena said, nodding. "I saw it all. I *felt* it all, for it is cut deep into the print of time. And once you see something with your own eyes, once you *feel* something, it becomes part of you. But my father didn't just kill *your* family. He killed many of the catamounts in your tribe. You may be the only one of your clan who survived. But you must remember what your grandmother taught you about injury and rebirth. It is the way of our kind—the catamounts and the owls and the other shifters—that when we are severely injured, we fight through it, we suffer, but we come back stronger than we were before, changed, but more powerful . . . more who we are."

"Yes, I understand . . ." Waysa said, as he moved closer to her. They were just a few feet from each other now.

"You saw the peregrine falcon strike me from the sky," Rowena continued. "I was close to death, but I did not die. You saw what was left of me after my father punished me for losing the Black Cloak to our enemies. Again, I was close to death, but I did not die. With each and every wound, every moment of pain, every night of suffering, I got stronger inside. I *changed*. Injury and rebirth, struggle and ascendance, these are the cycles of our kin. What I've been trying to say is that my powers have changed, Waysa. And my soul has changed as well. I am becoming more of who I am."

Waysa was listening to everything she said. "My grand-mother called it *ta-li-ne u-de-nv*, second birth."

"Yes, that's it," Rowena said.

"But you spoke of new powers . . ."

"I can see visions of the past, and I have the power to hear and speak."

"You mean with those who have gone on—"

"—and those who are in between."

"You're talking about Serafina . . ." Waysa whispered in astonishment. "Her *a-da-nv-do* . . . She's lingering . . ."

Rowena nodded very slowly. "Now you're truly beginning to understand."

"Where is she?" Waysa said. Suddenly, there was so much hope in his eyes.

"Do not worry, she is close, here with us," Rowena said softly.

"She's here with us now?" Waysa asked in surprise, looking around them. Unlike Braeden, who had resisted the idea, Waysa didn't seem to doubt that it was possible that spirits existed.

"Serafina and I have spoken with Braeden, and the three of us need your help," Rowena said.

"Tell me what I need to do," Waysa said.

Rowena hesitated.

"Tell him what I said or it's off," Serafina demanded.

"Understand that your instructions come from Serafina, not from me," Rowena said. "She asked that you go to Biltmore tonight and join Braeden. Watch over him. Protect him from my father. But more than anything, protect him from me. If I begin to do anything at all that might harm him or you, then you are to immediately claw my eyes out."

Waysa smiled. "That sounds like the Serafina I know."

"Those are her words," Rowena said.

"I'll do it," Waysa said.

"Good, he's with us," Serafina said in relief.

"Serafina says she's happy to hear that," Rowena said.

"You're speaking to her now?" Waysa looked up excitedly. "Can you tell her something for me?"

"She can already hear you," Rowena said.

Waysa looked around up into the sky where he imagined an *a-da-nv-do* might float.

"No matter what happens, Serafina, you stay fierce, my friend, you stay bold! You hear me?"

As tears welled up in her eyes, Serafina said, "Tell him that I hear him."

But wanting to say more, she moved her hand just so, and a gentle breeze of air blew through Waysa's long dark hair, lifting it for just a moment, then letting it drop down again. *I hear you.*

36

A few hours later, Serafina sat and waited in the darkness on Biltmore's front steps. The summer ball had ended. The Vanderbilts and all the guests who were staying in the house had gone up to their rooms to bed. The others had departed in their carriages. The servants had cleared the tables, and the musicians had packed up their cases and gone home. The house was dark and quiet now. Everything seemed so different from before.

But in her heart, she felt a new sense of contentment. She had finally managed to talk to Braeden and Waysa, and she had seen the smiles on their faces when they came to understand that she was still here. She realized there were many more challenges ahead, and she knew full well that some of them might be insurmountable, at least for her, but at least they were climbing together now. At least they were on the same side, come what may, and as long as that was true, she could keep going wherever she had to go.

Braeden emerged from the house, slipping quietly out the front doors and closing them gently behind him, carrying an old leather knapsack slung over his shoulder. By the size and shape of it, she thought he must have the cloak inside. Braeden stood alone in the darkness on the front terrace, gazing out as if he wasn't sure if he should proceed.

Serafina was relieved that he'd come like they'd agreed, but she felt qualmish in her stomach. It was a grave and dangerous plan to ask him to trust Rowena and give her the Black Cloak. There were a thousand ways it could go wrong. But Serafina knew that she'd run out of time. "Get the cloak tonight or I'll kill the boy myself!" Uriah had blared at Rowena when he attacked her in the bog. Rowena had been holding her father back by telling him that if he killed Braeden he'd never find the hidden cloak, but Rowena's threat had run dry now. Uriah had grown impatient. There was no doubt in Serafina's mind that, one way or another, Uriah was coming for Braeden.

She wished she could talk to Braeden here and now, but without Rowena she couldn't. All she could do was follow him.

Braeden sighed in discouragement when he gazed across the long expanse of the Esplanade and up toward Diana Hill in the distance, where she had asked him to meet her. Serafina knew what he was thinking. Before he'd been injured, he had climbed that hill easily. He'd had fun doing it. But with his bad leg, it was going to be a long way to the top. She wished she had picked an easier spot for him to reach.

Braeden's hands trembled as he tried to fix and adjust the metal brace on his leg. It appeared that one of the metal brackets had broken, making it even more difficult for him to walk.

Pulling in a deep breath, Braeden began his journey. He made his way along the length of the Esplanade, then started the climb up Diana Hill. He breathed heavily and his pace slowed as he trudged, one step at a time, dragging his bad leg behind him.

Then the dark shape of a catamount emerged from the forest.

"Waysa!" Braeden said in surprise. "What are you doing here?" And then he realized. "Serafina asked you to come . . ."

Serafina smiled, glad that Braeden had figured it out so quickly.

Waysa walked in lion form over to Braeden's side, and in a gesture of friendship, hunched down.

"Thank you," Braeden said appreciatively, and climbed onto his back.

Waysa leapt forward with a great bounding leap and ran. Braeden clung to the lion's back as Waysa sprinted straight up the slope of the hill, the cat's powerful legs nothing but a blur.

Now that's the way to travel, Serafina thought, jealous of her friends. She broke into a run in pursuit.

When a breeze stirred, she felt herself getting light on her feet. There was a part of her that thought she might be able to turn into wind the way she had turned into water the night

Braeden put on the cloak, but she was too worried that it would only hasten her fade.

She missed running as a panther, racing Waysa through the forest. But she was happy to see her friends together again, and to be with them, at least in spirit.

With the Black Cloak strapped into Braeden's knapsack as he rode on Waysa's back, and her running along behind, the three of them made their way toward Rowena's lair deep in the forest bog.

A haze of white feathery clouds shrouded the glowing moon as it slowly set and disappeared behind the western mountains. As the darkest shadows of the night fell through the forest trees, Serafina crept with Waysa and Braeden into Rowena's encampment.

The small habitation had been damaged by Uriah's attack a few nights before, and many of the surrounding trees had been destroyed, a grim reminder of why the four of them were there.

The sorceress emerged from the ravaged remnants of her lair wearing the dark hood and robes of her ancient druid kin.

Waysa waited with claws out just a few feet away, as Braeden stepped toward her.

"We've come as you asked," Braeden said. "So what do we do now?"

"You can watch everything I do, but you'll need to give me the cloak . . ." Rowena said.

"What are you going to do with it?" Braeden asked, stepping back from her. "How do we know this is what Serafina wants us to do?"

"Tell him that chicken and no grits is my favorite food," Serafina said, "and that raspberry spoon bread is his."

When Rowena repeated the words, Braeden said, "But tell me what you're going to do with it."

"I am going to try to repair it," Rowena said.

"Repair it?" Braeden asked in confusion. "Are you going to give the cloak to your father?"

"That would be the end of us all," Rowena said.

"Then what? What will happen when you repair it?"

"If all goes well, then it will begin to function the way it was designed."

"Which means what?" Braeden asked. "You're going to start sucking in people's souls and stealing their powers for yourself?"

As Rowena and Braeden talked, a dark and foreboding fear soaked slowly into Serafina. She was beginning to see Rowena's plan.

"When the cloak was torn during the battle on the Loggia, Serafina was splintered out into the world along with the black fragments," Rowena said. "They are the remnants of the cloak's innermost darkness. If I can repair the cloak properly, then it may pull those remnants and Serafina's soul back into its black folds."

"I don't understand, what do you mean *may*?" Braeden asked. "Aren't you sure?"

"No, I'm not," Rowena said. "The cloak is severely damaged."

"And if it doesn't work, what happens to Serafina?"

"If I fail," Rowena said, "I suspect that her spirit will disappear and she'll be lost forever."

"But if you succeed, it's even worse!" Braeden said. "Her soul will be trapped in the cloak."

"Yes," Rowena said.

The frightening image of Clara Brahms's stricken face flashed through Serafina's mind. The girl in the yellow dress had screamed in horror when the cloak absorbed her. Serafina didn't want to do this. She *definitely* didn't want to do this. She hated this plan. She had been running and fighting, biting and clawing, all this time to escape the Black Cloak, to rescue people from it, to protect people from it, to defeat it. There was no way she was going to let herself get sucked into it. She couldn't imagine anything worse than being trapped inside the Black Cloak. She'd rather die. She immediately started trying to figure out how she could communicate with Braeden and Waysa, how she could stop this.

"But if Serafina's spirit gets pulled back into the Black Cloak, then what's going to happen?" Braeden asked, his voice trembling with the same fear that was enveloping Serafina.

"I warned you about this," Rowena said harshly. "I told you this was going to frighten you. You have to trust me."

"But what's going to happen next?" Serafina asked Rowena. "That's what we need to know. Are you going to keep the cloak for yourself? Are you going to steal my strengths and capabilities? Or are you going to give the cloak back to your father? Do you think that will satisfy him and he'll leave you alone? Do you think that will win back his approval? With the cloak, you'll have everything! You'll have all the power and all the choices!"

Rowena suddenly hissed like an owl and turned away, clicking her throat in disgust. "It's impossible to explain it to you," she said again.

"Explain what?" Braeden asked in confusion, not realizing that Rowena was talking to Serafina.

"You keep saying that, Rowena!" Serafina shouted at her. "But you have to explain it, or we're not going to do it! Swear to me that you're not going to hurt Braeden."

"Are you talking to Serafina?" Braeden asked in confusion. "What is she saying?"

"Nothing of consequence," Rowena muttered and began to walk away, the angry flick of her hand casting a blast of force tearing through the forest and snapping branches. Waysa moved rapidly between Rowena and Braeden, ready to lunge at the sorceress.

Bitter-tasting bile rose up in Serafina's throat. This whole thing was beginning to feel like a trick. But then she remembered the night in the graveyard long ago. She had lured the

Man in the Black Cloak into a trap. After the battle, she had tried to tear the cloak's fabric with her hands, but the fabric had been far too strong. Then she tried to pierce it with a dagger. But the cloak could not be harmed by a normal blade. That night in the graveyard, she had pierced the cloak on the sharp point of the angel's steel sword. She had cut the cloak to pieces. That was how she had destroyed it. And when she did, it released its magic in a great cataclysm of heat and smoke and haze, and all the victims that had been captured in the cloak were suddenly set free. She remembered seeing Clara Brahms's body lying in the leaves on the ground. When the girl twitched and began to rise, Serafina had feared that she was a zombie rising from the dead, but she wasn't. She was a little girl, freed from the dark folds of the cloak. And Serafina remembered that she had freed her mother the same way that same night.

"You're going to repair the cloak . . ." Serafina said, "but then you're going to destroy it on the angel's sword . . ."

Rowena stopped and turned, relieved that she finally understood. "I do not know if I can succeed, but I am going to try . . ."

"You're going to try what?" Braeden asked, confused and frightened.

Serafina thought about how she had crawled from the grave and had been living in the spirit world, what she could and couldn't do, who she could and couldn't touch, what paths she could and couldn't take. Dust and water and wind, she wasn't long for this world. She thought about Braeden and Waysa fighting for her with all their hearts, and her pa with his deadened soul going through the motions of his life, and her mother who had lost all hope. She thought about Rowena's father, the coming storms, the raging rivers, his lust for vengeance against the Vanderbilts. He would not rest until Biltmore was destroyed. Then she started thinking about everything she'd seen Rowena do, how they'd first met, all the tricks and betrayals, and all the battles they had fought against each other. Rowena had followed many paths, twisting and intertwining, and there were many ways she could turn.

Through all this, Serafina realized that maybe the most difficult thing wasn't to trust your friend, or even your enemy, but to trust yourself. She had to trust that no matter how dark her future became, she was strong enough, that whatever happened, whether she passed away forever or somehow found her way through to the other side, she had to trust herself, trust her own soul, her own wisdom, her own strength, to pass through the darkness and unknown. She had to trust that she could become who she was meant to be.

Her hands were trembling. Her legs were shaking. Even her voice was unsteady when she spoke. "I have one last request," Serafina said to Rowena. "If I agree to do this, I need you to give me your word that no matter what happens to me, you'll protect Braeden and my pa and Waysa and everyone at Biltmore from your father. Give me your word."

Rowena paused. There was no grimace, no smile, but a face as stone and immobile as the angel's face in the graveyard.

Serafina studied her, trying to figure out what she was

thinking. Was she reluctant to give her word? Or was she actually, in a strange way, satisfied with what Serafina was asking her to do? Had this been what she wanted all along, to join them, to have friends that would fight for her, and that she would fight for in return?

But if Serafina died, Rowena would have to defend all of Biltmore from her father. It was not a fight she could win on her own. She could barely hide herself in the bog to escape him. There was no way she could protect everyone at Biltmore. The friendship Rowena sought came with an almost impossible price, but without that friendship, what chance did Rowena have to survive?

"I need your word, Rowena," Serafina said, but even as she pressed, she realized she didn't know what Rowena's word meant. This could all be a trick. But she could see no other choice. "If you don't help me," Serafina pressed her, "what will happen to you, Rowena?"

"I will survive alone," Rowena said.

"You know that's not true. Is that why you came to talk to me at my grave that night? Maybe you'll survive for a little while against your father. Maybe you can keep hiding from him. But will you truly live? If we trust you to help us, then you have to trust us to help you."

Rowena did not reply at first, but after a long moment, she nodded in agreement. "If you don't make it through, I will do everything in my power to protect them. You have my solemn word."

Serafina studied Rowena. She looked at her face, her eyes, the way she moved when she said the words. How do you know when someone's lying to you, or if they will keep their promise?

"What's going on?" Braeden asked. "What have you given your word to do?"

"We are running out of time, cat," Rowena said, ignoring Braeden.

A cold, black fear like nothing Serafina had ever felt before vibrated through her body. The last thing she wanted to do in the world was to get sucked into the Black Cloak, but she knew she had to do it.

"I'm ready," she said. "I trust you, Rowena. Tell Braeden and Waysa what we're going to do."

38

Serafina, Braeden, and Waysa watched Rowena work. The sorceress sat down in her lair and took the Black Cloak into her lap. The cloak's dark folds roiled and seethed of their own accord when she moved the fabric with her hands, as if she were holding not a garment but a massive, living snake.

She drew out a long, thin needle of bone and began to sew, slowly stitching the tears of the Black Cloak's torn fabric.

"The outside of the cloak is goat's wool woven with the skin of timber rattlesnakes," Rowena said, "so I've used a fine goat's wool thread for the stitchings. But the lining of the cloak, where its most important power lies, is black satin made from the silk of black widow spiders."

Braeden's face wrinkled in revulsion. "Spiders? The Black

Cloak is made from spider silk? How do you get usable silk from a spider?"

"It is very difficult," Rowena admitted as she worked, "but it is possible if you know the spell."

"A *coercion* spell . . ." Braeden grumbled.

"Yes, obviously, coercion is required," Rowena said, annoyed at the accusation. "Black widow spiders aren't the most willing allies, believe me, and their venom is exceedingly unpleasant. But their silk is much stronger than the silk of many other spiders. Spiders can make six different types of silk: strong silk for dangling, sticky silk for catching prey, flat silk for flying in the wind, and the others, each for their purpose. It takes all of the black widow's silks twined together to create the thread we need. I use a coercion spell to make the spiders do what I need them to do, and a twining spell to spin the thread."

"But isn't a spider's silk white or clear?" Braeden asked, appalled by it all, but beguiled by the gruesome details of the process. It seemed to fascinate him that spiders and other animals were part of the cloak's construction.

"It is the twining process that turns the thread black," Rowena said.

As hour after hour went by with Rowena clutching the twisting cloak, Braeden grew restless. Sometimes, he paced back and forth through the muck outside the lair, dragging his braced leg behind him. Waysa just watched and waited, his claws out, his tail flicking impatiently, as if he were more than ready should battle come.

Serafina watched Rowena carefully, determined to not let the sorceress trick her. She had to stay vigilant, but the truth was, she didn't know how or at what moment Rowena might betray her.

Rowena had gone quiet in her work. Her body began to rock back and forth like she was in some sort of trance, the cloak turning and coiling in her hands. But even as she rocked, she kept mumbling and hissing, casting spell after spell as she stitched the torn fabric, rocking and stitching, a witch knitting a dark and wicked curse, the Black Cloak slithering with power beneath her.

Serafina felt her lungs getting tighter, her breaths getting more difficult. As she watched the sorceress, a dark fear grew within her. She pulled her mesmerized eyes away from Rowena and looked out of the lair's damaged door to Braeden and Waysa, but suddenly they were gone. They had disappeared.

Serafina blinked and rubbed her eyes in confusion, then looked again. Braeden and Waysa were still gone.

As she gazed out at the forest, she realized that the trees seemed to be fading before her eyes, as if darkness darker than darkest night were blotting them out in a terrible black fog. It wasn't just her friends who were missing now, but the entire forest.

Serafina looked down at the ground she was standing on. It was gone, nothing but darkness.

She could not feel it.

She could not see it.

Everything was going!

She pulled in a breath. She could no longer smell the plants of the bog. She could no longer hear the insects.

She turned to Rowena in hot panic. All she could see now was the sorceress, her hooded head down, her face shrouded, the Black Cloak glowing and writhing in her lap as she stitched the last tear closed.

Serafina's world went black.

Serafina could not move.

She could not touch or feel.

All she could see around her was a black, swirling darkness, like she was inside a storm of soot.

All she could hear were the winds of moving fabric.

And all she could smell was ash.

It felt as if the whole world had disappeared and she was all that was left, utterly alone now and forever. Everything she had known, everything she had loved, was gone, incinerated by a prison of incessant darkness.

She tried to be brave. She tried to be bold. But she couldn't do it. She screamed in terror. "Rowena!"

"Do not fight it . . ." came a raspy voice.

Confusion flooded into Serafina's mind. Was it the cloak speaking to her?

Serafina screamed and she fought. She would *not* give up. She would *not* stop fighting. She would tear and tear and tear.

She wanted her mother and Braeden and her pa and everyone she loved. She wanted to see moonlight and sunlight and starlight and every kind of light there was, the light from inside a friend's soul when they smiled and the light from the dawn of a new idea. She wanted it all!

"You have to let everything go . . ." the voice came.

She wanted to hear the rustle of wind in the trees and the sound of music and the murmur of soft voices.

"Just let everything go . . ."

But she wasn't going to give up. She wanted to feel the coolness of the misty night on her skin and the warmth of the morning sun.

"Trust me, cat, just let everything go . . ."

Cat, Serafina thought suddenly. The voice had said *cat.* It wasn't the Black Cloak speaking to her, but Rowena! She was trying to guide her, to show her the way.

The sorceress had been her enemy. They had attacked each other, tricked each other, and slashed each other with wounds. But was she *still* her enemy? Or had Rowena truly switched sides?

And then a different kind of thought came into Serafina's mind.

She knew that despite the many vicious and deceitful

deeds Uriah had forced his daughter to do, Rowena had always wanted Braeden as her friend.

"You don't even know what friendship is!" Rowena had screamed at her in frustration. "I've seen it!"

She's seen it, and she wants it, Serafina thought. *And now I've forced Rowena to promise that if I don't make it, then she'd join with Braeden at Biltmore . . .*

Serafina had thought she had exacted a difficult promise from Rowena, but now she realized that it might have suited Rowena just fine.

All that time playing the role of "Lady Rowena" the sorceress had been pretending to like Braeden, but maybe the trick was that she wasn't pretending.

Was that Rowena's plan now, to get rid of her, and have Braeden's friendship to herself? By persuading Serafina to go into the cloak, had Rowena finally managed to trick her rival out of existence?

Serafina didn't know what was in Rowena's heart, but she saw two paths before her. She could trust Rowena, stop fighting, and let her soul be pulled entirely into the Black Cloak. Or she could try to keep fighting in this storm of oblivion.

She thought about how important it was that Braeden had learned from Rowena's deceit months before that sometimes he shouldn't trust people. And she thought how she herself had learned that sometimes she *should* trust people. Despite all of Rowena's duplicitous shifts and caustic moods, she had helped her talk to Braeden, she had helped her spell the letters in ash in front of the fireplace, and she had revealed the secrets of the Black Cloak. Was it possible that Rowena might have feelings for Braeden, but convincing Serafina to get pulled back into the Black Cloak wasn't necessarily a malicious trick designed to eliminate her? Was it possible that both of those things could be true at the same time?

Serafina realized that she didn't know the answers to the questions. It was a terrifying feeling, but there was no way to know. But she did know that here, in this dark, swirling place, and in the spirit world where she'd been wandering, there was no good path. There was nothing there. Even if she fought back to the place she'd been, *there was nothing there*. No voice. No touch. No love. Her only hope was *forward*. Her only hope was the *unknown*.

Trust me, Rowena had said. *Trust me.*

Serafina knew that she might not return to the land of the living. She might not ever see the world again. In her mind, she began to say good-bye to Braeden and to Waysa. She said good-bye to her pa and to her mother, and the cubs, and Mr. and Mrs. Vanderbilt, and everyone else she knew. One by one, she said good-bye to all of them. Her only hope was that she had somehow helped them.

Finally, she shut her eyes and pulled in a long, deep breath, her chest rising, filling her lungs with the sooty black void. She held her breath for as long as she could, knowing that it would be her last, like a person trapped underwater knows the inhalation that will finally drown her lungs in a watery death.

Then she exhaled, and her mind unfurled as the cloak sucked her soul deep into its void.

And she disappeared into the black folds that she had seen take so many souls before her.

She had no body. She had no wandering spirit. All she had was consciousness, churning through the black prison.

She finally knew what Clara Brahms, Anastasia Rostonova, her mother, and all the other victims of the Black Cloak had experienced.

She had no perception of time or change. Each moment might be a fleeting second—a drop of water as it falls to the floor and splashes into nothingness. Or it might be a whole year of bountiful experience lost—every moment she'd ever spent with the people she loved.

She did not know.

There was no up or down, no action or effect. No hard or soft, no brightness or color, no movement or sensation, no voice or touch, no shape or beauty or love or compassion.

Rowena had trapped her in a black, empty world.

Serafina opened her eyes and saw nothing but black. It was as if she hadn't opened her eyes at all.

She had been deep in the darkened void of a swirling, half-dreaming world when she was awoken to the sound of a muffled voice, but now there was no voice, no sound, no movement of any kind.

Just black.

She closed her eyes and reopened them. But it made no difference. It was still pitch-dark.

But she wasn't floating in the black void of the cloak anymore. She was lying on her back on a long, flat, cold surface.

Where am I? she thought. *How did I get here?*

Then a sound finally came: a thudding in her ears that was more real, more pressing, than anything she had ever heard.

Thump-thump.

For a moment that was all there was.

Thump-thump, thump-thump.

The beat of her heart and the pulse of her blood.

Thump-thump, thump-thump, thump-thump.

As she slowly moved her tongue to moisten her cracked, dry lips, she detected the faint taste of metal in her mouth.

But it wasn't metal.

It was blood—her own blood flowing through her veins into her tongue and her lips.

She tried to clear her throat, but then all at once she took in a sudden, violent, jerking breath and sucked in a great gasp of air, as if it was the very first breath she had ever taken. As her blood flowed, a tingling feeling flooded into her arms and legs and all through her body.

My body . . . she thought, trying to comprehend it. *I'm in my body . . . I'm alive . . . I'm truly alive . . .*

She frantically tried to think back and remember what had happened to her, but it was like trying to grasp the fleeting details of a powerful dream that drifts away the moment you wake.

She pulled air into her nostrils, hoping to draw a clue from what she could smell around her.

Dirt, she thought. *I'm surrounded by damp, rotting dirt.*

Serafina quickly twisted around inside the coffin that surrounded her, pressing her hands against the cold, hard wood.

Her palms were sweating. Her breaths were getting shorter. Her lungs tightened, making it more and more difficult to breathe. A surge of panic poured through her. Her soul had reunited with her body. She was alive! But now she was going to run out of air and die!

She kicked her feet against the end of the coffin. She pounded her fists. She scratched and she scurried, she twisted and she pried, but she could not escape. Just as before, the boards surrounded her on all sides, close and narrow and low.

She hissed with frustration. After all she'd been through, she was going to suffocate in a black coffin buried six feet under the ground! It wasn't right! It wasn't fair! She wanted to scream and cry!

"Quit your mewling, girl, and get on with makin' yourself useful!" she imagined her pa telling her. "Figure out what needs to be done and do it!"

Gritting her teeth, she tore off her dress and wrapped it around her head to protect her nose and mouth. Then she spun around onto her stomach, put her shoulder to the center of the coffin's lid and pushed. She pushed and she kept pushing, over and over again, hammering her shoulder against the center board, *bang, bang, bang.*

When she finally felt the board cracking, she spun around and pulled at the edge of it with her fingers. A massive heap of dirt poured on top of her, crushing her down.

She shoved the dirt into the corners of the coffin until she had packed away as much of it as she could. Then she pushed her head up into the hole and started digging, scraping frantically with her bare hands. The loose earth poured down around her head and shoulders, collapsing onto her faster than she could dig it away.

She felt the pressing, suffocating weight of it all around her, closing in on her, crushing her chest, trapping her legs, but she kept clawing, kicking, squirming her way blindly up through the darkness, desperately trying to breathe.

She dug frantically toward the surface, but she knew she wasn't going to make it. She was too small, too weak, too frail, too dull. Her puny, soft, skin-covered fingers were nothing against the dirt. She was going to die.

"No! No! No!" she growled deep in her throat, until she was making one continuous growl.

She had one moment, and the moment was now. She could stop moving, stop breathing, let the earth win. Or she could envision what she wanted to be and become it.

She growled and she kept growling, the anger building inside her. She felt it coming now. She felt her whole body beginning to change. It was unstoppable now.

She envisioned her mountain lion mother and her black panther father. She was a catamount through and through. She was the *Black One*, the warrior-leader of the forest. It came like a great volcano, exploding from deep within her.

Suddenly, the earth around her expanded with a great heave, giving way to her newly muscled girth. She felt her tail twisting, her four feet clenching and clawing against the dirt. She began digging anew, filled with panther strength and power.

Her claws tore into the earth, ripping it away with lion ferocity. Her powerful legs pushed her upward toward the surface, toward air, toward life.

Her face and whiskers pushed against the dirt, her panther ears pressed back against her head as she shoved herself upward. Her powerful chest filled with a deep, dark, throbbing growl, like the roll of thunder through the ancient mountains where she'd been born into the darkened world.

As she dug, she heard a frenzy of scratching noises, digging down toward her.

Her upstretched claws clacked with the claws of another

catamount. It was Waysa, digging frantically, and Gidean digging at his side!

"You're almost there!" Braeden shouted as he dug toward her.

"Come on, cat, dig!" Rowena urged as she pulled handfuls of dirt away.

Finally, Serafina thrust her panther head up into the air and took in a long, deep, desperately needed breath. She felt the warm night air pouring into her mouth and down her throat and into her lungs. She felt her lungs filling with blessed air, expanding like a great bellows, her chest heaving, pushing easily against the loose dirt still around her. She felt her heart pumping, her bones pushing, and every muscle in her body at her beck and call.

"You made it!" Braeden shouted, as she clambered the rest of the way out. "You made it!"

Standing on four feet now, she threw the dirt from her black coat with a mighty shake. The entire world loomed large. She saw the angel's glade and the forest, and the stars above the trees. Her lungs could finally breathe! She was alive in the world, whole and complete! She was alive! She lifted her yellow panther eyes, and gazed at the smiling faces of her friends all around her.

Serafina shifted into human form and looked around her at the angel's glade, trying to understand what had happened.

"We destroyed it," Braeden told her excitedly.

Serafina looked over at the statue of the angel and saw the molten remnants of the Black Cloak lying in a pile on the ground below the angel's sword. The tight spider weave and binding spells of the cloak's fabric had disintegrated into a hot, smoldering heap as it released the energy within it. The smoky effluent drifted across the angel's glade and the graveyard beyond. They had pierced the cloak on the angel's sword, just as she had done months before when she freed Clara Brahms and the other victims trapped inside the cloak. Even though she knew she should have been expecting it, it took Serafina several seconds to comprehend that destroying the cloak had broken its spell, reunited her three splintered parts, and freed her from its dark imprisonment.

"When we destroyed the cloak, we thought we would find you lying on the ground, like when you freed Clara and the other children," Braeden said. "But we didn't."

"The damaged cloak had torn you apart," Rowena said. "When the spell broke, your freed spirit fled to your human body in the grave."

"And the essence of your panther body was pulled in as well," Waysa said. "It wasn't until I heard you digging that I realized what happened and told the others."

"We all started digging as fast as we could!" Braeden said.

Serafina was amazed. Their plan hadn't worked exactly the way they had expected, but it *did* work.

She looked at Braeden. She could see the exhilaration and relief sparkling in his eyes, a large smile on his face.

"I can't believe it!" he said. "You made it! After all this time, you're truly here! You're alive!" He moved toward her and embraced her, so pleased that he lifted her off her feet and swung her around.

She laughed in joy at his enthusiasm. It felt amazingly good to wrap her arms around him and hug him, to finally embrace him, to truly feel her friend's warm, living body.

As she held on to him, she could feel the rapid beat of his heart against her chest, the movement of air through his lungs as he breathed, and the tremble in his hands as he held her. She could feel everything, and she knew he could feel her. This was the world, she thought, the true and living world, and she was *in* it. In the distance over Braeden's shoulder, a blaze of falling stars streaked across the glistening darkness of the nighttime sky. Down in her soul she felt as infinite as the heavens upon which she gazed, filled with a deep gratitude just to be back with the people she loved.

"Thank you for not giving up on me, Braeden," she said as she held him, unable to control the quiver of appreciation in her voice.

"You're welcome," he said. "I knew that if we could find a way, you'd come back to us."

As she slowly separated from Braeden, she looked at Waysa, who had shifted into human form. Waysa stood before her now, tall and grinning and happy.

"Welcome back," he said, and they embraced. She felt the strength in her friend's arms and the pride in his chest. She felt the warrior in him, the satisfaction of finally winning a battle against their enemy. And she felt the serenity in him, the happiness that they were finally back together. She and Waysa had shared so much together. They had run through the forest, slept behind waterfalls, and swam in mountain pools, but nothing compared to the joy of this moment.

She gazed at Braeden and Waysa and she smiled. Her two friends had waited for her, fought for her, did everything they could to make this night happen, and they had finally succeeded.

Finally, Serafina turned and looked at Rowena. The sorceress in her dark robes, with her hood and her long red hair coiled loosely around her shoulders, stood quietly nearby. She was watching them, her green eyes bright and alive, but flickering with an uncertain wariness.

"I'm not going to embrace you if that's what you're thinking, cat," Rowena said.

Serafina smiled and nodded. "I know," she said. "But thank you, Rowena. Thank you from the bottom of my heart. You saved me."

"I put you there," Rowena said, reminding her. "And now I brought you back."

Serafina wasn't sure if she was saying that she had righted the wrong, or that they were even, or maybe something else, but either way, Serafina said, "I thank you for what you did tonight."

As Serafina spoke with her friends, she couldn't help but take in the world around her. She felt her two feet firmly on the ground, so simple, but so profound, to have weight, to have effect, to not be floating in the air or disintegrating into vapor, but to have substance, to have *presence*, to truly be in a place and in command of her body. She smelled the willow trees around the glade and heard the soft orchestra of buzzing insects. Gone was the feeling of being a droplet of water or a mote of dust. Gone was the feeling of being a gust of wind that might drift away at any moment. She was *alive*, truly alive. She was whole again, solid and firm, body and soul, and had never felt better in her life.

And as she stood there looking around her in amazement, she slowly began to realize there was something else, too, something new. When she tuned her ears just right, she could hear the gentle movement of the breeze in the boughs of the trees far above her. She could sense a drop of dew clinging to a leaf, feel it falling through the vibrating air, and hear it hit the ground and soak into the dusty soil. She could see the breath of the trees with her eyes and the rise of water to the clouds. Everything around her felt closer, finer, more acute.

The rising of the moon, the falling of the stars, ashes to ashes, dust to dust—she knew she'd come close to dying. She had walked *in between*. Her spirit had lingered in the world . . . but now she sensed that the *world* lingered in *her*. She felt the quiet rocks of the earth, the flow of distant rivers, and the drift of the clouds above—she could see and feel the spirit of the world all around her.

As she gazed from one point to the next, trying to understand her new senses and powers, she noticed a faint glint of moonlight on the ground over by the destroyed remnants of the Black Cloak. It was but a small reflection of light at first, but as she walked toward it, the glint became so bright that it was almost blinding to her.

She reached down beside the black pile of the ruined fabric and picked up the cloak's silver clasp. It felt heavy in her hand. In the past, the clasp's design had been a twisting weave of thorny vines. She'd even seen the little faces of children behind the vines. But tonight, the clasp was blank, without any design at all.

Serafina turned and walked back toward Braeden. He smiled at her, still elated with their success.

"You better hide this," she said as she slipped the clasp into his hand.

It still amazed her to think that Braeden had hid the damaged cloak from their enemies all that time, fearing its black, hissing power, but clinging to the hope that one day, somehow, someway, he would be able to bring her back into the world. And tonight was that night. He'd done it!

She moved toward him to embrace him again, but Rowena stepped between them.

"This is a sweet reunion and all, we'll be sure to all have tea together sometime," Rowena said in a biting tone. "But my father is going to sense the destruction of the cloak. He's going to come, and when he does, he'll be bent on a black vengeance like nothing you've ever seen, angry that the cat has escaped, but even angrier that I helped her do it."

Serafina knew Rowena was right. She gazed around at her friends. "Whatever happens, the four of us are in this together now."

As soon as she arrived at Biltmore, Serafina ran down to the workshop. She stopped to catch her breath just outside the door. Then she stepped slowly into the room and gazed upon her pa.

He was near his cot behind the supply racks, the cot he'd slept in for all the years she could remember. He was performing a simple task, straightening the blanket on his bed, but to her it seemed to be the most profound of actions.

Here was the man who had raised her, who had fed her and cared for her all her life, who had taught her all that he could teach her, who had guarded and protected her, and held her close every night.

She was so quiet, so still, standing there behind him, that

for a moment, she almost wasn't sure whether she was spirit or whole.

But then, with hot tears welling up in her eyes, she finally said, "I came home as soon as I could, Pa."

Her pa froze in his movement. He did not turn or say a word.

For several seconds it was as if he had not heard her at all. Or perhaps he did not believe what he had heard.

But then he slowly turned his head to the side, as if waiting for the sound to come again. And then he turned his body and looked at her.

He gazed upon her with awe, like a believing man who has come face-to-face with a winged angel. At first, he was unable to speak, but finally, he smiled, and his face wrinkled, and he wiped tears from his eyes, and he said, "Now you come on over here and see your pa."

She walked forward and collapsed into his arms, not just crying, but bawling.

"I'm sorry, Pa, I'm so sorry, I couldn't get home, I tried and tried, but I couldn't get home," she wailed.

He pulled her against his barrel chest, wrapped his thick arms around her, and held her tight.

She pressed her head against his chest and she held him in her trembling arms. As she let herself fall into him, she pulled in a long, dreaming breath, her chest heaving with the exhilaration of being there with him at this moment. She felt the warmth of his embrace and heard the sigh of his breathing as he held her. It was a miracle. She could *feel* him, truly *feel* him, and he could feel her.

Around her, she smelled the cotton fabric of his shirt, and the grease he'd worked with that day, and the familiar musk of his body, all mixed with the smells of the workshop, the solid oak benches and the half-burned coal in the little stove where they cooked their meals and the gritty stone of the floor and the oiled metal of the hammers, wrenches, and other tools. She was alive. And she was finally, finally, finally back—back in the workshop, back in her pa's arms. She was finally *home*.

In the time that followed, she took a long, warm bath, washed off the grave dirt and the bloodstains, and changed into a simple, clean dress. It felt as if she was living in the lap of luxury.

As they settled in for the night, it seemed like neither of them could quite believe that it was truly real. They kept looking at each other, touching each other, as if constantly wanting to make sure.

Her pa cooked an elaborate supper of chicken and dumplings with his favorite gravy, fried okra, and grits smothered with warm butter and cheese. She was so famished that she ate it all and wanted more. Whether it was drinking a glass full of cool, clear water or eating a meal with her pa, the simplest routines of her life had become the most glorious pleasures.

"You're doin' a good fine job on your supper there," her pa said happily as she scraped down to the bottom of the metal plate.

"It just tastes so good," she said, meaning it true, and it brought a smile to his face.

Over supper, her pa started talking, not with any particular purpose in mind, but just to talk, just to celebrate, like everything was all right again. He spun his usual tales of mending machines and solving the challenges of his day-to-day life. She had always loved his stories in which he was the humble hero fighting against impossible odds with wrench and hammer in hand, and she had never loved the stories more than on this night.

She wanted to tell him that she had seen the beautiful faerie lights he had strung in the garden on the night of the evening party, his shining beacon for her to follow home. And she wanted to tell him how proud she was of him the night she'd seen him smiling, dressed in his suit, in the glow of the glittering summer ball.

Later on, as they washed their dishes, her pa took on a more serious tone.

"I know ya might not be too keen on talkin' about it just yet, Sera," he said, "but what happened to you all this time?"

It was difficult to know how to answer his question in a way that he, or anyone, could understand, but she did the best she could.

She was pretty sure that her pa had an inkling that somehow her mother was a mountain lion, but she didn't think he knew that she too walked on four feet when she wanted to. If he did suspect it, it was something he didn't like to think about, like he didn't like to think about haints and demons and other creatures of the night. To him, she was his daughter, a human being, a twelve-year-old little girl that he cherished more than anything in the world, and he didn't like to think of her in any other way. And she was sure that it would come as quite a shock to him if he ever saw her as a crouched, snarling, clawing, leaping black panther. But she knew he had some idea of the strange and unusual things that happened in the dark of night, for he had warned her of them many times.

"You remember our old enemies . . ." Serafina began.

"The ones who captured the animals in the cages up in the pine forest a few months ago," he said, and she nodded her head.

"They came back, Pa. They attacked me, and I was wounded somethin' awful."

As her pa listened, she could tell by the expression in his eyes that it was difficult for him to hear.

"They caught me in a dark place and I couldn't escape," she said.

As she continued her story, telling him what she could and leaving out what she could not, he listened intently. She had been around him all her life, so she knew it wasn't the kind of story he wanted to hear, but he listened anyway for he knew he must. He knew that what he was hearing was what had happened to her, and she could see in his eyes and his expression that he wanted to understand. He'd been waiting and imagining and praying for her safe return for so long that now he wanted to know everything he could. He wanted to have that bond between them, the bond of *knowing*.

"So it was the young master who finally helped you to escape," he said.

She nodded. "Yes, it was."

"He was a gone miserable lad while you were away," her pa said, recounting a bit of how it was from his side of it all. "The master and I, the two of us as doleful as cold poke, used to talk about it, trying to figure out what we could do for the lad, but I think our talks did more for the pair of us menfolk than they did the poor boy. But in the end, I reckon he figured a way through it all on his own."

"I reckon he did," she said in agreement, but refrained from saying more. Her fondness for Braeden had become immeasurable, but it wasn't something she could easily talk about with her pa.

"And you thanked him kindly for what he did . . ." he said, always wanting to make sure she was doing right by other folk.

She nodded, assuring him that she had thanked Braeden, and that she would again.

"And what about your mother?" her pa asked. He didn't know her personally, but he knew that her mother was important to her. "Have you been able to see her since you returned?"

Serafina's heart clouded in sadness. "No," she said. "She went away and I have no way to reach her."

"Well, I hope she's all right," her pa said, but it was clear that he didn't know what else to say.

Serafina's thoughts lingered. She didn't quite know how to ask the question that had been swirling around in her mind since she'd crawled from the grave, but she thought that if anyone could help her, maybe her pa could.

"Pa, does it feel to you like so much has changed since I've been gone? Everything feels so different . . . but in other ways . . ." Her words dwindled off. She could see right away that she wasn't going to be able to express it the way she wanted to.

But he looked at her and said, "I think I understand what you're gettin' at. The way I see it, everything is always changing and everything is always staying the same."

His words shouldn't have made sense to her, but somehow they almost did.

"You see, everything around us is always changing," he continued, "the machines and the inventions, the people coming and going through our lives, even our own bodies over time—yours is growing up and mine is getting old. The trees in the forest are changing and the courses of the rivers. Even our own minds are changing, growing and learning, finding new paths to follow, shifting and shaping over time."

"But if everything is always changing, what can we hold on to?" she asked.

"That's where the rest of it comes in, Sera," her pa said. "Everything is always changing, but everything is always staying the same, too. The trees are growing and dying, but the forest remains. No matter how the river changes course from year to year, it always keeps flowing. Your body and your mind are changing, but deep down, your soul, your inner spirit, stays the same. I'm the same deep down inside that I was when I was twelve years old, and the spirit you feel inside you tonight will be with you fifty years from now. Yes, you'll be different, the whole world will be different, but the spirit inside you—the thing that makes you you—will still be there."

"But if we're always growing and changing, I don't understand how that can be," she said.

"Look at Mr. Vanderbilt," her pa said. "When he was your age, he was a kind but quiet little boy who loved to read books, study art, and travel to faraway places. Now he's a great man of wealth and power . . ."

". . . but he's a kind and quiet man, who loves to read books, study art, and travel to faraway places," she said, finishing his thoughts.

"That's right," her pa said, smiling. "The twelve-year-old little boy will be the fifty-year-old man. It's been him the whole time, all the way through. His body has changed, and everything around him has changed, but his spirit has always been with him."

Serafina nodded, feeling like she was beginning to understand.

"You asked me what we can hold on to," her pa said. "I'll tell you this: you hold on to the people around you, Sera, to your friends and family, to the people you love, and you hold on to that spirit deep down inside that never leaves you, that spirit that's always flowing, like a river inside you."

Finally, her pa paused. He looked at the floor for a moment, as if thinking about his own words a bit longer, and then looked at her. "Does any of my blither-blather feel like it makes any kind of sense to ya?"

Serafina smiled and nodded. It did indeed. She was pretty sure that her pa couldn't reckon the soul-splitting, haint-walking horror of what she'd been through, but somehow he seemed to have sensed just the right words to say to her.

"There's one more thing, Pa," she said, "that I need your help with tonight."

"Another question?" he asked gently.

"No," she said sheepishly. "I need you to help me make something."

"Make something?" he said in surprise, for in all her life with him in the workshop, she had never expressed any interest to fix something or make something. She was absolutely the least mechanically inclined person who had ever prowled the night.

"You've seen how Braeden wears a brace on his bad leg," she said.

"Yes," he said, a twinge of sadness in his voice.

"One of the metal pieces at the joint broke," she said. "I would like to see if we can come up with some way not just to fix it, but to improve it, maybe something that's less like a bone and more like a tendon."

Her pa looked at her and smiled a broad and happy smile. That was definitely something he could do.

Over the next few hours they worked together shoulder to shoulder in the workshop, long into the night, making little test pieces, and discussing and exploring different ideas, until they constructed a design they liked. She had never worked at her pa's side before, not like this. She had never had a need for man-made constructions. So it was an entirely new experience for her, and it brought her great joy, the act of actually *creating* something with her pa at her side.

Later that night, when they finally went to sleep, she curled up between her sheets, her head on the pillow, and it felt just about as fine as anything she had ever felt. She knew there were dark and terrible dangers out there in the forest. She knew there was still a fight ahead of her, but tonight, she was home with her pa, and for a little while, that's all she wanted. Everything is always changing and everything is always staying the same.

The next morning, Serafina went upstairs straightaway to find Braeden.

All the guests that had come for the ball had fled in their carriages to escape the heavy rains flooding the roads, so the house and grounds felt empty. She passed Mr. McNamee, the estate superintendent, gathering a large group of workers in the stable courtyard to repair the damage caused by the nightly storms.

Out back behind the stables, she spotted Braeden in the distance, walking alone into a pasture toward four black horses. The horses had been his companions for years, but in the months she had been gone, Braeden had fallen into such despair that he had drifted away from his friends. As he approached them for the first time in a long time, the horses stood in the field and stared at him as if he was a stranger.

Braeden folded his leg brace at the knee, and sat in the middle of the field. The horses studied him from a distance for a long time. Finally, they began walking slowly toward him.

The four black horses surrounded Braeden, lowered their heads to his, and gently nuzzled him, as horses in the field who have not seen each other in far too long will do.

Then the lead horse extended his front leg, bowed his head low with a bending neck, and knelt down onto one knee so that Braeden could climb onto his bare back. When the horse rose up again, Braeden was astride him, on four strong legs.

Serafina watched Braeden ride out into the rolling, grassy fields with his horses, up to the top of a great hill where there was a large white oak tree with a huge crown and thick splaying limbs. As the horses grazed at the top of the hill, Braeden stayed among them, once again a trusted member of their herd.

Serafina was about to climb the hill to catch up with them, but then she paused. The golden morning light shone down through the mist rising from the tall grass, and for a moment she felt the coolness of the mist, and the heat of the sun, and the touch of the breeze on her skin. She knew she had returned to the living, but at this moment it felt as if the separation between her and the world around her had slipped away. *We are made of the world, and the world is made of us,* she thought.

Wondering what she could do, she slowly raised her hand

in front of her, shaping her fingers until the mist around her began to move. The mist flowed outward, swirling and turning in a long tendril, propelled by her will. She guided the tendril of mist up the hill, toward Braeden and the horses, then up through the branches of the tree until the tendril of mist met the sun and disappeared. Serafina smiled, sensing that there was much for her to learn.

But she knew she didn't have time to linger. She had won one battle by escaping the cloak, but she knew the real war was yet to come. She continued on up the hill to join Braeden and the horses, but then something happened.

Black crows began flying in, strong and hard, from all directions. Soon, hundreds of crows were flying about the tree at the top of the hill, landing and taking off again, wheeling about the sky, croaking and cawing, as if they were engaged in some sort of raucous, noisy conclave.

When she saw Braeden standing below, looking up at the crows, she thought he was just watching them like she was, but then she realized that he was actually calling them in, trying to speak with them, his voice filled with urgency. As the crows flew in great circles around the top of the tree, he talked to them, sometimes struggling with the phrasing of his words, other times correcting himself, like someone who is gradually finding his way.

Finally, one of the crows flew down and perched on a branch near Braeden, tilted its black shining head, and made clicking-gurgling noises. It appeared that Braeden actually understood what the crow was saying to him, and when Braeden spoke back to the crow in English, the bird seemed to somehow understand him. Many of the other crows came closer and joined in their conversation until there were crows in the lower branches all around him.

As Serafina moved quickly up the hill, she was worried about scaring the crows off, but the birds seemed to have no shortage of boisterous, brazen confidence in themselves, flying all around, buzzing and cawing, flapping their great black wings, as they conversed with the boy.

Braeden seemed unfamiliar with the crows' language at first, as if he didn't understand everything they were saying, but he seemed to become more used to the cadence of it. Serafina had never given much thought to the cawing of crows, but as she watched them now, she began to hear just how many different kinds of sounds they made—long, castigating rattles, impatient clacks, triumphant caws, rowdy jeers and playful chortles, warnings and signals, praise and encouragement, and urgent calls to flight. She realized that the crows had an entire language of their own. And with powers she did not understand, Braeden was learning it.

Finally, he said a few last words to the crows, and they all launched up into the air at once. One flock of the crows flapped forcefully away on strong and steady wings, flying west toward the mountains in the distance. The other crows flew in small flocks in different directions, some toward the house, others the gardens, and still others into the nearby forests.

"Where have you sent them all?" she asked, making her presence known for the first time.

Braeden turned in surprise and smiled at the sight of her. "Serafina . . ." he said, his voice filled with gentle contentment. She was just happy that he could actually see her.

"Did you sleep well?" she asked.

"Better than I have in a long time," he said, nodding vigorously.

"Me too," she said, smiling. "It's good to be home. I was going to come up here and tell you that we have work to do, but I think you've already begun."

"I'm afraid I'm out of practice, so it took me a while to figure out how to speak to them."

She looked toward the flock flying west, their black silhouettes receding into the blue sky beneath a striking, sunlit formation of tumbling white clouds.

"And where is that particular flock going?"

"I asked them to head to the Smoky Mountains."

The sound of that name brought a pang of sadness to her heart.

Looking at Braeden and then the crows again, Serafina wondered what it was all about. "Why so far?" she asked. "What will they find there?"

"They're going to find your mother," he said. "To let her know that you've returned so that she'll come back, and you'll be able to see her again."

Serafina looked at Braeden and felt a deep warmth filling her chest. "That's so kind of you," she said, "to think of that, I mean, to ask them to do that. Thank you. I hope they find her, and the cubs, too. I'd love to see them all again."

"You're very welcome," Braeden said, pleased that she was happy with what he'd done. "Now that you're back, your mother and the cubs belong here with us, in our forests."

Serafina couldn't agree more, and she liked the way he said *our forests.*

As they were talking, she noticed that he was standing in an awkward position, favoring his bad leg. She glanced down and saw that the bracket on the brace was still broken.

"How's your leg?" she asked.

"It's been feeling much better," he said, trying to stay cheerful, but as his trembling fingers began fumbling with the straps and buckles, tightening them the best he could, it was clear that his leg was still sore. "I guess this rickety old brace does need some work," he admitted. "It was brand-new when my uncle got it for me, but after all it's been through, it's definitely suffered some wear and tear. This metal piece here broke off completely, and it's been causing me no end of trouble."

She shyly put out her hand and said, "Maybe this will help."

In her open palm were the two kidney-shaped, multi-holed leather straps that she and her pa had made.

"What are those?" Braeden asked with fascination as he leaned toward her and took a closer look.

"One for each side of your knee," she said, "to replace the metal bracket that broke. My pa and I made them."

"You did?" he asked in amazement, looking up at her. "Thank you!"

"Try them on."

"Yes," he said excitedly. "Let's see how they work . . ."

He took the leather straps out of her hands, his fingers brushing her open palm as he did so, sending a jolt of energy up her arm and down her spine. Then he folded himself to the ground, tore off the broken bracket, and began attaching the new straps.

"I hope they fit," she said.

"They seem like they're going to work very well," he said, standing up and flexing his knee back and forth as if someone had just given him a new, fully functional leg.

Seeing his happiness, Serafina smiled.

She glanced westward across the mountains. The westbound crows had disappeared on their journey.

"Do you think they will succeed?" she asked wistfully. "It's a big forest out there, and she's very good at hiding."

"The crows don't have the eyesight of a hawk, the nose of a vulture, or the speed of a falcon, but they are the smartest birds I know, and they will work together to find her."

"Are the crows always so noisy?" she asked, still a little amused by all the racket they'd been making. It seemed so quiet now up on the hill with only the horses grazing nearby.

"Oh yes," Braeden said. "They love to argue, those crows, and boy, are they quick to take offense. But they're good birds all the same."

"What about all the other crows that flew off in the different directions?"

"Each flock is a small family group that trusts each other, hunts and scavenges together, calling each other when they find something good, and warning each other when danger approaches. Each flock protects their own territory where they've learned to find food, roost at night, and stay safe. I asked all the different flocks in the area to post sentinels all around Biltmore's grounds and keep guard, to warn us if they see anything suspicious. Uriah has been their hated enemy for many years."

Serafina marveled at Braeden's story of the crows, but her gut twisted at the sound of her enemy's name. "And have they seen him?"

"They say he's moving every night, circling Biltmore."

Serafina couldn't help but take a swallow. "I don't like the sound of that one bit."

"Me neither," Braeden agreed. "The crows will be able to give us a short warning, but that's all."

Serafina gazed back at the house and the surrounding gardens, her heart filling with a dark foreboding. Noticing a change in the wind direction, she glanced up at the sky.

In what form would Uriah attack? Would it be a sudden strike like a rattlesnake's bite? Or would the storms and floods come gradually, doing his work for him, sweeping everything away in their destructive path?

"Last night Waysa told me that the rivers are getting worse," Braeden said. "Whole areas of the forest in the mountains above Biltmore are flooded with water and mudslides."

"When Uriah sees his best opportunity, he will attack," Serafina said.

"But what are we going to do?"

"We need to find the others."

"They're down by the spillway of the pond." Seeing her look

of surprise at his quick answer, Braeden said, "Crows have long memories, so they keep a watchful eye on Rowena wherever she goes. They don't trust her any more than they trust her father."

"What about you?" Serafina asked. "Do *you* trust her?"

"Yes, I think she's on our side now," Braeden said. "With the four of us working together, we can defeat him."

Serafina wanted to agree, but wasn't too sure what to make of Braeden's new optimism. A death struggle with a powerful sorcerer loomed ahead, but he seemed happier than he had been in a long time. But he wasn't just returning to his old self. There was something different about him, more focused and determined.

"Let's go," he said, touching her arm, "they're going to be looking for us," and they started down the hill toward the pond, his newly repaired leg brace seeming to provide a new smoothness to his gait.

She felt an unusual sense of satisfaction as she walked at Braeden's side. *This,* she thought, *this is how it should be.* She enjoyed being with him. His leather boot still dragged a little in the grass, and his hands were still trembling, but he seemed stronger and more at ease than he ever had before.

She wanted to keep this sense of peace and belonging for as long as she could, but as she and Braeden reached the bottom of the hill, she felt an unusual stirring in the air. A small flurry of wind swept by her. She might not have noticed such a thing in the past, but her senses were too keen now to ignore it. Suddenly, she caught the scent of a coming storm.

She looked around at the wind blowing in the tops of the

trees. A storm seemed to be moving in with unnatural speed. Even as the light of the sun withdrew from everything around them, a flash of lightning lit up the sky.

"So much for the sunny day," Braeden said. And she knew he wasn't just talking about the weather.

Rolling over the ridge of the closest mountain, a dark bank of clouds loomed like a great wave.

"It's coming this way," she said, eyeing the black front of the storm. "He's attacking now."

By the time they reached the pond, it had begun to rain, like a warm summer shower at first, with the sun still shining bright on the distant eastern horizon, but as the clouds passed directly overhead, the sky grew dark and malevolent, and the heavy rain came pouring down.

"It's been raining like this almost every night," Braeden complained, as they made their way miserably through the deluge.

Serafina was about to reply when her whole body jolted in surprise. A blistering white light blazed in her eyes as a bolt of lightning struck the top of the hill. The oak tree where they'd just been standing exploded into a thousand pieces, sending shards of burning wood hurtling in all directions, whizzing past her head, as the crack of thunder boomed in her chest and rolled across the blackened sky. Braeden's four horses reared up in panic and charged away across the field.

"Serafina!" Braeden said, grabbing her arm and pointing into the distance toward the grassy slope of Diana Hill in front of the house. The hillsides around Biltmore were running with dark rivers of storm water. Rushing currents tore at the earth, and great areas of mud were sliding down toward the house and gardens.

"Gad night a-livin', will you look at that," Serafina gasped. "I hope everyone's holdin' on down there."

As they ran down to the pond, they saw that the small inlet stream had become a turbulent river. The pond was so full that the water had breached the banks and flooded the nearby trees.

Sloshing through inches of water, they made their way toward the stone dam at the outlet of the pond. Normally, the small amount of overflow was nothing more than a trickle, but now a roaring waterfall poured out of the pond and over the spillway, dumping into the ravine below.

"We need to cross before it's too late," Serafina shouted, pointing toward the small wooden footbridge that traversed the top of the waterfall.

As they clambered across the bridge, the driving spray of the rain and the waterfall flew into her face. The blowing wind howled like a horde of ghouls. The wood planking beneath her feet swayed as the pushing current rocked the bridge's supports back and forth. She grabbed the side rail as her eyes darted to the rushing water below her. She felt the bridge suddenly jerk to the side, then tilt violently with the sound of cracking wood.

"Braeden, jump!" she shouted.

Just as she and Braeden leapt to the ground on the other side, the entire bridge split apart and came crashing down, then rolled over the falls in a great heap of broken, twisted boards.

"We made it," Braeden gasped, as Serafina scanned the path ahead for Waysa and Rowena. She spotted them running toward her and Braeden.

"This storm is my father's doing," Rowena yelled through the rain as the last of the bridge's wreckage went over the falls. "It's going to get worse from here."

"Let's get to cover!" Serafina shouted.

As the four of them ran through the rain toward the house, a great mass of mud was sliding into the outer edge of the gardens, tearing through the plants and knocking down the marble Greek statues.

Squinting through the rain, Serafina looked toward the house. A gushing river of water ripped down a side gulley, tearing at Biltmore's foundation.

"There's my uncle!" Braeden shouted.

The wind-torn figures of Mr. Vanderbilt and Superintendent McNamee stood in the middle of the blowing storm, shouting orders to what looked like more than fifty men as they worked frantically to stanch the flow of the water tearing at the house. Serafina watched in horror as a man was pulled into the current and swept away screaming for help.

"What are we going to do?" Braeden shouted, his voice filled with fear and confusion. "We can't battle a thunderstorm!"

Reaching the main house, Serafina led her friends through the side door into the circular room at the base of the Grand Staircase. She and her companions were breathless, sopping wet, and bedraggled from the storm. As she looked around at them, she could see the fear and uncertainty in their faces, and their relief to be in the shelter of the house. She felt it, too. The last thing she wanted to do was go back out there.

And then she realized something.

This was exactly what Uriah wanted, she thought, for them to hunker down and hide. He was pushing them, pressing them back, as he wreaked havoc on the estate.

"We need to attack," Serafina said.

"Now?" Braeden said in surprise. "In the middle of the storm?"

"Exactly," Serafina said. "This is our opportunity. He'll think we'll be hiding, taking cover. The last thing he's going to expect is for us to attack in the middle of the storm."

"Serafina is right," Waysa said.

"I don't think you realize how difficult he is going to be to kill," Rowena said.

"Do you know where he's hiding?" Serafina asked Rowena.

"I suspect he's up on one of the mountain peaks, looking toward Biltmore, directing this storm, but there's no way to tell for certain where he's going to be."

Serafina went over to the door and looked out into the blowing wind and rain. "Braeden, can your crows fly in this?"

"They normally take cover during a storm," he said, gazing

up at the darkened sky, "but they're strong fliers, and they'll jump at the chance to get into a fracas with an enemy they hate as much as Uriah."

"Talk to them and your other friends," she said. "I want to attack Uriah with all our allies at once."

"I'm sure they'll join us," Braeden said. "They've been fighting against Uriah for even longer than we have."

Encouraged, Serafina nodded and then looked at Rowena.

"I will load my satchel with potions and spells," Rowena said. Serafina could see the fear and determination in her eyes. Rowena, more than any of them, knew her father's wrath. She had felt his attacks. She had suffered his blows. She had thrown spells at him only to have them buffeted back. But Serafina could see that Rowena knew the time had come to stand up and fight him.

"You understand that we have to take him by surprise," Rowena warned.

Waysa stepped forward. "I'll attack him first."

Serafina could see the fierceness blazing in Waysa's eyes. She knew her friend wouldn't give up until either he or Uriah was dead. He was honor bound to avenge his family or die trying.

She looked around at her three companions. "Attacking now, in the middle of his attack, is going to be the most dangerous thing we've ever done. But there will be no peace in these mountains for any of us until we destroy him."

"But how are we going to do it?" Rowena asked.

"We'll plan it all out, every detail," Serafina said. "We'll use the crows to find him. Then Waysa and I will lead the attack, charging at him from two different directions at once. Braeden will bring in our animal allies at the same time, and Rowena, you'll attack with every spell you have. We have to hit him so fast and so hard that he never gains his footing."

Serafina looked around at her three companions. They were ready to fight. She waved her hand up at the sky. "Forget about this weather, this rain, this wind. This is nothing to us. We attack now, right through all this. *We* are the storm."

As night fell, Serafina and her companions made their way up into the rugged terrain of the mountains. She traveled in panther form with Waysa, the two of them slinking quickly and quietly through the underbrush. Rowena traveled on foot, her dark robes and hood gathered around her against the wind. Braeden rode his horse, with Gidean at his side.

Braeden made a dashing sight, a lionhearted boy in a dark outdoor coat riding atop his black horse, with his black Doberman dog at his side, and his black crows flying above him, and she herself a black panther gliding alongside. She was beginning to notice a trend in his choice of friends.

As they moved up the slope of the mountain, the wind was

still blowing, but they had left the rain and lightning of the storm in the valley behind them. They moved quickly through the highland forest, following the crows that led the way. The crows didn't normally fly at night, but tonight they flew with purpose. They flapped hard through the blowing wind, some of them tumbling in the air, others diving headlong through the buffeting gale, all of them cawing to each other, pressing each other on.

As Serafina and her allies began to reach the top of the mountain, the wind finally died down and the air became deathly still. They entered a forest crowded with large, slanting, jagged rocks. Many of the rocks towered over their heads, jutting up from the ground, cracked and crumbling as if they had been broken by powerful earthen forces. Mottled gray lichen and dark greenish moss covered the rocks, and gnarled trees grew from the cracks, their roots clinging to the stone like the long black, creeping legs of giant spiders.

Making their way slowly up through the denseness of the rocky forest, they came to a bank of fog so thick that they couldn't see ahead. Just as Serafina was wondering how they were going to get through it, she felt a stinging in her eyes and a bad sulfurous taste in her mouth. Suddenly, her nostrils burned. Her throat hurt. A wave of confusion and dizziness came over her. Braeden was suffering as well, coughing badly, his horse throwing its head in agitation as it tried to turn away.

"The fog is poisonous," Rowena said.

Serafina shifted into human form. "Everyone pull back!"

she shouted, coughing and rubbing her stinging eyes as she stumbled down the hill.

"What is going on?" Braeden asked, covering his mouth.

"He's using a spell to protect the top of the mountain," Rowena said in frustration, "but I don't know how to counter it."

Once they retreated down to a safe position, Serafina looked toward the ring of fog that surrounded the peak. "It's a line of defense," she said. "He must be up there."

"But there's no way to get through it," Braeden said.

"Not like this," she agreed. "But I have an idea. Everyone stay here."

As she made her way alone back up the slope of the mountain, she remembered all she had learned. She raised her hand in front of her and pushed it through the air. When she felt the air around her moving, she smiled and tried it again.

She walked slowly up into the poisonous fog, sweeping her hands back and forth, concentrating on the movement and the flow, the wisps of air and vapor, pushing and sliding, until rivers of fog moved to her will through the sky.

She cut a swath through the fog, clearing a narrow path, then called her friends forward to follow close behind her, Braeden on his horse, Gidean at his side, Waysa and Rowena coming up behind.

When they finally reached the other side, the air was clear and the fog behind them. They took cover in a thicket of heath behind a large rock.

"How in the world did you do that?" Braeden whispered to her in astonishment.

"Just something I picked up in my travels," Serafina said, pleased that she was able to hone her powers to useful purpose. But as she looked up toward the mountaintop, she grew more serious.

Like many of the Blue Ridge Mountains, which were some of the oldest mountains in the world, the top of this particular mountain wasn't a sharply pointed peak but a rocky dome, what the mountain folk called a *bald*, worn down by millions of years of wind and rain. Hundreds of the forest's spruce and fir trees lay on the ground like they'd been blown down by the high mountain winds or struck by the vengeance of a sorcerer. The trunks of the fallen trees lay crisscrossed over one another, their limbs broken and twisted, like a hundred titan soldiers lying dead on a hilltop battlefield.

"This is the place," Rowena whispered, as they crouched behind the cracked and weathered rock. "He's close. I can feel him."

Serafina looked back at Braeden on his horse just down the slope from them. "Call in our other friends now. We'll do everything just like we planned."

"There he is!" Rowena whispered, ducking down.

Serafina's arms and legs jolted with sudden strength. The battle was near.

Taking a deep breath, she slowly peeked up over the edge of the rock.

The dark and giant figure of the storm-creech Uriah loomed in the clearing, with the smoky-white haze hanging about him like the fog of the graveyard. He did not appear to be aware of their presence. He wore a long, ragged dark coat so shredded and torn that it looked like the rotting carcass of a dead animal. He stood on two long, bent legs like a gangly man, but he was impossibly tall, grotesquely hunched over, with his long, crooked arms in front of him and his white scaly clawed hands protruding from the ragged sleeves of his coat. The oily strands of his gray hair hung stringy and twisting down the side of his skull. His cracked and leathery face had been slashed by Serafina's four claws months before, and the open wounds still bled and festered after all this time. Uriah paced, lanky and stooping, in the center of the clearing, rocking back and forth as he gazed impatiently toward Biltmore, far in the distant valley, watching over the storm that he had sent to rip it from the earth.

When Serafina had first spotted the clawed creature in the forest, she hadn't been sure what it was, but now she could see that the storm-creech was indeed a man, or at least had been a man before he was consumed by a black and twisting vengeance. *With every injury, we become more of who we are,* Rowena had said. And here was *Uriah,* the sorcerer, the enslaver of wild animals, the murderer of her panther father and many others, the man who had set himself to destroy everything she loved.

By moving in on him the way they had, during the storm and slipping through his ring of poisonous fog, she'd caught him by surprise, and all her allies were ready. *We've got him,* she thought. But just as she turned to signal the attack, a fireball came hurtling over her head, snapping and boiling with terrific force, a long tail of thick black smoke trailing behind it.

It was headed straight for Braeden.

"Watch out, Braeden!" Rowena screamed as she leapt out from behind the rock and threw her arms up into an explosion of ice and frost. It came too late to destroy the fireball, but she managed to deflect it. Instead of hitting Braeden, the fireball struck Braeden's horse, sending it up rearing and striking against the burning flames, killing it almost instantly, collapsing the horse to the ground, and slamming Braeden down with his clothes on fire.

Enraged that Rowena had defended the boy, Uriah struck his arms forward and threw a violent blow across the distance, knocking her through the air with tremendous force and smashing her against a rock. Her lifeless body slid like a bloodied rag doll down to the ground.

Serafina shifted into her panther form and charged into an attack, running straight at Uriah.

Uriah waved his long, gangly arms around him. Suddenly, the branches of the fallen trees began to thrash back and forth, clicking and clacking. The moss hanging down from the limbs of the trees began to smoke. The bark on the trunks began to slowly peel off, as if the trees were burning. The grass turned brown and crackled beneath her running feet.

As Serafina charged toward him, Uriah did not flee or duck.

He threw his hands in one direction and then the other. A mighty wind kicked up, casting out dark, swirling tornadoes that tore up sticks, leaves, and other debris from the ground in front of her. A horrible, loud rushing sound overtook everything else.

Uriah looked straight at her, ready for her attack.

"Are you surprised to see me, Black One?" he roared. "Did you think the swat of a little cat could kill me?" His voice boomed so loudly that it pierced her ears and shook her to the core. "You can't kill me!"

Serafina knew that Uriah wouldn't be standing so fearless if he didn't think he could sustain her attack, and it was foolish to attack him straight on. But it was all part of the trick. She spotted Waysa charging out of the forest at full speed toward Uriah's back. And she knew they had him.

She leapt straight at Uriah's face. Waysa leapt on his back at the same moment. The two catamounts landed upon the man, ripping into him with their tearing claws.

Screaming in outrage, Uriah reached back and grabbed Waysa, pulled him over his shoulder, and threw him off with incredible strength, heaving him so far that Waysa went tumbling across the clearing. Uriah had always been strong, but nothing like this.

Their well-thought-out plan of having Rowena cast her spells, Braeden charge in with their animal allies, and the two catamounts attack from two different directions at once had already gone wrong. Their plans had been wrecked. There was nothing left for Serafina to do but *fight*!

Clinging to Uriah's chest and legs with all four of her clawed paws, Serafina pulled her head back and slammed her long, curved fangs into Uriah's neck. Uriah screamed in pain and grabbed at her, but Waysa came tearing back into the battle and leapt upon his arms with teeth and claws. On the ground, Gidean charged in, chomped onto Uriah's leg, and pulled viciously, snarling and biting, trying to yank Uriah off his feet.

As Uriah struggled to pull Serafina from his chest, she pulled back and bit again, this time, aiming straight for his throat. Her teeth clamped onto his windpipe and cut off his air. Her mother had taught her that big cats kill their prey not just by tearing into them with claws, or breaking their necks, but by blocking their windpipes and asphyxiating them, and that was what she was determined to do now. This time, she couldn't just wound him, she had to kill him. For her peace, for Braeden, for Biltmore, for all that she'd fought for, she had to destroy him. She clenched her teeth and would not let go.

47

As Serafina fought she glanced back toward Braeden.

He'd been struck down from his horse and hit the ground hard, but he rolled and quickly put out his burning clothes. He immediately scrambled over to his wounded horse lying on the ground. He put his open hands on the horse's body, desperately trying to heal his oldest friend, but his face clouded with anguish as he realized it was too late. His friend was already dead.

Braeden wiped his eyes and ran over to Rowena. It was hard for Serafina to see as she struggled with Uriah, but she made out the silhouette of what looked like some kind of stag with a rack of horns kneeling down, as Braeden dragged the bloody and unconscious Rowena onto its back.

"Take her to safety," he told the animal, as it rose to its feet and drove into the depth of the forest.

A pack of a dozen wolves emerged from the trees, snarling and snapping, as they charged into battle against the sorcerer.

"Attack his arms," Braeden yelled, pointing toward Uriah. "Protect Serafina. Bring him down!"

Uriah thrashed wildly to dislodge her, but Serafina held fast, her panther teeth clamped onto his throat. He grabbed at her with his clacking clawed hands, but Gidean, Waysa, and the wolves attacked him from all directions, biting his arms and legs, preventing him from pulling her away.

If she could just hold on for a few more seconds, they'd kill Uriah once and for all.

Serafina knew this was the ultimate battle. All the allies of the forest had come together at this moment to fight. It was like the battle that her mother and father had fought and lost twelve years before. But this time, she was going to *win*. They were going to finally defeat the most dangerous enemy the forest had ever faced.

Uriah struck Waysa with a heavy blow, knocking him away with his arm. Waysa went tumbling across the ground, but before the catamount even stopped rolling, he spun around and leapt back at Uriah with a vicious snarl, hitting him with such force that it tackled him to the ground with Serafina still attached.

Serafina buried her fangs deeper into Uriah's throat. Through the nerves in the base of her teeth, she could feel the force clamping onto his windpipe, and the slowing of the air to his lungs. He was the storm-creech, the clawed creature, but he still had to breathe. She could feel his struggle diminishing beneath her as she slowly cut off his life.

But suddenly, Serafina felt Uriah's body shaking beneath her, like he'd become possessed by a horrible spirit. His chest expanded with new strength and he began to rise to his feet. He kicked Gidean away from him, sending the dog somersaulting across the ground. Then he grabbed Waysa, tore his claws out of his skin, and hurled the catamount away like an empty sack.

Uriah kicked the wolves off his legs and threw them off his arms. The wolves fell away from him with blazing eyes as he stood to his full height. Then a black, dirty wind began to rip into the wolves around him.

"Now!" Braeden shouted. "Attack him!" A massive bear charged in and slammed into Uriah. Serafina's body swung hard with the force of the blow, her legs and tail dangling now. It took all her strength to hold on as her enemy struck desperately at her side and tore at her head and tried to pull her away.

Yes, pull! she urged him in her mind. *Pull! Yank me away and rip out your own throat!*

And through all this, Serafina held on. No matter what happened, she wasn't going to let go.

But then Uriah burst forth with a deafening explosion that shocked everything around them.

Braeden and the wolves were thrown to the ground. Even the bear went down.

Waysa was hurled through the air, hit a tree, and collapsed, his limp body dangling in the branches, his eyes closed.

Gidean tumbled away, his body dragging through the dirt, biting and twisting, until he finally lay still.

With a terrible new strength, Uriah grabbed Serafina's head and fangs with his hands, and began prying her teeth slowly out of his neck, his fingers dripping with his own blood.

"I told you, you can never kill me!" he spat at her.

She growled and bit harder and tried to stop him from dislodging her teeth, but there was nothing she could do. He tore her off him and slammed her to the ground so hard that it knocked the wind out of her. Then he burst away in an explosion of black air, leaving great flares of orange flame rising all around them.

They had ambushed him with their fiercest allies and all their strength, but he had escaped their attack.

Serafina lay on the ground, stunned. She lifted her head, her eyes looking frantically through the smoke, trying to make sense of the destruction. Was Waysa still alive? Was Braeden still fighting?

The dead and wounded wolves lay strewn across the clearing, their bodies burned and broken.

She glimpsed the bear barreling away through the burning forest, his fur singed by the flames as he ran.

Her heart lurched when she saw Waysa's long lion body hanging in the tree, dangling down from the branches. She still couldn't see if he was alive or dead, but he wasn't moving.

She had to get herself up. Through all the shock and pain of it, through all the strikes and bruises, she had to rise. But as she began to move and breathe again, the blazing-hot air of the burning trees around her scorched her throat and lungs. The forest was on fire.

She gazed through the orange, hazy, firelit clearing. A jolt of fear ripped through her when she spotted Braeden's body lying on the ground, crumpled and still.

Powered by a new surge of energy, she shifted into human form and scrambled toward him, pushing her way through the swirling smoke and embers. When she finally reached him, his eyes were closed. His wounded dog lay beside him. Piles of dead crows and wolves lay all around him.

She dropped to her knees at Braeden's side.

"Braeden, wake up!" she shouted as she grabbed him by his coat and pulled him up.

Finally, he started awake with a violent gasp, and looked around at his fallen friends in horror.

"So many of them are dead!" Braeden said in despair, overwhelmed and disoriented.

"We've got to move, Braeden!" Serafina shouted, trying to shake him out of it as she coughed from the smoke. "We've got to help who we can and get out of here!"

Her chest filled with new hope when Braeden came to his senses and started pulling wolves up onto their feet.

She scanned back through the smoke toward Waysa. Where the fire was burning across the flat ground, it moved slowly, but on the steep slopes around them, the flames tore through the thick vegetation in blinding blazes, sparks and flames swirling upward into the glowing orange sky. She heard the sharp crackling of burning branches all around them, and as the sap within the trees boiled, the tree trunks exploded. Her heart was racing with fear, but there was no time to lose.

She ran over to the tree where Waysa's body was hanging and started climbing. Its trunk was so hot that the sap was popping and steaming, dripping out of it like blood. She knew the tree was going to explode, but she had to keep going.

She climbed frantically out onto the branches. She held Waysa's catamount head in her hands. The concussion of the blast had knocked him unconscious.

"Waysa!" she shouted, pushing hard at his body. "We've got to go!"

She felt a sudden flare of intense heat below her. Flames were spiraling up the trunk of the tree. There was no way to climb down. The sap-filled branches around her began to hiss and boil. Every breath she took from the hot, smoky air felt like she was sucking fire down her throat.

She had no choice. As the flames burned into the creaking, collapsing branches, she wrapped her arms around Waysa's body and jumped.

A sledgehammer of pain thundered through her shoulder and ribs when she hit the ground with a heavy grunt. But she scrambled to her feet. She grabbed Waysa by the shoulders and tried to drag him, pulling and heaving, as the burning tree collapsed around them. She fell to the ground as Waysa finally woke and looked around him in confusion.

"We've got to go!" she shouted at him, and Waysa rose to his feet.

On her way back to Braeden, she pulled Gidean up onto

his unsteady legs. "Come on, boy, let's go, come on!" And the wounded dog sluggishly, obediently, tried to follow her.

"Everyone get up!" she shouted at the surviving wolves as the flames burned around them and the clearing filled with hot choking smoke.

But they had only moments to live before the fire engulfed them. The trees that surrounded them were all aflame and there was no way out.

She wanted to use the wind to blow the flames away, but sensed that it would just make the fire burn faster. She thought about trying to draw water out of the rocky ground, but she knew it wouldn't work. She looked up at the clouds, but she had no idea how to reach up there and make them pour down with rain.

It seemed so hopeless. She looked all around her at the walls of orange fire. The smoke choked her throat. Her eyes stung. The heat burned her skin. They were completely surrounded by flames.

"If we don't find a way out of this, we're going to die here," she shouted to Braeden as she peered through the burning forest looking for a path through.

"No we're not," Braeden said fiercely.

Serafina turned in the direction he was looking. The night sky above them was suddenly full of birds. Hawks and eagles and ospreys.

"Lie down," Braeden said.

"What?" she said in confusion.

"Lie down!" he ordered her. "Waysa, you too. Lie down!"

Waysa came stumbling over to them in human form. As she and Waysa lay down on the ground, Braeden kept shouting at them. "Now spread out your hands and legs. Splay yourself out!"

Serafina had no idea why Braeden wanted her to do these things, but she did as he said. Suddenly, she felt the brush of moving air above her. Many pairs of large, powerful talons gripped her arms and legs, her wrists and her ankles.

"Go!" Braeden shouted to the birds. "Take them!"

Serafina felt her limbs lifting upward, then her body. She couldn't keep the panic from sweeping through her. They were lifting her off the ground. But she didn't want to leave the ground! She liked the ground!

But suddenly, she was in the air, she was floating, she was flying. As she flew upward, she saw the intensity of the forest fire all around them. The mountain was on fire. Braeden's figure standing in the center of the tiny clearing became smaller and smaller as the birds lifted her. Then she was flying across the canopy of the forest like a hawk, above the flames and the smoke.

Waysa was flying beside her, hanging from the talons of the hawks and ospreys like she was.

Within seconds, the blaze of the forest fire fell behind them. The night became dark and cool again as they flew up into the clear moonlit sky over the dark green canopy of the untouched forest.

Serafina craned her neck and looked behind her, searching for Braeden. She could see him in the clearing surrounded by the fire. He was shouting commands as hundreds of hawks and other birds grabbed hold of Gidean and the surviving wolves. The flames were pressing in, the smoke choking him, but he wouldn't leave his friends behind. He was determined to save them all.

"Get out of there, Braeden," Serafina said, but she knew it was useless.

When she looked back a final time, the flames had engulfed the clearing. There was nothing left but fire and great torrents of sparks rising up from the top of the burning mountain.

"Wait," she called to the hawks that were carrying her. "Wait! Go back! Go back for Braeden!"

But they didn't understand her. And they didn't turn.

The birds carried her and Waysa high over the trees and the mountains, which rolled dark and quiet below them. The sorcerer's storm had cleared. Up in the sky, a feathery scattering of white clouds drifted past an impossibly bright moon, with a crush of glittering stars above. Looking down again, she spotted what she knew must be the French Broad River, dark and shimmering, as it wound through the mountains.

As they flew slowly up the valley of the great river, she saw Biltmore House on top of the hill, its gray towers striking up into the sky, the moonlight touching its sides.

But all she could think about was the valiant friend they had left behind.

48

Serafina fell to her knees on the ground in front of Biltmore, her chest heaving with anguish. But she quickly got herself up to her feet again and looked toward the mountain in the distance. She could no longer see the flames. The top of the mountain where they had been fighting had burned black, a thick cloud of smoke pouring from its heights.

Waysa stood beside her, gazing up at the mountain with her, his face filled with dread.

Biltmore's grounds had been badly damaged by the floods, and some of the house's foundation had been torn away, but for now the storm had receded, and the sun was coming up.

"I'm going back up there to find him," Serafina announced and started on foot toward the mountain.

"Wait," Waysa said, grabbing her arm.

Serafina's stomach felt like it was twisting into knots. She hated standing still when she could be moving. "We can't wait here, Waysa. Come on, we've got to help him."

But Waysa turned and looked at something in the distance.

Waves of morning mist were rolling through the trees and across the wide expanse of grass in front of Biltmore, the rising sun casting rays of light between the waves, dappling the front of the house in moving bands of gold.

"The *a-wi-e-qua* have brought him home," Waysa said softly, his voice filled with awe.

Serafina didn't understand what Waysa said until she saw the herd of elk emerging slowly and silently from the mist of the forest.

The elk of the Blue Ridge were large and magnificent forest creatures of old that Serafina knew only from the drawings in Mr. Vanderbilt's books. Seeing the elk here, now, was impossible, for the last of the mountain elk had been killed by hunters more than a hundred years before. Then she remembered the large, stag-like animal that Braeden had called in to carry Rowena to safety the night before.

Was it possible that a few had survived all these years, hidden deep in the mountain coves and the shaded marshes where no one could find them? Had they come out now because Braeden had asked for their help?

The lead elk was an enormous, thousand-pound beast with a massive rack of antlers rising some four feet above his head like the majestic crown of a forest king. Braeden rode on the elk king's back, holding the thick, dark brown mane with one hand and the wounded Rowena draped over the elk's neck with the other. The elk king led the herd in a slow procession across the grass toward her and Waysa.

Serafina felt a swoosh of relief crash through her. She rushed forward and helped her tired, bruised, soot-stained friend down from the elk's back. His clothes were burned and torn, but it appeared that he hadn't suffered any major wounds.

Waysa gently pulled Rowena's limp body from the elk's back and carried her in his arms, her long hair hanging loosely toward the ground.

Braeden turned to the elk king. "Thank you, my friend," he whispered.

As the elk herd turned slowly back into the forest and gradually disappeared into the morning mist, Serafina knew that she would probably never see them again.

She wrapped Braeden in her arms. "I was so worried about you," she said. "What were you doing up there? You almost got yourself killed!"

"I had to save as many of the wolves as I could," he said, shaking his head. "But finally the hawks pulled me out. I still can't believe we lost. I thought we finally had him, but . . . we lost so many of our friends. My horse, and many of the crows and the wolves . . ."

"I'm so sorry," she said. She knew he was hurting.

He shook his head sadly, even as he held her. "I told them

all how dangerous it was going to be, but they wanted to fight anyway. They were very brave."

She hugged him a little tighter before she let him go.

"Our friends fought with great honor, and you led them well," Serafina said. "We fought against our enemy the very best we could."

She and Braeden followed Waysa as he carried Rowena toward the house. Braeden went ahead and opened the front door for him, and then led them upstairs.

Serafina had seen many strange and wondrous things at Biltmore, but this was a sight she had never imagined: a dark-haired Cherokee catamount boy carrying a redheaded young English sorceress up the Grand Staircase of Biltmore Estate at sunrise.

"Let's take her up to the South Tower Room on the third floor," Braeden said, leading the way. "My uncle was worried about my aunt's condition, so he took her into Asheville while the road was still partially clear. We have most of the house to ourselves."

But just as he was saying this, a young dark-haired maid in a black-and-white uniform came bustling down the staircase, clearly not expecting to encounter anyone so early in the morning. Serafina was delighted to see that it was her old friend Essie Walker. Essie seemed so flush and full of life as she bustled down the stairs.

"Oh dear, y'all, pardon me," Essie said in surprise, catching herself up short as she came to an abrupt stop in front of them. Essie caught eyes with Waysa first, and seemed to snag there for a moment, but then she immediately moved her attention to the unconscious girl he was carrying. "Oh my, what's happened to the poor girl? Is she badly hurt?"

But then in the next instant, as Essie's eyes lifted, she noticed the young master Braeden and then Serafina beside him. Essie's eyes widened, like she was seeing a haint. *Not anymore*, Serafina thought.

"Essie, it's me," Serafina said, smiling as she moved toward her old friend.

Essie's face lit up. "Eh law, Miss Serafina, it's you!" she cried. "Where'd you get off to all this time, girl? It's been so long! I'm so glad you're all right! Your poor old pa is going to weep buckets when he sees you!"

Braeden quickly led them all up to the South Tower Room. It was a large, elegant, oval bedroom with an elaborate crown-canopied bed, hand-carved ivory-white molding running along the arc of its curved walls, and a domed ceiling.

As Waysa set Rowena gently down on the bed, Serafina noticed that Essie was staring at him intently. When the catamount boy stepped away from Rowena, Essie's eyes followed him. It was like she had never seen anything like him—neither inside the hallowed walls of Biltmore or out in the wider world—and what she saw now fascinated her.

When Waysa lifted his brown eyes and looked at Essie, she said, "Oh lord, pardon me," and turned aside, her face red. "I'll fetch some warm water and towels right away," she said as she hurried out of the room.

Braeden sat on the edge of the bed beside Rowena, attending

to her the best he could as he tried to examine her wounds. Her head was bleeding and there was a scrape on her shoulder, but there were no gaping cuts or obviously broken bones.

"She's been unconscious since Uriah threw her against the rock, but otherwise, she doesn't seem to be too badly hurt," Braeden said.

When Essie returned with the supplies, Braeden dipped one of the towels in the basin and then wiped Rowena's head and face thoroughly with the wet cloth, trying to clear some of the blood away.

Serafina gazed at Rowena lying unconscious in the bed. Through all the riddles and sharp talk, in the end, Rowena had been true to her word: the sorceress had brought her back into the living world. And Rowena had betrayed her father. But what struck Serafina most was the memory of Rowena leaping into the path of the fireball to save Braeden's life. There seemed to be far more to Rowena than Serafina had realized.

The passing of time and Braeden's attentions with the damp cloth seemed to have an effect on Rowena. She stirred with a groan, and then appeared as if she was slowly coming to. Finally, she opened her eyes and looked around at the four people staring at her.

"What happened?" she asked. "Did the plan work? Is he dead?"

We failed, Serafina thought as she sat in the South Tower Room with the others. *We failed to defeat Uriah.* They had developed a plan, gathered all their allies, and attacked in force, but they had still failed.

Serafina looked around at her three companions.

Rowena, battered and disoriented, rose from her bed and began to pace back and forth, rubbing her face anxiously, worried that her father was still alive.

Waysa went over to one of the room's three sunlit bays, pulled aside the elegant curtains, and opened the window to the outside. He stood looking out across the forested valley of the great river to the misty blue mountains of the southern range. In the distance, toward the rising peak of Mount Pisgah, the dark shapes of storm clouds gathered on the horizon. Serafina thought that he must be keeping a watchful eye for their enemy, but ever since their arrival at Biltmore that morning, Waysa had been restless. As a catamount who had lived all his life with his family in the forest, he wasn't used to being indoors. He didn't trust the smooth, flat ground or the closed-in walls in these unnaturally quiet caves, this place without tree or fern, without the sound of birds or insects, without the feel of the wind in his hair, and he hated not being able to see the sun or moon.

For her part, Serafina was happy to take advantage of the shelter of the room. When Essie brought in a tray of food for them and set it on the fine mahogany table in the sitting area in the center of the room, Serafina gobbled it down with the others.

"Essie, this is my friend," Serafina said. "His name is Waysa."

As Waysa turned and stepped toward her, Essie said, "Howdayado," and curtsied nervously.

"It's very good to meet you, Miss," Waysa said, clearly trying to sound as kind as possible.

"I'm so happy to see you, Essie," Serafina said smiling and hugging her. "I looked for you earlier. Why weren't you in your room on the fourth floor?"

"I've been promoted!" Essie said, filled with pride, but then she quickly remembered everyone else. "I'll tell you all about it, but I'll let y'all talk first."

"Thank you for everything, Essie," Braeden said, as Essie left the room. He, too, seemed relieved to be back in the comfortable routine and relative safety of Biltmore's sunlit rooms.

But they all knew they couldn't truly rest here.

"So, now what are we going to do?" Braeden asked, looking around at the others.

"We have to go back out there," Waysa urged.

When Braeden lowered his head, Serafina knew that he was thinking about his horse and the wolves and his other friends who had died in the battle during the night.

Seeing Braeden's sadness, Waysa said, "I don't wish to fight, but none of us—including our allies in the forest—are safe until we destroy him."

Serafina glanced over at Rowena, who had stopped pacing and was looking at them now, her face clouded with fear and uncertainty. She glanced at the door and then the windows as if she thought her father was going to crash into the room at any moment.

Serafina tried to think about what they should do. She knew that if she stood up right now and called for an immediate attack against Uriah that they would probably join her, and she wanted to do just that, she wanted to fight, but deep down, she knew it would be a mistake.

Finally, she turned to the sorceress.

"What about you, Rowena?" she asked gently. "What do you want to do?"

Rowena shook her head, clenching her jaw, but did not reply.

"Tell me what you're thinking," Serafina urged her.

"It doesn't matter what I'm thinking," Rowena said.

"But I can see you're gnawing on something . . ."

Rowena shook her head again, annoyed that Serafina was pressing her. But then she began to speak.

"I didn't know my father for the first thirteen years of my life," she said. "When I was four or five years old, my mother used to tell me stories about him, that he was traveling in other countries searching for the ancient lore, but I didn't understand what her words truly meant, and she died before I was old enough to ask."

"So you were born with . . ." Serafina began to say.

"I sensed there was something inside me, but I didn't know what it was or how to control it," Rowena said. "All I knew was that I was different from others, that I could do things. When my mother died, the authorities put me into an orphanage, but the adults there couldn't raise me any more than a fly can raise a wasp."

As Rowena spoke, the others listened in silence.

"Years later, my father came to the orphanage and retrieved me. I didn't know him, but I thought that everything I had endured up to that point in my life had been the darkness, the twisting, painful birth of what I was, and that now, with my new father, my life would truly begin."

"Is that when you came to America?" Serafina asked.

"Not at first. First, he trained me how to use the powers within me that had been such a mystery to me all my life. Then he brought me here, back to these mountains where he was born. He'd come to fight his old enemy, and he set me on a path. I followed it gladly. I was appreciative of the chance to help him, hungry for his attention and approval. I wanted to become everything he wanted me to be."

Rowena hesitated, seemingly lost in the shadows of her own

story for a moment, but then she continued, her voice ragged with her determination not to falter. "Trapping animals in cages, killing a man with snakes, hurling a dog from a staircase, throwing a boy from his horse, dragging him over the stones, striking him with wounds, fighting, always fighting, and the blood on the Loggia . . ." Her words dwindled into nothingness and she looked down at the floor. And then, after a long pause, she lifted her eyes to them and said, "What do you do when you realize you are the monster in your own story?"

For a moment, they were all still. And then Serafina answered, "You rewrite the story."

Rowena looked at her sharply, almost malevolently. "The past cannot be changed."

"But the future can," Serafina shot back.

"It doesn't matter now," Rowena said, turning away from her.

Just as Serafina was about to argue that it *does* matter, she realized that Rowena didn't actually believe the words she had just said. It wasn't a trick or a lie, but a shield, and Serafina had heard these words before. *It doesn't matter now,* Rowena had said when they first spoke at her lair, *just the ramblings of a troubled soul, nothing of consequence.*

Serafina looked up at Rowena. "It *was* you. You came to my grave to speak to me about all this . . . The voice I heard . . . You were the one who woke me . . ."

Rowena did not turn, did not look at her. For a moment it seemed as if she was going to walk out the door and never come back.

But then Braeden stepped toward Rowena and touched her

arm. It was like he had cast a spell on her and she could not move. "What do you mean it doesn't matter?" he asked. "Of course it matters. What are you saying, Rowena? You're going to stay with us, aren't you?"

And that caught her. Rowena slowly turned and looked at him.

Serafina could see in Rowena's eyes an awareness of all the suffering she had caused. *A troubled soul, nothing of consequence,* she had said of herself. Somehow Rowena had found a path through it all. But Serafina could see a deep hopelessness in Rowena now, as if the sorceress knew there was no way to make things right, no way to protect Braeden or herself or any of them from her father, that feelings didn't matter, it was all going to end in the same way no matter what she did.

Serafina moved toward her. "You *change*, Rowena," she said firmly. "If you don't like the way you are, you make yourself different. That's what you've done. That's what you've been doing. You've been hiding from your father, finding a new way. I know you're discouraged and scared. We all are. But you *can* rewrite the story. You determine what needs to be done and you do it, whatever it is, no matter how difficult it seems. There's no choice here. You do what's right."

"No," Rowena snarled at her. "That's exactly my point, cat. There *is* a choice. You have a choice between right and wrong at every step you take . . . There's always a choice."

"And you've made your choice, and you're going to keep making it," Serafina said, refusing to back down. "You've chosen to fight with us."

"Yes, I made my choice," Rowena said, her voice strained. "And now we have a war. We surprised my father up there on the mountain. We wounded him. But he'll come back for us now, hunt us, because vengeance, more than anything else, is what drives him. He shifts, he adapts, that's what he does—he's a snake that sheds its skin—but I'm warning you: my father is going to come for us for what we did last night. And he will kill us all. Starting with me."

Waysa stepped toward her. "You are one of us now, Rowena. We'll all fight this together. We're going to stop him before he can hurt you or any of us."

Braeden listened to Waysa, and then looked at Serafina and Rowena. "But we've already fought him and struck him down repeatedly, and he keeps coming back. We threw everything we had at him last night, and lost many good friends, and he still defeated us. How are we going to kill an enemy who can't be killed?"

The room went quiet.

No one had an answer. The young sorceress didn't storm from the room, but she didn't speak, either. She seemed even more distressed by their failure to defeat her father than the rest of them.

When Rowena noticed that Serafina was looking at her, the sorceress turned toward her and said, "Mark my words, he's going to come after us."

50

Rowena's words echoed in Serafina's mind. She was sure
she was right. But Serafina had no solution to the problem, no
attack or defense, and neither did her companions. None of
them knew what to do.

While the others got cleaned up, found some more food in
the kitchen, and rested after the long, difficult night, Serafina
went downstairs to the workshop to see her pa. She found him
cooking up some breakfast in the black iron skillet.

"That was a jenny-wallop of a storm last night," he said,
as she walked in. "Me and the rest of the crew were workin'
most the night, repairin' what damage we could. Where'd you
hunker down?"

"Didn't get much sleep," she said, sitting down at the little
table where they ate their meals.

"Everything all right?" he asked, concerned. "You're lookin' a little worse for wear."

"I'm all right," she said.

"But I can see your gears are a-turnin'," he said as he put a plate of food in front of her.

"I just have a question, is all," she said, picking up and chewing on a piece of ham. "Somethin' I need your help with."

"Put me on the scent of it and I'll be off on the bay," he said, using his favorite expression about barking coon dogs to say he was happy to help if she told him what it was about.

"What do you do when you're working on a machine, or some other kind of problem, and you just can't fix it? It just seems impossible," she asked.

Her pa looked at her. She was pretty sure that he could see that it was something important to her.

"When I'm faced with what seems like an unsolvable problem," he said, "I do all that I can do, and when that's not enough, I stop, and I step back. I study it real careful-like, look at it from different angles, try to think about it in ways that I never thought of before, and maybe nobody else has either."

"And does it work?"

"Sometimes. But the main of it is that the most important tool in your toolbox isn't the screwdriver or the wrench. It's your imagination."

Serafina was listening to her pa's words, but he must have seen the quizzical expression on her face.

"Let's try it," he said. "Give me a 'for instance.'"

"Pa?"

"Put me in a fix and let's see how I get out of it."

"All right," she said. "Let's say you want to hammer a nail into a board. You line up the nail, you hold it with your fingers, and you hit the nail on the head with your hammer repeatedly. It goes in a little bit, just enough to stick, but it doesn't go in all the way. You strike the nail with your hammer again and again as hard as you can, and still it doesn't go in. You even get three of your friends to help you, but no matter what you do, no matter how hard you pound, the nail won't go in. So what do you do?"

"I set down the hammer," he said.

She smiled, thinking he was joking, telling her that he'd just give up, but then she realized he wasn't playing. He meant it.

"I set down the hammer," he said again. "I'd take a step back, you see, figure out what I'm truly tryin' to do, and figure out a mend that doesn't involve a hammer. Or maybe even a nail."

Serafina gazed at her pa and tried to reckon his words. She wasn't certain, but she thought she maybe understood.

As they finished their breakfast and washed up the plates, her pa said, "I gonna be fixin' one of the jammed-up coal chutes. It's been leakin' storm water somethin' awful down into the basement every time it rains. I don't know what the rest of the day holds, but I'll be around." Then he looked at her, his eyes steady on her. "What about you?"

"I'll find you," she said, and that was what he needed to hear to know that she'd do her best to keep herself safe, and that he'd see her soon.

Reluctant to separate, the two of them embraced, held each other for several seconds, and then said good-bye.

"I'm glad you're home, Sera," he said softly.

"Me too, Pa," she said in return. "Thanks for the help."

"You stay dry, now," he said.

As she went back upstairs to find Braeden and the others, her mind was filled with thoughts of her pa and what was ahead of her.

She knew Uriah was coming for her and her friends. She knew they had to defeat him. But how? The same question kept rattling around her head: How do you destroy an enemy who can't be destroyed?

She knew she had to stay bold no matter what, but the problem before her seemed impossible. She wasn't strong enough to fight Uriah, and neither were her friends.

But then, deep in the most shadowed recesses of her mind, something began to lurk. The faint movement of an unseen shape. The shaded trace of an idea. It was a dark path, fraught with dangers that could lead to the deaths of her and her friends, and ultimately the destruction of Biltmore.

In many ways, the idea seemed to make no sense at all.

And therein lay its beauty.

Set down the hammer, she thought.

Serafina and Braeden walked together toward the Conservatory, the greenhouse with its tall, arched windows and its slanted glass rooftops shining in the morning sun. Many of the glass panes had been broken by the night's storm, but the brick structure was still standing.

As they entered the thick heat and steaming moisture of the building, the sun filtered down through the palms, ferns, and bromeliads that grew all around them and up over their heads, shading them in a junglelike canopy.

Serafina and Braeden quickly made their way through the plants of the central palm house to join Rowena and Waysa in the orchid room, where they met in the shroud of hundreds of delicate blooms.

They all knew they were there to figure out their next move against Uriah, but Rowena repeated the challenge that they had already faced many times: "How are we going to kill an enemy who can't be killed?"

"I think the trick is that we don't," Serafina said.

They looked at her in confusion.

"We can only hide for so long before he comes for us," Waysa warned.

"I don't think that's what she has in mind," Rowena said as she studied Serafina.

"We can't hunt Uriah down and fight him with tooth and claw," Serafina explained. "We can't beat him in a battle. And even if we do, he won't stay dead."

"But we have no choice," Waysa said.

"I think there may be another way," Serafina said slowly. She looked at Braeden. "In the angel's glade, the night you freed my spirit, I gave you something to keep safe . . ."

"The silver clasp," Braeden said.

"Do you still have it?" Serafina asked.

"I asked a hellbender in the marsh to hide it in the mud where no one could find it."

"Oh dear," Rowena said, shaking her head. "My father's going to be looking for that."

But Serafina smiled. It was perfect. The hellbender was a gigantic, two-foot-long, atrociously ugly brown salamander. The mountain folk called it a grampus, a snot otter, or a mud-devil. If there was anything that could hide the silver clasp, it was the hellbender.

"But what are you thinking about, Serafina?" Waysa asked.

Serafina turned to the sorceress. "It depends on Rowena."

"Do tell," Rowena said.

"If Braeden can retrieve the silver clasp," Serafina asked, "can you use it?"

"Use it to do what?" Braeden asked in alarm.

But Serafina kept her eyes on the sorceress. "Can you do it, Rowena?"

Rowena stared back at her in disbelief. "Well, you little rat catcher . . ." she whispered, her voice filled with the devilish conspiracy of it.

"What?" Braeden asked. "What's going on?"

"You want to remake it . . ." Rowena said.

"Remake what?" Braeden asked, his voice strained with apprehension.

"The Black Cloak," Serafina said.

"I knew it!" Braeden said. "No, Serafina, not that! We just got rid of that infernal thing! We don't want it back again!"

Serafina expected Braeden's reaction, but she fixed her eyes on Rowena. "Can you do it? Can you use the silver clasp to restore the Black Cloak to its full power?"

Rowena held her gaze, as if gauging the depth of her conviction, but she did not speak.

"Serafina, what are you doing?" Waysa said, grabbing her arm. "We don't want to do this."

Serafina looked at him. "Waysa, think about it. The cycle of injury and rebirth, of struggle and rising, it must apply to the cloak as well . . . I destroyed the cloak once and it came back. That means it can come back again."

"The silver clasp is the heart of the cloak's darkness," Rowena said. "The cloth is but its skin."

"But can you do it?" Serafina asked her again, more forcefully this time.

Rowena looked at her. "We would need the wool of black goats, the sheddings of black rat snakes, the entrapping mucilage of pitcher plants, the skin of timber rattlesnakes, and the silk of black widow spiders."

Serafina swallowed. The list got worse as it went. "We should be able to find the goats and maybe the snakes . . ." she said, trying to think it through.

"But we need satin fabric made from the silk of black widow spiders," Rowena said.

"I can't believe you two are even talking about this," Braeden said. "It's way too dangerous to bring the Black Cloak back! What if it falls into the wrong hands?"

"Uriah's hands," Waysa said. "I agree with Braeden. It's far too dangerous."

"And it's also impossible," Rowena said firmly. "I was able to use spider silk thread to sew the areas of the cloak that had been torn, but only my father knows the spells that will force the black widow spiders to weave entirely new fabric."

Serafina's eyes widened in surprise. "Are you saying that the spiders don't just provide the silk for the thread, they actually weave the material?"

Rowena nodded. "The spiders weave the fabric, one spider's thread over the other, like a very tight web. I know the binding spells and the other spells we need, but only my father knows the spells to make the fabric itself."

"Then we're stopped before we've started," Waysa said. "We have no choice but to gather our allies, track Uriah down, and strike with everything we've got."

"We've already hammered that nail and it's not going in," Serafina said, bringing looks of bewilderment from her friends. She turned again to Rowena. "There has to be a way, Rowena."

Rowena shook her head. "There's no way for me to force the spiders to make the cloth we need."

Braeden looked around at his friends in obvious disbelief, incredulous that they would even be thinking about this dire course of action.

"This is a horrible idea," he said.

Serafina knew that he had far too much experience with the Black Cloak to want to bring it back into the world. But as they were talking, she saw Braeden's expression change, and he turned away from them.

"Braeden . . ." Serafina said.

"Is it wrong to use an evil weapon to fight against evil?" he asked, without turning toward them.

Serafina watched him in silence, unsure of where this path was leading him.

"Is this what it has come to?" he asked as he stared at the ground. She thought he was talking about the situation they were in, but then she began to understand.

ROBERT BEATTY

This was his talent. This was his *love*. Through the bond of friendship, he could commune with animals, speak with them. But just how far could he go? And even if he could, was it the right thing to do? Was it right to create a terrible weapon if it was meant to be used to fight evil? Or was the weapon itself too terrible a thing to bring into the world?

Finally, after a long time, Braeden slowly turned and looked around at the others.

"These black widow spiders you're talking about . . ." he said. "Has anyone actually tried *asking* them to make the silk fabric we need?"

Rowena stared at Braeden and then looked back at Serafina. "If Braeden can persuade the spiders to willingly weave the warp and weft of the black fabric, then it will create a much tighter intertwinement than a coercion spell. That means the Black Cloak will be far more powerful than it was before."

"More powerful?" Braeden said in dismay. "It was bad enough before!"

"We're going to need that power . . ." Serafina said.

"But hold on," Waysa said. "Even if we can remake the Black Cloak, how does that solve our problem? What are we going to do with it?"

Over the next few days and nights, the four companions worked and watched, knowing that Death was coming. A stolen breath, a crushing blow, a ball of fire, Death was surely coming.

All across the grounds, large crews of men worked to protect and repair the storm-damaged roads, bridges, house, and gardens, even when the rain poured down.

Each night, Serafina prowled the grounds with Waysa in feline form, patrolling the estate's boundaries, running together through the forest darkness, their eyes scanning every shadow and their ears prickling to every sound. She knew that their only hope was to be ready.

Serafina loved running through the night. Waysa was fast

and strong, always knowing the way. They often ran side by side, challenging each other to greater speed. Other times they hunkered down near a stream or at the edge of a rocky ledge and just listened to the night forest. When they were in their catamount forms, they were together in body and soul.

But she had learned from hunting rats that she should not follow the same pattern every night, lest her quarry learn to avoid her. So on the third night, as they walked outside for their nightly run, she said, "You follow our normal path tonight. But I'll go a different way, and we'll meet back here."

Waysa was reluctant to separate, but he nodded, understanding the reason. "Remember that we're only patrolling. If you see Uriah, do not approach him on your own. Run like the wind."

"I will," Serafina agreed.

Shifting into her panther form, she went out into the night. She traveled southward at speed, through Biltmore's mud-damaged gardens, past the flooded bass pond, then down along the swollen creek. The area that had once been a small and secluded lagoon where the swans flew was now a large, flooded lake. Whole hills had disappeared. It was frightening how much the landscape had changed and was still changing.

From there she crept through the forest to the flood-breached shore of the mighty French Broad River. She stopped and gazed across the water, looking for any sign of their enemy.

She followed the river northward, wary of mists and shadows and creaks in the night.

Near midnight, she went up into the low, flat ground in

the bend of the great river, into Biltmore's vast farm fields. The fields were flooded. She crossed through acre after acre of ruined corn, potatoes, spinach, and dozens of other crops. She skulked quietly through the darkness past where Biltmore's barns should have been. The rushing water had torn the barns into twisted heaps of broken lumber and washed them away. The farmers had moved the animals to the highest reachable ground, but many were still in danger. The herds of tan Jersey milk cows that Mr. Vanderbilt had imported from England were standing in their pastures in a foot of water. The black Angus cows were huddled together in groups on the mud-wrecked hills that rose like small islands out of the lake that had once been their pasture. The chickens, sheep, and goats were stranded on small strips of rocky ground. But for all the disruption, the animals of the farm were quiet tonight, just a soft rustle of movement in the distance, as if they knew there were more dangers to come.

It made her sad to see Biltmore's once proud and productive farms brought to these conditions. The farms had always been such an important part of life at Biltmore. Mr. Vanderbilt had told her that his vision wasn't just to build a pretty house, but to create a self-sustaining estate that provided its own food for the family, the guests, the staff, and the workers and their families. In a time when the rest of the country was moving into cities, building great factories, and steaming quickly through their lives on black machines, Biltmore was meant to be a community all unto itself, a quiet, pastoral place where people lived close to the earth.

Mr. Vanderbilt had been so successful in his goal that he began donating hundreds of gallons of milk to the hospital, orphanage, and other establishments in Asheville. Biltmore's milk, butter, and cream became famous for its rich taste and high quality. And a new business was born.

Soon, hundreds of horse-drawn wagons emblazoned with "Biltmore Farms" were delivering fresh milk in glass bottles to doorsteps throughout the region. Serafina had sometimes seen the milk wagons trundling down the road in the early mornings.

But now the milk wagons were toppled over and broken to pieces by the storm, and the roads flowed like rivers.

Leaving the farms behind her, she came to where the Swannanoa River met with the French Broad, but instead of one river flowing into another, there was a flooded lake for as far as she could see.

As she traveled eastward, skirting the edge of the lake, she came to Biltmore Village, where years before Mr. Vanderbilt had created a small community for Biltmore's artisans, crafts-men, and other workers. There were many shops and cottages in the village, a school, a train depot, and a beautiful parish church, which Mr. Vanderbilt had named All Souls Church because he wanted folk of all walks of life to join him and his family in worship each Sunday. The village streets were lined with lovely trees, wrought-iron streetlamps, and fine brick side-walks for its citizens, but tonight, she could see that the village had been ravaged by the recent storms. Most of the cottages had been flooded or outright destroyed. Many of the trees had been toppled to the ground, their great trunks and branches lying across the streets. The once smooth brick sidewalks were wrinkled and broken with strange, snakelike patterns, as if the tree roots beneath had coiled and twisted.

Still in panther form, Serafina prowled through the darkened and abandoned streets of the village. Instead of joyous neighbors out and about enjoying the summer evening, or houses lit up with family warmth, the streets were empty and the houses dark. Slips of whispery ghost fog drifted through the village. Just out of town, she came upon a massive black iron beast half-buried under the wet shifting earth. She stared at the hissing hunk of iron with her panther eyes for several seconds until she finally understood what it was: a train locomotive, knocked on its side, the coals still burning in its belly, half-buried in mud. She could not tell if the train's engineer had managed to escape the iron wreckage or not.

Feeling far more disturbed than she expected by the sight of it all, Serafina turned and started heading southward again, back toward home. She was more sure than ever that somehow she had to stop Uriah. What had started out as a blood feud against Mr. Vanderbilt and his estate years before had become a war not just against her and her companions, but against *everything*. Uriah wanted to destroy it all, and if she didn't fight him, he would soon succeed.

She dove back into the forest again and traveled over the hill and dale of the land back toward the house. Finally, she passed through the house's main gates, coming upon the mansion much like the line of carriages had a few nights before. But tonight was a very different kind of night, still and quiet.

As she looked upon the house, it was dark—not a single lantern, Edison light, or candle was lit. For the first time in her entire life, the house actually looked abandoned.

As she walked toward the house in panther form, she marveled at how quickly its spirit could change, how it could be the brightest, most vibrant and dazzling display of grandiosity one had ever seen, then fall into a dark and moody slumber.

She and her companions had been locking all the doors of the house each night, so she slipped inside using one of her old secret ways through the air shaft in the foundation, then went upstairs.

Waysa had not yet returned. Braeden, her pa, Rowena, and the servants were all asleep. The main floor of the house was empty, dark, and quiet.

For a little while, she took the opportunity to walk the deserted halls of Biltmore in the form of a black panther, her long black body slipping through the shadows, her tail dangling behind her, her bright yellow eyes scanning the darkness. It was a delicious feeling to finally be home in the form she was always meant to be. She remembered creeping through these darkened corridors at night as an eight-year-old girl, wondering why everyone had gone to bed. Back then, her bare feet had made a soft, almost undetectable noise as she walked, but tonight her furred paws were utterly silent on the smooth, shining floors. She had prowled these halls all her life, but never quite like this. It amused her to imagine one of the servants getting up in the middle of the night to use the water closet and coming face-to-face with a black panther.

Shifting back into human form, she continued walking from room to room, watching and listening. She was a twelve-year-old girl and the Guardian of Biltmore.

As she stood in the darkness of the unlit Entrance Hall, the main room in the center of the house, she heard movement down toward the Library.

She walked slowly down the length of the Tapestry Gallery, listening and scanning the shadows ahead, the moonlight falling through the windows casting white slanting rectangles across the floor. The colors in the tapestries that covered the wall and the intricately painted beams on the ceiling seemed to glow in the light.

Then she heard the sound again. Something touching the glass windows. The shuffle of footsteps. Voices. It sounded as if someone outside was trying to get into the Library.

Serafina crouched down, her heart beating heavy in her chest. Her lungs pulled in slow, full breaths, readying her for whatever was about to happen.

She crept forward, using the fine chairs and other furniture in the Tapestry Gallery for cover, but always looking ahead through the archway that led into the darkened Library.

She heard a click and then the movement of a hinge.

Her fingers clung to the top of a settee as she peeked over its edge and watched the French doors. One of the doors swung slowly open into the Library.

Serafina felt the hair on the back of her neck rising.

She spotted a dark hooded figure slipping into the room.

She knew she shouldn't be scared. She was the Guardian of

Biltmore! She had been expecting this! But it didn't matter. She was terrified.

Her heart pounded now. Her chest tightened something fierce, her lungs started pumping, wanting more air, and the muscles in her arms and legs bunched for action.

The dark figure coming into the house pulled back its hood and looked quickly around the room to make sure it was empty. It was Rowena. Her hair lay in a jumble around her shoulders in an unusually unkempt fashion. Her face was smudged with soot and slime. Her eyes scanned the darkness. Serafina could see that it was the sorceress, so she knew she shouldn't be frightened, but she was. Every pore of her body was slowly filling with dread. Rowena looked so different from the last time they had spoken. Everything about her reminded Serafina not of the ally she'd been working with over the last few days, but the dark and mysterious druid girl she'd seen by the river, the young sorceress of the forest, the caster of spider spells, and the speaker to the dead. Serafina knew she should trust her new friend, knew that they had come up with the plan together, but she couldn't stop thinking that everything about the girl she was seeing now oozed a dark and wicked treachery.

Rowena whispered something to someone just outside the door. The sorceress wasn't alone.

Just stay steady, Serafina told herself. *Just stay very still.* But her heart was pounding so hard that it felt like it was going to give her away.

Rowena whispered again, bringing the person with her slowly into the house.

As she watched it, Serafina couldn't believe that it was actually happening. Her hands balled into tight, shaking fists.

She smelled the rotting, earthy stench of the creature first, and then heard the *tick-tick-tick*ing sound of its gnashing teeth. Then she saw the long, dark, ragged coat, and the clawed hands protruding from the tattered sleeves. The mangled, bleeding face came into the room with glowing silver eyes. Serafina's body flooded with cold fear. It was him! It was Uriah, coming right into the house!

"Come this way, Father," Rowena whispered. "They're all asleep . . ."

53

Serafina watched from behind the settee as Uriah looked slowly around the Library of Biltmore Estate, gazing up and around at all the books and fine furnishings—the secret inner sanctuary of his despised enemy.

Before Uriah had become the bent and hissing creature he was now, he had been the bearded man of the forest, a shrouded hermit whom day folk seldom saw. He had gathered his curses into sap-fueled cauldron fires up in the barren pinelands, but avoided face-to-face battles with his enemies. He never endangered himself. He was like a sniveling rat, a stinking polecat that stays hidden in the darkest depths of the forest. To attack his enemy, he would cast his spells from afar and send his demons into Biltmore to do his bidding. But this night, he had come.

He was entering the very place he most wanted to destroy.

As Rowena led her father quietly into the darkened house, Uriah spoke in his low, gravelly voice. "Have you done everything we talked about?"

"Everything and more, Father," Rowena said in an excited whisper. "It's even better than we hoped."

"Tell me," Uriah rasped.

"You were exactly right. The cat and the boy had the silver clasp all along. But more than that, I now know that the boy can control the spiders."

"What?" Uriah said harshly as he turned angrily toward his daughter in surprise and grabbed her by the throat. "You taught him how to cast the weaving spell?"

"No, no," she gasped, clutching at his scaly hands, tightened around her neck. "Father, listen to me. I swear I didn't! The boy doesn't use spells. He has the power to befriend the creatures of the forest."

"Like he did with the hawks and the wolves . . ." Uriah rasped as he released his daughter's neck.

Still in human form, Serafina watched in amazement as Uriah and Rowena spoke. She knew that Uriah could cast powerful spells and that the Twisted Staff he had created had allowed him to control animals by force at close range, but he seemed to envy Braeden's natural power. He and his daughter had once enslaved many of the forest's creatures, but even he couldn't claim the true and constant alliance of the wolves, the elk, and the other animals.

"Who's inside the house now?" Uriah asked. "Where is the usurper and his woman?"

"The Vanderbilts have gone, Father," she said. "Your storms have pushed them out."

"What about the Black One and the other catamount?"

"They're out patrolling the grounds, but I know the path they take. I waited until they were on the other side of the estate, miles away, before I brought you in."

"So, it is just the boy," Uriah said greedily. "We'll leave his bloody dead body on the floor for the usurpers to find when they return."

"We need to make them suffer, Father," Rowena hissed, "for all that they have done to us."

"And do these others trust you?" Uriah asked.

"They're fools, Father," the young sorceress said. "Even the cat trusts me this time. I pretended like I was conflicted about right and wrong, like I didn't know which path to follow, and then when I told them the secret of the black widow spiders, that clinched it."

"What about the cloak?"

"The boy and I have been working on it day and night," Rowena said. "The boy and his spiders have made the fabric, and I have used the spells you taught me to bind the darkness and suck in souls. But I must tell you, Father, the cloak is far more powerful than anything we've made before."

"More powerful?" he asked, his eyes widening. Serafina could hear the envy seething in his voice. "Where is the cloak now?"

"It's here in the house, Father, but they've locked it away. I can't get to it on my own. I need your help."

Uriah nodded, very pleased. "We'll take the cloak first and then we'll kill the boy."

"This way," Rowena whispered, leading him out of the Library and into the Tapestry Gallery.

As they walked, Uriah put his hand on his daughter's shoulder, a glint of pride contorting his nasty face. He looked as if he was more than pleased with his daughter's talent for treachery, her ruthless and conniving ability to change herself into whatever he needed her to be. Good or evil, dark-haired or fair, human or animal, she was the consummate shifter. His other demons and devices had been flawed, but his apprentice daughter! She was his most perfect creation.

Serafina ducked down into the darkest shadow she could find as Uriah and Rowena walked past her, his earthen stench wafting toward her like the odorous, twisting branches of a diseased and rotting tree.

Suddenly, Uriah stopped in midstride and looked around him.

Serafina froze, her heart pounding.

"What is it, Father?" Rowena whispered.

"Stay quiet," Uriah ordered her, as he listened into the darkness.

Serafina watched from her hiding spot behind the settee as he slowly turned his head and his silver eyes scanned each and every shadow in the long moonlit gallery.

She wanted to flee, right then, just get up and run like the dickens, but she knew she mustn't move or make a sound. She stayed exactly where she was, watching from the shadows of the room.

Uriah tilted his head and sniffed the air, like a predator picking up the scent of its prey.

A pain filled Serafina's chest. Her lungs wanted to breathe, to gasp in rapid gulps of air, but she could not let them, for a hurried breath would kill her now.

Stay very still, she told herself.

She pulled back just a little farther into the darkness, trying to settle her thumping heart and her buzzing legs so that he could not feel her there.

He sniffed the air again.

"She's here . . ." he rasped in a low, hissing whisper.

"Who's here?" Rowena asked.

"The Black One . . ." he said.

"Where?" Rowena asked, looking around them.

"She's here, in this house right now . . ." he whispered. He began moving with a slow and creeping deliberateness among the low tables and soft chairs where she was hiding, his scaly clawed hands raised and crooked like a praying mantis.

"She's in this very room . . ." he rasped.

He began to search behind each piece of furniture, dragging it aside, then going to the next.

He was coming her way.

"THERE!" he screamed, pointing to her.

Serafina broke cover and tried to run.

54

Serafina burst away and sprinted down the length of the gallery, running as fast as she could. Uriah rushed toward her with terrifying speed. The air around her concussed with shaking force. All she could hear behind her was the pushing of the furniture as he shoved it aside and the violent clicking of his gnashing teeth.

As she turned the corner out of the room and dashed across the main hall, she felt a blast of burning air fly past her. The glass on the old grandfather clock cracked, and the wood sides caught on fire.

She ducked down the corridor and darted across the Salon, jumping a chaise lounge as Uriah came barreling around the corner and threw a spell that smashed through the room, toppling everything in its path, and crashed through the far windows with an explosion of glass.

Her chest heaved in rapid breaths as she ran. Her arms pumped. Her legs buzzed with speed. She wanted to change into panther form so bad, but the time had not yet come.

Behind her, she heard the ferocious, attacking growl of Waysa tearing into the room. She glanced back just in time to see the fanged catamount leap upon Uriah's back, biting him and clawing him, pulling at him.

Waysa slowed Uriah down just enough to let Serafina get ahead. But then Uriah slammed Waysa's body into a stone pillar and the catamount collapsed to the floor.

Serafina's heart wrenched when she saw Waysa go down, but she knew he had done what he'd come for, and now the rest was up to her.

She raced away as fast as she could in the moments Waysa had given her. As she scurried through the Breakfast Room, the creature came right behind her, throwing a fireball that lit up the room with blazing orange light and set the leather wallpaper on fire.

There was less than a second between life and death.

Finally, she darted through the door that led into the Banquet Hall.

She'd made it!

She was exactly where she needed to be at exactly the right moment.

As she turned the corner out of sight and ran past the room's three giant fireplaces, she shifted into panther form. She leapt straight up the far wall, clung to the priceless Flemish tapestry with her claws, climbed it with tearing speed, and sprang through the air toward the window, which Braeden had opened for her just moments before.

But the window was far too small for a panther, so she shifted into human form in midair and landed on the windowsill. Unlike normal windows, these small, seldom-noticed windows at the top of the Banquet Hall didn't go *outside*, but to a back corridor of an upper floor high above.

"Here it is," Braeden said, handing her the coiling, hissing Black Cloak, just like they had planned. "Go!"

Grabbing the cloak, she sprinted down the length of the upper corridor, looping back behind where she expected Uriah to be, and came to a second window that looked down into the Banquet Hall. It was similar to the window she'd leapt *into*, but there was a reason she'd chosen this spot in the house.

Rowena had lured Uriah into Biltmore just as they had planned. Waysa had attacked him at just the right moment to slow him down. Braeden had been ready with the cloak right where they had agreed. And now Serafina was positioned directly over the door that Uriah was coming through as he entered the Banquet Hall in search of her.

Seeing Uriah below her, Serafina leapt.

As she fell through the air she stretched out the Black Cloak in her arms, coming down on Uriah like a giant black bat. But as she came down, she realized her timing was off and she was going to miss him. If she'd been in her panther form she could have used the twist of her tail to change the angle of her attack in midair, but she needed to be in her human form to hold the cloak. And now she was going to fall uselessly to the floor behind him. But in the moment of her fall, she used her new powers to shift the air around her with a violent push, and for a split second she wasn't just controlling the movement of the air, she was the air itself. *Ashes to ashes, dust to dust,* she thought. *I am human and panther. I am body and spirit. I am all things in the darkness.*

Her timing was perfect. Just as Uriah came through the doorway, she fell directly upon him and pulled the inner folds of the open cloak over his head and shoulders.

Uriah screamed in rage.

As Serafina landed on his back, he thrashed and struggled, and then heaved himself backward, slamming her into the stone of the fireplace, but she held on to him for dear life. *I am spirit!* she thought, pushing through the crushing pain. *I am power!*

She hung on and she kept hanging on. It was like grabbing a huge, wriggling, biting rat: once you had it, you couldn't let go. You had to grip it, strangle it, do anything you had to do, but you *COULD NOT LET GO*!

She pulled and pulled the cloak, Uriah's head tossing wildly, his arms pushing, his scaly clawed hands clutching blindly around him as he screamed in outrage. He was Uriah, the sorcerer, the master of the forest, the controller of all! He was not going to let this happen!

Suddenly, he began to spin around and around, roaring with a terrible sound as a dirty swirl of darkness poured out of his mouth. He was going to rip himself free. But Serafina pulled in the power of the elements around her, drawing forth a forceful wind from the air, lifting the ashes from the fireplaces up and around them in a great whirling motion.

Their two swirling forces crashed against each other, pushing in opposite directions, each one spinning and twisting against the other until the swirling motion came to a shuddering stop. She held Uriah as still as death with nothing but the force of her will.

Then she heard it.

I'm not going to hurt you, child . . . the cloak said in its hissing, raspy voice.

The folds of the cloak slithered around Uriah like the tentacles of a hungry serpent. The cloak moved of its own accord, wrapping, twisting, accompanied by a disturbing rattling noise, like the hissing threats of a hundred rattlesnakes. Uriah's horrified face looked out at her from within the folds of the enveloping cloak. She realized then that everything had come full circle. It was just as she had once seen Clara Brahms vanish into the Black Cloak. But instead of Clara's innocent bright blue eyes looking desperately out at her for help, Uriah's eyes were consumed with hatred and streaked with all-consuming fear. Then the folds closed over him, the scream went silent, and the man disappeared, body and soul.

Serafina and the cloak fell to the floor. She quickly scurried away from it so that its greedy black folds couldn't get her.

For several seconds, the cloak vibrated violently, and a ghoulish aura glowed in a dark, shimmering haze. A horribly foul smell of rotting guts invaded Serafina's nostrils, forcing her head to jerk back. She wrinkled her nose and tried not to breathe it in.

Suddenly, the cloak clenched into a tight wrenching coil, and an explosion of magical spells burst into the room, sending fireballs and lightning bolts and explosions of ice-cold air in all directions at once. The spears and shields on the walls clattered to the floor. The panther-torn tapestry and its cousins crumpled down. The flags caught fire. The statues tumbled. The entire room filled with a thick, choking smoke.

And then it was finally done.

Serafina jumped up to her feet, still panting, still filled with fear, and she looked around the room. Uriah was gone. She had captured him in the endless void of the Black Cloak. She had finally defeated the man who could not be killed!

She pulled in a long, shaky breath and exhaled, trying not to burst into tears of relief. A pure cool pleasure poured through the cavities of her lungs and the muscles of her legs. She looked around at the devastated, ash-filled, burning room and all she could feel was joy.

"We did it!" Braeden cheered, leaning out the window above her head and pumping his fist triumphantly even as he stamped out one of the burning wall tapestries with a towel.

That was when she came to her senses enough to realize that the room was truly on fire.

She did not run. She did not panic. Her powers had been growing within her, and she felt stronger now than she ever had.

She concentrated her mind, raised her hand into a fist above her, then threw her hand down in a sudden opening motion, and shouted, "Enough!"

The entire room burst with cold air. Every speck of ashen dust hit the floor. Every flame blew out. And the room was still.

"That worked a lot better than my towel!" Braeden shouted happily from the window.

Waysa came limping into the room, bleeding, but with a grin on his face. "I told you to run like the wind, Serafina! I thought for sure he was going to get you there at the last second!"

"Not with you on his back, my friend," Serafina said happily.

Behind Waysa, Rowena was walking into the room as well. Seeing that the sorceress and her other friends were all right, Serafina smiled and then laughed, euphoric with the realization that they had all survived.

But Rowena looked warily at the Black Cloak lying in a heap on the floor of the Banquet Hall right where Serafina had left it.

"It's done now," Serafina said, trying to reassure her.

Rowena slowly lifted her eyes and looked at Serafina. When she spoke, there was no sarcasm in her tone, no aloofness or airs, no whispers or seething voice, just a flat, steady seriousness. "Now we must make certain that this cloak never sees the light of day."

"Or the darkness of night," Serafina said, nodding. "I swear to you, we will hide the cloak well. We'll make sure that your father will never threaten you or anyone at Biltmore again."

Braeden walked into the room through the butler's door that came from the back stairs.

"I wish we could destroy the terrible thing," Braeden said.

"Destroying the cloak will free its prisoner," Serafina said. "We can never destroy it. We must put it somewhere it will never be found, and lock it up forever."

"I know just the place," Braeden said.

And Serafina knew exactly where he had in mind.

When she looked back at Rowena, and saw the sorceress still staring at the Black Cloak in stunned disbelief, Serafina thought she must be thinking about her father.

"It is done," Rowena said, as if trying to convince herself.

"And what will you do now, Rowena?" Serafina asked her gently.

Rowena paused, as if she was thinking about that profound question for the very first time. And then she looked at Serafina and said, "I will *live*."

Serafina smiled a little bit at the corner of her mouth. Rowena was just beginning to realize that she had *survived*. She would go on, free, into a very different world. She would truly live.

"But don't just live," Waysa said, looking at Rowena with kind eyes. "Live *well*. Make all this worth it."

Rowena nodded, appreciating his words. "And you do the same."

Serafina gazed around at her friends, all happy and smiling, looking back at her. They had saved Biltmore. And they had saved each other.

It was hard to take it all in, but they had finally defeated Uriah, the old man of the forest, the conjurer, the bearded man, the sorcerer, the wielder of the Twisted Staff, the creator of the Black Cloak, the enemy who could not be killed.

And through all of this, Serafina thought about her pa working on his machines, and Essie bustling from room to room, and Mr. and Mrs. Vanderbilt and the coming baby, and all the daytime folk at Biltmore. She thought about the wolves, and the crows, and the other animals of the forest, and she thought: *We're finally safe now.*

Serafina carefully gathered the Black Cloak up from the floor of the Banquet Hall. The cloak writhed and twisted in her hands.

There are other paths to follow . . . the cloak hissed as it tried to coil up her arms, as if it knew what she was planning to do with it. It wasn't the prisoner within speaking to her, but the cloak itself.

Serafina wanted to drop it, get away from it, but she knew she couldn't. She held the cloak tighter and looked at Braeden. "Get the trowel and mortar."

As Braeden grabbed the equipment, she noticed that the design on the Black Cloak's silver clasp was no longer blank, but entwined with thorny, binding vines twisting around the shadows of a single face.

She and Braeden headed outside with the cloak on their own. They wanted as few people as possible to know where they were going to put it.

They made their way through the darkened gardens and down toward the pond.

With me on your shoulders, you'd have strength beyond imagining . . . you could fly . . . you could live in ways that you never dreamed of . . . the cloak hissed.

She could feel the pull of the cloak on her mind, an aching desire to give in to its hissing pleas. She wanted to put it on, to *wear* it, to *use* it. By sucking in human souls, the cloak provided the wearer the ultimate power, but she knew she must resist it.

"Here it is," Braeden said as they came to the inlet of the pond.

She and Braeden crawled through the metal chute and into the flume.

Together, we could be all-knowing, Serafina . . .

"Don't you dare use my name!" Serafina snarled. She gripped the cloak in her tightly balled fists, refusing to listen.

Braeden carried the lantern, shovel, and tools as they followed the narrow brick tunnel beneath the pond. There was no water running through the tunnel, but it was dripping wet with the sludge of the black algae that coated the walls.

Think about what you've enslaved, the cloak rasped. *It's all in your hands now . . .*

Clenching the cloak tighter, Serafina led the way, delving

ROBERT BEATTY

deeper and deeper into the tunnel, until they reached its lowest and darkest point.

"This is the spot," Braeden said.

"Hurry," Serafina said.

Just put me on, and all of Uriah's power will be yours, Serafina . . . the cloak whispered.

Serafina tried not to imagine the knowledge and power she'd attain, but she could feel her hands shaking as she held the writhing thing. She wanted so bad to put the cloak on her shoulders.

"Braeden, please hurry!" she cried.

Braeden quickly pried up the bricks with the shovel, then got down on his knees and pulled the bricks away with his hands. There was already a shallow hole where he had stored the Black Cloak before, but Serafina said, "Dig it deeper."

Braeden grabbed the shovel and went to work, digging down into the gravel another two feet.

Together, we shall know a thousand spells . . . the cloak hissed.

"Deeper," Serafina said.

Together, we shall never die . . .

"Deeper!" Serafina told Braeden.

Braeden's hands began to bleed with blisters from the oak handle of the shovel, but he did not argue or complain. He could see Serafina's shaking body, and the anguish tearing through her face, and he kept digging.

"How far?" he asked, but he did not stop.

"Six feet," Serafina said. "Six feet under."

When Braeden had finally finished digging, Serafina

337

crawled down in and shoved the Black Cloak into the bottom of the hole. She pushed the folds of the material as deep as she could make them go, then pressed them down with the palms of her hands. The cloak hissed and rattled like a snake fighting against her.

"Bury it!" Serafina snapped harshly at Braeden, her voice sounding disturbingly like to the cloak itself.

"Bury it, Braeden, bury it . . ." she hissed, the voice of the cloak coming through her.

His eyes wide with fear, Braeden hurried to push the loose gravel into the hole, handfuls at first, then using the shovel. The dirt began to fill the grave. As Serafina held the cloak down, it felt like she was drowning it. She could feel the sensation of the dirt pressing more and more around her.

"You've got to get out of there, Serafina!" Braeden shouted.

Just put me on . . . the cloak hissed.

"Keep shoveling!" she screamed, holding the cloak down beneath the dirt as it writhed in her hands. *"Bury it!"*

Finally, when the dirt was all around her, and the cloak was buried, she clambered out. Braeden heaved her up to him.

She and Braeden filled in the rest of the dirt, packed it down, and stamped on it with their feet until it was hard.

Then, back down on their hands and knees, they used the trowel to spread a thick layer of mortar over the dirt.

"More," Serafina urged. "As thick as we can make it."

When the mortar was finally down, they pushed the bricks into place. The gray mortar oozed up into the thin spaces between the bricks as they laid them.

Brick by brick, they closed the Black Cloak in.

Brick by brick, they silenced the raspy voice.

And brick by brick they buried their enemy below.

When they were finally done and the mortar had hardened, Serafina stared suspiciously at the brick floor, half expecting to see the insidious black fabric squeezing up through the mortared cracks like little creeping fingers, its voice hissing for her to put it on.

But there was no sound or movement.

They had buried the Black Cloak and Uriah once and for all.

Here the Black Cloak and its prisoner would remain beneath the pond, buried in an unmarked grave and bricked in, seething in the darkness below the darkness.

56

The following day, as Serafina walked through the forested highlands that overlooked Biltmore, she saw a figure moving slowly through the trees. It took her several seconds to realize that it was Rowena coming toward her.

The sorceress was wearing the dark robes and hood of her ancient kindred, and she was carrying a long laurel staff. She wore a twisting bronze-and-silver torc around her neck, and her red hair was tied into a thick braid that fell down into the folds of her hood.

Rowena stopped a few feet in front of Serafina. As the sorceress gazed at her, her green eyes glistened in the sunlight that came down through the forest leaves.

"Have you hidden it?" Rowena asked her.

"We have," Serafina replied, nodding.

"Good," Rowena said, relieved.

The sorceress looked down at the ground for a moment as if collecting her thoughts, then she lifted her eyes and looked at Serafina once more. "Then this is where our paths finally part."

Serafina hesitated, not sure what to say to the girl who had been her enemy and her friend.

"You've decided on what you're going to do . . ." Serafina said.

Rowena nodded. "I am going to follow Waysa's advice. I'm going to live well."

"And where are you going?"

"Once long ago these dark forests and jagged mountains were the hidden domain of a great conjurer, the old man of the forest. As I see it, somewhere out there, there's a vacancy now. And a girl to fill it. In her own way."

Serafina nodded, understanding Rowena's words.

Rowena gazed toward Biltmore visible in the distance and then looked back at Serafina. "You are the protector of that place," she said. "Protect it well, and everyone within."

Serafina nodded, knowing exactly who she meant.

"Live well, sorceress," Serafina said.

"Live well, cat," Rowena said in return.

That night, Serafina slipped out of Biltmore just as the moon was rising in the eastern sky, her four feet trundling easily, silently, along the front terrace, then down the steps, and across the grass toward the trees.

When Waysa spotted her coming, he flicked his tail and ran.

So you want to race . . . Serafina thought, and lunged into a powerful run.

She chased Waysa through the forest, tearing through the ferns, leaping over creeks, dodging between rocks, her heart filling with the joy that only motion can bring.

Waysa doubled back around behind her, crouched at the top of a boulder, and leapt upon her as she ran past. The two catamounts somersaulted in mock battle across the forest floor, then Serafina burst out of it and sprinted away, forcing Waysa to chase after her.

She loved running through the forest with Waysa, her senses alive, and her muscles blazing with power. She loved the speed of it and the rushing wind, the feel of her furred feet flying across the ground, the grace of her tail steering her quick changes in course. When she ran as a black panther, she was everything she had ever dreamed of being.

After the chase, she and Waysa came to the cliff that looked out across the great river. They stopped there at the edge, panting and happy, and gazed out across the moonlit view. The flooding was already receding, the rivers and the forest slowly returning to their natural state.

Serafina's heart skipped a beat when she spotted movement on the high ground in the distance.

She glanced at Waysa. He saw it, too.

The dark figures were far away, and she couldn't quite tell what they were. They were but shadows and a slinking, skulking movement among the rocks of the ridge. Then it became more clear.

The silhouettes of three mountain lions came up over the distant ridge, backlit by the light of the rising moon.

Serafina's heart swelled. One of the lions looked larger than the other two younger, leaner cats.

Filled with excitement, Serafina and Waysa ran toward the ridge to meet them.

The five lions came together, rubbing their heads and their shoulders against each other and purring. Her mother was strong and powerful, and the cubs had grown so much!

Serafina, her mother, and Waysa shifted into human form.

Serafina gazed at her mother's beautiful face with its high, angular cheekbones, her long, lion-colored hair, and her tearful golden-amber eyes looking back at her, and then they moved toward each other and embraced.

"Serafina . . ." her mother purred as she held her.

"Momma . . ." Serafina whispered in return, pressing herself into the warmth of her mother's chest as she wrapped her arms around her.

"When I heard you were alive, I wept with joy and came as fast as I could," her mother said.

Serafina held her mother tight. She could feel the warmth of her mother's love pouring through her body. After all their nights apart, they were finally back together again.

Suddenly, she remembered being a little girl prowling unseen through Biltmore's upstairs rooms looking into the face of every woman she saw, wondering if it was the face of her mother. And she remembered that first night in the forest she saw her mother's eyes and knew who she was. It seemed so long ago now, but the feeling, the love she felt in her heart, was the same.

Months before, when she was first united with her mother, she had learned so much from her, about the lore of the forest and the lives of the catamount. She had learned so much about what it meant to be *Serafina*. But she knew now, even with all that she'd been through since then, that there was still so much more for her to learn. She was just beginning in the world, and she needed her mother to guide her. The spirit and the body, the heart and the soul, the light and the darkness, she wanted to learn it all.

Knowing that it was all ahead of her, Serafina found a great sense of peace.

All through the night, the five cats ran, leaping and diving through the forest, down into valleys and up along the ridges. The night was their domain. Serafina had found her kindred, her family, the primordial creatures to whom she was born.

Deep in the night, they finally returned to the place they began, at the edge of the high ground that looked out across the river to the distant mountains. When Waysa shifted into human form, Serafina did as well.

There was a strange look in her friend's eyes that worried her. She could see there was something on his mind.

Serafina looked at Waysa, but he did not want to look at her. She stepped toward him and touched his arm.

Finally, he lifted his eyes.

"I need to talk to you, Serafina," he said, a sad tone in his voice.

A sinking feeling poured through her. "Tell me what it is," she said softly, her voice trembling.

"Now that you're safe, and your mother is back, I . . ." Waysa's voice faltered.

"What is it, Waysa?" she asked him again, but she didn't truly want to know the answer. She wanted to pull back time, to go back, back to the way it was before.

"I think it's time for me to go," he said.

Her eyes watered as she looked at him. "No, Waysa . . ."

"When I finally avenged my family, I thought it would restore the balance. I thought it would heal my heart. But when I think of my sister and my brothers . . . my mother and my father . . . there's still . . . an emptiness inside me. My family is dead, I have to accept that, but I want to know if any other Cherokee catamounts survived. Uriah scattered my people. I need to find them. I need to tell them what's happened here, that there's no more need to fear. I need to bring them back together . . ."

Serafina stared at Waysa. She did not want to agree with him. She did not want to let him go. She wanted to yell at him and demand that he stay. She wanted to grab hold of him and *make* him stay.

But she knew she shouldn't. She knew that she should let him go, that it was right for him to go. If his people were still out there, he had to find them, he had to bring them together. That's what he did. He *saved* people, just like he'd saved her.

"I understand," she said softly.

Waysa slowly took her into his arms and held her, and she held him in return, and for a moment she and her friend were of one spirit. She suddenly remembered the wild-haired feral boy fighting for her against the wolfhounds, the pang of loneliness she had felt when she realized he had disappeared into the darkness and she might not ever see him again. She remembered hiding in the cave with the boy who had left her the riddle so that she could find him, how he'd pushed her through the waterfall so that he could teach her to swim, how they'd fought together, run together, how he'd told her that she could be anything she envisioned herself to be.

"You stay bold, Serafina," he said now, his voice shaking with emotion.

"Stay bold, Waysa," she said in return. "Go find your people. And remember, no matter what happens, you have your family here. You have my mother, and my brother and sister, and you have *me*."

He nodded silently as he slowly turned away from her. He shifted into lion form and disappeared into the forest.

Standing with her mother and the cubs at her side, the last she saw of him he was running along the ridge, and then he faded into the silver light of the glowing moon.

On a sunny afternoon a few days later, well after Braeden and Serafina had cleaned up the mess and repaired what damage they could in the house, the carriages returned from Asheville with Mr. and Mrs. Vanderbilt and the servants who had been traveling with them.

The footmen carried the luggage up to their rooms. Mrs. Vanderbilt's maid and Mr. Vanderbilt's valet began the process of unpacking. And soon Biltmore was filled with the normal sounds of the house, the bustling of the servants, the tinkling of teacups, Mr. Vanderbilt's St. Bernard, Cedric, following him from room to room. The whole family was home again. The house resumed its old patterns, with tea at four and dinner at eight.

Upon hearing the good news that Serafina had returned to Biltmore, Mr. Vanderbilt asked Braeden to have her join the family for dinner.

As was his tradition, Braeden presented Serafina with a dress to wear. She had no idea where he got this one, or how he'd gotten it so quickly. Maybe he'd persuaded one of his feathered friends to deliver it from a distant city by air. She just hoped he hadn't asked the black widow spiders to make it.

Wherever the dress came from, Serafina loved the lustrous deep-blue fabric, which reminded her of a certain mountain stream she knew. It wasn't a full, old-fashioned ball gown like she had seen the ladies wearing at the summer ball, or a light, lacy dress for an evening garden party. Those would have to wait until next year. This dress wasn't for any particular occasion, but a lean and formal dress for wearing to dinner with the family each night. And when she thought about that, it made her smile. That was just about perfect. This was her home now and her life.

She took a lovely warm bath, washed her hair, and then dressed for dinner in the red-and-gold Louis XVI room on the second floor like she had before, with Essie doing her hair. "Aw, Miss," Essie said, as Serafina stood before her for inspection. "The dress goes so well with your black hair. You look right lovely tonight, with the biggest smile that I've ever seen on you."

Serafina and Braeden arrived at dinner together arm in arm. Mr. and Mrs. Vanderbilt smiled and hugged Serafina, overjoyed to see her, and asked her how she'd been. As they sat down to dinner, Serafina was happy to talk with them.

Mr. and Mrs. Vanderbilt seemed to be in warm and pleasant moods, relieved that the storms were over and looking forward to the coming of their child. As there were no guests in the house, it was just the four of them this evening, with Cedric and Gidean lying nearby. Nothing felt out of the ordinary or awkward about any of it. It just felt right. She had to remember where to place her napkin and which fork to use, but her pa had trained her well, and facing a new challenge always did excite her.

Braeden seemed pleased to be sitting at the table with her and his aunt and uncle, content that everything was as it should be. He'd gone out riding in the forest earlier that morning, making sure that everyone was on the mend. She noticed a new brightness in his eyes, and a new confidence in his smile and his manner.

"I was talking to Mr. McNamee this morning about the plans for repairing the gardens," Braeden said. "It all sounds very interesting."

"I'm glad those awful storms have stopped," Mrs. Vanderbilt said.

Mr. Vanderbilt nodded his agreement as he dabbed his mustache with his napkin. "Time to rebuild."

"You're going to rebuild?" Serafina asked, looking at him with interest as she thought about the farms and the village and the other areas that had been damaged.

"Oh, yes, we'll rebuild," Mr. Vanderbilt said. "No matter what happens, we always rebuild."

"I'm going to help," Braeden interjected. "I'll be working on the plans and the reconstruction with Mr. McNamee, learning everything I can. I'm looking forward to it."

"We'll make everything even better than it was before," Mr. Vanderbilt said, nodding. "That's how we keep moving forward. Especially now."

When he said these words, he smiled a little and looked at his wife, who touched her hand to her belly. "We've decided on a name for our little one here," she said happily. "Shall we share it with you two?"

"Oh, yes!" Serafina said excitedly before Braeden could reply.

"Can you keep a secret?" Mrs. Vanderbilt asked, winking at Serafina.

"Believe me," Braeden said. "She can definitely keep a secret. And so can I."

"Well," Mrs. Vanderbilt said happily, "we're going to name our little darling after George's beloved grandfather, Cornelius Vanderbilt. So if it's a baby boy, he'll be Cornelius. But if it's a baby girl, she'll be Cornelia. But no one knows about any of this, so you mustn't tell anyone until it's official."

"That's a wonderful name," Serafina said.

"Yes, we thought so, too," Mrs. Vanderbilt said with satisfaction.

"And what did you two get up to while we were gone?" Mr. Vanderbilt asked Braeden and Serafina.

"Oh, the same old thing," Braeden replied, never wanting to lie to his uncle. For him and Serafina, "the same old thing" meant prowling through the night, fighting sinister demons, and living on the edge of constant death.

"I hope not," Mr. Vanderbilt said, knowing all too well the kind of trouble they were capable of getting into.

It was clear to Serafina by the keen look in Mr. Vanderbilt's eye that he had figured out that something significant had occurred while he was gone. Mr. Vanderbilt knew she had been the one who found the missing children a few months back, and that she'd helped rescue Cedric and Gidean from the cages up in the pine forest. Now that he'd returned from his trip, she was pretty sure that he had noticed the strange scratches on the windowsill above the Banquet Hall and the tears in the room's Flemish tapestry.

"Well, for my part," Mr. Vanderbilt said finally, "I'm just glad that you're back, Serafina. Your home is here with us at Biltmore. And I must say, I feel that Biltmore is a safer place for it."

"Thank you, sir," she said, nodding slowly to him. "I truly appreciate it. I was gone for far too long, but in my heart, it felt like I never left you and Mrs. Vanderbilt and Braeden."

Later that night, Serafina and Braeden walked up the Grand Staircase to the fourth floor and then into the Observatory. From there they climbed the circular wrought-iron staircase to the room's upper level, opened the window, and climbed out onto the roof.

Serafina remained quiet as they walked in the moonlight past the copper dome of the Grand Staircase, among the mansion's tallest towers and slanted slate rooftops, its many reaching chimneys, and its carved stone gargoyles of mythical beasts.

"Do you think we've actually defeated him for good, Serafina?" Braeden asked her. "Is it truly all over?"

"Yes, I think it is," Serafina said, nodding. "But you and I are both the Guardians of Biltmore now, the protectors of this house, its people, and the forest all around, so we must keep a watchful eye and stay ready for whatever danger comes."

"Do you think there's other evil out there?"

"I'm sure there is," she said.

"But what will it be? What form will it take?"

"I don't know," she admitted. "But whatever it is, we'll face it together."

She and Braeden sat on the rooftop to enjoy the warm evening with its graceful breeze rolling through the tops of the trees. She could feel it lifting her long hair and gently touching the skin of her neck. She thought about the wind and earth and water. For a little while, she had caught a glimpse into the movement and flow of the world, and the power of her own soul, and she looked forward to learning more about what she could do.

They gazed across the sweeping lawns, and the gently flowering gardens, and the deep forests that surrounded the house, with the glass of the Conservatory below them glinting in the moonlight and the glow of the house's lights touching everything around. They looked out across the darkened canopy of the trees and the layers of rolling mountains in the distance, with the glistening sweep of the glowing stars and planets rising above.

Suddenly, she remembered a moment from the previous autumn. It seemed so long ago now. She was just a lonely little girl, so small and quiet, standing in the basement at the bottom of the stairs listening to the crowd of fancy folk above, wondering whether she should go up there and tell them that she had seen a girl in a yellow dress get captured by a sinister man in a black cloak.

She remembered that all she wanted to do at that moment was to help.

From that very first moment, with her looking up at that stairway that led from the darkness of the basement to the brightness of the world above, all she wanted to do was to be part of something. That was all she *ever* wanted, not just to see, but to be seen. Not just to hear, but to be heard. Not just to feel, but to be felt by other people, to touch them, affect them in some way, to make their lives different, and to be made different by them. And here, on this night, at this moment, on this rooftop, she knew that time had finally come.

She remembered how it felt when her soul was split from the rest of her, when she was but a lost spirit wandering the living world, but never truly touching it, never truly feeling it or engaging with it.

And she thought back to the conversation she'd had with her pa, that many things changed over time, always becoming something new and always becoming something old. She realized now that the physical things were always changing. Even we ourselves change, learning and growing, getting pulled down and then rebuilding ourselves again.

But for all that, there was a rare and hidden thing, maybe the most important thing, that never changed, and that was the spirit deep inside us, the thing we were when we were a child, and the thing we were when we grow up, the thing we are when we're at home, and the thing we are when we go out into the world—it's always with us—that inner spirit stays with us through it all, no matter how our body changes from year to year or how the world changes around us.

And through all of this, there is one thing we seek. To be connected to the people around us, to touch and be touched, to have a true family and friends of all kinds with which we share the world and its changes. Like our own spirit within us, our family is the hidden, inner core that deep down never changes, the river that is always flowing.

She turned and looked at Braeden. She studied his face, his hair, his eyes, the way he gazed off into the distant forest.

Her heart began to beat strong and steady in her chest.

Her hand began to tremble.

Then she slowly reached over and put her hand on his.

She felt the warmth of it, the living pulse of it, the soft skin and the bones beneath. This was her ally, her friend, the boy she fought her battles with.

Braeden turned and looked at her, somewhat surprised.

Nervous, she felt like she needed to give him a little bit of an explanation of why she had touched him in this way.

Thinking back on everything they had been through, she said, "I just wanted to make sure that I was truly here."

Braeden smiled, understanding.

"You are," he said. "We both are."

Author's Note

Thank you for reading this third book in the Serafina series. I hope you enjoyed it. This concludes the story of the conjurer Uriah and the Black Cloak, but it is not the last you'll hear from me, or from Serafina and Braeden.

Disney Hyperion will be publishing my next book, which is called *Willa of the Wood*. This next story takes place in Serafina's world in the Blue Ridge Mountains, but is focused on a new character named Willa, a twelve-year-old forest girl with special powers that I think you're going to like. In the future, Willa's story will blend and intermingle with Serafina and Braeden's story. I hope you'll join us for these future books.

If you enjoyed *Serafina and the Splintered Heart*, I encourage you to let people know about it, post reviews and comments online, and share your impressions with others. Thank you for helping to spread the word. But please avoid revealing how the story starts with Serafina in spirit form, the appearance of Rowena and the Black Cloak, and other details. Enjoying this book depends on the reader knowing no more than Serafina does at any particular moment, so it's important to avoid spoilers.

I would like to touch on a few elements of this story. The Cherokee are an important part of our community here in Western North Carolina today. I would like to thank the Eastern Band of the Cherokee Indians (EBCI), the Museum of the Cherokee Indian, Western North Carolina University, and members of the Cherokee tribe for their assistance with the depiction of Waysa, the Cherokee people, and the Kituhwa dialect of the Cherokee language that is spoken here in the mountains of Western North Carolina.

When you read this story, you may have thought that the idea of making fabric from spider silk sounds a bit far-fetched, but in reality, spider silk is an exciting new area of textile research. This includes using natural spider silk, creating synthetic spider silk, and gene-splicing spider silk DNA into other animals to achieve enhanced qualities. One of the most impressive uses of natural spider silk is a golden-colored cape made from silk harvested sustainably from thousands of golden orb spiders. Creepy but true.

As I've mentioned in my previous author notes, Biltmore Estate is a real place, which you can visit and explore. I've worked hard to be historically accurate with my depiction of the house and grounds. I would like to thank Biltmore Estate and the descendants of George and Edith Vanderbilt for their continued support and encouragement of my writing efforts, and for all they are doing to preserve and protect an important part of our American history.

I write at home, nearly every day, and work in close connection with my family. I would like to thank my daughters, Camille, Genevieve, and Elizabeth, for helping me to create this story and improve many of its details. And I would like to thank my wife, Jennifer, for working closely with me to refine the writing. My family is an integral part of my writing process.

And once again, I would like to extend my thanks to my agent, my beta readers and consulting editors, and everyone on the Serafina Team in Asheville and around the country who have helped make the Serafina series what it is.

I would also like to give my sincere gratitude to Laura Schreiber and Emily Meehan, my editors at Disney Hyperion, and the rest of the wonderful Disney Hyperion team. I am so honored to be part of your efforts to bring high-quality, imaginative books to readers of all ages.

Finally, I would like to thank *you*, the reader. In an era of easy distraction, I am so thankful for your willingness to journey with me into the heart and imagination of Serafina's world. Thank you for reading my stories, and for all your support and encouragement.

Stay Bold,

—Robert Beatty
Asheville, North Carolina

SERAFINA
and the
TWISTED STAFF

SERAFINA
and the
TWISTED STAFF

ROBERT BEATTY

DISNEP·HYPERION

LOS ANGELES   NEW YORK

All rights reserved. Published by Disney•Hyperion, an imprint of
Disney Book Group. No part of this book may be reproduced or transmitted
in any form or by any means, electronic or mechanical, including photocopying,
recording, or by any information storage and retrieval system, without
written permission from the publisher. For information address
Disney•Hyperion, 125 West End Avenue, New York, New York 10023.

First Edition, July 2016
3 5 7 9 10 8 6 4 2
FAC-020093-19200

Printed in the United States of America

This book is set in Adobe Garamond Pro
Designed by Maria Elias

Library of Congress Cataloging-in-Publication Data
Names: Beatty, Robert, 1963–
Title: Serafina and the Twisted Staff / Robert Beatty.
Description: First edition. | Los Angeles ; New York : Disney-Hyperion,
[2016] | ?2015 | Sequel to: Serafina and the black cloak. | Summary: In
1899, when an evil threatens all the humans and animals of the Blue
Ridge Mountains, twelve-year-old Serafina, rat catcher for the Biltmore
estate and the daughter of a shapeshifting mountain lion, must search
deep inside herself and embrace the destiny that awaits her.
Identifiers: LCCN 2016006654 (print) | LCCN 2016012155 (ebook) |
ISBN 9781484775035 (hardback) | ISBN 9781484778692 ()
Subjects: LCSH: Biltmore Estate (Asheville, N.C.)—Juvenile fiction. |
CYAC: Biltmore Estate (Asheville, N.C.)—Fiction. | Good and evil—Fiction. |
Supernatural—Fiction. | Shapeshifting—Fiction. | Identity—Fiction. | Horror stories.
| BISAC: JUVENILE FICTION / Action & Adventure / General. | JUVENILE
FICTION / Horror & Ghost Stories. | JUVENILE FICTION / Animals / General.
Classification: LCC PZ7.1.B4347 Sh 2016 (print) | LCC PZ7.1.B4347 (ebook) |
DDC [Fic]—dc23
LC record available at http://lccn.loc.gov/2016006654

Reinforced binding

Visit www.DisneyBooks.com

SUSTAINABLE FORESTRY INITIATIVE   Certified Sourcing
www.sfiprogram.org
SFI-00993

THIS LABEL APPLIES TO TEXT STOCK

This book is dedicated to you, the readers who helped
spread the word about *Serafina and the Black Cloak*
and, in so doing, made this second book possible.

And to Jennifer, Camille, Genevieve, and Elizabeth:
my co-conspirators, co-creators, and the loves of my life.

Biltmore Estate
Asheville, North Carolina
1899

**Three weeks after defeating
the Man in the Black Cloak**

$\mathcal{S}$erafina stalked through the underbrush of the moonlit forest, slinking low to the ground, her eyes fixed on her prey. Just a few feet in front of her, a large wood rat gnawed on a beetle he'd dug up. Her heart beat strong and steady in her chest, marking her slow and quiet creep toward the rat. Her muscles buzzed, ready to pounce. But she did not rush. Swiveling her shoulders back and forth to fine-tune the angle of her attack, she waited for just the right moment. When the rat bent down to pick up another beetle, she leapt.

The rat caught a glimpse of her out of the corner of his eye just as she sprang. It was beyond her ken why so many animals of the forest froze in terror when she pounced. If death by tooth and claw came leaping at *her* out of the darkness, she'd fight.

Or she'd run. She'd do *something*. Little woodland creatures like rats and rabbits and chipmunks weren't known for their boldness of heart, but what was freezing in sheer terror going to do?

As she dropped onto the rat, she snatched him up quicker than a whiskerblink and clutched him in her hand. And now that it was well past too late, he started squirming, biting, and scratching, his furry little body becoming a wriggling snake, his tiny heart racing at a terrific pace. *There it is,* she thought, feeling the *thumpty-thumpty* of his heartbeat in her bare hand. *There's the fight.* It quickened her pulse and stirred her senses. Suddenly, she could detect everything in the forest around her—the sound of a tree frog moving on a branch thirty feet behind her, the reedy buzz of a lonely timberdoodle in the distance, and the glimpse of a bat swishing through the starlit sky above the broken canopy of the trees.

It was all for practice, of course, the prowling and the pouncing, the stalking of prey and the snatching hold. She didn't kill the wild things she hunted, didn't need to, but they didn't know that, darn it! She was terror! She was death! So why at the last moment of her attack did they freeze? Why didn't they flee?

Serafina sat down on the forest floor with her back against an old, gnarled, lichen-covered oak tree and held the rat in her clenched fist on her lap.

Then she slowly opened her hand.

The rat darted away as fast as he could, but she snatched him up and brought him back to her lap again.

She held the rat tight for several seconds and then opened her hand once more.

This time, the rat did not run. He sat on her hand, trembling and panting, too confused and exhausted to move.

She lifted the terrified rodent a little closer on her open hand, tilted her head, and studied him. The wood rat didn't look like the nasty gray sewer varmints she was used to catching in the basement of Biltmore Estate. This particular rat had a scarred tear in his left ear. He'd encountered some trouble before. And with his dark little eyes and the tremulous whiskers of his long, pointy nose, he seemed more like a cute, chubby brown mouse than the proper vermin on which she had earned her title. She could almost imagine a little hat on his head and a buttoned vest. She felt a pang of guilt that she'd caught him, but she also knew that if he tried to run again, her hand would snatch him up before she even thought about it. It wasn't a decision. It was a reflex.

As the little rat tried to catch his breath, his eyes darted to and fro for a way out. But he didn't dare. He knew that as soon as he tried to run, she'd grab him again, that it was the nature of her kind to play with him, to paw him, to claw him, until he was finally dead.

But she looked at the rat and then set him on the forest floor. "Sorry, little fellow—just practicing my skills."

The rat gazed up at her in confusion.

"Go ahead," she said gently.

The rat glanced toward the thistle thicket.

"There ain't no trick in it," she said.

The rat didn't seem to believe her.

"You go on home, now," she told him. "Just move slowly away at first, not too fast—that's the way of it. And keep your eyes and ears open next time, even if you got a beetle to chew on, you hear? There are far meaner things in these woods than me."

Astonished, the torn-eared wood rat rubbed his little hands over his face repeatedly and bobbed his head, almost as if he was bowing. She snorted a little laugh through her nose, which finally startled the rat into action. He quickly got his wits about him and scampered into the thicket.

"Have a good evenin', now," she said. She reckoned he'd bolster his memory of his courage the farther he got away from her and have a good story to tell his wife and little ones by the time he got home for supper. She smiled as she imagined him telling a great and twisty tale with his family gathered around, how he was in the forest just minding his own business, gnawing on a beetle, when a vicious predator pounced upon him and he had to fight for his every breath. She wondered if she'd be a beast of ferocious power in the story. Or just a girl.

At that moment, she heard a sound from above like an autumn breeze flowing through the tops of the trees. But there wasn't a breeze. The midnight air was chilled and quiet and perfectly still, like God was holding his breath.

She heard a delicate, almost gossamer, whisper-like murmur. She looked up, but all she could see were the branches of the trees. Rising to her feet, she brushed off the simple green work dress that Mrs. Vanderbilt had given her the day before and walked through the forest, listening for the sound. She tried to determine the direction it was coming from. She tilted her head left and then right, but the sound seemed to have no position. She made her way over to a rocky outcropping, where the ground fell steeply away into a forested valley. From here she could see a great distance, miles yonder across the mist to the silhouettes of the Blue Ridge Mountains on the other side. A thin layer of silvery white clouds glowing with light passed slowly in front of the moon. The brightness of the moon cast a wide-arcing halo in the feathery clouds, shone through them, and threw a long, jagged shadow onto the ground behind her.

She stood on the rocky ledge and scanned the valley in front of her. In the distance, the pointed towers and slate-covered rooftops of the grand Biltmore Estate rose from the darkness of the surrounding forest. The pale gray limestone walls were adorned with gargoyles of mythical beasts and fine sculptures of the warriors of old. The stars reflected in the slanting windowpanes, and the mansion's gold- and copper-trimmed roofline glinted in the moonlight. There in the great house, Mr. and Mrs. Vanderbilt slept on the second floor, along with their nephew, her friend, Braeden Vanderbilt. The Vanderbilts' guests—family members from out of town, businessmen, dignitaries, famous artists—slept on the third floor, each in their own luxuriously appointed room.

Serafina's pa maintained the steam heating system, the electric dynamo, the laundry machines powered by spinning leather straps, and all the other newfangled devices on the estate. She and her pa lived in the workshop in the basement down the

5

corridor from the kitchens, laundry rooms, and storerooms. But while all the people she knew and loved slept through the night, Serafina did not. She napped on and off during the day, curled up in a window or hidden in some dark nook in the basement. At night she prowled the corridors of Biltmore, both upstairs and down, a silent, unseen watcher. She explored the winding paths of the estate's vast gardens and the darkened dells of the surrounding forest, and she hunted.

She was a twelve-year-old girl, but she had never lived what anyone other than herself would call a normal life. She had spent her time creeping through the estate's vast basement catching rats. Her pa, half joking when he'd said it, had dubbed her the C.R.C.: the Chief Rat Catcher. But she'd taken on the title with pride.

Her pa had always loved her and did the best he could to raise her, in his own rough-hewn way. She certainly hadn't been unhappy eating supper with her pa each evening and sneaking through the darkness at night ridding the great house of rodents. Who would be? But deep down, she'd been a fair bit lonely and mighty confused. She had never been able to square why most folk carried a lantern in the dark, or why they made so much noise when they walked, or what compelled them to sleep through the night just when all manner of things were at their most beautiful. She'd spied on enough of the estate's children from a distance to know she wasn't one of them. When she gazed into a mirror, she saw a girl with large amber eyes, deeply angled cheekbones, and a shaggy mane of streaked brown hair.

No, she wasn't a normal, everyday child. She wasn't an *any* day child. She was a creature of the night.

As she stood at the edge of the valley, she heard again the sound that had brought her there, a gentle fluttering, like a river of whispers traveling on the currents of wind that flowed high above her. The stars and planets hung in the blackened sky, scintillating as if they were alive with the spirits of ten thousand souls, but they offered no answers to the mystery.

A small, dark shape crossed in front of the moon and disappeared. Her heart skipped a beat. What was it?

She watched. Another shape passed the moon, and then another. At first, she thought they must be bats, but bats didn't fly in straight lines like these.

She frowned, confused and fascinated.

Tiny shape after tiny shape crossed in front of the moon. She looked up high into the sky and saw the stars disappearing. Her eyes widened in alarm. But then the realization of what she was seeing slowly crept into her. Squinting her eyes just right, she could see great flocks of songbirds flying over the valley. Not just one or two, or a dozen, but long, seemingly endless streams of them—clouds of them. The birds filled the sky. The sound she was hearing was the soft murmur of thousands of tiny wings of sparrows, wrens, and waxwings making their fall journey. They were like jewels, green and gold, yellow and black, striped and spotted, thousands upon thousands of them. It seemed far too late in the year for them to be migrating, but here they were. They hurried across the sky, their little wings fluttering, heading southward for the winter, traveling secretly at night to avoid the hawks that hunted in the day, using the ridges of the mountains below and the alignment of the glinting stars above to find their way.

The flighty, twitching movement of birds had always tantalized her, had always quickened her pulse, but this was different. Tonight the boldness and beauty of these little birds' trek down the mountainous spine of the continent flowed through her heart. It felt as if she was seeing a once-in-a-lifetime event, but then she realized that the birds were following the path that their parents and grandparents had taught them, that they'd been flying this path for millions of years. The only thing "once in a lifetime" about this was *her,* that she was here, that she was seeing it. And it amazed her.

Seeing the birds made her think of Braeden. He loved birds and other animals of all kinds.

"I wish you could see this," she whispered, as if he was lying awake in his bed and could hear her across the miles of distance between them. She longed to share the moment with her friend. She wished he was standing beside her, gazing up at the stars and the birds and the silver-edged clouds and the shining moon in all its glory. She knew she'd tell him all about it the next time she saw him. But daytime words could never capture the beauty of the night.

A few weeks before, she and Braeden had defeated the Man in the Black Cloak and had torn the Black Cloak asunder. She and Braeden had been allies, and good friends, but it sank in once again, this time even deeper than before, that she hadn't seen him in several nights. With every passing night, she expected a visit at the workshop. But every morning she went to bed disappointed, and it left her with biting doubts. What was he doing? Was something keeping him from her? Was he purposefully avoiding her? She'd been so happy to finally have a friend to talk to. It made her burn inside to think that maybe she was just a novelty to him that had worn off, and now she was left to return to her lonely nights of prowling on her own. They were friends. She was sure of it. But she worried that she didn't fit in upstairs in the daylight, that she didn't belong there. Could he have forgotten about her so quickly?

As the birds thinned out and the moment passed, she looked out across the valley and wondered. After defeating the Man in the Black Cloak, she reckoned herself one of the Guardians, the marble lions that stood on either side of Biltmore's front doors, protecting the house from demons and evil spirits. She imagined herself the C.R.C. of not just the small, four-legged vermin, but of intruders of all kinds. Her pa had always warned her about the world, of the dangers that could ensnare her soul, and after everything that had happened, she was sure there were more demons out there.

For weeks now, she'd been watching and waiting, like a guard on a watchtower, but she had no idea when or in what shape the demons would come. Her darkest worry, deep down, when she faced it true, was whether she'd be strong enough, smart enough—whether she'd end up the predator or the prey. Maybe the little animals like the wood rat and the chipmunk knew that death was just a pounce away. Did they think of themselves as prey? Maybe they were almost expecting to die, ready to die. But she sure wasn't. She had things to do.

Her friendship with Braeden had just begun, and she wasn't going to give up on it just because they'd hit a snag. And she had only just started to understand her connection to the forest, to figure out who and what she was. And now that she'd met the Vanderbilts face-to-face, her pa had been pressuring her to start acting like a proper daytime girl. Mrs. V was taking her in, always talking to her with a gentle word. Now she had the basement and the forest and the upstairs—she'd gone from having too few kin to having too many, getting pulled in three directions at once. But after years of living without any family besides her pa, it felt good to be getting started with her new life.

All that was fine and good. When danger came, she wanted to fight, she wanted to live. Who didn't? But what if the danger came so fast she never saw it coming? What if, like an owl attacking a mouse, the claws dropped from the sky and killed her before she even knew they were there? What if the real danger wasn't just whether she could fight whatever threat that came, but whether she even recognized it before it was too late?

The more she thought about the flocks of birds she'd seen, the more it rankled her peace of mind. It was plenty warm, but she couldn't stop thinking that December seemed far too late in the year for birds to be coming and going. She frowned and searched the sky for the North Star. When she found it, she realized that the birds hadn't even been flying in the right direction. She wasn't even sure they were the kinds of birds that flew south for the winter.

As she stood on the rocky edge of the high ground, the dark ooze of dread seeped into her bones.

She looked up at where the birds had been flying, and then she looked in the direction they came from. She gazed out across the top of the darkened forest. Her mind tried to work it through. And then she realized what was happening.

The birds weren't migrating.

They were *fleeing*.

She pulled in a long, deep breath as her body readied itself. Her heart began to pound. The muscles of her arms and legs tightened.

Whatever it was, it was coming.

And it was coming now.

A moment later, a sound in the distance tickled Serafina's ear. It wasn't sparrow wings, like she'd heard before, but something earthbound. She tilted her head and listened for it again. It seemed to be coming from down in the valley.

She stood, faced the sound, and cupped her hands around the back of her ears, a trick she'd learned from mimicking a bat.

She heard the faint jangle of harnesses and the clip-clop of hooves. Her stomach tightened. It was a strange sound to encounter in the middle of the night. A team of horses pulling a carriage was making its way up the three-mile-long winding road toward the house. In the daytime, there would be nothing unusual about that. But no one ever came to Biltmore at night. Something was wrong. Was it a messenger bearing bad news? Had someone died? Was the North going to war with the South again? What calamity had befallen the world?

Pulling back from the rocky ledge, she hurried down into the valley and made her way through the forest to one of the arched brick bridges where the road crossed over the stream. She watched from the concealing leaves of the mountain laurel as an old, road-beaten carriage passed by. Most carriages had one or two horses, but this carriage was pulled by four dark brown stallions with powerful, bulging muscles, their hides glistening with sweat in the moonlight and their nostrils flaring.

She swallowed hard. *That isn't a messenger.*

Braeden had told her that stallions were wild and notoriously difficult to deal with—they kicked their handlers and bit people, and especially hated other stallions—but here were four of them pulling a carriage in unison.

When she looked at who was driving the carriage, the hairs on the back of her neck stood on end. The carriage bench was empty. The horses were all cantering together in a forceful rhythm, as if by the rein of a master, but there was no driver to be seen.

Serafina clenched her teeth. This was all wrong. She could feel it in her core. The carriage was heading straight for Biltmore, where everyone was fast asleep and had no idea it was coming.

As the carriage rounded a bend and went out of sight, Serafina broke into a run and followed.

She ran through the forest, tracking the carriage as it traveled down the winding road. The cotton dress Mrs. Vanderbilt had given her wasn't too long, so it was easy to run in, but keeping pace with the horses was surprisingly difficult. She tore through the forest, leaping over fallen logs and bounding over ferns. She jumped gullies and climbed hills. She took short-cuts, taking advantage of the road's meandering path. Her chest began to heave as she pulled in great gulps of air. Despite the trepidation she had felt moments before, the challenge of keeping up with the horses made her smile and then made her laugh, which made it all the more difficult to breathe when she was trying to run. Leaping and darting, she loved the thrill of the chase.

Then, all of a sudden, the horses slowed.

She pulled herself short and hunkered down.

The horses came to a stop.

She ducked behind a clump of rhododendrons a stone's throw from the carriage and concealed herself as she tried to catch her breath.

Why is the carriage stopping?

The horses anxiously shifted their hooves, and steam poured from their nostrils.

Her heart pounded as she watched the carriage.

The handle of the carriage door turned.

She crouched low to the ground.

The carriage door swung slowly open.

She thought she could see two figures inside, but then there was a roil of darkness like she'd never seen before—a shadow so black and fleeting that it was impossible for even *her* eyes to make it out.

A tall and sinewy man in a wide-brimmed leather hat and a dark, weather-beaten coat emerged from the carriage. He had long, knotty gray hair and a gray mustache and beard that reminded her of moss hanging from a craggy tree. As he climbed down from the carriage and stood on the road, he held a gnarled walking stick and gazed out into the forest.

Behind him, a vicious-looking wolfhound slunk down from the carriage onto the ground. Then another followed. The hounds had large, lanky bodies, massive heads with black eyes, and ratty, thick blackish-gray fur. Five dogs in all came forth from the carriage and stood together, scanning the forest for something to kill.

Afraid to make even the slightest sound, Serafina took in a slow, ragged breath as carefully and quietly as she possibly could. The beat of her heart pounded in her chest. She wanted to run. *Just stay still,* she ordered herself. *Stay very still.* She was sure that as long as she didn't break cover, they wouldn't see her.

She wasn't certain what it was—maybe his long, frayed coat and the worn state of his carriage—but the man seemed as if he'd traveled a long distance. It surprised her when he shut the carriage door, stepped away, and looked at the horses. The stallions immediately broke into a run like they had been whipped. The carriage soon disappeared down the road, taking whoever remained inside onward toward Biltmore but leaving the bearded man and his dogs behind in the forest. The man did not appear to be dismayed or upset by this, but acted as though this forest was exactly where he wanted to be.

Saying words Serafina could not understand, the man gathered his pack of dogs around him. They were foul beasts with massive paws and thick claws. They didn't seem like normal dogs that sniffed the ground and explored the forest. They all looked up at their master, as if waiting for his instructions.

The man's face was shrouded by the bent brim of his hat. But when he tilted his head upward toward the moon, Serafina sucked in a breath. The man's silvery eyes glinted with power, peering out from his weathered, craggy face. His mouth came slowly open like he was trying to suck in the moonlight. Just when she thought he was going to utter words, he let out the most terrifying hissing scream she had ever heard. It was a long, raspy screech. And right at that moment, a ghostly white barn owl appeared out of the trees, flying overhead, the beat of its wings utterly silent, but then it answered the man's call with a bloodcurdling scream in return. The sound sent a terrible burst of shivers down Serafina's spine. And as the owl flew by her, its eerie, flat-faced head pivoted toward her, as if searching, hunting. She ducked to the ground like a frightened mouse.

As the owl disappeared into the midnight gloom, Serafina peeked back toward the road. Her heart stopped cold. The bearded man and his five hounds were now looking out into the forest in her direction, the man's eyes still gleaming with an unnatural light despite the fact that he had turned away from the moon. She tried to convince herself that it was impossible for the man and his dogs to see her concealed in the leaves. But she couldn't shake the horrible fear that they knew exactly where she was. The ground beneath her seemed to become slippery with some unknown dampness. The ivy on the forest floor seemed to be moving. She heard a *tick-tick-ticking* sound, followed by a long, raspy hiss. Suddenly, she felt the touch of the man's breath on the back of her neck, and she spun around, cringing violently, but there was nothing there but blackness.

The man reached into his pocket with one of his knobby, leathery-skinned hands and took out what appeared to be a scrap of torn, dark-colored cloth.

"Breathe it in," he ordered his dogs, his voice low and sinister. There was something about the stranger's rugged face and beard, his rustic clothing, and the way he said his words that made her think he was an Appalachian man, born and raised in the rocky ravines and thorny coves of these very mountains.

The first wolfhound pushed its muzzle into the folds of the dark cloth. When it drew its nose out again, its mouth gaped open, its teeth bared and chattering, dripping with saliva. The dog began to growl. Then the second dog and the third nosed the dark cloth, until all five had taken the scent. The wicked, snarling malevolence of the hounds stabbed her stomach with fear. Her only hope was that the trail of the cloth's scent would take them in the opposite direction.

The man looked down at his pack of hounds. "Our quarry is near," he told them, his voice filled with menacing command. "Follow the scent! Find the Black One!"

Suddenly, the dogs howled, savage like wolves. All five of them burst from their haunches and lunged into the forest. Serafina jumped despite herself. Her legs wanted to run so bad that she could barely keep herself still. But she had to stay hidden. It was her only chance to survive. But to her horror, the hounds were running straight toward her.

She couldn't understand it. Should she keep hiding? Should she fight? Should she run? The dogs were going to tear her to pieces.

Just when she knew she had to run, she realized it was too late. She didn't have a chance. Her chest seized. Her legs locked. She froze in terror.

No! No! No! Don't do it! You're not a rat! You're not a chipmunk! You've got to move!

Faced with certain death, she did what any sensible creature of the forest would do: She leapt ten feet straight up into a tree. She landed on a branch, then scurried along its length and hurled herself like a flying squirrel in a desperate leap to the next tree. From there, she bounded to the ground and ran like the dickens.

With howls of outrage, the hounds gave chase, running and snapping at her. They coursed her like a pack of wolves on a deer. But they were *wolfhounds,* so they weren't born and bred to chase down and kill anything as small as a deer. They were born and bred to chase down and kill *wolves.*

As she ran, Serafina glanced back over her shoulder toward the road. The craggy-faced man looked up at the owl as the haunting creature came circling back around. Then, to Serafina's astonishment, he threw his walking stick up into the sky. It tumbled end over end toward the owl. But it did not strike the bird. It seemed to blur and then disappear into the darkness, just as the owl flew into the cover of the trees. Serafina had no idea who the man was or what she had seen, but it didn't matter now. She had to run for her life.

Fighting off a single jumping, biting, snapping, snarling wolfhound was bad enough, but fighting five was impossible. She sprinted through the forest as fast as she could, her muscles punched with the power of fear. She wasn't going to let these growling beasts defeat her. The cold forest air shot into her pumping lungs, every sense in her body exploding with a lightning bolt of panic. Coming up behind her, the first hound reached out its ragged neck, opened its toothy maw, and bit the back of her leg. She spun and struck the dog, screaming in anger and searing pain as the dog's fangs punctured her flesh. The smell of the blood excited the other hounds into even more of a frenzy. The second dog leapt upon her and bit her shoulder, tearing into her with growling determination as she slammed her fist into its face. The third clamped its teeth onto her wrist as she tried to pull it away. The three of them pulled her down and dragged her across the ground. Then the other two dogs came in for the kill, their fangs bared as they lunged straight for her throat.

As the wolfhound charged in, Serafina threw her arm across her neck. Instead of tearing through her throat, the dog's fangs chomped down on her forearm, shooting spikes of pain through her bone as she screamed. The second dog pressed in for the killing bite, but a fist-size stone slammed into its head, knocking it back. Then another stone hit one of the other dogs, and it whirled to defend itself.

"Haaaa!" came a violent shout out of the darkness as a boy with long, wild hair leapt into the fray, striking and punching and clawing, flailing his arms in a spinning, growling attack.

Fierce with pain, Serafina slammed the heel of her hand into the nose of the dog clamped on her arm, pushing the dog away.

"Get up! Stay bold! Run!" the boy shouted at her as he attacked two of the dogs and cleared the way for her.

Serafina scrambled up onto her feet, ready to flee. But just when she thought she and the boy were gaining the advantage and might actually be able to escape, one of the dogs came leaping out of darkness, slammed into the boy's chest, and knocked him off his feet. The boy and the dog rolled to the ground in a somersault of snarling, biting ferocity.

The next dog lunged at Serafina. She dodged it, but another dog came at her from the other side.

"You can't outrun these things for long," the boy shouted. "You've got to get to cover!"

She dodged a lunging bite, and then a second and a third, but the snapping mouths kept coming at her. She slammed a dog in the head and punched one in the shoulder, but the dogs just kept biting, biting, biting.

She ran backward, defending herself from the incoming bites, but then she slammed into a face of sheer rock wall and could retreat no farther. She crouched into an attack position, hissing like an animal caught in a trap.

Just as a dog leapt at her, the boy tackled it to the ground.

"Now!" he shouted. "Climb!"

Serafina turned and tried to scramble up the craggy rock face, but the rock was dripping with water and too slippery to climb. Emboldened by her attempt to escape, two of the dogs immediately charged. She kicked their heads away repeatedly with her feet. She swatted and punched with her fists.

"Don't fight, you fool! Climb!" the boy shouted. "You've got to run!"

Just as she turned to climb, another dog lunged at her, but the boy leapt onto its back, biting and scratching like a wild animal. The hound howled in vicious indignation and twisted around, snapping furiously at the boy. They went tumbling onto the ground in a fierce ball of battle. Two more dogs dove fang-first into the melee.

Seeing her chance, she jumped up and grabbed the branch of a rhododendron, then hoisted herself up the face of the rock. She quickly found a foothold and another branch. Using the rhododendron bushes as a ladder, she climbed as fast as she could up the cliff. *Try that, you handless mutts!*

When she had climbed out of reach of the dogs, she looked back. Two of the dogs ran back and forth at the base of the cliff, growling as they tried to find a way up. The braver and stupider of the two tried repeatedly to run up the sheer wall, only to fall back down again. "Go on back to your master, you nasty dogs!" she spat at them, remembering the dark and shadowy figure.

But as she looked out across the woods, it wasn't their master she was looking for. She couldn't see the other three dogs or the boy. The last time she saw him, he'd been consumed in a terrible battle. She hadn't been able to tell who was winning and who was losing, but it seemed impossible that he could fight off all three of them at once.

She waited and listened out into the forest, but there was nothing. The two dogs that had been on her had disappeared.

They were running along the base of the cliff. *Those mongrels are looking for another way up,* she thought.

She had to keep moving before it was too late. She climbed another fifteen feet until she reached the top edge of the cliff.

Panting and exhausted, and bleeding from her head, arms, and calves, she crumpled to the ground. She scanned the trees below her, searching for the boy.

She looked and looked, but there was nothing moving out there, nothing making a sound. How had they moved away from her so quickly? Was the boy all right? Did he get away? Or was he hurt?

She'd never laid eyes on the boy before, never seen anything like him, the way he moved and fought. He had brownish skin, a lithe, muscled body, and long, shaggy dark brown hair, but it was his speed and his ferocity that struck her most. She reckoned he must be one of the local mountain folk, like her pa, who were well known for being tough as nails and twice as sharp, but the boy had fought as hard as a rabid bobcat. There was something almost *feral* about him, like he'd lived in these woods all his life.

She stood and scanned the terrain behind her—flat, rocky ground and a thicket of shrublike vegetation leading down into a larger ravine. She was pretty sure she knew where she was and how to get home, but she turned and looked out over the cliff again. The feral boy had saved her life. How could she just leave him?

The pain of the bites and scratches she'd suffered in the

battle burned something fierce, like sharp, twisting barbed wire puncturing her flesh. Blood dripped down into her eyes from the wound to her head. She needed to get home.

She looked out across the tops of the trees in the direction she had last seen the boy. She waited and listened, thinking she'd hear signs of battle or maybe see him looking up at her. Or, God forbid, she would see his bloody, torn body lying lifeless on the ground.

Don't fight, you fool! Climb! His words came ringing in her ears like he was still there. *Run!* he'd shouted.

Should she flee like he'd told her to, or should she look for him like she wanted to?

She hated making noise, making herself known to whatever lurked in the forest around her, but she couldn't think of anything else to do: She cupped her hands around her mouth and whispered "Hello! Can you hear me?" over the tops of the trees.

And then she waited.

There was nothing but the crickets and frogs and the other sounds of the night forest.

She could feel the battle-pound of her heart slowing down, her breaths getting weaker, and her arms and legs getting heavier. If she was going to make it home, she had to go soon.

She didn't want to just leave him out there fighting on his own. She wasn't the leaving kind—or the forgetting kind, either.

She wanted to talk to him, find out his name and where he

lived, or at least know he was safe. Who was he? Why was he in the forest in the middle of the night? And why was he willing to leap into a pack of vicious dogs to defend her?

She whispered once more out into the trees, "Are you out there?"

Serafina knew she'd waited for the feral boy too long when she heard the two wolfhounds coming toward her from the north. They had found a way up and around the cliff.

She looked around her. She glanced up at a tree, wondering if she could climb high enough. Then she thought about scaling back down the cliff again to confuse them. But she knew she couldn't survive out here all night on her own. *Get out of here!* the feral boy had told her.

Finally, she gathered herself up.

Whoever the boy was, she hoped he'd be all right. *Stay strong, my friend.*

She ducked into a dense boscage of spruce and fir, the evergreens packed so tightly together that it was like swimming through an ocean of green foliage. As she pushed her way through the thicket, she found her strength giving way to confusion. Her knees kept buckling beneath her, and she couldn't focus on the terrain in front of her. She raised her hand to her head and realized that she was bleeding badly from a tear in her scalp. The blood was dripping down her forehead and into her eyes.

She stumbled through the sea of trees, knowing there was no way to elude the dogs now. Spasms of pain radiated from the puncture wounds in her arms and legs. She had to wipe the blood out of her eyes to see where she was going. The needled branches of the trees were so thick and high that she could no longer see the moon and stars. Her racing feet cracked sticks on the ground, making noise that she wouldn't normally make, but it didn't matter now. She had to run like she'd never run before. But even as she ducked and darted between the trees, she kept hearing the feral boy's voice: *You can't outrun these things for long!* She wanted to turn and fight them, but if they caught her here in the thicket of trees, it'd be impossible to see their attacks. They'd kill her for sure. She had to keep running.

Suddenly, the trees opened up and she nearly fell headlong over a cliff edge into a rocky crash of whitewater rapids below. She pulled herself back from the edge with a gasp and grabbed onto the branches of a tree.

Looking over the edge of the cliff, she could see there was no way to cross the river here. The cliff was too high, the rapids too dangerous. *There ain't nothin' but bad choices,* she thought.

She knew she had to get to cover, but right now, the cover she needed was to conceal her scent.

Pushing herself on, she ran along the cliff as it led down toward the river.

When she came to the stretch below the rapids, she tried to wade quickly across what looked like the safest and shallowest point. She'd never been in deep water before and didn't know how to swim. She pushed hard through the drag of the rushing, knee-deep water, desperate to reach the other side and escape the wolfhounds. The mountain river was so cold that her legs ached. The current ran swift and strong. As she placed each step against the tearing force of the current, she felt the round, algae-covered rocks turning and slipping beneath her searching feet.

She reached the center of the river. The water ripped around her thighs, making it more and more difficult to push against it. She was making headway. But just when she thought she was going to make it across, she felt the current lifting her body away from the rocks beneath her feet. She lost her balance and crashed down into the icy-cold water. She flailed wildly, desperately kicking her legs in search of footing, but the bottom of the river disappeared as the current swept her into deep water. Coughing and spitting, she thrashed and leapt and gasped frantically for air as the river carried her downstream toward the next set of rapids.

The current sucked her into a rifling chute between two giant boulders, then shot her out the other side, tumbling end over end underwater through a dark green pool. As her head broke the surface, she managed to steal another gasp of air before the river grabbed hold of her again, heaving her and yanking her through a spiral of rushing water. She found herself spinning submerged in a whirlpool so deep that she said good-bye to her pa. But then her body hit a jagged rock. She tried to cling to it, but the rushing flow immediately pulled her away again. She'd always thought she was strong, but compared to the force of the river, she was nothing more than a kitten tossed into the water. When the rapids finally spat her out into the calm water downstream, she crawled from the river, wet and bedraggled, and collapsed onto the rocky shore, exhausted.

She had made it across.

She knew that if the dogs followed her downstream and saw her across the river, then they would pursue her. She had to get up, had to keep running, but she couldn't get her arms and legs to move. She couldn't even lift her head. The freezing-cold water and pounding force of the river had sapped all the remaining strength from her muscles. Her limbs were shaking. As she lay on the watery stones at the edge of the river, the protection of Biltmore seemed impossibly far away, beyond her reach. Her body was so tired she could barely get a few *feet*, let alone the miles she needed to go. The small puddles of water among the stones where she lay began to turn dark one by one. She felt so cold.

She wondered if the feral boy was lying mortally wounded in the forest back where she'd left him, or still fighting the wolfhounds. Or maybe he had escaped them. She could hear his voice in her mind. *Run!* he had shouted to her. *Run!* But she could not run. She could not move.

A wave of black calm passed through her, inviting her to simply shut her eyes and let everything go. A cloud of sickening colors veiled her eyes. She could feel herself passing out. How easy it would be to simply drift away. But a fierceness boiled in her heart. *Get up!* she told herself. *Run! Get home!* She struggled to rouse herself, to get onto her feet, to at least raise her head.

She opened her eyes and squinted through the blood. The terrain on this side of the river was low and gentle, dotted with ferns and birch trees, so different from the rocky cliffs that she had left behind on the other side. She saw a light coming toward her in the darkness. At first she thought it must be a twinkling star, for the sky was clear, but it wasn't one light. It was many lights.

She felt her chest trying helplessly to suck in air in anticipation of an attack, but even in the haze of her fear, she hoped that it might be a torch or lantern, her pa coming in search of her like he did once before.

But then she saw that the lights weren't the flickering flames of a lantern, but the scintillating dance of living creatures floating in the air and coming toward her down the river.

Are they fireflies? she wondered as they came closer.

But these were much larger and bright green in color, their wings slowly flashing white and green, white and green, as they flew, like the wings of luminescent butterflies.

But they're not butterflies, either, she thought with a smile. *They're luna moths.*

It was an entire eclipse of moths, each one pale green in color and glowing in the moonlight, hundreds of them flying together down the length of the river, their long tails streaming behind their silent, gently fluttering wings.

She had found her first luna moth in Biltmore's gardens one midsummer's night when she was a little girl. She remembered the luna moth's almost magical glow in the starlit darkness as she held it in her open hand, its wings moving gently up and down. But it was so strange to see so many of them traveling together. Was she imagining this? Was this how death came? A distant memory from the midnights of her past?

But as she watched the luna moths flying over the water, it struck her again that they weren't just hovering. They were traveling down the length of the stream, as if they would follow this river to the one that it flowed into, and then onward to the next river, and the next, through the mountains, and all the way to the sea. They were leaving this place. Just like the birds.

She heard the wolfhounds barking and howling to each other on the cliff on the other side of the river. They were coming.

As the last of the luna moths disappeared, she tried to push herself up onto her weakened arms, but she didn't have the strength. She tried to get her legs underneath her, but she couldn't.

But she'd seen the luna moths for a reason. She was sure of it.

She looked around for a place to take cover and noticed a grove of birch trees just a few feet away. As she tried to figure out how she was going to reach the trees, she saw a pair of eyes glinting in the darkness.

The eyes were keeping their distance, studying her.

Serafina held the eyes in her gaze and breathed as steadily as she could.

At first, she thought she had misjudged the position of the wolfhounds, that they had already crossed the river and were now surrounding her. But they weren't the searing black eyes of the wolfhounds. The eyes were golden brown.

A flood of relief flowed into her.

She knew who it must be.

"I need your help," she whispered.

But what emerged from the forest jolted her with a shock of fear. A mountain lion she had never seen before came straight at her. He was a young lion, with dark fur, but he looked strong, unafraid, and hungry. He was not at all the creature she was expecting.

Serafina tried to get up to defend herself, but it was no use. The beast could easily kill her.

But even as she tried to figure out how she was going to fight this unknown lion, a second lion emerged from the trees.

She breathed a sigh of relief. It was a lioness, full grown and full of power, a lioness she knew well.

When her mother was in her lion form, she was more beautiful than ever, with a thick tan coat, huge paws, and the muscles of many hunts. Her striking face and golden eyes glowed with intelligence.

"I'm so glad it's you, Momma," Serafina said, surprised by the tearful desperation in her own voice.

But in that moment, before Serafina could make out any

sort of answer in her mother's eyes, the lioness suddenly turned her head and looked across the river.

Then Serafina heard it, too. The wolfhounds were upon them. And it wasn't just two anymore. The five were united again, growling and barking and snarling. They would be here in seconds.

Serafina's mother moved quickly toward her and flattened herself beside her. Serafina didn't understand what she was doing. Then the darker lion came and nudged Serafina's body with his head. At first, she thought the lions were trying to rub against her and disguise her scent with theirs, but then she realized their true intention.

Serafina climbed onto her mother's back, clutching her neck and shoulders. With the lioness carrying her and the dark lion close at her side, the three of them moved into the trees, slowly at first, and then more quickly. Serafina felt her mother's fur against her face, and the force of her mother's lungs, and the power of her muscles. The lioness began to move more swiftly through the forest. Soon they were running.

It was the most incredible feeling, streaming through the

night at high speed, propelled by the undulating rhythm of the lioness's bounding stride, so strong and quiet and fast, the dark lion running beside her. Serafina had dreamed of running like this many times, but she had never moved this fast in her entire life. What amazed her was how smooth it was, how agile her mother's movements, how quickly she could change direction and speed, with both grace and power at her command.

When they reached a prominence of high ground, the two lions paused and looked down toward the river. They watched as the five wolfhounds followed Serafina's scent to the edge of the river, then crossed it. But they went straight across, not realizing she had been swept far downstream by the powerful current. At the time, it had felt like a catastrophe that the river had pulled her off her feet and carried her downstream, but now she realized that it had saved her. The wolfhounds sniffed the ground, circling in confusion. They'd lost her scent. And when they ran up and down the edge of the river looking to find her trail, their confusion mounted.

They can't find me, Serafina thought with a smile as she clung to her mother's back. *All they can smell is mountain lion.*

Suddenly, the lions were moving again, running through the forest at high speed, leaping small ravines and creeks, dashing through ferns. The branches and trunks of the trees flashed by. The whistle of the wind filled her ears.

They ran for so long through the night that Serafina's eyes closed, and all she could feel was the movement of the running, the coolness of the air above her, and the warmth of her mother beneath her.

$\mathcal{S}$erafina awoke a short time later on a bed of soft bright-green grass glowing in the moonlight. She felt the warmth of nuzzling fur and the deep and gentle vibration of purring. Her mother's two cubs snuggled up against her, kneading her back with their tiny paws, so happy to see her that they were giving her a back rub. She couldn't help but smile. She could feel their little noses pressing against her shoulders and their whiskers tickling her neck. Over the last few weeks that she'd been visiting the cubs at her mother's den, she had come to love her half brother and half sister, and she knew they had come to love her.

She reached up to feel the cut on her head. It had been dressed with a leafy compress that had stopped the bleeding and numbed the pain. The wounds on her arms and legs had been treated with poultices of forest herbs. She didn't want to, but she was pretty sure she could move if she needed to. She had noticed in the past that pain didn't slow her down like it did many other people. She had surprised her pa in this regard more than once. Cold weather didn't affect her either. Like her kin, she seemed to have been born with a natural toughness, the ability to keep going even when she had been battered and bloodied. But even so, the medicine on her cuts and punctures was a welcome relief.

Feeling a gentle hand on her shoulder, she looked up. Her mother was in her human form—with her golden feline eyes, strikingly angled cheekbones, and long light brown hair. But the most striking feature was that whenever Serafina looked into her mother's face, she knew that her mother loved her with all her heart.

"You're safe, Serafina," her mother said as she checked the dressing on her head.

"Momma," she said, her voice weak and ragged.

Looking around her, Serafina saw that her mother had brought her deep into the forest, to the angel's glade at the edge of the old, overgrown cemetery. Beneath the cemetery's dark cloak of twisted and gnarled trees, thick vines strangled the cracked, lichen-covered gravestones. Straggly moss hung down from the dead branches of the trees, and the darkened earth oozed with a ghostly mist. But the mist did not seep into the angel's glade itself, and a small circle of lush grass always remained perfect and green, even in winter. In the center of the glade stood a stone monument, a sculpture of a beautiful winged angel with a glinting steel sword. It was as if the angel protected the glade in a cusp of time, making it a place of eternal spring.

Her mother had been raising her two new cubs in a den beneath the roots of a large willow tree at the edge of the glade. And on a very different night than tonight, it had been the battleground on which Serafina and her allies had defeated Mr. Thorne, the Man in the Black Cloak.

Find the Black One! the bearded man with the wolfhounds had said earlier that night. She could not help but gaze around the glade for signs of the Black Cloak that she had torn to pieces on the razor-sharp edge of the angel's sword. She'd been sure that she had destroyed it, but she should have smashed its silver clasp and burned the leftover scraps of cloth. She looked toward the graveyard, with its tilting headstones and its broken coffins, and wondered what might have happened to the last remnants of the cloak.

For as long as she could remember, she had prowled through Biltmore's darkened corridors on her own. All her life, she'd hunted. It had been her instinct. She had never known why she had a long, curving spine, detached collarbones, and four toes on each foot. She had never known why she could see in the dark and others could not. But when she finally met her mother, she understood. Her mother was a *catamount*, a shape-shifting cat of the mountains. Serafina had come to understand that she wasn't just a child. She was a *cub*.

Desperate to learn more, she had hunted with her mother in the forest every night for the last several weeks, not just learning the lore of the forest, but what it meant to be a catamount. She had listened diligently to her mother's teachings and studied her mother when she was in her lion form. She had concentrated with all her mind and all her heart just like her mother had taught her. She had tried countless times to envision what she would look like, what it would feel like, but nothing ever happened. She was never able to change. She stayed just who she was. She wanted so badly to ask her mother to help her try again right now, but she had a sick feeling in her stomach that her mother wouldn't do it.

As the cubs trundled around in front of Serafina and nuzzled her face, she petted them and snuggled them, pressing their little ears back with her hands. The cubs were pure mountain lions, not shape-shifters, but they had accepted her from the beginning, never seeming to notice or care that her teeth were short and her tail was missing.

She wondered where the dark lion had gone. He was too young to be the father of her mother's cubs, so why had he been with her?

"Who was that other lion, Momma?" she asked. "The young one—"

"Never mind about him," her mother snarled. "I've told him to keep his distance from all of us, especially you. This isn't his territory and he knows it. He's only passing through with the others."

Serafina looked up at her in quick surprise. "What others?"

Her mother touched her cheek. "You need to rest, little one," she said, and then began to pull away.

"Please, tell me what's happening," Serafina pleaded, grabbing her mother's arm. "What others are you talking about? Why are the animals leaving? Who was that man in the forest? Why has he come?"

Her mother turned and looked into her eyes. "Never let yourself be seen or heard in the forest, Serafina. Always stay low and quiet. You must keep yourself safe."

"But I don't want to be *safe*. I want to know what's happening," she said before she could stop herself, realizing how childish she sounded.

"I understand your curiosity. Believe me, I do," her mother said gently as she reached out and touched her arm. "But how many lives do you think you have, little one? The forest is too dangerous for you. One of these nights I might not be there in time to save you."

"I want to be able to change like you, Momma."

"I know you do, kitten. I'm sorry," her mother said, wiping Serafina's cheek.

"Tell me what I need to do," Serafina begged. "I'll keep practicing."

Her mother shook her head. "Catamount kittens change with their mothers when they are very young, before they walk or run or speak. It becomes so much a part of how they envision themselves that they cannot even remember it being any other way. They see themselves as a catamount, and a catamount they become. I'm so sorry that I wasn't there to teach you when you were young."

"Teach me now, Momma."

"We've been trying every night—you know we have," her

mother said. "But I'm afraid it's too late for you. You won't ever be able to change."

Serafina shook her head fiercely, almost growling at her mother, she was so frustrated and hurt by her words. "I *know* I can do it. Don't give up on me."

"The forest is too dangerous for you to be here," her mother said, her eyes filled with sadness.

"You can come back with me to Biltmore in your human form," Serafina said excitedly. "We can be together."

"Serafina," her mother said, her tone both soft and firm at the same time, like she knew the loneliness and confusion that Serafina must be feeling. "I was trapped in my lion form for twelve years. I can't even imagine going back into the world of humans again, not yet. You have to understand. My soul was cleaved. I need time to heal, to understand what I am. I'm so sorry, but right now I belong in the forest, and I need to take care of the cubs."

"But—" Serafina tried to say.

"Wait," her mother said softly. "Let me finish what I was saying. I need to tell you this." Her mother paused, filled with emotion. "During those same twelve years that I was a lion, you were as trapped as I was. You were trapped in your human form." Her mother wiped a tear from her own eye. "That is what you are now. That is what you've grown up to be. You're a human. And I'm a catamount." Her mother looked down at the ground and pulled in a long, ragged breath. And then she lifted her eyes and looked at Serafina again. "I am so thankful that we had this time together, that I got to know you and see what a wonderful girl you've grown up to be. I love you with all my heart, Serafina, but I can't be your mother the way I know I should be."

"Momma, please don't say that. . . ." Serafina said.

"No, Serafina," her mother said, holding her with trembling hands. "Listen to me. You almost died tonight. I should have never let you wander the forest alone. I almost lost you." Her mother's voice cracked. "You have no idea how much you mean to me . . . and you have no idea how dark a force has been stirred. I want you to go back to Biltmore and stay there. That is your home. You're safe inside those walls. Things are changing here. I must take the cubs and go. The forest is far too dangerous for you, especially now."

Serafina looked up at her. "You're going? What do you mean, 'especially now'? Tell me what's happening, Momma. Why are all the animals leaving?"

"This is not your battle to fight, Serafina. With your two legs, you can't run fast enough to escape this danger. And you can't claw hard enough to fight against it. Once you've rested, I want you to go home. Be very careful. Stay clear of everything you see. Go straight back to Biltmore."

Serafina tried to keep from crying. "Momma, I want to be here with you in the forest. Please."

"Serafina, you don't be—"

"Don't say that!"

"You have to listen to what I'm saying," her mother said more forcefully. "You don't belong here, Serafina."

Serafina rubbed the tears out of her eyes in fury. She

wanted to belong. She wanted to belong more than anything. Her mother's words were splitting her heart in two. She wanted to keep arguing, but her mother would say no more.

Her mother laid Serafina's head down in the grass. "I've given you something to help you sleep. You'll feel better when you wake."

Serafina lay quietly as her mother told her to, but it was all so confusing. Whether house or forest, she just wanted to find a place to be. She seemed to have friends who weren't her friends, kin who weren't her kin. It felt like a dark force was gathering in the forest and seeping into her heart, like the Black Cloak slowly wrapping itself around her soul.

Lying at the base of the angel, she felt herself drifting into a deep and blackened sleep, as if she was falling into a bottomless pit, and there was nothing she could do to stop it.

When she woke a few hours later, she was no longer lying in the grass. She found herself in total darkness. She felt dirt all around her—below her, above her, and on all sides.

It took Serafina several seconds to realize that she was lying in her mother's earthen den. Her mother must have picked her up and carried her into the den when she was sleeping.

She felt warmer and stronger than she had before. She got herself up onto her hands and knees and crawled out of the den, then stood in the moonlight of the angel's glade. Looking up at the stars, it felt like a few hours had passed.

Her bleeding had stopped and her wounds did not hurt as badly as they did before. But as she looked around her, her heart sank, for her mother and the cubs and the dark lion were gone. They had left her here alone.

She found words traced into the dirt.

IF YOU NEED ME, WINTER, SPRING, OR FALL,

COME WHERE WHAT YOU CLIMBED IS FLOOR AND RAIN

IS WALL.

Serafina frowned. She didn't know what the words meant or even if they had been left for her.

She gazed around the angel's glade and then out into the trees. The forest was utter stillness, nothing but a mist drifting through the wet and glistening branches, and she could not hear a single living thing. It was as if the entire world outside the glade had disappeared.

She thought about her mother, and the cubs, and the dark lion, and what her mother had said: *You don't belong here, Serafina!* Of all the wounds she'd suffered, that one hurt the most.

Then she thought about Braeden, and her pa, and Mr. and Mrs. Vanderbilt, and everyone at Biltmore living their daytime lives so separate from her own.

You don't belong there, either.

Standing in the center of the angel's glade, she came to a slow and aching realization.

She was once again alone.

Just alone.

When she thought about what her mother had told her she would never be able to do, an aching, broken, throbbing part of her just wanted to kneel down and cry. She didn't understand. She had been so hopeful with all the changes that were happening in her life, but now she felt like she was caught in between, like she didn't belong anywhere. She was neither forest nor house, neither night nor day.

After a long time, she turned and looked at the beautiful, silent stone angel, with her graceful and powerful wings and her long steel sword. Serafina read the inscription on the pedestal.

OUR CHARACTER ISN'T DEFINED
BY THE BATTLES WE WIN OR LOSE,
BUT BY THE BATTLES WE DARE TO FIGHT.

Then she looked back out into the forest once more. She decided that no matter what she could or couldn't do, no matter who did or didn't want her, she was still the C.R.C. That much she knew for sure. And she'd seen things in the forest tonight that she couldn't account for. She didn't know who the bearded man was, except that he was something so dark that the animals fled before him, something so dangerous that even her mother believed that he could not be fought. Her mother was sure the darkest dangers lurked in the forest, and no doubt they did, but Serafina knew from experience that sometimes they crept into the house. She remembered the driverless carriage and the four stallions going onward up the road toward Biltmore. She could swear there had been someone else in that carriage. In what guise would this new stranger arrive and slither his way into Mr. and Mrs. Vanderbilt's home? Into *her* home. And what had he come for? Was he a thief? Was he a spy?

Standing there in the angel's glade, Serafina came to a decision. If there was a rat in the house, she was going to find it.

Serafina stopped at the edge of Biltmore's lagoon, crouched down in the undergrowth, and scanned the horizon for danger.

She waited and she watched.

From her current vantage point, she didn't see any signs of trouble. Everything looked peaceful and serene.

The mirrorlike surface of the lagoon reflected the last of the shimmering stars that would soon give way to dawn. A family of swans flew low over the smooth water, then circled around and came in for a landing, shattering the reflection of the starlit sky.

In the distance, Biltmore House sat majestically atop a great hill, seeming to rise up out of the trees of the parkland that surrounded it. The windows glinted as the first light of the rising sun touched its walls. With its slate-blue roof, elegant arches, and spired towers, it looked like a fairy-tale castle of old, the kind she had read about in the mansion's library when everyone else was asleep.

As she gazed upon the house, a gentle warmth filled her heart. She was glad to be coming home. She decided that she would try to rekindle her friendship with Braeden, and she'd make sure she thanked Mrs. Vanderbilt again for the dress she'd given her. And she would do her best to mind her pa. But the first thing she had to do was to make sure she watched out for any strangers who had arrived at Biltmore during the night. The pain of her wounds had lessened, but the frightening images of the bearded man in the forest and the other figure in the carriage blazed in her mind. And she kept wondering what had happened to the feral boy who had helped her and then disappeared.

She headed toward the house, making her way up the slope through an area of open grassland dotted with large trees. She slinked from tree to tree, careful to stay hidden.

When she spotted two men and a dog in the distance walking toward the edge of the forest, she crouched low and took cover. She immediately recognized the lean, dark-haired figure of Mr. Vanderbilt, the master of Biltmore Estate, in his calf-high boots, woodsman jacket, and fedora hat. Like most gentlemen, he often carried a stylish cane when he was out and about on formal occasions, but today he had equipped himself with his usual chestnut hiking stave with its spiked metal ferrule and leather wrist strap. Cedric, his huge white-and-brown Saint Bernard, walked loyally beside him. Over the last few weeks, she'd gotten to know Mr. Vanderbilt better than she had before. There was much about the quiet man that was still a mystery to her, but she'd come to appreciate him, and hoped he felt the same about her. She was relieved to see him safe and out for what looked like an early-morning walk. This was surely a good sign that all was well at Biltmore.

But then she saw the man walking with him.

He wore a long tannish-brown coat over his light gray gentleman's suit, and carried a walking stick with a brass knob that glinted in the sun as he moved. He had an old face, a balding head, and a thick gray beard. Serafina narrowed her eyes suspiciously. She immediately thought of the terrifying man she'd seen in the forest, with his silvery glinting eyes and his craggy face. They were disturbingly similar figures. But as she watched, she decided that this wasn't him.

The man walking with Mr. Vanderbilt was older, slower in movement, more bent of frame. She could not see his face well enough to know who he was, but he seemed familiar. And she remembered that the man with the dogs had exited the carriage and sent it on toward Biltmore. Was this the second occupant of the carriage? Maybe it was one of the bearded man's servants sent ahead to spy. Or was he a demon like the Man in the Black Cloak? She knew that someone had come to Biltmore during the night. She just needed to find out who it was.

She slipped behind a large black walnut tree and watched the two men. As they walked slowly into the forest, the stranger poked a hole in the ground with the tip of his cane. Then he took something out of his leather shoulder satchel, knelt down, and seemed to bury it in the dirt. Serafina thought that this was very peculiar behavior.

The two men and the dog finally disappeared into the foliage, leaving Serafina with nothing but lingering doubt about who this stranger was and how he was connected to the man she'd seen the night before.

As she puzzled through what she'd seen, she continued up the slope toward the house. Her heart leapt when she saw Braeden by the stables saddling one of his horses.

Seeing her friend safe and sound, Serafina smiled and felt her muscles relaxing. She could see now that whoever or whatever had come to Biltmore in the carriage during the night hadn't hurt her friend. But the first thing she was going to do was tell Braeden what happened to her in the forest and warn him about what she saw.

Braeden was wearing his usual brown tweed hacking jacket and vest, with a white shirt and beige cravat. He moved around easily in his leather riding boots. His tussle of brown hair was blowing in the breeze a little bit. It did not surprise her to see Gidean, his Doberman, at his side. Braeden seemed to make a lasting bond with whatever animal he met. He had befriended the unusual, pointed-eared black dog while traveling in Germany with his family a few years ago. After the tragic death of his family in a house fire, the boy and his dog had become inseparable. In some ways, Gidean was the last remaining member of Braeden's family before he came to Biltmore to live with his uncle, and he had found few other friends.

Serafina knew that Braeden rode every day. He'd gallop

across the fields like the wind, his horse running so fast that it was like they weren't even attached to the earth. It was good to see him here.

She broke from her cover and ran toward him, thinking that she'd pounce on him and knock him to the ground in fun. She was just about to shout *Hey, Braeden!* when a second figure stepped out from behind the horse. Serafina dropped quickly into the tall grass.

When she didn't hear anyone shout *Hey, there's a peculiar girl in the grass over there!* she crawled over to the base of a nearby tree and peeked out.

A tall girl about fourteen years old with long, curly red hair stood waiting for Braeden to adjust the stirrup on her horse's sidesaddle. She wore a fitted emerald-green velvet riding jacket with an upturned collar, triangular lapels, and turn-back cuffs. The jacket's gold buttons glinted in the sunlight whenever she turned her body or lifted her wrist. Her trim green-and-white-striped waistcoat and long skirt matched her jacket in every detail.

Serafina frowned in irritation. Braeden normally rode alone. His aunt and uncle must have asked him to entertain this young guest. But what should she do now? Should she brush off her ripped, dirtied, bloodstained, fang-shredded dress, and walk over to Braeden and the girl and introduce herself? She imagined an exaggerated, backwoods version of herself coming out of the brush toward them. *Mornin', y'all. I'm just back from catchin' some wood rats and nearly gettin' eaten up by a pack of wolfhounds. How you two doin' this mornin'?*

She thought about approaching them, but maybe interrupting Braeden and the girl would be a rude, unwelcome imposition.

She had no idea.

Out of instinct more than anything else, she stayed hidden where she was and watched.

The girl allowed Braeden to help her up into the saddle, then rearranged her legs and the long folds of her riding skirt to drape over the left side of the horse. That was when Serafina noticed that she was wearing beautiful dove-gray suede, laced-up, flower-embroidered ankle boots. They were completely ridiculous for horseback riding, and Serafina couldn't even imagine running through the forest in such delicate things, but they sure were pretty.

Along with her fancy attire, the girl carried a finely made riding cane with a silver topper and a leather whip end. Serafina smirked a little. It seemed like all the fancy folk liked to carry some sort of cane or walking stick or other accoutrement whenever they went outside, but she preferred to have her hands free at all times.

Seeing the whip, Braeden said, "You won't need anything like that."

"But it goes with my outfit!" the girl insisted.

"If you say so," Braeden said. "But please don't touch the horse with it."

"Very well," the girl agreed. She spoke in a grand and mannerly tone, as if she'd been raised in the way of a proper lady and she wanted people to know it. And Serafina noticed that she had an accent like Mrs. King, Biltmore's head housekeeper, who was from England.

"So, do tell," the girl said. "How do I stop this beast if it runs away with me?"

Serafina chuckled at the thought of the horse bolting with the screaming, frilly-dressed girl, jumping a few fences in wild abandon, and then landing in a mud pit with a glorious splat.

"You just need to pull back on the reins a little bit," Braeden said politely. It was clear that he didn't know this girl too well, which further reinforced Serafina's theory that Braeden's aunt and uncle were putting him up to this.

Beyond all the girl's fanciness and airs, there was something that bothered Serafina about her. A highfalutin fashion plate like her would certainly know how to ride a horse, but she seemed to be pretending that she didn't. Why would she do that? Why would she feign helplessness? Was that what a girl did to attract a boy's attention?

Seemingly unmoved by the girl's ploy, Braeden walked over to his horse without further comment. He slipped effortlessly onto his horse's bare back. A week ago, he had explained to Serafina that he didn't use a bridle and reins to control his horse but signaled the speed and direction he wanted to go by adjusting the pressure and angle of his legs.

"Now, we mustn't go too fast," the girl said daintily as the two young riders rode their horses at a walk out onto the grounds of the estate. Serafina could tell she wasn't scared of the horse but simply pretending to be a delicate soul.

"Actually, I thought we might do a bit of high-speed racing," Braeden said facetiously.

Seeming to realize that Braeden wasn't falling for her precious-princess routine, the English girl changed her tone as fast as a rattlesnake changes the direction of its wind.

"I would race you," she replied haughtily, "but I might get a speck of mud on my skirt from my horse kicking up dirt into your face as I passed you."

Braeden laughed, and Serafina couldn't help but smile as well. The girl had a bit of spunk in her after all!

As Braeden and the girl rode away down the path, Serafina could hear them talking pleasantly to each other, Braeden telling her about his horses and his dog, Gidean, and the girl listing the particulars of the gown she'd be wearing to dinner that evening.

Serafina noticed that as Braeden and the girl entered the trees, the girl looked warily around her. The wilds of North Carolina must seem a dark and foreboding place to a civilized girl like her. She urged her horse forward to move closer to Braeden.

Braeden looked at the girl as she came up alongside him. Serafina could no longer tell if Braeden was simply being polite or if he actually wanted to be this girl's friend, but as they rode out into the trees, she felt a strange queasiness in her stomach that she'd never felt before.

Serafina could have easily followed them without their knowing it, but she didn't. She had a job to do.

Last night she'd seen the man in the forest send the carriage

to Biltmore. She reckoned that the sensible place to look for signs that the intruder had arrived was the stables.

She crept in through the back door, wary of Mr. Rinaldi, the fiery-tempered Italian stable boss who didn't take kindly to sneakers-about who might spook his horses. It was easy for her to move quietly on the perfectly clean redbrick floor, and even in the daytime there were plenty of shadows in the stables to take advantage of. The horse stalls consisted of lacquered oak boards trimmed in black railing with curving black grills along the top. She began checking each of the stalls. Along with the Vanderbilts' several dozen horses, she found a dozen others that belonged to the guests.

Ga-bang!

Serafina hit the floor. Her heart pounded. It sounded like a sledgehammer had hit the side of a stall. Having no idea what she was going to see, she peered down the stable's central aisle. Disturbed dust floated from the ceiling down toward the floor, as if the earth itself had shaken, but otherwise the aisle was empty. She could see that four of the stalls at the end had been boarded up all the way to the ceiling. They were completely closed in, as if to make sure that whatever they held had no possibility of escape.

She gathered herself up onto her feet and moved slowly down the aisle toward the boarded stalls. She could feel the sweat on her palms.

The oak boards blocked her view of what was inside the stalls, so she crept up close, put her face to the boards, and peered through the cracks.

A massive beast hurled itself at the boards of the stall. The flexing wood struck Serafina in the head. The surprise of it sent her tripping backward in fear. The beast kicked the stall boards and slammed them with its shoulders, snorting and thrashing. The boards bent and creaked under the pressure of the pounding animal.

When she heard the stable boss and a gang of stablemen running toward the disturbance she'd caused, she scrambled into an empty stall, ducked down, and hid in a shadow.

She gasped for breath, trying to figure out what she'd just seen—a massive dark shape, black eyes, flaring nostrils, and pounding hooves.

A storm of questions flooded her mind as Mr. Rinaldi and

his men came charging down the aisle. The beast continued its terrible pounding and thrashing. The stable boss shouted instructions to his men to reinforce the boards. Serafina quickly climbed out the back of the stall and darted from the stables before they caught sight of her.

Those were the stallions! There was no question now. Whoever he was, the second occupant of the carriage was here.

She scurried along the stone foundation at the rear of the house, pushed her body through the air shaft, crawled through the passage, pushed aside the wire mesh, and entered the basement. Her presence at the estate had become known to the Vanderbilts a few weeks before, so she could theoretically use the doors like normal people, but she seldom did.

She went down the basement corridor, through a door, and then down another passageway. As she stepped into the workshop, her pa turned toward her.

"Good mornin'," he began to say in a pleased, casual fashion, but when he got a look at her bedraggled state, he lurched back in surprise. "Eh, law! What happened to you, child?" His hands guided her gently to a stool for her to sit. "Aw, Sera," he said as he looked at her wounds. "I said you could go out into the forest at night to spend time with your mother, but you're breakin' my heart, comin' home lookin' like this. What've you been doin' out there in them woods?"

Her pa had found her in the forest the night she was born, so she reckoned he must have had an inkling of what she was, but he didn't like dark talk of demons and shifters and things that go bump in the night. It was as if he thought that as long as they didn't talk about those things, they would not be real or come into their lives. She had told herself many times that she wouldn't bother her pa with the details of what happened at night when she went out, and normally she kept that promise, but the moment her pa asked, it all just started gushing out of her before she could stop it.

"I had a terrible run-in with a pack of dogs, Pa!" she said, choking up.

"It's all right, Sera, you're safe here," her pa said as he took her into his thick arms and huge chest and held her. "But what dogs are you talking about? It wasn't the young master's dog, was it?"

"No, Pa. Gidean would never hurt me. There was a strange man in the forest with a pack of wolfhounds. He sicced 'em on me somethin' fierce!"

"But where did he come from?" her pa asked. "Was he a bear hunter?"

She shook her head. "I don't know. After he got out of the carriage, he sent the carriage on toward Biltmore. I think I saw the horses in the stables. And I saw a strange man with Mr. Vanderbilt this morning. Did anyone unusual arrive at the house last night?"

"The servants have been jabbering on about all the folk comin' in for Christmastime, but I doubt the man you saw was one of the Vanderbilts' guests. I'll wager it was one of those poachers from Mills Gap that we ran off the estate two years ago."

Serafina could hear the anger seething in her pa's voice. He was riled up that someone had done his little girl harm. He kept talking as he examined the crusted blood on her head. "I'll go speak with Superintendent McNamee first thing. We'll take a party out there to confront this fella, whoever he is. But first off, let's get you patched up. Then you rest a spell. Your lesson can wait."

"My lesson?" she asked, confused.

"For them table manners of yourn."

"Not again, Pa, please. I've got to figure out who's come to Biltmore."

"I told ya. We're fixing to hammer that nail till it's sunk in deep."

"Sunk in my head, you mean."

"Yeah, in your head. Where else do ya learn things? Now that you and the young master are gettin' on, you need to behave proper."

"I know how to behave just fine, Pa."

"You're 'bout as civilized as a weasel, girl. I shoulda been schoolin' ya more about the folk upstairs and how they go 'bout things, 'cause it hain't like us."

"Braeden is my friend, Pa. He likes me just fine the way I am, if that's what you're pokin' at," she said. Although, as she heard herself defending Braeden's opinion of her, it felt suspiciously like she was lying not just to her pa but to herself. Truth was, she didn't know if she was or wasn't Braeden's friend anymore, and she was becoming increasingly less certain of it every day.

"It's not directly the young master I'm concerned about,"

her pa continued as he got a clean, wet cloth and started look-ing after her wounds. "It's the master and the mistress, and especially their guests come city way. You can't sit at their table if you don't know the difference between the napkin and the tablecloth."

"Why would I need to know the difference between—"

"The butler told me that Mr. Vanderbilt was going to be looking for you upstairs later today. And everyone in the kitchen is fixin' for a big supper tonight."

"A supper? What kind of supper? Is the stranger going to be there? Is that what this is all about? And what about Braeden— is he going to be there?"

"That's a bushel more questions than I got answers for," her pa said. "I don't know anything about it, truth be told. But other than the young master, I can't figure any other reason why the Vanderbilts would be a-looking for you. I just know there's a big shindig tonight, and the master sent word, and it didn't sound so much like an invitation as an instruction, if ya get my meaning."

"Did they say it was a supper or a shindig, Pa?" Serafina said, getting confused, and realizing as she said it that the Vanderbilts didn't have events by either of those names.

"It's all the same up there, hain't it?" her pa said.

Serafina knew that she had to go to the event her pa was telling her about. For one thing, it'd be the best way to see all the new people who had arrived at the house. But the obstacles immediately sprang into her mind. "How can I go up there,

Pa?" she said in alarm, looking at the bite marks and scratches all over her arms and legs. They didn't hurt too badly, but they looked something awful.

"We'll clean the mud off ya, get the sticks and blood outten your hair, and you'll be fine. Your dress will cover them there scratches."

"My dress has more holes in it than me," she protested as she examined the bloodstained, tattered pieces of the dress Mrs. V had given her. She couldn't show up in that.

"Them toothy mongrels sure did a number on you," he said as he examined the tear in her lower ear. "Don't that hurt?"

"Naw, not no more," she said, her mind on other things. "Where's that old work shirt of yours that I used to wear?"

"I threw that thing out as soon as I saw that Mrs. Vanderbilt gave you something nice to wear."

"Aw, Pa, now I ain't got nothin' at all!"

"Don't fuss. I'll make ya somethin' outta what we got up in here."

Serafina shook her head in dismay. "What we got around here is mostly sackcloth and sandpaper!"

"Look," her pa said, taking her by the shoulders and looking into her eyes. "You're alive, ain't ya? So toughen up. Bless the Lord and get on with things. In your entire life, has the master of the house ever demanded your presence upstairs? No, he has not. So, yes, ma'am, if the master wants you there, you're gonna be there. With bells on."

"Bells?" she asked in horror. "Why do I have to wear bells?"

How could she sneak and hide if she was wearing noisy bells around her neck? Or did they go on her feet?

"It's just an expression, girl," her pa said, shaking his head. Then, after a moment, he muttered to himself, "At least I think it is."

10

Serafina sat, mad and miserable, on the cot while her pa did his level best to clean and bandage her wounds. As usual, she and her pa were surrounded by the workshop's supply shelves, tool racks, and workbenches. But her pa seemed to have forgotten the work he was supposed to be doing that morning. His mind had become consumed with her.

Some of the copper piping and brass fittings from the kitchen's cold box sat in a twisted clump on the bench. The previous day, her pa had explained something about an ammonia-gas brine system, intake pipes, and cooling coils, but none of it took. He'd raised her in his workshop, but she had no talent with machines. She couldn't remember anything about the contraption other than it was complicated, kept food cold, and was one of the few refrigeration systems in the country. The mountain folk kept their food cold by sticking it in a cold spring tumbling down into a creek, which seemed far more sensible to her.

As soon as her pa was done fussing with her, she slipped off the bed, hoping he'd forget his threat to make her rest. "I've gotta go, Pa," she said. "I'm gonna sneak upstairs and see if I can spot the intruder."

"Now, listen here," he said, holding her arm. "I don't want you confrontin' anybody up there."

She nodded. "I'm with ya, Pa. No confrontin'. I just want to see who's up there and make sure everyone is all right. No one will ever see me."

"I'm needin' your word on this," he said.

"You got my word, Pa."

Off she went to the main floor. She spotted a few guests strolling this way and that or lounging in the parlors, but nobody suspicious. She moved up to the second floor next, but she didn't see anything out of the ordinary there, either. She scoured the house from top to bottom, but there was no sign of the stranger she'd seen with Mr. Vanderbilt or anyone else who seemed like they might have been the second passenger in the carriage. She listened for scuttlebutt from the servants as they prepared for the event in the Banquet Hall that evening, but she didn't pick up anything other than how many cucumbers the cook wanted the scullery maid to fetch and how many silver platters the butler needed for his footmen.

She tried to think through everything she had seen the night before, wondering if she'd missed any clues. What had she actually seen when the bearded man threw his walking stick up into the air toward the owl? And who was the second passenger who remained in the shadows of the carriage? Was it the stranger she'd seen walking with Mr. Vanderbilt? And who was the feral boy who had helped her? Was he still alive? How could she find him again?

Another bushel of questions I don't have answers to, she thought in frustration, remembering her pa's words.

Later that afternoon, when she walked back into the workshop, her pa asked, "What did you find out?"

"A whole lot of nothin'," she grumbled. "No sign of anyone suspicious at all."

"I spoke to Superintendent McNamee. He's sendin' out a group of his best horsemen to hunt down the poachers." As he spoke, her pa wiped his grease-smeared hands with a rag.

"Elevator actin' up again, Pa?" she asked.

Her pa had often boasted that Biltmore had the first and finest electric elevator in the South, but he seemed a mite less keen on the machine today.

"The gears in the basement keep gettin' all gaumed up when it hits the fourth floor," he said. "Everwho installed the thing got them shafts all sigogglin, this way and that. I swear it ain't gonna work proper till I tear out the whole thing and start again." He waved her over to him. "But take a look at this. This is interestin'." He showed her a thin piece of sheet metal that looked like it hadn't just broken, but had been torn. It was odd to see metal torn like that. She didn't even know how that was possible.

"What is that, Pa?" she asked.

"This here little bracket was supposed to be a-holdin' the main gear in place, but whenever the elevator ran, it kept flexing back and forth, you see?" As he spoke, he showed her the flexing motion by bending the sheet metal with his fingers. "The metal is plenty strong at first. Seems unbreakable, don't it? But when ya bend it back and forth over and over again like this, watch what happens. It gets weaker and weaker, these little cracks start, and then it finally breaks." Just as he said the words, the metal snapped in his fingers. "You see that?"

Serafina looked up at her pa and smiled. Some days, he had a special kind of magic about him.

Then she looked over at the other workbench. Somewhere between mending the elevator, fixing the cold box, and tending to his other duties, her pa had cobbled together a dress for her made out of a burlap tow sack and discarded scraps of leather.

"Pa . . ." she said, horrified by the sight of it.

"Try it on," he said. He seemed rather proud of the stitching he'd done with fibrous twine and the leather-working needle he sometimes used to patch holes in the leather apron he wore. Her pa liked the idea that he could make or mend just about anything.

Serafina walked glumly behind the supply racks, took off her tattered green dress, and put on the thing her pa had made.

"Looks as fine as a Sunday mornin'," her pa said cheerfully

as she stepped out from behind the racks, but she could tell he was lying through his teeth. Even he knew it was the most god-awful, ugly thing that ever done walked the earth. But it worked. And to her pa, that's what counted. It was functional. It clothed her body. The dress had longish sleeves that covered most of the punctures and scratches on her arms, and a close-fitting collar that hid at least part of the gruesome cut on her throat. So at least the fancy ladies at the shindig or the supper, or whatever it was, wouldn't swoon at the corpsy sight of her.

"Now, sit down here," her pa said. "I'll show you how to behave proper at the table."

She sat reluctantly on the stool he placed in front of an old work board that was meant to represent the forty-foot-long for-mal dining table in Mr. and Mrs. Vanderbilt's grand Banquet Hall.

"Sit up straight, girl, not all curvy-spined like that," her pa said.

Serafina straightened her back.

"Get your head up, not hunched all over your food like you gotta fight for it."

Serafina leaned back in the way he instructed.

"Get them elbows offen the table," he said.

"I ain't no banjo, Pa, so quit pickin' on me."

"I ain't pickin' on you. I'm tryin' to teach ya somethin', but you're too stubborn-born to learn it."

"Ain't as stubborn as you," she grumbled.

"Don't get briggity with the sass, girl. Now, listen. When you eat your supper, you need to use your forks. You see here?

These screwdrivers are your forks. The mortar trowel there is your spoon. And my whittlin' blade is your dinner knife. From what I've heard, you gotta use the right fork for the job."

"What job?" she asked in confusion.

"For what you're eatin'. Understand?"

"No, I don't understand," she admitted.

"Now, look straight ahead," he said, "not all shifty-eyed like you're gonna pounce on somethin' and kill it at any second. The salad fork here is on the outside. The dinner fork is on the inside. Sera, you hearin' me?"

She didn't normally enjoy her pa's etiquette lessons, but it felt kind of good to be home, safe and sound, suffering through yet another one.

"You got it?" he asked when he finished explaining about the various utensils.

"Got it. Dinner fork on the inside. Salad fork on the outside. I just have one question."

"Yes?"

"What's a salad?"

"Botheration, Serafina!"

"I'm askin' a question!"

"It's a bowl of, ya know . . . greenery. Lettuce, cabbage, carrots, that sort of thing."

"So it's rabbit food."

"No, ma'am, it is not," her pa said firmly.

"It's poke sallet."

"No, it ain't."

"It's food that prey eats."

"I don't want to hear no talk like that, and you know it."

As her pa schooled her in the fineries of supper etiquette, she got the notion that he'd never actually sat at the table with the Vanderbilts. She could see that he was going more on what he imagined than live experience, and she was particularly suspicious of his understanding of salads.

"Why would rich and proper folk like the Vanderbilts eat leaves when they could afford to eat something good? Why don't they eat chicken all day? If I was them, I'd eat so much chicken I'd get fat and slow."

"Sera, you need to take this seriously."

"I am!" she said.

"Look, you've got a friend in the young master now, and that's a good'n. But if you're gonna be his friend for long, you need to learn the rudiments."

"The rudiments?"

"How to behave like a daytime girl."

"I ain't no Vanderbilt, Pa. He knows that."

"I know. It's just that when you're up there, I don't want you to—"

"To what? Horrify them?"

"Well, now, Sera, you know you ain't the daintiest flower in the garden, is all. I love ya heaps, but there ain't no denying it—you're a sight feral, talkin' about prey and hunting rats. With me, that's all fine and good, but—"

"I understand, Pa," she said glumly, wanting him to stop. "I'll be on my best behavior when I'm up there."

When she heard someone coming down the corridor, she

flinched and almost darted. After years of hiding, it still made her scurry when she heard the sound of footsteps approaching.

"Someone's comin', Pa," she whispered.

"Naw, hain't nobody a-comin'. Just pay attention to what I'm tellin' ya. We've got to—"

"Pardon me, sir," a young maid said as she stepped into the workshop.

"Lordy, girl," Serafina's pa said as he turned around and looked at the maid. "Don't sneak up on a man like that."

"Sorry, sir," the maid said, curtsying.

The maid was a young girl, a couple of years older than Serafina, with a pleasant face and strands of dark hair curling out from beneath her white cap. Like the other maids, she wore a black cotton dress with a starched white collar, white cuffs, and a long white lace apron. But from the look of her and the sound of her words, it seemed like she was one of the local mountain folk.

"Well, spit it out, girl," Serafina's pa told her.

"Yes, sir," she said, and glanced at Serafina self-consciously. "I have a note from the young master for the little miss."

As the maid said these words, she eyed Serafina. Serafina could see the girl trying to make sense of the weird angles of her face and the amber color of her eyes. Or maybe she was notic- ing the bloody wounds peeking out from beneath the edges of the burlap gunnysack she was wearing. Whatever it was, there was apparently plenty to stare at, and the girl couldn't quite resist availing herself of the opportunity.

"Ah, ya see, Sera," her pa said. "I told ya. Good thing we've been a-practicin'. The young master is sending you a proper invitation to the supper this evening."

"Here you go, miss," the maid said as she stretched out her hand with the note toward Serafina as if she didn't want to get any closer to her.

"Thank you," Serafina said quietly. She took the note from the maid slowly so as not to startle the girl with too quick a movement.

"Thank you, miss," the maid said, but instead of then leaving, she froze, transfixed, as she studied Serafina's streaked hair and odd clothing.

"Was there something else?" Serafina's pa said to the maid.

"Oh no, I'm sorry, pardon me," the maid said as she pulled herself out of her stare, curtsied in embarrassment to Serafina, and then quickly excused herself from the room.

"Well, what's it say, then?" Serafina's pa said, gesturing toward the note.

As Serafina carefully opened the small piece of paper, her hands trembled. Whatever it was, it felt important. As she read Braeden's words, the first thing she understood was that her pa had been wrong. She wasn't receiving an invitation to a dancing party or a formal dinner. The note dealt with a far darker subject. Just the first sentence tightened her chest with fear. Suddenly, she remembered seeing the black-cloaked Mr. Thorne falling dead to the ground, killed by her and her companions. Then another image flashed through her mind: her and Braeden at the gallows, hanging by their necks for the crime of murder. But as she read the frightening note, there was another emotion as well. She glowed with the knowledge that it was Braeden who was telling her these words. At long last, it was her old friend and ally.

S,

A murder investigator has arrived at Biltmore. He's the strangest man I have ever seen. You and I have been summoned at 6:00 p.m. for questioning about the disappearance of Mr. Thorne. Be careful.

—B.

11

Serafina suspected that the murder investigator was the second man in the carriage. It appeared that she didn't need to look for him, because he was looking for her. She thought, too, that he must have been the stranger she'd seen with Mr. Vanderbilt earlier that morning. But no matter who he was, getting interrogated by the police couldn't be a good thing. What was she going to say when he asked about Mr. Thorne's disappearance? "Oh, him? Yes, I remember him. I led him into a trap by my mother's den, and my allies killed him. Do you want me to show you where it all happened?"

As she headed up the narrow, unlit back stairway toward the main floor, it felt like her head was filled with more thoughts than her mind could hold.

It was half past five in the afternoon. She had half an hour to spy on the house and gather clues before she had to report for the interrogation. But she ran into an immediate problem.

The young maid who had stared at her earlier was waiting for her at the top of the stairs, blocking her path.

Serafina stopped and narrowed her eyes at her. "What do you want?"

When the girl stepped toward her, Serafina stepped back warily.

"I need to talk to you, miss. . . ."

Serafina did not reply.

"Beggin' your pardon, miss," the maid said, "but you don't want to go up there lookin' like that."

"This is the way I look," Serafina said fiercely as she gazed steadily at the girl.

"I mean your dress, miss," the girl said.

"It's the only one I have," Serafina said.

The maid nodded, seeming to understand. "Then let me lend you something. My day-off dress or my Sunday dress, anything. But not . . ."

"But not this," Serafina said, gesturing toward the burlap sack she was wearing.

"I ain't heard nothin' but good things about your pa," the maid said sheepishly. "People say he can fix just about anything round here. But, beggin' your pardon, miss, I think we can agree that he ain't no dress designer."

Serafina smiled. She was absolutely right about that. "And you're going to help me?" she asked tentatively.

"If you want me to," the girl said, smiling a little.

"What's your name?" Serafina asked.

"I'm Essie Walker."

"I'm Serafina."

"The girl who brought the children back," Essie said, nodding. She already knew who she was and seemed pleased to meet her.

Serafina smiled and nodded in return. T.G.W.B.T.C.B. wasn't quite as catchy as C.R.C., but she liked it.

As she looked at Essie more closely, it seemed to her that she had a gentle face, without any deceit or guile, and a warm, friendly smile.

"Where do your people bury, Essie?" Serafina asked, which was how she'd heard her pa ask other mountain folk where they were from.

"I don't rightly know," Essie said. "My ma and pa passed away when I was but one or two. My nanny and papaw raised me for a while, out on a farm up Madison County way, pert nigh Walnut, but when they passed, I didn't have nowhere to go. Mrs. Vanderbilt heard about me and took me in and gave me a bed to sleep in. I told her I wanted to make myself useful."

"You're pretty young for being a maid at Biltmore," Serafina said.

"Youngest maid ever," Essie said, smiling proudly. "Come on, let's go. We'll get ya sorted out." Essie reached for Serafina's hand, but Serafina reflexively pulled away, snapping her whole body back before Essie was even close to touching her.

Essie caught her breath, startled by Serafina's quick movement.

"You're a mite skittish, aren't ya?" Essie said.

"I'm sorry," Serafina said, embarrassed.

"It's all right," Essie said. "We've all got somethin' that spooks us, right? But come on. Time's a-tickin'."

Essie turned and bolted up the stairs. Serafina followed easily right behind her. The two of them ran up three flights, then darted through a small doorway that led to a back corridor, then up another stairway to the fourth floor. Essie led them down a tight passage that ran beneath the North Tower, past a cluster of maids' rooms, around a corner, down six steps, and through the main Servant Hall, where three maids and a house girl were gathered around the fireplace on their break.

"Don't pay us no mind," Essie called as she and Serafina ran through the room. They dashed down a long, narrow corridor with a Gothic arched ceiling wedged beneath the steep angle of the mansion's slanted rooftop. There were twenty-one rooms on the fourth floor for the maids and other female servants. And Essie's room was the third on the right.

"We'll duck in here, miss," Essie said as Serafina followed her in.

During her nightly prowls, Serafina had sometimes snuck into one of the maids' rooms when the maid went down the hall to the water closet, so she had seen the clean, plainly finished rooms before. But Essie had made up her room's simple white metal bed with soft pillows and an autumn quilt. To Serafina, it looked like a perfect warm spot for curling up in the late-afternoon sun. But she had a feeling Essie didn't get much time for napping. A clump of wrinkled clothing lay across the splint-reed chair, two of the drawers on the chestnut dresser were pulled out, and there was water left over in the basin on the washstand.

"Pardon the mess, miss," Essie said, quickly picking up the underclothing from the floor and pushing the dresser drawers shut. "Lord protect me if Mrs. King comes up for an inspection this afternoon, but five o'clock comes awful early some mornin's. Wasn't thinkin' on company when I left."

"It's all right," Serafina said. "You should see where I sleep."

"I was all blurry-eyed this mornin' on account of I stayed up with that awful Mr. Scrooge," Essie said as she moved the clothes off the chair. Hearing these words, Serafina's ears perked right up. Who was this evil Mr. Scrooge? But then she saw a copy of *A Christmas Carol* by Charles Dickens on Essie's nightstand, piled with some Asheville newspapers, a Bible, and a scrap of what looked like Mrs. King's weekly work schedule. Serafina realized with a bit of a shock that Christmas was only a week away. The tan leather-bound book with gold-leaf lettering on the front looked suspiciously like the same edition of *A Christmas Carol* that Serafina had "borrowed" from Mr. Vanderbilt's collection the year before. *So I'm not the only one who steals Mr. Vanderbilt's books,* Serafina thought with a smile.

Across Essie's dresser lay all manner of feminine accoutrements: hairbrushes, hairpins, little tins of ointment, and a glass bottle of Essie's lemon scent, which Serafina could smell from a country mile. The room's cream-colored walls were cluttered with scraps of Essie's sketches of flowers and fall leaves. Serafina knew that she should be doing her job, creeping through the shadows, and spying on Biltmore's guests, or at least worrying about the interrogation that was minutes away, but she could not resist the temptation of seeing a little bit of Biltmore up close in a way she never had before.

In the center of one of the room's walls was mounted a single Edison lightbulb. Serafina's pa had told her with a swell in his chest that Mr. V was friends with Mr. Thomas Edison and liked using all the latest scientific advancements.

Seeing all this amazed Serafina. Essie had her own lightbulb! Serafina knew from her pa that many of the mountain folk of western North Carolina were living in clapboard shacks and log cabins without electricity, central heating, or indoor plumbing. Many of them had never even *seen* a lightbulb, let alone have one for their own particular use. But Essie had made herself a cozy little den up here on the fourth floor, like a tiny mouse nesting up in the attic, where no one would ever find her.

A window set into the room's roof-slanted wall provided something that Serafina, a denizen of the basement, seldom beheld from this height: a mesmerizing westward view across the Blue Ridge Mountains. The clear sight of Mount Pisgah rising in the distance above the other peaks caught her eye. A few nights after she and Braeden had defeated the Man in the Black Cloak, they had snuck up onto the rooftop to celebrate their victory. She remembered sitting under the stars with him, looking across the mountains, as Braeden explained how that peak was more than nineteen miles away, but it was still on the estate. He had marveled at how it took a day to get there on horseback, following twisting, rocky trails through the mountains, but a hawk soaring on the wind could simply tilt its wing and be there in a moment.

Smiling, Serafina turned and looked around Essie's room as Essie watched her with interest. "I ain't got it too bad, do I, miss?"

"Not too bad at all," Serafina agreed. "I like it here."

Essie pulled a nicely made beige day dress off one of the hooks on the wall. "It's my Sunday best," she said, handing it to over to Serafina. "It ain't nothing fancy compared to what the ladies wear, but—"

"Thank you, Essie," Serafina said, gently taking it from her. "It's perfect."

Essie kept talking as she turned around so Serafina could change.

"I'm a chambermaid now, but I'm fixed on being a lady's maid someday," Essie said. "Maybe serve the lady guests when they come, or even Mrs. Vanderbilt herself. Do you know Mrs. V?"

"Yes," Serafina said as she pulled off her burlap dress. Goose bumps rose up on her bare legs and arms, half chill and half nervousness. It felt so odd to be undressing when there was someone else in the room.

"I thought you must know her, you being you and all," Essie continued.

The fact was that Serafina had become very fond of Mrs. Vanderbilt over the last few weeks and had enjoyed their talks together, but she hadn't seen her around the house in several days.

"My friend's been a-goin' to the girls' school Mrs. V set up, learning how to do her numbers and weave fabric on the loom," Essie said. "Mrs. V wants all the girls to get some kind of education so that they can fend for themselves if they have to."

"I think she's very kind," Serafina agreed as she tried to figure out how to get into the dress. It seemed to have a bewildering array of buttons and drawstrings and other complications.

"Kind as kind can be," Essie continued. "Did you hear about the dairy boy? Two weeks ago, a dairyman and his eldest boy got awful puny, real bad sick, liketa died, so Mrs. V went on over to their cabin with a basket of food to help the family get through for a while. When she saw the boy was on the down-go, she had the menfolk haul him into her carriage, and she carted him all the way to the hospital in Asheville."

"What happened to the boy?" Serafina asked as she finally figured out how to slip into the dress and fasten up the last of the buttons.

"He's still mighty sick," Essie said. "But I hear they're taking good care of him down there."

"You can turn around now," Serafina said.

"Oh, miss!" Essie said. "That's a whole heap better, believe me. Come over to the mirror and take a look while I fix your hair."

Essie didn't seem to care that Serafina was different from everyone else, that her face was scratched, her eyes too large, and the angle of her cheeks unusually severe. She just went straight to work. "This hair of yourn!" she said, and started tugging away at it like it was a bushel of misbehaving ferrets. "We ain't got time for me to do a proper job, but we'll get it wrangled up."

As Essie worked, Serafina found herself looking into the mirror and noticed something odd. There appeared to be chunks of long black hair growing among the rest that she'd never seen before.

"What's wrong, miss?" Essie said, seeing her frown.

"My hair is brown, not black," she said, mystified as she raised her hand slowly up to her head and touched the black strands.

"You want 'em gone, miss? I used to cut my mamaw's gray hairs out all the time. They'd come in all long and wiry like they'd drunk too much moonshine, and we'd cut 'em out quick as they came."

"Just yank 'em," Serafina said.

"That's gonna hurt, miss. There's a lot of 'em."

"Just grab 'em hard and yank 'em out," Serafina insisted. If she'd didn't have enough problems going to the main floor for all to see, now she had strange things growing out of her head. She looked hideous.

Essie selected the strands of black hair and pulled so hard that it tugged Serafina's head back.

"Sorry, miss," Essie said.

"Keep going," she said. As Essie worked, Serafina decided to ask a question about what she'd seen earlier that morning.

"You said you're fixin' to be a lady's maid. Have you served that new girl who's been visiting?"

"The English girl," Essie groaned, making it pretty clear she was none too keen on her.

"You don't like her?" Serafina asked, amused.

"I don't trust that girl any farther than I can throw her, coming in here with all her fancy high-and-mighty airs and puttin' a bead on the young master first thing."

Serafina wasn't sure exactly what she meant by all that, but it occurred to her that someone in Essie's position, working in the rooms on the second and third floors, might see things that she herself did not.

"What about the murder investigator who came in last night?" she asked. "Have you seen him?"

"Not yet, but I heard from one of the footmen that he had all sorts of trunks and cases hauled up to this room, filled with strange instruments of some kind. He's been giving all the servants orders, demanding this and that."

That doesn't sound good, Serafina thought.

Having yanked out several chunks of black strands, Essie picked up her brush and started brushing Serafina's hair in long, pulling strokes. It felt so strange but so oddly pleasant to have someone pull a brush through her hair, the sensation of the drag on her roots, and the detangling of her hair, and the gentle rake of the soft bristles against her scalp. She had to do everything she could to keep from purring.

"Can I ask you a question, miss?" Essie asked as she brushed. "Ya know, Mrs. King keeps tellin' all of us girls to mind our own business, but everyone's been talking about it all the same. We all want to know what's going on."

"Going on with what?" Serafina asked uncertainly.

"With Mrs. V," Essie said. "She didn't come out of her room for breakfast this morning, and she's been feeling so poorly lately that we hardly see her. I'm sure she'll get through it, whatever it is, but I was just wondering if you've heard anything."

"I didn't realize she was down sick," Serafina said as a knot formed slowly in her stomach. That explained why she hadn't seen her.

"She's been sick as a dog some days," Essie continued. "Then other times she perks up for a while. We seen the doctor a-comin' and a-goin'. We all just want to know if she's going to be all right."

"I honestly don't know, Essie. I'm sorry," Serafina said. The news that Mrs. Vanderbilt was sick hung heavy in her heart. "But when I hear something, I'll be sure to tell you."

"I'd be much obliged," Essie said, nodding. "And I'll do likewise."

Finally, Essie set down the hairbrush. She took Serafina's hair in her hands, wrapped it around, and rolled it up into a loose twist on her head. Then she fastened it in place.

"There you go, miss," Essie said. "I think that will do ya for a little while."

When Serafina looked in the mirror, she saw a new girl staring back at her. Her own face was still there, still looking back at herself, but with the dress Essie had lent her and her hair pulled up, she almost looked presentable.

Essie smiled, proud of her handiwork. "You're a right proper girl now," she said, nodding with satisfaction.

"I think I am," Serafina said in astonishment.

Serafina turned toward Essie and, remembering how she had recoiled from her touch when they first met on the stairs, she reached out and slowly put her hand on Essie's arm like she had seen other people sometimes do. The gesture felt unnatural to her, to actually be touching someone in this way, and she wasn't sure it was the right kind of moment for it, but when she did, Essie's face glowed with happiness.

"Aw, miss, it hain't nothin'—just helpin' out another girl, is all."

"I truly appreciate it, Essie," Serafina said.

Then Serafina paused and decided to ask one more question before she went. "A little bit ago, you said everybody's got somethin' that spooks them."

"I think that's about right, don't you?"

"It sounded like you were thinking about something in particular. For you, is it the fear of getting sick like the dairyman's boy?"

"No, miss."

"Then, what is it? What spooks you?"

"Well, I ain't too keen on haints, of course—don't suppose anyone is, people comin' back from the dead and all that—but what sends me a-runnin' are the stories my papaw used to tell round the fire at night to scare us little ones."

"About what?"

"Oh, you know, how when a wind kicks up on a calm day and blows something over, or you find an animal dead in the woods for no good reason, people always say, 'It's just the old man of the forest playing his tricks again.'"

Serafina felt her lips getting dry as she listened to Essie's story. She could hear the fear creeping into the girl's voice. "What old man?" Serafina asked.

"I'm sure you've heard the stories same as me, an old man with a walking stick wandering the shadows of the forest, drifting in and out of the mist, leading folk off the road and getting them lost in the swamps. Sometimes they say he causes mischief around the cabin, curdled milk and dead chickens in the yard. My papaw used to love tellin' stories, but them ones scared me half to death. Still do, truth be told."

"But who is the old man in the stories? Where'd he come from? What's he want?" Serafina asked, mystified.

Essie shook her head and shrugged. "Knock me cold if I know!" She laughed. "It's just some old stupid story, but for some reason it scares the livin' daylights out me like nothin' else. If I find myself out in the woods at night and hear the break of a stick or a gust of wind, half time I just run on home as fast as I can. I'm so bad awful scared of the dark it ain't even funny! That's why I love it here."

"Here? Why?" Serafina asked, unable to fathom the mysterious connection.

"Indoor plumbing," Essie said, laughing. "Ain't gotta go out to the outhouse every night in the dark!"

Serafina smiled. Her new companion was a daytime girl through and through, but there was something about Essie Walker that she was growing mighty fond of.

"But truly, miss," Essie said, turning more serious. "You've gotta get going back downstairs, and I gotta get back to work. If we stay holed up in here like a couple of treed coons much longer, they're gonna send the dogs out for us."

"The dogs?" Serafina said in alarm.

"You know, the bloodhounds, the coon dogs. It's just an expression."

"Yes, of course," Serafina said, realizing that, like Essie, there was maybe more than a few things in the world that spooked her.

As Serafina said good-bye, she was sorry to go, especially to what awaited her downstairs, but she was glad to have made a new friend.

Serafina flew down the stairway, barely touching every fifth step, one flight, two flights, three flights down. Hitting the main floor, she dashed past a startled footman at the butler's pantry door, then headed down the narrow passage through another door, across the Breakfast Room, then another corridor, and finally stopped, took a breath, and stepped calmly into the Winter Garden.

Tall, dangling palms, ficus trees, and other exotic plants filled the room. Sunshine poured down through the arched dome of ornate beams that held the Winter Garden's glass ceiling aloft. Fine pieces of ceramic art were displayed on small viewing stands throughout the tiled room, and French rattan furniture provided places for the fancy folk to lounge.

She'd come here to this central room in the house hoping to meet Braeden before being questioned by the investigator, but she felt so vulnerable walking openly into this grand place where once she had only prowled.

She kept checking for places to hide, her muscles pulsing, first this way, then that, as if she'd need to flee at any moment. Then she spotted Braeden and the English girl standing together. Serafina hesitated. Her body tensed.

The two citizens of the upstairs had changed out of their riding outfits—he into his afternoon black coat, trousers, and tie, and she into a sky-blue dress with a narrow-waist corset, capped puffy sleeves, and silk chiffon covering her forearms. The girl's chestnut-red tresses were piled high on her head, swept back in soft, neat waves, held in place by a twined wooden shawl pin, then spilling down on one side in twisted rolls, sausage curls so tight and perfectly formed they reminded Serafina of coiled springs in her pa's workshop. Whoever they had assigned to be the girl's lady's maid that afternoon must have spent hours curling her hair with a fire-heated curling iron. Serafina had guessed before that the girl was about fourteen years old, but she could see now that she was clearly trying to act older. She wore finely wrought, dangling silver earrings and a black velvet ribbon choker necklace with a cameo pendant. Serafina had to admit that she was an elegant-looking girl, with striking eyes the color of the forest.

As Serafina stepped closer to them, her heart pounded far harder than if she'd been entering a battle with the wolfhounds.

Out of habit, she walked silently. Neither of the humans noticed her. But Gidean's sharply pointed black ears perked up, then dropped down in relief when he recognized her. He wagged his tail nub excitedly. Serafina smiled, warmed by the dog's enthusiasm.

The English girl was facing in Serafina's direction, but she didn't take notice of her until it became quite obvious that Serafina was walking straight toward them. The girl was clearly startled by Serafina's appearance. Her eyes widened and she tilted her head. She looked almost scared. But as Serafina came closer, the girl seemed to compose herself more firmly. She looked at Serafina with a withering gaze, as if to say, *Why in the world is someone dressed like you walking toward someone dressed like me?*

If you don't like this, you should have seen what I was going *to wear,* Serafina thought.

Pausing just short of them, Serafina stood between the bronze fountain in the center of the room and a beautiful blue-and-white Ming vase on a small wooden table beneath a collection of graceful palms. Serafina remembered overhearing that Mr. Vanderbilt had purchased the vase on his travels to the Orient, that it was over four hundred years old and one of the most valuable works of art in the house. Serafina stood so still and out in the open that for a moment she almost felt like one of the pieces of furniture.

When Braeden finally turned and saw her there, his face lit up, and he smiled. "Hello, Serafina!" he said without hesitation.

Serafina's body filled with a wave of relief and happiness. "Hello, Braeden," she said, hoping she sounded at least somewhat normal.

Even though he should have been expecting her, Braeden seemed so surprised and happy to see her there. Had he been worried about her? Or was it simply because she so seldom visited the main floor in the daytime?

"I . . ." she began, not sure how to say it properly. "I am in receipt of your note," she said, trying to sound as sophisticated as possible but wanting to make it clear she understood the seriousness of the interrogation.

He nodded knowingly, stepped toward her, and spoke to her in a low voice. "I don't know what we're walking into here, but I think we need to be very careful."

"What's the investigator's name?" she asked. "Where does he come from?"

"I don't know," Braeden said. "He came in late last night."

"And what does your uncle say about all this?"

"If the authorities determine that Mr. Thorne was murdered, then the murderer will be hanged."

"He actually said that?" Serafina asked, taken aback, but even as she and Braeden talked, she felt the air bristling around her. When Braeden first saw her and greeted her with such warmth, she had noticed that the English girl stepped back a little, her chin raised and her face tense with uncertainty. Now she was just standing there, waiting quietly. The situation was becoming increasingly awkward for her. Braeden should have been introducing her, but he wasn't. He seemed to have forgotten her. Serafina couldn't imagine that was a pleasant feeling.

It dawned on her that the girl might be as uncomfortable with her surroundings at Biltmore as Serafina was. The girl was a newcomer, still trying to find her place to fit in, and now here was the one boy she knew whispering with some strange, shaggy-haired, tooth-marked vagrant. Despite the sharpness Serafina had felt for the girl the first time she saw her, she almost felt sorry for her.

"Oh yes," Braeden said, seeming to read Serafina's mind and suddenly remember his responsibilities. "Serafina, this is—"

But at that moment, Mrs. Vanderbilt came sweeping down the steps into the Winter Garden. "Ah, I see that you're all here. Good. I'll take you down to the Library to speak with Mr. Vanderbilt and the detective."

The lady of the house wore a handsome afternoon dress, and she was putting on a good front, but Serafina could see she did indeed look a bit peaked. Her cheeks were pale, but her brow was flushed. She seemed to be trying to soldier on through her day with a positive attitude despite her poor health.

"Serafina, before we go down, I would like you to meet someone," Mrs. Vanderbilt said, bringing her with a soft gesture of her hand toward the English girl. "I would like to present Lady Rowena Fox-Pemberton, who is visiting us from very far away. I hope the two of you can become good friends during her time here at Biltmore. We must do all we can to make her feel as if Biltmore is her home."

"It's good to meet you, miss," Serafina said politely to the girl.

"My lady," Lady Rowena said as she looked Serafina up and down in surprise.

"Excuse me?" Serafina asked, genuinely confused.

"You are to address me not as 'miss', but as 'my lady,'" Lady Rowena corrected Serafina, in her formal English accent.

"I see," Serafina said. "Is that how they do it in England? And will you be addressing me as 'my lady' also, then?"

"Of course not!" the girl said in astonishment as color rose to her cheeks.

"All right," Mrs. Vanderbilt said, reaching out and touching each of the girls with an open hand in an attempt to smooth over the situation. "I'm sure we'll get the English-American relations sorted out. . . ."

But as Mrs. Vanderbilt reached gently toward her, Serafina reflexively stepped back and felt the brush of a tall, dangling palm frond against her cheek. The palm leaf seemed to actually move of its own accord and get tangled in her hair. Startled, Serafina reached up and spun quickly to brush it away, thinking that it must be a tree snake or something, for that was exactly how it felt. She snapped around so fast that she bumped into the furniture behind her.

"Oh, do be careful there, Serafina!" Mrs. Vanderbilt cried out in panicked dismay, reaching toward the thing behind Serafina.

That was when Serafina realized that her sudden movement had bumped the small wooden stand that held the Ming vase.

The vase tipped off the stand and fell. Serafina watched in horror as the priceless piece of art plummeted toward the hard tiled floor. She tried to reach for it, but she was too late. It hit the floor with a crash and shattered into a thousand pieces. The sight of the exploding porcelain took Serafina's breath away. The sound of it echoing through the house churned a sickness in her stomach.

Everyone stared at the shattered vase in shock and then looked at her.

Serafina's cheeks burned with heat, and her eyes filled with tears. "I'm so, so sorry, Mrs. Vanderbilt," she said, moving toward her. "I did not mean to do that. I'm so sorry."

"Maybe we can glue it," Braeden said, dropping to his knees and trying to pick up the shards as Lady Rowena Fox-Pemberton stared balefully at Serafina and shook her head as if to say, *I knew you didn't belong in the house.*

"George is going to be heartbroken," Mrs. Vanderbilt muttered to herself, her hand over her mouth as she stared in stunned disbelief at the broken pieces on the floor. "It was one of his favorites. . . ."

"I'm so sorry," Serafina said again, her heart filled with an aching, shameful pain. "I don't know what happened. The plant attacked me." But even as the words slipped out, she knew how immature they sounded. Lady Rowena just stared at her, taking it all in, too smart and well poised to actually smile, but seeming to be on the edge of it. Serafina looked around her at the plants and the other objects in the room. She didn't understand it. She had spent her whole life prowling in this house, ducking and darting, and never once had she ever knocked over or broken anything. And now, just as she was starting to come out into the upstairs world, just as she was wanting to show Mrs. Vanderbilt how much she appreciated her friendship, she did this horrible, stupid, clumsy thing. She wanted to run back down to the basement and cry. It took every ounce of her courage to remain standing there in her shame.

Finally, Mrs. Vanderbilt looked at her nephew kneeling on the floor trying to clean up the mess. "Braeden," she said, "I'm afraid it's not going to work."

Sensing the gravity of his aunt's mood, Braeden slowly stopped his efforts.

"You do not have time for this," Mrs. Vanderbilt said. "You and Serafina are expected to speak with Detective Grathan."

Serafina had never seen Mrs. Vanderbilt act so cold and businesslike to Braeden or anyone else, and it was totally her fault.

"I'll take Lady Rowena for a walk to the Conservatory," Mrs. Vanderbilt said. "You and Serafina go down to the Library immediately."

Mrs. King, the head housekeeper, entered the Winter Garden and spoke directly to Mrs. Vanderbilt. "I've asked a maid to get a broom and dustpan to clean up the broken vase," she said, her voice level and professional. As the highest-ranking servant at Biltmore, the matron possessed a commanding presence. Wearing a practical olive-green dress with mother-of-pearl buttons and a sash around her waist, she kept her hair pulled back in a tightly controlled bun behind her head.

"Thank you, Mrs. King," Mrs. Vanderbilt said appreciatively. "Please take the children to the Library."

When Mrs. Vanderbilt called her and Braeden "children," Serafina saw the satisfaction in Lady Rowena's face.

"Come this way," Mrs. King instructed Braeden and Serafina. It was the kind of voice that was used to being obeyed.

Mrs. King had been running Biltmore for years, even before Mr. Vanderbilt married and Mrs. Vanderbilt arrived. As Serafina followed the matron through the Entrance Hall, she wiped her teary eyes and tried to think about what her pa would tell her at this moment. *Quit yer snifflin' and get your wits about ya, girl,* he'd say, and he'd be right. If she was going to be questioned by an investigator for a murder that she'd been a part of, she had to pull herself together.

Serafina studied Mrs. King as she followed her down the long length of the Tapestry Galley toward the Library, for she had seldom been this close to her.

One of the things that had always mystified Serafina about Mrs. King was that she lived in an area of Biltmore that Serafina had never seen. She was the one and only inhabitant of the mysterious second-and-a-half floor. Serafina couldn't imagine how a whole floor, or even half of one, could exist between two other floors. But she'd learned long ago that all manner of both grand and wicked things were possible at Biltmore. The palm trees, for example, were particularly untrustworthy.

She couldn't help but notice the key ring hanging on Mrs. King's sash. It was a large brass ring with all the keys of the house, for every door, cupboard, and secret hatch, from the basement to the top floor. Serafina had always been mesmerized by the jingling, jangling sound of the hanging keys. But just as she was looking at it, something tiny pulled a key from the ring, darted down Mrs. King's dress, and shot along the floor quicker than two blinks and a sneeze. The brown little creature had been so small and had moved so fast that Serafina barely saw it. And she was quite sure that no one else had. But she'd been C.R.C. long enough to know what it was: a mouse. Sometimes mice move so fast that they're just a flash and then they're gone. Already, she started doubting that she'd actually seen it. How in the world could a live mouse run down Mrs. King's dress? And what was it doing? Stealing a key to the cheese cupboard?

But she had bigger problems to face. As she and Braeden plodded along behind Mrs. King, Serafina looked over at Braeden. His lips were pressed together, his face filled with worry. It felt like Mrs. King was taking her and Braeden to their trial, sentencing, and execution. She had half a mind to turn and run, just get out of there while she still had the chance. She'd be as gone as yesterday's breeze before Mrs. King even noticed she was missing. But she knew she couldn't leave poor Braeden behind, so she trudged glumly along beside him, not knowing what else to do. She felt like she was tied up in a poke sack and was just about to get chucked into the river.

As they entered the Library, Serafina gazed across the familiar room. Thousands of Mr. Vanderbilt's leather-bound books lined the walls of intricately carved wood and sculpted marble-work. The books reached all the way up to the angelic Italian painting on the ceiling some thirty-five feet above their heads.

But there was no one in the room. The globes of the brass lamps were lit, and a fire burned in the massive black marble fireplace, but the Library Room was completely empty.

When she glanced at Braeden, it was clear that he was as confused as she was. But the stalwart Mrs. King appeared undeterred. She led them along the bookcases built into the western wall, then turned right and stopped. They were now looking at a section of the room's oak paneling. It took Serafina nearly a second to recognize that it wasn't just a wall. It was a door. And the carving on the door's center panel is what disturbed her: a robed man holding a finger to his mouth as if to say *Shhh!* There was blood dripping down his head and a knife stuck in his back.

"You may step through the door," the matron said. "They are expecting you."

Serafina stepped cautiously into the dimly lit room. It was a cramped, closed-in den with leather furniture, shades blocking out the setting sun, and a dark ceiling patterned like the bones of a bat's wing. This was not his usual office, but Mr. Vanderbilt sat behind the desk.

She had been watching the master of Biltmore all her life, but she'd never been able to figure him out. He was a man of immense wealth but quiet word, a refined, bookish gentleman with a slight frame and slender hands. He had shrewd, dark eyes, black hair, and a black mustache.

"Come into the room," he said gravely. He seemed to be in a grim and unforgiving mood.

As she and Braeden stepped slowly forward, she saw

something out of the corner of her eye: a man sitting in the shadows, unmoving, studying her. She couldn't help but pull in a breath. Her heart began to beat heavy in her chest, marking time like a slow, powerful drum.

As her eyes adjusted to the darkness of the room, she began to see the stranger's features. To her surprise, it wasn't the elderly man she'd seen walking into the forest with Mr. Vanderbilt. This man's straggly rat-brown hair fell to his shoulders, and he had a short goatee. He stared at her with intense, unrelenting eyes. He might have been handsome in the past, but so many raised gray scars traced his face that she could see an entire history of battle there, against both blade and claw—it was a wonder that he had survived them. His brown woolen coat and shoulder cape were matted and wind-worn, tattered at the edges, like he'd been on the road for many years.

As the man looked at the scratches on her face and the bite wounds on her hands, it felt like something was crawling up her spine. The muscles in her body twitched and tensed, wanting to fight or flee. He could see too much. Terrifying images flashed through her mind: the gray-bearded man in a wide-brimmed hat stepping onto the road, the snapping jaws of the white-fanged hounds, the black silhouette of a figure sitting in the carriage as it pulled away.

Had this man looked out from the carriage and seen her? If he had seen her at all, he could have only caught a glimpse of her as she ran away. She was wearing different clothes now, and her hair had changed. Whatever it was, he seemed as uncertain about her as she was about him.

In his hand, he held a cane with a spiraling shaft and a curving antler handle. There was something about the cane that made her think it was far more dangerous than it appeared. But it seemed to be a different style than the one she'd seen the night before. It was like there were little flaws in her memory. Had she seen a gnarly stick or a more formal, spiraling cane with a hooked horn handle like this one? Could it change shape?

"Sit down," Mr. Vanderbilt instructed. He pointed to the two small, bare, wooden chairs in the middle of the room. Serafina had seldom heard Mr. Vanderbilt so stern, so sharp of tone, but she couldn't tell if it was because he was angry with her and Braeden or because of this detective's unexpected presence in his home. Mr. Vanderbilt had welcomed all sorts of guests to entertain themselves in the magnificent mansion he had built for that purpose, but he himself had a tendency to withdraw from revelry. He often sat in a quiet room by himself and read rather than imbibe with others. He was a man of his own spirit. And now here was a stranger, a detective, a man of the road, come to call with words of murder, and Mr. Vanderbilt seemed none too pleased about it.

As she and Braeden sat down in the two chairs, she glanced over at her friend. He looked scared and alone. Mrs. King had instructed him to leave Gidean outside the room. He seemed vulnerable without his canine protector at his side, which made Serafina more determined than ever to make sure this Detective Grathan did not get the better of them.

Mr. Vanderbilt looked at her and Braeden. "Detective Grathan is investigating the disappearance of Mr. Thorne. He theorizes that Mr. Thorne did not take his leave of Biltmore of his own accord but encountered foul play while he was here."

"Yes, sir," Braeden said, trying to sound steady, but Serafina could hear the quiver in his voice. There was no doubt in her mind, either, that if they made a mistake here, they might be arrested and charged with conspiring to murder Mr. Thorne. She had led him into the trap. And Braeden owned the dog that helped kill him.

"I recommend that you answer all his questions truthfully," Mr. Vanderbilt said.

Serafina glanced at Mr. Vanderbilt, for the tone in his voice had an unexpected edge to it. On the face of it, he was telling her and Braeden to do the right thing, to cooperate with the detective's investigation. But in another way, it seemed to her that he was signaling them, warning them that they needed to be very careful, like the man might possess the power to discern truth from lie.

"Detective Grathan," Mr. Vanderbilt said as he turned to the man, "everyone at Biltmore will, of course, cooperate with your investigation. This is my nephew Braeden Vanderbilt, my late brother's son, and his friend Serafina. Along with the others you've already spoken to, they were present on the day of Mr. Thorne's disappearance. You are free to ask them any questions you deem necessary to complete your investigation."

The detective nodded, then spoke to Mr. Vanderbilt in a serious tone. "You do not have to be present for this questioning."

Whoa, Serafina thought. He just asked Mr. Vanderbilt to leave the room. *No one* asked Mr. Vanderbilt to leave anywhere.

It was *his* house. Serafina could sense the tension increasing between the two men.

"I will remain," Mr. Vanderbilt said unequivocally.

Detective Grathan looked at him and seemed to decide that for the moment he would not argue with the master of Biltmore. Instead, he pivoted his head slowly toward Serafina. She swore she could hear the sound of ticking cartilage as his head turned. The man studied her for several seconds, seeming to pull every detail of her apart, bit by bit. She noticed his fingers wrapped slowly around the antler handle of his cane. Then he spoke.

"Your name is Serafina, is that correct?" he asked.

"Yes," she said. *And your name is Mr. Grathan,* she wanted to say in return. *Do you and your master own five mangy, overgrown tracking hounds with teeth like daggers?*

"Did you know Mr. Thorne?" he asked.

"Yes, I knew him," she replied truthfully, "but I only spoke to him a few times."

The man studied her. He held his cane—or staff or stick or whatever it was—as he spoke to her. Then he slowly pivoted his head and looked at Braeden. "And did you know Mr. Thorne as well?"

"He was my friend," Braeden said, which was also the truth.

"When did you last see him?"

"At the party on the night of his disappearance," Braeden said. It seemed that he, too, had picked up on his uncle's warning. When Braeden glanced at her with a knowing look, she was sure of it. In that moment, the two friends silently agreed what course they must take: to give the detective no advantage, to speak the careful truth but nothing more.

The detective turned his head slowly back to Serafina. "And when was the last time you saw Mr. Thorne?"

The last time she'd seen him, he'd been lying dead on the ground in the graveyard, his blood leaking out of him, and then his body decomposed before her eyes, his worldly carcass becoming nothing but blood-soaked earth.

"I believe it was the last day we all saw him," she said. "The day he disappeared."

"At what *time* did you last see him?"

"As I recall, it was after dark," she said, but *midnight* would have been more accurate.

"So you were one of the last people to see him here at Biltmore."

"I believe I must have been."

"And what was he doing when you saw him last?"

"The last time I saw him here at Biltmore, he was putting on his cloak and going out the door."

"You saw him leave Biltmore?"

"Yes, very clearly. He was running out the door."

"Running?" the detective asked in surprise.

"Yes. Running." *He was chasing me,* she thought, *and I led him to his death.*

The detective's head pivoted to Braeden.

"And did you see this as well?"

"No," Braeden said. "I went to bed after the party."

The detective's eyes held steady on Braeden for several

seconds as if he did not believe his answer. Then he said, "The black dog is yours." Serafina had no idea how he knew this, because Gidean wasn't even in the room.

"Yes," Braeden replied uncertainly.

"The dog is almost always with you, but you say you went to bed early that night. How and when did the dog suffer a wound to its right shoulder?"

"I . . ." Braeden said, confused and disturbed by the question.

"How was the dog wounded?" the detective pressed.

"I did not see him get hurt," Braeden said truthfully.

"But when did it happen?"

"It was the morning we discovered that another child had gone missing. I sent Gidean out into the woods to track the child," Braeden said.

Serafina thought it was clever the way Braeden said *another child had gone missing*, disguising the fact that it had actually been *she* who had gone missing. She had gone out to trap Mr. Thorne. And she liked the way Braeden described it as *the morning*, which was technically correct because it had been after midnight, but gave the impression that it was the next day.

"And did the dog find the missing child?" the detective asked.

"Yes, he did," Braeden said. Then he looked at Mr. Vanderbilt. "Uncle, why is he asking me all these questions about Gidean? Does he think Gidean and I did something wrong?"

Serafina couldn't tell if Braeden was faking his expression

of fear and bewilderment or whether it was genuine, but either way, it was convincing.

"No, of course not, Braeden," Mr. Vanderbilt said, looking firmly at the detective when he said these words. "He's just doing his job." It was clear that Mr. Vanderbilt would brook little more of this imposition. "Just answer his questions truthfully," he said again, and this time Serafina was sure of it—he was helping them. He was on their side. *Choose your words carefully,* he was telling them. She knew that the key was to avoid and deflect the difficult questions.

The detective turned his head with a sharp scrape of his neck and looked at Serafina. "Do you know what happened to Mr. Thorne on the night about which we speak?"

How in the world was she going to avoid that question without lying through her teeth? She could already see them erecting the gallows and tying the noose for her neck.

"God rest his soul," she said abruptly.

"Then you think that he's not just missing but actually dead?" the man said, leaning forward and peering at her.

"Yes."

"How do you know this?"

"Because he has not returned."

"But do you know *how* he died? Did you see a body? Was there some sort of unnatural force involved?"

In those last few words, the rat betrayed himself. What was he truly looking for? When he said *unnatural force,* did he mean black magic? The man in the forest had instructed his dogs to hunt down what he had called the Black One. This man wasn't just looking for Mr. Thorne's murderer. He was looking for the Black Cloak!

"You haven't answered my question," he pressed her.

"I believe a powerful force must have surprised him and killed him," she said. "Everyone in the mountains knows that the forest is filled with many dangers." And then she remembered the expression that Essie had said always spooked her. "Maybe the old man of the forest is up to his old tricks again."

The detective's expression widened when she said these words. "What kind of powerful force are you talking about?"

"I think there are forces both good and evil in the forest."

"And you believe it was these forces that killed Mr. Thorne?" the detective asked.

"It could be," she said. What she wasn't saying was that it had been the *good* forces rather than the evil ones that had killed Mr. Thorne.

Mr. Vanderbilt leaned forward. "I don't know where your questions are going, Mr. Grathan. I suggest we proceed with the other people on your list."

"I have more questions for these two," the detective said sharply, not looking at Mr. Vanderbilt. Serafina could feel the barely controlled intensity rising within the detective. It was as if he had come in the *disguise* of a civilized person, a police investigator, but now his true character was beginning to show itself.

He thrust his hand into his pocket and brought out a silver

clasp engraved with an intricate design: a tight bundle of twisting vines and thorns.

Serafina's heart began to pound in her chest. Now there was no doubt. The detective had found the remnants of the Black Cloak. That meant he had indeed been out to the area of her mother's den. A flash of new fears flooded her mind. She could feel the heat rising in her body.

"Do you recognize this?" the detective asked her.

The pulse of her blood thumped in her temples. She could barely hear his words.

"Do you recognize this?" he asked again.

"It appears to be a clasp from an article of clothing," she said, trying to keep her voice as flat and undisturbed as possible.

"But you're not answering the question!" he pressed her.

"Mr. Grathan, calm yourself," Mr. Vanderbilt warned him.

"Do you recognize it?" Mr. Grathan asked her, ignoring him.

"It looks as if whatever it once held is now set free," she said.

"But have you seen it before?" he asked again, gripping the handle of his cane like he was going to swing it around and wield it like a weapon at any moment.

She felt a great weight pressing in on her. But as she pretended to examine the clasp, she noticed that something was different: the tiny faces that had been behind the thorns were gone now.

"I have never seen a silver clasp with this design," she said, at last finding a way to hew to the truth.

The detective stared at her for a long time as if he knew she was deceiving him but could not quite frame the words to trap her.

"Detective, we need to move on," Mr. Vanderbilt pushed him.

"I have more questions!" the detective insisted, his voice filled with aggravation, his eyes locked on Serafina. "Do you know which room Mr. Thorne slept in during his stay at Biltmore?"

"It was on the third floor," she said.

"Do you live here at Biltmore?"

"Yes, I do."

"With the female servants on the fourth floor?"

"No."

"Then where do you sleep at night?"

"I do not."

The detective stopped and looked at her in surprise. "You do not sleep?"

"I do not sleep at night."

The man frowned. "Are you a night maid?"

"No."

"Then what are you?"

She looked him straight in the eyes and said, "I'm the Chief Rat Catcher. I track down vermin."

He stared right back at her and said, "Then we have that much in common."

14

$\mathcal{S}$erafina glanced at Braeden as the two of them quickly left Mr. Vanderbilt's den and crossed through the Library.

"We have to stay away from that man," Braeden whispered to her.

"No, we need to get rid of him!" Serafina said fiercely. She was still breathing heavily from her exchange with him.

"If my uncle hadn't stopped everything and dismissed us, were you going to fight the detective right there?"

Serafina just shook her head. "I don't know," she admitted. As they walked toward the Entrance Hall, Gidean followed at their side.

"Did you see his face? All those scars?" Braeden said. "That man's scary! What's he been fighting?"

"His neck creaked every time he turned his head," Serafina said.

"He was horrible. And he just kept asking question after question. I thought it would never end! What's going to happen if he finds out we were involved in Mr. Thorne's death? Is he going to arrest us?"

"Worse than that, I think," Serafina said. "I'm not sure he is who he says he is."

"What do you mean?" Braeden asked in alarm. Looking at her wounds, he said, "What happened to you last night?"

She desperately wanted to talk to him, but as they reached the Entrance Hall, she heard Mrs. Vanderbilt and Lady Rowena coming in through the Vestibule.

"One of the servants must have notified them that we were done," Braeden muttered. She couldn't be sure, but it almost sounded like there was sadness in his voice.

"Do you have to go?" Serafina asked quietly, glancing at him. She knew he probably did.

"Come on!" he said suddenly, and pulled her in the opposite direction.

Laughing, Serafina ran with Braeden up the Grand Staircase, the wide, magnificent circular stairway that led to the upper floors. She wasn't sure where Braeden was taking her, other than just to escape, but when they reached the third floor, she had an idea where they could go and talk in secret. There was much she had to tell him.

"This way!" she said as they ran through the living hall past several smartly dressed ladies and gentlemen enjoying tea.

"Hello, everybody!" Braeden called cheerfully as they blazed through.

"Oh, good evening, Master Braeden," one of the gentlemen said, as if it weren't unusual at all for two children and a dog to be dashing through the living hall.

"Where are we going?" Braeden asked breathlessly as they darted down a back corridor.

"You'll see," she said.

At the end of the hallway, she stopped just where it dog-legged up toward the North Tower Room. Two small bronze sculptures and a gathering of books sat atop a built-in oak cabinet. The first bronze sculpture depicted a horse being spooked by a rattlesnake. The second was a lean and muscular leopardess, her ears pinned back and her fangs bared as she sank her teeth and claws into some sort of wild beast.

Serafina had noticed over the years that there were sculptures and paintings of great cats everywhere at Biltmore: two bronze lionesses prowled on the mantel above the billiard table, and two rampant lions raised their claws above the fireplace where guests enjoyed their breakfast. She knew it was silly now, but when she was younger, she had always imagined that these were her aunts and uncles, her grandmothers and grandfathers, like family portraits on the wall. An old woodcarving print of a proud, great-grandfatherly lion was displayed in the Library, and there were cousin-like lion faces carved into the decorative corbels in the Banquet Hall. The statues on the house gates depicted the head and upper body of a woman, but if you looked very carefully, which she always did, you could see the lower body of a lion. The one that had always perplexed her the most was the white marble statue leading into the Italian Garden: a woman with a lion draped over her back and a little girl at her side. Even the doorbell at Biltmore's front door depicted a great cat. She had often wondered why Mr. Vanderbilt had collected so many tributes to the feline race. But of all the cats at Biltmore, this small bronze sculpture of a leopardess in the throes of a ferocious attack had always been her favorite.

"What are we doing?" Braeden asked, staring in confusion at the sculptures.

Serafina bent down and opened the cabinet door. Inside were more of Mr. Vanderbilt's books. Getting down on her hands and knees, she moved the volumes aside and gained access to the back of the cabinet. She pushed hard on the wooden panel like she remembered doing before, but it didn't budge.

"What are you doing that for?" Braeden asked.

"Come on, help me," Serafina said, and soon she and Braeden were working shoulder to shoulder. The back panel of the cabinet finally pushed through, opening into a dark hole.

"Follow me," Serafina said, her voice echoing a little as she crawled into the darkness. She hadn't been in here in years, but when she was younger, it had been one of her favorite places.

"I'm not going in there until you . . ." Braeden was saying behind her, but she kept going into the darkness.

"Serafina?" Braeden asked from out in the corridor. "Fine, I'm coming." He must have turned and petted Gidean, because in the next moment his voice became softer. "You wait here, boy," he said. "This doesn't look like a good place for a dog."

Gidean whined a little, not wanting to be left behind again.

Serafina crawled through the cramped, dusty, darkened tunnel until she came to the bottom rungs of a ladder.

"Be careful here, Braeden," she whispered as she heard him coming up behind her on his hands and knees.

"Here we go," she said. She grabbed the first rung and started climbing. The ladder was not straight like a normal ladder. It curved, climbing upward into the darkness. The space around her opened up into a black void: no walls, no ceiling, no floor, just the ladder she was climbing and darkness all around. As she climbed farther and farther, her muscles tensed and her skin tingled. Falling meant certain death.

"Where on earth are we?" Braeden asked as he climbed up the ladder behind her, his voice sounding small in the vast space they were entering. "It's terribly dark in here!"

"We're in the attic above the ceiling of the Banquet Hall."

"Oh my God, do you realize how high that is? That ceiling is seventy feet high!"

"Yes, so don't fall," Serafina advised. "It's open along the sides."

"How do you know about this place?"

"I'm the C.R.C.," she said. "It's my job to know everything there is to know about Biltmore, especially its secret rooms and passages."

As they climbed the ladder into the darkness, it became more and more clear that the ladder was curving up and over the arc of the Banquet Hall's soaring barrel-vaulted ceiling. It felt like they were climbing along one of the rib bones inside the body of a giant wooden whale.

Finally, they reached a lattice of steel girders and joists suspended high above the ceiling. Serafina climbed up onto the top edge of one of the beams, just a few inches wide, and walked along its length. It was a dark and treacherous place. A single misplaced step meant a fatal fall into the darkness. The top side of the Banquet Hall's ceiling hovered below them, but if they fell from the girders, they would hit the ceiling and then tumble along the curve until they disappeared into the black chasm that ran along the side.

"I can't see anything!" Braeden complained as he inched his way slowly and unsteadily along the top of one of the narrow girders. The only light came from a few tiny pinholes in the slate shingles of the roof. It was plenty of light for Serafina, but it left Braeden nearly blind. She reached back and guided him along until they found a good spot and sat on the girder with their legs hanging down into the darkness.

"Well, this is a nice place for evening tea," Braeden said cheerfully. "It's nearly pitch dark, and if I move in any direction, I'll die, but besides that, I love the ambience."

Braeden could not see it, but Serafina smiled. It was good to be at her friend's side again. But then her thoughts turned more serious. After they defeated the Man in the Black Cloak, she had told Braeden about how her pa adopted her and who her mother was, and they'd been sharing with each other the truth of their lives ever since.

"Braeden, I need to tell you what happened," Serafina said.

Over the next half hour, she recounted the night before. She had told some of what happened to her pa earlier that morning, but when she told the story to Braeden, she left nothing out. It felt good to finally tell her friend everything that had happened. Sometimes it felt as if things weren't real, weren't complete, until she shared them with Braeden.

"That sounds terrifying," Braeden said. "You were lucky to get out of there alive, Serafina."

She nodded in agreement. It had been a close call, and she was glad to be home.

"And are you sure Detective Grathan is the second man you saw in the carriage?" Braeden asked.

Serafina shook her head. "I don't know," she admitted. "I think he must be, but I didn't get a good look at him. There are four horses in the Biltmore stables that look like the stallions I saw. Could you find out who they belong to?"

"I'll ask Mr. Rinaldi, the stable master," Braeden said. "Whoever this Detective Grathan is, I don't like him. What are we going to do now? We can't let him find out anything more about us, that's for sure."

It was a good question, and Serafina tried to think it through. "We need to keep low and hidden, and figure out exactly who he is," she said. "We'll watch him very carefully and see what he does."

"Did you see what he had?" Braeden exclaimed. "The Black Cloak's silver clasp!"

"Which probably means he went out to my mother's den. I

saw her just last night, so I think she and the cubs are all right, but he might have come dangerously close to discovering them. Maybe that's why she was so anxious to leave."

"If he discovered your mother's den, it might have been *his* life in danger rather than hers."

"It's those nasty wolfhounds I'm worried about," she said. "They were truly vicious beasts."

"What about that feral boy you described? Do you think he escaped? Who do you think he was? It sounds like he fought very hard."

"I don't know," she said, "but I have to find out. He saved my life."

"We could ask around about him," Braeden suggested. "Maybe one of the mountain folk who work on the estate knows who he is. But why do you think the animals are leaving the mountains? There's been a family of otters living in the river for years, but two days ago, when I was out riding, I saw them leaving, all of them. Yesterday when I checked their holt, they were gone. The den was empty."

"My mother said there were other animals leaving, too, besides the luna moths and the birds I saw, but I couldn't get her to tell me about it."

"Even the ducks that normally live on the pond are gone," Braeden said.

At that moment, Serafina thought she heard something, like a faint scratching noise. She swiveled toward the noise.

"What's wrong?" Braeden asked.

She paused and listened but didn't hear anything.

"Nothing, I guess," she said, realizing that she was still a bit jumpy after her confrontation with Detective Grathan.

"This is a good hiding spot," Braeden said with satisfaction. "We should use it more often. Detective Grathan will never be able to find us in here. But it's probably getting late. They're going to be ringing the bell for dinner soon. I should go."

Serafina remembered that her pa had been excited that the Vanderbilts had sent her a message requesting her presence. But in the end, it hadn't been an invitation to dinner. It had been a summons to an interrogation.

"Yes, you better go," Serafina agreed, a bit too sadly.

"My aunt will be looking for me," Braeden said.

"And Lady Rowena, too, I reckon," she said.

Braeden looked at her and squinted, trying to see her face. "You know, she's not as bad as she seems."

"All right," Serafina said, realizing she had poked her friend a bit too hard.

"Her father sent her here all alone while he travels on business," Braeden continued. "He's some sort of important man, but it seems kind of mean of him to leave her here all by herself where she doesn't know anyone."

"I agree," Serafina said. She could see that the two of them had been talking.

"Rowena's mother passed away when she was seven," Braeden said. "And her father doesn't pay much attention to her. Before coming here, Rowena had barely been outside

London. I know she comes across like she's conceited, and maybe she is—I don't know—but she worries about things just like everyone else."

"What do you mean?" she asked.

"She said she worries that she brought all the wrong kind of clothes to be at a country estate, so she doesn't have anything to wear. She also thinks some of the other guests have been making comments about her accent."

Serafina frowned. It never even occurred to her that *Lady Rowena* would worry about her clothes and the way she spoke.

"I don't know," Braeden said. "I don't think she's a bad person. She's just not used to it here. It seems like she needs our help. My aunt asked me to look after her until her father comes. But that doesn't mean I'm not your friend."

"I understand," Serafina replied finally. And she did. She'd always known Braeden to be a kind person and a gentleman. "Just don't forget about me," she said, smiling a little, then realized again that he couldn't see her smile.

"Serafina . . ." Braeden scolded her.

"I will tell you the truth of it," she said. "Over the last week, sometimes it's felt like you didn't want anything to do with me anymore."

"What about you?" Braeden protested, getting at least as emotional as she was. "What have you been doing? You're always asleep when I'm awake and you go out every night on your own! Sometimes I think that one of these days you're going to turn into a wild creature or something. . . ."

Not likely, Serafina thought glumly.

"So you're not trying to avoid me?" she asked.

"Avoid you?" Braeden said in surprise. "You're just about my only friend."

Serafina smiled to hear him say that. And then she laughed a little. "What are you talking about? You have many friends. Gidean, Cedric, your horses . . ."

Braeden smiled. "And I have a new friend, too."

"Oh, yes?"

"When my uncle and I rode out to Chimney Rock the other day, I found a beautiful peregrine falcon with a broken wing at the base of the cliffs. I don't know what happened to her. Maybe a hunter shot her or she got into some kind of battle, but she was badly hurt. I wrapped her up in my coat and brought her home. Her name is Kess. She's incredible."

Serafina nodded as she felt a gentle and reassuring warmth filling her chest. This was the Braeden she knew. "I can't wait to meet her."

"I bandaged her wing, and I've been trying to help her eat."

"Do you think her wing will heal over time and she'll be able to fly again?"

"No, I'm afraid not," Braeden said sadly. "My uncle gave me a book on birds from his library. It said that if a bird of prey's wing is broken below the bend, it can sometimes heal, but if it's broken above the bend, like Kess's is, then it's impossible. She'll never fly again."

"That's too bad," Serafina said, trying to imagine how

terrible it would be for a falcon not to be able to fly, and for a moment she thought about her own situation, her own limitations. "But at least she'll have you as her friend."

"I'm going to take good care of her," Braeden said. "Peregrine falcons are amazing birds. The book says that they can fly anywhere on earth they want to. The word *peregrine* actually means 'wanderer' or 'traveler.' Sometimes, two peregrine falcons will hunt together. And they're the fastest animal on the planet. Scientists estimate that they dive at over two hundred miles an hour, but it's so fast that no one has ever been able to measure it exactly."

"That's amazing," Serafina said, smiling. She enjoyed listening to Braeden talk about his birds and his other animals. *This is how it should be,* she thought, the two of them sitting in a dark and secret place, just talking. This was the kind of friend she had always dreamed of, someone who was eager to hear her stories and excited to tell her things and content to be with her for a little while.

But she knew it couldn't last. He was right when he said he had to go.

She guided him through the darkness across the beam and over to the top of the ladder. As he began to climb down, he stopped, seeming to wonder why she wasn't climbing down with him.

"Just stay alert tonight," she told him. "Stay well clear of Grathan and don't let him corner you alone. Be safe."

"You too," Braeden said, nodding. "But aren't you coming out?"

120

"You go on ahead," she said. "I'll stay here awhile."

After he had started down, she wondered why she had let him go without her, why she had decided to stay here in the darkness. She'd accused him of not caring about their friendship, but he'd turned around and accused her right back. Maybe there was more truth in his accusation than hers. Mr. and Mrs. Vanderbilt knew who she was now. She could live openly at Biltmore if she wanted to. She might not have an invitation to dinner, but she could go out there with him into the house. Still, she didn't. Why? She sat in the darkness and thought about it for a long time. She had lived in the darkness all her life. This was where she felt most comfortable.

Her momma had said that she belonged with the folk at Biltmore, and perhaps that was true, but it still didn't change who she was.

Sitting in the darkness for a long while, she barely noticed the time passing. She knew that elsewhere in the house, the Vanderbilts and their guests must have eaten their dinner and gone to bed. The house was quiet and dark.

All her life, she had napped here and there for short periods throughout the day and night, so to her there were no separate, distinct days—time was continuous. She wondered what it would be like to sleep for a long period when the sun went down and wake up new each morning.

It was only the starlight now that filtered down through the pinprick holes in the rooftop, but to her eyes, the starlight-filled holes created a constellation of new stars all their own.

She stood and walked among the rafters in the attic,

hopping across the void from one joist to another, the darkness her domain.

But at that moment, she heard something out of the ordinary and stopped.

She stood in the darkness and waited, listening.

At first, all she could hear was the gentle beat of her own heart. Then she heard it again.

It was a scratching noise, like long claws or fingernails being dragged slowly along the inside of the wall.

She swallowed.

She almost couldn't believe what she had just heard.

She looked all around her, up at the ridge of the roof and along the edges of the walls, but she couldn't see anything that shouldn't be there.

Then she heard a *tick-tick-ticking* sound, followed by a long, raspy hiss. Someone's hot breath touched the back of her neck. She startled wildly and spun around, ready to fight. But there was no one there.

What's going on? she thought desperately, looking around her, but even as she did so, the pinprick stars in the roof above her began to go out.

She frowned in confusion.

It was like the holes were being blocked by something.

What's happening?

There was something . . . or many somethings . . . crawling on the ceiling.

Suddenly it was nearly pitch dark. Even she couldn't see.

Frightened, she ran along the top edge of a girder toward

the ladder. A single misstep and she'd fall to her death, but she had to get out of here.

Some sort of small living creature struck her head with a hard thump. She ducked down, her arms protecting her head, and kept running. Another creature landed in her hair, twisting wildly and screeching. When she tried to grab it with her hands, she felt its razor-sharp bites into her skin. Then a third creature hit her in the face, and she lost her balance and fell. She plummeted into the darkness.

15

As Serafina fell through midair, she reached out and grabbed
desperately. She caught hold of the girder's edge just in time,
stopping her fall. She hung down into the darkness above the
chasm, clinging to the girder by her fingers. The black void
loomed below her like a giant mouth waiting for her to drop
into it. The cold, gritty, sharp edge of the steel girder felt like
it was going to cut her fingers off, but letting go would be the
end of her. All the while, hundreds of creatures flew around her,
hissing and clicking, swarming through the attic like a black
tornado. Gritting her teeth, she swung her legs and wrapped
them around the girder. She hung there upside down. She
pulled herself up onto the top edge of the girder, then crouched
down to defend herself from the flying creatures.

The hissing grew in intensity. One creature struck the side of her head with a thump, clinging to her scalp and hair, its wings batting. Then another struck her in the face, and she swatted it away. Three more clung to her back. Another struck her neck and bit into her skin. Snarling in pain and anger, Serafina grabbed it against her neck and crushed it in her hand. Then she looked at the dead body she held.

She couldn't believe it. It made no sense. They were chimney swifts! These flying creatures were akin to bats in many ways, but they were actually dark, scaly, hissing little birds. They spent most of their time in the air at dusk, but when they landed, they couldn't perch. Instead they clung to the inside of chimneys and caves with their tiny, sharp feet. Their tails were not feathers but spines. The swifts had filled the attic, thousands of them coating the girders and the walls, like a gray, spiny-feathered, hissing, chattering skin.

Suddenly, the sibilation of the swifts rose into a crescendo of rasping sound, and they all burst into the air inside the attic. A great swirling cloud of them swarmed around her. They hurled their bodies against her, clinging at her with their tiny scaly feet, pecking at her with their sharp beaks, their spiny tails digging into her face, their wings batting and tangling up her hair.

The torrent of swifts was so thick around her that she could not hear or see. She would soon lose track of her position. She wanted to hunker down, curl into a ball, and cover her face and head, but she knew if she did that, she'd never get out. So she kept fighting, flailing her arms, and pulling the creatures off her. Eyes almost closed for protection, she desperately looked around for an escape. Seeing a girder between her and the ladder, she took a leap and managed to just land on it. From there, she pushed her way along the girder through the cloud of birds. She finally came to the ladder and climbed down as fast as she could, fighting the attacking birds all the way.

At last, she pushed her way through the panel at the back of the cabinet and came rolling out, breathless and terrified, into the third-floor corridor. She spun around and slammed the panel shut with her shoulder, closing the swifts behind her.

For several seconds, she just lay there, catching her breath, trying to comprehend what had just happened. Chimney swifts were strange, crepuscular little creatures, but they were normally harmless. She'd seen them flying their cheerful, chirping, mosquito-catching acrobatics above Biltmore's roofs at sunset many times. Why did they now swarm and attack her? She'd been living in this house, crawling in these passages her entire life, and they'd always left her alone. Why was this happening now? Was the house itself turning against her?

She looked around her. The house was dark and quiet. It was well after midnight, and everyone was asleep.

Still feeling scared and shaky from what had happened, she got up onto her feet. She stood unsteadily for a moment, recovering. Then she brushed herself off and pulled the feathers and dead swifts out of her hair.

When she heard a creak in the distance, she stopped, half in a panic that the attack was going to start all over again, but nothing came.

She started walking through the darkness. She followed the

corridor and passed through the living hall with its sofas, chairs, and tables. Earlier, several of the guests had been enjoying their tea here, but now it was eerily dark, empty, and still. It was like they had all disappeared. A terrible chill went down her spine. What if Braeden was gone, and Mr. and Mrs. Vanderbilt, and all the guests? What if they were *all* gone? Maybe she was the last one, the only one to survive the attack. What if everyone else in the house was dead?

She heard another sound. It wasn't a creak this time, but a footstep, and then another. Somewhere in the house, someone was awake. It felt like someone was following her, lingering in the shadows behind her.

When she reached the top of the Grand Staircase, moonlight shone through the rising cascade of slanting, leaded-glass windows, casting silver-blue light across the wide, gently arcing steps and the filigreed railing that spiraled up through Biltmore's floors. Attached to a copper dome at the very top of the staircase, an ornate wrought-iron chandelier hung down through the center of the magnificent spiral. As she headed down the staircase, the black shadow of her body in the moonlight moved along the outer wall like a strange, crawling animal. Then she heard something coming up the stairway toward her.

She stopped, uncertain what she was hearing. Her heart beat faster, and her breaths grew shorter and more intense. It wasn't a small noise or a single step or two. Someone was definitely coming up the stairs. Her muscles jittered, preparing her for battle. Her mind kept telling her to get ahold of herself—it could be one of Biltmore's guests or a servant. But then she realized that her instincts were telling her something: the sound wasn't human. She sucked in a breath and crouched down, ready to leap.

Whatever it was, she could hear the creature's feet clicking and scraping on the limestone steps.

It had four legs.

And claws.

Her chest pulled in air at a steady, rapid race. She could feel every muscle in her body coming alive, ready to fight.

She began backing slowly up the stairs until she reached the upper landing, making as little noise as possible.

But it was coming fast, gaining on her. She could hear it growling now, coming faster.

Its multilegged shadow traveled up the outer wall like a giant spider.

Just when she was about to turn and run, it came up onto the landing and into sight.

But it wasn't a spider.

It was a black dog.

The dog paused and then began to move slowly toward her, stalking her, its head low as it snarled and growled. She backed up as it came toward her.

As it approached, she realized it wasn't one of the wolfhounds or some other dog. It was her friend Gidean.

Much relieved, she let out a long breath. She smiled and relaxed. "Gidean," she said happily, thinking that he must have mistaken her for an intruder.

But the dog snarled and kept moving toward her, his body

tense and coiled, ready to spring. A new fear grew within her. Her chest tightened.

"Gidean, it's me," she said again, rising desperation in her voice. "Come on, Gidean, it's me."

But Gidean did not recognize her.

Her body flushed with heat.

The large black dog with its pointed ears kept coming slowly toward her, snarling, its teeth bared now, its canines snapping. It was the most terrifying snarl she'd ever heard.

Gidean burst into an attack, growling as he leapt into the air straight at her.

He slammed into her body, biting into her shoulder and knocking her backward off her feet. She hit the stone floor with a painful slam, her head hitting so hard that she nearly blacked out. Then she twisted and spun and punched her way out from under the dog's legs.

"Stop this, Gidean!" she cried as she leapt away. "Gidean, it's me! It's Serafina!"

But the dog leapt again, biting her arm and shaking her as he growled. The only other time she'd ever seen Gidean this fierce was when he was fighting the Man in the Black Cloak. It was like *she* had suddenly become the evil one.

"Gidean, no! Stop!" she cried as she smashed her fists into the dog's face to get him to release her. She kicked and screamed and finally twisted away from him. He immediately pressed the attack, snapping at her legs as she scurried away. She ducked and darted, but wherever she went, he followed. He was incredibly fast. She kept dodging him, but she could not shake him.

She didn't want to fight him, but he just kept coming. He bit her again, his canines clamping onto her leg. With a ferocious tug, he pulled her off her feet, then charged in at her throat. She blocked her neck and rolled away, then leapt to her feet, and he immediately struck her and took her down again.

She didn't want to hurt her friend, but she didn't want to die, either. She couldn't keep going. She couldn't keep fighting him. He was an incredible warrior and filled with a terrific rage, the likes of which she'd never seen. Something had twisted him, deranged him, turned him into a rabid beast that did not recognize her. And he was wearing her down. She could tell that she wasn't going to last much longer.

She fended off one more attack and then turned and fled back toward the top of the stairs as fast as she could.

Outraged by her attempt to escape, the growling Doberman charged after her with shocking speed. Just as she reached the railing, the dog leapt through the air, its fang-filled mouth opened wide for the bite.

16

Gidean slammed into Serafina's body and sent them both somersaulting over the railing, falling, falling, fifty feet to the marble floor below.

As she fell through the open air, the shock of what had happened screamed through her mind, her limbs flailing, nothing to grab onto. She was falling upside down, looking up toward the ceiling. She could see the floors of the house flashing by in the rings of the four-story-high chandelier. The domed ceiling at the top of the Grand Staircase kept getting smaller and smaller as she fell.

She was going to die. When she hit the floor, her bones would break. Her head would crack open. Blood would splash everywhere. And she'd die.

And there was absolutely nothing she could do about it.

She could not jump or bite or run or scream to save herself this time. No clever idea or special trick would save her. Her mother couldn't save her. Her pa couldn't save her. There was no trap she could set to defeat her enemy.

And she didn't even understand who her enemy was or why. Just as she'd feared, the claws of doom had reached down out of the sky and snatched her life away before she even knew they were there.

It felt like it was taking an impossibly long time to fall, like every second was a hundred seconds long. She thought about prowling through the basement at night, and eating chicken and grits with her pa, and looking up at the stars with Braeden. She thought about all the mysteries that would never be solved. Why were the animals leaving? Who was the bearded man? Why had the feral boy helped her? From where would the danger come to Biltmore, and what form would it take?

Then something peculiar happened.

She didn't think about it and *decide* to do it. It just happened. Her body snapped. She tucked in her arms, twisted her spine, and flung out her legs, righting herself in midair. Then she stretched out her arms and pulled in her legs to stop her spin and position her limbs in the direction of her fall. It was an instinct, a split-second reflex, like snatching a rat the instant it tried to run away.

She hit the floor hard but strong, bracing her landing with the bending, crouching muscles of her legs and arms until she was down low on her curled feet and extended hands, her body finally still and unharmed.

She landed on her feet.

But Gidean did not.

His body slammed onto the floor beside her. She didn't just see it and hear it; she felt the crushing blow, the crack of bones, and the whimper of the dog. She knew immediately that the battle was over.

Gidean lay beside her, his head down and bleeding, his body broken in a thousand places. He was nearly dead.

Gidean had been Braeden's constant companion and closest friend since Braeden had lost his family. The dog had walked at Braeden's side wherever he went, ran with him when he rode his horse, and guarded his door at night. There had been a time when she didn't like dogs and dogs didn't like her, but she and this dog had worked together, fought together, and defended each other. Gidean had attacked the Man in the Black Cloak and saved her life. But now Gidean lay dying on the marble floor beside her.

When a shadow moved across the moonlit floor, she thought it must be an owl or some other creature of the night outside the Grand Staircase's windows. She turned and looked up. It was Rowena in a white nightgown, standing on the second floor, looking down at her in shock. Rowena's hair was long, loose, and unbrushed, her eyes wide with fear. She gripped what looked like a pencil in her hand, or perhaps a hairpin, brandishing it in front of her like a weapon.

"Rowena!" Serafina shouted to her. "Go get the veterinarian! Run!"

Rowena did not move. She stared in horrified shock at the sight of Gidean lying on the floor in a pool of blood and Serafina standing over him with blood all over her hands. The girl did not seem to understand Serafina's words. She did not run to get the veterinarian. Instead, she turned and slowly walked in the direction of Braeden's room.

What was she doing? What did she think she saw?

When Rowena returned a few moments later, Serafina heard the rush of frantic footsteps, but it wasn't the veterinarian. Braeden came running down the stairs.

"What's happened?" Braeden screamed as he came. He was beyond distraught.

Braeden ran to Gidean's side and collapsed to his knees at his dog's side. "He's badly hurt!" he cried. "Serafina, what did you do?"

Serafina was too overwhelmed to answer him.

Tears streamed down his face as he hugged his dying dog. In all she and Braeden had been through together, she'd never seen him cry before. "Aw, Gidean, boy, please don't go . . . don't go . . . please, boy . . . no . . . don't leave me. . . ."

Serafina burst into tears. But as she cried, she tilted her head upward and saw Rowena standing there again. Rowena was just staring at her. She hadn't retrieved the veterinarian; she'd gone to Braeden.

Rowena slowly lifted her arm and pointed at Serafina. "I

saw her," she said, her voice filled with trembling. "I saw her do it! She hurled the dog over the railing!"

"That's not true!" Serafina shouted back at her.

Guests and servants flooded down the stairs from the floors above. Mr. and Mrs. Vanderbilt came, utterly shocked by what was happening. The balding, gray-bearded elderly man she'd seen walking in the forest with Mr. Vanderbilt made his way slowly down the steps with his cane, studying the scene. Mrs. King came hurrying into the hall, along with Essie and many of the other maids, but no one seemed to know what to do.

"Get the veterinarian!" Mr. Vanderbilt shouted, and the butler ran to fetch him.

Serafina wiped the tears from her eyes as she looked up at the people of Biltmore. Then she saw the dark figure of Detective Grathan standing on the third floor high above. His long brown hair hung around his head like a dark hood. Holding his spiraling antler cane in his hand, he looked down at her and the crying boy and the bloody dog on the floor between them. She wanted to snarl up at him, to bite him, but he just stared at her, as if it was a scene he'd seen many times before. There wasn't fear in his expression like the others. There was a knowingness in his eyes.

Braeden looked at Serafina, his eyes filled with agony. She knew he could see the fresh blood on her face and the scratches on her body. It was obvious that she and Gidean had fought. "What happened, Serafina?" he cried, tears streaming down his face.

"I don't know, Braeden," Serafina said.

"She's lying," Lady Rowena said as she came down the stairs and stood behind Braeden. "She was fighting the dog and then tricked it so that it jumped over the railing."

"Braeden, please believe me. That's not what happened," Serafina pleaded. "Gidean attacked me. We both fell."

"She didn't fall," Lady Rowena said. "She couldn't have fallen. She's standing right in front of us."

"Gidean would never attack you," Braeden said hopelessly to Serafina as he dropped his head and looked at his wounded dog.

"I—I didn't do this!" Serafina stammered, tears pouring out of her eyes again as she furiously wiped them away. She couldn't understand how this could happen. How could she be in this situation? Braeden had to believe her. She reached out to hold his arm.

"Leave him alone! You have done enough!" Rowena shouted, blocking her. Serafina snarled at the girl, then turned back to her friend.

"I swear to you, Braeden, I did not do this."

Braeden looked desperately at her. "He's hurt bad, Serafina."

"You should leave," Rowena said to Serafina, her voice filled with fear and anger. "You don't belong with civilized people. Look at you! You're like some kind of wild creature! You don't belong here!" Then she looked around at all the frightened onlookers. "How can you live with her in this house? Something's going to happen! It won't just be a dog next time. She's going to hurt someone!"

"Braeden, no . . ." Serafina begged him, clutching his arm.

Out of the corner of her eye, Serafina saw two footmen moving in to protect the young master.

"Braeden, please . . ."

As Mr. Vanderbilt came toward her and Braeden, he gestured for his footmen to take control. She had no idea what Mr. Vanderbilt and the footmen were going to do, but when a footman grabbed her from behind, it startled her badly. In all her anger and confusion, she twisted around hissing and bit him on the hand before she could stop herself. It was pure and utter reflex, an instinct over which she had no control. Her teeth sank into the man's hand, drawing blood. He leapt back, screaming in pain. She could see the horrified faces of everyone around her as they backed away from her. Mr. and Mrs. Vanderbilt stared at her in disbelief, barely able to comprehend what she'd just done. She'd become the very wild beast that Rowena was screaming about.

Filled with shame and anguish, tears streaming down her face, she leapt to her feet. The Vanderbilts and the guests and servants shrank away from her in fear. Gazing around at their horrified faces, she couldn't stand it any longer. She ran. The crowd recoiled in panic as she fled through them across the Entrance Hall. One of the women screamed. Serafina escaped through the front doors and plunged into the darkness outside. It felt like it took forever to run across the open lawn and reach the trees. She kept running, just running, her heart pouring out of her, and still running, into the forest, into the mountains, crying and distraught, more confused than she had ever been in her life. She had bitten a footman and snarled at everyone.

Blood all over her hands, she had snapped and hissed like a trapped animal.

You don't belong here! Rowena's words screamed through her mind as she ran, echoes of her mother's words the night before. She had been cast unwanted from place to place and had nowhere to go.

But worst of all, she'd hurt Gidean terribly bad, and she'd broken Braeden's heart. It felt like she'd betrayed the only two friends she had ever known.

Serafina ran into the forest and just kept running, hot tears of anguish pouring from her eyes. Her lungs gasped frantically for breath, her chest filled with shaking emotion. She wasn't running with direction; she was running *away*—away from the injured Gidean, away from the sight of her best friend in anguish, away from the shame of what she'd done.

When she finally slowed to a walk, she sniffled and wiped her nose with the back of her hand and kept walking fast and hard. As she crossed through the great oaks of the forest and Biltmore disappeared farther and farther behind her, her stomach churned. The magnitude of what she was doing began to sink in. She was leaving her pa and Braeden, and Mr. and Mrs.

Vanderbilt, and Essie, and everyone else she knew at Biltmore. She was leaving them all behind.

When she thought about how she hadn't even said goodbye to her pa, she started crying all over again. It broke her heart that he'd hear about this shameful, horrible incident from the servants and from Mr. Vanderbilt, that her pa would hear that she'd hurt the young master's dog and that they'd thrown her out of the house. She could still feel in her teeth the sensation of biting into that footman's hand. She could still see the horrified looks on all their faces when she ran through the crowd of people. Maybe Lady Rowena was right. Maybe she truly was a terrible and wild creature. She didn't belong in a civilized home.

But her mother had told her that she didn't belong in the forest, either. The words still echoed in her mind. She was too human, too slow and weak to fight off attackers. *You don't belong here, Serafina,* her mother had said.

She didn't belong in the forest or at Biltmore. She didn't belong *anywhere*.

She walked for miles, driven by nothing but burning emotion. When she saw a glow of light in a valley below her, she finally slowed down, curious. Tall, rectangular shapes rose up among the trees, some of them dotted with dim points of light, others entirely dark. The sound of a whistle startled her, and then she saw a long, dark chain of boxes curving along the mountainside. The metal snake weaved in and out of the trees, but as it crossed a trestle bridge over a river, a plume of white steam roiled up into the moonlit clouds. *It's a train,* she thought. *A real train.*

She'd learned about locomotives, with their fireboxes and their piston rods, from her pa, and she'd heard tell of Mr. Vanderbilt's grandpa who'd spread his ships and trains across America. Even from this great distance, she could feel the iron beast's rumble in the earth beneath her feet and the pressure of its hurtling movement in her chest. She couldn't even imagine being up close to such a thing. But she wondered fleetingly what it would be like to leap upon such a monster and fly to distant places on long, shining tracks. It was a foreign world down there in the city of Asheville, filled with people and machines and ways of life she did not understand, and from there, an entire country spread out in all directions. What would she become if that was the path she took?

As the sun rose, she kept moving, trekking far up into the Craggy Mountains, mile after mile. She drank from a stream when she was thirsty. She hunted when she hungered. When she was tired, she slept tucked into a crevice of rock. A wild creature she became, full and earnest, if not in body, then in spirit whole.

Later the next evening, as she crossed through a forested cove between two spurs of a mountain ridge, the scent of a campfire drifted on the crisp autumn air. Drawn to it, she came upon a small collection of log cabins where several families gathered around a little fire roasting corn on the cob and grilling trout caught from the nearby stream. She marveled that a boy about her age was playing a gentle melody on a banjo while his younger sister accompanied him on a fiddle. Others were singing soft and dancing slow, like the quiet river by which they lived.

Serafina did not approach the mountain folk, but she sat in the trees on the hillside just above them and, for a little while, listened to their music and let her heart go free.

She watched and listened as the mountain folk played song after song, all of them singing along and dancing in each other's arms. Some of their songs were fast jigs and reels, everyone hooting and hollering, but mostly, as the night wore on, they played the softer songs, songs of the gentle heart and the deepened soul. They drank their white lightning and their autumn cider and rocked in their chairs, telling their stories around the campfire, stories of long-lost loves and heroic deeds, of strange occurrences and dark mysteries. When everyone started drifting off to their beds beneath their cabin roofs or sleeping on the ground beneath the stars, she knew it was time for her to go as well, for this was not her home tonight, this was not her bed. She reluctantly pulled herself up onto her feet and slipped away from the smoldering campfire's glowing light.

She kept traveling, but slower now, less and less anxious to get away from what was behind her. High up into the Black Mountains she climbed, following a ridge of craggy gardens where only rhododendrons and alpine grasses grew. She walked along a stony reach where the moonlit mist fell down the mountains like the waves of a silver sea. She trekked over a highland bald with no trees, just the moonlight, and the geese flying across the dark blue sky. She followed a jagged-edged river and gazed upon a waterfall that fell, and fell, and fell, down one rock after another, splashing and turning, until it disappeared into the misty forest below.

As she was about to carry on, she looked over and saw movement on a ridge that ran parallel to her own. It was a red wolf, long and lean and beautiful, trotting along a path. When the wolf stopped and looked at her, it startled her. But then she realized that she recognized the wolf and the wolf recognized her.

She had seen him a few weeks before along the river, the night she was lost in the forest. So much had happened in her life since then.

She stared at the young wolf for a long time, and the wolf stared at her. He had thick, reddish-brown fur, pointed ears, and incredibly keen eyes. She wondered how he had fared since last they met. The wound he had suffered that night had healed and he looked stronger now.

Then she saw something behind him. Another wolf trotted along the path. Then another. She soon saw that there were many wolves with him, male and female, pups and elders, all traveling with him. But some of them glistened with fresh wounds. Others were limping. She could see that they had fought a great battle against a terrible enemy. Her wolf friend had become one of the leaders of his pack. The pack of wolves wasn't hunting but traveling a long distance. She could see it in the way they moved, the way they held their heads and tails down as they trotted. They were leaving these mountains, like the luna moths and songbirds, and they were leaving them for good.

When she looked at the red wolf again, he seemed to see the sadness in her face, for now she saw it reflected in his.

Something deep down in her began to burn. Her wolf friend had found his kin. He had found his place. The wolves of the pack stuck together. They fought together. That's what a family was. That's what it meant to be kin. You didn't give up on that.

She felt the heat rising in her cheeks against the midnight chill. She thought about Biltmore and her family there. She didn't want to leave them, to be separated from them. She wanted to stick together. She wanted to be a pack of wolves, a pride of lions. She wanted to be a family.

She thought about her mother, and the cubs, and the dark lion, and the feral boy who had saved her life. She wanted to be with them, to hunt with them, to run with them, to be part of their lives in the forest.

They were all her folk. And she was theirs.

Standing there on top of the mountain, she knew what she had to do.

The running would get her to a distant city or to the top of a mountain, but in the end, the running would get her nowhere. There was nowhere to go when you didn't have a family to go home to, to share it with.

As the wolf and his pack disappeared into the trees, she sat down in the gravel right where she had been standing and looked out across the mountains beneath the stars.

Something was wrong. She could feel it.

Why would her mother send her away? That wasn't right.

Why would chimney swifts swarm her?

Why would Gidean attack her?

Why was she running away from Biltmore?

Why were the wolves leaving?

The more questions she asked herself, the fiercer she felt. All these things seemed wildly separate, but maybe all the questions were connected. Maybe they all had the same answer.

She didn't know if Gidean had lived or died after the fall from the railing. She didn't know if Braeden would ever be able to forgive her. But she wasn't going to give up on her family. Families were supposed to stick together no matter what. No argument or terrible event should break them apart. Her pa had shown her time and time again that if something was broken, you fixed it. And the one thing Serafina had learned in the twelve years of her life was that if the rat wasn't dead, then whack it again until it was. You didn't give up. She was going to fight, and she was going to keep fighting until her family understood her.

She was convinced now that something was wrong in the forest. Something was wrong at Biltmore. And she was going to find out what it was and fix it.

She stood, brushed herself off, and headed back down the mountain.

She knew what she must do.

18

Serafina made her way back along the mountain ridge through the thick, scrubby vegetation that grew among the rocks, then down the slopes of Graybeard Mountain into the forest trees of the lower elevations. She rested when she needed to but tried to keep moving. She was determined to find her mother and learn everything she could about the dark force that had invaded the mountains. She had seen the terrifying man in the forest with his dogs, and she had come up against Grathan at Biltmore. She didn't know who or what these men were, or exactly what dark powers they possessed, but she knew she had to fight them.

Her mother and the cubs had abandoned the den at the angel's glade, so the only clue she had to follow was the cryptic words her mother had scratched into the dirt.

"'If you need me, winter, spring, or fall,'" Serafina said, "'come where what you climbed is floor and rain is wall.'"

She imagined it must be a riddle, something she could solve but their enemies could not. But it confused her. Her mother had wanted her to go back to Biltmore, not follow her, so why did she leave any message at all?

As she descended the mountain, she came to a dark stand of decrepit old pine trees with thick, straight trunks coated in black mold, all the lower limbs of the trees withered and rotted, the roots growing along the ground like long, treacherous fingers. The smell of damp earth and rotting wood filled her nostrils. Everything around her was sticky with black pinesap. There were no other plants growing here—no saplings or bushes could survive in the perennial shadow of the blackened pines. Nothing but dark bloodred pine needles covered the ground.

Disturbed by this deadened place, she crouched down and tried to see ahead of her through the murkiness of the night. She wondered if there was a path through it or if she had to find a way around it. She could hear the pinesap dripping from the branches of the trees. A foreboding crept into her. On the ground, beneath the twisted limbs of the pine trees, she saw a dark, unnatural shape.

Her instinct urged her to turn around and go the other direction, put distance between her and whatever this place was. But her curiosity would not let her leave. She crept slowly toward the shape, pulling deep drafts of air into her lungs.

It appeared to be a worn, flat, rectangular stone, and beside it, a low, elongated, heavy iron cage buried in the ground. She

SERAFINA and the TWISTED STAFF

took a hard swallow. She studied the cage, trying to understand what it was for. It was no more than a foot or two high. A small door had been fabricated into the end of the cage, with a latch on the outside. *To lock something in,* she thought. It appeared to be a cage for an animal of some kind. Then she found another cage, and then another. As she crept along, low and quiet, she felt a sickening in her stomach. There were hundreds of cages for as far as she could see.

She found a small hut made of twisted branches and gnarly vines. She had seen woodsmen make lean-tos and shelters from branches before, but this shelter did not look like the branches had been cut and gathered, but as if they had grown or slithered into that spot to form walls and roof. The vines and branches interlaced into an unnatural weave, like the hide of a perverse beast. Pinesap dripped from the tree limbs onto the roof of the hut, coating it in a black and stinking ooze. The gray remnants of a campfire smoldered in front of the hut. A black iron pot sat in the smoking ashes. Dozens of dead crows and vultures lay on the ground, their clawed feet cramped into balls.

Serafina's limbs trembled. Her heart pounded. She was frightened by what she was going to find within this dark place. But she had to find out. She had to keep going.

She crept closer to the shelter. She watched and listened. There appeared to be no movement, no sound, other than the constant dripping of the sap.

She crept inside.

There were bundles of wire inside the foul hut but no inhabitant. She found wire cutters, gloves, and other tools, but

no indication what all this was for except for a pile of furred animal skins lying on the hut's dirt floor. Black furs and brown, gray and white. She couldn't help but clench her teeth at the sight of it and snarl her nose away from the rancid smell of the dead skin. It felt like spiders were crawling all over her shoulders and neck.

She hurriedly backed out of the hut and scanned the area for danger. This was a deeply disturbing place. She quickly turned to leave. Then she heard a sound that stopped her in her tracks.

A whimper.

19

$\mathcal{S}$erafina turned.

Back behind the shelter, there were more cages.

She heard the whimper again—a long, pleading, mournful whine.

As she glanced warily around her, her legs buzzed with tension. Her temples pounded. Every sensation in her body was telling her she should not linger here, but her heart was telling her she must go toward the sound.

She crept slowly forward. The other cages had been empty, but to her horror, she found several inhabited cages behind the shelter.

She saw brownish fur inside one of the cages, but she still couldn't tell what the creature was.

She crept closer.

The mound of fur in the cage was a few feet long, and it was shaking.

Then she heard the whimpering sound again.

Serafina tried to stay steady and strong, but she started trembling as badly as the poor animal in the cage. She couldn't help it. She looked behind her, then scanned the forest to make sure no one was near. It felt like a terribly dangerous place. The pine trees grew so close together, and the area beneath the upper limbs was so dark that it was difficult to see any distance at all.

Crawling on her hands and knees, she crept around to the front of the cage.

She peered through the cage's iron bars.

There she saw it.

Serafina looked into the face of one of the most beautiful animals she had ever seen: a young female bobcat. She had large, striking eyes, long whiskers, and a white-marked face with wide ruffs of hair that extended outward from her cheeks and around her head, all the way to her tufted, black-tipped ears. She had grayish-brown black-spotted fur, with black streaks on her body and dark bars on her legs.

But as beautiful as the bobcat was, she was in terrible shape. It was clear that she'd been drooling and clawing, chewing at the metal cage, frantic to escape.

As Serafina approached her, the bobcat became quiet and still, staring at her with big, round eyes. She seemed to understand that Serafina was not her enemy.

Serafina saw that there were other animals in the cages,

too—a woodchuck, a porcupine, even a pair of river otters. One of the saddest of all was a red-tailed hawk with its talons lacerated and bloody, its feathers torn and broken from batting its wings against the wire mesh in its fight to escape.

Serafina quickly glanced around her, frightened that the owner of this camp would arrive at any moment. These terrible cages didn't belong to her, so she had no right to do what she wanted to do. But did she need someone's permission to do what was right?

She looked behind her and then scanned the trees for danger. Her heart began to pound in her chest so hard that she could barely breathe.

She knew she should run, but how could she leave?

She inched closer to the bobcat's cage, unfastened the latch, and opened the door.

"Come on out," she whispered.

The bobcat crept out slowly, afraid of everything around her. Serafina touched the cat's fur with her bare hand. The bobcat looked at her with her huge eyes, then slunk quickly off into the forest. Once the bobcat had escaped the pine trees and was in the safety of the distant undergrowth, she turned and looked at Serafina.

Thank you, she seemed to be thinking. Then the cat finally made its escape, disappearing into the brush.

"Stay bold," Serafina said quietly, remembering the expression the feral boy had used when he had helped her. She didn't know why, but for some reason those two simple words had meant a lot to her.

She quickly released the woodchuck, porcupine, and otters. They all looked strong enough to get home. She was sure the otters would know the way to the nearest river. But the hawk was in a bad way. She thought that he could probably fly, but a red-tailed hawk out at night was in grave danger from its natural enemy, the great horned owl.

She reached into the cage, carefully grabbed the hawk with both hands, and pulled him out. He lifted his wings and tried to pull away, none too happy to be handled. She expected he would hiss and snap at her, but he did not. He stared at her with his powerful raptor eyes and clamped onto her wrist with one of his talons, squeezing so hard that she thought he was going to break her bones. It was as if he somehow understood she wanted to help him, but at the same time, he wasn't going to give up control.

She left the pine forest and the terrible cages behind her, carrying the wounded hawk clutched in her hands.

When she and the hawk had finally escaped the pine trees and entered a better part of the forest, she slowed down. She wished she could carry the hawk all the way back to Biltmore and give it to Braeden to take care of, but she couldn't travel fast enough with a hawk in her hands, and she was pretty sure the hawk wasn't too happy about being carried around by somebody like her. She found a safe thicket of tree brush and stuffed the hawk inside where it could hide from the marauding owls until daylight came. "Rest here, then fly strong, my friend," she whispered.

From there, she tried to move quickly away. She wanted to

put as much distance between her and those terrible cages as she could. She knew that the forest was a wild, untamed place, with all sorts of life-and-death struggles, but what kind of person would trap and capture animals like that? Why would he leave them there, starving and afraid, hidden beneath the darkened trees?

A mist drifted through the branches of the forest and made it difficult for her to find her way, but she kept moving downhill the best she could. She felt a tightness in her stomach. She couldn't escape the feeling that she had just avoided a dark and terrible danger.

Through the mist she saw something out of the corner of her eye. When she looked over, she spotted a figure in the distance walking through the trees. At first she thought it might be the man she'd seen entering the forest with Mr. Vanderbilt. She felt a sudden hope. Maybe she was far closer to Biltmore than she realized. But a heaviness rolled into her chest. She crouched in the underbrush and watched the figure at a distance. He was wearing a long, dark, weather-beaten coat and a wide-brimmed hat. It was the bearded man she'd seen in the forest a few nights before! She hit the dirt in sudden panic.

She tried to stay quiet, but her chest pulled in rapid breaths as she looked toward him. He had a heavy, dark gray beard, not long and scraggly white like many of the mountain men, but thick and wavy like an animal's coat. His face was craggy with cracks and wrinkles, wind-worn like he'd been in the forest for fifty years. She scanned the area, looking for signs of the wolfhounds, but didn't see them. Nor did he seem to be carrying the walking stick he had before. But she knew it was him.

Staying low and quiet and very still, she watched him. He seemed to drift into and out of the mist, in and among the trees, disappearing and then reappearing in the swirls of the fog. He drifted farther away, then closer, as if the trees themselves were playing tricks on her eyes. He seemed more like a ghostly haint than a mortal man. As she felt the goose bumps rising on her arms, she wanted to run, but she was afraid the sound of her flight would draw his attention.

But she had to get out of here. Just as she started to back away and go in the opposite direction, the man stopped dead in his tracks. He pivoted his head toward her with a startling, inhuman quickness—like an owl spotting prey. His terrible silver eyes peered right at her.

She ducked down to the ground and pressed her back to the base of a gnarled, old fir tree, hiding. The image of his pivoting head threw a shiver down her spine.

She heard him moving rapidly toward her.

She had to run, but her chest tightened and her legs clamped. A sharp pain attacked her throat like someone's fingers had grabbed hold of her windpipe. Her whole body started shaking violently with something beyond fear, something beyond her control. Panic set in. She couldn't get any air into her lungs. She tried to scream, but she couldn't get sound of any kind to pass through her constricted throat.

The footsteps came rapidly closer as the man in the long

dark coat came toward her. She could hear his boots sinking into the damp earth as he walked. She became aware of a sudden coldness on the ground beneath her and around her. When she looked down, she saw that the earth had become soaked with blood.

Serafina tried to leap up from the ground and flee, but the man had cast some sort of spell on her. Her muscles were rigid. They would not move.

As the man bore down on her, Serafina watched in horrified amazement as the roots of the tree erupted out of the blood-soaked earth, grew rapidly around her wrists, and clamped her hands to the ground. Without her hands to fight, she was completely defenseless.

Like a desperate mink caught in a trap, she bent down and chewed at the roots that held her hands. When another root started slithering like a snake around her ankles, she kicked it angrily away.

Suddenly, the forest that had always been her ally and concealment had become her enemy.

As the man came around the tree, his face was shrouded in darkness save for the silver blaze of his eyes. He grabbed at her with two bony, clutching bare hands, grasping like the talons of an owl. As his long, clawlike fingernails sank into her, she twisted wildly and broke herself free. She thrashed her legs, then darted away.

She ran as fast as she could, until she thought she must have put some distance between herself and her pursuer. But just as she turned her head to look behind her, she heard a *tick-tick-ticking* sound. A terrible, hissing scream erupted a few feet above her left shoulder. The sound scared her so badly that she leapt back and hit a tree. A large, nasty-looking white barn owl flew right over her head, its horrible black eyes peering at her, its mouth open as it let out its bloodcurdling scream.

She dove into a thicket of vine-strangled brambles where the barn owl could not fly. She thought she was very clever. But then the barn owl disappeared and the bearded man began tearing the branches away, pushing into the thicket toward her. She got down on her hands and knees and crawled through the vines into the deepest part of the thicket. She hoped it might provide her some form of protection from the bearded man's spells. But instead, the vines started moving, snaking, twisting themselves around her limbs and neck.

She screamed and thrashed and yanked at the vines as she crawled out the other side of the thicket. From there, she stood up and ran across the open ground.

She wanted to turn, she wanted to fight, she wanted to attack this horrible man, but there was nothing she could do but run for her life. She ran fast through the cover of the forest. She thought she was doing it. She thought she was escaping.

When she glanced back, she saw that the man had not chased her. He was still standing where he had been. He simply flattened his hand to his mouth and blew across his palm in her direction. It was like the cold, corpsy breath of Death himself had struck her. The blood rushed from her head. Her lungs went cold. Her muscles went limp, and her body involuntarily collapsed, somersaulting down a small incline, dead weight and lifeless, until her body came to rest in the dirt.

Her whole body had gone pale and cold. Her lungs had stopped pulling in air. Her heart had stopped pumping blood. She had a few seconds of thought left as the blood drained from her head, but she was a dead girl, a cadaver, lying facedown on the ground.

The man made his way down to her, grabbed her limp body like a rag doll, and pulled her up onto an old stump. But even as he dragged her lifeless body against the cold earth, she could feel the effects of his spell wearing off—like pins and needles in her limbs. She did not understand it, but she was apparently a far tougher creature than he had accounted for in his spell. Her chest tingled with the slip of new air into her lungs. Her heart suddenly thumped to life again, and warm blood flowed through her like waves.

"Now, let's get a good look at you," the man said as he brought her into the moonlight. "Just what kind of little girl are you, sneaking up on me like that?"

When he flipped her limp body around so that he could

see her face, she was terrified, but she kept her eyes closed and pretended to be dead.

"Ah, I see," the man said when he saw her face. "It's you again. I should have known. You've been a nuisance to us already, haven't you? And I've seen enough of your kith and kin to know that it's only going to get worse if I let you grow up."

As Serafina felt her strength coming back into her muscles and the saliva wetting her mouth, she knew she only had one chance. The old rat trick. Bursting alive, she twisted around and bit the man's right hand as deeply and fiercely as she could.

The man reflexively yanked back his hand. But she didn't let go at first. His arm's yanking motion pulled her entire body up. At that moment, she released her bite and went flying through the air. She landed on the ground, rolled to her feet, and ran.

Serafina ran for miles, and then walked, and then ran some more, traveling as far from that place as she could.

She tried to think through everything she had seen. She knew it had been the same bearded man she had encountered in the forest a few nights before. He had seemed to be drifting in and out of the trees with an almost specter-like quality, like an apparition in the mist. Was he the old man of the forest that the mountain folk spoke of? He seemed to know her. He had said that she was a nuisance, like she was getting in his way. But in the way of what? What was his goal? Was it truly to find the Black Cloak? Or was it more than that? She thought about the stallions pulling the driverless carriage, and the swifts swarming her in the attack, and Gidean attacking her on the stairs. . . . Was he somehow controlling these animals? Whoever he was, he could use his hands to throw deathly spells that Serafina never wanted to experience again.

When she had come down from the craggy gardens, she'd intended to find her mother and make her tell her everything she knew, and then from there, go on to Biltmore. But what if the bearded man had already found her mother and the cubs? What if he had killed them? It was too terrible to think about. She ran faster. Now more than ever, she had to find them.

As the sun rose and she traveled through the forest, she tried to think about where her mother might have gone. But other questions crept into her mind, too. Did her mother know this intruder was invading her territory? Had her mother sent her away to keep her safe?

Serafina thought again about the message her mother had left for her.

It didn't seem to make any sense.

"What you climbed is floor"?

She racked her brain. "What did I climb?" she asked herself.

Was it a tree of some kind? A floor of wood?

She thought about her battle against the wolfhounds. She had leapt into a tree, then ran along a branch, then fought the dogs on the ground until they backed her against the rock face at the bottom of the cliff.

And then she got it.

She had climbed up the rock wall.

So maybe she was looking for something that had a rock floor.

What kind of room has a rock floor?

Then she smiled. Not a room. "A cave," she said.

But there were many caves in the mountains. She thought about the next line of the riddle.

"What does 'rain is wall' mean? That makes no sense."

As she walked through the forest, she kept repeating "where rain is wall."

"How could rain be a wall?" she said to herself. "Rain is water. . . . You drink water. You wash with water. You swim in water. . . ." The possibilities were endless.

And pointless.

There was water everywhere. She looked at the clouds. There was even water up there. Water started out in a cloud, and then fell as rain, and then flowed across the earth into the rivers. She thought about rivers.

When is a river a wall?

Walls are vertical.

Then it came to her.

"A waterfall," she said with satisfaction. A wall of water, a wall of rain.

There were no lakes or ponds in these mountains, but there were plenty of waterfalls. The mountains were alive with moving water. The mountains had been *carved* by moving water, in all its forms and spirits: great rivers that roared headlong over cliffs, and tiny streamlets that trickled through the deepest woods. There were triple-tiered falls that slipped across cascading stone and falls that poured over sliding rocks to icy-cold pools below. There were tall, narrow falls that plummeted from jagged heights and low, quiet falls that smoothed their boulders round.

But what she needed was a waterfall with a cave. She knew of several. But one was far too wet. The other far too easy to find. Her mind settled on a waterfall she knew of that was hidden in a small, protected cove. Is that where her mother had gone?

There was only one way to find out, so she headed for it.

"What you climb is floor and rain is wall," she said as she walked. It made sense. It made perfect sense. And it felt good that something in the world finally did.

When she arrived at the waterfall several hours later, late in the morning, she studied it from a distance, wary of the danger it might contain. The water flowed smooth and straight over the edge of rock. She could smell the crash of the clear blue water into the pool below, and feel the droplets floating on the breeze as the mist touched her cheeks.

She didn't want to go right inside the cave, because she wasn't sure what was in there, but she crept slowly, carefully, toward the entrance, staying low to the ground and very quiet.

"I was hoping you'd come," said a loud male voice immediately behind her.

Startled beyond her wits, she arched her back and jumped straight up, hissing and spinning around to defend herself.

Serafina landed on all fours on a tree limb and looked down at her attacker.

She stared for a moment and then blinked, unsure of what she was seeing.

The feral boy was sitting casually on the ground just a few feet behind where she had been.

"Do you want to climb trees?" he asked, smiling. "Or are you hungry?"

Still feeling the jolt of fear tingling through her body, she studied the boy. He had an uncanny stealth to him. She had not heard him or sensed him in any way.

He was a thin, well-muscled boy with light brown skin and dark shaggy hair just the way she remembered him. His chest was bare, as were his feet; he wore nothing but a simple pair of worn trousers.

"Come on, let's eat," he said matter-of-factly, standing up and walking along a barely discernible path toward the waterfall. She noticed the taut muscles of his back as he moved.

"Wait," she said.

The boy stopped and looked at her. His eyes were chestnut brown with traces of gold. "I'm Waysa," he said. "And you're Serafina."

"How do you—" she began to ask, in confusion.

"We'll be safe here, at least for now," he said. "We're pretty sure he doesn't know about this spot."

She looked at him in amazement. How did he know so much about her and her situation? And who was the "we"?

Her brow furrowed. "So you were the one who left the message for me?"

"Of course," he said with the slightest hint of a shrug.

"And you were the one who saved my life against the wolfhounds. . . ."

"You weren't doing too bad yourself," he said, smiling. "You're very bold. You might have made it."

"Thank you kindly for what you did," she said seriously, remembering his bravery and how close she had come to death.

"You're more than welcome," he said. "Come on, we have to get out of sight."

Although she knew she should be cautious, she felt comfortable and at home with this boy in a way that she had never felt at home with anyone in her life.

She climbed down onto the ground, looked around her, and then followed him into the cave behind the waterfall.

She'd seen such caves where the river came down in a deafening roar of churning whitewater, but here, the water poured down in a smooth, even flow, with sunlight passing through it, creating a shimmering silver wall.

Sometimes it seemed to her as if the whole world was made of light: the shine of moonlight through the clouds, the green glow of luna moths, the silver light of midnight on a river, the blue light of dawn—and now the blaze of a sunlit wall made of rain. And, of course, there could be no light without darkness, no waterfall without stone.

As she stepped farther into the cave, she saw that the back wall was encrusted with dark purple amethysts. When she turned in the direction she had come, and looked out through the opening beneath the waterfall, she saw a most magnificent phenomenon. The sunlight shining through the mist rising from the falls cast a collage of rainbows across the opening. She couldn't help but smile.

"You don't see that every day," she said in awe.

Her mind was bursting with a hundred questions for this boy, but there was a part of her that felt a gentle calmness to be here, to be someplace that felt safe and protected, and finally rest for a moment.

As she turned back around and cast her gaze across the sandy rock floor, she saw that there wasn't much inside the cave, but it looked dry and comfortable, and the boy did have several blankets, some food, and a small campfire.

"You want your meat cooked?" he asked, glancing toward her as he squatted near the fire.

"Yes, please," she said. She hadn't answered him earlier, but the truth was that she was as hungry as a spring bear, and very tired.

As Waysa cupped his hands around his mouth and blew into the fire, the embers came to life with his breath, then he added a few more sticks.

Once he had the fire going strong, he lifted up two choices from the night's hunting. "I've got a rabbit and a drummer."

The brownish chickenlike bird he was calling a drummer looked like what the folks at Biltmore called a grouse, a game bird known for thumping its chest with its wings. "The drummer looks good," she said.

"Good choice," he agreed. "Tastes even better than chicken."

She looked around the cave and wondered exactly where and how this boy lived. Was he one of the mountain folk or was he wild?

"So you've eaten chicken, then. . . ." she said.

"I tend to stay clear of cabins, but I'm not above the occasional snatch, if that's what you're asking."

"And this is your home?" she asked.

"No. Your mother wouldn't let me live here even if I wanted to. This isn't my territory. It's hers, or at least it was. I'm in between."

"My mother?" she asked, turning toward him.

"She's all right. Don't worry. We all survived."

A wave of relief passed through her, and she could feel herself relaxing.

"Your mother is scouting ahead, looking for new territory," Waysa said.

He pulled his lips back from his teeth and uttered three guttural sounds.

Something rustled behind her. When she turned, she noticed for the first time a small, jagged hole in the rock at the back of the cave. And something was crawling out of it.

The small, spotted, furry head of Serafina's half brother popped from the hole and meowed. He pushed his way out, and his whole body emerged. He came trundling toward her, all proud of himself and happy to see her, purring and meowing. She knelt down and pulled him into her chest and purred with him as he rubbed his body against her.

When Waysa gave another call, Serafina's half sister came running out at full blast and crashed into Serafina with joy. Serafina laughed, swept her half sister up into her arms, rolled onto the rock floor of the cave, and let the cubs leap upon her.

"You're here! You're all right!" she said, her chest filling with happiness.

The cubs swatted her with their soft paws, tackled her,

pretended to bite her arms, and wrestled with her. Then they turned on each other, and a whole new mock battle began.

Waysa soon had the grouse cooked, and the two of them ate it around the campfire. The food was delicious, and she enjoyed sharing pieces with the cubs.

"You're a fine cook," she said, looking at Waysa. He was at home in the forest, hunting his food, living in a cave. She remembered how fiercely he had fought, how brave he had been, how silently he had moved through the forest when he snuck up behind her. She had sensed it all along, but she hadn't been allowing herself to hope—Waysa wasn't just the feral boy who had saved her from the wolfhounds. He didn't just disappear. He had gone to get her mother. He had come back for her, found her lying at the edge of the river, nudged her onto her mother's back, and run with her through the forest. He was the dark lion! He was the one her mother had warned to leave her alone. This meant that her mother wasn't the only catamount in the world. There were others!

"You said that you're in between, that you're just passing through," she said. "So where do you come from?"

"Cherokee, southwest of here."

"Are your kinfolk from there?"

"Originally, but not anymore," he said bitterly. He rose and turned his back to her, and for a moment she was frightened that he was going to leave the cave completely.

"I'm right sorry," she said, realizing that something terrible must have happened. Waysa had been so casual, so bold, so full of life, but now a darkness clouded his spirit.

He paused and shook his head, unable to continue for a moment, then began to speak in a slow and serious tone. "It was three weeks ago. We had just completed a hunt together. We were happy and safe, and soon my brothers and sister and I would be going out to find territories of our own. But then the conjurer came upon us. He killed my older brother first, before any of us even knew he was attacking. My father fought him with every muscle in his body, but finally fell. My mother was killed as well, and then my two younger brothers. I was almost able to save my young sister." Waysa stopped, his hand covering his face as he shook his head and turned away. "We all fought him," he said, his voice ragged with emotion. "But his spells were far too strong."

"I'm sorry, Waysa," Serafina said softly, tears brimming in her eyes. She tried to stay fierce and strong, for his benefit if not her own, but seeing Waysa's pain cleaved a fissure in her heart as deep as wounds of old.

"I fled," he said, his voice quivering with shame. "When I saw my sister die, I didn't know what else to do. There was no one left. There was no one else to fight for. I felt like I just wanted to die. I ran and kept running and didn't stop for days. Then I entered your mother's territory, and she nearly killed me."

Serafina nodded, remembering how her mother had attacked her the first she met her. "She's like that," she said. "She defends her territory somethin' fierce."

He nodded. "As it should be. My mother had her own

territory, and my father his. And soon my brothers and sister would have had theirs, too. My sister was . . ."

Waysa's words drifted off. He didn't want to continue whatever he was going to say.

"So my mother ran you off the first time you came into her territory," Serafina said, standing and trying to change the subject. "But now you're looking after her cubs."

"She saw that I helped you against the conjurer's dogs. And when he attacked the cubs last night, I fought at her side to defend them. We've decided to work together now, come what may. This is the safest place we know, so I agreed to hide here and protect the cubs while she scouts ahead. She hated to leave them, but she can travel so much faster without them, and she wasn't sure what she'd find where she's going."

As more questions flooded Serafina's mind, she looked over at her half brother and half sister. They were her family, so close to her in so many ways, and yet so different from her as well. They were forever mountain lions. And she was forever human. They shared the same affliction: to always be what they were born.

"You look exhausted," Waysa said, "and like you've been dragged through a mud pit. You need to rest. But before you do, we should get you cleaned up."

"What do you mean?" she asked, turning toward him.

But in one quick moment, he rushed her and tackled her headlong through the waterfall. The shock of the icy-cold water hit her first, then she felt herself tumbling downward.

Serafina felt a swoop in her stomach as she fell through the rush of the waterfall, her body plummeting toward the rocks and water below. Her mind exploded with fear of what was going to happen when she hit the bottom.

She had tried to cross that one river at its most shallow point to escape the wolfhounds, and it had nearly killed her. She'd never swum in deep water. She wasn't even sure she could. And she certainly didn't want to find out like this.

But at that instant, her whole body plunged with a great, enveloping crash into an ice-cold pool of deep blue. The biting cold was the most immediate shock she felt. But the force of her fall sank her down, down, down into the churning water, surrounded by clouds of swirling bubbles. She tried to flail her arms and legs, but she just kept sinking. Her lungs were going to burst, desperate to take a breath.

A hand grabbed her wrist and pulled her up.

As soon as her face broke the surface, she heaved in a great, gasping breath of air and started flailing and splashing.

Waysa held her to keep her afloat. "Don't panic! I've got you!"

"I can't swim!" she sputtered.

"Paddle your legs," Waysa told her, and she started pushing her legs rapidly against the water. "All right, good. Now paddle your arms in front of you, close to your chest, like this. Good. You see, you paddle your arms and your legs together, like you're crawling as fast as you possibly can."

Serafina had no choice but to listen to everything he was telling her to do. "Keep paddling!" he ordered. "Good. Now I'm going to let you go."

"Don't let me go!" she screamed.

"I'm letting go. . . ."

When Waysa released her, she paddled furiously and kicked her legs and held her head above the water in front of her, terrified at every breath that it would be her last. But she soon found herself holding her own. She wasn't immediately sinking! She could swim. She could actually swim!

"That's it! You've got it!" Waysa shouted.

It turned out that swimming was like falling and landing on her feet without getting hurt. For her and her kind, it was a reflex. It wasn't something she would have ever chosen to do, but now that she had to do it, she could do it almost instinctively. She paddled around in the pool, filled with joy. She could actually swim!

"It's so cold!" she complained, half angry and half laughing.

"Just keep paddling. You'll get used to it," Waysa said, swimming beside her.

Serafina swam one way and then another. She tried turning her body this way and that, feeling the water rush over her skin. It felt like she was flying slowly through soft, thickened, ice-cold air.

When they were done, Waysa climbed out of the pool onto the rocks and boulders at the edge of the river. Then he turned and put out his hand.

She grabbed hold and he hoisted her up onto a boulder. From there, they climbed together, hand over hand, back up to the cave. They threw more sticks onto the fire, gathered the warm, fuzzy cubs into their arms, and huddled around the flames.

"You could have given me a warning!" she said.

"Would you have done it if I had?" he said, laughing.

"No!"

"You see," he said, gloating. "You're going to find swimming useful for crossing rivers on long journeys."

It felt good to be warm and clean again, her hair lying around her shoulders, and her body strong. The icy water seemed to have a powerful and rejuvenating effect.

For a little while, as they sat by the fire, she and Waysa talked about their lives. She knew she should ask him about the bearded man he had called the conjurer, and where her mother had gone, and all the other questions on her mind. But she'd been running and fighting for so long that, for a little while, she just wanted to feel like things were going to be all right. In the cave, it was like it was just the two of them in the world, and the world was good. She asked him questions about his sister and the other members of his family, and he seemed grateful to have a chance to talk about them. He asked her about her life at Biltmore, about her pa and her younger days. She told him about Braeden, and what had happened to Gidean, and how she'd fled in shame. Talking to Waysa was easy. It felt like a salve on the wounds of her heart.

When she and Waysa curled up in their blankets on opposite sides of the campfire, she was relieved to finally sleep for a few moments. She dreamed of forests—of tall, beautiful trees and flowing water, rocky slopes and deep ravines. And she dreamed of swimming.

A short time later, she awoke curled up in a little ball with the two sleeping cubs. They were warm and soft, breathing quietly with little purring sounds, their heads tucked into her chest and legs.

Waysa was awake as well, gazing at her from across the fire.

For a long time, she did not speak, and neither did he.

When she finally did say something, her words were soft. "You fled your home from far away. You've been running. When you came here, you could have kept running. What kept you here, Waysa?"

Waysa turned away from her and gazed at the waterfall.

"Why did you stay?" she asked, her voice low and gentle.

"I've been waiting for you," he said softly.

She felt her brows furrow as she looked at him. "I don't understand."

"I would have passed through and kept going days ago, but after I saw you in the forest that night . . ."

"What?" she urged him. "After you saw me in the forest, what happened?"

"I wanted to wait for you," he said.

"What do you mean, wait for me?" she asked gently, narrowing her eyes at him.

"I thought we could leave here together."

Serafina could hear the seriousness in his voice.

"You don't truly know me," she said.

"You're right," he said. "I don't. I don't know anyone anymore, not a single living soul other than you, and your mother, and the cubs."

Serafina didn't know what to say. It was the way of a young mountain lion to leave his mother and find a territory of his own, but it was the way of a human to want a friend and a family.

As Serafina stared at Waysa, she realized that there was far more to this boy than she thought. He was asking her to leave this place with him, to go live in the forest and run through the ferns and hunt drummers and swim in pools together. He'd been hoping to find her again. He'd been waiting for her.

She watched him for a long moment, just holding his gaze, and then she said, "You realize I can't change."

"Of course you can," he said.

"I've tried. I can't do it."

"You're just not seeing what you want to be."

"I don't understand."

"Once you envision what you want to be, then you'll find a way to get there."

"I don't think so," she said.

"I'll teach you," he said, and his voice had such confidence, such kindness, that it was almost impossible not to believe him.

As she turned away from him and cuddled with the cubs, she thought about what Waysa had said. She slowly realized that there was a new path opening up in front of her now. It awed her to think about it. One path would take her home to Biltmore like she'd planned, to people she knew and loved, but to conflict and pain and uncertainty as well. But this other path, with Waysa, would take her away, maybe forever. She knew she would miss her pa and Braeden, but she wondered what starting over would be like. Would she come to know Waysa in the way she knew them? Would she go on to see new mountains and new waterfalls? Were there different kinds of trees and animals in those distant places? Would she finally find a place to belong? What would become of her? With Waysa's help, could she truly learn to change?

As she tried to envision her future, she realized there were many paths, many different ways to go, and part of growing up, part of *living,* was choosing which paths to follow. Two main paths lay before her, leading to two very different lives.

She slowly got up to her feet and tried to think it through. She knew that she had to be smart and she had to be bold. But more than anything, she knew she had to follow the path of her heart.

Standing in the cave with Waysa, Serafina tried to imagine all that had happened when the conjurer attacked her mother and the cubs—the bearded man casting his spells and twisting vines. The cubs must have been terrified.

"Is that why he attacked?" she asked Waysa. "Did he want the cubs?"

"He's been capturing animals of all kinds," he said. "That's why they're fleeing. They sense the coming danger. And that's why you and I must take the cubs and leave this place, Serafina. As soon as you are rested enough to travel at speed, we must follow your mother's path and join her."

Waysa's words were a shock to her. She longed to see her mother again, but her heart ached painfully at the thought of leaving.

"We can't fight this darkness, Serafina," Waysa warned, seeming to sense what she was thinking. "We must flee these mountains."

"But I don't understand," Serafina said. "Tell me what's going on. Why is all this happening? Why did my mother send me back to Biltmore?"

"Your mother loves you and her cubs more than anything in the world. She thought you'd be safe at Biltmore. But she was wrong."

"Is Biltmore in danger?" Serafina asked in alarm.

"Everything's in danger. Especially Biltmore."

"What?" Serafina said. "Then we need to help them, Waysa."

"We can't," he said, shaking his head. "He's far stronger than we realized. He's even stronger than when he killed my family three weeks ago. He's gathering more and more power as he comes this way. His power is tied to the land, to the forest and the people and animals he controls within it. But Vanderbilt and his vast estate stand in his way of controlling this region for himself."

"But who is he? Who is this man?" she asked, panic building up inside her.

"He's a shifter, like the catamounts. He can shift into a white-faced owl at will. But he uses his power for evil, to try to control the forest, to steal from it, to take its animals and its trees and the magic within it and bend them to his will. My people call him the Darkness, for he is a future through which they cannot see. Shifters inherit their gift, pass it down from one generation to the next, but he has taken his power further.

He has spent years learning to twist the world we know, to throw curses and cast spells. He wants to control this forest, to make slaves of us all, from the smallest mouse to the largest bear, and everything in between. He hates the catamounts most of all because he cannot control us. We stand against him. He will destroy anything in these mountains that gets in his way."

"Are you saying that he's going to attack Biltmore?"

"I don't know by what path or trickery he will come," Waysa said. "He's a conjurer of the dark arts. He does not fight with tooth and claw like you and me. He does not fight straight on. He uses subterfuge and deceit to weave his way. He flies silent. He watches like an owl and keeps himself hidden at a safe distance. He concentrates his power into weapons and then sends in his demons to do his bidding."

Serafina tried to understand. "Do you mean . . . a weapon like the Black Cloak?"

Waysa nodded. "The Black Cloak was a collector of souls, one of the first concentrators of dark power that he ever created. I do not know all the different spells he will cast this time, but the tearing of the Black Cloak wrought a terrible new fury in him. That's what started all this. That's what brought him here."

"Are you saying the creator of the Black Cloak has come alive? Not Mr. Thorne, but the cloak's actual *creator*?"

"He's never been dead," Waysa said.

"I don't understand. Where does he come from?"

"My father told me that the old man of the forest lived in these mountains long ago. He was born with unusual powers, but he yearned to develop and control the powers he possessed.

He traveled to the Old World, where he learned the dark arts from the necromancers there. By the time he returned, he had become a powerful conjurer. He found a shadowed cave in which to live, like a spider building a nest. He cast spells on the people in the nearby village and enslaved the animals of the forest. He—"

"Why didn't anyone try to stop him?" Serafina interrupted.

"They did. The catamounts rose up against him and fought him in a great battle. They nearly defeated him. He lost his strength and became but a ghost of what he was. He's been far away from here, gathering new skills and powers in foreign lands, but now he's come back, more powerful than ever. Even as we speak, he's hiding like a rattlesnake beneath a log, letting his venom build up within him, biding his time before he strikes again."

"Then we need to fight him!" Serafina said.

Waysa grabbed her by the shoulders so quickly it startled her. "Listen to me, Serafina," he said, looking into her face. "He's made a staff of twisted purpose to focus his power. It allows its wielder to control animals, to do his bidding against their will. And not only that, he has a new ally, a conjurer with power frighteningly similar to his own. The two of them working together will be unstoppable. They see this as their land—their forest and their mountains—and they plan to take it all back. And the more they take, the more powerful they become. We cannot fight them!"

"My mother will beat them!" Serafina blurted out before she could stop herself. But even as she said it, her chest filled with a dreadful realization. "My mother already fought the conjurer before, didn't she . . ."

Waysa nodded slowly.

"That's why she won't fight him again. . . ." Serafina said.

"That's right," Waysa said, but then hesitated.

She looked at him. "What is it? Tell me."

Waysa lifted his eyes and met her gaze. "Twelve years ago, the conjurer killed your father," Waysa said softly.

"My father?" Serafina asked in astonishment. "My true father?" She couldn't even imagine this. "But how? Why? How do you know about my father?"

"Your father was a catamount like us. All the catamounts knew him. Your mother hid it from you because she didn't want you to follow in his footsteps, but he was a great warrior, the fiercest fighter and strongest leader the catamounts have ever seen. My mother and father and all the creatures of the forest fought at his side against the conjurer twelve years ago. That was when the conjurer was nearly defeated. Your father led the fight against him. He was the one who taught my father the expression that my father taught me."

"The expression?" Serafina asked in confusion. "What expression?"

" 'Stay bold!' your father used to say when the others lost heart. It has been the mantra of the catamounts ever since. 'Stay bold!' "

"My father started that?" Serafina asked in bewilderment. "But what happened to him?"

Waysa shook his head in regret. "Your mother and father

rallied all the allies of the forest and led an attack against the conjurer. They weakened him severely, draining nearly all of his power. They almost destroyed him entirely. But it is the way of his kind that even when he seems to be dead, he is not. His spirit lives on. He hides in a darkness the rest of us cannot see. At the very last moment of the battle, your mother was absorbed into the Black Cloak and your father was struck down. Your father stayed bold to the very end. He saved the catamounts and the other creatures of the forest in that battle. But he lost his own life."

"What?" Serafina said. "How could all this be true? My mother did not tell me any of this."

"Your mother wanted to protect you, Serafina. She didn't want you to fight battles that you couldn't win. She thought you would be hidden and safe within Biltmore's walls. But it's clear now that all is lost there, too. We cannot win this war."

"But who is he, Waysa?" she asked again. "Who is the old man of the forest? And who is this Mr. Grathan? Is that the other conjurer you spoke of? Or is it one of his demons?"

"I do not know by what names or forms he and his allies come this time," Waysa said, "but I know the conjurer has returned. And he will kill anyone who resists him. As fiercely as your mother has always defended her territory, she knew that no matter how dangerous it was, she must leave this place behind, that she must go forth as quickly as she could to search out a new territory for her and her cubs. She has gone deep into the Smoky Mountains, scouting ahead into unknown forests, talking with the catamounts there, looking for a new place for us to live. We shall find new territory in those distant mountains, a place bright and free, and we shall guard it well. The Great Smoky Mountains will be the last bastion of our kindred, Serafina, the last homeland for those few of us who have survived."

Serafina listened to Waysa's words in amazement. She knew the danger he was talking about. She'd experienced the conjurer's spells firsthand. She remembered what it felt like to have the air pulled from her lungs. And she'd witnessed his staff of power at work. But as tantalizing as it was to go with Waysa and the cubs to join her mother in the mountains far away, the path with them was like the city she'd seen in the valley, and the train on the mountainside, and the wolves traveling the ridge to distant peaks: even as these new paths opened up to her, she knew they were not the paths of her heart. She wanted to go back to her pa and Braeden, and to Essie and Mr. and Mrs. Vanderbilt. Biltmore was her home. If the old man of the forest could steal breath and control animals, there was no end to the harm he could do. He could force Cedric to turn on Braeden. He could kill Mr. Vanderbilt with the bite of a wolf. His spy, Mr. Grathan, had already squirmed his way into the house like a rat through a sewer pipe. Maybe it was Grathan who wielded the staff of power that Waysa spoke of, like Mr. Thorne had wielded the Black Cloak. She didn't know exactly what their plan was, but she had to stop them.

"Somehow, we must figure out a way to fight," she said fiercely. "I will not turn my back on the people of Biltmore."

"Serafina, you've seen his spells and his demons," Waysa

argued. "We cannot fight that. I saw the very breath pulled from my sister's lungs even as she tried to say good-bye to me. Come with me and the cubs to find your mother. We'll go up into the Smoky Mountains, and we'll be safe there. There are trees and valleys and rivers for hundreds of miles."

"I'm sorry, Waysa," Serafina said, shaking her head. "I have to go back."

"You told me that the people of Biltmore said you don't belong with them," Waysa said. "You told me that you ran away from there. You're a catamount, Serafina. You have *us* now. You don't need them anymore!"

Waysa's words crashed into her, but she tried not to listen. She *couldn't* listen. She knelt down and hugged her little siblings. "Go without me," she told Waysa. "Take care of the cubs. Follow my mother's path like you planned."

"Serafina," Waysa said, his voice strong, "you don't need them!"

Serafina felt the emotion welling up inside her, almost too much to bear. She stood and embraced Waysa. She held him tight for a long moment. And then she let him go, knowing that it might be the last time she ever saw him. "But I *do* need them," she said. "And more than that, they need me."

She looked at her catamount kin one last time, then turned and headed toward Biltmore.

"You can't save Biltmore all by yourself!" Waysa shouted after her as she slipped into the underbrush.

"I won't be alone," she said.

26

Just before dawn, Serafina crept through the darkened forest that surrounded Biltmore. In the morning's slow change from darkness to light, there was no breeze, no sound, just a stillness in the cold air and the breathing of the earth. The mist floated like long-stretching gray clouds among the branches of the trees. She was eager to find her way up to the house. But then she spotted the silhouette of what looked like a robed, hooded figure in the haze. She ducked down, squinting through the morning fog, trying to figure out who or what she was seeing. Was she too late? Was the conjurer already here?

The figure appeared to be a gray-bearded man with a walking stick moving slowly through the trees. As she studied him, he seemed to drift in and out of the mist, disappearing for several beats of her heart, then reemerging again. Was it the old man of the forest? Then she saw him poke his walking stick into the ground, take something small out of his satchel, kneel down, and bury it.

As she crept closer, she saw that he wasn't wearing the robes that she thought she'd seen before, but a long, lightweight coat against the morning chill. It was the elderly stranger she'd seen walking into the forest with Mr. Vanderbilt. And she'd seen him again standing with the other guests the night she fled.

She watched him, trying to understand what he was doing. He walked another twenty feet, then looked around, seemed to make a decision, and then knelt down again. It took her several seconds to realize that the small things he was pulling out of his satchel were acorns. He was planting trees.

Memories flooded into her brain like water that had been blocked behind a dam for many years. He wasn't a stranger at all. She had watched this man years before. His named was Mr. Frederick Law Olmsted. He was the landscape architect who had designed the grounds of Biltmore Estate, and he was one of Mr. Vanderbilt's closest friends and mentors. Biltmore had been his last and most ambitious project before he retired. She tried to remember the last time she'd seen him. Was it three years ago? Four? Mr. Olmsted's face was far older than she remembered, and his body more frail, like something had happened to him while he was gone.

When she was just learning to prowl the grounds, she had

seen Mr. Olmsted supervising hundreds of men constructing the gardens and the grounds according to his design. But there had been other times, quieter moments like this, when she saw him by himself, when he didn't think anyone else was watching, walking alone with his knobby cane in his hand and his leather satchel over his shoulder, seeming to wander the fields and woodlands, planting tree after tree after tree, as if shaping the very future of the forest. It was as if he could envision in his mind what it would look like a hundred years hence. And while he was a famous man who worked on a grand scale with hundreds of workers at his command, sometimes, secretly, he still liked to plant certain seeds and saplings himself, as if to touch the soil for touching's sake. A hickory here. A rhododendron bush there. Somehow, he could see the future.

It was hard to imagine now, years later, with Mr. Olmsted's young forest flourishing all around them, but when Mr. Vanderbilt and Mr. Olmsted first came to this area, most of the trees had been cut down, the farms had been spoiled, and the terrain had been what her pa called a *scald*—treeless, ruined land. Her pa had told her that it was Mr. Olmsted and Mr. Vanderbilt who had decided to change all that.

As Mr. Olmsted made his way through the forest, she realized that he must be heading out toward the Squatter's Clearing, one of the few remaining areas of the estate that had not yet been planted with either garden, farm, or forest. She was relieved that the elderly wanderer was Mr. Olmsted, but she wondered why he had come back to visit Biltmore again after all his years away. And what was this normally peaceful man so determined to do that it got him up in the morning before the sun even rose?

Leaving Mr. Olmsted behind her, Serafina slipped quietly through the darkness into the Biltmore gardens, past the pond, along the azalea path, and to the Conservatory, its thousands of steamed glass panes glistening in the morning starlight. She remembered one time, when she was eight years old, her pa had come over to repair the hothouse's boiler and she had prowled among the exotic plants, pretending to be a jaguar in the jungles of South America.

Making her way up into the shrub garden with its meandering, crisscrossing paths, she smelled the winter bloom of the Carolina jessamine. Coming with the season's crisp air, and the explosion of green and red holly and mistletoe in the surrounding woods, the yellow flower of the jessamine always reminded her that Christmas would soon arrive. But never mind gentle Mr. Olmsted, and the mistletoe, and Christmas, she thought, catching herself. There'd be no Biltmore at all if she didn't stop Mr. Grathan and the dark forces she'd seen in the forest.

She crawled through the air shaft at the rear foundation of Biltmore House and climbed up through the metal grate. After being away for several nights, the dark, quiet, secluded corridors of the basement were a welcoming home.

The smell of the pastry kitchen and the warm sheets in the laundry and all the other things she'd grown up with brought a swirl of fond memories back into her heart.

She made her way to the workshop, past the benches and tools, and back into the supply racks, where she found her pa sleeping on his mattress, gently snoring. She thought about going to her own mattress to sleep, but she didn't. Without making a sound or disturbing him in any way, she curled up beside her pa. She'd never been so happy to be home in her life.

She did not wake him, because she still felt ashamed of the incident that had caused her to run away. She didn't know how he would react to her when he woke. But she was sure that as he slept, he somehow knew that she was there, curled up beside him, that she was still alive, still prowling the shadows of the house and forest, and that she still loved him with all her heart.

When her pa opened his eyes, he roused himself from his cot and looked at her as if to be sure that he wasn't dreaming.

"Pa . . ." she said softly.

He swept her up into his arms and pulled her into his great chest and swooshed her around the room, as if to capture her and never let her go. "I was so worried about you," he said, relief flowing through his words. As she felt her heart breaking free with joy, she knew she was finally home.

When they settled down, she explained to her pa everything that had caused her to leave, that she never meant to hurt anyone. And as her pa started making their breakfast, he gave her a bit of a gentle talking-to.

"When somethin' bad happens, Sera, no matter how foul and painful it is, ya don't go runnin' off," he told her. "Ya come home, girl. Ya come to me and we talk about it, whatever it is. That's what kin are for. You got it?"

She nodded. She knew he was right. "I got it, Pa."

As they ate their breakfast, Serafina turned to darker

thoughts. "Tell me what's been happening here, Pa. Is everyone all right? How is Braeden?"

Her pa shook his head. "I'm afraid the boy's been having a hard time of it."

"Did Gidean die?" she asked, her voice quivering.

"The dog was terribly wounded, beyond the veterinarian's help. I don't know if they finally decided to put him outten his misery."

A flash of heat seared Serafina's face. She pressed her lips tight together to keep the hot tears from bursting into her eyes. She took in a breath and covered her face with her hands, and then, after several seconds, she tried to continue. "Is everyone else all right?"

"No, there's other bad news," he said. "Unfortunately, the stable master, Mr. Rinaldi, passed away while you were gone."

"What happened to him?" Serafina asked. "Was he sick?"

Her pa shook his head like he still couldn't believe it. "He was kicked by a horse and killed."

Serafina looked at him in alarm. "Was it one of those stallions?"

"I don't know which horse it was, but it was the darnedest thing. Everyone was shocked by it."

"I'm sorry about Mr. Rinaldi," Serafina said.

"But other than that, more guests have arrived for the Christmas jubilee, and Mr. Vanderbilt has been very busy."

"What about Mrs. Vanderbilt? Is she feeling better?"

"She's been up and around on some days, but other days I don't see her at all."

"Is Detective Grathan still here?" Serafina asked.

"He came down here yesterday a-looking for you," her pa said.

"What did you say to him?" Serafina asked in surprise.

"I told him you were good and gone and that I didn't know where you were, which was the truth."

"Good," she said. That was the best thing her pa could have said. The less Grathan knew about her the better. "Whatever he says, whatever he does, do not trust that man, Pa."

She glanced around the room to see what her pa was working on. "Were you able to get the elevator gears fixed like you wanted to?"

Her pa nodded with satisfaction. "Them gears are fit as a fiddle now, working well and fine, just like I knew they could. But your vermin have been mommucking again."

"What do you mean?" Serafina asked, confused.

He stepped over to one of his benches and showed her a bundle of black-coated wire.

"What's that?" she asked, moving toward him.

"The house is protected by a fire alarm system that's all tied in to a central point by these here wires, but take a look. . . ."

At first, Serafina thought he was showing her a wire that had been cut by snippers, but when she looked at it more closely, she saw tiny tooth marks. The wire had been *chewed*.

"I guess, when you're away, the rats will play," her pa said. "Them darn varmints chewed the insulation clean off, then bit right through the copper core. Never seen anything like it. If I hadn't noticed this and fixed it, the whole system woulda been useless. We might woulda had a fire start up and get total out-ten hand before we had time to put out the flames. And worse yet, people wouldn't have had time to get out."

"I'll see to them rats, Pa," Serafina promised, furious that she'd only been off the job for a short time and the rats were already back.

As she and her pa caught up on things, she realized how foolish she'd been to feel ashamed to see him. He had no reproach, no anger, nothing but love and concern for her.

"You were gone for a few long days," he said, seeming to sense what was on her mind. "How far'd ya go?"

"Up into the Black Mountains," she said.

"The Blacks?" he said in surprise. "That's way back up in through there to them rocks. Musta been awful bad cold this time a year."

"Not too bad," she said. "Did Superintendent McNamee and his men go out into the forest to look for that poacher?"

He pa nodded. "They went out, came back, didn't see nothin', but they found all manner of tracks out there."

"There's something bad comin', Pa," she told him.

"What are you talking about?" he asked, looking at her with a seriousness in his eyes. There had been a time when he didn't have ears for her stories, but that time had passed.

But even as he laid out the question before her, she realized how difficult it was going to be to explain everything she'd learned. "I got a glimpse of something nasty in the forest, and it's comin' this way," she said. "Just be careful, Pa. And tell me if you see anything unusual, all right?"

Her pa stared at her, silent and unblinking, not liking her answer one bit. She'd gotten his attention full and earnest now. "You're acting like you saw a haint or some such," he said quietly.

"I did, Pa," she said. "I did."

She didn't mean that she had literally seen a ghost, but it was the only way she could get to the gist of it. A man, a haint, a demon, a spirit—she had no idea what he truly was, but she knew he would come. And Grathan was already crawling beneath their very noses. The first thing she needed to do was to somehow gain Braeden's trust again, warn him about what she'd learned, and develop a plan of attack. It made her all qualmish in her gut whenever she tried to think about what she was going to say to Braeden about what had happened with Gidean, but she knew she had to do it.

When they heard the first sounds of the servants down the hall, she and her pa realized it was time for them to start their day.

She said good-bye to him and went down the corridor.

As she passed the open door of the servants' washroom, she saw her reflection in the little mirror above the basin. She gave it nothing but a glance as she walked by, but then she stopped, backed up, and looked again, surprised by what she saw.

Given how she'd occupied herself while she was away, it didn't surprise her that the dress that Essie had lent her was torn and stained. She'd need to apologize to Essie and somehow replace it. And she saw, too, that her face had been marked by a rather gruesome variety of cuts and scratches to go along with the vicious scar from the neck wound she'd suffered a few weeks before. She was not a pretty sight. But what truly gave her pause were her eyes. All her life, her eyes had been a soft golden amber color, but now they looked bright yellow. She frowned and growled a little in frustration. She seemed to be evolving from merely peculiar-looking to positively hideous.

She went up the back stairs to the main floor, ducked into a heating register, then shimmied her way up a vertical metal shaft to the second floor. Crawling through the air shaft down to Braeden's end of the house reminded her of their adventures a few weeks before. She came to the register that supplied Braeden's bedroom and peered through the decorative metal wall grate beneath his desk and into his room.

Her heart swelled when she saw that Braeden was there. She so desperately wanted to push open the grate and speak with him, explain what had happened, and try to convince him one more time that she never meant to hurt Gidean. But then she saw something that shocked her. Gidean was lying on the floor next to Braeden. He was alive! She didn't know how that was possible, but she was so glad and relieved. Gidean lay in a soft bed of pillows that Braeden had made for him, his eyes shut as Braeden stroked his head. He was clearly gravely wounded, but he was alive!

"I'm here with you, boy," Braeden said to his dog as he gently petted his ears.

When the tears seeped out of Serafina's eyes, she quickly pulled back from the grate and crawled down the shaft a few feet. Sitting alone in the darkness, she hugged her knees to her body and covered her face. If she watched Braeden and Gidean any longer, she'd start sobbing—from sadness, but mostly from relief that he was still alive—and no one wanted to hear sobbing in their heating register.

Serafina heard the faint sound of approaching footsteps. She crawled to the adjacent register, which looked into the hallway.

Whoever it was had stopped walking. He was just standing there outside Braeden's door. What was he doing?

She could see his shoes and trousers, but she couldn't see his face because of her low position. She knew it wasn't Mr. Vanderbilt, for she knew his shoes well. She pressed herself to the floor and tried to look upward. Now she could see that the man standing outside Braeden's door was holding a spiraling wooden cane with a hooked antler handle and he had straggly rat-brown hair.

Suddenly, she felt the closeness of the shaft she was hiding in, the dusty air moving in and out of her lungs. She tried to stay calm, but her chest rose and fell more and more heavily as she waited and watched.

She expected the man to knock, but he did not.

He leaned forward, pressed his ear against the door, and listened.

The rat was spying on Braeden.

27

Serafina watched, her heart beating strong and steady in her chest, marking time. When Braeden came out of his room, the spy stepped back into the shadow of an alcove and hid from him.

Serafina sucked in a breath and readied herself to push open the register cover and leap into action, but as Braeden walked by, the man remained hidden. He did not attack.

To Serafina's astonishment, Gidean walked at Braeden's side. The dog moved slowly, carefully, but he was walking on his own. Serafina couldn't believe it. How was this possible? She'd only been gone a few days. How could the dog's broken bones have healed so quickly?

The spy waited until Braeden was gone, then quietly slipped into his room.

That dirty rotten rat, Serafina thought as she crawled back to the other register to watch him.

The intruder rummaged hurriedly through Braeden's desk and opened his dresser drawers. She worried that he'd pull back the register cover and see her there, or maybe hear her breathing, but she had to stay and see what he was doing. As he bent down to look under Braeden's bed, she saw the side of his scarred face. Just as she'd suspected, it was Grathan.

She felt the fear rising up in her stomach.

Why was he rummaging through Braeden's belongings? Was he truly looking for evidence of Mr. Thorne's murder? Or was he looking for clues to the whereabouts of the Black Cloak?

Or did Braeden have some other connection to all this that she didn't understand?

Grathan found a small map of the riding trails that Braeden had been working on, but seemed frustrated that he couldn't find anything else. When he finally left Braeden's room, Serafina breathed a sigh of relief, but she couldn't rest.

She dropped down through the vent shaft to the main floor and looked through a register just in time to see Gidean lying down in the morning sun in the Entrance Hall with the master's huge Saint Bernard, Cedric. That meant Braeden couldn't be too far away. But finding him and staying undetected wasn't going to be easy.

Many of the fancy-dressed guests were taking their strolls. Servants bustled about the house attending to their various duties upstairs and down. Several families of Vanderbilts were arriving from New York to spend the holidays. Serafina prowled from spot to spot, avoiding a gaggle of housemaids and then sneaking past a pair of footmen, one of whom had a bandaged hand from her bite a few days before.

By afternoon, the house was so busy that she had to take refuge in the hidden compartment beneath the stairway on the south side of the second floor. When she overheard two chambermaids saying that the young master had gone out to the South Terrace, she ran for it.

Slipping out a side door, she darted along the columns at the front of the house, beneath the strange creatures carved into the tops of the columns and the gargoyles mounted along the edge of the roof. Few people seemed to notice them, but she had always been fascinated by the menagerie of Gothic carvings that adorned the house—weird dragons and chimeras, sea horses and sea serpents, bearded men and fanged beasts, strange girls with wings, mysterious figures in cloak and hood, and a hundred other fantastical creatures of the imagination. She had always wondered where Biltmore's stone carvers had come up with their ideas.

She ran down the steps to the long, wisteria-covered Pergola that bordered the South Terrace, a flat, open, grass-covered courtyard with a picturesque view of the river valley and the mountains beyond. Braeden and Lady Rowena stood on the terrace alone, gazing out at the scenery. Serafina had been hoping that Lady Rowena's father had finally arrived and taken her away, but clearly that hadn't happened.

Serafina desperately wanted to talk to Braeden, to warn him about what she'd learned in the mountains, but she couldn't do it with Lady Rowena there. She ran down the length of the Pergola, came up the steps that approached from the other side, and then peeked across the terrace.

Lady Rowena wore a peacock-blue walking dress with an elaborate triple lapel, a black-laced throat, and a collar that stood high around the back of her neck, as if holding the tumble of her red hair. She carried a matching parasol casually over her shoulder to protect herself from the sun. She reminded Serafina of the girls depicted in the hand-colored fashion plates of the ladies' magazines. She seemed to have a new dress or outfit for every activity and time of day.

But the sight of Braeden and Lady Rowena together wasn't the most startling thing. What surprised Serafina was that Braeden was carrying a large bird of prey on his leather-gloved left hand. *That must be Kess, Braeden's peregrine falcon with the broken wing.*

Kess was a strikingly handsome bird, with blue-gray wings and back, and a pale breast streaked with dark bars. Her throat was pure white, but much of her head was black, like she was wearing a helmet and mask, ready for aerial battle. But what Serafina loved most of all were Kess's powerful yellow talons with long, curving black claws, perfect for raking her prey from the sky.

"It's a rather menacing-looking creature, isn't it?" Lady Rowena remarked to Braeden.

When Serafina heard Lady Rowena say this about such a

beautiful bird of prey, she struggled to keep herself calm. She wanted to yell *That's the stupidest thing I've ever heard!* but she was pretty sure that at least one of them would figure out who it was hiding in the bushes.

"I think she's beautiful," Braeden said calmly.

There was something about his tone that caught Serafina. He didn't seem angry or annoyed like she thought he should be. If anything, he seemed a bit distant, like he had other things on his mind. But then he seemed to slowly bring himself around and focus on the moment at hand.

"Well," he said, "let's see what she can do today. . . ."

Braeden had told her that the falcon would never be able to fly again. She thought it was kind of him to bring Kess out into the sunlight, at least so that she could look around and remember better days. But then, to Serafina's amazement, Braeden lowered his arm and threw the falcon up into the sky. Kess didn't just fly; she flapped up into the breeze and soared, calling out in pure joy. Serafina could see the smile on Braeden's face as he pointed to the bird and talked to Lady Rowena, excitedly sharing all the different facts he knew about hawks and falcons. Kess's flight had changed his mood entirely.

The flying peregrine had long, pointed wings that pumped her through the sky, and a long tail that she used for steering and braking. Serafina could tell that she was still favoring her damaged wing, but she seemed so happy to be in the sky even for a little while. But it bewildered her. How did Braeden fix a broken wing that could not be fixed?

Lady Rowena watched the flying falcon in silence as if

nothing she was seeing impressed her. Serafina wanted to scratch her eyes out more than ever. But right at that moment, something extraordinary happened. A red fox ran up the steps, brushed past Serafina, and trotted across the South Terrace toward Braeden and Lady Rowena. The fox had a beautiful red-and-silver coat, with black legs, a white underside, and a huge, puffy red tail. Its ears were perked up, its nose pointed, and its eyes alert.

When Lady Rowena saw the fox coming toward her and Braeden, she screamed, "An animal!"

The startled fox paused and sat a few yards away from them as if he was sorry that he had scared the girl in the fancy dress.

But Braeden squatted down and faced the fox. "Come on, little guy. We won't hurt you," he said, stretching out his hand. "You're welcome to join us. How's your paw doing?"

The fox walked up to Braeden and sat at his feet.

Serafina watched in amazement. A dog or a horse was one thing, but how could Braeden befriend a wild fox?

Keeping low, she crawled up a few more steps to get a closer look.

The falcon continued to circle in the open air out beyond the wall where Braeden and Lady Rowena were standing. When Braeden whistled, the bird tilted her wing and looked at him.

Braeden smiled. "Did you see that? Did you see how she looked over at us? She's so happy!"

"Well, I must say, it does seem to like you," Lady Rowena said with a smile, finally giving in to Braeden's enthusiasm as she watched the bird fly around them.

"She's a girl," Braeden said gently. "Her name is Kess."

He seemed to be so willing to teach Lady Rowena about animals and show her a better way of thinking, like he understood that she was from the city and didn't understand animals the way he did. Serafina thought he was far more patient than she could ever be.

"Can you get her to do whatever you tell her to do?" Lady Rowena asked. "Does it follow your commands?"

"No," Braeden said. "She's my friend. I do things for her and she does things for me."

"I see. . . ." Lady Rowena said thoughtfully, looking up at the bird. Suddenly, this interested her. She turned and pointed toward the ridge of the house. "Can you have it kill one of those pigeons up there?"

"Actually, those are mourning doves, not pigeons," Braeden said, but he looked toward the doves and then looked toward the falcon. "I suppose," he said uncertainly, "but I don't want her to stress her wing. And I don't think she's hungry. I fed her some chicken à la crème this afternoon, and she seemed to like that very much."

Serafina smiled. Classic Braeden. Stealing gourmet meals from under the nose of Biltmore's French chef to feed to his animal friends. When Serafina's stomach growled, she realized she wouldn't have minded some of that chicken something-something herself.

"So she can't actually do anything useful, then," Lady Rowena said. "You haven't taught her any tricks."

Braeden quietly knelt down and petted the fox's head and

ears. He finally seemed a little discouraged by Lady Rowena's words. "I have an idea," he said, standing once more. "Let's try this. . . ." He walked a few feet and picked up a stick.

"What are you going to do with that?" Lady Rowena asked.

"Kess's wing is still on the mend, but let's see if she wants to play a little."

Braeden hurled the stick up into the sky, then gave a long, whistling call.

The whistle and the flashing, somersaulting stick caught the falcon's attention immediately. She rolled, tucked her wings, and plunged into a stoop. She dove, plummeting at high speed through the air. At the last second, she pulled back her wings, thrust out her talons, and grabbed the stick.

"She got it!" Braeden exclaimed.

Serafina's heart leapt with the thrill of seeing the bird in action.

"Well, look at that," Lady Rowena said.

Even Miss Hoity-Toity is impressed, Serafina thought with a smile.

But then the falcon came gliding toward Lady Rowena at head level.

"What is it doing?" Lady Rowena asked, cowering back and shielding herself with her parasol. "Why is it flying at me? Tell it to stop!"

The falcon flew over her head and dropped the stick on her. "Help! It's attacking me!" Lady Rowena screamed as the stick bounced harmlessly off her parasol and fell to the ground. The fox darted in, grabbed it, and trotted over to Braeden as if they were all playing a grand game of fetch.

"They're just playing with you," Braeden assured Lady Rowena.

As he knelt down and petted the fox again, he gazed up at the flying falcon. "She's such a wonderful bird," he said. Serafina could hear the admiration in his voice, and maybe a little sadness. "Once her wing has healed all the way, she'll be ready to fly long distances again, and she'll continue her migration to South America. Can you imagine flying all the way to the jungles of Peru?"

"Well, I have to say, it seems a shame to let it go after all the work you've put into it," Lady Rowena said. "You don't want to lose it. Perhaps you can use a rope to tie it to a branch so it can't get away."

"If you tied her with a rope, she couldn't fly," Braeden said, horrified by the thought.

"A string, then, or a steel wire, something to control it. A steel wire would definitely work."

As Serafina fumed over Lady Rowena's horrible suggestion, Braeden whistled a low warbling call.

The falcon turned and flew toward him.

"Watch out!" Lady Rowena cried.

But the bird came in for a nearly perfect landing on his arm.

"Kess is my friend," Braeden said. "Friendship is more powerful than the strongest wire."

As the fox trotted into the woods, and Braeden and Lady

Rowena walked back toward the house, Braeden carried Kess on his arm. "Would you like to come to the stables with me while I put Kess away?"

"Of course not," Lady Rowena said, wrinkling her nose.

"Come with me," Braeden urged her. "I'll show you the mew we built for Kess."

"I don't go into stables of any kind. I might get my clothes dirty," Lady Rowena said haughtily. "I shall go upstairs and change for our stroll." With this, Lady Rowena separated from Braeden and went into the house.

Serafina quickly followed Braeden as he walked toward the stables. She hoped she could talk to him alone. But as she came up behind him, her stomach felt like it was spinning. What could she say that would make any difference to him? How could she explain what happened? Before she could work up the courage to say something, the stablemen came into view and she lost her chance.

A few minutes later, as the sun was beginning to set, Braeden met Lady Rowena out in front of the house again.

Serafina was surprised to see that the English girl had completely changed her appearance in a short amount of time. Her hair, her clothing, and her accoutrements were all different. Apparently, going for a walk on the wooded paths of the estate required a completely different outfit from what she'd had on while standing on the terrace.

Lady Rowena now wore what looked like a girl's hiking outfit from a grand shop in London, with a formfitting buttoned jacket, a long dark skirt, and jaunty leather ankle boots.

And, of course, the outfit came complete with a matching hat, a small pair of opera glasses, presumably to better enjoy the natural scenery, and a fancy, obviously useless feather-adorned hiking staff.

Braeden and Lady Rowena walked side by side down the estate's wide, perfectly manicured paths. These were just the type of fancy folk that Mr. Olmsted had designed the paths for, to give them the feeling that they were in nature, that they were in the deep parts of the forest, but without the inconvenience or discomfort. Serafina followed at a safe distance, trying to figure out what to do. She needed to talk to Braeden, but here Lady Rowena was again, blocking her way! As they passed through a grove of hemlock, oak, and maple trees, she couldn't quite manage to hear what they were saying, but they seemed to be deep in conversation about something.

As Braeden continued to talk with Lady Rowena, Serafina felt an itch creeping up her spine. At first she thought it might be the aggravating tone of Lady Rowena's high and mighty accent or the annoying tilt of her overly stylish hat, but she slowly realized that it was something far more serious than that.

Serafina scanned the forest. She spotted a dark shape on a branch, high up in a nearby tree. The sight of it put a lump in her throat and she became very still, not wanting to move another inch lest it notice her. It was deep in the cover of branches and difficult to see, but from its silhouette, it appeared it might be an owl or some other type of large bird. She couldn't make out the details or colors of the creature, but she could see that it had a rounded head and no ear tufts. Owls normally slept in the day, of course, but as night came on, this one seemed to be perched there in the canopy of the trees, silently watching Braeden and Rowena on the forest floor below.

Serafina decided that she could wait no longer, whether Rowena was there or not. She had to talk to Braeden.

As she rose to approach him, she remembered Braeden on his knees crying in anguish in a pool of blood at Gidean's side and Rowena screaming at her to get out of Biltmore. She remembered biting the footman and running away in shame. A hot flash flushed through her body. Her legs wobbled beneath her. But she pushed herself on. She stepped out of the bushes, walked up behind Braeden and Rowena, and spoke.

"Braeden, it's me. . . ."

28

"Serafina . . ." Braeden said gently. He did not move toward her or say more. It was as if he was gazing upon some sort of rare animal in the forest and he didn't want to scare her off.

She did not move. "Hello, Braeden . . ." she said, her voice trembling. All the emotions she was feeling were in those two simple words—the sadness for what had happened to Gidean, the sorriness for her part in it, and the fear of his reaction.

"You've come back. . . ." Braeden said. When she heard the faint, uncertain trace of surprise and hope in his voice, she realized that he did not hate her; he had *missed* her, and that was far more than she had hoped for.

She nodded to let him know, that yes, it was her intention

to come back. "I'm right sorry about everything that happened," she said.

Just as Braeden started to move toward her, Serafina noticed Lady Rowena again, standing behind him. Serafina expected the girl to be angry, maybe even start yelling at her to go back to the forest where she belonged, but she didn't. Rowena's face was white with fear. "What are you doing here?" she asked warily. "Why have you come back here after what you did?"

"Rowena," Braeden said, lifting his hand to assuage her.

"You are not wanted here," Rowena said to Serafina.

"Rowena, stop," Braeden said, touching her arm. "You're wrong. She *is* wanted here."

"Thank you," Serafina said softly to Braeden. She knew she didn't deserve his loyalty, but she was relieved to have it. "I think I know what happened to Gidean, why he attacked me."

Braeden did not seem to absorb her words. "Did you hear what happened to Mr. Rinaldi?" he asked her, his voice trembling with misery and confusion.

"My pa told me that he was kicked by a horse. Was it one of those stallions?"

"No . . ." Braeden said, the shame in his voice so heartbreaking that she wanted to hug him. "It was one of *my* horses," he said.

"It wasn't your fault, Braeden," Serafina said emphatically.

"But I was the one who trained them," he said, lowering his head. "I never thought one of my horses would ever do something like that."

"That's exactly what I'm saying," Serafina said. "It wasn't

your horse's fault. And it wasn't Gidean who attacked me. Those animals were under someone else's control."

Braeden raised his head. "What do you mean?"

Rowena suddenly stepped between them. "She's talking about witchcraft. She's trying to trick us!"

"She's not trying to trick us," Braeden said.

"You can't possibly want this creature here," Rowena said.

"Yes, I do want her here," Braeden said. "She's my friend."

"But you saw her," Rowena said. "She bites!"

"Many of my friends do when they're cornered," Braeden said.

Serafina smiled. But Rowena stopped and looked at Braeden, confused, her brows furrowed. Serafina could see by the expression on her face that Rowena was truly struggling to understand what was going on. But how could she? So many awful, incomprehensible things were happening at Biltmore.

Serafina turned toward her. "I know this must all seem very strange, Rowena," she said. "But I didn't mean to hurt Gidean. I would never do anything to harm him or Braeden, or anyone else at Biltmore, including you."

Rowena looked at her and seemed to take in what she said, but she was still suspicious. She looked uncertainly at Braeden. "What she's telling you about the animals can't be true," she said. "Black magic isn't real."

"Trust me," Braeden said firmly. "Sometimes it is."

"Are you saying you actually believe her?" Rowena asked. It wasn't anger but genuine astonishment.

"I do," he said. "It all fits."

"This all makes sense to you?" Lady Rowena said in disbelief, shaking her head.

"Braeden and I have been through this together before, Lady Rowena," Serafina said. "We've learned to trust each other."

"And we've learned to trust what we see even when what we see seems impossible," Braeden said.

Rowena looked at Braeden. "But is this truly what you want, Braeden? You want to be around this ragged girl?"

"Yes, I do," Braeden said. "I should have never doubted her. She's my closest friend, Rowena. But that doesn't mean Serafina and I can't be your friend as well."

Rowena's face roiled in dismay, and she turned away. She took several steps down the path. For a moment, Serafina thought she was going to walk back to Biltmore on her own even as night fell.

But then Rowena hesitated.

Serafina had disliked Rowena from the first moment she'd seen her horseback riding with Braeden, and she hated the way Rowena was frightened of the things she didn't understand, and the girl had definitely jumped to all the wrong conclusions about *her*. But as Serafina watched Rowena standing there in the path, she thought maybe Rowena was far smarter and tougher than she first appeared. Maybe she wasn't the only one who had jumped to conclusions. Rowena seemed to be thinking everything through now, trying to understand the situation she was in.

Serafina watched as Rowena exhaled a long, uneven breath, then turned and looked at her and Braeden.

The aloofness and disdain that had always been Rowena's armor had broken down a little bit and molded into something else. There was a seriousness in her eyes that Serafina hadn't seen before. She looked like a girl who wasn't going to give up, who was determined to figure out where she fit in, where she belonged. And that was a girl Serafina could relate to.

Serafina stepped slowly toward her.

"I know that you and I are very different," Serafina said, "but I am not your enemy."

Lady Rowena did not reply, but for the first time she was looking at her and truly listening to her.

"We have both said things and done things around each other that we shouldn't have," Serafina said, "but there's a danger at Biltmore far more important than any of that. Black magic, evil spells, whatever you want to call it. But it's very real. And we've got to stop it."

Rowena studied her without saying a word for several seconds. Serafina could not tell if it was suspicion or wariness or fear, or if somehow she'd managed to get through to her. But then Rowena spoke.

"You know," Lady Rowena said to her, "you're a rather fierce person."

"And you're altogether too well dressed," Serafina said. "We all have our faults."

As Lady Rowena looked at Serafina, the edge of her mouth curled into a little smile. "We do indeed," she said finally.

While they were talking, the setting sun had been gradually withdrawing its light from the trees, slowly pulling the colors from the world around them, and bringing the details of the forest to life in the way that Serafina was used to.

"Now, tell us what you found out, Serafina," Braeden said. "What's going on with the animals?"

"First, tell me about Gideon," Serafina said. "How is it possible that he's walking?"

29

"Gidean is still weak, but he's healing very quickly," Braeden answered Serafina's question.

"I've never seen anything like it," Rowena said.

"That's such good news," Serafina said, relieved, but she sensed Braeden's confusion.

"When I saw Gidean lying there on the floor in all that blood," Braeden said, "I swear he was dead—or just about to die. His body was broken. His eyes were closed. I got down on my knees, and I leaned forward to say my last words to him. When I put my hands on him, his body was so still, so lifeless. I thought I was too late, he would never hear my words to him, he was already gone. But then I felt his heart start beating. And a few seconds later, he opened his eyes and looked at me with such emotion in his eyes."

Serafina swallowed hard. "How is that possible?"

"I don't know," Braeden admitted.

Feeling a shiver run down her spine, Serafina glanced up into the trees just in time to see the owl open its wings and disappear into the darkness.

"Do you remember what happened before, Braeden, with the Black Cloak . . ." she said. "I think it's happening again— not the cloak itself, but something else like it. I encountered the bearded man again. He's some sort of conjurer. The mountain folk call him the old man of the forest. The Cherokee call him the Darkness. I think that Grathan is his spy here at Biltmore. Or maybe one of his demons or his apprentice. I'm not sure. But they're working together. We need to watch Grathan and figure out how we can defeat him."

Braeden nodded. "We should find out what room he's staying in, and when we're sure he's not there, we should search it."

"Are you talking about Detective Grathan?" Lady Rowena said. "He's staying in the Van Dyck Room on the third floor."

Serafina and Braeden both looked at Lady Rowena, surprised that she knew something about their enemy that they did not.

"I overhead him telling the staff that he'd be going out this evening and he wouldn't be back until the morning," Rowena said.

Braeden smiled, obviously impressed.

"I could be much more useful if I actually understood what we're talking about," Rowena said.

"If what you say is true, then you've already been useful," Braeden said.

"But hold on," Serafina said doubtfully. "You said he was going out *tonight*?"

"Yes," Lady Rowena said confidently.

"But why?" Serafina asked. "What reason did he give for going out at night? The house is surrounded by nothing but gardens and forest for miles."

"He told the staff that he would be taking his carriage into town," she said. "But of course I knew he was lying."

"You did?" Serafina asked in surprise. "How?"

"He had the wrong kind of shoes. He had his old, cracked muddy boots on. Positively dreadful. No one in their right mind would wear such hideous things into town."

Serafina smiled. She was liking Rowena more and more. "Tell us what else you noticed."

"Well, he's an extremely poorly dressed person—that I can tell you without hesitation. His coat is badly worn and altogether of the wrong season. Someone needs to tell that man that it's 1899."

Serafina nodded. The fashion critique was expected, but then Lady Rowena continued.

"Yesterday, the nasty man followed me through the Rose Garden. He probably thought I didn't know he was there, but a lady knows when a man is following her, whether he's a proper gentleman or a commoner like Mr. Grathan. He's been watching Braeden very carefully as well. And he's been looking for you, Serafina. Did you know that? He asked me at dinner two nights ago if I knew if you had truly left Biltmore. He stays well clear of Mr. Vanderbilt and Mrs. King, but he's been cornering the servants and asking questions about somebody called Mr. Thorne and something about a sculpture of a stone angel in the forest. I don't know what it all means, but at dinner every night, he pulls guests aside and practically interrogates them."

Serafina stared at Lady Rowena in stunned disbelief. The girl was a walking encyclopedia of house gossip and intrigue.

"Well," Lady Rowena said in response to Serafina's look of surprise, "I've been rather bored here all alone. I had to take up *some* sort of hobby, didn't I?"

"What about Mr. Olmsted?" Serafina prompted her.

"What does he have to do with any of this?" Braeden asked.

"What have you seen, Rowena?" Serafina persisted.

"He lurks in his gardens late in the afternoon. After dinner, he spends endless hours in the library looking over old sketches and photographs as if he's pining for the bygone days. But every morning at breakfast, Mr. Vanderbilt asks where he's going for a walk that day, and he says he's just wandering, going wherever the wind takes him. But he's lying, just like Mr. Grathan."

"Lying?" Braeden asked.

"Mr. Olmsted is lying to Mr. Vanderbilt?" Serafina asked.

"Oh, yes. Definitely. He says he's going for a leisurely stroll, but he goes straight out like a shot in the same direction every day, like he's on some sort of mission out there in the woods."

"She seems to be a fount of observations," Braeden said, amused by this sudden turn.

Serafina took in everything Rowena had said, then focused on the next step. "Braeden, do you remember the four stallions I told you about?"

Braeden nodded. "I went to the stables and checked into it, but the stallions were gone. The stablemen told me that they were only here for a short time, and they hadn't seen them since."

Serafina frowned. "Can you find out exactly who they belonged to?"

"Normally, I would ask Mr. Rinaldi, may he rest in peace. But I could go back and see if he registered the horses' owners in his logbook."

"Good, please do that," Serafina said. "It might provide us more clues about how all this fits together."

"And what about me?" Lady Rowena asked. "If Braeden has a job, then so should I."

Serafina studied her. It was hard to believe that this was the same Rowena as before, but she truly did seem like she wanted to help and be part of their group.

"If there's spying to be done, then I'm your girl," Rowena said. "What do you want me to find out?"

Serafina wasn't sure how far she could trust Rowena, but she'd give her an assignment as a test.

"I want you to get a list of all the guests staying at Biltmore and what rooms they're in. Every bedroom has a name, so learn them, just like you did with Mr. Grathan's room. And if anyone new arrives, we definitely need to know that. We also need to know everything that's talked about at dinner, especially involving Mr. Grathan."

"Absolutely," Rowena said. "I'm chuffed about this. This is so much more interesting than sitting around with the old ladies, sipping tea. Are we going to have a secret handshake?"

"A what?" Serafina asked in confusion.

"You know, like real spies."

"I don't understand," Serafina said.

"What about secret code names?"

Amused, Braeden looked at Serafina and smiled. "Yes, what about secret code names, Serafina?"

"Look," Serafina said. "If anyone sees anything unusual, like the arrival of a new stranger or an unexplained shadow in the garden, anything like that, then you need to find me and tell me right away."

"Got it," Braeden agreed.

"You can count on me," Rowena said.

"And, Lady Rowena," Serafina said, "this is important. You can't tell anyone else about what we're doing. No one. Do you understand?"

"Yes."

"Do you swear?"

"I swear," Rowena said.

"For any of us, at any time, if something happens and it's an emergency, then stop the master clock and the other two will see it."

222

Braeden nodded, liking the plan.

"For heaven's sake, how are we supposed to do that?" Rowena asked in bewilderment.

"There's a large clock in the carriage house courtyard," Braeden explained. "It runs on gears. It controls fourteen other clocks throughout the house so that every room is on Standard Time, just like in my great-grandpa's train stations."

"What a marvelous way to make sure the servants don't have any excuses for being late!" Lady Rowena exclaimed.

Serafina shook her head.

"So, how do I set this signal?" Rowena asked.

"On the third floor of the carriage house, there's a small room with the clock's gear mechanism inside," Braeden explained. "Simply pull the lever to stop the clock. But don't break anything or there'll be hell to pay from Serafina's pa."

"Not to mention your uncle," Serafina added. "If anyone sets the signal, then we'll all meet out on the roof right away. But only use the signal in case of extreme emergency."

"On the roof?" Lady Rowena exclaimed. "How do I get on the roof?"

"Take the stairs up to the fourth floor, cross through the hall, go down the corridor on the left, and climb out the second window," Braeden said, as if this was the simplest thing in the world.

"Remember, don't stop the clock unless it's an extreme emerg—" Serafina began, but before she could finish her sentence, she heard someone coming up the darkened path. The hairs on the back of her neck stood on end.

"Get down!" she said, pulling Lady Rowena and Braeden into the bushes.

"What are you doing?" Lady Rowena complained. "My dress might get snagged on a thistle!"

"Sssshh!" Serafina said as she dragged the girl to the ground and covered her mouth with her hand.

Serafina spotted the flicker of approaching torchlight on the leaves of the surrounding trees. She heard the sound of coming footsteps, heavy boots treading across the ground.

A dark figure came toward them up the path. Her chest tightened when she saw the man's long, weathered coat. Then she saw his spiraling cane and his dark hair. Her heart pounded. It was him! It was the rat-fiend Grathan. Rowena had been right. He wasn't going into town for the evening. He was coming right toward them!

As he strode rapidly up the path, a murderous determination clenched Grathan's scarred face. It was as if he'd uncovered some new piece of information. He was no longer going to investigate, interrogate, or spy. He was going to *kill*. He gripped his cane in his hand as if he could transform it into a savage weapon at any moment.

Serafina glanced at Braeden as he hunched low to the ground, his eyes fixed on their enemy. Lady Rowena began to squirm in panic, her chest rising and falling in her corset, but Serafina held her tight. She tried to keep them all quiet, but *her* chest was pulling in air, too, now, fast and hard, preparing her body for battle. Her muscles buzzed, ready to explode.

Grathan was thirty feet away, moving quickly. She could

hear the shift of his clothes along with the pounding of his feet.

Twenty feet away now . . .

If it came to it, she thought she could run fast enough to escape him, but Rowena couldn't in her long dress.

Ten feet away now . . .

Serafina decided that if Grathan spotted any one of them, she must immediately attack.

He was right on top of them now. She crouched down, poised for the lunge.

For a moment, nothing happened. She thought he was going to pass them right by without ever seeing them hiding in the bushes just a few feet off the path. But then a beast howled in the distance.

Braeden and Lady Rowena both startled, their eyes flaring wide. Serafina grabbed their arms and held them in place.

Do.

Not.

Move.

Hearing the howl, Grathan stopped abruptly on the path. All Serafina could hear now was the sound of his breathing and the flame of his torch. Peering up through the ferns at him, she slowed her breaths until she was perfectly quiet, not moving in any way. But around her, her companions shifted nervously. Even their rustling clothes made too much noise.

Grathan gazed up the path in the direction of the howl. The scars on his face looked like the claw marks of a wild animal. When she saw the glisten of the torch's flame reflected in his eyes, she felt a twist of fear coiling through her body.

Serafina watched Grathan as he stood on the path. He tilted his head as if listening for the sound of another howl. Then, after several long seconds, he hurried up the path with new urgency.

When Grathan finally went around a bend in the path and disappeared, Serafina held her position. She sensed that Braeden and Rowena were anxious to move. They weren't used to long periods of stillness like she was, but she kept them there, her hands holding them in place for several minutes longer, until she was sure it was truly safe.

Finally, she looked at her companions, lifted her finger to her lips, and then pointed toward Biltmore. The three of them ran home without saying a word.

Serafina could easily run faster than both of them, but she took up the rear, watching behind them to make sure Grathan hadn't doubled back. She knew there would come a point in the near future when she would have to fight him, but the last thing she wanted was to confront him now, unprepared, in the darkened forest with her two companions. She had to find a way to gain an advantage over him.

As they reached the outer edge of the gardens, she was glad to see the faint lights of Biltmore in the distance.

"Did you see that?" Lady Rowena said proudly as they hurried toward the mansion's side door. "He walked right past us and didn't even see us!" She crouched down and moved her hands in front of her like she was a master of stealth. "I was totally invisible! I was like a thief in the night!"

Serafina smiled, but Braeden looked confused. "Where was he going?" he asked. "What's out there in the woods?"

"I told you we can't trust that man," Rowena said.

"Let's hurry back to the house," Serafina said as they crossed the lawn.

"There's a formal dinner tonight," Braeden said, seeming to sense what she was thinking, "so the house is going to be very busy."

"As soon as things quiet down, after dinner is over and everyone goes to bed," Serafina said, "I'll sneak up to the third floor and search Grathan's room."

Serafina took them through the side door, and then they hid in the shadows beneath the Grand Staircase and gazed out across the Entrance Hall.

The house was softly lit with candles placed here and there on the mantels and tables, which gave the rooms an almost ethereal feeling. It was very quiet, save for the gentle music of violins and cellos playing in the Banquet Hall. It was good to see the Vanderbilt families and all their friends celebrating together. Serafina loved all the ladies' sparkling dresses. Christmas Eve was just a few nights away.

A beautiful, formally dressed young lady in her early twenties and a handsome young gentleman slowly descended the Grand Staircase arm in arm. The young man wore black tails, a white tie, and white gloves. Serafina loved the way the silver buttons on his shirt and vest glinted in the candlelight and matched the watch chain dangling from his pocket. The young lady on his arm wore a voluminous silvery dress with capped shoulders, a taut corset, and a long train that swished as it dropped from step to step as she came majestically down the stairs. She wore graceful white satin gloves and carried a silvery folding fan that matched her dress. A ring of shimmering pearls encircled her neck. Her dark hair had been swept up and arranged into the most elaborate coiffure Serafina had ever seen.

"Who's that?" Lady Rowena asked, entranced.

"Her Grace Consuelo Vanderbilt, Duchess of Marlborough," Braeden said quietly. "And her husband, Charles Richard John Spencer-Churchill, the ninth Duke of Marlborough. My cousins."

Serafina smiled. She had no idea how he remembered

names like that, but the girl sure was pretty. She loved the way Duchess Consuelo lilted her fan as she walked.

Serafina watched breathlessly as the young couple sauntered through the Entrance Hall and around the Winter Garden on their way to the evening meal.

In the Banquet Hall, the servants were preparing the forty-foot-long main table for the eight o'clock dinner as all the gentlemen in their black tails and white ties escorted their ladies in their long, formal dinner gowns. The shine of silver platters and the sparkle of crystal glasses in the candlelight seemed bright compared to the darkness from which she and Braeden and Lady Rowena had just come.

"Y'all better go on upstairs and get changed for dinner," Serafina whispered to her companions. "When you go to bed tonight, stay safe. Lock your doors. Tomorrow, get that information we talked about. And keep your eyes peeled for new clues."

"Got it," Braeden said.

"Will do," Lady Rowena agreed.

As Lady Rowena split off and went up the Grand Staircase, Serafina couldn't help but feel surprised by the girl. She was not at all what Serafina had expected.

"What are you going to do now, Serafina?" Braeden asked when Lady Rowena was gone.

"I'm going to keep watch," she said.

"I'll watch with you," he said.

Serafina looked at him. "You don't have to do that, Braeden.

Go to dinner with your family and then go on to bed. Get some sleep. I'm just glad I'm home."

"I couldn't sleep when you were gone, and I'm sure not going to sleep now that you're back," he said.

She looked at him and felt the warmth of his words moving through her. "Thank you, Braeden," she said. "It was the same way for me. I'm none too eager to run away again—believe me."

Smiling, Braeden said, "Let me go tell my uncle that I'm back, and then I'll meet you here."

"What about your dinner?" she asked, gesturing toward the glittering folk gathering in the Banquet Hall in the distance.

"What about yours?" he asked, moving his hand in an inviting way toward the gathering. "I'm sure we can find a gown for you to wear."

Serafina smiled uncomfortably, feeling a new kind of fear roiling up inside her. "Thank you," she said hesitantly, "but I'm not quite ready for that."

He nodded, understanding. "Then where are you going to eat your dinner?"

"My pa grills chicken on the cookstove in the workshop," she said.

"Sounds good, if you and your pa wouldn't mind another mouth to feed," he said.

"Um . . . yes . . . that would be . . . fine," she stammered, surprised and a little scared of the idea of Braeden eating supper with her and her pa. "What about Lady Rowena—won't she miss you at dinner?"

"Oh, Lady Rowena may need us in the woods, but she

doesn't need us at a dinner party. That's her home territory, and she'll do fine without us. Let me just go ask my uncle to excuse me from joining the dinner tonight, and I'll send a message on to Rowena so that she doesn't think I got absorbed into a black cloak or something."

Serafina smiled, and before she could stop him, he walked away and did exactly what he said he would. He spoke briefly to his uncle and, to Serafina's amazement, walked right back to her. There was no conflict or argument.

"Lead the way," he said, grinning. "I'm starving."

When she walked into the workshop with Braeden at her side, her pa nearly dropped dead from shock, but he made the best of the situation as quickly as he could. He pulled up a bench stool and wiped it off for Braeden to sit on. He gave Braeden his sharpest pocketknife to cut his chicken with. And he even managed to cobble together what looked impressively similar to a napkin for Braeden's lap. Serafina just sat back, ate her chicken, and smiled at the sight of the two of them sitting together and trying to chat.

Braeden used such refined English and her pa used such mountain talk that sometimes she had to help them understand each other. For the first time in her life, she felt like she didn't just *belong*, but like she was the glue that held the world together.

After dinner, Serafina invited Braeden to do what she imagined friends all over America did after a good meal together. They went rat catching.

"My pa told me that some sort of rodent has been chewing at the wires," Serafina explained.

"Then let's get to it," Braeden agreed.

As the last of the gilded ladies and gentlemen upstairs retired to their bedrooms for the evening, and as the servants cleaned up the Banquet Hall, Serafina led Braeden through the back rooms of the basement. In an hour or so, when everyone was asleep, she'd sneak up to Grathan's room on the third floor and search it, but until then, the hunt was afoot. They prowled the darkened corridors and shadowed storage rooms of her old domain, bringing back memories of her life in the world below.

After all that had happened to her over the last few weeks, she thought catching a couple of wire-chewing rats would make for easy pickings. But she and Braeden searched and searched and they couldn't find them. As the night wore on, it became more and more perplexing. She used her eyes and her ears and her nose just as she always did, but the rats were nowhere to be found. Her pa had said there were rats in the house. And she was the Chief Rat Catcher. She always found her rats. But for some reason, she could not find them tonight.

"Is it me?" Braeden asked. "Am I making too much noise?"

"No, I don't think that's it," Serafina said. "We're checking all their favorite hiding spots. If they're down here, we should at least be seeing them."

"What about upstairs?"

She shook her head. "There aren't any rats upstairs. I never let them get that far." She frowned, not sure what to do.

"Maybe your pa was mistaken about the rats," Braeden said.

"It's possible," she said, "but I saw the wires, and they definitely looked like they'd been chewed."

Just after midnight, she and Braeden gave up the hunt and went back upstairs to the main floor. There was no one there. All the lights were off and the candles had been extinguished. The servants had gone to their rooms upstairs and down. The musicians had closed up their cases and gone home for the night. The Banquet Hall and all the other rooms on the main floor were dark and empty.

"Come on," she said, waving for him to follow her as she crept up the darkened Grand Staircase. "We'll search Grathan's room."

At the top of the second floor, they hunkered down and looked upward to make sure the stairs were clear, then padded quietly up to the next level.

When they reached the third floor, they crouched down once more, protected by nothing but darkness and the sweep of the staircase. At that moment, Serafina realized they were in the exact location where she and Gidean had gone over the railing. She looked over into the dark, empty living hall. The moon shone in through the windows, casting the room in an eerie silver light.

A shiver ran through her.

She heard something on the other side of the living hall.

When she looked at Braeden, she could tell by his expression that he had heard it, too.

It was faint and difficult to make it out. She cupped her hands behind her ears to amplify the sound.

Then she heard it again.

A faint slithering just ahead.

The scrabbling of tiny feet on bare floor.

She touched Braeden rather than use her voice, and together they crept forward along the wall.

When the sound stopped, they stopped as well. When the sound resumed, they crept forward once more.

Now she could hear the creatures breathing, the scratching of their toenails on the floor, and the dragging of their tails. She felt the familiar trembling in her fingers and the tightness in her legs.

"It's the rats," she whispered to Braeden.

They crept slowly and quietly across the darkened living hall until they reached the corridor between the North Tower and the South. When she peeked around the corner, a dark fear boomed in her chest. At the end of this corridor was the cabinet with the hidden door that led to the attic where the chimney swifts had attacked her.

Were the rats in there?

She stepped slowly forward, still listening, still trying to figure out exactly where the rodents were. She heard what sounded like the grinding teeth of a hundred rats.

She was now standing in the exact spot where Gidean had attacked her that night.

"Serafina . . ." Braeden whispered, his voice filled with terror, as his trembling hand searched for and then touched her arm.

And then she saw it. Attached to the wall was a large wooden fire alarm box with a glass front and brass instrumentation inside. It had been there for years. But crammed inside the box tonight was a mass of roiling dark fur and scaly tails.

Their gnawing teeth clicked like the sound of a thousand cockroaches. The rats were chewing on the electrical wires.

She watched the rats in horror, too shocked to move. Braeden clutched her arm tighter.

Then the sound stopped abruptly.

All at once, all the rats craned their necks and looked at her.

A large, grisly looking rat crawled out of the box. Then another followed it. The rats, seemingly half out of their minds, rose up onto their back legs and stared at Serafina. Then they all started moving toward her.

She couldn't believe what she was seeing. She wasn't hunting them—they were hunting her!

Filled with fierceness, she charged toward them, wondering how she was going to catch them all. But they weren't moving like normal rats moved. They weren't scurrying away in fear at the sight of her. They ran *toward* her.

"Serafina!" Braeden whispered in terror, looking around them.

When Serafina looked down, she saw what he was seeing: hundreds of spiders and centipedes crawling out of the woodwork.

"Serafina!" Braeden cried again as he frantically wiped the spiders off his legs.

Serafina heard a terrible *tick-tick-ticking* sound and a long, raspy hiss. She felt the hot air of a breath on the back of her neck. She spun around in panic, but there was nothing there except a darkened corridor.

"Braeden, run!" she shouted.

They turned and ran. They tore through the living hall and down the Grand Staircase. She glanced over her shoulder. A brown slithering carpet of hundreds of rats flooded down the staircase behind her. It was like a waterfall of rats. She burst forward with speed, but Braeden couldn't run nearly as fast as she could. The rats were going to eat him alive.

But just as she slowed down to wait for him, something flashed by her.

"Come on, slowpoke!" Braeden shouted as he slid at incredible speed down the endless, smooth wooden railing of the spiral staircase.

The wave of rats slammed into her feet and scratched their way up her bare legs. She tried to tear them away, but it was no use—there were too many of them. She took a flying leap onto the rail, grabbed on, and went sliding down behind Braeden.

It felt like she'd been dropped off the edge of a cliff. The swoosh of her spinning descent made her insides float. She and Braeden slid down, down, spiraling down to the next level, then ran and leapt, and slid again, following the great curve of the railing all the way down to the main floor. When they reached the bottom, they leapt off the rail and ran down into the basement.

Serafina knew she shouldn't, but at the bottom of the basement stairs, she turned and looked behind her.

T he rats were gone.

Those dirty, awful, insane creatures had chased her three floors down and then simply disappeared.

Had they vanished into thin air, or had they slunk back into the walls? Had the rats been some sort of conjuration?

She growled in frustration, angered by what had just happened. She was the Chief Rat Catcher! There weren't supposed to be rats in Biltmore House. She had made sure of it for years. And now all of a sudden there were hundreds of huge vicious ones, the likes of which she'd never seen before!

And since when did spiders crawl out of walls and attack? It was as if the animals' only purpose was to scare her off the third floor.

Braeden sat on the floor beside her, panting, his back against the wall as he tried desperately to catch his breath.

"Good night!" he exclaimed, shaking his head. "If this is what rat catching is like, you can count me out next time!"

"Come on," she said, touching his shoulder.

"Tell me where we're going," he said as he got up off the floor.

"We're going back up there."

"What?" he said, holding his ground. "Please say we're not."

"Don't you want to see if they're still up there? That was Biltmore's Grand Staircase! How can there be rats on it?"

"I swear, your curiosity is going to get you killed one of these days, Serafina. And me, too, I think."

"Come on," she said. "We've got to see."

Gathering their courage, they crept up the basement stairs to the main floor, then came slowly and carefully around, and looked up the Grand Staircase. There were no rats or spiders or centipedes. There was no sign of them at all. They were gone.

The moonlight lit the Grand Staircase in a silver glow, as if inviting them to ascend once more. But as they stared at the foreboding threat of the empty staircase and felt the hairs on the backs of their necks tingling, they both knew there was no way they were going to try to get back up to the third floor tonight. That was just about the last place on earth they wanted to go.

"There shouldn't be that many rats in the house," Braeden whispered.

"There shouldn't be *any* rats in the house!" Serafina said

fiercely, smoothing down the back of her neck with her hand. "Something isn't right, Braeden."

"A lot of four-legged nasty somethings," Braeden agreed. "Come on, let's find someplace safe to rest."

Avoiding the Grand Staircase, they used the back stairs to reach the second floor, then padded quietly to Braeden's room.

Gidean greeted Braeden happily at the door, then came over to Serafina, his tail nub wagging. She knelt down. Her eyes closed, she hugged him and petted his head, feeling a warmth in her heart. She was so glad that he seemed to have no memory or confusion about the battle they'd fought against each other that terrible night.

While Braeden slept in his bed, Serafina was happy to curl up with Gidean in the warm glow of the fireplace and try not to have nightmares of rats that didn't flee.

She awoke a few hours later, just before dawn. She had reconnected with Braeden and her pa, and even Lady Rowena now, but after everything that had happened—breaking the Ming vase, her fight with Gidean, biting the footman, terrifying the guests, and all the rest—she wasn't sure if everyone in the house would be glad to see her, so she had stayed low and quiet. But there was one more person she thought she could trust. And it might be a perfect, sneaky way to get safely into Detective Grathan's room when he wasn't there.

She quickly ran up the back stairs to the fourth floor, snuck down the hall, and slipped into the third room on the right.

"Oh, miss, it's you!" Essie said, smiling in surprise. Freshly dressed in her maid's uniform and getting ready to start her workday, Essie set down her hairbrush and went to Serafina. "I heard tell about everything that happened. I've been so worried about you! Where'd ya go?"

"I ran away up into the mountains," Serafina said.

"Oh, miss, you shouldn't have done that," Essie said. "That's far too dangerous for a little thing like you. There are panthers up there!"

Serafina smiled. "Those were the least of my problems."

"What? What happened?" Essie said, clutching her arm.

"I'm all right," Serafina said. But then she stepped back and presented her sorry state. "I'm sorry about ruining your nice dress, Essie."

"Oh, you never mind about that, miss," Essie said, pulling her back toward her. "Come sit down here on the bed. I can see you're mulling over somethin'."

"Do you know that man Detective Grathan?"

"Yes, I've seen him," Essie said. "He's been asking all sorts of questions about Mr. Vanderbilt and Mr. Olmsted, and about you, too, and Master Braeden, and the dogs."

"He asked about Gidean and Cedric?"

"Oh, yes! He's been asking after the young master's dog in particular. I can tell you one thing for sure: everyone is mighty tired of that man."

The night before, Serafina hadn't known for sure if she should trust Lady Rowena, but so far what the girl had said about Detective Grathan had turned out to be true.

"Do you clean Detective Grathan's room?" Serafina asked, finally coming to the purpose of her visit.

Essie scowled. "Maggie and me are supposed to be cleaning it, but he ain't been givin' us the chance."

"What do you mean?"

"He always locks his door, and he's given us strict instructions to never enter his room. He could have a dead cat in there for all we know, and there'd be nothin' we could do about it."

"A dead cat?" Serafina asked in alarm.

"It's just an expression," Essie said.

"Do you have a master key or anything like that?"

"Oh, no, miss, I ain't got permission for that. Most guests don't lock their doors. No reason to. But Mrs. King says if a guest wants privacy, then we should give it to them."

Serafina shook her head in frustration. This seemed like another dead end.

"So what's the big interest in Detective Grathan?" Essie asked.

"I think he's up to no good, and I want to catch him at it," Serafina said, which was the God's honest truth.

"Well, you be careful," Essie warned gravely. "He strikes me as a bad awful man."

Serafina nodded. Remembering the rats the night before, she said, "I'll do my best." Then one more thought came into her mind.

"Which room is Detective Grathan in?" she asked Essie. She thought it would be good to double-check what she'd learned from Rowena.

"Well, when he first arrived, Mrs. Vanderbilt told us to put him in the Sheraton Room, which is a very nice room, but Detective Grathan had some sort of problem with it."

"What did he say?"

"No one could understand what he was yammering on about, but he complained high and low about it so much that they finally just give in and put him where he wanted to be. I mean, how rude, to be a guest in someone's house and then to demand a particular room!"

"What room did he demand?" she asked.

"The Van Dyck Room at the top of the stairs on the third floor."

This was the same room that Lady Rowena had named, so this wasn't new information in itself, but when Serafina heard Essie say these words, her heart began to thump. *The room at the top of the stairs on the third floor.* That was right where she and Braeden had encountered the rats, and right where Gidean had attacked her, and before that, the chimney swifts. Then she remembered that the black-cloaked Mr. Thorne had used the same room.

"On my way back from the water closet this mornin'," Essie continued, "I heard the other girls talkin' about Detective Grathan."

"What did they say?"

"Well, you know he missed dinner last night, which was extremely rude to Mr. and Mrs. Vanderbilt. He came in late, went straight up to his room, tracking mud all the way, which poor Betsy had to clean up before Mrs. King saw it in the morning, and then he rang his bell. He had the gall to demand his dinner be brought up to him in his room. The cook had to get hisself out of bed, reopen the kitchen, warm up a plate for him, and send a footman all the way up there. That would have been no problem at all if he'd showed a speck of gratitude, but he wouldn't even let the footman in his room. He shouted at him to set the tray on the floor outside the door and go away."

Serafina listened with fascination. "So Detective Grathan is back in the house. . . ."

"Oh, yes, he's back, but I wouldn't cry none if Mr. Vanderbilt kicked him right on out again. All the other guests are so friendly and appreciative, especially round the holidays, but he's just a very rude and demanding man."

"Thank you for all the information, Essie," Serafina said, clutching her arm. "You've been a good friend to me. I'll pay you back for your dress as soon as I can."

"I know you will, miss," Essie said. "I've got a few minutes before I have to go. Do you want me to do your hair? It looks like you've been through a right lot of trouble."

Serafina smiled and nodded appreciatively. "Yes, that would be nice."

"How would you like me to do it?" Essie said, standing behind Serafina and gathering her hair up into her hands.

"Have you seen Consuelo Vanderbilt, the Duchess of Marlborough?" Serafina asked with a twinkle in her eye.

"Oh, miss, that would take an hour!" Essie said. "I'm a-fixing to get to work!"

"All right, a roll and a twist it is," Serafina said, laughing.

After talking with Essie, Serafina ventured down to the

lower floors. Moving from one hiding spot to another, she watched the comings and goings of the bustling house for the rest of the morning, but she didn't see anything suspicious or out of the ordinary. There was no sign of Detective Grathan. The rat seemed to have gone to ground. She wondered if her two allies had spotted anything. Somehow, they had to come up with a plan to defeat Grathan once and for all. They couldn't keep dodging him. But so far, they hadn't even been able to get into his room. Something terrible happened every time she tried. She felt like she needed some sort of trap.

That afternoon, she went outside to patrol the perimeter of the grounds. She wondered if there was a point at which the old man of the forest would attack head-on. From what direction and in what form would he come? Or would the attack come from Grathan himself, within the house?

She spotted Mr. Vanderbilt and Mr. Olmsted walking down a path together in the gardens, and hurried to listen in on their conversation.

"Have you checked in on the planting crews working down along the river?" Mr. Vanderbilt asked Mr. Olmsted.

"They're making good progress," Mr. Olmsted said. "Mr. Schenck has a good eye for the land." Serafina recognized the name of the chief forester they had hired to manage Biltmore's woodlands.

"All we need now are a few more decades, and we'll have a lovely forest again," Mr. Olmsted said.

The two men laughed a little, but Serafina could see a seriousness in Mr. Olmsted's expression, in the wrinkles around his eyes. The old man was hiding something from Mr. Vanderbilt, just as Lady Rowena had said.

"I just want to keep making progress," Mr. Vanderbilt said to Mr. Olmsted as the two friends walked together.

"Don't worry, George. We'll keep at it," Mr. Olmsted assured him. "We're going to make it so beautiful at Biltmore that no one will ever know what it was like before. You and your family and your guests will be able to enjoy the bounty of nature for years to come."

"I appreciate that, Frederick," Mr. Vanderbilt said.

"I learned long ago," Mr. Olmsted continued, "that whether it's a delicate tea rose or a three-foot oak, planting and growing requires an immeasurable amount of patience."

"I don't always have it," Mr. Vanderbilt said.

"Neither do I," Mr. Olmsted admitted.

Serafina thought that Mr. Olmsted should have chuckled or smiled when he said that, but he didn't. There was a darkness in him that she did not understand. There were thoughts on his mind that he was not sharing with Mr. Vanderbilt. She wondered again why he'd come back to Biltmore now, at this particular time.

As she watched and listened to these two men, she thought about her own life. Years ago, she had often seen these two friends together, walking and planting, talking about what species of trees would grow in each area, how they could bring in more water here or protect an area from the wind there, like shepherds of the forest. She had never thought about it before, but lately she had started to realize that all the comforts, buildings, and machines around her were once nothing more than someone's dream. In the not-too-distant past, these things had just been an idea in someone's head. When Mr. Vanderbilt's grandfather grew up, people had to walk or ride horses to travel great distances, but he'd imagined trains crisscrossing America. It was only by those trains that his grandson was able to venture from New York to the wilds of western North Carolina. And then his grandson had dreams of his own and built a great house in the mountains. Mr. Edison had imagined a lightbulb that would bring light to the darkest nights. Other people had imagined the elevator, and the dynamo, and all the other inventions her pa worked on every day. But unlike the men of iron, Mr. Olmsted had dreamed of vast gardens and endless forests. Those were the things he'd brought into the world. Thinking back in time, she wondered if the mountains, and the rivers, and the clouds, and even human beings, had been *God's* dream a million years before.

As she thought about all this, she couldn't help but wonder about herself. *Envision what you want to be, then you'll find a way to get there,* Waysa had told her in the cave behind the waterfall. She knew she wasn't going to invent a machine or build a great building, but she had to figure out who and what she wanted to be. She had to envision her future, and then she had to get there.

When she snuck back into the house that evening, she hunkered down in the second-floor air shaft and tried to think about what she could do. What trick could she use to trap Grathan? She had tried to get into his room and failed. She

could barely keep track of where he was. But he had to have some kind of weakness.

Restless for some sort of plan, she crawled through the shaft and checked Braeden's room, which was empty. So she made her way down to the Library. As usual, she entered through the vent near the ceiling. Just as she began climbing down the bookshelves to the Library's second-floor walkway, Serafina heard footsteps approaching. She scurried into a hiding spot, crouched down, and waited for someone to enter the room.

But no one did.

She kept waiting, curious. She was sure she had heard something. It was like the person had paused just outside the door and wasn't coming in. The longer it went on, the more curious she became. Was she mistaken?

Suddenly, a figure appeared in the room, but not through the main door like she'd expected. Someone stepped out from behind the upper portion of the room's massive fireplace mantel. It was Lady Rowena! Serafina realized she must have used the hidden passageway that led from the house's second floor directly into the top level of the Library.

Serafina thought she should reveal herself to Rowena, but there was something furtive about the girl's movements, so she crouched down and watched her.

Rowena quickly ran down the finely wrought spiral staircase to the Library's main floor, her lavish, dusky-rose dress billowing behind her. She looked around as if to make sure no one else was in the room, then darted over to the walnut wall panels just to the left of the fireplace.

Serafina crept along the railing, but before she could get to a better vantage point, she heard a faint metallic ratcheting, a turning sound, and then a distinct *click*. This was followed by the squeak of what sounded like a hinge. Rowena must have found some sort of small hidden compartment in the wall. There was a rustling of paper and then a long sliding sound.

Rowena came back into view with a bundle of rolled documents in her hands. She took them over to one of the tables and opened them up. It was hard to tell from a distance what the rolls contained, but they seemed to be architectural drawings of some kind.

What was Rowena looking for? Was she studying a diagram of the house so that she would know it as well as Serafina and Braeden did? Or maybe she'd found the list of guests and was now matching them to the various rooms of the house like Serafina had told her to. It seemed wrong for Rowena to be snooping around in the Library when no one else was there, but then Serafina realized that she herself was doing the exact same thing. Maybe Rowena had some theory she was pursuing about Detective Grathan. When Serafina asked Rowena to join her and Braeden, she had no idea the girl would be so committed. She seemed to truly enjoy playing spy. Serafina was eager to hear what she had learned.

Just as she thought about revealing herself to Rowena, Serafina heard the sound of footsteps walking down the Tapestry Gallery toward the main door of the Library. Lady Rowena quickly stuffed the drawings back into the hidden compartment in the wall, sat down on the sofa in front of the fire, and pretended to read a book.

This girl is good, Serafina thought as she watched with a smile. That was a trick she'd never thought of before. The old act-like-everything-is-fine-here trick.

A footman came into the room. "I beg your pardon, my lady," the footman said, bowing slightly. "Dinner will be served at the normal hour of eight o'clock this evening, but please be advised that most of the clocks in the house have stopped, so we are letting our guests know that it's currently seven o'clock and they may wish to start getting dressed for dinner at this time. Thank you."

Serafina's body jolted when she heard the footman's words. The clocks had stopped! Lady Rowena was here in the Library, so that meant Braeden had sounded the alarm! He was in trouble!

Rowena seemed to understand this as well, for she immediately brushed past the footman and hurried out of the room.

Serafina darted from her hiding spot and ran for the rooftop.

Serafina climbed through the fourth-floor window onto the roof of Biltmore House and hurried along the top side of the Grand Staircase's copper dome. She made her way between the slanting slate roofs, rising chimneys, pointed towers, and sculpted stone gargoyles of Biltmore's rooftop realm. The ridges of the roof were capped with ornate copper trim embossed with patterns of oak leaves, acorns, and George Vanderbilt's gold-gilded initials burning bright in the moonlit night.

As she came to the edge of the roof, she had a nighthawk's view of the Winter Garden's glass rooftop and the estate's many courtyards and gardens far below her. With the glistening stars above and the forested mountains rolling into the distance, the roof provided her a breathtaking view of her world.

She heard a tremendous racket coming her way and spun around.

"The clocks have all stopped!" Lady Rowena said breathlessly as she tried to climb through the window out onto the roof in her fancy dress.

Serafina went over to help her. Lady Rowena's dress, which was decorated with a profusion of silk taffeta roses, was so long and cumbersome that when she tried to clamber through the opening, her legs became entangled. The two of them worked together to push the fabric aside, avoid stepping on the flower-encrusted skirt hem, and pull her through the small window without tearing anything.

"We've almost got it," Lady Rowena groaned. "Just a little more."

Finally, she popped through the opening and fell onto the rooftop.

"I'm here," she said, gathering herself up like a soldier standing at attention. "Someone stopped the clock!"

"I stopped it," Braeden said as he stepped easily through the window and onto the roof.

"What's happened?" Serafina asked him. "Did you see something?"

"Gidean and Cedric are missing," Braeden said, his voice cracking.

"What do you mean, they're missing?" Serafina asked. Some dogs were natural wanderers, but losing track of a wounded Doberman and a giant Saint Bernard seemed almost impossible to her.

"We've searched all over the house and the grounds. Cedric seldom leaves my uncle's side and Gidean has never gone missing before, but no one can find either of them," Braeden said in dismay.

Serafina tried to think it through. She walked to the edge of the roof and looked down, first at the gardens, with their many statues and paths, and then outward, across the forest.

She remembered what she had seen in the dark shadows of the pines the last time she'd gone out there.

She didn't want to think about it.

She didn't want it to be true.

But the memory kept rising up in her mind.

"I think I may know where they are. . . ." she said, feeling a sickness in her stomach even as she said it. It was the last place on earth she wanted to go.

"Thank you for meeting with us, sir," Serafina said as Mr. Vanderbilt walked into the Library.

"Braeden told me that you had important information regarding the disappearance of the dogs," Mr. Vanderbilt said, his voice grave. She could not tell whether he was angry with her for what had happened a few nights before, when Gidean was injured, but he was obviously deeply worried about Cedric's disappearance.

"Serafina can help us, Uncle," Braeden said. "I trust her with my life, and with Gidean's and Cedric's, too. The strange things that have been happening at Biltmore, the way Gidean attacked Serafina, Mr. Rinaldi's death, Cedric and Gidean's disappearance . . . they're all related."

"In what way?" he asked.

"Mr. Vanderbilt," Serafina began, "you met me for the first time a few weeks ago when the children disappeared."

Mr. Vanderbilt's face turned even darker than it already was. "Yes," he said, looking at her. "Is this the same?"

"No, not exactly," she said. "But you saw then that you could trust me."

"Yes, I remember," he said, studying her.

Serafina looked at Mr. Vanderbilt and held his eyes. "I never meant to hurt Gidean. And I don't believe he ever meant to hurt me. I'm not sure, but I think I might know where the dogs are. They're in the forest. But I don't want to go there alone. I think we should form a hunting party with men and horses and weapons, and I'll lead us there. Whatever this turns out to be, we'll fight it together this time."

Mr. Vanderbilt looked at her for a long time, clearly taken aback by what she was saying. He seemed to fathom how frightened she was. "This is *that* dangerous. . . ." he said quietly, thinking it through.

Still looking at him, she slowly nodded.

Mr. Vanderbilt contemplated everything she'd said, then looked over at Braeden.

"We need to go get the dogs, Uncle," he said. "And Serafina is the only one who can take us to them."

"What will we encounter when we get to this place you speak of?" Mr. Vanderbilt asked her.

"I do not know for sure," she said, "but I think there will be animals in cages."

"Cages . . ." he repeated, his face clouding with dismay as he tried to imagine it. "When would you want to do this?"

Serafina swallowed. "Now, sir," she said, feeling sick to her stomach even as she said it.

"It's pitch dark," he said.

"I don't think we have time to wait, sir. If my suspicions are right, then the dogs are in terrible danger. I think he's going to kill them, sir. We have to go tonight. And one more thing: it should only be yourself and your most trusted men."

"There are many men here who will want to help," Mr. Vanderbilt said. "And if there is something criminal going on, Detective Grathan will insist on coming."

Serafina pursed her lips. "He's the main one who should *not* come, sir. I believe Mr. Grathan to be a grave danger to us."

Mr. Vanderbilt stared at her with his penetrating dark eyes for several long seconds, seeming to take in everything she'd told him. She held his gaze, waiting for him to reply.

"I understand," he said, slowly nodding. "We'll do it exactly as you say."

A half hour later, Mr. Vanderbilt had assembled the rescue party in the courtyard just as he'd promised, including eleven handpicked men on horseback, and Serafina on foot along with two trackers and their dogs. Many of the men carried torches, the flames snapping and flickering in the darkness. When Serafina saw Braeden enter the courtyard on his thorough-bred, her heart sank, but she could tell by the determined look on his face that she couldn't prevent him from coming. And Lady Rowena rode beside him, seeming just as determined. She no longer rode sidesaddle, but astride, the pretense of courtly daintiness set aside. Her cheeks were flush in the chill air. She wore a fashionable riding coat, but it was dark and heavy and well suited to the task. She had pulled her red hair back and tucked it into the coat's hood. Her hands were covered in leather gloves, and she carried a riding stick, like many of the men. She looked the part. Serafina wasn't surprised that the girl had insisted on coming—she just hoped Lady Rowena wouldn't be sorry when they got there.

Mr. Vanderbilt and the hunt master called everyone forward, and the horses set off at a trot. The hunting party rode out of Biltmore just after midnight under the dying glow of a clouded moon.

As Serafina walked through the forest with the mounted hunting party all around her, she felt like a general leading an invading army into battle. But the thudding hooves, shifting saddles, jangling bridles, and breathing men made so much noise that it was impossible for her to hear anything else. She split off from the others and traveled ahead of them through the trees so she could better hear the forest around them.

She knew she shouldn't get too far ahead of the others. A swirling mist floated in the low areas of the land and in the boughs of the trees, moving through the forest like waves of ghosts, one after the other, dancing among the rocks and the trunks of the trees, sometimes blocking her view of the horses and the men.

She glanced back at Braeden, Rowena, and Mr. Vanderbilt riding on their horses with the men in a loose wedge formation. She knew that the master of Biltmore had always loved the beauty of the outdoors, but he was not a hunter, in spirit or experience, and he had asked the estate's hunt master to lead the horsemen and the trackers during the search. The hunt master rode in front of the two Vanderbilts and all the other riders. He was a large, commanding man with a gruff voice and stout demeanor, and looked like he had spent most of his life in a saddle. She could see the hunt master watching her with steady eyes, following her movement through the brush ahead of them. She was the only one who knew the way.

The trackers—two rugged-looking men in heavy coats—traveled on foot like she did, holding a pack of six Plott hounds: large and lanky black and brindled dogs that had been bred for hunting bear in these mountains since the seventeen hundreds.

But as she led the search party up the mountain toward the stand of pines where the cages were located, the trackers looked confounded. Their dogs had their noses to the ground but seemed confused, barking and agitated, and sniffing all around. Rather than picking up a distinct scent that they could follow, the Plotts started growling.

"Steady the hounds!" the hunt master ordered the trackers sternly.

"Jesse there is acting like he's on a wildcat," one of the trackers said as he gestured at the dogs on their leashes. "Bax is lookin' like he's on a bear. And old Roamer is snarling like there's somethin' over yonder hill that he's never smelled before."

The hunt master glanced at Serafina.

They had finally come to the stand of pines that she was looking for, but the trees were so thick and the limbs so low that there was no way for them to get their horses through. And she knew enough about hunting to know that there was nothing the hunt master liked less then ordering his riders to get off their horses. He'd rather go around something than dismount, but she was certain that the cages were *through* the pines.

"Straight through these trees," she said, signaling with her hand.

She had no authority to be telling the man how to manage his hunt, but she had to tell him what she knew. She glanced toward Mr. Vanderbilt, who had reined his horse up beside the hunt master.

But before the hunt master could give the call to dismount, an explosion of strange howls erupted from the trees. The barking, yipping, screaming howls put a shiver down Serafina's spine. They weren't the howls of wolfhounds or wolves, but something else. The men looked all around, their eyes white with fear as their horses shifted and turned, crashing into one another.

Pairs of glowing eyes came at them through the darkness, at least fifty, moving this way and that.

The Plott hounds barked and snarled, ready to fight.

"Hold steady, men!" the hunt master shouted, trying to bring order to the rapidly deteriorating situation. "Keep your seat beneath you!"

A snarling, twisting wolflike creature lunged out of the

darkness and attacked the hunt master's horse. The panicked horse went screaming onto its hind legs, rearing and striking.

"Pull back!" the hunt master shouted as more of the wolflike creatures came charging in, biting at the horses' legs, leaping onto the riders and pulling them from their saddles.

Fear exploded in Serafina. These weren't dogs or wolves. They were *coyotes*, a massive band of them, brought into the mountains by an unnatural force. Coyotes didn't normally come to these forests, for the wolves were their enemies.

Filled with panic, she sprinted toward Braeden, Rowena, and Mr. Vanderbilt through kicking horses, snarling coyotes, and screaming men. Her legs burst her forward, propelling her into the mayhem. She ducked and dove, dodging the vicious lunges of the coyotes as she ran.

The coyotes took down the two trackers even as the Plott hounds tore into the coyotes, but there were far too many of the coyotes for the hounds to battle them all.

Braeden and Mr. Vanderbilt were expert riders and had been alert to danger, so neither of them had fallen from their saddles in the initial surprise of the attack. But Mr. Vanderbilt's horse was bucking and shifting and throwing itself around, smashing into tree limbs, nearly knocking poor Mr. Vanderbilt from its back. It seemed as if even their horses had become their enemies now.

"Pull back!" the hunt master shouted as he struck a coyote in the snout with his torch.

"Braeden, come on!" Rowena called, shouting for them to retreat as she struggled to rein in her terrified, thrashing horse.

"We have to keep going!" Braeden screamed, desperately determined to help Cedric and Gidean, but finally even he was forced to pull back with the others.

Many of the men who had been thrown from their horses fled in terror on foot. Those who managed to stay in their saddles yanked their reins around and charged away. But the coyotes pursued them, snapping at their horses' legs and haunches, trying to corner and trap the lumbering horses in the heavy brush.

As the hunting party retreated in disarray back toward Biltmore, Serafina hunkered down to the ground at the base of a tree. She didn't know what to do. She found herself in a dark, quiet patch of the forest, all alone. She watched and listened to the chaos as it receded into the cloak of the forest's mist. A bout of hopelessness swirled through her. She couldn't fight off an entire band of coyotes. She couldn't settle the spirits of those panicked horses or bring calm to those struggling men. A lump formed in her throat as she caught one last glimpse of Braeden, Rowena, and Mr. Vanderbilt as they pulled away. She desperately wanted to follow them home. The thought of being left behind in this place terrified her.

But she did not move.

A dark and frightening thought crept into her mind. The only way she could save Gidean and Cedric was if she carried on alone, sneaking and crawling beneath the black limbs of the pitch-covered trees while the men battled the coyotes in the distance. Her only hope was to creep unseen and unheard into the dark lair of her enemy.

As she developed her plan in her mind, she heard something moving slowly toward her. At first she thought she heard four feet on the ground, but then she realized it wasn't a stalking coyote or wolfhound. The front two legs were softer of foot, more careful. The back two trudged along, sounding heavier. It wasn't *four feet*. It was two hands and two knees.

Braeden's head poked through the underbrush.

"Aw, Braeden, you shouldn't have come back!" Serafina said in exasperation. "What did you do?"

"I fell off my horse," he said, trying to sound innocent.

"You liar," she said. "You never fall off your horse!"

"But coyotes were attacking!"

She shook her head. "No, that wasn't it. I saw you, Braeden. You didn't fall off your horse!"

"Fine," he admitted finally. "I broke off from the main party, but my horse was too scared to come back up here. I couldn't convince him to go any farther, but I didn't want to leave you out here, so I slipped off and let him go back with the others. He'll be all right."

"It's not the horse I'm worried about!" she said, perturbed. "You should've stayed with the others."

"I didn't want to leave you alone out here in this terrible place in the dark."

"The darkness is where I belong," she said. "But you don't."

Braeden gestured toward the stand of pines. "I may not be able to see in the dark like you, Serafina, but if our dogs are in there, then I have to help them."

"What happened to Lady Rowena and your uncle? Are they all right?"

"Yes. They stayed with the rest of the hunting party."

"And that's where you should be." She stared at him, angry at his stubbornness. He had no idea what he was getting himself into. But she knew there was no talking him out of it.

"All right," she said finally, and crawled over to him. "We'll go in together, but you must stay close to me, and you must be absolutely quiet."

The two of them ducked below the lowest limbs and crept together into the thick stand of pines. The trunks and the branches and the ground itself were coated with sticky black sap that exuded like dark blood from the bark of the trees. The sap permeated everything with a reeking, sickeningly sweet smell. The upper boughs of the trees blocked the moon and the stars, cloaking the area beneath into a murky black world. Even she had trouble seeing.

She had to put her hand out in front of her to keep from running into dead hanging branches, but each time her fingers touched something in the darkness, the viscid pitch stuck to her fingertips, slowly coating her hands with an oily mucus. Her feet and hands kept sticking to the ground, making little sucking and snapping noises as she moved.

She knew that Braeden must be utterly blind, so she took his hand and put it on her shoulder. "Just hold on to me as we go through," she whispered. She could feel his hand trembling even as he held her. She couldn't imagine how terrifying it must be for him to creep blindly into this terrible place.

As they crept forward, moving from tree trunk to tree trunk along the pitch-coated ground, her nostrils wrinkled at a foul smell. At first she thought it must be the smell of rotting pinesap, but then she realized that it was the smell of animals, of animal waste. Then the smell got much worse.

She heard a hissing, gurgling, boiling sound just ahead and saw the orange flickering light of some sort of cooking fire in the distance.

"What is that?" Braeden whispered uncertainly, finally able to see something.

"That's where we're going," she said.

As they crawled forward into the smoky haze of the fire, Serafina's hand inadvertently touched a cold, flat, slimy surface that she thought was a rock. Looking down, it took her several seconds to realize that it wasn't. It was a gravestone, flat in the ground, so old that the letters and numbers had worn off and nothing was left but a blank surface.

In front of the gravestone, in the area of ground where the body lay below, there was an old mortsafe—a heavy, bolted iron cage, sunk low into the ground, long and narrow like the proportions of a body. She didn't know whether mortsafes were intended to keep grave robbers out or dead bodies in, but it was now being used for an even more horrifying purpose. A small door had been constructed at the end of the iron cage. Inside the cage lay a doe and two spotted fawns, staring out at her, crumpled down so low that they couldn't even stand.

Looking to the right and to the left, she saw that there were many of these old gravestones and iron cages, hundreds of them for as far as she could see. She had encountered the cages here a few nights before, but she hadn't realized they'd been constructed from the iron mortsafes of an old graveyard. There was an entire cemetery beneath the thick forest of pine trees. The graveyard had been abandoned long ago, and the forest of pines had grown on top of it. She looked around her. The cages were filled with animals of all kinds. In the next cage over, a mink ran back and forth, back and forth, desperately looking for a way out. The cage near Braeden held a friend of his: a small red fox, curled up tight and trembling in fear, its eyes staring at Braeden pleadingly.

"We have to let them go!" Braeden said, his voice shaking.

"Wait," she whispered. Seeing all these caged animals, she knew her enemy must be near. They had only so much time to do what they'd come to do. As they crept through the cages toward the fire, they passed a weasel and a family of raccoons. She could feel her pulse starting to pound in her temples, and her limbs starting to shake. She looked all around her, scanning the cages. Somewhere out there in the swirling mist, trapped in the cages beneath the low, dripping limbs of the pine trees, she knew that Gidean and Cedric lay helpless.

Suddenly, Braeden's hand gripped her shoulder so tightly that it hurt. She caught her breath when she saw the silhouette of the man walking in the distance. It was the gray-bearded man of the forest in his boots and his long, weather-beaten coat. He moved with strength and purpose, focused on his work. As he pushed handfuls of branches into the fire, swirls of sparks roiled upward. The blaze snapped and hissed with the new supply of burning sap. Then she saw the source of the terrible smell: the man was boiling something in the black iron pot resting in the fire.

Serafina's muscles jumped and buzzed. She wanted to run away. But at that moment, she heard a *tick-tick-ticking* sound, and then the terrible hissing scream as a barn owl flew in. She shoved Braeden flat to the ground, cowering in fear beneath the searching eyes of the owl as it flew low beneath the branches of the pines, right past them, and over to the fire and the bearded man. The owl dropped a crooked twig at the man's feet and then kept flying.

In response to the passing owl, the bearded man raised his chin and chattered a frightening cry, uttering the *tick-tick-ticking* sound followed by a low, self-satisfied hiss. She saw now that the owl wasn't just his familiar, or a servant under his command. There was alliance in that hiss, a dark and horrible love.

"We shall burn that place down!" he shouted to the owl. She could see his leathery, craggy face. He was a man possessed by a hatred and insanity more murderous than she had ever seen.

Braeden trembled beside her, his face as white as a ghost, his mouth gasping for breath. She clutched him to give him courage.

The man bent down and picked up the twig the owl had dropped. She thought he was going to throw it into the fire with the rest, but in the next moment, there was a trick in her eye, she flinched, and the small twig became as long and stout as a walking stick. It was the staff of power that Waysa had told her about. The Twisted Staff was blackish, thorned, and deeply gnarled, with what looked like a slithering snake or vine curling around and twisting along its length. And at this moment, the staff seemed to possess a seething, pulsing, demonic power, as if it sensed that soon it would gain even more.

At the man's feet lay a dark pile of skinned fur, black and brown and white, the remnants of animals that he had used in his terrible concoction. She couldn't imagine what horrible thing he was doing, but then he raised the Twisted Staff upward and dipped it into the pot, coating it over and over again with the thick, viscous liquid as he mumbled words she could not understand.

Then he drew the dripping staff from the putrid mixture and went over to one of the nearby cages. Serafina looked over and saw with horror what was inside. It was Gidean! Her friend crumpled down onto his haunches, his teeth snarling with anger, but his eyes filled with fear as the man approached the cage. The man pointed the staff at the cage. The cage door flung open. Gidean, his whole body trembling, crawled out of the cage toward the man. *Bite him, Gidean!* she wanted to scream. *Bite him and run!* But Gidean could not. The man was using the Twisted Staff to control him.

As she reached back to clamp her hand over Braeden's mouth, she knew it was too late. Seeing Gidean under the staff's control, Braeden made a sound of anguish. The bearded man's neck snapped around, and he looked straight at Braeden, his silver eyes blazing.

Serafina sprang into attack. She charged straight at him, knowing that her only chance was to take him down before he could lift his hand and throw a spell.

But the man raised his hand to his lips and blew across his open palm.

She felt the breath of death shoot through her. Her body went cold. Her muscles went limp. And she collapsed to the ground.

Braeden collapsed behind her.

Lying on the ground with her breath stolen and her heart stopped, the side of her face in the dirt, she gazed out through unblinking eyes. Braeden lay flat out on the ground beside her, just a few inches away, his eyes wide open, glazed and unmoving, staring at her in terror. She could not turn her head, but on the trunks of the pitch-blackened trees, she saw the flickering shadow of the bearded man moving toward them.

Serafina slowly became aware that she was awake, but she could not open her eyes, and she could not move. She could feel the cold earth beneath her and air moving ever so slowly into and out of her lungs, but she could not utter a sound.

She smelled dead pine needles and the sap-covered earth where her face lay against the ground. She tasted dirt in her mouth.

She was lying on her side, her right arm up by her head, her left arm bent beneath her body, twisted behind her at an unnatural angle, her legs crumpled up close to her. She sensed the crawling sensation of the wet sticky pitch on the bare skin of her legs, her arms, and her face, but she could not lift herself from it.

She could hear nothing but the faint and desolate sound of wind in the trees.

Is this how I'm going to die? she thought. And then she thought that it must be. She felt herself sinking down into darkness.

"Serafina!" someone whispered urgently to her, as if determined not to let her lose hope. The voice had no body, no face. It was not Braeden's voice, nor her pa's. And soon her certainty that she had heard the voice drifted away with the wind.

She lost consciousness again and then came back. Time went by. She wasn't sure how long. It could have been a few seconds, or a few minutes or a few hours.

When she was finally able to open her eyes, she still couldn't lift her head. She saw mostly blackened ground, and just above that, a crisscross of bolted iron bars and wire mesh, and through the cage to another cage that contained one of the white swans she had seen on Biltmore's lagoon a few nights before.

"Serafina!" the voice called again.

The sound was coming from the other side of the swan.

She slowly managed to lift her head.

It broke her heart to see a brown-skinned boy with long, shaggy dark hair in the cage there. He looked so small and weak in the cage that she almost didn't recognize him, but his brown eyes were looking back at her, his spirit fierce and unbroken, like a caged feral cat.

"Stay bold, Serafina!" he said, his voice filled with ragged emotion.

"Waysa . . ." she tried to say, but she barely heard her own dry, croaking voice. As she tried to get up, her head bumped against iron bars that held her to the ground. The bearded man had caged her to a grave in an iron mortsafe like all the other animals.

Craning her neck and peering between the iron bars, she looked out of her cage. She could see the bearded man working in his camp a short distance away. Her body jolted with fear at the sight of him, but the cage held her. She could not escape. The hissing, crackling fire glowed with flickering orange light, the sparks rising upward in a swirl and the haze of smoke drifting through the crooked branches of the trees.

The man moved around the fire, slowly feeding it fuel as he tended the iron pot. Splinters of scattered images poured into her mind as she remembered everything she had seen: the owl, the staff, the wolfhounds, the carriage, the horses, the rats, the coyotes. What did it all mean? The man dipped the Twisted Staff into the mixture over and over again, infusing it with its terrible power.

"What happened to you, Waysa?" she whispered. "How did you get here?"

"I had to save the cubs," he said, his voice grave. Serafina imagined that when the bearded man attacked, Waysa had turned to fight him rather than run from him, giving her mother and the cubs the split second they needed to escape.

A fierce wave of emotion filled her muscles with a little bit of strength. She tried to turn her body.

The eyes of a wolf peered at her through the iron bars of one of the adjacent cages. It was her old companion that she'd seen on the mountain ridge. Despite his valiant efforts to lead his pack to the safety of the highlands, they never made it out of the forest. As the wolf gazed at her from behind the bars, her heart sank. There was nothing she could do for him, nor he for her.

She was both relieved and heartbroken that Braeden lay in the cage next to her, his body facedown and outstretched beneath the iron bars of the mortsafe. He looked like the corpse of a boy who had crawled out of his grave but could get no farther, trapped beneath the bars. His body looked utterly lifeless, his skin pale and clammy, but his eyes were open, staring out in bewilderment.

"It's me, Braeden," she whispered over to him, trying to bring him around. She was pretty sure he was alive, but the conjurer's spell had hit him hard. "Wake up! It's me! It's Serafina!"

But even as she tried to rouse him, she wondered what they would do. What would come next? She was surrounded by caged animals. She *was* a caged animal. The bolted iron bars and the wire mesh in between were far too strong for her to break through. She pushed and pulled against the cage. She kicked at it and rammed it with her shoulder. But it made no difference. She could not get out.

Serafina tried digging down into the ground, past the pine needles into the dirt. She dug until her fingers bled, but it was no use. The mortsafe went deep into the ground. If she dug down deep enough, she'd find nothing but rotted boards, bones, and body.

The iron bars of the mortsafes were close enough together to keep an adult human from getting through, but on many of the cages, including the one she was in, the bearded man had installed wire mesh to make sure smaller animals could not fit between the iron bars and escape.

"I've tried to get through the wire," Waysa said as she examined the mesh on her cage. He started kicking the wire mesh with all his strength. It barely moved, but as Serafina saw the wire mesh flexing from the pressure of his kicks, she had an idea.

She pressed herself close up against the lower side of her cage. The wire mesh consisted of squares just big enough to fit several fingers through. She grabbed one strand of the mesh tightly in her fingers and bent it. Then she bent it back. She bent it again. And then back again. Over and over again.

"What are you doing?" Waysa whispered.

Serafina did not answer, she just kept bending that one strand of wire back and forth, back and forth. Her fingers were getting raw and her muscles ached. But finally, she felt the wire heating up. She kept bending and bending as fast as she could. Then it snapped! She'd broken the strand!

She couldn't help but smile when she saw the astonished look on Waysa's face. She had just broken metal with her bare hands. She was *magic*.

She immediately started on the next wire, bending, bending, bending, until it snapped in her fingers. "Thank you, Pa!" she whispered to herself as she moved on to the next wire. Working on one strand at a time, she slowly peeled back an area of the wire mesh close to the ground where the space between the iron bars was largest. She tried to crawl through the hole, but it was very tight. She couldn't get through.

"Get down, Serafina!" Waysa whispered a warning.

Serafina froze where she was, clinging to the dirt like a frightened animal as she heard the *tick-tick-ticking* sound and the raspy scream of the owl. It flew right over their heads as it came into the camp. The man hurled the staff up into the sky. It blurred into a twig. The owl caught it in midair with its claws, then disappeared into the trees.

Serafina didn't understand what was happening, but she was more determined than ever to get out. She pressed her face into the dirt and shoved her head into the hole. Buttressing her feet against the other side of the mortsafe, she used the strength of her legs and torso to push her head through the hole, scraping her ears so close that they tore and bled. She shifted her neck, bent in her shoulder blade at her detached collarbone, and wriggled herself into the hole. Once she got some of her head, shoulder, and arm through the hole, she reached out for something to grab onto so she could pull her whole body though, but there was nothing to grab, nothing to pull on. She clawed at the earth, but she found no purchase. Now she was stuck, wedged in the hole. She could move neither back nor forward.

When she looked around for a branch or a rock or something to hold on to, she saw Braeden in the cage next to her working furiously to bend the strands of the wire mesh like she had.

"Hold on, Serafina!" Braeden whispered, but she knew it was no use. His body was larger than hers. Even if he got through the mesh, he couldn't fit between the bars.

Nothing was working. Feeling the panic of entrapment, Serafina started gasping for air. Her heart pounded. She tried to keep her wits about her, but she breathed faster and faster. She looked toward the fire in the distance. How much time did they have before the bearded man came for them?

Finally, Braeden managed to break a small hole through the wire mesh of his cage. Just as she'd suspected, he couldn't fit his body through the narrow gap between the iron bars. But he put his hand through the hole and stretched his arm out toward her. At first, Serafina didn't understand what he was doing, but then she got it. She pressed herself up against the bars of her cage and stretched her arm out toward him. She pushed and pushed, her fingers outstretched. Reaching across the space between the cages, their hands finally clamped together in the middle. "Gotcha!" he said as he grabbed her hand. Then he pulled her toward him.

Now, with Braeden pulling on her arm and her pushing with her legs, she found the leverage she needed. She managed to wriggle herself all the way through the hole and crawled out on the other side. She made it through! She had escaped!

She quickly crawled over to Braeden's cage and tried to open the latch from the outside.

"He's coming!" Waysa whispered frantically.

Serafina heard the thrashing sound of the bearded man's footsteps heading in their direction.

She finally got Braeden's cage open and pulled him out. "Go free the dogs!" she whispered to him. Then she hurried over to Waysa's cage and unlatched it.

The bearded man would be here in a matter of seconds.

As Waysa crawled free, Serafina glanced over. Gidean and Cedric were down on their haunches, excitedly looking at Braeden as he opened their cages. Serafina used the last moment to quickly unlatch the wolf's cage. Her young wolf friend looked at her with gratefulness in his eyes. Then she raced away, knowing that the bearded man was just steps behind her.

She and Braeden and the others fled the cages, ducking low beneath the limbs of the pines as they ran.

Behind her, she heard the snarling attack of the freed wolf as it leapt from its cage at the bearded man. She had no idea what would happen next, but at least the wolf had a fighting chance.

Serafina, Braeden, Waysa, and the two dogs fled into the cover of the pines. Waysa led the way, often scouting ahead for danger. Serafina didn't know how it was possible, but Gidean seemed to have regained some of his old strength and speed. Cedric was a heavy dog, unused to running long distances, but he was determined to keep up. Serafina ran at Braeden's side, making sure he didn't fall behind. They finally escaped the blackened pines and entered the oaks, but they did not slow down. Their fear pushed them onward. They ran for miles.

But partway back to Biltmore, Braeden collapsed, too tired to continue. She let him rest for ten seconds, but then pulled him back up onto his feet. "Get up, Braeden!" she told him. "We've got to get home!"

They ran some more, but Braeden finally crumpled in exhaustion. Too tired to run any farther, he did not give up or ask the others to slow down. He called Cedric over to him. "I need your help, my friend," he said as he climbed onto the Saint Bernard's back and held on.

"Come on, Cedric! Come on, boy! Let's go!" Serafina called the dog, and together they ran. Coming from a long line of rescue dogs, Cedric seemed to understand exactly what they wanted. He charged forward with new speed and purpose, carrying the young master along with him.

They ran through the hickory and the hemlock, through the alder and the elm. They crossed thickets and meadows, streams and ravines, pushed by a fear darker than they had ever known.

As the faint light of Biltmore House finally came into view near dawn, Serafina sensed that they had escaped the horror behind them. She slowed and looked over at Waysa. They breathed heavily as they walked beside each other.

"I have to go back to Biltmore," she said.

Waysa nodded. "I'll go find your mother and the cubs and make sure they're safe." Then he stopped her with his hand and looked at her with new ferocity in his eyes. "You were right. We can't run from this fight. I will rejoin you later. Stay bold, Serafina."

"Stay bold, Waysa," she said in return as they quickly embraced, and then Waysa dove into the underbrush and disappeared.

Braeden watched her say good-bye to Waysa, and then said, "I see you found the boy from the forest."

"He joined with my mother and the cubs. His name is Waysa."

"He reminds me of you," Braeden said, his voice weak and tired, but filled with a kindness that she did not expect.

"Me too," she agreed.

"Do you want to go with him?" Braeden asked uncertainly. He looked toward the house in the distance. "The dogs and I can make it to Biltmore on our own from here."

"No," she said. "I want to go home with you."

Braeden nodded, and they continued on together toward Biltmore with Gidean and Cedric at their sides.

"Look," Serafina said when she saw a rider galloping at high speed across the large lawn in front of the house. The rider was up on her stirrups, leaning forward in the saddle, galloping at incredible speed, her long red hair flowing behind her. It was Lady Rowena!

Rowena rode into the stable courtyard.

When Serafina and Braeden and the two dogs walked into the courtyard a few moments later, a force of thirty men were gathering, some on foot, some with horses.

"Mount up, men," Mr. Vanderbilt shouted from atop his horse. "We're going back out."

Serafina and Braeden looked around at the ragged group. Many of the men from the original hunting party were wounded and exhausted. They had been fighting the coyotes in the forest all night. The horses had suffered the worst, and the trackers had lost all but one of the Plott hounds. The badly shaken hunt master, who had dismounted from his sweating, terrified horse and now sat collapsed on the ground, appeared too shocked by what they'd been through to even rouse himself. But most of the men were mounting fresh horses, and new men were joining the effort.

Rowena was right there with Mr. Vanderbilt, on a new horse and ready to ride. Her hair was hanging down, her face was scratched, and she looked exhausted, but she seemed determined to help in the search.

"Come on, hurry," Rowena was calling to the others as she wheeled her horse around. "We have to go and look for them!"

Serafina's pa, several of the stablemen, and a dozen other servants were also joining the group.

But when Mr. Vanderbilt pulled his horse around, he saw Braeden and Serafina and the dogs coming toward him.

"Thank God," Mr. Vanderbilt said. He dismounted, dropped his reins, and took the exhausted Braeden into his arms.

"Serafina," her pa said, relieved, as he came toward her and pulled her into his chest.

"I'm all right, Pa," she said. "I'm not hurt."

As she hugged her pa, Serafina saw Rowena dismount and

embrace Braeden, obviously relieved that he was still alive. The other men were patting the young master's back and welcoming him home.

Mr. Vanderbilt knelt down and scruffed Cedric's neck. "It's good to see you, boy," he said as he petted his dog. Then Mr. Vanderbilt's dark eyes rose up and looked at Serafina.

"I'm sorry, sir," she said, her voice shaking, fearful that he'd be angry at her for leading them into such a catastrophe. As she and her pa turned toward Mr. Vanderbilt, she said, "I had no idea that was going to happen."

"None of us have ever seen anything like that," he said. He wasn't angry with her. His voice was filled with a sense of common purpose. They were a pack. They were in this together.

"Could the coyotes have been infected with rabies?" her pa asked.

"I hope to God not," the veterinarian said, overhearing their conversation as he tended to the slashed leg of a nearby horse. "If it's rabies, then all the men, horses, and dogs who were bitten last night will be dead within days, and there's nothing we can do about it."

"It didn't look like rabies to me," Mr. Vanderbilt said, shaking his head. "There had to be fifty coyotes, and they had a deliberateness in their eyes."

The hunt master shook his head. "Those animals were possessed," he mumbled, his eyes glazed with disbelief.

"We need to go back, Uncle," Braeden said.

"Go back?" Mr. Vanderbilt said in surprise.

"There are still animals up there that need our help."

Mr. Vanderbilt shook his head. "I'm sorry, Braeden. We're not going back out right now. We can't risk it. Everyone is exhausted. We need to rest and regroup."

"It was awful, Uncle," Braeden said, and then proceeded to describe the bearded man and the animals in the cages. "Serafina got me and the dogs out of there, and then we ran."

When Mr. Vanderbilt looked at Serafina, she could see the gratitude in his expression, but she knew the fight wasn't over. "We need to find Mr. Grathan, sir," she said. "He's involved in this."

"I was suspicious of him from the start," Mr. Vanderbilt said. "He represented himself as an officer of the law, so I didn't think I should interfere with his investigation, but I hired a private detective to check into his credentials."

"What did you find out?" Braeden asked.

"Mr. Grathan has no association with any city or state agency. He's a fraud."

"What are we going to do, Uncle?" Braeden asked.

"I've sent word for the Asheville police to come at once. They'll arrest him."

"But where is Grathan now?" Serafina asked.

"We've searched for him. He's not in the house," Mr. Vanderbilt said. "But he may still be on the grounds."

"I think Grathan is far more dangerous than he seems, sir," Serafina said. "And I fear that the police will be coming on horseback or carriage and will run into the same type of problem we did."

Mr. Vanderbilt nodded. "We'll arm several groups of men

and start looking for Grathan on the grounds. If and when the police arrive, we'll go back up into that area, free those animals, and destroy the cages. Until then, I want all of you to stay in the house and stay safe."

As the men continued talking, Serafina, Braeden, and Rowena huddled beneath the arch of the Porte Cochere, the carriage entrance that led into the house.

"What happened?" Rowena asked, her voice quivering.

"We're all right," Braeden said. "We got the dogs. That's the important thing."

"I was so worried about you," she said, looking at both Braeden and Serafina. Serafina realized that danger and death seemed to erase the lines of class. Suddenly, everyone was the same, fighting to hold on to their lives and the people around them. She saw it in Mr. Vanderbilt, her pa, the hunt master, the trackers, and the men on their horses willing to go out into fearsome dangers to rescue her and Braeden. And now she saw it in Lady Rowena.

"Thank you for helping us, Rowena," Braeden said.

"When my father sent me here to Biltmore, he told me to make friends," Lady Rowena said, looking at the two of them and smiling wanly. "I think maybe I have."

"You definitely have," Braeden said.

"Will your father be coming to Biltmore soon?" Braeden asked.

"I believe he'll be here rather sooner than we all expect," Rowena said. "He's coming for Christmas."

Serafina thought she sensed something strange in Rowena

when she said this. Was it sadness? Worry? She couldn't quite place it.

"Are you eager to see him?" Serafina asked.

"The truth is," Rowena said, "my father thinks I am a rather silly little girl."

"I'm sure that's not true," Braeden said.

Rowena shook her head. "No, it's true. I'm afraid my father has never thought too much of me. But pretty soon, one way or another, he's going to have to start."

"He'd be very proud of you if he knew how brave you were last night," Serafina said, trying to encourage her.

But as they were talking, Rowena looked like she was going to keel over right where she stood. Exhaustion had finally begun to catch up with the poor girl. Braeden reached out to steady her.

"If you will excuse me," Lady Rowena said finally, touching Braeden's arm and closing her eyes for a moment like she was going to faint, "I'm feeling rather tired. I'm going to my room to take a bath and change into some clean clothes."

Braeden nodded. "Get some rest and we'll do the same. My uncle and the men will take care of things now."

As two of the maids helped the bedraggled, mud-splattered Lady Rowena limp slowly back to the house, Serafina heard her mutter in bewildered shock, "Oh dear, I think I may have gotten dirt on my dress." She was so exhausted she was nearly delirious.

Serafina stayed with Braeden. As she looked over at Mr. Vanderbilt talking to her pa and the other men, she knew they were making sensible decisions, but she couldn't get over the feeling that it wasn't enough, that everyone, including her, was missing something. It was as if they were putting together a puzzle, and they thought they were almost done, but there was a whole other box of pieces that they didn't even know about.

She watched as the stablemen washed the blood from the courtyard bricks and the maids cleaned the mud from the steps that led into the house.

"Come on," Serafina said to Braeden, and they began to walk along the front of the house. "We need to figure this out."

"Whoever that man was last night, he seemed insane," Braeden said.

"Like he was consumed by some sort of feud or blood vengeance."

"He said he was going to burn the place down," Braeden said.

Serafina remembered the chilling words.

"What do you think he was talking about?" Braeden asked.

"I'm not sure," she said.

"Do you think he was talking about Biltmore?" Braeden asked.

As they reached the front entrance of the house, Serafina glanced up at the carved stone archway above the front door. It depicted a strange-looking bearded man brandishing a long spear or staff of some kind.

"I don't know. It's definitely possible. Does the Vanderbilt family have enemies?" she asked. "What about your uncle? Does anyone hate him or want to do him harm?"

"No, I don't think so," Braeden said. "He's a good man."

"I know he is," Serafina said. "But is there something from his past that we don't know? What do we know about his life back in New York before he came here? Or all his trips to Europe and all over the world? Could it be that he came to the remote mountains of North Carolina for a reason?"

"You think he was trying to escape something?"

"Or maybe *someone*? I don't know," she said.

"Come on," Braeden said, leading her into the house. "I have an idea."

The two of them were tired, dirty, and hungry, but they were too intent on solving the mystery to stop now. Serafina followed Braeden down the gallery and into the Library.

"What are we looking for?" Serafina asked as they entered, not sure how Mr. Vanderbilt's collection of books could help them.

"My uncle keeps his travel records here," Braeden said as he went over to one of the cabinets. "Maybe we'll find something."

Serafina went to Braeden's side and tried to help him look. But she wasn't sure what they were looking for.

She found a set of black leather-bound journals entitled *Books I Have Read—G.W.V.* As she flipped through the pages, she saw that Mr. Vanderbilt had been recording the title and author of every book he'd read since 1875, when he was twelve years old. There were thousands of entries over the years, in English, French, and other languages.

Braeden found evidence of his uncle's many trips throughout the United States and abroad, to England, France, Italy,

China, Japan, and many other countries. And she knew that the house was full of art, sculpture, and artifacts from his travels. In fact, she'd just shattered one of them. Any one of those artifacts could have been haunted or cursed in some way, which might explain a blood vengeance against Mr. Vanderbilt.

But the more she thought about it, the more one particular thought came to her mind. The man she'd seen on the road that first night hadn't struck her as a New Yorker or any other kind of northerner or foreigner. His skin was craggy with the weathered cracks of these mountain winds, his mustache and beard were long and gray like many of the local elders', and his voice was tinged with the sound of the mountain folk. She could not be sure from their brief and terrifying encounters, but he seemed like an Appalachian man.

She remembered the disturbing words he'd screamed to the owl: "We shall burn that place down!"

"Let's look into the records of Biltmore House," she said.

"Not my uncle's travels?"

"No, let's focus on Biltmore," she said, more confident now.

"Those are over here," he said, leading her to a different set of boxes.

As they dug through the papers, it was hard to imagine finding any answers there, but when Braeden opened a box of scratchy old photographs, she leaned in closer.

The first photograph she examined showed a vast stretch of clear-cut land with nothing but stumps and weeds, a team of twenty or thirty mules, a couple of wagons piled with firewood, and a score of scroungers with axes. It was hard to imagine, but judging by the view of the mountains in the background, it appeared to be the hilltop on which Biltmore was constructed. The clearing was so open and bare and treeless. There were no gardens, no woods, just scarred and empty land. This was how it had looked when Mr. Vanderbilt bought the land years before.

The next photograph showed hundreds of stonemasons, bricklayers, carpenters, and other craftsmen building the lower floors of Biltmore House. There were men and women, white folk and black folk, Americans and foreigners, northerners and southerners, and many mountain folk. Her heart warmed when she spotted her pa in one of the photographs, working on a geared crane system among many other men. She smiled, for in her mind, she'd always imagined her pa working alone, building Biltmore almost by himself, for that was how she'd always seen him working. She realized how foolish she had been. He had been but one of thousands of men who had worked for six years. It was amazing to see the scaffolded walls of Biltmore rising from nothingness in photograph after photograph.

A while later, as she searched through the documents of Biltmore trying to find the clues they needed, Serafina looked over at Braeden. Exhausted, he had fallen asleep in one of the cushioned chairs. Serafina let him sleep, but she kept looking.

"I'm starving," Braeden announced when he awoke. They quickly retrieved some food from the kitchen. But as soon as they'd eaten and washed up, they went back to work.

Later that afternoon, as Braeden was digging through yet another box, he handed her a photograph. "Look at this one."

Something about it caught Serafina's eye. Like the other photographs, this one was filled with men and wooden scaffolding, and the half-built Biltmore rising in the background. She wasn't even sure what the photographer had been trying to make a picture of, other than the construction site itself. Some of the men in the picture were working, some talking, some looking at the camera, others not. When she studied the photograph more closely, one of the men drew her attention. The image was so small it was difficult to tell, but he had a heavily wrinkled face and a long gray mustache and beard. He was not wearing a long coat or carrying a walking stick, but he was gazing into the camera and his eyes looked like dots of silver. It was their enemy—the man she'd seen in the forest. This was him. She was sure of it. That meant he wasn't a forest haint or nightmarish specter, but a real person. At least, he had been years before.

"Braeden, look at this," Serafina said, showing him the photograph. "We need to know who this man is."

"Then we need to talk to Mr. Olmsted," Braeden said.

As Braeden led Mr. Olmsted into the Library, Serafina watched the balding, gray-bearded old man carefully.

"How can I help the two of you?" he asked as he made his way into the room, using his wooden cane for balance. "Sounds like it was a bad business all around last night, especially for you two."

A little startled that Mr. Olmsted was so aware of what was going on, Braeden looked over at Serafina, who was standing by the giant globe.

Serafina shook her head slowly to Braeden. *Don't talk about it. Just get on with our question.*

"Sir," Braeden said, "since you were in charge of many of

the work crews during Biltmore's construction, we were wondering if you could help us with some photographs we found."

"I can certainly try, Master Braeden," he said as he settled onto the sofa in front of the fireplace. "This looks like a nice, warm spot."

"So here is the photograph that we—"

"Perhaps we should have a nice hot cup of tea before we get started," Mr. Olmsted said, seeming not to hear that Braeden had already started talking.

"Uhhh . . ." Braeden hesitated, glancing again at Serafina. "Certainly, of course," he said as he went over to the wall and pressed the button for the butler's pantry.

"While we're waiting for the tea, perhaps we can look at this photograph," Serafina said, taking the photo from Braeden and walking over to Mr. Olmsted.

"We certainly can, Serafina," Mr. Olmsted said. It startled her when Mr. Olmsted used her name. She didn't even realize that he knew she existed. But then he patted the cushion next to him and invited her to sit beside him. Surprised, she sat on the sofa with him and put the photograph in his hands.

"Oh, this is an old one. . . ." Mr. Olmsted said, studying the photograph with interest. His hands trembled as he held it.

"Do you recognize this man here?" Serafina asked, pointing.

"You rang, sir?" the footman said as he came into the Library in his black-and-white livery.

"Mr. Olmsted would like a cup of tea, please," Braeden said.

"Right away, sir," the footman said, and exited.

Serafina watched as Mr. Olmsted studied the face in the photograph. His expression started out mildly curious, as if he was remembering the fond days of old when he was designing the gardens, sculpting the land, and supervising the crews as they planted thousands upon thousands of trees, bushes, and flowers. But then his expression shifted. He narrowed his eyes and brought the photograph up close to his face.

"Maybe this will help, sir," Braeden said, handing him a magnifying glass he'd pulled from a nearby table.

"Oh, yes, thank you, Master Braeden," Mr. Olmsted said, and studied the photograph. "Yes, I remember this fellow," he said finally.

"Who was he?" Serafina asked.

For several seconds, Mr. Olmsted seemed lost in thought, as if he was trying to figure out how to answer her question. "Well, I will tell you a story about a piece of land not too far from here," he said finally. "Years ago, George Vanderbilt was traveling the country with his mother. He was still a young man, just twenty-six years old. He went out riding his horse one day in the mountains, and he drew rein at the top of a hill. He thought the prospect of the distant scenery very fine. It occurred to him that one day he would like to build a house in that location. He bid his lawyer to see if it was possible to purchase that particular parcel of land. Finding the price to be cheap and the owner anxious to sell, he instructed his lawyer to buy that land and all around it. After securing many thousands of acres, George finally invited me to the location and took me out to that spot on the hill. He said to me, 'Now, I have brought you here to examine this land and tell me if I have been doing anything very foolish.'"

Mr. Olmsted smiled as he remembered his friend's words.

"What did you tell him?" Braeden asked. "Was it foolish?"

"Well, I told him the hard truth of it. The site had a good distant outlook, but the land itself had been abused by scavengers and subsistence farming for many years, the soil was depleted, and the woods were miserable, the very hillsides eroding for lack of trees and undergrowth. The squatters who occupied the area didn't own the land, but they had cut down the trees for their cabins and fuel, and most especially to sell the wood in the city. I watched as these squatters drew jags of hickory cordwood to the city in their carts, selling the wood to the highest bidder. You see, back then, wood was almost a form of currency, and these men were stealing it right out of the forest until there was no forest left, and then they'd go on to the next mountain. They had chopped and burned most of the forest in the area."

"Burned?" Braeden asked in dismay.

Mr. Olmsted nodded. "After cutting down all the trees, they made grazing fields for their cattle and hogs. The native cherry, tulip, black walnut, locust, and birch that were so vital to these mountains had all been destroyed. Corn, grain, and tobacco had been grown year after year until the soil was worn out. This was not unusual for the cotton states after the war. Much of the land had been ravaged and lay in a most desperate state."

"So my uncle had made a terrible mistake just like he

feared," Braeden said in astonishment. "Did he abandon that property and come and find the Biltmore land with all its beautiful trees?"

Mr. Olmsted smiled a slight but devilish grin beneath his mustache, as if Braeden's words had pleased him. "Not exactly. I told your uncle that the hilltop on which he hoped to build a house did indeed have a lovely view, and the distant acres had potential. I explained that with extensive planting, I thought we could rebuild the natural environment that had been lost. It would take time and money, thousands upon thousands of plantings, and years to grow. It had never been done on this scale before, but if we could do it, then it would set an example for reforestation throughout the South and, indeed, throughout all of America. We would show the way to conserve and build our forests, rather than just cut them down."

"Wait," Braeden said. "I don't understand. Are you saying that was *Biltmore*?"

Mr. Olmsted smiled. "You are currently standing in the exact spot on which your uncle sat on his horse, looked across the mountain view, and decided he wanted to build a house."

"But all the beautiful trees and the gardens . . ." Braeden said.

"We planted them," Mr. Olmsted said simply.

Serafina sat mesmerized, listening to Mr. Olmsted. Unlike Braeden, who was a relative newcomer to the estate, she had grown up here from the very beginning with her pa, so she knew the story, but she still enjoyed hearing it. It amazed her the way Mr. Olmsted thought about things on such a vast scale, across the mountains and the whole country, and over decades of time. It seemed like she spent most of her time trying to survive the next few seconds. She couldn't even imagine what it must be like to envision the landscape decades in advance.

But her thoughts soon turned to the dark business that had brought them to this moment.

"But who is the man in the photograph, Mr. Olmsted?" she asked.

"Ah, yes," Mr. Olmsted said, turning more serious. "That's where our story continues. That same year, as we began the reclamation work, we soon learned that the clear-cutting and selling of the wood wasn't just happenstance. It wasn't just individual scavengers passing through. There was a depraved and conniving man named Uriah organizing it all. He didn't have any more right to this land than the other squatters, but he was a trickster, a deceiver. He did favors for people and then held them accountable. He lent money on ill terms. Most of the squatters in the area were obligated to him in some way or another, and the others feared him, for those who opposed him met with violent ends. By the time we arrived, he controlled them all. I think he must have been an old slaver or something because he seemed to relish having power over other people. He seemed obsessed with controlling *everything*."

"But my uncle had bought the land," Braeden said, confused.

"That's right, he had. Over a hundred twenty-five thousand acres, covering four counties. He had bought it lawfully from its original owners, but these marauders of the forest did not care who legally owned the land, and neither did Uriah. They had been cutting these trees for years and no one was going to stop them. To Uriah, this land was his domain and his alone."

His domain and his alone, Serafina thought.

"None of us realized when we started the reclamation of the land and the construction of the house that we'd have to deal with this Uriah fellow. Despite the power he had held over the local squatters for many years, it was obvious to us that Uriah's better days were behind him. I think he might have been injured in the war or weakened by a devastating disease. He was in bad shape. He seemed desperate in his dealings with us, like he was barely hanging on to the last vestiges of the corrupted empire he'd built here. We couldn't figure out why he didn't just give up his illegal claims and go away. It was like his very life depended on it. In any case, he obviously wasn't the type of man to go easily. He started putting up a serious fight."

"What did my uncle do?" Braeden asked.

"Well, we wouldn't let a man like Uriah get anywhere near your uncle, of course. But Mr. McNamee, the estate superintendent, had plenty of run-ins with the wretch, as did Mr. Hunt, the house's architect, and I. One confrontation after another. We began bypassing Uriah and dealing with the squatters directly. We gave them jobs and farmland to work. We needed the help and they were happy to join us. Many of them settled into cabins on the property or found homes in town. But Uriah hated us, challenged us constantly, telling us what we could and couldn't do, what boundaries we could and couldn't cross, as if he himself owned the land. We were in the right by morals and the law, so it would have been easy to discount the man, but I tried to deal with him fairly. I never trusted him, but I sensed that he was far more sinister than he seemed, and I was loath to make him too sharp an enemy. There's nothing more dangerous than a desperate man. But Mr. Hunt didn't share my trepidation of Uriah. He treated him with all the respect he deserved. Which is to say, none at all. And Uriah despised Mr. Hunt for it."

"But Uriah didn't know Mr. Vanderbilt?" Serafina asked, confused.

"Not personally, no, but he definitely knew *of* him. Uriah hated George Vanderbilt most of all, for he saw George as the master of all his misfortune."

"But it wasn't my uncle's fault!" Braeden insisted.

"No, it wasn't," Mr. Olmsted agreed. "But Uriah didn't see it that way."

Serafina and Braeden remained quiet as the footman entered the room with a silver tray of fine Biltmore-monogrammed china, and then proceeded to serve Mr. Olmsted his tea. Slowly, one by one, he set out a finely decorated saucer, a teacup, a teapot, a bowl of sugar, a teaspoon, and a creamer, and then he slowly poured the steaming tea while they all waited in silence. It seemed like it was taking forever. When the footman was finally gone, Serafina jumped right back into the conversation.

"What happened to Uriah in the end?" Serafina asked.

Mr. Olmsted took a sip of his tea and then set the cup down on its saucer with a light *tink*. "Well, he confronted us one too many times, and we all lost our patience. I'm afraid we had a most violent exchange of words. Finally, Mr. McNamee ordered his security men, more than twenty armed men on horseback, to tie his hands and take Uriah away by force."

"What did they do to him?" Braeden asked.

"They took him by train to the coast. I believe they mentioned something about putting him on a ship bound for foreign lands. In any case, we were glad to see the back of him."

"Uriah must have been very angry about that," Serafina said.

"Anger doesn't begin to describe his state of mind. I won't repeat all the obscenities he cast at us, but he cursed us up and down and vowed he'd return and kill us all. 'Even if it takes me a hundred years,' he screamed, 'I'm going to come back here and burn your house to the ground!' "

"Wait," Serafina said. "Is that actually what he said, those exact words?" A lump formed in her throat, for she already knew the answer. She could just imagine hearing him scream those words. In fact, she was pretty sure she already had.

She sucked in a breath. At long last, she had finally marked her enemy. This man, Uriah, was a shifter and a conjurer like Waysa had said, kin to the white-faced owl, sorcerer of the dark arts, his power tied to the land. He was the old man of the forest that the mountain folk told stories about around their fires at night. He was the deceiver and master of the tree-killing squatters that Mr. Olmsted had seen. And he was the enemy that her mother and father and the other catamounts had fought against and weakened twelve years before. By the time of Biltmore's construction, Uriah could no longer hold on to his malicious realm. But when he was cast out into the world, he began regathering his strength, finding new dark arts to wield, turning his pain and his hatred into a black and sinister magic more powerful than ever before—all so that one day he could come back to these mountains, burn Biltmore to the ground, and reclaim his dark domain.

She knew now that when she put on the Black Cloak, it had deceived her, tried to convince her that it had been created for good, but it hadn't. Uriah had pulled Mr. Thorne into his web of deceit and sent him into Biltmore to gather souls, to gather power. And now Uriah was making the Twisted Staff to give him control over the animals. Uriah wanted the people, and the animals, and the forest, and the land, and he was going to use his demons and his devices to do it. He wanted to control it all.

"Are you all right?" Braeden asked, touching her arm.

She blinked and pulled herself out of her thoughts and looked at him. "Yes, I'm all right, I'm sorry, go ahead."

"Mr. Olmsted," Braeden asked, "would it truly be possible for someone to burn down Biltmore?"

"I'm not the architect, but I can tell you what I know."

"Pardon me, Mr. Olmsted," Serafina interjected suddenly as a thought came into her mind. "What happened to Mr. Hunt?"

"In the last year of the house's construction, just a few months before the greatest work of his life was completed, our friend Mr. Hunt sadly passed away."

"He died?" Braeden asked.

"Yes, I'm afraid so. We were all very shocked and devastated by the terrible turn of events."

"How did he die?" Serafina asked.

"He got a cold first, and then a bad cough, and then his gout flared up. The doctors weren't sure, but in the end, it appeared that he died of heart failure."

"A cold?" Braeden said, shocked. "It started with a cold?"

This news seized Serafina with new fear. No one died from a cold. Was this what was happening to Mrs. Vanderbilt? Was it the same sickness? Had Uriah cast a spell on the mistress of Biltmore?

"You were going to tell us about the possibility of fire," Braeden urged Mr. Olmsted.

"As you can imagine, Mr. Hunt was very concerned about fire at Biltmore, and being a shrewd man, he incorporated many defenses against it. First, he built the entire underlying structure of the house from steel girders, brick walls, and stone, rather than wood. Second, the house is divided into six separate sections so that if a fire did start, it could not spread. And third, there are fire detectors throughout the house—all tied together by an electric alarm system."

When Mr. Olmsted said these words, Serafina looked at Braeden and Braeden looked at her. *The rats . . .*

"It was all beyond me, of course," Mr. Olmsted continued. "I'm a planter of trees, not an electrical engineer, but I remember that it was all very advanced."

"But what if someone lit the fire on purpose?" Serafina asked.

Mr. Olmsted shook his head. "They might try, but thanks to Mr. Hunt, it would be difficult to succeed. First, they would need to defeat the fire alarm, and second, they would need to know the internal details of the house's six sections to know exactly where to light the fires."

"Did Uriah see all that when the house was being built?" Braeden asked.

"Oh, no, he had no access to such information."

"Is there a way someone could find out about it?" Braeden asked.

"Well, I suppose. The details of Mr. Hunt's construction are described in his drawings."

"Where are those?" Serafina asked.

"Don't worry," Mr. Olmsted said. "No one could ever reach those plans. They are kept hidden and protected under lock and key in this very room."

After Mr. Olmsted left the Library, Braeden looked at Serafina. "What are we going to do?"

"First, you need to tell your uncle about what we've learned. I'll go ask my pa to make sure the fire alarm system is working. But before I do that, do you remember the night we were attacked by the horde of rats?"

"We were going to search Grathan's room."

"But the rats stopped us," she said. "Then the dogs went missing. I don't know where Grathan has gone to, but I'm going to sneak into his room and search it."

"You be careful," Braeden said as he nodded his agreement. He glanced out the window toward the setting sun. "When I talk to my uncle, I'll also find Rowena. She'll be wondering where we are."

"Lady Rowena was very brave last night," Serafina said. "You go find her. Let's meet on the back Loggia in half an hour."

"Got it," Braeden said.

As she headed up the back stairs to the third floor, she tried to think everything through. It was clear that Uriah had conjured the Twisted Staff to help him destroy Biltmore and the Vanderbilts. But just as Waysa had said, Uriah didn't fight straight on. He wasn't wielding the staff himself. He had sent in Grathan, his apprentice and spy. When she came to the hallway that led to the Van Dyck Room, she paused and took a deep breath. She'd tried to get into this room multiple times before and failed, but this time she was determined to do it.

She crept down the hallway and pressed her ear to the door, listening for movement within. When she didn't hear anything, she slowly turned the doorknob. It was locked. She wished she had Mrs. King's master key ring, but she didn't.

She ran down the corridor, slipped into a heating vent, and climbed through the wall. It took her a while to find her way through the shafts, but she finally found the brass register she was looking for and pushed into Mr. Grathan's room.

She felt like she was crawling into a dragon's lair. But she found herself in an elegantly attired chamber, with goldenrod damask wallpaper, a parquet wood floor, a Persian rug, a small fireplace, and chestnut furniture. The walls were adorned with Van Dyck prints hanging on the wall by long steel wires. It surprised her, but there was nothing obviously wrong or out of place about the room. *I guess there's no dead cat,* she thought, remembering Essie's expression.

But the room wasn't entirely empty, either. A worn shirt and a wrinkled pair of trousers lay draped over one of the chairs. Three leather suitcases sat on the floor. It made her palms sweat to think about it, but Mr. Grathan could come back at any moment.

She searched the room as fast as she could, looking for shoes and clothing stained with pinesap or the black smudges of fire coals. It crossed her mind that she might even find incriminating containers of the highly flammable sap itself. She reckoned the pine forest wasn't just a way for Uriah and Grathan to conceal themselves, but part of their plan to destroy Biltmore. Her pa had told her once that there was nothing hotter than a forest fire burning through a stand of pines, that the trunks of the trees actually exploded when the sap boiled. It would be an ideal way to start a fire inside a house, even one that was designed not to burn.

When she didn't find what she was looking for, she opened one of his leather suitcases and rummaged through it. Nothing but clothes. She opened up the next suitcase. Still nothing. After checking the third, she finally stopped. She gazed around the room, frustrated.

There's nothing here. . . .

From what she could find, Mr. Grathan appeared to be a normal, everyday man. She pursed her lips and breathed through her nose, perturbed.

This doesn't make sense. . . .

Where were the fire matches and containers of pinesap? Where were the books filled with pentagrams, runes, and evil spells? Grathan had been so determined to make sure no one entered his room, but what had he been doing? Hiding his stupid toothbrush?

There has to be something here. . . .

She went back and double-checked the leather suitcases. She searched them more thoroughly this time, looking for unusual seams or details that seemed out of place. Then she found it. There was a small hidden compartment in the lining of one of the cases.

Now, this is interesting. . . .

Inside, she found newspaper clippings—some tattered, going back years, others more recent—but they were all articles about hauntings, strange disappearances, and gruesome murders. Many of the names and cities in the articles were underlined.

What are you doing, Mr. Grathan?

Along with the clippings, she found an old, tattered map of the United States. Each of the locations mentioned in the various articles was circled and also marked with what looked like a small *X*. But then she realized they weren't *X*'s. They were little crosses. And even more disturbing, some of the locations were marked with more than one.

Her first thought was that he was obsessed with following reports of occult and supernatural phenomenon. But then she realized that maybe he wasn't just a follower. Maybe he was the *cause* of these events.

Wherever he goes, people die.

Her heart began to pound. She dug through the clippings again, checking the date on each one. The headline of the most recent one read, *The Mysterious Disappearance of Montgomery Thorne.*

Grathan truly had come to investigate Mr. Thorne's disappearance, but he wasn't a police detective. Why had he come?

Besides Mr. Thorne, three names were mentioned in the article, the known residents of Biltmore Estate: George, Edith, and Braeden Vanderbilt.

This isn't good. . . .

Most of the circles on the map were worn and faded, but there was one that stood out: the circle that marked the location of Biltmore Estate. There was no cross beside it.

After going to all these other places, he's come here. . . .

She gazed around the room, trying to think.

The room is so empty, so few clues. But there has to be a way . . .

She stood and she turned.

How can I see what can't be seen?

She noticed a slight discoloration on the floor in front of one of the upholstered chairs. She got down on her hands and knees and put her nose to that area of the carpet.

It's dirt from a shoe. . . . It's a scuff mark. . . . Mr. Grathan sat in this chair. . . .

She moved upward and ran her nose slowly along the arm of the chair, sniffing for scents. At first she couldn't pick up anything other than the fabric itself. Then she caught a faint but extremely distinct smell.

I've smelled this before. . . .

It was the scent of some kind of powdery stone. And she could smell the lingering trace of metal. It seemed so familiar. She could picture it in her mind, but she couldn't think of its name. It was a small, rectangular, smooth gray stone.

It's a whetstone! That's what my pa called it.

She'd seen her pa use a whetstone in the workshop to scrape a steel blade until its gleaming edges were razor sharp.

She swallowed.

Grathan sat in this chair and sharpened a bladed weapon. . . .

Her chest began to rise and fall more heavily, her lungs wanting more air. She tried to think it through.

Uriah summoned Grathan here. But Grathan isn't just spy. . . . He's an assassin!

He isn't just a murder investigator. He's the murderer!

She couldn't help but look around the room, but she'd already searched it. There was no weapon to be found.

How does he carry the weapon and conceal it?

And more important, who has he come to kill?

She remembered that Essie and Rowena had told her that Grathan had asked many questions about Mr. Thorne, Gidean, and Braeden. One was already dead. One was a dog.

There was only one name remaining. . . .

When she heard a noise outside the room, she hit the floor and slid under the bed.

She waited and listened, her chest rapidly pulling air into her lungs.

She heard the muffled sounds.

There was some sort of commotion out in the corridor, people talking, a sense of alarm.

Her chest filled with panic. She sniffed the air for the smell of smoke, but didn't detect any.

She quickly crawled out from under the bed and went over to the door. When she heard Essie's voice, she quickly stepped out of the room.

"Oh, miss, it's you!" Essie said in surprise. "What are you doing here?"

"Is there a fire?" Serafina asked. "What's happening?"

"We came up lookin' for *you*, miss," Essie said.

"Me? Why me?"

"Someone told Master Braeden that you were seen in the gardens badly injured. Master Braeden was all a-jumble about where you were, so he sent us up here to look for you while he searched outside."

"Injured?" Serafina said in bewilderment. "I'm not injured. Who told him that?"

At that moment, Serafina remembered the night she'd caught the wood rat: every time it tried to run away, her reflex had been to snatch it up again. When she fell from the Grand Staircase, her reflex had landed her on her feet. Reflexes were a powerful and useful force. But they could be used against you. She knew it because she'd done it. A few weeks ago, she had walked the corridors of Biltmore dressed as a defenseless victim in a fancy red dress. She had used Mr. Thorne's reflex against him and lured him to his demise.

But now here she was.

Someone was in control and it wasn't her.

If she was suddenly discovered to be missing and thought to be injured, who was the first person at Biltmore who would react? Who would immediately jump onto his horse and ride blindly out into the darkness of the night all by himself to save her?

She imagined running out into the gardens and finding Braeden's lifeless body lying on the ground, ambushed and stabbed to death by a man with a sharpened blade.

She grabbed Essie's arm. "I'm going to go out and find Braeden and bring him back. But you need to do something very important. Run downstairs as fast as you can and get my pa, Mr. Olmsted, and Mr. Vanderbilt. I want you to tell them to check the plans of the house and find the places it's most vulnerable to fire. Go to those places and look for pinesap on the floor and walls, or any kind of flammable material. They should station guards to protect those areas. Make sure no one can light a fire."

"I'll do it. I'll do it right away!" Essie said.

Serafina touched Essie one last time and then she ran. She didn't care who saw her or heard her now. She ran frantically through the house and down the stairs, her lungs gasping for air.

As she sprinted through the Entrance Hall, she heard the hooves of Braeden's horse clattering across the courtyard in front of the house. She burst out the front door just in time to see Braeden gallop by. He was leaning forward on the horse, filled with panicked urgency. She'd never seen him go so fast. But he was riding headlong into darkness toward the gardens.

"Braeden!" she shouted after him. "Come back! I'm here! I'm alive!" But he didn't hear her.

Serafina ran after him. As she went out into the night, she heard the loud, bloodcurdling howl of a wolfhound in the nearby trees. A flood of dread poured into her mind. It sounded like a wolfhound sentinel in the woods had spotted Braeden and was sounding the call for his white-fanged brothers to join him.

Then she heard the long, yipping, yelping, snapping howl of a single coyote. The howling answer of a hundred other coyotes rose up from all around Biltmore's grounds.

A terrible thought struck her mind. All this deception and disguise wasn't just about finding the Black Cloak and burning down Biltmore. Now they wanted *Braeden*. Braeden in particular. And soon they would have the boy in their jaws.

She heard another sound in the distance. She knew the wraithy racket all too well: the clatter of four horses and a carriage on the road to Biltmore.

They were coming. They were all coming.

Then she spotted movement ahead at the edge of the gardens. She sucked in a breath. The black silhouette of a figure lurked in the shadows, hunched and slinking in a long dark coat. It was Grathan. He was wielding his cane like a weapon.

"Braeden!" Serafina screamed as he and his horse disappeared into Biltmore's vast gardens, but he was too far away to hear her.

As Grathan ducked into the gardens behind Braeden, he

gripped his cane in two hands and drew out a long, pointed, swordlike dagger. There it was. The weapon he had been hiding had finally come forth! The freshly sharpened edges of the blade shone in the moonlight with gleaming power. Brandishing the blade in front of him, Grathan followed Braeden down the path into the gardens. He was going to kill him!

Serafina burst forward with new speed. When she finally reached the path, she caught something out of the corner of her eye: A white-faced owl glided low across the courtyard and then disappeared into the garden trees.

Her chest tightened with fear.

Grathan, the wolfhounds, the coyotes, the stallions, the owl—everything was coming together.

The trap had sprung. And she and Braeden were the mice.

41

Serafina raced down the path that Braeden and Grathan had taken, but as she rounded a bend, she came upon an unexpected sight.

Grathan stood frozen in the path. His back was to her as he stared at the ground in front of him. Whatever it was, it had stopped him dead in his tracks.

"Don't move," he said, his voice trembling, as he glanced back at her.

Serafina didn't understand what was happening until she saw the timber rattlesnake coiled up on the path in front of him. It was a thick, dangerous-looking snake, nearly five feet long, brown and patterned with jagged bars. Its nasty wedged-shaped head was raised up off the ground, its yellow eyes staring at him, and its black tongue flicking.

She felt so confused. Why had he warned her?

"Just don't move, Serafina," he said again as the snake began to rattle.

Then Serafina saw that it wasn't just one rattlesnake. There were many of them, lying all over the path and the surrounding grass. One of the loathsome pit vipers coiled mere inches from her bare legs, its head moving back and forth as if it was angling for an attack.

Grathan gripped his cane in one hand and his dagger in the other.

He tried to step backward, but as soon as his legs moved, the closest rattlesnake struck like the snap of a whip, leaving two bleeding holes in his leg, so fast that even Serafina barely saw it. Grathan tried to leap back from the terrifying strike, but he landed off the path, right onto a second rattlesnake. That rattlesnake lunged forward, its mouth spread, and sank its venomous fangs deep into his calf. As he cried out and tried to jerk away, a third snake struck his thigh. Grathan screamed in pain and tripped backward, dropping his dagger. The other snakes converged upon him, striking him in the face and throat and chest. Their fangs pumped venom into his bloodstream. Grathan's arms and legs and his entire body were shaking. Serafina had no idea whether she should fight the snakes or run. There was nothing she could do but stand there in horror and watch.

Grathan lay flat on the ground now, faceup, with his limbs splayed, the snakes draping and coiling around him. The man's face was dark and swollen with poison, but his eyes were open and he looked at her.

"She's . . . not . . . who . . . she . . . seems. . . ." he gasped in a weak, raspy voice, barely able to speak.

"What?" Serafina asked in confusion. "I don't understand!"

"Run!" he gasped.

"Tell me what you're talking about!" she cried. She wanted to get closer to the man and hear what he was trying to tell her, but she had to keep her distance from the snakes. She knew she was in danger, but she had to have to answers. "Who are you? Who are talking about?" she asked him.

But Grathan's eyes closed and he was gone. He died right before her eyes.

Serafina stepped back, then stepped back again, aghast with what she saw.

She had thought that Grathan was her mortal enemy, the second occupant of the carriage, Uriah's spy and assassin. But she suddenly felt a strange sadness that something had just happened that shouldn't have happened and that it was all her fault. She looked down at the poor dead man on the ground. Had she made a terrible mistake about him? It seemed like he was trying to help her at the end, like he was trying to tell her something.

The silver clasp of the Black Cloak lay in his open, dead hand. She wanted to grab it, but the snakes coiled around his arm.

As horrified as she was by what she'd just seen, she tried to tell herself that what had happened was good, that these snakes had just killed her enemy. It was over! Her enemy was dead.

But she shook her head and growled. There weren't rattle-snakes in Biltmore's gardens. Vipers didn't hunt in groups and attack people on paths in the shrub garden. They'd been brought here by an unnatural power. But if he was evil, Grathan should have been *controlling* these snakes, not getting killed by them! The puzzle wasn't *solved*. There were just more pieces!

At that moment, she heard a *tick-tick-ticking* sound behind her, followed by a long, raspy hiss, not a rattle like a snake's, but the clicking sound of a barn owl. She felt the hot air of a breath on the back of her neck.

"I thought I got rid of you," said a voice behind her.

Serafina spun, ready to fight.

But it was Lady Rowena standing a few feet behind her. Serafina's first thought was that she must have been mistaken in what she had heard and felt. Lady Rowena stood before her holding a twig in her hand, as if to defend herself with it. Serafina was just about to ask her what she was doing there, when Rowena spoke.

"I see . . . the Black One is here," Rowena said in a peculiar voice. When she said the words, Serafina couldn't help but glance at the Black Cloak's silver clasp, which still lay in Grathan's dead hand.

Following her glance, Rowena's eyes opened wide. Then she smiled. "Oh. Thank you. We'd misplaced that."

Rowena moved toward Grathan's body, seemingly undisturbed by the fact that he was lying dead on the ground and that he was draped with rattlesnakes. She stepped among the snakes as they coiled and raised their heads and watched her with their searing yellow eyes, but they did not rattle or bite her. She bent down and picked up the silver clasp. "I'll take that off your hand," she said to Grathan's dead, swollen face.

As Rowena spoke, Serafina realized that she sounded different than she had before. Her snobbish English accent seemed to have decayed into a casual, snarling tone, as if she'd grown weary of the ruse.

"I'm afraid Detective Grathan here had been doing a bit too much detecting," Rowena said, "and he was getting dangerously close to telling Vanderbilt his theories. I guess the poor, lost soul saw himself as some sort of demon-killer, a fighter against evil. The fool thought he was going to kill me with a dagger."

A loud and sudden howl erupted from the woods, the call of a wolfhound, so close that it startled Serafina into pivoting toward it. But Rowena didn't seem bothered by the howl at all.

When Serafina looked back at her, the small stick in her hand had become a gnarled and twisted wooden staff. In that moment, Serafina remembered Lady Rowena's riding crop, and the wooden pin in her hair, and the parasol on the South Terrace, and the hiking staff in the woods. *It goes with my outfit!* she had insisted in her snobby tone. Every time she'd seen Rowena, the girl had been in different clothes, but she'd always been carrying something long and wooden.

Serafina realized now that Mr. Grathan hadn't snuck into

the garden to kill Braeden with his dagger, but to kill Rowena. He wasn't a police detective like he was pretending to be, but an occultist, a hunter of the strange and unusual. And he'd found it.

"There and there," Rowena said, pointing the staff to two positions along the garden path and the snakes slithered to where she pointed.

Finally, Rowena turned and looked at Serafina. "Yes, I thought I got rid of you."

"When was that, exactly?" Serafina said, trying to stay bold despite her confusion and her fear.

"When you and the dog went over the stair rail."

"Eight to go, I guess," Serafina said, her eyes locked on Rowena.

"I was none too pleased, believe me."

"Actually, you looked scared."

"Don't flatter yourself," Rowena scowled. "I was just surprised. You're a tougher little creature than you look. But I should have known with your kind."

As they spoke, Serafina couldn't help glancing toward the house to make sure there were no signs of smoke or flame, but she immediately regretted it.

"What are you looking for?" Rowena asked her. "It's too late, you know. I already lit the fires. There's nothing you can do to stop it now. Your precious house is going to burn. I told you I was going to finally do something to make my father proud."

Serafina tried to leap away and run, but she couldn't move

her feet. She looked down at the ground. To her astonishment, vines of ivy were growing rapidly around her ankles and up her legs.

Before she could tear the ivy away, she heard the sound of a single horse coming swiftly down the path.

The image of Biltmore's bronze statue of a rattlesnake-spooked horse flashed in her mind.

Rowena turned toward the sound of the horse.

Braeden came around the corner on horseback. "Serafina, I've been looking all—"

"Braeden, run!" Serafina screamed as loud as she could as Rowena raised the Twisted Staff.

43

The rattlesnakes struck out and sank their fangs into the horse's legs. The horse squealed as it went up rearing and striking, its head thrashing and its eyes wild with panic. Braeden fell from the horse, making a horrible cracking sound when he hit the ground.

Serafina tried to leap to Braeden's defense, but she immediately fell headlong, the ivy tentacles clamping her feet to the ground.

As she frantically ripped the ivy away, a snake rose up in front of her face, hissing and rattling, preparing to strike. With a quick flash of her hand, she whapped it on the head so fast that it never knew what hit it. Rattlesnakes were fast, but she was faster. When a second snake lashed at her with its fanged strike, she leapt straight up into the air to dodge it, then pounced on it and crushed its head.

But even as she killed the snakes, the ivy grew around her feet again, entrapping her. As Serafina tried to tear the vines away, she glanced up to see thick plumes of dark smoke roiling up from the walls of the house. Biltmore was on fire!

Serafina saw Braeden squirming out of the way of the rearing, stomping horse. The horse wasn't just frightened of the rattlesnakes. Suddenly, it wanted to kill him. The earth shook every time it hit the ground with its huge black hooves, Braeden frantically rolling this way and that, barely escaping being crushed. One stomp and Braeden would die. There was nothing she could do to save him.

But at that moment, a lean, dark mountain lion leapt out of the darkness and tackled the horse in a tumbling, screaming collision of wild beasts. Waysa had arrived. The catamount wasn't large compared to the massive size of the horse, but he fought with a lion's speed and power, moving so fast that sometimes he was nothing but a brown blur.

The five wolfhounds came running into the battle. Rowena pointed the Twisted Staff at Braeden, who was trying to get himself up onto his feet. The dogs attacked him, easily bringing him down. They clamped onto him with their fangs and dragged him screaming across the ground.

Serafina snarled and hissed in frustration as she tore the twisting ivy from her legs. Waysa's arrival gave her new hope. The second she was free, she ran toward Braeden, grabbed one of the wolfhounds by its haunches, and yanked it away. When the angry dog spun around and lunged at her with its snapping jaws, she dodged the strike and struck its head.

"Get her staff!" she screamed to Braeden, but he was on the ground, kicking and screaming, fighting for his life. One wolfhound had hold of his right hand. Another, his left wrist. And a third had hold of his leg. They weren't just biting him, or trying to kill him, they were dragging him away. Serafina knew that Braeden had barely even seen Rowena, let alone understood the complexity of what was happening. Serafina had seen the whole thing, and even she didn't understand what was going on. The snakes could strike him. The dogs could rip out his throat. But they weren't. The dogs were dragging him away.

It wasn't until Serafina heard the terrible clatter of the four stallions' hooves in Biltmore's courtyard that she began to understand. The wolfhounds, the Twisted Staff, the stallions and the carriage. Uriah and Rowena wanted Serafina dead and out of the way. But they wanted Braeden *alive*!

Waysa charged out of the bushes at the staff-wielding Rowena. When she pointed her weapon at two of the wolfhounds, they hurled themselves into the lion's charge. The catamount and the two wolfhounds exploded into a vicious battle of tearing fangs and ripping claws.

Rowena slashed the staff out into the forest and shouted something Serafina didn't understand. Sensing that she was bringing in more animals twisted to her command, Serafina rushed toward her. The only way she was going to defeat Rowena was to get the staff.

A massive bear came charging out of the trees. Serafina

gasped, barely able to believe her eyes. Black bears were normally such quiet, unaggressive creatures of the forest. She had no idea how she could fight the snarling five-hundred-pound beast.

The bear hurled itself at her with its great maw of teeth. She dodged its first attack, but the animal spun around with startling agility and lunged again, roaring with anger, swiping at her with its massive paws, its teeth clacking. She dodged again, and then again, surprising even herself with how fast she could move when her life depended on it. She knew if the bear got hold of her, it'd be the end of her. She darted this way and that, beneath it and around it, so close to it that she could smell its fur. Even when its claws missed her, the force of its bruising shoulders against her chest shot lightning bolts through her ribs.

As she kicked and screamed and thrashed and dodged the bear, the wolfhounds dragged Braeden's body up to the carriage with the four dark stallions waiting at Rowena's command. Serafina didn't understand what was happening, but she knew she had to help him or she was going to lose him forever. But she couldn't save him. She couldn't even save herself!

Rowena and the wolfhounds pulled Braeden's now limp, unconscious body into the black carriage and disappeared inside. The stallions reared up with terrifying neighs, like they'd been prodded by a painful goad. Gusts of steam poured from their mouths and nostrils. The horses burst into a run, pulling the carriage behind them. And in the distance, great clouds of smoke filled the sky.

Serafina scurried and rolled, dodged and darted between the swipes of the bear's slashing paws and the snaps of its deadly teeth, but she could not escape.

She caught a glimpse of Waysa battling the wolfhounds. Rowena could control many things, but she could not control *him*. His soul was still half human, which made the catamounts a particularly dangerous enemy to Rowena and her Twisted Staff.

The bear threw itself into its next attack. Serafina ducked to the side and tried to dart away. When it spun around and lunged at her with a mighty swipe of its paw, she leapt up a steep incline. Bears could run much faster than humans, so she couldn't outrun it. They climbed trees with great speed, so that was no good, either. Playing dead was certain death. Nor did she have the strength or claws to damage the bear, or a weapon to fight it with. All she had was her agility and her mind. She darted into the sticks of a bush, thinking that the steep incline and dense thicket would give her a chance to escape. But that meant nothing to the bear. It charged up the slope and crashed through the brush like it wasn't even there, roaring and swiping as it came.

Serafina knew that she was outmatched by the bear in almost every way, but then an idea sprang into her mind. There were still a few things she could do better than a bear.

She turned and she ran. Just as she knew it would, the bear dropped down onto all fours and chased after her. She knew she only had so many steps before the bear caught up with her and attacked her from behind. It would drag her to the ground and maul her with its teeth and claws until she was dead. She heard the pound of its running feet and the bellows of its breath coming up behind her. Terrified, she glanced over her shoulder as she ran. There it was, charging toward her at full speed, its muscles rolling beneath its heavy black fur. Her short, frantic breaths exploded through her. She was running as fast as she could, but it would overtake her in half a second.

Finally, she came to what she was running for and jumped. *Thank God for Mr. Olmsted,* she thought as she fell through the air. She landed in the crushed stone of the long, formal, rectangular Italian Garden, which was sunk deep into the natural terrain and surrounded by a twelve-foot-high stone wall.

The moment she hit the ground, she turned around and looked up. The bear did not stop. It came barreling over the drop-off and leapt into the Italian Garden right behind her, determined to catch her and kill her. She scrambled out of the way just as its huge form hit the ground with a great crash beside her, shaking the earth. It immediately swiped at her with a mighty swing of its paw, then lunged with snapping jaws. She scurried up the white marble statue of a Greek goddess next to the garden's wall, climbed to the top of its head, and then leapt.

"It's not an Italian Garden, Mr. Olmsted," she said as she landed on the top edge of the wall, clinging to it with her hands and feet. "It's a bear pit!"

The bear roared and charged forward to follow her, but as it tried to climb the statue, its flailing paws and massive weight broke the Greek goddess into pieces, and the beast came tumbling down. The bear sprang to its feet and looked up at her and roared again, but it could not climb the stone wall or leap to the top. The bear could jump *into* the walled garden, but not *out* of it.

She'd done it. She'd escaped.

Serafina quickly ran along the top edge of the wall and disappeared into the bushes before the bear found its way out on the other side. Leaving the Italian Garden behind her, she ran through the shrubs and came to the road. But it was empty. The carriage was long gone. Serafina's mind had been filled with confusion since the moment Rowena had appeared. Who was she? And where was Uriah?

She looked toward the rooftops of Biltmore in the distance, and her heart sank in dread. Dark smoke and mist roiled across the hilltop, blurring her view of the house. It looked as if the towers and the rooftops were being enveloped by a conjurer's spell. Rowena's fires were burning! Serafina wanted to run to the house and scream for help, but she couldn't. She had to put her faith in Essie and go save Braeden.

Pulling herself away, she ran down the road in the direction that Rowena had taken him. But even as she ran, she knew it was no use. The stallions pulling the carriage were fast. She'd never catch up with them. She could hear the sound of their hooves receding in the distance.

Once again, she needed far more speed than her lousy two feet could give her. As she ran down the road and the immediate fear of the bear began to wear off, she couldn't believe how foolish she'd been to not know that Rowena wasn't who she had pretended to be. She felt angry and disgusted with herself. She was stupid. She was weak. She was slow. It felt like her feet were heavy, like she was plodding down the road.

But, somehow, she had to save Braeden!

I want to be fast, she thought in frustration as she ran. *I want to be strong! I want to be fierce!*

Waysa's words came into her mind. *Once you envision what you want to be, then you'll find a way to get there.*

She had envisioned her mother in her lion form many, many times, and it never did her any good, but as she ran desperately down the road to catch up with the carriage carrying her friend away, a flash of memories splintered through her mind.

She remembered Uriah saying *Find the Black One!* as he offered the wolfhounds a scrap of cloth.

She remembered the black strands that Essie had cut out of her hair.

As she ran after the carriage, she could feel her feet hitting the ground and her lungs gasping for more air.

She remembered seeing the reflection of her yellow eyes in the mirror.

She remembered Rowena saying *the Black One is here,* then moving her eyes to what was in Grathan's hand only *after* Serafina had looked there.

A fierce emotion poured through her. She had to run and run and keep running, driving all her anguish and her pain down into her muscles, pumping her chest, pulling air into her lungs, pounding blood through her heart, and driving strength into her legs.

She had been trying to envision her mother in her mind all this time, but she realized now that it wasn't her mother she had to see.

She felt her speed doubling, then tripling, her muscles rippling with sudden power. She leapt off the road and tore through the forest. She bounded a ravine and burst into new speed on the other side.

As she came around a bend in the road, she saw the carriage in the distance, pulled by the raging stallions, their shoulders and haunches bunching and bulging as their hooves clattered across the road. Their steel horseshoes threw flashes of sparks beneath their feet as they ran.

She found herself catching up. She heard herself growling. She felt the length and sharpness of her fangs. She felt her claws ripping across the earth. The powerful bellows of her lungs pumped in air.

And even as she ran full tilt, her eyes and ears sensed everything around her, behind her, and ahead of her.

She saw flashes of gray and brown coming toward her from the left and the right. They were fast runners. Long tails. The flash of snarling teeth. Dozens of coyotes charged in at her, biting at her sides.

Serafina wanted to turn and fight them, but she knew that if she did, she'd lose the carriage. She'd lose Braeden. So she kept running, blazing through the forest. Two of the coyotes dove in and clamped onto her sides. Then a third bit her haunch, holding on to her with its teeth. She stumbled and regained her balance and kept running, but then another coyote clamped onto her.

Suddenly, a tan-colored flash burst beside her, and a half-dozen coyotes went tumbling away, whining in pain and fear, many of them bleeding as they went down. Serafina's mother ran beside her, fighting her way through, clearing her path. Her mother had returned! The lioness leapt onto the closest coyote, sank in her claws, and took it down in a whining, snapping, somersaulting ball. Serafina kept on running, driving through, gaining speed now. Her mother reappeared and took down another coyote, and then another. Soon she and her mother were running side by side unopposed, two catamounts at full speed through the forest, the coyotes well behind them.

Just as the carriage crossed a stone bridge, Serafina leapt onto the backs of the four stallions, her claws ripping into their bodies as they tried to rear up and fight her. They bent their necks in their leather harnesses and snapped at her with their crushing teeth, but they were no match for her saber-toothed fangs and razor-sharp claws. Their panicked, flailing struggles pulled the four horses wildly off-kilter. The carriage careened off the road and went tumbling down, Serafina and the stallions battling all the way, until it finally crashed into the bottom of the ravine.

She could only become what she could envision.

And finally she had envisioned it.

Find the Black One! Uriah had told his dogs. But it wasn't the Black Cloak he had been searching for.

It was *her*.

He knew she was going to get in his way.

She realized as she leapt upon the backs of the stallions and tumbled down into the ravine that her father hadn't been a mountain lion like her mother.

He had been a *black panther*.

And now, so was she.

It all came together in her mind. Her mother and father had fought Uriah twelve years before. Her father had been the Black One, the warrior-leader of the forest who had almost defeated Uriah and whose descendants could never be allowed to rise again.

But now his daughter—the new Black One—had come into her own. And her name was Serafina.

45

Serafina clawed her way out of the wreckage. She leapt easily up onto a large rock and looked down at the pieces of the broken carriage, desperately searching for Braeden.

She was relieved when he crawled slowly out of the debris, battered and disoriented but still alive. When he glanced up at Serafina, his eyes widened in surprise. He was startled for a moment, but then Serafina saw the recognition flood through his expression and he smiled. He knew exactly who she was.

But he did not take the time to speak or approach her. He immediately dug through the debris and found the Twisted Staff.

"Braeden, give that to me. . . ." Rowena said, her voice seething as she clambered from beneath the broken boards of the carriage. "We don't have to fight each other," she said. "Just like you said, we're friends. Join me and all this will be over."

Braeden gripped the staff at each end and slammed it over his knee, but it did not bend or break.

"You aren't strong enough to destroy it," Rowena said. She stepped toward him and slowly put out her hand. "Just give the staff to me, Braeden, and we'll work together. I'll show you how to use it. We'll combine your powers with my powers, and we'll control everything in these mountains. No one will be able to stop us, not even the catamounts."

Braeden looked at her silently.

"These aren't your people, Braeden. You know that," Rowena said. "Haven't you felt the pull I'm talking about? You came to these mountains two years ago and you've been searching ever since, but you won't find the home you're looking for at Biltmore." Rowena's lip curled a little bit. "It's filled with nothing but humans."

Finally, Braeden turned. It looked like he was going to simply walk away from her.

"Braeden, I'm warning you one last time. . . ." Rowena said, her voice rising.

But at that moment, Braeden stopped. Now it seemed as if he was going to turn toward her. But he lowered his arm and then hurled the staff way up into the sky.

Rowena frowned, looking both annoyed and perplexed by his action. "You know it's going to come back down," she said condescendingly.

But Braeden just smiled and gave a long whistling call. "Not necessarily," he said.

At that moment, something came swooping in across the darkened sky.

"What is that?" Rowena snapped in surprise. "What are you doing?"

"Just a friend of mine," Braeden said. "No wire."

The peregrine falcon came in high, but then tilted and rolled. She reached out and grabbed the Twisted Staff out of midair with her talons. Then, with several quick flaps of her wings, Kess propelled herself upward. She seemed to drift across the moonlit sky almost effortlessly.

"Bring that bird back here right now, Braeden!" Rowena shouted. "Do you know what you've done?"

"Yes, I think I do," Braeden said, nodding as he turned from the falcon and looked at Rowena. "I want to make this very clear: I will never join you, Rowena."

"You're going to wish you had," Rowena spat.

But as the staff became more and more distant in the talons of the falcon, two of the wolfhounds emerged slowly from the trees, their hearts no longer twisted by its controlling power. The wolfhounds stalked toward Rowena, their heads low and their eyes filled with menace as they bared their teeth and growled.

"No," she ordered them, facing them uncertainly, thrusting her bare hands toward them. "No! Stop! Get out of here!"

But they did not go. And they did not stop.

"You're free now! Go!" she shouted at them.

Beasts of their own will, they continued to move toward her. They were indeed free.

The dogs leapt upon her. Her shouts turned to screams. She writhed and fought. One bit her leg. The other her side. Serafina leapt into the battle to help the wolfhounds fight her. But at that very instant, there was a blur of sight and sound, and Rowena disappeared from between the two dogs.

A barn owl flapped up into the sky. Serafina pulled back in surprise, startled by what she'd just seen.

She suddenly remembered the first night she saw Uriah in the forest. She had assumed that the owl had been his familiar, his eyes and ears of the forest, but it had been Rowena! He had passed her the shape-shifting staff that very night.

And now Rowena was flying straight toward the peregrine falcon.

Serafina thought it was strange that Kess wasn't flying high and fast like a falcon could. She was flying low and slow, down the length of the French Broad River, along an edge of jagged cliffs. Was the weight of the staff too much for her to carry, or did she have something else on her mind?

Then Serafina saw something that turned her heart cold. The gray-bearded man in the long, weather-beaten coat emerged from the trees at the top of a distant rocky hill. She could see his black silhouette in the moonlight. Serafina felt the hackles on the back of her neck rise up, the air pulling into her chest. It was Uriah. He'd finally come. The conjurer saw the peregrine falcon carrying his Twisted Staff away and the barn owl coming up behind the falcon in close pursuit.

Suddenly, Serafina understood.

She burst into a run, sprinting as fast as she could through the forest toward the cliffs that ran along the river. She knew exactly what Uriah was going to do next and where she needed to be when it happened.

Waysa had told her that Uriah had learned the dark arts during his travels in the Old World. And she remembered thinking that Uriah's call to the owl a few nights before had been filled not just with the sense of alliance she expected, but a dark and horrible love. And now she'd seen Rowena turn into an owl, just like Uriah. Rowena wasn't just the demon he'd sent into Biltmore to find its weaknesses. She wasn't just the conjurer's apprentice and the wielder of the Twisted Staff. Rowena was his *daughter*.

46

Serafina tore through the forest up the hill, straight for the rocky, hundred-foot-high cliff edge where Uriah was standing. As her black shape sprinted invisibly through the night, she kept her eyes fixed on the elusive conjurer. Just as she'd hoped, the man disappeared with a startling blur and turned into an owl. Uriah flew toward Rowena and Kess. It was the reflex she'd been counting on, that Uriah couldn't help but fight at his daughter's side and take back the stolen staff. Serafina knew that she couldn't defeat Uriah when he was in human form and able to use his hands to throw his spells. But as he flew down the length of the river along the jagged edge of the cliffs in pursuit of the falcon, she ran like she'd never run before, her yellow eyes locked onto Uriah as he flew. The flurry of her powerful legs pulled her rapidly across the terrain. Seeing the edge of the cliff in front of her, she drove forward with one last burst of power. And then she leapt.

Her timing was perfect. She sailed thirty feet off the edge of the cliff. As she soared through the air, she pulled back her paw, then slammed it forward with a mighty strike into Uriah as he flew by. Her deadly claws raked through the bird. Feathers exploded. The ravaged owl spun end over end from the force of the blow.

She'd done it.

She had defeated the man of the forest.

She had killed her enemy.

Her chest filled with relief and happiness, but then the momentum of her leap gave way to a different sensation. Free fall. She felt herself being pulled toward the earth, her fall picking up more and more speed. As she twisted her spine and righted herself, she caught a glimpse of a breathless Braeden reaching the rocky edge and looking out in terror as he realized she had jumped off the cliff.

She fell and fell. A hundred feet was too high for even her to survive, whether she landed on her feet or not. She had but one hope: that she had leapt out far enough.

She hit the water and it exploded all around her. She felt the great crash of it, and then it enveloped her. Her huge black body plunged deep into the river's dark currents. The force of the rapids immediately began to sweep her away.

Knowing what she had to do, she quickly started paddling. She rose to the surface in a flurry of bubbles, took a deep breath, shook off her whiskers, and then paddled steadily for the shore, using her long black tail to steer.

She spotted Uriah's bloodied white-feathered body floating down the river. She wanted to bite the owl, crush it, make sure it was dead, dead, dead, but the rapids took him away before she could catch him. She'd have to be satisfied with the havoc she had wrought.

She swam out of the rapids and hauled herself up onto the rocky shore. Waysa came trundling down the shoreline to meet her in mountain lion form, his jaunty steps making it clear that he was pretty pleased with himself, as if he was saying, *I knew that swimming lesson would save your life one day.*

The two catamounts quickly ran back up the path to the top of the cliff, where Braeden waited. He smiled in relief when he saw Serafina, but then he pointed.

Serafina looked into the distance. Rowena, still in owl form, was attacking the peregrine falcon with her talons, hitting Kess's body with strike after strike. Serafina didn't know if Rowena had seen her father die, but there was a new fierceness in the owl's attacks.

Normally, a falcon would flip claws-up to meet an incoming dive, but because Kess was carrying the staff, she could not, so she took the hits and flew on the best she could. But Rowena was relentless, striking again and again. Then Rowena finally grasped the Twisted Staff in her talons and tried to yank it away. The two intertwined raptors locked together, clawing and screeching, tumbling down through the air, fighting as they fell. But then suddenly the falcon flew upward again, pulling with powerful strokes toward the clouds, dragging the staff and the owl with her.

"What is Kess doing?" Braeden asked as he peered up into the sky.

Kess flew higher and higher, ignoring the owl's clawing talons, pecking beak, and battering wings.

The two birds went so high they disappeared, even to Serafina's eyes.

"What happened?" Braeden asked in astonishment. "Where'd they go?"

But Serafina could not reply.

Serafina could hear the two birds battling up in the sky. She heard the screeching and hissing noises of the owl, and the long *kak-kak-kak* of the peregrine, and then everything went quiet.

She peered up at the sky and took a breath. One of the birds finally came into view. It was flying alone, carrying the Twisted Staff in its talons. Serafina's heart sank when she saw that it was the owl. It was Rowena. Serafina kept looking, but there was no sign of Kess. It appeared the falcon had lost the battle.

The owl flew toward them now. Serafina dreaded what was going to happen next. Once Rowena changed back, she could use her staff to start the battle all over again, hurling god knows what kinds of animals at Serafina and her allies. And it was clear that Uriah had taught his daughter well. He might not have thought too much of her, but Rowena had become a powerful young conjurer in her own right.

"What happened?" Braeden asked as he looked all around,

his voice frantic and confused. "Is Kess dead? Did Rowena kill her?"

Serafina thought she must have. But then she spotted a tiny dot way up in the sky, hundreds of feet above the forest. It was Kess, flying strong, far higher than a barn owl could ever fly. Serafina wondered what she was doing way up there. Then Kess tipped into a barrel roll and dove.

47

Serafina watched as Kess dove through the sky toward the unsuspecting Rowena. The falcon tucked her wings close to her body and shot through the air in a striking stoop, moving faster than anything Serafina had ever seen in her entire life.

"There she is!" Braeden gasped at the last second, just as Kess came slashing into view.

The falcon struck the owl so hard that it popped with an explosion of feathers. Serafina could feel the force of the hit in her chest, like two stones striking against each other in mid-air. Then Kess pinwheeled around and raked Rowena with her talons in a second attack. The burst of white owl feathers swirled in the air. The stunned owl somersaulted lifelessly, falling toward the ground.

At the instant of the strike, the owl released the staff. It fell end over end through the air for a hundred feet. Then the falcon swooped down and grasped it in midair.

Serafina watched the body of the owl fall, dead weight all the way down, and then disappear into the trees on the other side of the river. After what had just happened, it seemed like Rowena had to be dead, but Serafina watched and waited to see if the owl flew back up again. It did not.

"Look!" Braeden said, pointing up into the sky.

It was Kess. The falcon was flying toward them. She came in low and steady. Serafina could see her black mask and her bold white chest with its black bars. She was flecked with her enemy's blood, but she looked healthy and strong. She gave a call, a cheerful *kak-kak-kak,* as she passed overhead, still carrying the Twisted Staff.

Kess flew out past the edge of the cliff and over the river. With a few strong pumps of her pointed wings, she rose higher.

Braeden whistled triumphantly to her. At first, Serafina thought he was calling her back to him to bring him the staff, but then she realized that he wasn't. He was calling his farewell.

"Good-bye, Kess," Braeden said softly. His dream that Kess would someday fly the world again was coming true. "Have a safe journey, my friend."

Serafina watched as the falcon flew across the valley of the great river, and then up and over the rising forest toward the peaks of the mountains in the distance. Kess pumped her wings and tilted her tail, and a few moments later, she disappeared, gliding over Mount Pisgah nineteen miles away.

Unlike the owls of the night and the hawks of the day, Kess flew and hunted both night and day. She was a peregrine, which meant she was the great wanderer of the sky. She could fly wherever and whenever she wanted to.

Tonight she would follow the rocky ridgelines of the southern mountains and the glint of the stars and find her way southward, continuing her long journey to the jungles of Peru. Along the way, she could drop the Twisted Staff into a blazing volcano or use it to build a nest on a cliff in the Andean clouds. But whatever she decided to do with it, it was gone.

"I couldn't figure out at first why Kess was flying so low down the length of the river," Braeden said. "But then I remembered that peregrine falcons sometimes hunt in pairs, cooperating with each other to bring down their prey. She must have known that you were on her side, Serafina."

Serafina took a long breath into her lungs and felt her heart swelling with wonder and hope.

She lifted her head and sniffed the air. There was no smell of smoke drifting through the forest. When she looked toward the house in the far distance, she didn't see the glow of flames rising up from its walls. Essie must have warned Mr. Vanderbilt and the others in time so they could put out the fires before the house was badly damaged. Essie had done it! Biltmore was saved.

It was over.

She and her allies had won.

Her enemies were finally dead.

Her mother emerged from the underbrush, bloodied and

limping from her war with the coyotes. But she had defeated them. She had cleared them from what was once again her territory. She carried Serafina's wriggling half sister by the scruff of her neck, while her half brother walked at his mother's side. The two cubs were muddy, matted, and stained with blood, but they were bold with life.

Relieved and exhausted, Serafina finally lay on the ground to rest, draping her long, lean black body in the grass. Her mother set down her half sister and came over to her. Serafina could see the love and admiration in her mother's eyes as she came toward her. Her mother brushed up against her and purred with happiness and pride. Serafina had finally done it. She'd finally become a full-whiskered catamount. Waysa sat down beside her, batting her playfully with his paws, as if to say *I told you that you could do it!* The catamounts were united. And they were here to stay.

Serafina gazed around her at the trees and the mighty river and the wreckage of the carriage, and tried to comprehend all that had happened. She remembered being so frustrated by her limitations, by what she could and couldn't do at that particular point in her life. She realized now that her life wasn't just about who she was, but about who she would become.

She looked at Braeden. He smiled and lay down on the ground with her and the other catamounts. He obviously felt quite at home with them, among the kith and kin of his heart.

Finally, he leaned his back against the long length of her panther body. He wiped the blood from a cut at his mouth, and then he shut his eyes, tilted his head back, and rested his head against her thick black fur.

"I don't know about you, Serafina," he said with a smile, "but I think we're getting rather good at this."

She could not smile in return, but she felt a warm and powerful gladness in her heart, and she swished her tail and gazed toward Biltmore Estate and the distant mountains. She had finally done it. She had finally envisioned what she wanted to be. And became it.

48

The next morning, when Serafina woke up in the workshop in her human form and walked outside onto the grounds, she looked out across the mountains and came to a realization. It was through the darkness of the blackest night that she had come to love the brightness of the rising sun.

That morning, Mr. Vanderbilt and Braeden formed a work crew with nearly a hundred men from the estate's stables, farms, and fields, and they went out to the animal cages. Serafina and her pa went with them.

The troop of men and horses encountered no difficulties on the way.

When they arrived at the pine forest, Mr. Vanderbilt and the other riders dismounted and entered by foot.

They found the animals still in the cages, but the campsite had been abandoned, the fire cold, nothing but gray ash. Serafina couldn't help but carefully scan the forest, looking for any evidence that Uriah might have somehow survived the battle the night before, but saw nothing. He appeared to be truly gone.

Braeden knelt down in front of one of the cages, opened it up, and helped the red fox crawl out of it. Recognizing him, the fox came to him immediately and crawled up into his lap. He held the fox in his arms and soothed it with strokes of his hands.

"Everything's all right now," Braeden said as he petted the fox. After a few moments, the fox seemed stronger of both body and spirit and trotted off into the forest.

Braeden went to the next cage and freed a beaver from its imprisonment. As he opened the cages, some of the animals immediately ran into the forest. Others needed his care. He knelt down with them and held them until they were strong enough to be on their way. He freed the raccoons and the bobcats, the otters and the deer, the swans and the geese, and the weasels and the wolves.

It filled Serafina with joy to see the animals running free and running strong. "Stay bold," she told them in a whisper.

As Braeden freed the animals one by one, Serafina's pa and the other workers in the crew used their crowbars, chisels, and hammers to tear out and destroy the cages so they could never be used again.

At the end of the day, as they traveled back to Biltmore

through the oaks and chestnuts, the elms and the spruce, Serafina thought that the character and spirit of the forest through which they traveled had changed.

Scurries of flying squirrels ran up and down the trunks and glided from tree to tree. Otters played in the streams.

"Look up there, Serafina!" Braeden said, grabbing her arm in excitement.

She gazed upward and saw thousands of birds, streams and streams of them flooding across the clear blue sky. There were skeins of geese flying in echelons of V's, swans and ducks in long lines, and clouds of fluttering waxwings, cardinals, and jays.

"Isn't it magnificent, Serafina?" Braeden asked her, his voice filled with wonder. "I'm so glad you're here to see this with me because I would have never been able to describe it. Did you ever think you would see something like this in your whole life?"

Serafina stood with Braeden watching the birds and she smiled. "Not like this," she said.

49

Serafina sat in a red damask-upholstered gold chair in front of a French-style vanity table and mirror in the Louis XVI Room on the second floor of Biltmore House. Light poured into the beautiful oval-shaped room, with its curving white walls, red draperies, and golden-brown wood floor. Essie stood behind her, brushing Serafina's long, silky black hair.

"I don't know what happened to your hair, miss, but it's beautiful," Essie said as she brushed it.

"Thank you," Serafina said, looking at herself in the mirror. All traces of the brown were gone. Only the black remained. And it wasn't shaggy and streaked like before, like a spotted cub's camouflage, but smooth and shiny and entirely black.

Her clean, bare neck and shoulders showed the scars of

her past, the jagged wound she'd taken to her neck when she destroyed the Black Cloak, the bites of wolfhounds on her arms and upper shoulders, and a new cut she'd suffered fighting Rowena and her animals: a long scratch across her cheek just below her eye. The appearance of the wounds did not bother her. They were the scars of battles fought and battles won.

But she still had one worry. "How has Mrs. Vanderbilt been?" she asked.

"She's been down sick on some days, but then she perks up. No one expects it of her this year, but ya know she likes to give Christmas presents to all the children of the estate workers. She's been sendin' me and the other girls hither and yon for all sorts of gifts. She and I spent the entire mornin' wrapping the presents and puttin' them under the tree."

"You must be excited about the Christmas jubilee tonight," Serafina said, smiling. It was good to hear that maybe Mrs. Vanderbilt was feeling a little better.

"Oh, yes, miss. I can't wait. But after all the ruckus last night, I hope it's quieter tonight, or old St. Nick might just look down on Biltmore's rooftop and keep on flyin'."

"Thank you again for everything you did, Essie," Serafina said. "You saved a lot of people's lives, and you saved the house, too."

"You should have seen the look on Mr. Vanderbilt's face when I told him everything you said. I've never seen him move so fast! He gathered up your pa and all the men, and the guests, and all the maids and cooks. We went to all the places in the basement and kitchen and pantries and the stables, and just like you said, there was pinesap and kerosene already aflame. Somebody had lit all those fires. It was so frightening! Your pa said someone cut the wires on the alarm boxes, so he sounded the alarm himself. Then he got the fire hoses throwing water, which was truly something to behold. Mr. Vanderbilt got the bucket brigades going real quick like. Everybody chipped in and worked together, and we put those fires out in no time at all. But it coulda been a disaster!"

Serafina smiled as she listened to Essie tell her story. "You're right," she agreed. "It could have been a disaster. But it wasn't. You saved us."

"It wasn't me. It was *everybody*—everybody working together."

Serafina nodded in agreement.

"But what about you, miss?" Essie said. "A lot of strange happenings last night."

"Strange happenings?"

"Oh, all the cats were a-caterwauling, and the coyotes were a-howlin', and the horses racing the moon. Noises, screams in the night, all sorts of commotion. Somebody actually crashed a carriage off the bridge by the river, smashed it to smithereens."

"Truly?" Serafina said.

"I heard that Mr. Vanderbilt checked into that peculiar Mr. Grathan. Turns out he was some sort of shady character who goes around the country investigating ghost stories and ever what. He was a complete charlatan. Maggie and me thinks he and that English girl tried to run off in the carriage together, that's what we think. No one's seen hide nor hair of either of 'em since last night, and I bet ya we're not a-gonna!"

"I bet you're right," Serafina said.

But deep down she felt a pang of sadness for poor Mr. Grathan. She remembered the scars on his face. They were not unlike her own. There were just many more of them. Mr. Grathan had been a demon killer, just like she was. But this time the demon had killed him first. Serafina realized that she had made a mistake in her judgment of both Mr. Grathan and Rowena in different ways, in part because of how they looked and dressed, and she vowed to be far more careful next time.

"You want to know what?" Essie said, leaning down to her and speaking in a low, conspiratorial tone. "You're not gonna believe this, but Maggie said she looked out her window last night and saw a black panther."

"Do you believe her?"

"Oh, sure. I saw one once, years ago."

"You did?" Serafina asked in surprise.

"I wasn't but five or six at the time, but I recall it like it was yestermorn. One of the clearest memories of my entire life. I was walking down the road with my nanny and my papaw, and this big old black panther crosses the road right in front of us. He stopped and turned and looked right at us. He had the most beautiful yellow eyes you ever did see. But I was afeared. I thought that panther was gonna eat us for sure, and he probably woulda done if it weren't for my pa. I wanted to take off a-runnin' and I woulda been halfway outta Madison County, but my papaw gripped my shoulder and held me in place and we just stared at that big cat. That panther stared right back at us, eyes keen like he was as knowin' as you and me. And then he turned and continued on his way. My pa said that them kind are very rare, that there can only be one black one at a time. So, if Maggie saw one last night, I guess a black one has returned to these parts. Don't want to get et, of course, but I sure would love to see him."

As Essie told her story, tears streamed down Serafina's cheeks, and then she began to sob. Essie had seen her father.

"Aw, miss, I'm sorry," Essie said. "What'd I say? I didn't mean to scare you! The panther ain't gonna hurt us none. You're such a delicate creature, aren't you?"

Serafina looked at Essie in the mirror, shook her head, and wiped her eyes. "I'm not scared," she said.

"Never mind about all that commotion last night. I'm sure it was nothin'. My papaw would say it was just the old man of the forest up to his tricks again, nothing to mind."

Serafina smiled and nodded and blew her nose into a silk handkerchief from the table.

"Don't fret none. We're gonna fix you up real nice for tonight," Essie said as she stood behind Serafina and worked on her hair. "We have plenty of time now. Do you want me to put your hair up into a fancy coiffure like Consuelo Vanderbilt's was the other night? It's very popular these days."

Serafina smiled and imagined it in her mind, but then she said, "Actually, I have another idea," and explained to Essie what she wanted.

She liked talking with Essie and spending time with her. There was something soothing about it that brought her home. But then Serafina saw Essie's expression change, maybe as she thought back on the unexplained happenings and the strange sounds she'd heard in the night.

"Do you believe in haints and spirits, miss?" Essie asked her.

"I believe in *everything*," Serafina said very seriously, remembering all that she had seen.

"Me, too," Essie said as she stroked Serafina's hair.

"Essie, do you remember when we first met a while back, you were fixed on becoming a lady's maid to Mrs. V's guests?" Serafina asked.

"Well, that's right," Essie said. "But ya know what I reckon?"

"What's that?" Serafina said.

"On special nights like this, at least, I reckon I'm *your* lady's maid, miss."

"I reckon you are." Serafina nodded and smiled, and reached up and touched Essie's hands with her own. "But you know what I want more than that, Essie? I want you as my friend."

"Aw, now," Essie complained, "you're gonna start me a-cryin' if we keep this up!"

At that moment, there came a gentle knocking.

"Who could that be?" Essie asked as she went over to the door. "Don't they know us girls are busy in—" As Essie opened the door and saw the young master standing there, she ran out of air to speak.

Serafina rose and went over to Braeden as the shocked Essie moved quietly backward into the room.

Braeden held in his arms two large white boxes with ribbons.

"What's this?" Serafina asked, studying the boxes as Braeden smiled.

"A Christmas present for each of you," Braeden said as he handed the first one to her. "Open it up."

"Truly?" Serafina said.

But she didn't wait for an answer. Inside the box, Serafina found a gorgeous creamy satin winter ball gown.

"It's beautiful, Braeden," Serafina said. "Thank you."

"Essie, you, too," Braeden said, handing the second box to her. "This is to cover Serafina's debt to you."

"Oh, my, will you look at that!" Essie said, beaming as she opened the box and saw the gown within.

"They're both beautiful," Serafina said, watching Essie.

Braeden stepped closer to them and spoke in a facetiously conspiratorial tone. "Now, between me, my aunt, and Essie, this is the third dress we've given you, Serafina. Perhaps you could try to be just a little bit more careful and not ruin this one right away."

"I'll do my best," Serafina said, smiling, and gave Braeden a hug as Essie wiped tears of joy from her eyes.

50

As Serafina and Braeden walked together through the house to the Christmas party, Braeden took her down several corridors to the Smoking Room. It was a richly appointed hideaway, with dark blue velvet chairs, fine blue wallpaper, and shelves of gold-leafed leather-bound books, where the gentlemen would retreat after dinner to smoke their cigars and talk in private. The room was empty at the moment, but Serafina could tell that Braeden had paused for a reason.

"I want to show you something I think you'll find interesting," he said. He took her by the arm and led her into the room. "One of the groundskeepers found something in the woods. He wasn't sure what to do with it, so he gave it to the taxidermist."

As Serafina walked into the room, she looked around her.

On the sculpted marble fireplace mantel sat a stuffed animal on a stand. There were other stuffed animals in the house, so this in itself wasn't unusual. But it wasn't just a pheasant or a grouse. It was a barn owl with its sharp talons clinging wishfully to a crooked stick and its wings splayed upward as if in sudden alarm. The owl seemed to have a particularly shocked look on its face.

"Ah," Serafina said, admiring the owl. She wasn't sure if it was a male or a female, wasn't even sure how to tell the difference, but she decided it looked like her old friend and nemesis. She gave the owl a slow and solemn nod. "Good evening, Rowena. Excuse me, I'm so sorry . . . *Lady* Rowena."

"Well," Braeden said, "my aunt Edith asked us to make her feel at home."

Serafina smiled and looked at the owl. "Rowena, you will always have a home here at Biltmore."

Serafina was pleased that she and Braeden and their allies had defeated Rowena, but the truth was that in some ways her father had twisted Rowena's heart as malevolently as his staff had twisted the minds of those poor animals. Serafina couldn't help but wonder what would have happened if Rowena had seen past her need to impress her father, had turned away from her father's vengeance, and had taken a different path.

After studying the owl for a moment, Serafina asked Braeden, "Did the groundskeeper find only one?"

"I'm afraid so," Braeden said. "But I asked him to gather some of the other men and go back out and keep looking, both in the forest and along the shore of the river, just in case."

"Good," Serafina said. "I would feel a lot better if we had two owls on the mantel rather than one," she said.

Leaving the room, Serafina and Braeden walked over to the Banquet Hall.

Before going in, Braeden paused at the door and looked at Serafina.

Serafina gazed into the soft glow of the candlelit Christmas party in the opulent room. Glittering ladies in their long, formal gowns and handsome gentlemen in their black jackets mingled about the room, talking and laughing warmly, holding their champagne in long crystal flutes. Along with the sparkling folk, most of the house servants were there as well, filled with a relaxed cheer and looking so different in their best day-off clothes, the formalities of work put aside for this special evening.

Many of the children of the servants were hovering by the Christmas tree, waiting excitedly to open their presents. Serafina remembered being a little child curled up in a ball in the darkness at the bottom of the basement stairway listening to the Christmas party above, longing to see and to share in the smiling faces of the other children. And here she was tonight, her first Christmas upstairs. As familiar as all this was to her, and as strange and foreign as well, this was the society she lived in. This was her home. These were her people, her kin, both distant and close.

Standing with Braeden in the doorway, Serafina could see their reflection in one of the mirrors on the wall. It was mesmerizing to see themselves there. Braeden wore the black jacket, white tie, and white gloves that were customary of a young gentleman of his station. His scrapes and bruises had been attended to, and his hair had been neatly combed. His face was lit up with happiness and his brown eyes sparkled with the reflection of the room's light.

Serafina wore the beautiful golden-cream satin gown that Braeden had given her for Christmas, with its magnificently embroidered pearl- and braid-trimmed corset and its long cascading train. As was customary of a young lady, she wore matching satin opera gloves, and glistening shoes adorned her feet. But unlike the other girls in the room, who wore their hair up and arranged, curled into tightly wound coiffures, she had decided to let her silky jet-black hair lay long and smooth over her shoulders, and her eyes were as yellow as a panther's.

A few nights before, Braeden had invited her to join the dinner party, and she had said that she wasn't quite ready, but now he posed the question to her again.

"Ready to go in?" he asked softly.

"I am," she said, and they stepped into the room together.

51

Serafina had spent all the Christmases of her life in the darkness of the basement. When she stepped into the grand room, it glowed with the soft light of hundreds of candles, bathing everyone's faces and their smiles in a golden hue. The women's silver-threaded dresses seemed to scintillate in the light of the Christmas tree. Everything in the room had been decorated with holly and mistletoe and poinsettias. Stockings hung on the mantels of the crackling fireplaces.

A score of foresters had used a wagon and a team of Belgian draft horses to pull the massive, thirty-five-foot Fraser fir tree up to Biltmore's front door. Then a crew of men, including her pa, had worked together with ropes, pulleys, and poles to erect the giant tree in the Banquet Hall. There, it had been decorated over days on end by servants and guests alike who stood on ladders, adorning it with velvet ribbons, sparkling orbs, and splendorous ornaments until its glow filled the entire room. Now beneath the tree lay a heap of Christmas presents for the children of the estate workers: dolls and balls, horns and chimes, trains and bicycles, harps and drums, wagons and pocket knives, and other toys of all kinds.

Serafina and Braeden made their way over to the Christmas tree and stood beside it. They watched with a smile as Mr. Vanderbilt called for everyone's attention and quieted the room. "Good evening, everyone, good evening. Merry Christmas to you all!"

"Merry Christmas!" everyone shouted in return.

"As you all know," Mr. Vanderbilt continued, "here at Biltmore, we pride ourselves on staying up to date with the latest advancements in science and technology. And tonight, on Christmas 1899, I would like to introduce to you what may in fact be the coming new century's most important invention."

With a mischievous look in his eyes, he waved in a dozen smiling maids, including Essie, carrying baskets full of candy canes, which they handed out to all the children and adults in attendance. But they weren't just normal all-white candy canes like they had all seen before. They were striped with a magnificent red spiral that brought loud cheers and laughter of delight from everyone in the room.

As the night slipped on, the servants laid out all sorts of food: ham and roast turkey, dressing and cranberries, and much more—all the bounty of the estate. For dessert they had plum pudding and fancy cakes, ice cream from the estate's dairies, and apple tarts from the estate's orchards.

Soon, Mr. Vanderbilt persuaded Mr. Olmsted to collect the children around the fireplace and read them a poem that began " 'Twas the night before Christmas . . ."

Serafina and Braeden gathered with the other children and listened to the poem with rapt attention.

She loved the part that said "when all through the house, not a creature was stirring, not even a mouse." She had felt that way many times as she prowled through Biltmore at night. And she loved the line "The moon on the breast of the new-fallen snow . . ." The author of the poem had finally found a way to use daytime words to capture nighttime beauty.

Halfway through the story, she looked over and saw her pa gazing at her. She remembered how he had found her in the forest when she was little. All he'd ever wanted in his life was to have a family, for her to be his daughter, and tonight he was filled with a happiness and a relief she had never seen in him before.

She rose and walked over to him. "At least there wasn't any salad tonight, Pa," she said.

"And none of them forks to learn on, thank goodness," he said, winking at her, and took her into his arms.

A few moments later, she overheard Mr. Vanderbilt, Mr. Olmsted, and the chief forester, Mr. Schenck, gathered around the fireplace talking about the Biltmore School of Forestry that they'd set up. Her pa told her that it was the first school like it in all of America, to share the knowledge of rebuilding and managing forests. From what she could tell, it sounded like the men of Biltmore were hatching grand plans for the future.

"Thank you so much, Frederick," Mr. Vanderbilt said warmly to Mr. Olmsted. "What a delightful Christmas present it was to go out to Squatter's Clearing with you this morning and see all the work you've been doing. I must say, you're very good at keeping a secret! I had no idea that you and the crews had made such good progress. You've planted the entire clearing! It's marvelous!"

"You're welcome, George," Mr. Olmsted said, smiling broadly beneath his gray beard. The deceit she'd seen in Mr. Olmsted's eyes days before was the surprise Christmas present that he'd been planning for his old friend.

And seeing his smiling face, she realized now that the seriousness she'd sensed in Mr. Olmsted since his arrival wasn't some nefarious plan, but an elderly man's awareness that he only had so much more time on this earth to finish his work. He was determined to make good on his promise to Mr. Vanderbilt to build him a property and a forest that people would cherish for generations to come. The expression she saw in the wrinkles around his eyes and his mouth was the realization that he had probably come to his favorite place on earth for the last time in his life, that this would be his last Christmas at Biltmore, and one of his last years in a world he so dearly loved.

As Serafina stepped away from the men by the fireplace, Mrs. Vanderbilt came over to her, and with a smile, handed her a small, wrapped present with a red bow.

"You forgot to open yours, Serafina," Mrs. Vanderbilt said gently.

"For me?" Serafina said in surprise. She tore away the wrapping paper and lifted the lid on a small wooden box. Inside, she found a finely painted porcelain miniature of a beautiful spotted jaguar. It was one of Biltmore's very own cats.

"Thank you, Mrs. Vanderbilt," she said, looking up at her as she wiped a tear from the corner of her eye. "I'll be very careful with it."

"It's just my way of saying thank you for everything you've done," Mrs. Vanderbilt said.

Hoping she wasn't being too forward, Serafina asked, "How have you been feeling, Mrs. Vanderbilt?"

"You needn't worry about me," Mrs. Vanderbilt said, touching her gently on the shoulder. "I'm going to be all right." But even as she said the words, Serafina sensed that there was something that Mrs. Vanderbilt wasn't saying.

At the end of the evening, Serafina stood with Braeden by the Christmas tree. She could feel that everything was good and right between them.

"Merry Christmas, Braeden," Serafina said.

"Merry Christmas to you as well, Serafina," Braeden said. "I'm glad we're finally home."

After a few seconds, her curiosity got the best of her, and she asked him the question that was on her mind.

"You know what you did for Gidean and Kess . . ." she began. "Has it always been that way?"

"I've loved animals all my life," he said, "but . . . I don't

know. . . . When I was little, I found a meadowlark with a broken leg. I fed it and took care of it, and a few days later, its leg
healed and the bird flew off. I just thought that was how it was
supposed to work. . . . But when I helped the peregrine falcon
and then Gidean, I began to realize . . . that maybe I was different. Kess's wing should not have healed."

"But it did," Serafina said, looking at him. "I need to ask
you something else, Braeden. Do you think it might work on
people?"

"I'm not sure," he said.

She paused and then finally asked the real question she
wanted to ask. "Do you think you could help your aunt Edith?"

"I don't think that's something I can heal," he said.

"I understand," Serafina said glumly, lowering her head.

But then Braeden smiled. "My uncle just told me that my
aunt isn't ill. She's with child."

Serafina looked at him in surprise. A wave of shock and
relief passed through Serafina. Mrs. Vanderbilt was going to be
all right—more than all right. She was going to have a baby!
That was such tremendous news.

But even as Serafina smiled, she could see that Braeden was
thinking about her earlier question, about everything that had
happened with Rowena and Gidean and the falcon.

"Honestly," Braeden said, "I don't truly understand what
power I have."

Serafina smiled. "None of us do."

52

Serafina lay on the front balcony of the Louis XV Room of Biltmore House, swishing her tail and looking out across the open grass of the Esplanade as the moon rose, casting its silver light over the tops of the distant trees. No one could see her there, for she was as black as the night itself. The daytime folk were in the house behind her, sleeping soundly in their beds.

Serafina could see the silhouette of the wolves passing through the moon's light on a distant hill. They were returning. And in the spring, the songbirds would come, just as they had for a million years. The dark spell on the forest had been broken. The Twisted Staff was gone.

A beautiful green luna moth fluttered by with its long tails streaming behind. She watched as it flew up past the balcony, then headed for the gardens. It was late in the year for luna moths, but the animals were coming home.

In the room behind her, Mrs. Vanderbilt and the baby within her lay sleeping. Serafina could sense their calm and steady heartbeats. She did not know why her mistress had decided to sleep this evening in the room they planned on turning into the nursery. It was as if she and her baby were eager for their meeting day to come.

Serafina gazed out across the lawn of the Esplanade to the hilltops, looking for unusual shapes in the mist, or a silhouette among the trees, or the silent passing of an owl.

She watched and she listened. She was the black sentinel in the night.

She did not know when, or in what form, but she knew that one day more demons would come.

She vowed to be watchful.

She vowed to be ready.

For the night was her domain and hers alone.

Just a few days before, she had thought that she had to decide between one path or the other, between the forest and the house, between the mountains and the gardens.

But now she knew she did not have to decide whether she was a creature of the night or the day, whether she was catamount or human, wild or tame. She was all these things. She could be whatever she wished to be. Like the peregrine falcon that flies both night and day, she would do whatever she wished to do. The C.R.C. and the Guardian. The human and the panther. She was all these things and more.

But just as she felt a dark and lovely peacefulness finally beginning to flow into her soul, she saw a black-cloaked figure moving through the trees in the distance. She couldn't make out the identity of the figure, couldn't even be sure it was entirely human, but whatever it was, it stopped, and turned, and looked at her with glowing eyes.

Serafina's heart pounded in her powerful chest as she stared back at the figure. She could feel her muscles beginning to bunch beneath her and her lungs filling with air.

As she rose to her four feet, she glanced behind her to make sure Mrs. Vanderbilt was still safe in the bedroom.

But when Serafina turned back to look at the figure in the distance once more, the figure was gone.

An Invitation to Biltmore

If you'd like to see and experience Serafina's world, I invite you and your family to visit Biltmore Estate, a wonderful real-life place nestled in the forested mountains of Asheville, North Carolina. My family and I live nearby and have been exploring it for years.

This story is fictional, but I've done my best to describe the house and other historical details accurately. When you visit Biltmore, you'll see the sunlit Winter Garden, the magnificent Grand Staircase, Mr. Vanderbilt's spectacular Library, and all the other main rooms featured in the book. You'll walk through the estate just as Serafina, Braeden, and Lady Rowena did. If you come at Christmastime, you'll be awed by the giant Christmas tree in the grand Banquet Hall. And if you know which one of Biltmore's 250 rooms to check, you may even spot a certain owl on the fireplace mantel.

I can also assure you from personal experience that the darkened attics, hidden doors, and secret passages described in the book are real. These aren't for visitors (they are *hidden* doors after all!), but you may be able to spot one or two!

Here and there in the story, I have used artistic license for reasons of pacing (I figure you didn't want to read an encyclopedia), but in general I've tried to stay true to the spirit and detail of the house.

If you enjoy the outdoors, you should explore the forests and mountains that surround Asheville. You can venture up past the Craggy Gardens to the tallest mountain in the eastern United States just as Serafina did during her journey. You can see the same waterfalls and swim in the same rivers.

Many of the characters depicted in the story were real-life people, including George and Edith Vanderbilt, the housekeeper Emily Rand King, and Frederick Law Olmsted, the father of landscape architecture in America. Even Cedric the Saint Bernard was real.

My goal in depicting Mr. Olmsted the way I did, including showing him planting trees, was to capture the spirit of his and George Vanderbilt's original vision for rebuilding and protecting the forest surrounding Biltmore, which would go on to become the birthplace of forest conservation in America. The conversation I depicted between the two men was inspired by Olmsted's personal letters. But I did use artistic license to bring him back to Biltmore for a visit in 1899, a few years after he retired. Given more room, I would have also liked to have described the roles of Gifford Pinchot, Carl Schenck, and others. Years later, after George Vanderbilt passed away unexpectedly, his wife, Edith, fulfilled his vision for the forest by selling the vast majority of their forested land to the government so that it would be protected by the public trust. It became what is today the Pisgah National Forest, one of America's first and finest national forests.

Whenever I see the unique beauty of Biltmore House and its surrounding gardens and trees, I can't help but marvel at the vision and power of the human spirit when it aspires to good purpose.

—Robert Beatty

Acknowledgments

First, I would like to thank you, the readers, for helping to spread the word about *Serafina and the Black Cloak*. It is because of your support on Book One that I was provided the opportunity to continue Serafina's story.

My deep thanks go to Laura Schreiber and Emily Meehan, my editors at Disney Hyperion, for their insight into storytelling and their commitment to the Serafina Series. And thank you to the rest of the wonderful team at Disney Hyperion in New York and LA.

Thank you to the middle-grade students and teachers of Carolina Day School, the ladies of the LLL Book Club, and all my other beta readers.

I would also like to thank the freelance editors who provided invaluable feedback on the manuscript: Jodie Renner, Sam Severn, Jenny Bowman, Kira Freed, Sheila Trask, Dianne Purdie, John Harten, and Misty Stiles.

Thank you to Dr. Bridget Anderson, an expert in turn-of-the-century southern mountain dialect. Having always enjoyed the different way people speak in our diverse country, I appreciate her assistance, helping me to honor the traditions of southern mountain talk.

Thank you to my Serafina home team in Asheville, including Scott Fowler and Lydia Carrington at Brucemont Communications, Robin McCollough for helping to spread the word, Paul Bonesteel and the talented team at Bonesteel Films, and everyone else in Asheville who helped make the book a success.

Thank you to Deborah Sloan and M.J. Rose for helping me to get the word out. And thank you to my agent, Bill Contardi, and my foreign-rights agent, Marianne Merola, at Brandt & Hochman in New York. And thank you to Egmont UK and my other foreign publishers.

I would also like to thank all the kind and supportive folks at Barnes & Noble in Asheville and throughout the southeastern region, and Malaprop's Bookstore, and all the other bookstores throughout the country who have believed in me, supported me, and been such gracious hosts. And thank you to all the teachers and librarians throughout the country who have used *Serafina and the Black Cloak* in their classrooms and work tirelessly every day to inspire reading in young people.

Thank you to my friends Dini Pickering, Chase Pickering,

and Ryan Cecil, fourth and fifth generation family members of George Vanderbilt. I am honored by your support and encouragement. And thank you to all the staff members and management at Biltmore Company, especially Ellen Rickman, Tim Rosebrock, and Kathleen Mosher.

Finally, I would like to thank my family, including my two brothers and my Jankowski in-laws, but most especially my wife and three daughters, who not only inspired this story, but helped create it, develop it, and bring it to the world. In the words of W. H. Auden, you are "my working week and my Sunday rest, my noon, my midnight, my talk, my song."

SERAFINA

and the

BLACK CLOAK

SERAFINA and the BLACK CLOAK

ROBERT BEATTY

DISNEP·HYPERION

LOS ANGELES   NEW YORK

First Edition, July 2015
9 10
FAC-020093-19200

Printed in the United States of America

This book is set in Adobe Garamond Pro
Designed by Maria Elias

Library of Congress Cataloging-in-Publication Data TK
ISBN 978-1-4847-0901-6

Reinforced binding

Visit www.DisneyBooks.com

To my wife, Jennifer, who helped shape
this story from the beginning,

and to our girls
—Camille, Genevieve, and Elizabeth—
who will always be our first and
most important audience

Biltmore Estate
Asheville, North Carolina
1899

1

Serafina opened her eyes and scanned the darkened work-shop, looking for any rats stupid enough to come into her territory while she slept. She knew they were out there, just beyond her nightly range, crawling in the cracks and shadows of the great house's sprawling basement, keen to steal whatever they could from the kitchens and storerooms. She had spent most of the day napping in her favorite out-of-the-way places, but it was here, curled up on the old mattress behind the rusty boiler in the protection of the workshop, that she felt most at home. Hammers, wrenches, and gears hung down from the rough-hewn beams, and the familiar smell of machinery oil filled the air. Her first thought as she looked around her and listened out into the reaching darkness was that it felt like a good night for hunting.

Her pa, who had worked on the construction of Biltmore Estate years before and had lived in the basement without permission ever since, lay sleeping on the cot he'd secretly built behind the supply racks. Embers glowed in the old metal barrel over which he had cooked their dinner of chicken and grits a few hours before. They had huddled around the cook fire for warmth as they ate. As usual, she had eaten the chicken but left the grits.

"Eat your supper," her pa had grumbled.

"Did," she had answered, setting down her half-empty tin plate.

"Your whole supper," he said, pushing the plate toward her, "or you're never gonna get any bigger than a little shoat."

Her pa likened her to a skinny baby pig when he wanted to get a rise out of her, figuring she'd get so furious with him that she'd wolf those nasty grits down her throat despite herself.

"I'm not gonna eat the grits, Pa," she said, smiling a little, "no matter how many times you put 'em in front of me."

"They ain't nothin' but ground-up corn, girl," he said, poking at the fire with a stick to arrange the other sticks the way he wanted them. "Everybody and his uncle likes corn 'cept you."

"You know I can't stomach anything green or yellow or disgusting like that, Pa, so quit hollering at me."

"If I was a-hollerin', you'd know it," he said, shoving his poker stick into the fire.

2

By and by, they soon forgot about the grits and went on to talk about something else.

It made Serafina smile to think about her dinner with her father. She couldn't imagine much else in the world—except maybe sleeping in the warmth of one of the basement's small sunlit windows—that was finer than a bit of banter with her pa.

Careful not to wake him, she slinked off her mattress, padded across the workshop's gritty stone floor, and snuck out into the winding passageway. While still rubbing the sleep out of her eyes and stretching out her arms and legs, she couldn't help but feel a trace of excitement. The tantalizing sensation of starting a brand-new night tingled through her body. She felt her muscles and her senses coming alive, as if she were an owl stirring its wings and flexing its talons before it flies off for its ghostly hunt.

She moved quietly through the darkness, past the laundry rooms, pantries, and kitchens. The basement had been bustling with servants all day, but the rooms were empty now, and dark, just the way she liked them. She knew that the Vanderbilts and their many guests were sleeping on the second and third floors above her, but here it was quiet. She loved to prowl through the endless corridors and shadowed storage rooms. She knew the touch and feel, the glint and gloom, of every nook and cranny. This was *her* domain at night, and hers alone.

She heard a faint slithering just ahead. The night was beginning quickly.

She stopped. She listened.

Two doors down, the scrabbling of tiny feet on bare floor.

She crept forward along the wall.

When the sound stopped, she stopped as well. When the sound resumed, she crept forward once more. It was a technique she'd taught herself by the age of seven: move when they're moving, stay still when they're still.

Now she could hear the creatures breathing, the scratching of their toenails on the stone, and the dragging of their tails. She felt the familiar trembling in her fingers and the tightness in her legs.

She slipped through the half-open door into the storeroom and saw them in the darkness: two huge rats covered in greasy brown fur had slithered one by one up through the drainpipe in the floor. The intruders were obviously newcomers, foolishly scrounging for cockroaches when they could've been slurping custard off the fresh-baked pastries just down the hall.

Without making a sound or even disturbing the air, she stalked slowly toward the rats. Her eyes focused on them. Her ears picked up every sound they made. She could even smell their foul sewer stench. All the while, they went about their rotten, ratty business and had no idea she was there.

She stopped just a few feet behind them, hidden in the blackness of a shadow, poised for the leap. This was the moment she loved, the moment just before she lunged. Her body swayed slightly back and forth, tuning her angle of attack. Then she pounced. In one quick, explosive movement, she grabbed the squealing, writhing rats with her bare hands.

"Gotcha, ya nasty varmints!" she hissed.

The smaller rat squirmed in terror, desperate to get away, but the larger one twisted around and bit her hand.

"There'll be none of that!" she snarled, clamping the rat's neck firmly between her finger and thumb.

The rats wriggled wildly, but she kept a good, hard hold on them and wouldn't let them go. It had taken her a while to learn that lesson when she was younger, that once you had them, you had to squeeze hard and hold on, no matter what, even if their little claws scratched you and their scaly tails curled around your hand like some sort of nasty gray snake.

Finally, after several seconds of vicious struggling, the exhausted rats realized they couldn't escape her. They went still and stared suspiciously at her with their beady black eyes. Their sniveling little noses and wickedly long whiskers vibrated with fear. The rat who'd bit her slowly slithered his long, scaly tail around her wrist, wrapping it two times, searching for new advantage to pry himself free.

"Don't even try it," she warned him. Still bleeding from his bite, she was in no mood for his ratty schemes. She'd been bitten before, but she never did like it much.

Carrying the grisly beasts in her clenched fists, she took them down the passageway. It felt good to get two rats before midnight, and they were particularly ugly characters, the kind that would chew straight through a burlap sack to get at the grain inside, or knock eggs off the shelf so they could lick the mess from the floor.

She climbed the old stone stairs that led outside, then

walked across the moonlit grounds of the estate all the way to the edge of the forest. There she hurled the rats into the leaves. "Now get on outta here, and don't come back!" she shouted at them. "I won't be so nice next time!"

The rats tumbled across the forest floor with the force of her fierce throw, then came to a trembling stop, expecting a killing blow. When it didn't come, they turned and looked up at her in astonishment.

"Get goin' before I change my mind," she said.

Hesitating no longer, the rats scurried into the underbrush.

There had been a time when the rats she caught weren't so lucky, when she'd leave their bodies next to her pa's bed to show him her night's work, but she hadn't done that in a coon's age.

Ever since she was a youngin, she'd studied the men and women who worked in the basement, so she knew that each one had a particular job. It was her father's responsibility to fix the elevators, dumbwaiters, window gears, steam heating systems, and all of the other mechanical contraptions on which the two-hundred-and-fifty-room mansion depended. He even made sure the pipe organ in the Grand Banquet Hall worked properly for Mr. and Mrs. Vanderbilt's fancy balls. Besides her pa, there were cooks, kitchen maids, coal shovelers, chimney sweeps, laundry women, pastry makers, housemaids, footmen, and countless others.

When she was ten years old, she had asked, "Do I have a job like everyone else, Pa?"

"Of course ya do," he said, but she suspected that it wasn't true. He just didn't want to hurt her feelings.

"What is it? What's my job?" she pressed him.

"It's actually an extremely important position around here, and there ain't no one who does it better than you, Sera."

"Tell me, Pa. What is it?"

"I reckon you're Biltmore Estate's C.R.C."

"What's that mean?" she asked in excitement.

"You're the Chief Rat Catcher," he said.

However the words were intended, they emblazoned themselves in her mind. She remembered even now, two years later, how her little chest had swelled and how she had smiled with pride when he'd said those words: Chief Rat Catcher. She had liked the sound of that. Everyone knew that rodents were a big problem in a place like Biltmore, with all its sheds and shelves and barns and whatnot. And it was true that she had shown a natural-born talent for snatching the cunning, food-stealing, dropping-leaving, disease-infected four-legged vermin that so eluded the adult folk with their crude traps and poisons. Mice, which were timid and prone to panic-induced mistakes at key moments, were no trouble at all for her to catch. It was the rats that gave her the scamper each night, and it was on the rats that she had honed her skills. She was twelve years old now. And that was who she was: Serafina, C.R.C.

But as she watched the two rats run into the forest, a strange and powerful feeling took hold of her. She wanted to follow them. She wanted to see what they saw beneath leaf and twig, to explore the rocks and dells, the streams and wonders. But her pa had forbidden her.

"Never go into the forest," he had told her many times. "There are dark forces there that no one understands, things that ain't natural and can do ya wicked harm."

She stood at the edge of the forest and looked as far as she could into the trees. For years, she'd heard stories of people who got lost in the forest and never returned. She wondered what dangers lurked there. Was it black magic, demons, or some sort of heinous beasts? What was her pa so afraid of?

She might bandy back and forth with her pa about all sorts of things just for the jump of it—like refusing her grits, sleeping all day and hunting all night, and spying on the Vanderbilts and their guests—but she never argued about this. She knew when he said those words he was as serious as her dead momma. For all the spiny talk and all the sneak-about, sometimes you just stayed quiet and did what you were told because you sensed it was a good way to keep breathing.

Feeling strangely lonesome, she turned away from the forest and gazed back at the estate. The moon rose above the steeply pitched slate roofs of the house and reflected in the panes of glass that domed the Winter Garden. The stars sparkled above the mountains. The grass and trees and flowers of the beautiful manicured grounds glowed in the midnight light. She could see every detail, every toad and snail and all the other creatures of the night. A lone mockingbird sang its evening song from a magnolia tree, and the baby hummingbirds, tucked into their tiny nest among the climbing wisteria, rustled in their sleep.

It lifted her chin a bit to think that her pa had helped build all this. He'd been one of the hundreds of stonemasons, wood-carvers, and other craftsmen who had come to Asheville from the surrounding mountains to construct Biltmore Estate years before. He had stayed on to maintain the machinery. But when all the other basement workers went home to their families each night, he and Serafina hid among the steaming pipes and metal tools in the workshop like stowaways in the engine room of a great ship. The truth was they had no place else to go, no kin to go home to. Whenever she asked about her momma, her father refused to talk about her. So, there wasn't anyone else besides her and her pa, and they'd made the basement their home for as long as she could remember.

"How come we don't live in the servants' quarters or in town like the other workers, Pa?" she had asked many times.

"Never ya mind about that," he would grumble in reply.

Over the years, her pa had taught her how to read and write pretty well, and told her plenty of stories about the world, but he was never too keen on talking about what she wanted to talk about, which was what was going on deep down in his heart, and what happened to her momma, and why she didn't have any brothers and sisters, and why she and her pa didn't have any friends who came 'round to call. Sometimes, she wanted to reach down inside him and shake him up to see what would happen, but most of the time her pa just slept all night and worked all day, and cooked their dinner in the evening, and told her stories, and they had a pretty good life, the two of them, and she didn't shake him because she knew he didn't want to be shook, so she just let him be.

At night, when everyone else in the house went to sleep, she crept upstairs and snatched books to read in the moonlight. She'd overheard the butler boast to a visiting writer that Mr. Vanderbilt had collected twenty-two thousand books, only half of which fit in the Library Room. The others were stored on tables and shelves throughout the house, and to Serafina, these were like Juneberries ripe for the picking, too tempting to resist. No one seemed to notice when a book went missing and was back in its place a few days later.

She had read about the great battles between the states with tattered flags flying and she had read of the steaming iron beasts that hurtled people hither and yon. She wanted to sneak into the graveyard at night with Tom and Huck and be shipwrecked with the Swiss Family Robinson. Some nights, she longed to be one of the four sisters with their loving mother in *Little Women*. Other nights, she imagined meeting the ghosts of Sleepy Hollow or tapping, tapping, tapping with Poe's black raven. She liked to tell her pa about the books she read, and she often made up stories of her own, filled with imaginary friends and strange families and ghosts in the night, but he was never interested in her tales of fancy and fright. He was far too sensible a man for all that and didn't like to believe in anything but bricks and bolts and solid things.

More and more she wondered what it would be like to have some sort of secret friend who her pa didn't know about, someone she could talk to about things, but she didn't tend to meet too many children her age skulking through the basement in the dead of night.

A few of the low-level kitchen scullions and boiler tenders who worked in the basement and went home each night had seen her darting here or there and knew vaguely who she was, but the maids and manservants who worked on the main floors did not. And certainly the master and mistress of the house didn't know she existed.

"The Vanderbilts are a good kind of folk, Sera," her pa had told her, "but they ain't *our* kind of folk. You keep yourself scarce when they come about. Don't let anyone get a good look at you. And whatever you do, don't tell anyone your name or who you are. You hear?"

Serafina *did* hear. She heard very well. She could hear a mouse change his mind. Yet she didn't know exactly why she and her pa lived the way they did. She didn't know why her father hid her away from the world, why he was ashamed of her, but she knew one thing for sure: that she loved him with all her heart, and the last thing she ever wanted to do was to cause him trouble.

So she had become an expert at moving undetected, not just to catch the rats, but to avoid the people, too. When she was feeling particularly brave or lonely, she darted upstairs into the comings and goings of the sparkling folk. She snuck and crept and hid. She was small for her age and light of foot. The shadows were her friends. She spied on the fancy-dressed guests as they arrived in their splendid horse-drawn carriages. No one upstairs ever saw her hiding beneath the bed or behind the door. No one noticed her in the back of the closet when they put their coats inside. When the ladies and gentlemen went on their walks around the grounds, she slinked up right next to them without them knowing and listened to everything they were saying. She loved seeing the young girls in their blue and yellow dresses with ribbons fluttering in their hair, and she ran along with them when they frolicked through the garden. When the children played hide-and-seek, they never realized there was another player. Sometimes she'd even see Mr. and Mrs. Vanderbilt walking arm in arm, or she'd see their twelve-year-old nephew riding his horse across the grounds, with his sleek black dog running alongside.

She had watched them all, but none of them ever saw her—not even the dog. Lately she'd been wondering just what would happen if they did. What if the boy glimpsed her? What would she do? What if his dog chased her? Could she get up a tree in time? Sometimes she liked to imagine what she would say if she met Mrs. Vanderbilt face-to-face. *Hello, Mrs. V. I catch your rats for you. Would you like them killed or just chucked out?* Sometimes she dreamed of wearing fancy dresses and ribbons in her hair and shiny shoes on her feet. And sometimes, just sometimes, she longed not just to listen secretly to the people around her, but to talk to them. Not just to see them, but to be *seen*.

As she walked through the moonlight across the open grass and back to the main house, she wondered what would happen if one of the guests, or perhaps the young master in his bedroom on the second floor, happened to wake and look out the window and see a mysterious girl walking alone in the night.

Her pa never spoke of it, but she knew she wasn't exactly normal looking. She had a skinny little body, nothing but muscle, bone, and sinew.

She didn't own a dress, so she wore one of her pa's old work shirts, which she cinched around her narrow waist with a length of fibrous twine she'd scavenged from the workshop. He didn't buy her any clothes because he didn't want people in town to ask questions and start meddling; meddling was something he could never brook.

Her long hair wasn't a single color like normal people had, but varying shades of gold and light brown. Her face had a peculiar angularity in the cheeks. And she had large, steady amber eyes. She could see at night as well as she could during the day. Even her soundless hunting skills weren't exactly normal. Every person she'd ever encountered, especially her pa, made so much noise when they walked that it was like they were one of the big Belgian draft horses that pulled the farm equipment in Mr. Vanderbilt's fields.

And it all made her wonder, looking up at the windows of the great house. What did the people sleeping in those rooms dream of, with their one-colored hair, and their long, pointy noses, and their big bodies lying in their soft beds all through the glorious darkness of the night? What did they long for? What made them laugh or jump? What did they feel inside? When they had dinner at night, did the children eat the grits or just the chicken?

As she glided down the stairs and back into the basement, she heard something in a distant corridor. She stopped and listened, but she couldn't quite make it out. It wasn't a rat. That much was certain. Something much larger. But what was it?

Curious, she moved toward the sound.

She went past her pa's workshop, the kitchens, and the other rooms she knew well, and into the deeper areas where she hunted less often. She heard doors closing, then the fall of footsteps and muffled noises. Her heart began to thump lightly in her chest. Someone was walking through the corridors of the basement. *Her* basement.

She moved closer.

It wasn't the servant who collected the garbage each night, or one of the footmen fetching a late-night snack for a guest— she knew the sound of their footsteps well. Sometimes the butler's assistant, who was eleven, would stop in the corridor and gobble down a few of the cookies from the silver tray that the butler had sent him to retrieve. She'd stand just around the corner from him in the darkness and pretend that they were friends just talking and enjoying each other's company for a while. Then the boy would wipe the powdered sugar off his lips, and off he'd go, hurrying up the stairs to catch up on the time he'd lost. But this wasn't him.

Whoever it was, he wore what sounded like hard-soled shoes—*expensive* shoes. But a gentleman proper had no business coming down into this area of the house. Why was he wandering through the dark passages in the middle of the night?

Increasingly curious, she followed the stranger, careful to avoid being seen. Whenever she snuck up close enough to almost see him, all she could make out was the shadow of a tall black shape carrying a dimly lit lantern. And there was another shadow there, too, someone or something with him, but she didn't dare creep close enough to see who or what it was.

It was a vast basement with many different rooms, corridors, and levels, which had been built into the slope of the earth beneath the house. Some areas, like the kitchens and the laundry, had smooth plaster walls and windows. The rooms there were plainly finished, but clean and dry, and well-suited to the daily work of the servants. The more distant reaches of the understructure delved deep into the damp and earthen burrows of the house's massive foundation. Here the dark, hardened mortar oozed out from between the roughly hewn stone blocks that formed the walls and ceiling, and she seldom went there because it was cold, dirty, and dank.

Suddenly, the footsteps changed direction. They came toward her. Five screeching rats came running down the corridor ahead of the footfalls, more terrified than any rodents she had ever seen. Spiders crawled out of the cracks in the walls. Cockroaches and centipedes erupted from the earthen floor. Astounded by what she was seeing, she caught her breath and pressed herself to the wall, frozen in fear like a little rabbit kit trembling beneath the shadow of a passing hawk.

As the man walked toward her, she heard another sound, too. It was a shuffling agitation like a small person—slippered feet, perhaps a child—but there was something wrong. The child's feet were scraping on the stone, sometimes sliding . . . the child was crippled . . . no . . . the child was being *dragged*.

"No, sir! Please! No!" the girl whimpered, her voice trembling with despair. "We're not supposed to be down here." The girl spoke like someone who had been raised in a well-heeled family and attended a fancy school.

"Don't worry. We're going right in here . . ." the man said, stopping at the door just around the corner from Serafina. Now she could hear his breathing, the movement of his hands, and the rustle of his clothing. Flashes of heat scorched through her. She wanted to run, to flee, but she couldn't get her legs to move.

"There's nothing to be frightened of, child," he said to the girl. "I'm not going to hurt you . . ."

The way he said these words caused the hairs on the back of Serafina's neck to rise. *Don't go with him,* she thought. *Don't go!*

The girl sounded like she was just a little younger than her, and Serafina wanted to help her, but she couldn't find the courage. She pressed herself against the wall, certain that she would be heard or seen. Her legs trembled, feeling as if they would crumble beneath her. She couldn't see what happened next, but suddenly the girl let out a bloodcurdling scream. The piercing sound caused Serafina to jump, and she had to stifle her own scream. Then she heard a struggle as the girl tore away from the man and fled down the corridor. *Run, girl! Run!* Serafina thought.

The man's steps faded into the distance as he went after her. Serafina could tell that he wasn't running full-out but moving steadily, relentlessly, like he knew the girl couldn't escape him. Serafina's pa had told her that's how the red wolves chase down and kill deer in the mountains—with dogged stamina rather than bursts of speed.

Serafina didn't know what to do. Should she hide in a dark corner and hope he didn't find her? Should she flee with the terror-stricken rats and spiders while she had the chance? She wanted to run back to her father, but what about the child? The girl was so helpless, so slow and weak and frightened, and more than anything, she needed a friend to help her fight. Serafina wanted to be that friend; she wanted to help her, but she couldn't bring herself to move in that direction.

Then she heard the girl scream again. *That dirty, rotten rat's gonna kill her,* Serafina thought. *He's gonna kill her.*

With a burst of anger and courage, she raced toward the sound. Her legs felt like explosions of speed. Her mind blazed with fear and exhilaration. She turned corner after corner. But when she came to the mossy stone stairway that led down into the deepest bowels of the subbasement, she stopped, gasping for breath, and shook her head. It was a cold, wet, slimy, horrible place that she had always done her best to avoid—especially in the winter. She'd heard stories that they stored dead bodies in the subbasement in the winter, when the ground was too frozen to dig a grave. Why in the world had the girl gone down *there*?

Serafina made her way haltingly down the wet, sticky stairs, lifting and shaking off her foot after each slimy step she took. When at last she reached the bottom, she followed a long, slanting corridor where the ceiling dripped with brown sludge. The whole dank, disgusting place gave her the jitters something fierce, but she kept going. *You've got to help her,* she told herself again. *You can't turn back.* She wound her way through a labyrinth of twisting tunnels. She turned right, then left, then left, then right until she lost track of how far she'd gone. Then she heard the sound of fighting and shouting just around the corner ahead of her. She was very close.

She hesitated, frightened, her heart pounding so hard it felt like it was going to burst. Her body shook all over. She didn't want to go another step, but friends had to help friends. She didn't know much about life, but she did know that, knew that for sure, and she wasn't going to run away like a scared-out-of-her-wits squirrel just when somebody needed her most.

Trembling all over, she steadied herself the best she could, sucked in a deep breath, and pushed herself around the corner.

A broken lantern lay tipped on the stone floor, its glass shattered but the flame still burning. In its halo of faltering light, a girl in a yellow dress struggled for her life. A tall man in a black cloak and hood, his hands stained with blood, grabbed the girl by the wrists. The girl tried to pull away. "No! Let me go!" she screamed.

"Quiet down," the man told her, his voice seething in a dark, unworldly tone. "I'm not going to hurt you, child . . ." he said for the second time.

The girl had curly blond hair and pale white skin. She fought to escape, but the man in the black cloak pulled her toward him. He tangled her in his arms. She flailed and struck him in the face with her tiny fists.

"Just stay still, and it will all be over," he said, pulling her toward him.

Serafina suddenly realized that she'd made a dreadful mistake. This was far more than she could handle. She knew that she should help the girl, but she was so scared that her feet stuck to the floor. She couldn't even breathe, let alone fight.

Help her! Serafina's mind screamed at her. *Help her! Attack the rat! Attack the rat!*

She finally plucked up her courage and charged forward, but just at that moment, the man's black satin cloak floated upward as if possessed by a smoky spirit. The girl screamed. The folds of the cloak slithered around her like the tentacles of a hungry serpent. The cloak seemed to move of its own accord, wrapping, twisting, accompanied by a disturbing rattling noise, like the hissing threats of a hundred rattlesnakes. Serafina saw the girl's horrified face looking at her from within the folds of the enveloping cloak, the girl's pleading blue eyes wide with fear. *Help me! Help me!* Then the folds closed over her, the scream went silent, and the girl disappeared, leaving nothing but the blackness of the cloak.

Serafina gasped in shock. One moment the girl was struggling to get free, and the next she vanished into thin air. The cloak had consumed her. Overwhelmed with confusion, grief, and fear, Serafina just stood there in stunned bewilderment.

For several seconds, the man seemed to vibrate violently, and a ghoulish aura glowed around him in a dark, shimmering haze. A horribly foul smell of rotting guts invaded Serafina's nostrils, forcing her head to jerk back. She wrinkled her nose and squinched her mouth and tried not to breathe it in.

She must have made some sort of involuntary gagging noise, for the man in the black cloak suddenly turned and looked at her, seeing her for the first time. It felt like a giant claw gripped her around her chest. The folds of the man's hood shrouded his face, but she could see that his eyes blazed with an unnatural light.

She stood frozen, utterly terrified.

The man whispered in a raspy voice. "I'm not going to hurt you, child . . ."

earing those eerie words jolted Serafina into action. She had just seen what those words led to. *Not this time, rat!* With a burst of new energy, she turned and ran.

She tore through the labyrinth of crisscrossing tunnels, running and running, certain that she was leaving him far in the distance. But when she glanced over her shoulder, the hooded man was flying through the air right behind her, levitated by the power of the billowing black cloak, his bloody hands reaching toward her.

Serafina tried to run faster, but just as she came to the bottom of the stairs that led up to the main level of the basement, the man in the black cloak grabbed her. One hand clamped her shoulder. The other locked on to her neck. She turned and hissed like a snared animal. She whirled and clawed in a wild circle and broke herself free.

She bounded up the stairs three at a time, but he followed right behind her. He reached out and yanked her head back by her hair. She screamed in pain.

"Time to give up now, little child," he said calmly, even as the tightening of his fist slowly tore strands of her hair from her head.

"I ain't never!" she snarled, and bit his arm. She fought as hard as she could, scratching and clawing with her fingernails, but it didn't matter. The man in the black cloak was far too strong. He pulled her into his chest, entangling her in his arms.

The folds of the black cloak rose up around her, pulsing with gray smoke. The awful rotting odor made her gag. All she could hear was that loathsome rattling noise as the cloak slithered and twisted its way around her body. She felt like she was being crushed in the coil of a boa constrictor.

"I'm not going to hurt you, child . . ." came the hideous rasping voice again, as if the man wasn't of his own mind but possessed by a demented, ravenous demon.

The folds of the cloak cast a wretched pall over her, drenching her in a dripping, suffocating sickness. She felt her soul slipping away from her—not just slipping, but being yanked, being extracted. Death was so near that she could see its blackness with her own eyes and she could hear the screams of the children who had gone before her.

"No! No! No!" she screamed in defiance. She didn't want to go. Hissing wildly, she reached up and clutched his face, clawing at his eyes. She kicked his chest with her feet. She bit him repeatedly, snapping like a snarling, rabid beast, and she tasted his blood in her mouth. The girl in the yellow dress had fought, but nothing like this. Finally, Serafina twisted out of his grip and spun to the ground. She landed on her feet and leapt away.

She wanted to get back to her pa, but she couldn't make it that far. She fled down the corridor and dashed into the main kitchen. There were a dozen places to hide. Should she slip behind the black cast-iron ovens? Or crawl up among the copper pots hanging from the ceiling rack? No. She knew she had to find a better place.

She was back in her territory now, and she knew it well. She knew the darkness and she knew the light. She knew the left and the right. She had killed rats in every corner of this place, and there was no way she was going to let herself become one of those rats. She was the C.R.C. No trap or weapon or evil man was going to catch her. Like a wild creature, she ran and jumped and crawled.

When she reached the linen storage room, with all its wooden shelves and stacks of folded white sheets and blankets, she scampered into a crumbling break in the wall, in the back corner beneath the lowest shelf. Even if the man did notice the hole, it would seem impossibly small for anyone to fit through. But she knew it provided a shortcut into the back of the laundry.

She came out in the room where they hung and dried the

fancy folks' bedsheets. The moon had risen outside, and its light shone through the basement windows. Hundreds of flowing white sheets hung from the ceiling like ghosts, the silver moonlight casting them into an eerie glow. She slipped slowly between the hanging sheets, wondering if they would provide her the concealment she needed. But she thought better of it and kept going.

For good or ill, she had an idea. She knew that Mr. Vanderbilt prided himself on installing the most advanced equipment at Biltmore. Her pa had constructed special drying racks that rolled on metal ceiling tracks that tucked into narrow chambers where the sheets and clothes were dried with the radiant heat of well-sealed steam pipes. Determined to find the best possible hiding place, she made herself small and pressed herself through the narrow slot of one of the machines.

When Serafina was born, there had been a number of things physically different about her. She had four toes on each foot rather than five, and although it was not noticeable just by looking at her, her collarbones were malformed such that they didn't connect properly to her other bones. This allowed her to fit into some pretty tight spots. The opening in the machine was no more than a few inches wide, but as long as she could fit her head into something, she could push her whole body through. She wedged herself inside, into a dark little spot where she hoped the man in the black cloak wouldn't find her.

She tried to be quiet, she tried to be still, but she panted like a little animal. She was exhausted, breathless, and frightened beyond her wits. She'd seen the girl in the yellow dress consumed by the shadow-filled folds and knew the man in the black cloak was coming for her next. Her only hope was that he couldn't hear the deafening pound of her heartbeat.

She heard him walking slowly down the hallway outside the kitchen. He'd lost her in the darkness, but he moved methodically from room to room, looking for her.

She heard him in the main kitchen, opening the doors of the cast-iron ovens. *If I'd hidden there,* she thought, *I'd be dead now.*

Then she heard him clanging through the copper pots, looking for her in the ceiling rack. *If I'd hidden there,* she thought, *I'd be dead again.*

"There's nothing to be frightened of," he whispered, trying to coax her out.

She listened and waited, trembling like a field mouse.

Finally, the man in the black cloak made his way into the laundry room.

Mice are timid and prone to panic-induced mistakes at key moments.

She heard the man moving from place to place, rummaging beneath the sinks, opening and closing the cabinets.

Just stay still, little mouse. Just stay still, she told herself. She wanted to break cover and flee so bad, but she knew that the dead mice were the dumb mice that panicked and ran. She told herself over and over again, *Don't be a dumb mouse. Don't be a dumb mouse.*

25

Then he came into the drying area where she was and moved slowly through the room, running his hands over the ghostly sheets.

If I'd hidden there . . .

He was just a few feet away from her now, looking around the room. Even though he couldn't see her, he seemed to sense that she was there.

Serafina held her breath and stayed perfectly, perfectly, perfectly still.

Serafina slowly opened her eyes.

She didn't know how long she'd been asleep or even where she was. She found herself crammed into a tight, dark space, her face pressed up against metal.

She heard the sound of footsteps approaching. She stayed quiet and listened.

It was a man in work boots, tools jangling. Feeling a burst of happiness, she wriggled her way out of the machine and into the morning sunlight pouring through the laundry windows.

"Here I am, Pa!" she cried, her voice parched and weak.

"I've been gnawin' on leather lookin' for you," her pa scolded. "You weren't in your bed this mornin'."

She ran forward and hugged him, pressing herself into his chest. He was a large and hardened man with thick arms and rough, calloused hands. His tools hung from his leather apron, and he smelled faintly of metal, oil, and the leather straps that drove the workshop's machines.

In the distance, she heard the sounds of the staff arriving for the morning, the clanking of pots in the kitchen, and the conversations of the workers. It was a glorious sound to her ears. The danger of the night was gone. She had survived!

Wrapped in her father's arms, she felt safe and at home. He was more accustomed to mallets and rivets than a kind word, but he'd always taken care of her, always loved and protected her. She couldn't hold back the tears of relief stinging her eyes.

"Where've ya been, Sera?" her father asked.

"He tried to get me, Pa! He tried to kill me!"

"What are you goin' on about, girl?" her pa said suspiciously, holding her by the shoulders with his huge hands. He looked intently into her face. "Is this another one of your wild stories?"

"No, Pa," she said, shaking her head.

"I ain't in any kinda mood for stories."

"A man in a black cloak took a little girl, and then he came after me. I fought him, Pa! I bit him a good one! I spun 'round and clawed him, and I ran and ran and I got away and I hid. I crawled into your machine, Pa. That's how I got away. It saved me!"

"Whatcha mean, he took a girl?" her pa said, narrowing his eyes. "What girl?"

"He . . . he made her . . . She was right in front of me, and then she vanished before my eyes!"

"Come on now, Sera," he said doubtfully. "You sound like you don't know whether you're washin' the clothes or hangin' 'em out."

"I swear, Pa," she said. "Just listen to me." She took a good, hard swallow and started at the beginning. As the story poured out of her, she realized how brave she'd actually been.

But her pa just shook his head. "You've had a bad dream is all. Been readin' too many of them ghost stories. I told ya to stay away from Mr. Poe. Now look at ya. You're all scruffed up like a cornered possum."

Her heart sank. She was telling him the God's honest truth, and he didn't believe a word of it. She tried to keep from crying, but it was hard. She was going on thirteen and he was still treating her like a child.

"I wasn't dreamin', Pa," she said, wiping a sniffle from her nose.

"Just calm yourself down," he grumbled. He hated it when she cried. She'd known since she was little that he'd rather wrangle with a good piece of sheet metal than deal with a weepy girl.

"I've gotta go to work," he said gruffly as he separated from her. "The dynamo busted somethin' bad last night. Now get on back to the workshop, and get some proper sleep in ya."

Hot frustration flashed through her and she clenched her fists in anger, but she could hear the seriousness in his voice and knew there was no point in arguing with him. The Edison dynamo was an iron machine with copper coils and spinning wheels that generated a new thing called "electricity." She knew from the books she'd read that most homes in America didn't have running water, indoor toilets, refrigeration, or even heating. But Biltmore had all of these things. It was one of the few homes in America that had electric lighting in some of the rooms. But if her pa couldn't get the dynamo working by nightfall, the Vanderbilts and their guests would be plunged into darkness. She knew he had a lot of things on his mind, and she wasn't one of them.

A wave of resentment swept through her. She'd tried to save a girl from an evil black-cloaked demon-thing and almost got herself killed in the process, but her pa didn't care. All he cared about was his stupid machines. He never believed her about anything. To him, she was just a little girl, nothing important, nothing worth listening to, nothing anyone could count on for anything.

As she walked glumly back to the workshop, she fully intended to follow her pa's instructions, but when she passed the stairway that led up to Biltmore Estate's main floor, she stopped and looked up the stairs.

She knew she shouldn't do it.

She shouldn't even think about doing it.

But she couldn't help it.

Her pa had been telling her for years that she shouldn't go upstairs, and lately she'd been trying to follow his rules at least some of the time, but today she was furious that he hadn't believed her. *It'd serve him right if I didn't listen to him.*

She thought about the girl in the yellow dress. She tried to make sense of what she'd seen: the horrible black cloak and the wide-eyed fear in the girl's face as she disappeared. Where had the girl gone? Was she dead or somehow still alive? Was there still a chance she could be saved?

Snippets of conversation drifted down the stairs. There was some sort of commotion. Had they found a body? Were they all crying in despair? Were they searching for a murderer?

She didn't know if she was brave or stupid, but she had to tell someone what she'd seen. She had to figure out what happened. Most of all, she had to help the girl in the yellow dress.

She began to climb the stairs.

Staying as small and quiet as she could, she crept up the steps one by one. A cacophony of sounds floated down to her: the echo of people talking, the rustling of clothing, dozens of different footsteps—it was a crowd of many people. Something was definitely happening up there. *We've got to keep to ourselves, you and I.* Her pa's warning played in her mind as she climbed. *There ain't no sense in people seein' you and askin' questions.*

She slinked to the top of the stairway, then ducked into an alcove on the main floor that looked onto a huge room full of fancy-dressed people who seemed to be gathering for some type of grand social event.

Massive, ornately crafted wrought-iron-and-glass doors led into the Entrance Hall, with its polished marble floor and vaulted ceiling of hand-carved oak beams. Soaring limestone arches led from this central room to the various wings of the mansion. The ceiling was so high she had the urge to climb up there and peer down. She'd been here before, but she had always loved the room and couldn't help marveling at it again, especially in the daylight. She'd never seen so many glistening, beautiful things, so many soft surfaces to sit on, and so many interesting places to hide. Spotting an upholstered chair, she felt an overwhelming desire to run her fingernails over the plush fabric. All of the room's colors were so bright, and the surfaces were so clean and shiny. She didn't see any mud or grease or dirt anywhere. There were brightly colored vases filled with flowers—to think! Flowers, actually *inside* the house. Sunlight flooded in from the sparkling, leaded-glass windows of the spiraling, four-story-high Grand Staircase and the glass-domed Winter Garden, with its spraying fountain and tropical plants. She squinted her eyes against the brightness.

The Entrance Hall teemed with dozens of beautifully attired ladies and gentlemen along with manservants in black-and-white uniforms helping them to prepare for a morning of horseback riding. Serafina stared at a lady who wore a riding dress made of white-piped green velvet and cranberry-red damask. Another woman wore a lovely mauve habit with dark purple accents and a matching hat. There were even a few children

32

there, clothed as finely as their parents. Her eyes darted around the room as she tried to take it all in.

Serafina looked at the face of the lady in the green dress, and then she looked at the face of the lady in the mauve hat. She knew her momma was long dead, or at very least long gone, but all her life, whenever she saw a woman, she checked to see if the woman looked like her. She studied the faces of the children, too, wondering if there was a chance that any of them could be her brothers and sisters. When she was little, she used to tell herself a story that maybe she had come home one day to the house, muddy from her hunting, and her mother had taken her downstairs and stuck her in the belt-driven washing machine, and then went back upstairs and accidentally forgot about her, just spinning and spinning away down there. But when Serafina looked around at the women and the children in the Entrance Hall and saw their blond hair and their blue eyes, their black hair and their brown eyes, she knew that none of them were her kin. Her pa never talked about what her momma looked like, but Serafina searched for her in every face she saw.

Serafina had come upstairs with a purpose, but now that she was here, the thought of actually trying to talk to any of these fancy people put a rock in her stomach. She swallowed and inched forward a little, but the lump in her throat was so huge, she wasn't even sure she could get a word out. She wanted to tell them what she saw, but it suddenly seemed so foolish. They were all happy and carefree, like so many larks on a sunny day. She didn't understand. The girl was obviously one of these people, so why weren't they looking for her? It was like it never happened, like she had imagined the whole thing. What was she going to say to them? *Excuse me, everyone . . . I'm pretty sure I saw a horrible black-cloaked man make a little girl vanish into thin air. Has anyone seen her?* They'd lock her up like a cuckoo bird.

As a tall gentleman in a black suit coat walked by, she realized that one of these men might actually be the Man in the Black Cloak. With his shadowed face and glowing eyes, there was no doubt that the attacker had been some sort of specter, but she had sunk her teeth into him and tasted real blood, and he needed a lantern to see just like all the other people she'd followed over the years, which meant he was of this world too. She scanned the men in the crowd, keeping her breathing as steady as she could. Was it possible that he was here at this very moment?

Mrs. Edith Vanderbilt, the mistress of the house, walked into the room wearing a striking velvet dress and a wide-brimmed hat. Serafina couldn't take her eyes off the mesmerizing movement of the hat's feathers. A refined and attractive woman, Mrs. Vanderbilt had a pale complexion and a full head of dark hair, and she seemed at ease in her role as hostess as she moved through the room.

"While we wait for the servants to bring up our horses," she said happily to her guests, "I would like to invite everyone to join me in the Tapestry Gallery for a little bit of musical entertainment."

A pleasant murmur passed through the crowd. Delighted by the idea of a diversion, the ladies and gentlemen streamed into the gallery, an elegantly decorated room with its exquisitely hand-painted ceiling, intricate musical instruments, and delicate antique wall tapestries. Serafina loved to climb the tapestries at night and run her fingernails down through the soft fabric.

"I'm sure that most of you already know Mr. Montgomery Thorne," Mrs. Vanderbilt said with a gentle sweep of her arm toward a gentleman. "He has graciously offered to play for us today."

"Thank you, Mrs. Vanderbilt," Mr. Thorne said as he stepped forward with a smile. "This whole outing is such a wonderful idea, and I must say you're a most radiant hostess on this lovely morning."

"You're too kind, sir," Mrs. Vanderbilt said with a smile.

To Serafina, who'd been listening to Biltmore's visitors her entire life, he didn't sound like he came from the mountains of North Carolina, or from New York like the Vanderbilts. He spoke with the accent of a Southern gentleman, maybe from Georgia or South Carolina. She crept forward to get a better look at him. He wore a white satin cravat around his neck, a brocade waistcoat, and pale gray gloves, all of which she thought went nicely with his silvery-black hair and perfectly trimmed sideburns.

He picked up a finely made violin and its bow from the table where it had been lying.

"Since when do you play the violin, Thorne?" called one of the gentlemen from New York in a friendly tone.

"Oh, I've been practicing here and there, Mr. Bendel," said Mr. Thorne as he lifted the instrument to his chin.

"When? On the carriage ride here?" Mr. Bendel retorted, and everyone laughed.

Serafina almost felt sorry for Mr. Thorne. It was clear from their playful banter that Mr. Bendel and Mr. Thorne were companions, but it was equally clear that Mr. Bendel had serious doubts as to whether his friend could actually play.

Serafina watched in nervous silence as Mr. Thorne prepared himself. Perhaps it was a new instrument to him and this was his first performance. She couldn't even imagine playing such a thing herself. At long last, he set the bow gently across the strings, paused for a moment to collect himself, and then began to play.

Suddenly, the vaulted rooms of the great house filled with the loveliest music she had ever heard, elegant and flowing, like a river of sound. He was wonderful. Spellbound by the beauty of his playing, the ladies and gentlemen and even the servants stood quietly and listened with rapt attention, and they let their hearts soak in every measure of the music he made.

Serafina enjoyed the sound of his playing, but she also watched his dexterous fingers. They moved so fast over the strings that they reminded her of little running mice, and she wanted to pounce on them.

When Mr. Thorne was done, everyone applauded and

congratulated him, especially Mr. Bendel, who laughed in disbelief. "You never cease to amaze me, Thorne. You shoot like a marksman, you speak fluent Russian, and now you play the violin like Vivaldi! Tell us, man, is there anything you're *not* good at?"

"Well, I'm certainly not as skilled a horseback rider as you are, Mr. Bendel," Mr. Thorne said as he set his violin aside. "And I must say it has always been most vexing to me."

"Well, stop the presses!" Mr. Bendel called. "The man has a chink in his armor after all!" Then he looked at Mrs. Vanderbilt with a smile. "So, when exactly are we going horseback riding?"

The other guests laughed at the two gentlemen as they quipped back and forth, and Serafina smiled. She enjoyed watching the camaraderie of these people. She envied the way they spoke to one another and touched each other and shared their lives. It was so different from her own world of shadow and solitude. She watched a young woman tilt her head and smile as she reached out and put her hand on the arm of a young gentleman. Serafina tried imitating the gesture herself.

"Are you lost?" someone said behind her.

Startled, Serafina whirled around and started to hiss, but then she stopped herself short. A young boy stood in front of her. A large black Doberman with sharply pointed ears sat at his side, staring intently at her.

The boy wore a fine tweed riding jacket, a buttoned vest, woolen jodhpurs, and knee-high leather boots. He was a little sickly looking, a little frail even, but he had watchful, sensitive brown eyes and a rather fetching tussle of wavy brown hair. He stood quietly, staring at her.

It took every ounce of her courage not to run. She didn't know what to do. Did he think she was a vagrant who had wandered in? Or perhaps she looked like a dazed servant—maybe a chimney sweep or window-washing girl. Either way, she knew she was stuck. He'd caught her dead to rights exactly where she wasn't supposed to be.

"Are you lost?" the boy asked again, but this time she heard what sounded strangely like kindness in his voice. "May I help you find your way?" He wasn't timid or shy, but he wasn't overconfident or arrogant, either. And it surprised her that he didn't seem angry at her for being there. There was a trace of curiosity in his tone.

"I-I-I'm not lost," she stammered. "I was just—"

"It's all right," he said as he stepped toward her. "I still get lost sometimes, and I've lived here for two years."

Serafina sucked in a breath. Suddenly, she realized that she was speaking face-to-face with the young master, Mr. Vanderbilt's nephew. She'd seen him many times before, standing at his bedroom window looking out at the mountains, or galloping his horse across the grounds, or walking alone on the footpaths with his dog—she'd watched him for years, but she'd never been this close to him.

Most of what she knew about him she'd overheard from the gossiping servants, and when it came to the young master, they sure did prattle on. When he was ten years old, his family died in a fire and he became an orphan. His uncle took him in. He became like a son to the Vanderbilts.

He was known as a loner. Some of the less charitable folks whispered that the young master preferred the company of his dog and his horse to most people. She'd overheard the men in the stables saying that he'd won many blue ribbons at equestrian events and was considered one of the most talented horseback riders around. The cooks, who prided themselves on preparing the most exquisite gourmet meals, complained that he always shared the food on his plate with his dog.

"I've explored pretty much every room on the first, second, and third floors," the young master said to her, "and the stables, of course, but the other parts of the house are like foreign lands to me."

As the boy spoke, she could tell he was trying to be polite, but his eyes kept studying her. It was nerve-racking. After all those years she'd been hiding, it felt so strange to have someone actually looking at her. It made her stomach twist, but at the same time, her skin tingled all over. She knew she must look completely ridiculous standing before him in the remnants of her pa's old work shirt, and he must have noticed her hands were dirty and there were smudges all over her face. Her hair was as wild as a banshee's, and there was no hiding its streaked color. How could he help but stare?

She reckoned he knew most of the guests and servants, and she could see him trying to figure out who she was. How out of place she must seem to him! She had two arms and legs like everyone else, but with her sharp cheekbones and her golden eyes, she knew she didn't look like a normal girl. No matter how much she ate, she couldn't put any weight on the feral leanness of her body. She wasn't sure if she looked more like a skinny little shoat to the Vanderbilt boy or like a savage little weasel, but neither of those animals belonged in the house.

There was a part of her—maybe the smart part—that wanted to turn tail and run, but she thought that maybe the young master might be the perfect person to tell about the girl in the yellow dress. The silky-laced adults with all their high-falutin airs wouldn't pay a smudge-faced girl any mind. But maybe *he* would.

"I'm Braeden," he said.

"I'm Serafina," she blurted out before she could help herself. *You fool! Why did you give him your name?* It was bad enough that she'd allowed herself to be seen, but now he had a name to go with her face. Her father was going to kill her!

"It's good to meet you, Serafina," he said, bowing, as if she deserved the same respect as a proper lady. "This is my friend Gidean," he said, introducing her to his dog, who continued to sit and study her malevolently with steady black eyes.

"Hello," she managed to say, but she didn't appreciate the way the dog stared at her like it was only his master's command that kept him from chomping on her with his gleaming white teeth.

Gathering her courage, she looked at Braeden Vanderbilt

nervously. "Master Braeden, I came up here to tell you something that I saw. . . ."

"Really? What'd you see?" he asked, full of curiosity.

"There was a girl, a pretty blond girl in a yellow dress, down in the basement last night, and I saw a man in a—"

As the coterie of ladies and gentlemen began to flow out of the Tapestry Gallery and move toward the main doors, the handsome Mr. Thorne broke away and approached Braeden, interrupting her.

"Are you coming, young master Vanderbilt?" he asked encouragingly in his Southern accent. "Our horses are ready, and I'm anxious to see your latest riding skills. Perhaps we can ride together."

Braden's face lit up with a smile. "Yes, sir, Mr. Thorne," he called. "I'd like that very much."

As soon as Mr. Thorne rejoined the others, the young master's eyes immediately returned to Serafina. "Excuse me, you were telling me what you saw. . . ."

At that moment, Mr. Boseman, the estate superintendent and her pa's boss, came stomping up the stairs. He'd always been a scowling-faced curmudgeon, and today was no exception. "You there, who are you?" he demanded, clutching Serafina's arm so hard that she winced. "What's your name, girl?"

Just when she thought it couldn't get any worse, a sudden commotion rose up in the main hall. A disheveled, overweight middle-aged woman still wearing her nightclothes came rushing down the Grand Staircase from the third floor. She crashed into the crowd in a flurry of hysterical panic.

"It's Mrs. Brahms," Mr. Boseman said, turning toward the disturbance.

"Has anyone seen my Clara?" Mrs. Brahms cried frantically, reaching out and grabbing the people around her. "Please help me—she's gone missing! I can't find her anywhere!"

Mrs. Vanderbilt moved forward and took the woman's hands in an attempt to calm her. "It's a very large house, Mrs. Brahms. I'm sure Clara is just off exploring."

Worried discussion spread through the crowd. All the ladies and gentlemen of the riding party began talking to one another in confusion, wondering what was happening.

Miss Clara Brahms, Serafina thought. *That's the girl in the yellow dress.*

The whole time, Mr. Boseman kept his hand clamped on her arm.

She wanted to leap forward and tell everyone what she'd seen, but then what would happen? *Where did you come from?* they'd demand. *What were you doing in the basement in the middle of the night?* There'd be all sorts of questions she couldn't answer.

All of a sudden, Mr. George Vanderbilt, the master of the house, walked into the center of the crowd and raised his hands. "Everyone, may I please have your attention," he said. All of the guests and servants immediately stopped talking and listened. "I'm sure you all agree that we need to delay our ride and search for Miss Brahms. Once we find her, we'll resume the activities of the day."

George Vanderbilt was a slender, dark-haired, intelligent-looking gentleman in his thirties with a thick black mustache and keen, dark, penetrating eyes. He was well known for his love of reading, but he was a fit and healthy-looking man, too, who seemed far younger than his years. And Serafina wasn't the only one who thought so. She had heard the servants in the kitchen joke that their master must have secretly discovered the Fountain of Youth. Mr. Vanderbilt was a meticulous dresser, and as she admired his commanding presence, she couldn't help but notice his clothes, too. In particular, his shoes. Like the other gentlemen present, he wore a gentleman's riding jacket, but instead of riding boots, he wore expensive black patent-leather shoes. As he strode across the hard surface of the marble floor, his shoes made a familiar clicking sound . . . the same sound that she'd heard in the corridors of the basement the night before.

She looked at the other men's shoes. Braeden, Mr. Thorne, and Mr. Bendel wore riding boots in preparation for their outing, but Mr. Vanderbilt was wearing his dress shoes.

He approached the lost girl's mother and consoled her. "We're going to search this place from top to bottom, Mrs. Brahms, and we'll keep looking until we find her." He turned to the ladies and gentlemen and waved over the footmen and maidservants as well. "We'll break up into five separate search parties," he explained. "We'll search the entire house, all four floors and also the basement. If anyone finds anything suspicious, report it immediately."

Mr. Vanderbilt's words struck fear into Serafina's heart. They were going to search the basement! The basement! That meant the workshop! With a mighty twist of her body, she yanked herself out of Mr. Boseman's grip and darted away before he could stop her. She bounded headlong down the stairs into the basement. She had to warn her pa. The leftovers from last night's dinner, the mattress she slept on . . . they had to hide it all.

Serafina rushed up to her father in the workshop and grabbed his arm. Trying to talk and catch her breath at the same time, she gasped, "Pa, there's a girl missing just like I said, and Mr. Vanderbilt's searching the whole house!" Her words tumbled out with a mixture of urgency and pride. As she hurriedly reminded him of what she'd seen the night before, she was sure that he'd see now that she wasn't dreaming or making up stories.

"They're searchin' the house?" he asked, ignoring everything else. He turned and quickly gathered his cooking supplies and razor from the bench, then dragged her mattress into the hidden area he'd constructed behind the tool rack. There could be no evidence of their living there when the search party came through.

"What about the girl I saw disappear?" she asked in confusion. She couldn't figure out why he wasn't more interested in what she was telling him.

"Children don't just disappear, Sera," he said as he continued his efforts.

Her heart sank. He still didn't believe her.

Her pa looked around the room one last time to make sure he hadn't missed anything, and then he looked at her. For a moment, she thought he was finally going to listen to what she was saying, but then he pointed at her hairbrush and snapped, "For God's sake, girl, pick up your things!"

"But what about the Man in the Black Cloak?" she argued.

"I don't want you thinking about anything like that," he barked. "It was nothing but a nightmare. Now hush up."

She flinched from the words. She couldn't understand why he was being so mean. But she could hear the worry in his voice along with the anger, and in the distance she could hear the search party coming down the stairs. She knew it wasn't just the threat of discovery that scared him. He hated any talk of the supernatural or any sort of dark and fiendish forces out in the world that he couldn't fix with his wrenches, hammers, and screwdrivers.

"But it's real!" she demanded. "The girl's actually gone, Pa. I'm telling the truth!"

"A little girl's gotten herself lost, that's it, and they're lookin' for her, so they'll find her, wherever she is. Get your wits about you. People don't just vanish. She's gotta be someplace."

She stood in the center of the room. "I think we should both go out there right now and tell them everything I saw," she declared boldly.

"No, Sera," he said. "They'll spit nails if they find me livin' down here. They'll fire me. Do you understand that? And God knows what they'll make of you. They don't even know you're alive, and we're gonna keep it that way. I'm talkin' to you dead straight now, girl. You hear me?"

The sound of the search party could be heard down the corridor, and it was coming their way.

Clenching her teeth, she shook her head in frustration and stood before him. "Why, Pa? Why? Why can't people see me?" She didn't have the courage to tell him that at least one Vanderbilt already had, and that he knew her name. "Just tell me, Pa, whatever it is. I'm twelve years old. I'm grown up. I deserve to know."

"Look, Sera," he said, "last night, somebody sabotaged the dynamo, did it some real damage that I'm not sure I can mend. If I don't get it fixed by nightfall, there's gonna be hell to pay from the boss, and rightly so. The lights, the elevators, the servant-call system—this whole place depends on the Edison machine."

She tried to imagine someone sneaking into the electrical room and damaging the equipment. "But why would someone do that, Pa?"

The search party was making its way through the kitchens and would arrive in the workshop at any moment.

"I ain't got time to think about it," he said, moving toward her with his huge body. "I just gotta get it workin', that's all. Now do what I tell ya!"

He charged around the room and hid things with such roughness and loudness and violence that it frightened her. She crept behind the boiler and watched him. She knew that when he was like this she couldn't get anywhere with him. He just wanted to be left alone to do his job and work on his machines. But it was gnawing at her, and the more she thought about it, the madder she got. She knew it wasn't the right time to talk to him about everything she'd been thinking and feeling, but she didn't care. She just blurted it out.

"I'm sorry, Pa," she said. "I know you're busy, but please just tell me why you don't want anyone to see me." She stepped out from behind the boiler and faced him, her voice getting louder now. "Why have you been hiding me all these years?" she demanded. "Just tell me what's wrong with me. I want to know. Why are you ashamed of me?"

By the time she was done, she was practically screaming at him. Her voice was so loud and shrill that it actually echoed.

Her pa stopped dead in his tracks and looked at her. She knew she had finally reached down inside him and grabbed that armored heart of his. She'd finally stirred him up. She felt a sudden impulse to take it all back and dart behind the boiler again to hide, but she didn't. She stood before him and looked at him as steadily as she could, her eyes watering.

He stood very still over by the bench, his huge hands balled into fists. A visible wave of pain and despair seemed to pass through him all at once, and for a moment he couldn't speak.

"I'm not ashamed of you," he said gruffly, his voice strangely hoarse. The searchers were now only one room away.

"You are," she shot back. She was trembling in fear, but she wasn't going to give up this time. She wanted to shake him. She wanted to shake him to the core. "You're ashamed of me," she said again.

He turned away from her so that she couldn't see his face, just the back of his head and huge, bulky body. Several seconds of silence went by. Then he shook his head like he was arguing with himself, or furious with her, or both—she wasn't sure.

"Just keep your mouth shut and follow me," he said as he turned and walked out of the room.

Scurrying after him, she caught up with him in the corridor. Her body felt queasy all over. She didn't know where he was taking her or what was going to happen. She could barely suck in breaths as he led her down the narrow stone stairs to the subbasement and into the electrical room with the iron dynamo and thick black wires that spidered up the walls. They had left the search party behind them, at least for a little while.

"We'll hole up in here," he said as he pulled the door shut with a heavy thud and locked them in. As he lit a lantern against the darkness, she'd never seen him look so serious, so grave and pale, and it frightened her.

"What's happening, Pa?" she asked, her voice shaking.

"Sit down," he said. "Ya ain't gonna like what I got to tell ya, but it might help ya understand."

Serafina swallowed, sat on an old wooden spool of copper wire, and prepared herself to listen. Her pa sat on the floor facing her, with his back against the wall. Staring down at the floor and deep in thought, he began to talk.

"Years ago, I was workin' as a mechanic in the train yard in Asheville," he said. "The foreman and his wife had just had their third baby boy and their home was full of joy, but while everyone else celebrated, I sat alone in a kind of self-made misery. I ain't proud of it, the way I was soppin' around that night, but things just weren't workin' out for me the way they were supposed to in a man's life. I wanted to meet a good woman, build a house in town, and have children of my own, but years had gone by and it hadn't happened. I was a big man and not much to look at. I sweated all day on the engines, and those few times I encountered any womenfolk, I could never find my words. I could talk about nuts and bolts till the mornin' come, but not much else."

She opened her mouth to ask a question, but she didn't want to disrupt the story that was finally pouring out of her pa.

"That night, while everyone was tipping the jug," he continued, "I was feelin' pretty poor, and I headed out. I went for a long walk, just walkin' like ya do when you got too much on your mind to do naught else. I went deep into the forest, up through River's Gap, and into the mountains. When night came, I just kept walkin'."

It was hard for her to picture her father traveling through the forest. All those times he had warned her had led her to believe that he would never set foot in the forest. He hated the forest. At least he did now.

"Were you scared, Pa?"

"Naw, I weren't," he said, shaking his head and still looking at the floor. "But I shoulda been."

"Why? What happened?" She couldn't even imagine what it was. The flicker of the lantern cast an eerie shadow on his face. She had always loved his stories, but this one felt closer to his heart than any story he had ever told.

"As I was walkin' through the woods, I heard a queer howlin' noise, like an animal in terrible, writhing pain. The bushes were movin' somethin' fierce, but I couldn't quite make out what it was."

"Was it somethin' dyin', Pa?" She leaned toward him.

"I don't think so," he said, looking up at her. "The ruckus in the bushes went on for a spell, then the noise stopped all sudden-like. I thought it was over, but then a pair of greenish-yellow eyes peered at me from the darkness. Whatever sort of man or beast it was, it circled slowly around me, taking one position and then another, studying me real careful, like it was trying to make a decision about me, whether I was worth eatin' or just lettin' be. I sensed a real power behind those eyes. But then the eyes disappeared. The beast was gone. And I heard a strange mewling, crying sound."

She straightened her back and looked at him. "Crying?" she asked in confusion. That definitely wasn't what she was expecting.

"I searched through the bushes. Blood covered the ground, and in the blood lay a pile of small creatures. Three of 'em were dead, but one remained just barely alive."

She got off the wooden spool and crouched down beside her pa. She stared at him, totally absorbed in his story. In her mind, she could see the bloody creatures on the ground.

"But what kind of creatures were they?" she asked in amazement.

He shook his head. "Like everyone else who lives in these mountains, I'd heard the stories of black magic, but I never gave them much credit until that night. I studied the one that was still alive the best I could in the darkness, but I still couldn't figure what kind of thing it was. Or more like my mind just couldn't believe it. But when I finally took up the creature in my bare hands and held it, I realized that it was actually a tiny human baby curled into a little ball."

Serafina's eyes opened wide in surprise. "What? Wait. I don't understand. What happened? How did a baby get there?"

"The same question was runnin' through my own mind, believe me, but one thing I knew for certain: regardless of how she came into the world, I had to get this baby some help. I bundled her up in my jacket, hiked back down the hill, and carried her out of the woods. I took her to the midwives at the convent and begged them to help, but they gasped at the sight of her, muttering that she was the devil's work. They said she was malformed, near to death, and that there was nothing they could do to help her."

"But why?" Serafina cried in outrage. "That's terrible! That's so mean!" Just because something looked different didn't mean you just threw it away. She couldn't help but wonder what kind of world it was out there. The attitude of the midwives almost bothered her more than the idea of a yellow-eyed beast lurking in the night. But she felt a renewed glimmer of admiration for her pa as she imagined his huge, warm hands wrapped around that tiny little baby's body, giving it heat, keeping it alive.

Her father took a long, deep, troubled breath as he remembered that night, and then he continued his story. "You have to understand the poor little thing had been born with her eyes closed, Sera, and the nuns said that she would never see. She'd been born deaf, and they said she would never hear. And it was plain enough to see that she had four toes on each foot instead of five, but that was the least of it. Her collarbones were malformed, and she had an unnaturally long, curving spine—all twisted-like—and she did not look like she could survive."

The shock hit her like a blow. She looked up at her father in astonishment. "I'm the baby!" she shouted, leaping to her feet. This wasn't just a story, this was *her* story. She'd been born in the forest. That meant her pa had *found* her and taken her in. She was like a baby fox who'd been raised by a coyote. She stood in front of her pa. "I'm the baby!" she said again.

Her father looked at her, and she saw the truth of it flickering in his eyes, but he didn't acknowledge it. He didn't say yes and didn't say no. It was like he couldn't reconcile his memory of that dark night with the daughter he had now, and he had to tell the story the only way he could: as if it wasn't her at all.

"The bones of the baby's back weren't connected to each other the way they should have been," he continued. "The nuns were half scared out of their wits at the idea of caring for this child, like it was some sort of demon spawn, but to me she was a little baby, a little chitlan, and you didn't abandon such a thing. Who cares how many toes she had!"

Serafina kneeled on the floor in front of him, trying to understand it all. She was beginning to see the kind of man her father was and maybe where she got some of her own stick-to-it-iveness. But it was all so confusing. How could she get anything from him if she wasn't even his?

"I took that baby away, fearin' them nuns would drown her," he said.

"I hate them nuns," she spat. "They're terrible!"

He shook his head, not in disagreement, but more like the nuns didn't mean anything at all because they were the least of his problems.

"I didn't have any proper food," he said, "so I crept into a farmer's barn and milked his goat—stole a bottle, too. Felt ashamed doin' these things, but I needed to get some food into her, and I couldn't see a better road. That night, I fed the little chitlan her first meal, and as bad off as she was, and with her eyes still closed, she drank it down real good, and I remember praying that somehow it'd help. The more I held her and watched her suck down that milk, the more I wanted her to live."

"Then what happened?" She slid closer to him. She knew that outside the locked door of the electrical room, somewhere above them, the lawful inhabitants of Biltmore Estate were searching from room to room, but she didn't care. "Keep goin', Pa," she nudged.

"I looked for a woman who could mother the baby proper, but none of them would do it. They was sure she was gonna die. But two weeks later, while I was fixin' an engine with one hand and bottle-feedin' the chitlan with the other, somethin' happened. She opened her eyes for the first time and stared straight at me. All I could do was stare right back at her. She had these big, beautiful yellow eyes that just didn't stop. I knew then and there that I was hers, and she was mine, that we were kin now, and there was no denyin' it."

Serafina was so mesmerized by his story that she barely blinked. The yellow eyes that her father spoke of were still looking at him, and they had been for twelve years.

He rubbed his mouth slowly with his hand, looked over at the dynamo, and then continued the story. "In the time that followed, I fed the little chitlan every morning and every night. I slept with her tucked under my arm. I nestled her in an open toolbox beside me when I worked. When she started growing up a little, I taught her how to crawl and run about. I was tryin' my best to take good care of her—she was mine now, you see—but people started askin' questions and government types started comin' around. Men with badges and guns. One night when I was out workin' in the train yard, three of 'em waited until she wandered off a bit, and then they cornered her, trapped her in real tight. They was gonna take her away and put her someplace, God knows where, or maybe worse. I hit the first officer so hard that he went down bleeding and he didn't get up, then I struck the second one and grabbed for the third, but he skedaddled on outta there. The little chitlan was all right, thank God, but I knew we were in trouble. They'd be comin' back with more men next time, chains for me, and a cage for the chitlan. I knew then that we had to go. We had to escape the pryin' eyes and yammerin' mouths in the city, so I quit the train yard and found a new job way up in the mountains, workin' the construction of a great house."

She gasped as she realized that he hadn't just been hiding *her*; he'd been hiding *them*. *That's why we're in the basement,* she thought as a wave of relief passed through her. He was protecting her.

"I took care of her through good times and bad," her pa continued, "just doin' everything I could, and over the years, the strange little creature that I found in the forest grew up into a fine little girl, and I did my best to forget how she came into the world or how I got her."

And here, finally, her father paused and looked at her in earnest. "And that's you now, Sera," he said. "That's you. It's plain to see that you're not like other girls, but you're not misshapen or hideous like them nuns said you'd be. You're remarkably graceful in your movements—fast and agile like I've never seen. You're not deaf and blind like they said, but real sharp in your senses. I've been protecting you every day for the last twelve years, and the God's truth: they've been the best twelve years of my life. You mean the world to me, girl. There's no shame here, none at all, just a strong desire to keep us both alive."

When he stopped and looked at her with his steady dark eyes, she realized that she'd been sobbing, and quickly wiped the tears off of her face before he got mad at her for crying. In some ways, she had never felt closer to her pa than at that moment, for his story had snagged her heart, but there was something else roiling up inside her, too: her father wasn't her father. He'd found her in the woods and taken her. He'd been lying to her and everyone else for her entire life. All these years he'd refused to talk about her mother, just let her wonder on and on, and now here it was. The truth. Tears kept streaming down her face. She felt so stupid imagining fancy ladies and her mother forgetting her in a washing machine and all that stuff she used to think about when she was little. She'd spent countless hours wondering where she came from and he had known all this the whole time.

"Why didn't you tell me?" she asked him.

He didn't answer her.

"Why didn't you tell me, Pa?" she asked again.

Staring at the ground, he shook his head slowly back and forth.

"Pa . . ."

Finally, he said, "Because I didn't want it to be true."

She stopped and looked at him in shock. "But it *is* true, Pa. You can't just wish things aren't true when they are true!"

"I'm sorry, Sera," he said. "I just wanted you to be my little girl."

She was angry, very angry, but she felt a lump in her throat. He had finally reached deep down into his heart and told her what he was thinking, what he was feeling, what he was frightened of, and what he dreamed of.

And what he dreamed of was *her*.

She clenched her teeth and breathed through her nose and looked at him.

She was angry and confused and amazed and excited and frightened all at the same time. She finally knew the truth. At least some of it.

Now she knew that she didn't just *feel* different, she *was* different.

The thought of it terrified her: she was a creature of the night.

She came from the very forest that her pa had taught her to fear all her life and had forbidden her to enter. The thought of coming from that place repulsed her, scared her, but at the same time there was a strange confirmation in it, almost a relief. It made a twisted kind of sense to her.

She looked at her father, sitting with his back against the wall. Now that he had finally told her the story, he seemed exhausted, like a man who had shared a great burden.

He picked himself up off the floor, brushed off his hands, and walked slowly to the other side of the room, deep in thought.

"I'm sorry, Sera," he said. "I reckon it ain't gonna do ya no good on the inside knowin' all that, but you're right, you're growin' up now, and ya deserved to know." He came over to her and squatted down and held her so that he could look into her face. "But whatever you do with it, I want you to remember this one thing: there's nothin' wrong with you, Sera, nothin' at all, you hear?"

"Yeah, I hear, Pa," she said, nodding and wiping the tears from her eyes. There was turmoil in her heart, but one thing she knew for sure: her father believed in her. But even as she stood there looking at him, thoughts and questions started weaving through her mind.

Would she have to stay hidden forever? Could she ever fit in with the people of Biltmore? Could she ever make any friends? She was a creature of the night, but what did that mean she could do? She looked down at her hand. If she grew out her fingernails, would they become claws?

In the distance she could hear the sound of the search party moving through the basement, and she tried to block it out. She looked over at her father again. After a long pause, she quietly asked the question that had been forming in her mind.

"What about my mother?"

Her pa shut his eyes for a second as he took a good, long breath, and then he opened his eyes, looked at her, and spoke to her with unusual softness. "I'm sorry, Sera. The truth is I don't rightly know. But when I see her in my mind, I think she must have been beautiful, both lovely and strong. She fought hard to bring you into the world, Sera, and she wanted to stay with you, but she knew she couldn't. I don't know why she couldn't. But she gave you to me to love and take care of, and for that I'm much obliged."

"So maybe she's still out there someplace. . . ." Her voice trembled, uncertain. Her pa's story had made it feel like there was a tornado twisting inside of her, but the thought of her momma felt like the bursting of the sun.

"Maybe she is," he relented, gently.

She looked at him. "Pa, do you . . . do you think that . . . do you know if she was human or—"

"I don't want to hear any talk 'bout that," he interrupted her, shaking his head. She could see in the tightness of his mouth how upset her question made him. "You're my little girl," he said. "That's what I believe."

"But in the forest—" she began.

"No," he cut off her, "I don't want you to think about that. You live here. With me. This is your home. I've told ya before, and I'll tell ya again, Sera: our world is filled with many mysteries, things we don't understand. Never go into the deep parts of the forest, for there are many dangers there, both dark and bright, and they will ensnare your soul."

She stared at her pa for a long time, trying to comprehend his words. She could see the seriousness in his eyes, and she felt it, too, deep down in her heart. Her pa was the only person she'd ever had in the world.

She heard men coming down the corridor outside the door. They were searching the rooms of the subbasement. The hair on her arms tingled, telling her to run.

She looked at her pa. After all he'd done for her by telling her this story, she didn't want to bring it up again, didn't want to make him angry, but she had to ask one last question.

"What about the man who took the girl in the yellow dress? What kind of demon is he, Pa? Does he come out of the forest, or do you think he's one of the fancy-dressed swells from upstairs?"

"I don't know," he said. "I've been prayin' to God in heaven that it was a figment of your imagination."

"It wasn't, Pa," she said softly.

He didn't want to argue with her anymore, but he looked straight at her. "Don't get it in your head you're gonna go out there, Sera," he said. "It's just too dangerous for us. You see why now. I know you're hankering to help her, and that does ya credit, but don't worry about the girl. She's their kin, not ours. They don't need our help. They'll find her. You stay out of it."

At that moment, someone pounded on the heavy wooden door to the electrical room.

"We're searching the house!" a man shouted.

Serafina glanced around even though she already knew there was no way out of the room.

"Open this door!" shouted another man. "Open up!"

5

The moment her pa opened the door, Mr. Boseman and two other men stormed into the electrical room. Serafina clung to the metal racks on the ceiling, hidden among the hundreds of thick copper wires that ran to the floors above.

While her pa launched into an elaborate explanation of exactly how a dynamo generated electricity to the bewildered men, Serafina crawled along the ceiling, dropped silently to the floor behind them, and darted out the open door.

She dashed down the corridor and crawled into a small coal chute, then curled up in the darkness and hunkered down.

She'd always had a hankering for sitting quietly in dark, confined spaces. As she peered out of the blackness through a small hole in the chute's iron door and watched the searchers go by one way and then the other, her mind kept going back to the story that her pa had told her about her birth. It infuriated her that he'd waited this long to tell her. Could it really be true? Had she actually been born on the ground one night out in the darkness of the forest? Her momma, whoever she was, must have been very brave.

But the more she thought about it, the more she reckoned that maybe her momma didn't just go sauntering into the forest that night to give birth. Maybe she already lived there. And if that was true, then what kind of creature had her mother been? And what kind of creature did that make her? What if her pa had been wrong to take her?

It was all so confusing. She felt more unsettled and disjointed than ever. Suddenly, her pa wasn't her pa and Biltmore wasn't her home. And she still didn't have a momma.

She knew now that her pa had been hiding her because he was scared of what people would do to her. But it still confused her because her pa loved her, so couldn't other people love her, too? What difference did it make when you slept and when you hunted? It seemed like everyone must love the feeling of lying in the warm sunlight of a window, or seeing a bird fly across the sky, or taking a walk on a cool, moonlit night when all the stars were overhead. She wasn't sure if most boys and girls her age could catch one rat or two with their bare hands, but she didn't think that it was too strange a thing either way.

As another search party moved past her, Serafina watched

them and shook her head. If Clara Brahms was alive and wanted to hide, there were plenty of places for her to do so. Adults, even a hundred of them running around in a panic, didn't seem to grasp all that was possible in a place like Biltmore. There were *thousands* of places to hide. She hoped they would somehow find Clara, despite what she had seen happen the night before, but she didn't think they would. Clara Brahms was *gone*.

You're too loud and moving too fast, she thought as the searchers went by. *You're never going to find her that way. You've got to catch the rat.*

Her pa had told her to leave them to it, that it wasn't any of her business, that they weren't her kin, but who was he to say who was kin and who wasn't? He stole babies out of the woods! What if Clara was still alive and needed her help? How could she just sit there and watch? What if the Man in the Black Cloak came again and took someone else? She resolved that she needed to find Braeden Vanderbilt again and tell him what she'd seen. It wouldn't be right not to. She'd always dreamed of having a friend, but what kind of friend was she going to be to Clara Brahms if she didn't try to help her?

When the corridor was clear, she crawled out of the chute and snuck away. Her plan was to creep upstairs, but when she passed the mossy stairway that led down to the lower levels of the basement, she wondered if there'd be any sign of what had happened the night before. The young master would be far more likely to believe her story if she could bring him some sort of evidence of what she'd seen.

She slinked down the stairs, down and down again, into the damp darkness of the subbasement until she came to the slanted, brown-dripping corridor.

She couldn't stop her breathing from getting heavier, but she kept going, telling herself that she'd be safe.

She crept through the darkness until she came to the spot where she'd seen the Man in the Black Cloak. There was no sign of Clara Brahms, but there were red drips on the wall. On the floor she found a tiny shard of glass. *From the broken lantern,* she thought.

She searched the area but found nothing else.

On her way back, she followed the same series of corridors she had used to escape the demon or whatever it was. She studied the areas where she had battled for her life. She spotted something lying at the base of the wall that, at first glance, looked like a dead, rotting rat. It had the size and color of one of the nasty vermin, but as she took a step closer, her nose wrinkled. It gave off a putrid, foul smell, but it wasn't a rat. She clenched her teeth and got down onto her hands and knees and examined it. It was a glove lying crumpled on the floor. Images of the Black Cloak swirling around her rose up in her mind, the cloak cutting her off from all she knew and loved.

It's just a glove, you silly fool, she thought, smiling at her scaredy-cat thoughts, but when she picked it up, her mouth curled in disgust. Inside the glove there were bloody patches of skin.

It was so disgusting, far worse than any rat carcass she'd

ever found, but she forced herself to examine it more closely. The glove was made out of a fine, thin, black satin material. The flakes and patches of skin inside appeared as if they had sloughed off the hand that had last worn the glove. The skin had black spots and gray hairs. It was as if the owner of the glove hadn't just been old, but aging rapidly, almost disintegrating. Her muscles twitched as she remembered fighting for her life. She had bitten and clawed in a wild frenzy. The glove must have fallen from his belt or pocket, for she remembered that his hands had been bare and bloody when she fought him.

Men's gloves were as common as top hats and canes, so it wasn't a very good clue. It didn't provide her evidence to show to the young master. But it did stiffen the idea that whoever or whatever the Man in the Black Cloak was, there was something wrong with him.

Anxious to get out of the damp and more determined than ever to find the young master, she scampered her way up to the main level of the basement.

Many of the rooms on this level had windows at the tops of the walls. Outside, she could see servants and guests searching the gardens, the Rambles maze, and the many footpaths. She couldn't help but hope to see Braeden Vanderbilt among them.

She wondered if she could think of Braeden as her friend now, or if she was fooling herself. The God's honest truth was that she didn't even know what a friend was, other than what she'd read in books. If you meet someone face-to-face and they don't hiss at you and bite you, does that mean you're friends?

But when she thought about it a little more, she remembered that she did in fact nearly hiss at the young master when they first met, so that wasn't ideal. Maybe they weren't friends at all. Maybe he thought she was nothing but a lowly dirt-scraper from the basement and she didn't warrant a second thought. She probably should have told him right off that she was the C.R.C. That would have been a lot more impressive. As it was, she just wasn't sure what sort of impression she'd made, except that she was dirty, rude, unkempt, and had bad hair.

She darted up the stairs to the first floor. She took advantage of the chaos of the search to scurry unseen from one hiding spot to another. She moved silently, padding swiftly on soft feet. The adults spoke so loudly and made such a galumphing noise when they stomped all over the place that they were easy to avoid.

She dashed over to the Winter Garden, where she hid beneath the fronds of the tropical plants.

As Mrs. Vanderbilt and two servants hurried down the corridor, Serafina scooted into the Billiard Room and made a narrow escape. She thought that even her rodent enemies would have been impressed by her quickness of foot on that particular maneuver.

Walled in rich oak paneling and appointed with soft leather chairs, the Billiard Room smelled of cigar smoke. Deep-hued Oriental carpets covered the floor. Black wrought-iron lamp fixtures hung down from the ceiling over the game tables. Animal heads and hunting trophies lined the walls. She liked those.

The trophies on the walls reminded her of the rats she'd killed and laid at her pa's feet. So she and the Vanderbilts had that much in common. On the other hand, she had stopped doing that when she realized that it was the catching she liked more than the killing.

Just as she was about to leave the room, a footman came in with one of the maids. Serafina quickly dove beneath the billiard table.

"Maybe she's been giving us the slip at every turn, Miss Whitney," the footman said, leaning down to look under the billiard table just as Serafina darted behind the sofa.

"She could be just about anywhere, Mr. Pratt," Miss Whitney agreed, looking behind the sofa just as Serafina hid in the green velvet curtains that adorned the windows.

"Do you know if anyone has checked the pipe organ?" Mr. Pratt asked. "There's a secret room back there."

"The girl is a pianist, so she might be curious about the organ," Miss Whitney agreed.

Taking a quick breath and using the curtain for cover, Serafina climbed up the window stile lickety-split, then wedged herself into the uppermost corner of the window. She had just enough time to see that Mr. Pratt was wearing white gloves, a black tie, and a black-and-white footman's livery, but she took special notice of his black patent-leather dress shoes.

"What do you mean, she's a pianist?" Mr. Pratt asked.

"Tilly, on the third floor, told me the girl's some sort of musical prodigy, gives piano concerts all over the country,"

Miss Whitney said, as she ran her hands through the curtains where Serafina had just been hiding.

Serafina held her breath and stayed very still. Miss Whitney was so close to her now that she could smell her sweet lavender-and-rose perfume. All Miss Whitney had to do was pull back the curtain and look up, and she'd see Serafina clinging there with a Cheshire smile. Despite her fear of being seen, Serafina couldn't resist noticing the details of the maid's outfit. She loved the pretty pink uniform with its white collar and cuffs, which the maids wore in the morning before changing into their more formal black-and-white uniforms in the afternoon.

"Come on. There's no one in here," Mr. Pratt said. "We'll check the pipe organ."

Serafina breathed a sigh of relief as Miss Whitney walked to the other side of the room.

Mr. Pratt pushed the oak-paneled wall just to the right of the fireplace.

"Oh my!" Miss Whitney said in surprise, laughing nervously as a concealed door opened up. "I've cleaned this room countless times, and I never knew that was there. You're always so clever, Mr. Pratt."

Serafina rolled her eyes at Miss Whitney's silliness. The maid was obviously besotted with this know-it-all footman. Serafina liked Miss Whitney, but she could sure use some help learning how to sniff out a rat. And that was exactly what Serafina thought about shiny-shoes Mr. Pratt.

Mr. Pratt laughed, clearly pleased with Miss Whitney's reaction to his little trick.

"How do you know about all these secret things?" Miss Whitney asked him. "Do you skulk through the rooms at night when everyone else is sleeping?"

"Oh, I'm full of surprises, Miss Whitney, and not just about a little girl in a yellow dress, you wait and see," he said. "Come on . . ."

Yellow dress? How did he know what Clara was wearing when she disappeared? There was something about this footman that Serafina didn't like. He was too slick, too flirty, too tricky in his hoity-toity black livery, and she didn't trust him any more than she trusted a rat in the pastry kitchen.

I wouldn't go in there if I were you! She wanted to shout to Miss Whitney as they passed through the concealed door, but instead she listened to the rat's footsteps. They were similar to the footsteps she'd heard in the basement the night before, but he and Miss Whitney disappeared into the wall too quickly for her to be sure one way or the other.

As soon as they were gone, she climbed down and checked the area to the right of the fireplace to make sure she'd be able to find the concealed door if she ever needed it. A concealed door could be a very useful thing to a girl of her particular occupation. Measuring three oak panels tall and two oak panels wide, the door was disguised to look exactly like the wall. There was even a framed picture hanging there, a weirdly realistic tintype of a white-haired old man that she guessed was probably Mr. Vanderbilt's long-dead grandfather, Cornelius Vanderbilt.

It pained her to think that not only did she not have a grandpa to tell her stories about the old times, she barely even had a pa anymore. He was just someone who found her in a bloody heap and decided to steal goat's milk to keep her alive in his toolbox. He could be anybody. And she was still mightily perturbed at him for not coming straight with her sooner.

Below the hunting trophies that loomed above, the wall was covered with portraits of Vanderbilts. Mother, father, grandmother, grandfather, brothers and sisters and cousins. She found herself instinctively searching the faces to see if any of them resembled her. Was Clara Brahms alive someplace, wondering if her mother had forgotten her, just as Serafina often wondered about her own? But the difference was that Mrs. Brahms hadn't forgotten her daughter, would never leave her behind. Clara Brahms's mother was still looking for her.

Serafina stepped closer to the wall of pictures. The last picture was another depiction of old Cornelius, the patriarch of the grand Vanderbilt family, walking proudly beside one of his iron steam trains, the blur of his motion giving him a ghostlike quality. It put shivers down her spine just looking at it. But the picture had gone a bit catawampus when Mr. Pratt and Miss Whitney went through, so she straightened it out. When she touched the door, it glided open on smooth, well-oiled hinges. She took a deep breath, then slipped through.

. . .

To her surprise, the secret door led to the Smoking Room. From there, she found a similar passage into the Gun Room, with its racks of rifles and shotguns protected by panes of glass. Seeing her reflection in the glass, she spit on the back of her hand and wiped her face until she got a few of the larger smudges off her cheeks and chin. Then she smoothed her long brown-streaked hair back behind her ears in a few quick movements. She stood there and just stared at herself, wondering.

If her momma saw her, would she recognize her? Would she hug her and kiss her or would she look the other way and just keep walking? When strangers saw her, what did they think? What did they see, a girl or a creature?

As a group of estate guests walked past the room, she heard them talking in hushed voices that perked up her ears.

"I'm telling you it's true!" a young man whispered.

"I heard about it, too," whispered another. "My grandmama told me that there's an old cemetery out there with hundreds of gravestones, but the bodies are missing!"

"I heard there's an old village," said a third voice. "It's all overgrown and taken back by the forest, like everyone who lived there abandoned their houses."

Serafina had heard the tall tales passed around among the kitchen folk at night, but she'd never been too sure whether she was supposed to believe them or not.

Every place she went in the house that day, she overheard conversations—gentlemen discussing whether detectives should be called in to investigate the missing child; servants trading stories about suspicious guests; and parents arguing about the best way to protect their sons and daughters from getting lost in the giant house without being rude to the Vanderbilts. And now they were talking about the old cemetery in the woods.

She kept thinking about the Man in the Black Cloak. If he was one of these people, he could be lurking in any corridor or room. How do you tell a friend from an enemy just by looking at him?

It seemed like the farther she went, the more questions she had. The only thing certain so far was that the search continued and they still hadn't found Clara Brahms. Either alive or dead.

Then she had an idea. If the Man in the Black Cloak was some sort of wraith that drifted out of the forest at night, or if he conjured himself out of the ether in the basement, then she probably wouldn't find very much evidence of him in the upper floors of the house. But if the Man in the Black Cloak was at least partially mortal and resided at Biltmore, then he'd have to stash his cloak someplace when he wasn't wearing it. If she could find the cloak, then maybe she could find the man.

The closets and storerooms throughout the house were some of her favorite hiding spots, so she knew them well. When ladies and gentlemen came to Biltmore, they usually exited from their carriages at the front door. But in bad weather, they used the covered porte cochere at the north end of the house, near the stables. Always just out of sight, darting and dodging, creeping and crawling, she made her way there.

The coatroom was dark and cramped, which suited her just fine. She loved closets. As she pushed her way through the thick forest of coats, cloaks, stoles, and capes, she searched the hangers one by one, looking for a long black satin cloak. When she reached the back wall of the coatroom without finding it, she couldn't help but feel a pang of disappointment.

As she crept out of the coatroom, she realized that she'd have to go to Braeden without any proof, but the truth was that she hadn't been able to find *him*, either.

You've got to think, girl, she heard her pa telling her in the tone he used when she couldn't reckon one of her lessons. *Use what you know, and think it through.*

An idea came to her. Knowing what she did about Braeden Vanderbilt, he'd either be with his dog or his horse or both. He loved horses. It would be the first thing he thought of. He'd go to the stables to help the stablemen look for Clara Brahms there. Or maybe he'd search the grounds on horseback. Either way, the stables seemed like the place to go.

The most direct path was through the porte cochere. There were quite a few people coming and going through this busy area, but she hoped that if anyone spotted her, they'd assume she was a scullery maid or a kindling girl going about her chores.

She took a deep breath and ran down the steps toward the archway that led to the stables. She moved fast. She thought she was going to make it. But just as she looked behind her to make sure no one was following her, she collided with a great smash into a large man in front of her. It knocked the wind out of her and nearly knocked her off her feet, but the man grabbed her by the shoulders and held her up with a brutal grip.

Her captor wore a full-length black rain cloak even though it wasn't raining. He had a peculiar pointed beard, crooked teeth, and an ugly, pockmarked face. She hadn't seen the face of the Man in the Black Cloak, but this is what she'd imagined he'd look like.

"What you lookin' at?" he demanded. "Who is you, anyway?"

"I ain't nobody!" she spat defiantly, trying desperately to tear herself free and run, but the man's hands clamped her so tight that she couldn't escape. Now it was her turn to be the biting rat with its neck squeezed between finger and thumb. She noticed that he was standing in front of the open door of an awaiting carriage.

"You the new pig girl?" the man demanded. "What you doin' up 'ere?" He tightened his grip so viciously on her arms that she let out a squeal of pain. "I said, what's your name, ya little scamp?"

"None of your business!" she said as she kicked and fought any way she could.

The man had a terrible smell, like he needed a bath really, really bad, and his breath stank with the huge wad of putrefied chewing tobacco that bulged in his cheek.

"Tell me your name, or I'm gonna shake ya," the man said even as he shook her. He shook her so violently that she couldn't catch her breath or get her feet on the ground. He just kept shaking her.

"Mr. Crankshod," a firm, authoritative voice said from behind her. It wasn't just a name. It was a command.

Startled, the ugly man stopped shaking her. He set her on her feet and began to smooth her hair, pretending that he had actually been taking care of her all along.

Gasping for breath, she turned to look at who had spoken.

There stood Braeden Vanderbilt at the top of the steps.

Serafina's heart sprang. Despite the terrible situation he'd caught her in and the angry expression on his face, she was glad to see Braeden.

The crab-crankedy Mr. Crankshod, however, was far less pleased. "Young Master Vanderbilt," he grumbled in surprise as he bowed, wiped the tobacco spittle from his lip, and stood at attention. "I beg your pardon, sir. I didn't see you there. Your coach is ready, sir."

Braeden looked at them both without speaking. Clearly, he wasn't pleased by what he'd just seen. The boy's Doberman appeared ready to attack whichever of them his master told him to, and Serafina hoped that it was going to be the sputum-faced Mr. Crankshod rather than her.

Braeden stared at Mr. Crankshod, then slowly moved his eyes to her. Her mind whirled with potential cover stories. He had stopped the mountainous brute from shaking the living daylights out of her, but what could she say to explain her presence here?

"I'm the new shoeshine girl," she said, stepping forward. "Your aunt asked me to make sure your boots were well shined for your trip, sir, spit and polished good, sir. That's what she said, all right, spit and polished good."

"No, no, no!" Mr. Crankshod shouted, knowing it was a ruse. "What's this, now, ya little beggar? You ain't no shoeshine girl! Who is ya? Where'd ya come from?"

But a smile of delicious conspiracy formed at the corner of Braeden's mouth. "Ah, yes, Aunt Edith did mention something about getting my boots shined. I had quite forgotten," he said, exaggerating the aristocratic air in his voice. Then he looked at her sharply and his eyebrows furrowed into a frown. "I'm on my way to the Vances', and I'm running late. I don't have time to wait on you, so you'll just have to come with me and do it in the carriage on the way."

Serafina felt the blood rush to her face. Was he serious? She couldn't go in a carriage with him! Her pa would kill her. And what was she gonna do all cooped up in there anyway, getting dragged around in a box by a bunch of four-legged black hoof-stompers?

"Well, come along, let's be quick about it," Braeden said, his voice filled with the impatience of a lordly gentleman as he gestured toward the carriage door.

She had never been in a carriage in her life. She didn't even know how to get in one or what to do once she did.

The ill-tempered, rat-faced Mr. Crankshod had no choice but to obey the young master's commands. He shoved Serafina toward the door, and she suddenly found herself in the dimly lit interior of the Vanderbilt carriage. As she crouched uncertainly on the floor, she could not help but marvel at the carriage's luxuriously appointed finery with its hand-carved woodwork, brass fixtures, beveled-glass windows, and plush, paisley, tufted seats.

Braeden followed her in with the grace of familiarity and took a seat. Gidean sat on the floor, eyeing her with fanged intent.

Mind your own business, dog, she thought as she stared back at him.

Mr. Crankshod shut the carriage door and climbed up onto the driver's bench with the other coachman.

Oh, great, rat face is driving us, Serafina thought. She had no idea how long a trip this would be or how she could send word back to her pa. He'd ordered her to hide in the basement, not get kidnapped by the young master and his stink-breathed henchman. But at least she'd finally be able to talk to Braeden alone about what she saw the night before.

The carriage seat looked too clean for her to sit on with her basement clothing, and she was supposed to be cleaning the young master's boots, so she knelt on the floor of the carriage and wondered how she was going to pretend to clean his boots when she didn't have any brushes or polish. Spit and polish was one thing, but just spit was another.

"You don't really have to clean my boots," Braeden said softly. "I was just going along with your story."

Just as Serafina looked up at him and their eyes were about to meet, the horses pulled and the carriage jounced forward. In a moment as unusual as it was mortifying, she actually lost her balance. "I'm sorry," she mumbled as she fell against Braeden's legs and then quickly straightened herself up.

She glanced at the seat that she suspected she was supposed to be sitting on, but the dog stared at her with his steely eyes. When she moved toward the seat, the dog growled, low and menacing, baring his teeth as if to say, *If I can't sit on the seat, then neither can you.*

"No, Gidean," Braeden chastised him. She couldn't decide if the young master had spoken the command because he wanted to protect her or if he just didn't want to get the inside of his carriage bloody. In any case, Gidean's ears crumpled and his head lowered under the force of his master's reprimand.

Seeing her chance, she slipped onto the seat opposite Braeden and as far away from the dog as possible.

As Gidean continued staring at her, she felt an overwhelming desire to hiss at him and make him back off, but she didn't think that would go over too well with the young master, so she held back the urge.

She had never liked dogs, and dogs had never liked her. Whenever they saw her, they barked. One time, she had to scurry up a tree to get away from a crazed foxhound, and her pa had to use a ladder to retrieve her.

When the carriage rumbled into a turn, Serafina looked out the window and saw the grand facade of the house. Biltmore Estate rose four stories high with its ornately carved gray stone walls. Gargoyles and ancient warriors adorned its dark copper edges. Chimneys, turrets, and towers formed the spires of its almost Gothic presence. Two giant statues of lions guarded the massive oak doors at the entrance, as if warding off evil spirits. She had marveled at those statues many times on her midnight prowls. She had always loved them. She imagined that those great cats were Biltmore's protectors, its guardians, and she could think of no more important job.

In the golden light of the setting sun, the mansion really could be quite startlingly lovely. But as the sun withdrew its brightness behind the surrounding mountains, it cast ominous shadows across the estate, which reminded her of griffins, chimeras, and other twisted creatures of the night that were half one thing and half another. The thought of it gave her a shudder. In one moment, the estate was the most beautiful home you had ever seen, but in the next, it was a dark and foreboding haunted castle.

"Lie down and be good," Braeden said.

She looked at him in surprise and then realized that he was talking to the dog, not to her.

Gidean complied with his master's request and lay down at his feet. The dog seemed a little more relaxed now, but when he looked at Serafina, his expression seemed to say, *Just because I'm lying down, don't think for a second that if you do something to my master I can't still kill you. . . .*

She smiled to herself. She couldn't help it—she was beginning to like this dog. She could understand him, his fierceness and his loyalty. She admired that.

As she tried to get used to the rumbling motion of the moving carriage, she noticed that Braeden was studying her.

"I've been looking for you . . ." he said.

She stole a quick glance at him and then looked away. When she looked into his eyes, it felt like he could tell what she was thinking. It was unnerving.

She tried to say something, but when she opened her mouth, she could barely breathe. Of course, she'd snuck around enough over the years to overhear people of all walks of life speaking to one another, so theoretically she knew how it was done. So many guests and servants had passed through Biltmore over the years that she could take on a rich lady's air or a mountain woman's twang or even a New York accent, but for some reason, she struggled mightily to find the right words—any words—to say to the young master.

"I—I'm sorry about all this," she said finally. The annoying constriction in her chest seemed to strangle her words as she spoke them. She wasn't sure if she sounded anything like a halfway normal person or not. "I mean, I'm sorry about being dumped into your carriage like luggage that wouldn't fit on the roof, and I don't know why your dog doesn't like me."

Braeden looked at Gidean and then back at her. "He normally likes people, especially girls. It's strange."

"There are plenty of strange things happening today," she said, her chest loosening up a bit as she began to realize that Braeden was going to actually talk to her.

"You think so, too?" he said, leaning toward her.

He wasn't anything like what she imagined the young master of the Vanderbilt mansion would be, especially as good-looking and well educated as he was. She had expected him to be snobbish, bossy, and aloof, but he was none of these things.

"I don't think Clara Brahms is hiding," he said in a conspiratorial tone. "Do you?"

"No," she said, raising her eyes and looking at him. "I definitely don't." She wanted to pour it all out and tell him everything she knew. That had been her plan all along. But her pa's words kept going through her mind: *They ain't our kind of folk, Sera.*

Whatever he was, Braeden seemed to be a good person. As he was talking to her, he didn't judge her or discount her. If anything, he actually seemed to like her. Or maybe he was just fascinated by her in the same way he would be by a weird species of insect he'd never seen before, but either way, he kept talking.

"She's not the first one, you know," he whispered.

"What do you mean?" she said, drawing closer to him.

"Two weeks ago, a fifteen-year-old girl named Anastasia Rostonova went out for a walk in the evening in the Rambles, and she didn't come back."

"Really?" she asked, hanging on his every word. She had thought she had something to tell him, but it turned out that he had just as much to tell her. A boy who whispered about kidnappings and skulduggery was the kind of boy she could learn to like. She knew the Rambles well, but she also knew that the shrubbery maze of crisscrossing paths caused many people great confusion.

"Everyone said Anastasia must have wandered into the forest and gotten lost," he continued, "or that she ran away from home. But I know they're wrong."

"How do you know?" she asked, keen to hear the details.

"The next morning, I found her little white dog wandering around the paths of the Rambles. The poor dog was frantic, desperately searching for her." Braeden looked at Gidean. "I didn't know Anastasia well—she'd only been visiting with her father for a couple of days when she disappeared—but I don't think she would have run away and left her dog behind."

Serafina thought that sounded about right. Braeden seemed as loyal to Gidean as Gidean was to him. They were friends, and she liked that. Then she thought about that poor girl and what might have happened to her.

"Anastasia Rostonova . . ." She repeated the funny-sounding name.

"She's the daughter of Mr. Rostonov, the Russian ambassador," Braeden explained. "She told me that Russian girls always put an *a* on the end of their last name."

"What did she look like?" she asked, wanting to make sure she hadn't gotten her kidnapped rich girls mixed up.

"She's tall and pretty, and she has long, curly black hair, and she wears elaborate red dresses that look really hard to walk in."

"Do you think she vanished like Clara Brahms?" Serafina asked.

Before he could answer, something caught her eye through the carriage windows. There were trees on either side of the carriage. They were traveling down a narrow dirt road that wound through a thick and darkened forest, the very forest that her pa had warned her to never enter. And the very forest where she had been born. She couldn't help but feel a pang of trepidation. "Where are we going, exactly?"

"My aunt and uncle are worried about me, so they're sending me to the Vances' in Asheville for the night to keep me out of harm's way. They ordered Crankshod to guard me."

"That wasn't very smart," she said before she could help herself. It wasn't a very polite thing to say, but for some reason, she was having a dickens of a time not telling Braeden the truth.

"I've always detested that man," Braeden agreed, "but my uncle depends on him."

As she looked out the window at the forest, she could no

longer see the horizon or the sun. All she could see was the thick density of the forest's huge old trees, black and decrepit, which grew so closely together that she could barely tell one from the other. It seemed a dark and foreboding place for anyone to even visit, let alone live, but there was something that excited her about it, too.

But then she felt a sinking sensation in her stomach. Somewhere, miles behind them, was Biltmore. Her pa would be wondering why she wasn't showing up for dinner. *No chicken or grits tonight, Pa. I'm sorry,* she thought. *Try not to worry about me.* A day ago, she had been leading a perfectly normal life catching rats in the basement, and now everything had turned so bizarre.

Pulling her gaze away from the forest, she finally turned to Braeden, swallowed hard, and began to say what she'd come for. "There is something I need to tell—"

"How come I've never seen you before?" he interrupted.

"What?" she asked, taken aback.

"Where do you come from?"

"Yeah, good question," she said before she could stop herself, imagining the bloody pile of dead creatures her pa had plucked her from.

"I'm serious," he said, staring at her. "Why haven't I seen you before?"

"Maybe you haven't been looking in the right places," she shot back at him, feeling cornered.

But when she saw his eyes, she realized that he wasn't going to give up. Her temples began to pound, and she couldn't think straight. Why was he asking all these infernal questions?

"Well, where do *you* come from?" she asked, trying to throw him off the trail.

"You know I live at Biltmore," he said gently. "I'm asking about you."

"I-I . . ." she stammered, staring at her lap. "Maybe you met me before and just forgot," she said.

"I would have remembered you," he said quietly.

"Well, maybe I'm just visiting for the weekend," she said weakly, looking at the floor.

He wasn't buying any of it. "Please tell me where you live, Serafina," he said firmly.

It surprised her when he said her name like that. It had tremendous power over her, like she had no choice but to look up at him and meet his gaze, which turned out to be a serious mistake. He was looking at her so intently that it felt as if he were casting a spell of truth on her.

"I live in your basement," she said, and was immediately shocked that she'd actually uttered it out loud. He had powers over her that she did not understand.

He stared at her as her words hung in the air. She could see the confusion in his face and sense the questions forming in his mind.

She had no idea why she said it. It had just come flying out of her mouth.

But she'd done it. She'd said it out loud, straight to his face. *Please forgive me, Pa.* She'd wrecked everything. She'd ruined their lives. Now her pa would be fired. They'd be kicked out of Biltmore. They'd be forced to wander the streets of Asheville, begging for scraps of food. No one would hire a man who'd lied to his employer, holed up in his basement, and stolen food from him for his eight-toed daughter. No one.

She looked at Braeden. "Please don't tell anyone . . ." she said quietly, but she knew there were no claws in that paw, nothing at all to protect her. If he wanted to, he could tell anyone—Mr. Crankshod, Mr. Boseman, even Mr. and Mrs. Vanderbilt—and then the life she and her pa had made together at Biltmore would be over. They might even go to prison for stealing food all those years.

Just as Braeden was about to speak, the horses screamed and the carriage slammed to a halt. She was hurled across the open space and crashed into him. Gidean leapt to his feet and began to bark wildly.

"Something has happened," Braeden said fiercely as he quickly untangled himself from her and opened the carriage door.

It was pitch-dark outside.

She tried to listen for what was out there, but her heart pounded so loudly that she couldn't hear a thing. She tried to calm herself down and really listen, but the forest was too quiet. There were no owls, no frogs, no insects, no birds—none of the normal night sounds she was used to hearing. Just silence.

It was like every living creature in the forest was hiding for its dear life. Or already dead.

"Mr. Crankshod?" Braeden asked uncertainly into the darkness.

No answer came.

The hairs on the back of Serafina's neck stood on end.

Braeden stepped partway out of the carriage and looked up at the driver's bench at the front. "There's no one there!" he said in astonishment. "They're both gone!"

The four horses were still in the harnesses, but the carriage had stopped dead in the road. Right in the middle of the forest.

7

Serafina climbed slowly out of the carriage and stood at Braeden's side. The forest surrounded them, black and impenetrable, the craggy-barked trees packed densely together. Her legs jittered beneath her, filled with nervous impulse. She tried to steady her breathing. Her whole body wanted to move, but she forced herself to stay with Braeden and Gidean.

She watched and listened to the unnaturally quiet forest, extending her senses out into the void. She couldn't hear a single toad or whip-poor-will. But it felt like there was something out there, something big but extremely quiet. She didn't even know how that was possible.

Gidean stood beside her on full alert, staring into the trees. Whatever it was, he sensed it, too.

Braeden looked warily into the darkness that surrounded them and walked forward a few feet in the direction the carriage was facing.

"I wish I had a lantern," he said. "I can't see anything at all."

The horses fidgeted in their harnesses, their hooves shifting uneasily in the gravel.

"When they're scared, they move their feet," Braeden said sympathetically. "They have no claws, no sharp teeth, no weapons. Their speed is their main defense."

She marveled at how Braeden didn't just see the horses but understood how they thought.

When a breeze passed through the woods and rattled the branches of the trees, the horses spooked. All four of them pulled and tugged against their harnesses. It was like they were being attacked by some invisible predator. Squealing, the front two horses reared up on their hind legs and struck the air with their hooves.

As Serafina shrank back from the danger in frightened dismay, Braeden rushed forward and put himself between her and the horses. Standing in front of them, he raised his open hands to calm them. They towered above him, their eyes white with fear, their heads thrashing and their hooves flying. She was sure they were going to kick him in the head, or slam him with a shoulder, or trample him to death, but he stood with his hands raised, speaking to them in soft, gentle tones. "It's all right. We're all here," he said to them. "We're all together."

To her astonishment, the horses were calmed by his presence and his words. He touched their shoulders with his outstretched hands and seemed to bring the rearing horses back to the ground. Then he held the head of the lead horse in his hands and pressed his forehead to the horse's forehead so that they were looking at each other eye to eye, and he spoke to the horse in quiet, reassuring tones. "We're in this together, my friend. We're going to be all right. . . . There's no need to run, no need to fight. . . ."

The lead horse breathed heavily through its nose as it listened to Braeden's words, then settled and became still. The other horses quieted as well, reassured by the young master.

"H-how did you . . . ?" she stammered.

"These horses and I have been friends for a long time," he replied, but said nothing more.

Still astounded by what he'd done, she looked around at their surroundings. "What do you think frightened them?"

"I don't know," he said. "I've never seen them so scared."

Braeden turned and looked down the road ahead of them. He squinted into the darkness and then he pointed. "What is that up there?" he asked. "I can't make it out. Does the road turn?"

She looked in the direction he pointed. It wasn't a turn in the road. A huge tree with thick, gnarly branches and a scattering of bloodred leaves lay across the road, completely blocking their path.

Suddenly, Mr. Crankshod emerged out of the darkness, trudging his way back to the carriage. "We're gonna need the ax," he grumbled angrily.

Serafina and Braeden looked at each other in surprise, then looked back at Mr. Crankshod.

"Where have you been?" Braeden asked.

"We're gonna need the ax," Mr. Crankshod said again, ignoring the question.

"I'll get it, sir," the assistant coachman said as he came running up from behind Mr. Crankshod.

She hadn't noticed him before, but the assistant coachman was just a skinny boy with a mop of curly hair. He stood no taller than the shoulder of the lead horse and had thin arms and legs, bony knees and elbows, and a coltish skittishness about him. He wore a coachman's jacket, but it was several sizes too big in the shoulders and the sleeves were too long. His black coachman's top hat seemed ridiculously tall on his little head. The boy couldn't have been older than ten. He ran to the rear of the carriage, opened the wooden storage box, and grabbed the ax, which looked huge in his hands.

"That's Nolan," Braeden said, leaning toward her. "He's actually one of the best carriage drivers we have, and he takes very good care of the horses."

"Give it to me," Mr. Crankshod barked as he grabbed the ax out of Nolan's hands and stomped over to the fallen tree.

"I can help, too, sir, I can," Nolan said, tagging along behind him with a small hatchet.

"Naw, ya can't. Just stay out of the way, boy," Mr. Crankshod shouted. He seemed irritated that Nolan was even there.

Mr. Crankshod heaved the ax behind him in a great, sweeping swing and slammed the blade into the center of the trunk. The leaves of the tree shuddered with the force of the blow, but it hardly made any dent at all in the thick bark.

He swung the ax again and again, and finally cut through the bark. The wood chips began to fly. Serafina couldn't help but notice the brute strength of the man, but it was hard for her to tell if this was the same type of strength the Man in the Black Cloak had possessed.

"At this rate, we're gonna be 'ere all night," Mr. Crankshod complained, and just kept chopping.

"I'm sure I can help, sir, I'm sure I can," Nolan said enthusiastically, standing by with his hatchet ready.

"I'm sure you can't! Now just get back and stay out of the way!" Mr. Crankshod shouted. "You're no use to anybody here, boy!"

As the grumpy Mr. Crankshod made war on the tree, Serafina noticed Braeden looking around them, trying to figure out if there was a way to navigate the carriage around the obstacle. But the trees of this wicked forest grew so closely together that a man could barely get through them, let alone a carriage with a team of horses.

"Where are we?" Serafina asked.

"I think we're about eleven or twelve miles from the estate, a place called Dardin Forest," Braeden said. "There used to be an old town nearby."

"Haven't been any people living in that village for years," Mr. Crankshod grumbled as he chopped at the tree. "Nothin' but ghosts and demons left in these woods now."

Serafina scanned the forest, filled with a sense of foreboding. It felt like they were being watched, but she couldn't figure out why she couldn't detect who or what was out there. Her ears twitched with nervousness. The trees slowly swayed back and forth in the wind. They were covered in strange gray lichen and strung with grayish-white moss, which hung down like the thin hair of an old dead woman. The branches buffeted and creaked, as if anxious in their plight. It appeared that many of the trees were dying.

She walked along the length of the fallen tree. She thought it was peculiar that the tree still held its red leaves this late in the year, but it was what she saw at the base of the trunk that truly disturbed her.

"Come look at this, Braeden," she said.

"What have you found?" he asked as he came up behind her.

"I thought the tree must be an old snag that had rotted and fallen over in the last storm, but take a look. . . ."

The stump of the tree didn't appear rotted, and it didn't have the fibrous appearance of a trunk that had been snapped by high winds. It was difficult to tell, but it almost appeared as if it had been gnawed by giant teeth or cut down with an ax.

"Look at the angle here," Braeden said, gesturing at the side of the stump in anger and confusion. "Someone purposely felled this tree so that it would block the road."

Gidean barked and made Serafina jump a mile. As the dog kept barking, Braeden knelt at his side and put his hands on the dog's back. "What's wrong, boy? What do you smell?"

"If it's all right with you," Mr. Crankshod said gruffly, "we're not gonna wait around to find out."

Spooked by the dog and apparently convinced that he'd cut through enough of the trunk, Mr. Crankshod dropped the ax, braced his heavy boots against the earth, and grabbed hold of the branches. He tried to drag the tree off the road, but it was far too large for him to budge.

Braeden and Nolan ran forward and tried to help. The whole time, Gidean just kept barking.

"Somebody hit that dog and shut it up!" Mr. Crankshod shouted, spittle flying from his mouth.

"Mr. Crankshod, I think we should turn the carriage around and go back the other way," Braeden said sharply, obviously perturbed by his comment about the dog.

Mr. Crankshod agreed, but at that moment, a loud cracking sound filled the forest air. Serafina crouched, prepared to spring. A great shattering of wood erupted into an explosive crash as a large tree fell across the road behind them.

The horses squealed in panic and went up rearing and striking, pulling on their leather harnesses and dragging the carriage across the ground even though the brake was engaged and the wheels wouldn't turn. Their instinct was to run, whether they were free of the harnesses or not.

Braeden ran forward to help them.

"No, Braeden!" Serafina cried as she reached to stop him. The boy seemed determined to get himself killed by a horse kick.

Braeden leapt in front of the horses. He was able to calm them with a few soft words and quickly got them under control. Seeing that he was safe, Serafina scanned the forest in the direction of the fallen tree. That's when she realized that the worst had happened: the carriage, its four horses, the four humans, and the dog were now trapped on a section of road between two trees.

Mr. Crankshod, gripping the ax, stomped to the back of the carriage and shouted furiously into the darkness, "Who's out there? Show yourselves, you rotten, filthy swine!"

Serafina looked into the darkness waiting for an answer to come, but Mr. Crankshod's words drifted out into the black nothingness without reply.

"Mr. Crankshod," Braeden said firmly, "we need to go back to cutting the tree in front of us. The safest course now is to press on to Asheville."

"I just hope we can get there," Mr. Crankshod carped beneath his breath, stomping back.

As Mr. Crankshod, Braeden, and Nolan worked on the tree, Serafina couldn't help but look behind the carriage where the most recent tree had fallen. Gidean was looking in that direction as well, his eyes black in the starlight.

"What do you think, boy?" she whispered as she crouched beside him and peered into the darkness. "Is there something out there?" She and the dog were on the same side now.

She wondered about the second fallen tree. It couldn't be a coincidence. Someone was deliberately blocking them in so that they could not escape.

She scanned the forest. She had good senses, but she knew she couldn't smell nearly as well as Gidean, and he seemed to smell something right now. He wasn't barking anymore, but was staring intently into the forest, waiting for something to appear. For all his faults as a dog, he was a brave defender.

But she hated this: the looking, the waiting, feeling like a trap was slowly surrounding them. She couldn't stand it. She didn't know how to defend; she knew how to *hunt*. And right now, it felt like they were the ones being hunted, and she didn't like the feeling one bit.

She took a few steps forward into the trees to see how it felt. Her skin crawled with equal parts fear and excitement. She was drawn into the forest. Her instinct was telling her to go deeper.

She took a few more steps.

Gidean looked at her and tilted his head as if to say, *Are you crazy? You can't go in there!*

But then she padded quietly into the trees and ducked into the underbrush. She wanted to move, to prowl, to see what was out there, whatever it was. She wanted to be the hunter, not the hunted.

Leaving Gidean to guard the carriage, she crept deeper and deeper into the darkness of the forest, the very same black forest that her father had told her never to enter, the very same dark forest that Crankshod had said was filled with ghosts and demons.

But she was calm. She was in the right place. She figured if her mother could move through the forest at night, then so could she.

Suddenly, she heard the sounds of footfalls in the brush in front of her, as clear as a rat's footsteps in the basement, but much louder, much *larger*, moving through the leaves and the dirt. She wasn't sure whether it was an animal or a human.

As she crept closer to the sound, she crouched down but kept moving slowly forward. Sound and sight and feeling and smell—her whole body felt alive with sensation. With all her senses working, all her muscles in play, she stalked so slowly, so quietly, that she didn't make a single sound.

She heard the footsteps ahead of her more closely now. Feet crunching through autumn leaves. Walking at first and then breaking into a run. A man running through the underbrush. Some fifty yards out into the woods. She ran toward the sound, knowing that when a rat was moving, it couldn't hear nearly as well as when it wasn't.

When the man suddenly stopped, she stopped as well and remained perfectly still, holding her breath.

She knew the man must be listening for her, but she made no sound.

As soon as he started moving again, she moved as well, shadowing him.

But then something happened. The footsteps stopped. She felt a swooshing sensation of air on her face and head, like the beat of a vulture's wing. And then suddenly she heard a second set of footsteps behind her, between her and the carriage. How was that possible? Were there multiple attackers?

The forest erupted in a cacophony of sound. Leaves crashing. Sticks breaking. The rush of rapid movement. Her muscles exploded to life. It was an attack coming in from all directions.

In the distance, Gidean started barking and snarling and gnashing his teeth as if he were facing down Satan himself.

The carriage, she thought. *They're attacking the carriage.* She turned and sprinted toward it, heedless of the sound she made. She glimpsed a flash of movement surge past her in the darkness but could not tell what it was. As she ran toward the carriage, she could see Braeden and Nolan. But where was Crankshod? He was the strongest person in their group, the man who was supposed to be protecting them.

"Look out, Braeden!" she shouted in warning. "They're coming. Look out!"

Hearing her call, Braeden turned just in time to dodge the flashing shape of the incoming attacker. But then, in a startling movement of whirling black shadow, the attacker turned and was upon him again. Gidean charged in, snarling and biting. Nolan punched and kicked. Fighting, shouting, striking—all was confusion in a swirl of motion and battle.

Just as Serafina came within striking distance, a large black shape floated past her. She flinched so hard that her back hit a tree. Giant centipedes poured out of logs. Worms oozed up out of the earth. The Man in the Black Cloak had come. He was here in these woods. There weren't multiple attackers. There was only one. He seemed to float on the violence of the battle, his decaying, blood-dripping hands reaching outward as he came upon Braeden. It was clear he wanted the boy in particular. Serafina leapt forward to defend her friend. Gidean charged as well, but it was little Nolan, in a desperate act of shouting courage, who threw himself in front of the young master and blocked the attack.

The Man in the Black Cloak opened his arms and pulled Nolan to his chest. The slithering folds of the cloak wrapped around the boy. Nolan's shouts turned to screams. The gray smoke filled the forest. The rattling shook the trees. And then Nolan disappeared.

It took her breath away to see it again. *"No!"* she cried out in anguish, anger, and frustration.

Then the shaking came, and the glowing, and the terrible stench that followed. Every leaf on every tree around them suddenly fell to the ground, drenched with blood, and the ground itself became a stinking, horrific mud.

Expanded in size and now seemingly more powerful than ever, the Man in the Black Cloak advanced, heading straight for Braeden once more.

Braeden needed to fight or flee, but he stood frozen in shock by what he'd just seen happen to Nolan. He stared at the Man in the Black Cloak, unable to move.

Without thinking, Serafina charged forward and pounced on the man's back. She caterwauled a wild and crazed screech of anger. Her hands and feet clawed at the man with snarling ferocity.

The Man in the Black Cloak had no choice but to turn and fight her. He tried to pull her off his back and wrap her in his voluminous black cloak like he had the others, but Braeden pulled back a mighty swing and slammed the man's head with a large branch. Gideon lunged forward and bit the attacker repeatedly. Serafina tore herself free, rolled to the ground, spun, and leapt back into the battle. All three of them pressed the attack.

The Man in the Black Cloak, his eyes still glowing with power, levitated upward. Three against one now, he had lost the element of surprise. He snapped the billowing folds of the Black Cloak with his arm, and a great explosion of air knocked Serafina off her feet. She went tumbling backward as the Man in the Black Cloak withdrew into the forest and then was gone.

Gasping to catch her breath, Serafina scrambled to her feet and readied herself for the next attack, but it never came.

The battle was over.

She looked at her hands. Her fingers were slippery with blood and her fingernails had torn at the Man in the Black Cloak's rotting skin, but it was more than just the remnants of the battle. It was like the skin in the glove. He was disintegrating.

Through the darkness, she saw Braeden lying on the ground. Frightened that he'd been wounded, she ran over to him. "Are you hurt?" she sputtered.

"I'm all right." He gasped as she helped him onto his feet. "What about you? Did he hurt you?"

"I'm all right," she said.

"I . . . I . . . I don't understand, Serafina. What was that thing? What happened to Nolan?"

"I don't know," she said, shaking her head in frustration.

"I mean, where did he go? Is he . . . is he . . . is he *dead*?"

She didn't know the answer to Braeden's questions. Thinking about poor little Nolan made her sick to her stomach, angry, frightened. He was just gone. How could she help him? It was the second time she'd battled the Man in the Black Cloak, and the second time she'd lost a friend.

"Come on. We gotta go before it comes back," she said, touching his shoulder.

"What happened to Crankshod?" Braeden asked as he and Gidean followed her back toward the carriage and horses.

"I never saw him," she answered.

"Do you think it got him, too?" She could hear the fear and confusion in his voice.

"No, there's a rattling noise when it does it, and there was only one rattle."

"You know what it is," he said, grabbing her arm and bringing her to a stop. "Tell me, Serafina."

"I saw it last night," she said. "It took Clara Brahms the same way."

"What? What do you mean? Where? Does this mean that Clara's dead? I don't understand what's going on."

"Neither do I," she said. "But we've gotta go."

Braeden picked up a stick from the ground and looked out into the forest. "Whatever it is, it's still out there. . . ."

She knew he was right. They had fought it off, but it was definitely still out there. She couldn't forget the image of Nolan leaping forward to save his master. She could still see the terror-stricken look on the boy's face right before he disappeared. As she looked at Braeden, she couldn't help the terrible sinking feeling that crept into her mind.

"Whatever it is," she said, "it didn't come for Nolan. It came for you. . . ."

8

"The ax is gone," Serafina said as she and Braeden searched the area around the carriage. Without the ax or anyone to help them move the trees, they couldn't clear the road in front of them or behind them. They were trapped.

"We can ride the horses," Braeden suggested. But the trees grew so closely together in this part of the forest that the horses couldn't pass between them, which was almost a relief to Serafina, because she couldn't imagine clawing her way up onto the back of one of those stompers and expecting it not to kill her.

"We can walk," she said.

"Eleven miles is a long way to walk in these woods," he said. "Especially at night . . ."

He kept looking around, obviously frustrated, and she was, too; but there was something she liked about the fact that they were in this together. He was thinking of her as an ally. She'd never spent much time with other people, but she was beginning to see why people liked it. Although she was pretty sure that not everyone was as clever and kind as Braeden Vanderbilt.

"If we stay here, we can use the carriage for shelter," he said. "My uncle sent a rider ahead to tell the Vances that I was on my way. When I don't arrive, they'll come looking for me. I'm sure of it. I think we should wait for help."

She didn't want to agree—she wanted to keep moving—but she knew he was probably right. She kept hearing the words he'd said to the horses: *We're in this together. We're going to be all right.* The words felt strangely reassuring to her as well.

She watched as Braeden unharnessed the horses for the night. The horses couldn't go far because of the fallen trees blocking the road, but at least they could move around. He gave them hay and water from the supply that Nolan had stowed in the back of the carriage. Prior to this, she had only seen horses from a distance, and they had always seemed like terribly wild and unpredictable beasts, but as she watched Braeden working with them, talking to them, and caring for them, they seemed to be such good-hearted creatures, far more intelligent than she realized.

"Horses usually sleep standing up," Braeden said. "And they always take shifts so that at least one of them is awake and alert for danger. If they sense something, they'll raise the alarm. You just have to know the signals."

"Excellent. We have watch-horses," she said with a smile, trying to cheer him up.

Braeden smiled in return, but she could see he was still very frightened by what had happened, and she was, too. When a gust of wind passed through the trees, she reflexively spun around, fearful that the flying specter had returned.

"What do you see?" Braeden asked.

"Nothing," she said. "It's just the wind."

The night's cold had settled onto the forest, and with the moonlight that filtered down through the trees, they could see their breath. When a screech owl gave an eerie trill in the distance, it startled Braeden, but the sound of the bird calmed Serafina. She had lived all her life hearing those sorts of sounds on her nightly prowls of Biltmore's grounds.

"Just an owl," Braeden said as he exhaled.

"Just an owl," she agreed.

As they climbed into the carriage, Braeden held the door open for her and helped her up the little steps, touching her back with his hand. It was as if they were entering the Grand Ballroom for the holiday dance. As a young gentleman, it was a natural gesture for him, probably just a habit, but it was a sensation she had never felt before. For a moment, that gentle touch of Braeden's hand against her back was all she could feel or think about. It was the first time in her life that anyone other than her pa had touched her in a kind and gentle way. She tried hard to tell herself that Braeden's touch probably meant a lot more to her than it did to him. He probably wasn't even aware that he'd touched her. She knew that he had danced and dined with many fancy-dressed girls. It was probably silly for her to think that he wanted to be friends with a girl who wore a shirt for a dress and couldn't ride a horse.

"Come on," Braeden said quietly to Gidean, and the dog hopped up into the carriage with them. Braeden shut and locked the wooden door and shook it a few times to make sure that it was secure. Gidean circled twice, then took his position on the floor guarding the door.

"I'm sorry there aren't any blankets," Braeden said, looking through the carriage's storage cabinets and trying to figure out how they were going to stay warm. "Not even a good cloak to sleep under."

"I'll pass on the cloak, thank you," Serafina said with a smile, and Braeden laughed a little, but he seemed almost as nervous as she was to be crammed inside the carriage together, with nothing to do but look at each other in the darkness.

Braeden sat down and patted the seat beside him. "Perhaps you should sit here, Serafina, on this side. We've got to stay warm somehow."

Despite the uncomfortable tightness forming in her chest, she slowly moved toward him.

She hoped she didn't smell like the basement. If he was

accustomed to ladies like Anastasia Rostonova, with her lavish dresses, or even Miss Whitney, with her rose-scented perfume, she couldn't imagine that her own scent would be too pleasant for him. *Excuse me, Miss Serafina,* he would say, gagging and coughing, *on second thought, perhaps you should indeed sleep on the floor with the dog. . . .*

But he didn't say that. She sat beside him, and the world didn't come to an end. As they snuggled together a little to stay warm, she fretted that he'd discover some bizarre characteristic about her that she didn't even realize was bizarre. She just hoped there wouldn't be a reason for her to take off her shoes in Braeden's presence and have him notice her missing toes. She didn't want him to get too close. Would he be able to feel her missing bones? She wasn't even sure which ones they were. How many bones did a person usually have, anyway?

She had always been content to snuggle into small places on her own, but she was surprised to find herself so comfortable cuddled up beside him. She was able to relax a little and breathe again.

Earlier that morning, when she'd woken up wedged in a metal drying rack in Biltmore's basement, the last place in the world she would have thought she'd spend her next evening was nestled in the velvet warmth between the Vanderbilt boy and his valiant guard dog. Gidean, for his part, seemed to have gotten over his initial reaction to her. They'd fought together on the same side, she and this dog, and maybe they were a little bit friends now, at least temporarily.

"Serafina, I need to ask you a question," Braeden said in the darkness.

"All right," she agreed, but she knew it wasn't going to be good.

"Why do you live in the basement?"

She didn't know if he considered her to be his friend or if they were just shoved together by happenstance and he was making the best out of a bad situation, but after all they'd been through together, it didn't seem right to lie to him. And she didn't want to.

"I'm the machine mechanic's daughter," she said finally. She just said it. Just like that. Out loud. Even as she said the words, she felt both pride and a sickening feeling of impending doom that she had betrayed her father.

"I've always liked him," Braeden said casually. "He fixed the buckle on my saddle and made it much more comfortable for my horse."

"He likes you, too," she said, although she remembered that her pa had spoken more about the buckle than the boy that day.

"So, have you been down there in the basement all this time?" Braeden asked in amazement.

"I'm good at staying out of the way," she said simply. She wanted to tell him that she was the Chief Rat Catcher, but she held her tongue, not sure how he would react to the thought of her grabbing rats. He might want to know when she had last washed her hands. She suddenly doubted if he even cared what she did. All sorts of rich and famous people and their children came to Biltmore, so why would Braeden care what she did all night?

"So you were down there in the basement when you saw the Man in the Black Cloak the first time . . ." he said. "Who do you think it is?"

"I don't know," she said. "I don't even know if he's a human or a haint."

"What's a haint?" Braeden asked, his eyebrows raised.

"A shade, a haint. You know, a ghost. The Man in the Black Cloak may be some sort of wraith that comes out of the woods at night. But I think he's a mortal man. I think he's one of the gentlemen at Biltmore."

"What makes you think that?" Braeden said in surprise.

"His satin cloak, his shoes, the way he walks, the way he talks. There's something about him . . . like he thinks he's better than everyone else . . ."

"Well, he's certainly scarier than anyone I've met," Braeden said, but then said no more.

She could tell that her theory that the Man in the Black Cloak was a gentleman at Biltmore had disturbed him.

They sat in silence for a long time. She could feel Braeden's warmth beside her, his breathing, and the beating of his heart. She could smell the faint scent of wool, leather, and horses on him. Regardless of what the two of them being in the carriage together might or might not really mean, for the moment, it brought her a wonderful sense of peace, a sense that she belonged, and that, despite everything that was going on, she was exactly where she was meant to be. It didn't make any sense to her, or even seem possible, but there was no denying that that was how she felt.

"I need to ask you to do me a favor," she said quietly.

"All right," he said.

"Please don't tell anyone about me and my father. He really needs his job. He loves Biltmore."

Braeden nodded his head. "I understand. I won't tell anyone, I swear."

"Thank you," she said, relieved.

It felt like she could trust Braeden. And his reputation among the kitchen staff for being a loner who preferred to spend time with his animal friends rather than human beings seemed totally unfair to her now.

As Braeden fell asleep, his breathing became slow and steady.

Remaining very still, Serafina turned to gaze upon him. She passed her eyes over his smooth, pale complexion. He was so clean. And his clothing fit so well. His woolen jacket must've been made just for him. Even the buttons had been wrought with his very own initials, *BV*, etched upon every one. Mr. and Mrs. Vanderbilt must have commissioned those buttons, she thought. Did that mean they loved and cherished Braeden? Or was it just so that he would fit into their elegant society?

Her pa had told her the story of Mr. Vanderbilt while they were washing up after supper one night in the workshop. Like many well-off gentlemen in society, George Vanderbilt used his inheritance to build a home. But he didn't build it in New York City like all the others. He built it in the remote wilds of western North Carolina, set deep in the densely forested mountains, miles and miles from the nearest town. The ladies and gentlemen of elite New York society thought this was extremely eccentric behavior. Why would such a highly educated man born and raised in the civilized luxury of New York City want to live in the wilderness of such a dark and forested place?

Biltmore Estate took years to build, but when it was finally finished and everyone saw what George Vanderbilt had done, they understood his dream. He had constructed the largest, most magnificent home in America, surrounded by a working, self-sustaining estate and the gentle beauty of the Blue Ridge Mountains. He married a few years later. And everyone who was fortunate enough to earn an invitation came to the city of Asheville to visit George and Edith Vanderbilt. They were the rich, the famous, and the powerful: senators, governors, great industrialists, leaders of foreign countries, favored musicians, talented writers, artists, and intellectuals of all kinds. And it was beneath this glittering world that her pa had raised her.

She looked at Braeden, and she remembered when he came to Biltmore two years before. The servants spoke of the tragedy in hushed tones. Mr. Vanderbilt's ten-year-old nephew was coming to live at Biltmore because his family had died in a house fire in New York. No one knew how it started, perhaps an oil lamp or a spark from the cook fire in the kitchen, but the house caught on fire in the middle of the night. Gidean woke Braeden in a smoke-filled bedroom, pulled at his arm with his teeth, and dragged him from his bed. With the walls and ceiling ablaze around them, they stumbled out of the burning house, choking and exhausted. They barely escaped with their lives. Gidean had saved him. It was only then that Braeden discovered that his mother, father, brothers, and sisters were all dead. His entire family had been consumed by the fire. It made Serafina shudder to think about it. She couldn't stand the thought of losing her pa. How sad and lost Braeden must have felt to lose his whole family.

She had heard the servants talk about how hundreds of ladies and gentlemen, servants, and folk of every ilk came out for the funeral. Four black horses pulled the black carriage stacked with eight coffins, as a little boy walked alongside, holding his uncle's hand.

She remembered watching the boy the day he arrived at Biltmore and wondering about him. The servants said he came with no luggage, no belongings whatsoever other than the four black horses, which his uncle agreed to ship by train from New York.

Moving closer to Braeden, she remembered what he'd said to her earlier that night: *These horses and I have been friends for a long time.*

From that day forward, she had kept a lookout for the boy. She often saw him walking the grounds in the morning. He spent long periods of time watching birds in the trees. He fished for trout in the streams, but much to the consternation of the cook, he always released whatever he caught. When she watched him in the house, he didn't seem comfortable around boys and girls his own age, or most of the adults, either. He loved his dog and his horses, but that was all. Those seemed to be his only friends.

She remembered overhearing his aunt speaking to a guest once. "He's just going through a phase," Mrs. Vanderbilt had said, trying to explain why he was so quiet at the dining table and so shy at parties. "He'll snap out of it."

But Serafina had a feeling that he never did.

His aunt and uncle lived in a world of extravagant parties, but from a distance, Braeden seemed to find more accomplishment in riding a horse or repairing the wing of a wounded hawk than dancing with the girls at the resplendent proms. She remembered prowling around outside the windows of the Winter Garden when it was all lit up for a ball one summer's eve. She watched the girls in their lovely gowns sashaying this way and that, dancing with the boys, and drinking sparkling punch from a giant fountain in the center of the room. She'd always wanted to be one of those girls in a fancy dress and shiny shoes. She remembered listening to the orchestra play and the people talking and laughing. Crouched down in the shadow beneath the windows, she could look over and see the silent gaze of the stone lions guarding the front doors of the house.

She didn't know how Braeden felt about her, but there was one thing for sure: she was *different*. Different from any girl he had seen before. She had no idea whether that fixed her as friend or enemy, but it was *something*.

It was the middle of the night now, and she knew that she should sleep, but she wasn't tired. The day hadn't left her exhausted. It had exhilarated her. Suddenly, the entire world was different than it had been the day before. She'd never felt so alive in her life. There were so many questions, so many mysteries to solve. She kept praying that somehow, some way, despite everything she had seen, Clara, Nolan, and Anastasia were still alive, and she could save them. She wanted to go outside and hunt through the woods in search of clues about the Man in the Black Cloak.

But she decided to stay where she was, content to remain curled up beside Braeden.

After a while, it began to rain a heavy rain, and she listened to the sound of it on the leaves of the trees and the roof of the carriage, and she thought it was a perfect sound.

Her eyes and ears open, she vowed that if the Man in the Black Cloak came again that night, she'd be ready.

When Serafina awoke the next morning, the gentle rays of the rising sun filtered through the carriage window, bathing her and Braeden in a soft golden light. Braeden slept soundly beside her. Gideon lay at their feet, quiet and restful.

Suddenly, the dog raised his head and perked his ears. Then she heard the sound as well: trotting horses, turning wheels, the rattle of approaching carriages . . .

She sprang up. She didn't know whether the carriages were bringing friends or enemies, but either way, she didn't want to be seen. If she stayed in the carriage, she was trapped; she needed space to watch, to move, to fight.

She hated to leave him, but she touched Braeden on the shoulder. "Wake up. Someone's here."

Then she slipped out of the carriage and darted into the forest before he had even awoken.

Hiding in the bushes and trees some distance into the undergrowth, she watched Braeden and Gidean exit the carriage. Braeden rubbed his eyes in the sunlight and looked around for her, obviously wondering where she'd disappeared to.

"Over here! I found the carriage!" a man shouted as he climbed through the branches of the tree that had fallen across the road. Several carriages and a dozen men on horseback had come from Biltmore in search of Braeden. As the gang of men went to work with great two-man saws and lumber axes to hack away the tree, Mr. Vanderbilt climbed his way through the branches, crossed over the fallen trunk, and hurried toward Braeden.

"Thank God you're safe," he said, his voice filled with emotion as they embraced.

Braeden was obviously glad and relieved to see his uncle. "Thank you for coming for me."

As they separated, Braeden pressed back his sleep-ruffled hair with his hands and scanned the trees. Then he looked toward the carriages and rescuers.

She knew he was looking for her, but she had hidden herself like a creature in the woods. She felt like a wild animal there, beneath the leaves of the rhododendrons and the mountain laurel. The forest wasn't something she feared, like she had the night before. It was her concealment, her protector.

"Tell me what happened, Braeden," Mr. Vanderbilt said, seeming to sense Braeden's anxiety.

"We were attacked in the night," Braeden said, his voice ragged and his face splotchy with emotion. "Nolan was taken. He's gone. Mr. Crankshod disappeared right when the battle started, and hasn't shown up since."

Mr. Vanderbilt frowned in confusion. He put his hand on Braeden's shoulder and turned him toward the gang of workers cutting through the tree and clearing the road. In addition to the servants, Serafina recognized a dozen other men from the house, including Mr. Bendel, Mr. Thorne, and Mr. Brahms. She let out a small gasp. There was Mr. Crankshod, working among them.

"Mr. Crankshod said a group of bandits attacked," Mr. Vanderbilt said. "He fended them off, but when he attempted to pursue them, he became separated from the carriage and decided it was best to head back to Biltmore as fast as possible to fetch help. I was furious he'd left you, but in the end, he was the one who led us here to you, so maybe he was right to do what he did."

Serafina saw Braeden look at Mr. Crankshod in surprise. The ugly man looked right back at him, his eyes betraying nothing.

"I'm not sure it was bandits, Uncle," Braeden said uncertainly. "I only saw one attacker. A man in a black cloak. He took Nolan. I've never seen anything like it. Nolan just vanished."

"We'll send a mounted search party up and down this road until we find the boy," Mr. Vanderbilt said, "but in the meantime, I want to get you back to the house."

As Braeden and Mr. Vanderbilt spoke, Serafina watched Mr. Crankshod. She wondered what the old rat was up to. Something wasn't right with him. He hadn't fought any bandits. He had simply disappeared. And now here he was again with a crooked tale of his own heroism.

The only good news was that it seemed like he hadn't spilled the grits about her existence to Mr. Vanderbilt. Was Crankshod a hero? A villain? Or was he nothing more than a common rat-faced coward? She looked around at Mr. Vanderbilt, Mr. Crankshod, and the other men. She was beginning to see how difficult it was to determine who was good and who was bad, who she could trust and who she had to watch out for. Every person was a hero in his own mind, fighting for what he thought was right, or just fighting to survive another day, but no one thought they were evil.

Gidean wasn't so forgiving. He charged toward Mr. Crankshod right away and started barking and snarling at him. *Maybe dogs really can smell fear,* Serafina thought. *Or at least cowardliness . . .* It didn't look like Gidean was actually going to bite Mr. Crankshod, but he wasn't going to let him off without a good barking-to. The other men watched in amusement, but Mr. Crankshod was none too pleased by the dog's attention.

"Oh, shut up, you stupid mutt!" Mr. Crankshod shouted, and raised his arms to strike the dog with his ax.

Braeden and Serafina were too far away to help, but Mr. Thorne clamped his hand onto Mr. Crankshod's arm and stopped him mid-blow. "Don't be a fool, Crankshod."

"Aw, what the . . . Just keep that mangy cur away from me," Mr. Crankshod grumbled and stomped away.

Braeden ran over to Gidean and Mr. Thorne. "Oh, thank you, sir, thank you so much."

"It's good to see you're all right, young master Vanderbilt," Mr. Thorne said cheerfully, patting Braeden's shoulder with his leather-gloved hand. "Sounds like you'll have some big stories to tell everyone at dinner tonight about your adventure through the forest."

"Did you see anyone else when you arrived?" Braeden asked him, still holding Gidean but looking around again for Serafina.

"Not to worry," Mr. Thorne said. "Those yellow-bellied sorts aren't the type of men to stick around after an attack. I'm sure they're long gone by now."

Despite his reassuring words, Serafina noticed that he was wearing an elegant dagger on his belt and wondered if he had half expected to encounter the bandits himself.

"I'm sure you're right, Mr. Thorne," Mr. Vanderbilt said, shaking his head angrily as he walked up to them. "But it's hard to believe that bandits would venture such a brazen attack so close to Biltmore. I'm going to ask the police to increase their patrols of the road."

Braeden didn't seem to be listening to much of any of this. He just kept looking out into the trees. Serafina wanted to let him know she was all right, but she couldn't let all those men see her, and she definitely didn't want to have to explain who she was or why she had been in the carriage with Braeden, so she stayed quiet and out of sight.

Braeden squatted down and put his hands on Gidean, who was looking out into the trees in her direction. "Can you smell her, boy?" he whispered.

"What are you doing?" Mr. Vanderbilt asked gruffly.

Braeden stood, knowing that he'd been caught out.

"Who are you looking for, Braeden?" Mr. Vanderbilt asked him.

Serafina sucked in her breath. That was the question she had been dreading. Who was Braeden looking for? This is where her and her pa's secret would come out. Braeden's answer to his uncle's question had the power to destroy her life.

When Braeden hesitated, Mr. Vanderbilt frowned. "What do you have to say, Braeden? Spit it out."

Braeden didn't want to lie to his uncle, but he shook his head and looked at the ground. "Nothing," he said.

Serafina breathed a sigh of relief. He'd kept his promise. He wasn't going to tell. *Thank you, Braeden. Thank you,* she thought, but then his uncle lit into him.

"You've got to buck up, son," Mr. Vanderbilt said. "You're twelve years old now, and that's plenty old enough to handle yourself properly. Don't be scared of what's going on here. You've got to take charge of yourself. Be a man. We're only dealing with bandits here, thieves."

"I don't think it was bandits," Braeden said again.

"Of course it was. This is nothing a Vanderbilt can't handle. Do you agree?"

"Yes, sir," Braeden said glumly, looking at the ground. "Just hungry, I guess."

Mr. Thorne stepped in to rescue him. "Well then, by all means, let's get some food in you," he said enthusiastically, putting his arm around Braeden. "Come on, I raided the kitchen on my way out. I brought a sack full of pulled-pork sandwiches, and if that doesn't suit, we'll dig right into the raspberry spoon bread."

Braeden glanced one more time into the forest, then turned and followed Mr. Thorne.

Serafina desperately wanted to give poor Braeden some clue that she was out there and that she was safe. If she had been any other kind of girl, she would have left some sort of token for him when she left, a signal of their connection—perhaps a silver locket, a lace handkerchief, or a charm from her bracelet—but she was a wild girl and didn't have any of those possessions to give.

As the men gathered around Braeden, happy and relieved that they'd found him, Serafina noticed Mr. Rostonov, the bearded and portly Russian ambassador, step away from the others and stand alone at the edge of the road. Braeden had told her that Mr. Rostonov didn't know English too well. The poor man gazed tearfully into the forest, as if wondering whether his dear Anastasia had been murdered by what lurked in its shadows. He took out a handkerchief, wiped his eyes, and blew his nose. Braeden had said that Mr. Rostonov and his daughter were only scheduled to stay at Biltmore Estate for a few days before they returned home to their family in Russia in time for Christmas. But when Anastasia disappeared, he had stayed on, continuing the search for her. Mr. Rostonov couldn't bear the thought of returning home to his wife without his daughter. Back over by the carriages, some of the men went over to Mr. Crankshod, who was still put out by the incident with the dog, and thanked him for leading the search party to Braeden. But there was something about Crankshod, all smiling and greasy, that raised Serafina's hackles. What was he *really* doing? Where was he when the Man in the Black Cloak attacked? Did he work for him? Or was he him?

She looked suspiciously at Mr. Vanderbilt, too. She didn't like the way he was so tough on Braeden, telling him what to do and not to do and how to feel. He had no idea what Braeden had been through. He didn't listen any better than her pa, and he seemed far too quick to accept Mr. Crankshod's story that it had been bandits.

Braeden had said that his aunt and uncle had secretly sent him away for the night, so few people would have known he was going to be on the road at that time. And he had said that his uncle trusted Mr. Crankshod. Were they working together?

She tried to think it through. Was it really possible that Mr. Vanderbilt was the Man in the Black Cloak? Did he have some terrible need to swallow up *all* the children at Biltmore?

After the men cleared the second tree from the road, those who weren't continuing on to search for Nolan climbed back into the carriages. The coachmen began the intricate task of turning all the carriages around in the tight quarters of the narrow road so that they could head back to Biltmore Estate.

"I want you to ride with me in my carriage, Braeden," Mr. Vanderbilt said. "Mr. Crankshod will drive us."

"Yes, sir," Braeden said, "I understand, but we need to bring my horses home." His horses had been harnessed, but there wasn't a coachman to drive them.

"I'll take care of it," Mr. Thorne volunteered. He walked over to the horses, patted their heads gently as they nuzzled him, then climbed up into the empty driver's seat and gathered the reins.

Serafina saw Braeden smile, relieved that Mr. Thorne was willing to help, but something struck her as a bit odd. Many gentlemen were accomplished riders, but few had any experience with driving a carriage, which was a servant's job.

Mr. Bendel, who was riding his thoroughbred, came up alongside Mr. Thorne. "Well, there you go, Thorne. You've got a fallback position if you ever lose your fortune."

"I have to get a fortune before I can lose it," Mr. Thorne said humbly.

The two gentlemen laughed with each other, but then Mr. Bendel became more serious, tipped his hat to Mr. Thorne and Mr. Vanderbilt, and joined the search party of half a dozen riders that was heading out to look for Nolan.

"Don't wait on supper for me," Mr. Bendel called back to his friends as he rode off with the other horsemen.

Soon the carriages were all moving and heading down the road toward home.

Serafina wanted desperately to go with them, but she knew she couldn't. She remained hidden in the bushes. She had to suppress a sense of panic that she was being left behind, that she'd never be able to find her way through the forest back to Biltmore. And she missed Braeden's company already. As she watched the carriages recede into the distance, she thought, *Good-bye, my friend,* and she hoped he was thinking the same.

But even as the carriages disappeared, she felt a tingling sensation course through her limbs. She should have been frightened to be in the forest alone. All her life she'd been told to stay away from it, but now here she was. Far from Biltmore. Alone in the trees. And she had an idea. She was downright keen on it. She just hoped that it wasn't going to get her lost. Or killed.

As she stepped onto the empty road and looked down the length of it, she had a weird and foreign feeling from being so far away from her pa and Biltmore and all the commotion there. She half expected to burst into tears, go running after the carriages, and wail, *Wait! Wait! You forgot about me!*

But she didn't. And she felt rather grown-up about it.

The sun was well up now and casting a lovely warm light on the trees. Birds were singing. There was a gentle breeze. Things weren't so bad in the forest.

But then she looked down the long road winding through the trees and remembered that she was eleven miles from home.

"I'll try to be home for dinner, Pa," she said with a pang of uncertainty in her stomach, and she started walking. But she wasn't exactly heading for home. Not directly.

The Man in the Black Cloak had seemed to know the forest very well, and she remembered the tales of folk going missing. She had a creeping suspicion that the Man in the Black Cloak might be in some way connected to the abandoned village that she'd heard tell about. She had decided she was going to find the old village and see if it gave her any clues. Why would all the people in a town abandon their homes and leave?

There was a part of her, too, that was anxious to delve into the shadows of the forest, to see this mysterious world. It drew her, not just because she'd been forbidden by her pa to come here, but by the thorny truth of her pa's own account: she'd been *born* here.

She decided to walk on down the road a spell and see what she could see. Perhaps there would be an old sign pointing to the abandoned village, or perhaps she'd meet someone along the road who might be able to tell her how to get there. One way or another, it seemed like it would be pretty easy to find an entire town.

As she walked, her mind kept drifting back to her pa. She wished she could get a message to him. He'd be worried sick about her, especially with the horrible tales of disappearing children. She wondered if he ever got the dynamo working.

It created the one thing that everyone other than her needed so desperately at night: light. Who in the world would purposely damage an electric generator? And who would even know how to do something like that? Her pa was the only man on the estate who knew how it worked. Him, and maybe George Vanderbilt if he referred to one of the books in his library.

She thought that it was interesting how just about everyone had a special talent or skill, something they were naturally drawn to and good at, and then they worked years to master it. Nobody knew how to do everything. It wasn't possible. There wasn't enough time in the night. But everyone knew something. And everyone was a little different. Some people did one thing. Others did another. It made her think that maybe God intended for them to all fit together, like a puzzle made whole.

It still stunned her when she tried to imagine her big, train mechanic pa carrying a newborn baby out of the forest and taking care of her all those years. It had never occurred to her until now that she belonged anywhere but in the basement with her father, but now her mind ran wild with questions and ideas. She was anxious to get home, but walking down that road, she felt a little exhilarated that she was free and on her own. She could go in any direction she chose.

She walked for an hour without seeing a soul, nothing but blue jays and chickadees twitching about her, a few squirrels chattering away at her, and a mink dashing across the road in front of her like his life depended on it. She wasn't even sure she was still heading in the right direction anymore, but she figured she couldn't go wrong if she stayed on the road.

Then she came to a three-way split.

The left road was the widest and seemed to be the most traveled. She got down on her hands and knees and studied the rocky ground. It was hard to tell, but she thought that maybe she could see the indention of carriage wheels. But the middle road was wide and clear as well, with occasional dents in the ground that might be from the hooves of horses. Either one of these roads could be the road to Biltmore.

Only the third road was different. It wasn't even right to call it a road, but what *used to be* a road. Two old, rotting fir trees had collapsed, making an X across the path. Thick vines of poison ivy and smothering creeper grew all around and seemed to strangle the two fallen trees. This road obviously hadn't been traveled by carriage or horseback in years. She wasn't even sure a person on foot could get through.

She didn't see any sign or marker that identified the road, but it seemed possible that an old, unused pathway like this might lead to the abandoned village. Maybe the state of the road choked off the town. Or maybe the forest took back the road when the townsfolk disappeared. In any case, if she had any hope of solving the mystery of the Man in the Black Cloak, she needed clues and information. Where did he come from? What was his story? How could she stop him?

Poison ivy had never affected her the way it did other people, but she still climbed carefully through the thicket of vines and thorns. On the other side of the two crossed trees, she came into a boscage of rotting, dead snags, with rocks on the ground as sharp as ax blades. The narrow, overgrown track twisted and turned, and dove down into a rocky ravine, and she couldn't see what lay beyond.

As she gazed at the darkened passage, a shiver went through her spine. She had no idea where it would lead her, but she started down the path.

10

$\mathcal{S}$erafina followed the shadowed path for a while, crawling over fallen trees and through nasty thickets, until she came to yet another split.

As she was trying to figure out which direction to go, she heard faint sounds drifting through the branches. The sounds had an eerie, unearthly quality to them. She thought it might be nothing more than the wind blowing through the trees, but when she listened very carefully it almost seemed like there were people calling to one another in the distance and children playing.

With no other clues to guide her, she decided to go toward the sounds and see what she could find. If she passed a house, then perhaps the inhabitants could point her in the right direction.

The path led her around a sharp curve and plummeted into a steep, bracken-choked ravine, then it climbed back out again, making its way among large moss-covered rocks and old trees twisted by wind and age. Desperate for soil, the trees' roots clung to the rocks like giant hands, their massive fingers plunging into the earth beneath them.

This place is terribly creepy, she thought, but she kept going, determined to keep moving forward.

Unlike normal trees, which grew upward toward the sunlight, these had gnarled, contorted branches, as if they had been twisted by agonizing pain. Many of the trees stood dead and bare, withered by disease or some other killing force. Still more of the trees lay dead on the ground, their trunks crisscrossing one another as if a giant had pushed them over.

As she made her way, a mist rose up from the leaf-covered forest floor, and a fog set in that obscured her view of the terrain around her.

Oh, great. If I can't see, I'm gonna get lost for sure. . . .

She turned around to head back toward the last split in the path, but the fog became so thick that even this simple navigation was impossible. She tried to control her fear, but she felt the panic rise up in her. She gulped for air as the mist surrounded her and she lost her sense of place and direction. She began to realize that she'd made a terrible mistake in leaving

the main road. *Stay calm,* she thought. *Just think it through. . . .*
Find your way home. . . .

Her foot hit a lump, and she tripped and fell forward onto
the ground. Her hands and face touched something wet and
slimy buried in the leaves. She gasped when she saw that it
was the bloody carcass of a deer or some other large animal.
Its body had been eviscerated, its guts ripped out. Its head and
hind legs were missing, but from what was left over, it appeared
that it had been purposely cached here.

She gagged as she got up onto her feet, wiped her hands on
the bark of a slimy tree, and moved on, desperate to find the
road.

When she heard voices ahead, she felt a swell of hope.
She moved quickly toward them. *Maybe they're travelers,* she
thought. *Perhaps there's a hunting shack ahead.*

But then she stopped in her tracks. They were the same
eerie noises she had heard before, but this time they were much
closer: hoarse, raucous calling sounds, but with a strange, almost
human quality, like some kind of weird children running and
playing in the forest. A surge of fear swept through her. Her
legs and hands buzzed with agitation. The sounds were above
her and all around her now, and still she couldn't see them.

"Show yourself!" she demanded.

Something brushed past her shoulder and she whirled,
crouching to the ground to defend herself. A burst of rushing
air made her skin crawl as a black shape flew over her and then
landed in a tree.

She looked around her. And then she saw them. First one, and then another. They were surrounding her. The hoarse croaking sounds came from a conspiracy of thirteen ravens moving through the branches of the trees, calling to one another, speaking in their ancient codes. But the ravens weren't just conversing with each other—they were looking at her, flying around her, trying to communicate with her. As if frustrated by her lack of understanding, several of the ravens began diving at her with their claws. Were they attacking her or were they warning her? She didn't know.

"Leave me alone!" she shouted. She covered her head with her arms and ran to escape them. She dove into a thicket of brush, where the large birds couldn't fly. Driven by fear, she just kept running.

When she finally stopped to catch her breath, she looked behind her to see if they were still following. She found herself standing on something hard—some sort of flat surface. She looked down and saw a long, straight edge of gray stone. *Now what?* she thought.

It was half buried, but she knelt on the ground and wiped away the dirt and leaves to expose the smooth, flat granite underneath.

Serafina read the words that someone had etched in blocky letters into the stone:

HERE LIES BLOOD, AND LET IT LIE,

SPEECHLESS STILL, AND NEVER CRY.

She felt a cold sweat pass over her. She looked around. There was another flat gray stone just a few feet away. She pulled the brush aside and read:

COME HITHER, COME HITHER, AND LAY WITH ME.
WE'LL MURDER THE MAN WHO MURDERED ME.
CLOVEN SMITH 1797–1843

All right, I don't like this place at all. These are graves. . . .

She wiped her clammy hands on her shirt, then she took a few more steps, finding more graves beneath the undergrowth of the forest. The graveyard seemed like it went on and on. There were graves as far as she could see, most of them overgrown with vines and trees.

Many of the headstones were so close together that they couldn't possibly have bodies beneath them, just like the stories she'd heard. It was as if people had gone missing, their bodies never found, and these were but markers of the lost.

But as she delved deeper into the oldest parts of the abandoned cemetery, she saw mounds where bodies had definitely been buried, and other graves that were empty holes, as if the coffins had been plundered or the dead had crawled out of the ground on their own.

She swallowed hard and tried to keep moving despite the trembling in her limbs.

In some places, the layers of earth appeared as if they had shifted, exposing broken, rotting coffins to the air. Some of the coffins jutted up out of the earth or were tangled beneath gnarled tree roots. She kept walking and reading the stones. A hundred years of old people, young people, brothers and sisters, friends and enemies, husbands and wives.

She had heard stories about this old cemetery, filled with hundreds of gravestones and monuments, even though no one alive could remember burying the people. Many of the local mountain folk wondered where all the dead people in this cemetery had come from. Whole families seemed to have perished in short spans of time.

There were tall tales that the mountain folk no longer used this cemetery because burying your loved ones here didn't necessarily guarantee that they would stay. The coffins shifted in the unstable earth. The bodies went missing. Your dead loved ones were seen wandering their old homes and streets, as if searching for a place to rest.

There were tales, too, of human beings shifting into the shape of wild animals, of sorcerers and witches with surpassing power, and horrible, disfigured creatures crawling through the forest.

She came upon two small mounds so close together, side by side, that they were nearly a single grave. One tombstone identified the two young sisters within:

OUR BED IS LOVELY, DARK, AND SWEET.

COME JOIN US NOW AND WE SHALL MEET.

MARY HEMLOCK AND MARGARET HEMLOCK

1782–1791 REST IN PEACE AND DON'T RETURN

When she read the words *don't return*, the hairs on the back of her neck tingled. What kind of strange place was this?

She had come in search of an old village, but all she'd found was its cemetery. She had a feeling that this was all that was left.

As Serafina walked, the dry autumn leaves crunched beneath her feet. Tree branches lay like emaciated dead fingers on the ground among the gravestones and monuments. Many of the monuments had toppled to the earth and lay broken and strewn while others had sunk deep into the ground. A few of the gravestones remained standing, sticking up several feet with spires or crosses, but they were so thickly covered in black and green moss and overgrown with vines that they were nearly indistinguishable from the wretched forest around them.

She read another:

DEATH IS A DEBT TO NATURE DUE,

WHICH I HAVE PAID, AND SO WILL YOU.

In another area, she found row upon row of crosses. An old, weathered plaque explained that these sixty-six crosses were the graves of an entire company of Confederate soldiers who were found dead one night, even though they never fought in any battle.

Farther on, Serafina came to a glade, a little clearing in the trees strangely without bushes, vines, or undergrowth of any kind. This one particular part of the cemetery had not become overgrown, but remained an area of perfect green grass. In the center of the glade stood a stone monument carved into the likeness of a winged angel. Stranger still was the fact that although there was fog all around the glade, there was no fog in the glade itself. Sunlight filtered through the mist and illuminated the angel's face and hair and wings with a gentle light.

"Now, she's pretty," Serafina said as she stepped closer and read the inscription on the pedestal of the statue:

OUR CHARACTER ISN'T DEFINED
BY THE BATTLES WE WIN OR LOSE,
BUT BY THE BATTLES WE DARE TO FIGHT.

Serafina looked up at the angel and studied her. Dappled layers of green and gray moss and lichen covered the angel, and the black streaks of a hundred years of aging stained her long dress and her beautiful face. Dark tears seemed to be falling down her cheeks, as if she had known great sadness. But her wings stretched upward into a fury, her head raised into an apocalyptic cry, as if calling those around her into a great battle. *What kind of battle?* Serafina wondered. In her right hand, the angel held a sword. The statue itself was made of stone, but the sword appeared to be made of steel, and the metal gleamed as if it was untouched by time. Curious, Serafina slowly reached out her hand and touched the edge of the blade. She gasped and pulled back, blood oozing from her finger. The edge of the sword was razor-sharp.

Then something caught her eye. She felt a pulse of fear.

Her muscles tightened, readying themselves to flee. At the edge of the glade, a gravestone had tumbled over where a gnarled old willow tree had fallen and its upturned roots had created a small cave. She wasn't sure, but she thought she saw one of the shadows slowly move.

Then she was sure of it.

There was something stirring by the old grave.

11

Serafina had to remind herself to keep breathing, to stay calm. She felt her chest tightening, her breaths getting shorter and shorter. She wanted to turn and run, but she stayed and watched, her curiosity too strong to overcome.

She crept quietly through the graveyard to get a closer look.

She feared it might be a corpse crawling out of the ground. She imagined its rotting white hands digging through the dirt as it broke the surface. But as she got closer, she realized it wasn't a corpse at all, but a very living creature.

It was some sort of small wildcat with yellowish-brown fur, black spots and markings, and a long tail. It took her several seconds to figure out that it was a baby mountain lion.

Suddenly, a second lion cub appeared. They charged each other, grabbing each other with their paws and tumbling in play, meowing and howling and swatting each other. They had the most adorable little yellow faces marked with black streaks and spots, and long white kitty whiskers.

Smiling, Serafina watched the cubs play in the bright green grass of the stone angel's sunlit glade. The fear she had felt just moments before began to melt away. She had always loved kittens.

She crouched down and moved a little closer. One of the cubs spotted her. Its ears perked up, and it stared at her, studying her. She thought that it would run away in fear. But it didn't. It gave her a raspy meow and ambled toward her as if it didn't have a care in the world.

She extended her arm, holding her hand still. The brave little cub slowed down, but it kept coming toward her, watching her, inching closer and closer. When it reached her, it sniffed her fingers and rubbed the side of its mouth along the length of her hand. Serafina smiled, almost giggled, pleased that the cub didn't fear her.

She sat down in the grass, and the cub climbed right into her lap, pawing playfully at her fingers. She wrapped her arms around the cub and hugged its warm, fuzzy little body to her chest. It was good to have some company that didn't scare the living daylights out of her. The other cub came over, and soon she was lovin' on both of them as they tumbled and rolled around her, and they rubbed themselves against her and purred.

"What are you sweet little babies doing here?" she asked. After all she'd been through, it felt more than agreeable to be accepted by these wonderful little creatures. It felt like a homecoming.

Soon, they were all up and about. She chased the cubs around the glade, pretending to swat at them with her paw, then they chased her. She got down on her hands and knees. One of the cubs ran behind the pedestal of the stone angel, came around the other side, and peeked at her, his dark little eyes blinking as he pretended to stalk her. He darted out playfully, running sideways with his back arched into a mock attack as he leapt upon her. Then the other cub joined in, grabbing her arms and legs, trying to tackle her, and soon they were all brawling and growling. The adorable, kittenish attack made Serafina laugh out loud.

And her laughter carried through the misty forest.

She kept playing and wrestling with the cubs, feeling a pure and oblivious childlike pleasure that she hadn't felt in a long time.

Then she sensed severe and immediate danger. She turned and saw something hurtling toward her out of the mist. At first, it seemed to be floating like a ghost, but then she realized it wasn't a ghost at all.

It was running. Fast. Straight toward her.

A wave of dread washed through her as she realized that by playing with these cubs she'd made a terrible, terrible error in judgment. The angry, full-grown mother mountain lion

SERAFINA and the BLACK CLOAK

charged toward her. The lioness would kill her to defend her cubs.

Fear jolted Serafina into motion. The lioness leapt through the air, her claws and teeth bared. Serafina knew she was going to die, but she tried to duck. The impact of the lioness's attack slammed into her so hard that it knocked her off her feet. She and the vicious beast tumbled across the grass in a brawling, snarling mass of hissing, teeth, and claws.

Serafina battled with all her strength. She had never in her life fought anything so physically powerful. She knew there was no way to defeat her; she was but a kitten compared to this wild beast. Her only hope was to get away as fast as she could. She kicked her feet and flailed her fists. She beat the lioness with a stick, screaming all the while.

When the lioness tried to bite her neck and deliver her deadly blow, Serafina slammed her hands into the lioness's face and tore at her eyes, then whirled herself into a wild, twisting frenzy. Her attacks distracted the big cat just long enough to break herself free. Then she sprang up and darted away like a scalded dog.

The lioness chased her, but Serafina sprinted with an incredible burst of fear-induced speed. She scrambled into the thick bushes like a squirrel and just kept running. She ran and she ran. She ran until her whole chest hurt with thumping pain.

She crossed a rocky stream, then went through a thick stand of pines, and then delved into a thicket of thistles and blackberry thorns. She climbed up hills and over rocks and just kept running as far as she could.

Finally, exhausted, she ducked beneath a bush like a rabbit and listened for the sounds of her pursuer. She did not hear her.

She imagined that the lioness, satisfied that she had chased off the intruder, had returned to her cubs. She could picture the mother lion scolding them for playing with a stranger and pushing them angrily back into their den beneath the roots of the tree.

Panting and wounded, Serafina pressed on through the forest, determined to put as much distance as possible between her, the cemetery, and the mountain lion's den. She vowed to never return to that terrifying place.

When she finally stopped for a moment to catch her breath, she looked around her. Nothing looked familiar. It was then that she realized that she was completely and utterly lost.

12

Serafina kept moving and soon found herself traveling along the top edge of a rocky, tree-covered ridge. In her panic to escape the lioness, it seemed that she'd run halfway up a mountain.

Exhausted, she finally stopped to rest and check her wounds. Her clothing had been torn. The length of twine that once held her pa's shirt around her body had broken and was gone. Claw marks sliced her arms and legs. Her head hurt. Several tooth marks punctured her chest. She was pretty torn up, but it wasn't nearly as bad as she had expected.

It hurts, but I'm gonna live, she thought. *Assuming I can find my way home.* She had thought that the forest couldn't be nearly as bad as her pa described, but it turned out to be a far darker, more dangerous place than she'd ever imagined. With everything she'd seen so far, she didn't think she could survive another night here. But she was still miles from the house, stuck on a ridge, and she didn't even know which direction to go.

She looked up at the dark, cloudy sky, trying to find the position of the sun, then she scanned the surrounding landscape for clues and landmarks. With no compass, no map, and no idea where she was in relation to Biltmore Estate, how could she make sure she was going in the right direction?

She was already cold when it started raining.

"Oh, great," she said, shouting up at the clouds. "Thank you! That's really nice, you stupid sky!"

She hated getting wet. This was a miserable place. She just wanted to get home. She missed her pa something awful. She longed for a glass of milk, a piece of fried catfish, a warm little cook fire in the workshop, and her dry, cozy bed behind the boiler. Yesterday she'd been slinking gracefully across the plush carpets of Biltmore's elegant rooms, and today she was stuck out in the cold, wet, stupid, raining world.

As the rain poured down, she tried to hide under the boughs of a pine tree, but it didn't help. The big drips onto her sopping head and neck just made her more miserable. Rivulets of water flowed across the rocky ground beneath her. Wet and bedraggled, she clung to the trunk of the tree, terrified that she'd slip down the steep slope of the mountainside. She wanted her pa to get his ladder and rescue her like he had when she was little, but she knew he wouldn't even know where to look for her.

Then, as she watched the water trickle across the ground, a thought occurred to her.

Water runs downhill. Downhill, and into rivers.

She had been following the contour of the ridge because it had been easiest, but now she had a different idea. What if she climbed straight down the steepest slope of the mountain and used the trunks of the trees and the branches of the rhododendrons as a sort of ladder? She'd get down a lot quicker.

She stepped closer to the edge and peered tentatively over the cliff. It was a long way down, but she grabbed the first branch to see if it would hold her. Suddenly, her foot slipped in the wet leaves, her fingers broke free from the branch, and she plummeted down the mountainside.

The swooping sensation of free fall instantly filled her entire body. She slid down feetfirst, screaming. She tried to stay upright and reached out for the bushes to break her fall, but then she hit a tree trunk, and it knocked the wind out of her. She pitched in one direction, then the next, hurtling down the mountain. She hit a branch. She spun. She hit a rock. She plunged. Suddenly, she was somersaulting end over end. All the while she fell, tumbling down the mountainside in a great wave of autumn leaves. The rush of speed and the wind against her face made her feel like she was flying, but then she hit another tree, the force slamming a painful grunt from her chest, and she flipped and rolled until she finally crashed, breathless and hurting, at the bottom of the ravine.

She lay there for several seconds, unable to move. Her whole body hurt. She'd been punched and battered and stabbed.

"Well, that was one way to get down," she groaned.

When she was finally able to get on her feet, she brushed herself off and limped on her way.

She followed a small stream that trickled into a creek. Thirsty, she lay flat at the stream's edge and lapped up the clear mountain water like an animal.

The stream led her to a waterfall that crashed into a tumultuous pool thirty feet below.

Does this waterfall have a name? she wondered. If she knew that, then maybe it would help her understand where she was and give her a better chance of finding her way home. *What river is this?*

But then she realized that it didn't matter exactly where she was. A river wasn't a place. A river was movement. She remembered something her pa had taught her. All the rivers in these mountains wound through complicated, twisting routes, but eventually they all flowed in one direction, into the mighty French Broad River.

The Blue Ridge Mountains were some of the oldest mountains in the world. The river had been flowing here for millions of years and had helped shape the mountains into what they were today. And, most importantly, she knew that the French Broad River flowed through the grounds of Biltmore Estate, right past the mansion. The river was the way home.

She climbed down the wet, slippery rocks at the edge of the

waterfall, then made her way along the craggy shoreline. Confident in her direction now, she traveled as fast as she could. She had to reach her pa, who she knew must be worried sick about her, and she wanted to see Braeden. She wasn't sure if she had abandoned him by sneaking into the woods, or if he'd abandoned her by going home in his uncle's carriage; but they'd separated, and it made her stomach hurt. The more time that went by, the less certain she became of how she should feel. Was Braeden actually her friend, or was her mind just imagining it, like when she imagined herself as being friends with the butler's assistant who stopped and ate the cookies? All her life, she had pretended that she had friends, but was it true this time?

She and Braeden had only known each other for a short while, but she let the memories of their time together wash over her. To someone like her, it felt like a lifetime of friendship. She was like a starved animal wolfing down a scrap and thinking it had eaten a full meal. But she had no idea if he missed her the way she missed him.

She walked for hours, following the river until it flowed into a much wider, flatter river that she hoped was the French Broad, but she wasn't sure. She was tired, hungry, and sore from her wounds. She just wanted to get home.

As the sun slowly withdrew behind the trees in the western sky, she tried to push herself faster. She didn't want to get caught in the forest another night, for that's when the mountain lion, the Man in the Black Cloak, and whatever other demons might crawl out of the cemetery would be on the prowl. But it was no use. The sun abandoned her, the birds and the other daytime sounds went dead, and the darkness settled into the trees like a black oil.

Exhausted, she stopped to catch her breath and rest a spell. She knew it was dangerous to linger in the open. Wet and shivering, she crawled into a hole beneath the hollowed roots of a tree at the river's edge, curled into a little ball, and peered out into the darkness.

She was a failure. That's what she thought. She had come to the forest to see the world, but all she'd found was wretchedness.

From her little cave beneath the roots, she looked downstream along the gravelly shore of the river. The air around her was cold and still, but the river rippled with a steady rushing sound, and she could taste its moisture on her lips. The waxing moon rising above the mountains cast a silvery light across the deep-flowing black water. Mist oozed out of the forest and drifted across the river like a legion of ghosts.

A wolf called in the distance, a long, plaintive, lonely howl that put a shiver up her spine. The wolf was miles away, up on the mountains. But then she nearly jumped out of her skin when a much closer wolf answered the call with a returning howl.

Red wolves were elusive, almost mythological beasts, seldom seen by anyone, but they were well known for being fierce warriors that fought in packs, tearing their enemies with their gleaming white fangs.

The wolf close to her howled again, and a dozen wolves on

the other side of the river lit up the air with a bloodcurdling chorus of howls. Goose bumps rose on her arms.

She did not hear it approach for it moved like a ghost through the mist, but she saw the wolf come slowly out of the forest and look out across the river. She stayed very still among the roots and watched it. She could smell the musky scent of its coat and see its moonlit breath in the air.

It was a young wolf, long and lean, with a deep coat of reddish-brown fur, a slender nose, and tall ears. The fur on its right shoulder was bloody from a wound.

She held her breath and stayed quiet. *The wolf doesn't know I'm here,* she thought. *I'm one with the forest. I'm camouflaged and silent.*

But then the wolf turned its head and looked straight at her, its eyes as keen and penetrating as any creature she had ever seen.

Her muscles bunched as she prepared herself for the attack.

But then the wolf's ear twitched. Serafina heard it, too. There was something large moving through the forest, traveling along the river shore toward them.

The wolf looked in the direction of the sound, and then he looked back at her. He stared at her for several seconds, even as the sound moved toward them. Then, to her astonishment, the wolf walked into the river. He kept walking until he was up to his shoulders in the water, then the river swept him away and all she could see was his head as he tried to fight against the current. He was swimming toward the howls of his brothers and sisters on the other side of the river. And he was swimming away from the thing coming toward her.

Suddenly, she felt abandoned, vulnerable.

The river made too much noise for her to hear exactly what was coming toward her, but it was getting closer. Sticks breaking. Footsteps. Two feet. It wasn't the mountain lion or another wolf that had scared the red wolf across the river, but a man. Was it the Man in the Black Cloak?

As she huddled down into the dirt, a hideous giant centipede crawled across her hand. She flinched and stifled a scream.

Her lungs demanded more air. Her legs tensed, wanting her to run. But it was too late. The attacker was too close. A smart rabbit doesn't break cover when the predator is upon her. She *hides*. She pushed herself farther back into the dark little hole beneath the roots.

A flickering light came through the trees. She heard the pushing of bushes and the scraping of bark and the muffled clanking of metal and wood.

It's a lantern, she thought. *The same kind of lantern the Man in the Black Cloak used the night he took Clara Brahms.*

Trembling, she crouched low and readied herself for battle.

Serafina watched the man raise his lantern and look around him as he broke through the underbrush. It was clear that he was searching for something, but more than that, he was *frightened*. Even with his lantern and the nearly full moon, he could not see as well in the forest's darkness as she could. When the man took another step, she recognized the familiar creak of his leather work boot. That's when she realized that it wasn't the Man in the Black Cloak. It was her pa, in a long, dark brown weather cloak. Despite his warnings, and despite his fear, he had delved deep into the forest to rescue her.

She gasped, crawled out of her hole, and ran toward him.

"I-I'm here, Pa! I'm here!" she stammered, crying as she threw her arms around him.

He squeezed her tight for a long time. It was like being hugged by a gentle bear. She clung to his huge, warm body.

As he exhaled in relief, she could feel the shattering worry pouring out of him. "Sera, aw, Sera, I . . . I thought you'd disappeared like the other children."

"I ain't disappeared, Pa," she said, her voice quivering like she was a little girl again.

Seeing her torn clothing and the scratches on her arms even in the poor light of his lantern, he asked, "What happened to you, Sera? You have another run-in with a raccoon?"

She didn't even know where to begin in telling him everything that had happened to her, and she knew he wouldn't believe her anyway. He would think it was just another one of her cockamamy stories.

"Got terribly lost," she said, shaking her head in shame, and it was the truth. Tears streamed down her face.

"But you're all right?" he said, looking her over. "Where's it hurt?"

"Just wanna get home," she said, burying her head in the folds of his cloak. She remembered how angry she'd been at him for not telling her about her birth, and how she'd convinced herself that he wasn't on her side, but she realized now how foolish she'd been. Nobody in the world had ever done more for her than her pa, and nobody in the world had ever loved her like he did.

When the wolves across the river exploded into howls, it made her pa flinch.

He looked around. "I hate wolves," he said with a shudder as he put his arm around her shoulders and pulled her along. "Come on. We've gotta get out of here."

She happily went with him, but as the wolves continued their howling, it sounded different to her than it had before. The howls weren't the lonely searching calls spread across the vast distances of mountain ridges, but excited yip-howls, all from the same location. She couldn't help but feel that they weren't howls of menace, but of joy and reunion. *You made it, brother.* She thought of the wounded red wolf crossing the river. *You made it home.*

Her pa held the lantern out in front of them as they traveled, like a guide leading them through the night. She was glad to let him lead the way.

"You got to the river and followed it like I taught ya," he said as they walked.

"I wouldn't have made it otherwise," she said.

Soon, they left the trees of the forest behind them and then continued for another mile. Finally, they climbed up the bank of the great river and saw the Biltmore mansion shining in the moonlight on the high ground in the distance. They still had a ways to go, but at least she could see it now. The faint smell of wood smoke drifted on the cold winter air and filled her with a powerful longing for home.

The local folk called the magnificent house "The Lady on the Hill," and tonight she could see why. Biltmore looked majestic with her light gray walls and slate-blue rooftops, her chimneys and towers stretching upward, and the reflection of the moon glistening on her gold and copper trim, like something out of a fairy tale. Serafina had never been so glad to see her home in all her life.

Her pa took her gently by the shoulders and looked into her face. "I know you're drawn to the woods, Sera," he said. "You've always been pulled by your curiosity, but you've got to stay outta there. You've got to keep yourself safe."

"I understand," she said. She sure couldn't argue with him that it wasn't dangerous.

"I know you're good in the dark," he said, "best I ever seen, but you gotta resist the urges, Sera. You're my little girl. I'd hate to lose you all the way."

When he said *all the way*, it haunted her. She realized then that he felt like he was already losing her. She could hear the despair in the raggedness of his voice and see it glistening in his eyes as he looked at her. This was his greatest fear; not just that she would be hurt or killed in the forest, but that her wildness would draw her in, that she'd become more and more wild. More wild than human.

She looked up at him and met his small brown eyes, and saw the reflection of her amber eyes in his. "I'm not gonna leave ya, Pa," she promised.

He nodded and wiped his mouth. "Come on, then," he said, wrapping his arm around her. "Let's get ya home and dry, and get some supper in ya."

• • •

By the time they reached the mansion, the workers had come in from the farms and fields. Most of the mansion's doors had been closed up and locked. The shutters and shades had been drawn against the demons that lurked in the night.

As Serafina and her pa headed for the basement, she was surprised to see that the stables were filled with people and activity. Oil lamps glowed brightly in the night.

She and her pa couldn't help but pause to see what the commotion was about. A returning mounted search party, a dozen riders strong, stormed into the inner courtyard, filling the air with the clatter of horse hooves striking the brick paving. They'd been looking for Clara Brahms and the other victims. As the riders dismounted and the stablemen hurried out to tend to the horses, the parents of the missing children gathered around.

Nolan's pa, who was the stable blacksmith, begged for news of his son, but the riders shook their heads. They'd found nothing.

Poor Mr. Rostonov was there as well, struggling to ask questions in his Russian-hindered English as he held on to his daughter's little white dog. The shaggy creature barked incessantly, growling at the horses as if chastising them for the failure of the search.

Watching Mr. Rostonov, the Brahmses, and Nolan's pa in their desperate struggle to find their children, Serafina's heart filled with an aching sadness. It made her guts churn to think about it, to think about her part in it all. She had to find the Man in the Black Cloak.

"Come on," her pa said as he pulled her away. "This whole place is comin' apart at the bolts, equipment breakin' for no reason, folks losin' their children. It's a bad business all around."

As they ate their dinner together huddled around their little cook fire in the workshop, her pa talked about his day. "I've been working on the dynamo, but I can't figure out how to fix it. The floors upstairs are pitch-black. The servants had to pass out lanterns and candles to all the guests, but there weren't enough of them to go around. Everyone's frightened. With all the guests in the house and the disappearance of the children, this couldn't have come at a worse time. . . ."

She could hear the pain in his voice. "What are you going to do, Pa?"

"I've gotta get back to it," he said. It was only then that she realized that he'd stopped his work in order to look for her. "And you need to go to bed. No hunting tonight. I mean it. Just hunker down and keep yourself safe."

She nodded her head. She knew he was right.

"No hunting," he said again firmly; then he grabbed his tool bag and headed out.

As her father's footsteps receded down the corridor, heading for the stairs that led down to the electrical room in the sub-basement, she said, "You'll figure it out, Pa. I know you will." She knew he would never hear the words from so far away, but she wanted to say them anyway.

She found herself sitting alone in the workshop. The Man in the Black Cloak had taken a victim each night for the last two nights in a row. With the dynamo broken, she imagined him walking through the darkness of Biltmore's unlit corridors tonight with a crooked smile on his face. It was going to be easy pickings for him.

She sat on the mattress behind the boiler. When she was out on the mountain ridge in the rain, this was all she wanted—to be dry and well fed and comfortable in her bed. But now that she was here, it wasn't where she wanted to be. Her pa had told her to go to sleep, and she knew she should—her body was tired and sore—but her mind was a swirl of memories and sensations, hopes and fears.

There was only one person in the world who would believe what had happened to her in the forest that day. There was only one person who'd understand everything she'd been through, and he lived in a room on the second floor at the far end of the house. She missed him. She was worried about him. And she wanted to see him.

When she and Braeden were stranded in the carriage, they were together, they were on the same side, they were as close as close could be. But now that they were both back home again, he in his bedroom and she in the basement, he seemed farther away than when she was lost in the mountains. There were too many forbidden stairs and doors and corridors between them.

They ain't our kind of folk, Sera, her pa had said, and she could only imagine what Mr. and Mrs. Vanderbilt would say about her if they knew she existed.

Using a wet rag she found in the workshop, she tended to

her wounds and cleaned herself up the best she could. Although she lived in a dirty place filled with grease and tools, she liked to keep herself clean, and her adventure in the mountains had left her as muddy as a mudpuppy on a rainy day. She took off her wet clothes, wiped her face and neck, her hands and arms, and all the way down her legs until she was spotless once more.

When she was done she changed into a dry shirt, but she'd lost her only belt. She found an old leather machine strap on one of the shelves and used a knife to slice it lengthwise so that it was about an inch wide. She poked holes in it and cut thinner strips of leather to fasten it. When she was done, she cinched the leather belt around her waist to see what it looked like on her. She was so thin that she could wrap it around her waist twice, but she thought it looked very nice. If her pa had been there, he would have said that it made her look halfway to half-grown. She had always wanted to wear a dress, too, like all the other girls, but she'd never been able to find a discarded one, and she didn't think it was right to steal one. For now, she was happy with her new belt. She bowed and pretended she was a young woman meeting a friend at the market. She smiled and twittered and pretended to tell a story that made her friend laugh.

Somewhere between washing the blood and mud off her face and seeing herself in her new belt, she decided that if she could survive a haunted forest, find her way through a misty cemetery, and narrowly escape a highly perturbed mountain lion, then maybe she could sneak into a Vanderbilt's bedroom while he was sleeping. One way or another, she needed to solve the mystery of the Man in the Black Cloak, and that wasn't going to get done with her taking a nap behind the boiler. The Man in the Black Cloak was going to walk again tonight. He was going to take another child. She was sure of it. And the one he wanted was Braeden Vanderbilt. She had to protect him.

The house was quiet and dark. There was a palpable fear in the air. With no electric lights, the Vanderbilts and their guests had gone to bed early, holing up in the safety of their rooms, next to their small brick fireplaces. A once bright and grand home had been robbed of light and had become a dark and haunted place.

She knew Mr. Vanderbilt's room and Mrs. Vanderbilt's room were both on the second floor, connected by the Oak Sitting Room, where they shared their breakfast each morning. She didn't want to go anywhere near there. She turned left down the corridor toward the southern end of the house, where she knew Braeden's bedroom overlooked the gardens.

She crept past door after door, but they all looked annoyingly similar. Finally, she came to one adorned with a running horse carved in relief in its center panel, and she smiled. She'd found him.

Crouched outside Braeden's door, she realized that the real risk she faced wasn't just that someone would catch her, but that Braeden wouldn't want her there. He hadn't invited her to his room that night. He hadn't even said he wanted to see her ever again. What if her whole theory of their friendship had been pure and utter imagination on her part? What if he was glad to get rid of her in the forest that morning? Maybe he didn't want anything to do with her anymore. He certainly wouldn't want her sneaking into his room late at night.

So she devised a plan. She would peek in, and if her presence there didn't feel right, she'd turn tail quick as a wink.

She slowly turned the knob and pushed on the door. When she slipped inside the room, Braeden lay fast asleep in his bed. He lay on his stomach beneath several layers of blankets, his cheek against the white pillow, his arms up around his head. He looked plum tuckered out, like there wasn't anything in the world that could wake him, and she was glad that he was able to sleep. Gidean slept on the floor beside him. She was relieved to see that they were both safe.

Sensing her entrance, Gidean opened his eyes and growled.

"Shh," she whispered. "You know me. . . ."

Gidean's ears went down in relief when he recognized her voice, and he stopped growling.

Now, that's a good dog, she thought. And it was a pretty good sign that her hopes for friendship with Braeden weren't on the completely wrong mountaintop. She'd get a chuckle out of that—if she became friends with the dog but not the boy.

She gently closed the door behind her and locked it. At first, she thought it was the foolish adults who had forgotten to lock the door and protect Braeden from whoever or whatever was making their children disappear, but then she realized that it was the type of door that could only be locked from the inside. She couldn't decide whether to be angry with him or pleased. She couldn't help but smile a little when she realized that maybe he'd left it unlocked for her. Maybe he was hoping that she would come.

Standing quietly by the door, she gazed around the room. The warm embers of the fire glowed in the fireplace. The red oak-paneled walls were covered with paintings of horses, cats, dogs, hawks, foxes, and otters. His shelves were filled with books about horseback riding and animals. Award plaques and blue ribbons from equestrian events were everywhere. Soon they would need to build the young master a new room for all his first-place finishes. Knowing the Vanderbilts, it wouldn't be just a room but a whole wing.

It felt good to be there with Braeden, to be in the warmth and darkness of his room. She could see that this was his refuge. But she had the feeling that maybe even here, in this seemingly protected place, they weren't completely safe. Something was telling her that she should stay on her guard, at least a little while longer.

Careful not to wake him, she moved quietly over to the window and scanned the grounds for signs of danger. The moon cast a ghostly silver light across the Rambles, a maze of giant azaleas, hollies, and other bushes. The branches of the trees swayed in the wind. It was in the Rambles that Anastasia Rostonova had disappeared, leaving her little white dog behind to search the empty paths for her.

As she looked down from the second floor to the moonlit gardens below her, she could almost imagine seeing herself a few nights before, walking across the grounds toward the forest's edge, two rats clenched in her fists.

She looked behind her at Braeden, lying in the bed. Then she looked out across the forest once more. An owl glided on silent wings across the canopy of trees and then disappeared.

I am a creature of the night, she thought.

When she finally began to feel tired, she pulled herself away from the window. She went over to the fireplace and felt the warmth of its glowing coals. Then she pulled a blanket off the leather chair and curled up on the fur rug on the floor in front of the fire. She fell asleep almost immediately. For the first time in what seemed like a long time, she slept soundly and dreamed deeply for hours. It felt good to be home.

In the middle of the night, she awoke slowly to the gentle sound of Braeden's voice. "I was hoping you would come," he said. It didn't seem to surprise him at all to wake and find her curled up by his fireplace. "I was worrying about you all day."

"I'm all right," she said, her heart filling with warmth as much from the tone of his voice as the words he spoke.

"How did you make it home?" he asked.

She told him everything, and for the first time, it all began to feel real in her mind and in her heart. It didn't feel like just a dream or a child's fantasy, but actually true.

Braeden turned onto his back and listened to her account with rapt attention. "That's amazing," he said several times.

When she was done, he paused for a long time, as if he was envisioning it all in his mind, and then he said, "You're so clever and brave, Serafina."

She couldn't suppress a sigh as all the fear, uncertainty, and helplessness that had built up inside her drifted away.

They sat quietly in the darkness for a long time, he in his bed and her by the fireplace, not moving or talking, and it felt good just to be there for a while.

She got up slowly, took a few steps over to the window, and then faced him. She could see his eyes looking at her as she stood in front of him in the moonlight. She imagined her skin must look very pale to him, almost ghostly, and her hair almost white in color.

"I'm going to ask you a question," she said.

"All right," he said softly, sitting up in his bed.

"When you look at me, what do you see?"

Braeden went quiet and did not answer. The question seemed to scare him. "What do you mean?"

"When you look at me, do you see . . . do you see . . . a normal girl?"

"Clara Brahms is different than Anastasia Rostonova, and you are different than both of them," he said. "We're all different in our own way."

"I understand what you're saying, but am I . . ." She faltered. She didn't know how to ask it. "Am I strange looking? Do I act strange? Am I some sort of weird creature or something?"

It stunned her when he did not reply right away, when he did not immediately deny it. He didn't say anything at all. He hesitated. For a long time. Every second that went by was like a dagger in her heart because she knew it was true. She felt like leaping out his window and running into the trees. His reaction confirmed that she was strange and contorted beyond reckoning!

"Let me ask you a question in return," he said. "Have you had a lot of friends during the course of your life?"

"No," she said soberly, thinking that now he was being particularly cruel if this was his way of explaining just how grotesque she was.

"Neither have I," he said. "The truth is, besides Gidean and my horses, I've never had a good friend my own age, someone I really trusted and wanted to be with through thick and thin. I've met a lot of girls and a lot of boys, and I've spent time with them, but . . ."

His voice faltered. He could not explain. And she could feel the hurt inside him, and her heart went out to him despite the fact that he'd practically called her a monster to her face just moments before. "Keep going . . ." she said softly.

"I-I don't know why, but I haven't made any friends that are . . . like . . . that are . . ."

"Human," she said.

He nodded. "Isn't that strange? I mean, isn't that *very* strange? After my family died, I didn't want to talk to anyone anymore or be with them. I didn't want to wonder when I was going to see them next. I just didn't want to. I wanted to be alone. My aunt and uncle have been very kind. They've brought all sorts of boys and girls here to see if I was interested in making friends. I sat with them at dinner because my aunt and uncle wanted me to sit with them. I danced with the girls because they wanted me to dance with them. I never said anything mean to any of the girls or the boys, and felt nothing but kindness toward them, and maybe they never even knew what I was feeling. There was nothing wrong with them, but for some reason, I would just rather be with Gidean, or taking a walk watching the birds, or looking for new things in the forest. My uncle brought my cousins here to explore the forests with me, but they started playing a game with a ball, and soon I drifted away from them. I don't understand it. There's nothing wrong with any of them. I think there's something wrong with *me*, Serafina."

Serafina looked at Braeden, and she spoke very softly, not sure she wanted to know the answer to the question she was about to ask. "Was it like that when you met me?"

"I don't . . . I . . ."

"Would you just as soon I go?" she said quietly, trying to understand.

"No, it's . . . it's hard to explain. . . ."

"Try," she said, praying that he wasn't just about to tell her that he felt nothing for her and just wanted to be alone.

"When I met you, it was *different*," he said. "I wanted to know who you were. When you ran down the stairs and disappeared, I was frantic to find you again. I searched all over, every floor. I checked every closet and looked under every bed. Everyone else was looking for Clara Brahms, may God be with her, but I was looking for *you*, Serafina. When my aunt and uncle decided to send me away to the Vances, I pitched a fit of temper like they'd never seen before. You should've seen the look on their faces. They had no idea what had gotten into me."

Serafina smiled. "You really didn't want to leave Biltmore that bad?" Still smiling, she took a few steps forward and sat on the edge of the bed beside him.

"You have no idea how my heart leapt when I saw stupid old Crankshod shaking the daylights out of you in the porte cochere," he said. "I thought: There she is! There she is! I can save her!"

Serafina laughed. "Well, you could have come a little earlier and saved me a good shaking!"

Braeden smiled, and it was good to see him smile, but then he remembered her question and turned more serious again as he looked at her. "But then, later, during the battle in the

forest, and in the carriage that night, and when you disappeared the next morning, that's when I realized how different
you really were from anyone I had ever met. Yes, you are different, Serafina . . . very different . . . maybe even strange, like
you say . . . I don't know . . . but . . ." His words faded, and he
did not continue.

"But maybe that's all right with you," she said tentatively,
thinking she understood him.

"Yes. I think it's what I like about you," he said, and there
was a long pause between them.

"So, we're friends," she said finally, her heart beating as she
waited for his answer. It was a statement, but it was also a question, to be confirmed or denied, and it was the first time in her
life she had ever asked someone that question.

"We're friends," he agreed, nodding his head. "Good
friends."

She smiled at him, and he smiled in return. Her chest filled
with a sensation like she was drinking warm milk.

"I also want to tell you this, Serafina," he said. "I don't
think there's anything wrong with you. And maybe there's
nothing wrong with me, either. I don't know. We're just different from the others, you and I, each in our own way. You know
what I mean?"

He climbed out of the bed. "I have a present for you," he
said as he lit an oil lamp on his nightstand. "I know you don't
need the light, but I do. Otherwise, I'm going to stub my toe
on the bed."

"A present? For me?" she said, not really hearing anything else he said.

Presents were something she'd read about in *Little Women* and other books, something people exchanged when they liked each other. She had never been able to figure out why her pa never celebrated her birthday, but now that he'd told her the story of her birth, she realized that it probably dug up dark and painful memories that he preferred to forget. It didn't help that buying sentimental presents that weren't useful was akin to a sin in his book. And the one time he tried to make her a gift, she ended up with a doll that looked suspiciously like a crescent wrench. The truth was she had never received an actual wrapped present in her life, but the thought of it excited her.

"Why do I deserve a present?" she asked Braeden as she crawled farther onto the bed.

"Because we're friends, right?" he said as he handed her a medium-size lightweight box wrapped in decorative paper and tied with a crimson velvet bow. "I hope you don't mind what it is."

She looked at him and raised an eyebrow. "Well, that's foreboding. What is it, a black satin cloak?"

"Just open it," he said, smiling.

She untied the bow, thinking of how different the soft velvet felt in her fingers compared to the rough twine that she once cinched around her waist. But having no practice at it, she didn't know how to unwrap the beautiful paper. Braeden had to show her how.

Finally, she lifted the lid off the box.

She gasped. What she saw in the box struck a deep chord in her heart. It was a gorgeous winter gown. It had long sleeves of dark maroon velvet and a corset of richly patterned charcoal-and-black velour, all trimmed in lynx-gray piping, its silver threads shimmering in the flickering light of the oil lamp.

"Oh, it's wonderful . . ." she said in amazement as she lifted the dress out of the box. The material felt so soft and warm that she kneaded it with her fingers and touched it to her face. She had never seen such a beautiful dress in her life.

She pulled her hair back behind her head and tied it with the red bow from her present. Then she went to the mirror and draped the dress in front of her to see what she looked like. When she saw her image, it almost seemed like a completely different person staring back at her. She wasn't a wild creature from the forest anymore, but a beautiful little girl who belonged wherever she went. She stared at the girl for a long time.

As she marveled at the exquisite details of her new gown, a dark thought crept into her mind. She didn't want to be rude, but her curiosity won that battle as fast as water running downhill. She turned to Braeden.

"I already know what you're going to ask," he said.

"We've only known each other for a short time, so how did you get this dress so quickly?"

He looked at the pictures on his wall.

"Where did it come from, Braeden?"

He looked at the floor.

"Braeden . . ."

Finally, he looked at her and answered, "My aunt had it made."

"But not for me."

"She wanted me to give it to Clara."

"Ah," Serafina said, trying to come to grips with it.

"I know, I know, I'm really sorry," he said. "She never wore it, though, I swear. She never even saw it. I just really wanted to give you something nice and I didn't have anything. I didn't mean any offense by it."

Serafina gently touched his arm. "It's a beautiful gown, Braeden. I love it. Thank you." She leaned toward him and kissed him on the cheek.

Braeden smiled, happy.

She enjoyed seeing him pleased, but the dress made her think of Clara again. "So, why were the Brahms invited to Biltmore?" she asked.

"I don't know," Braeden said. "I think my aunt and uncle heard that Clara was a prodigy and they thought it would be nice to meet her and have her play for the guests."

"And your aunt saw how sweet and pretty she was, how educated and talented, and she wanted you to be friends with her."

He nodded. "Part of my aunt's grand plan to find a friend for me. She really liked Clara, in particular, but I only spoke to her a few times so I didn't know her very well."

As Braeden spoke, Serafina's ears picked up the sound of someone approaching. She heard footsteps coming slowly down the hall. She set aside the dress. "Do you hear that?" she whispered. "Someone's coming!"

"I hear it," Braeden said in a low voice.

Gidean rose to his feet and went straight to the closed door.

"Douse the light!" she whispered.

Braeden quickly followed her suggestion, striking them into darkness.

Staying quiet, they stopped and listened.

From the sound of the shoes, she thought that it might be Mr. Vanderbilt coming to check in on his nephew. She'd been caught, she thought. She'd been caught bad and there wasn't going to be any way to get out of it! The shoeshine-girl ruse wasn't going to work this time. She wondered if she could hide under the bed, or fling some sort of crazy excuse at him and then skedaddle down the corridor before he got a good look at her. But then she heard the slithering noise.

It was the Man in the Black Cloak.

He was coming down the corridor.

He was searching.

Every night he came.

He was relentless.

"I have a secret way out," Braeden whispered.

"Let's just be real quiet," she said. "Stay very still." Leaving Braeden near the bed, she moved forward through the darkness and joined Gidean at the door, worried that he'd start barking and give their presence away. She touched the dog's shoulder, letting him know that if a fight came, they'd fight it together.

The sound came closer and closer until the Man in the Black Cloak was right outside the door.

He stopped there, listening, waiting, as if he could sense them inside the room. He knew they were in there.

She could hear him breathing. She picked up the foul scent of the cloak as the stench wafted through the crack under the door.

The Black Cloak began its slow, slithering, rattling motion.

Gidean growled.

The doorknob slowly turned.

15

Serafina watched the doorknob rotate a quarter turn and then come to a stop with a click of metal on metal. She had locked the door when she came in, and she remembered the weight of it, with its solid, inch-thick oak panels. It seemed nearly impossible for anyone to break the door. She just hoped that the Man in the Black Cloak couldn't pass through it using some sort of dark magic.

She could feel him breathing on the other side of the door, seething.

She waited, holding on to Gidean.

After several seconds, the doorknob returned to its normal position and the footsteps resumed, continuing slowly down the hallway. She let go of Gidean, and they all finally started breathing normally again. She looked at Braeden.

"That was a close one," she whispered.

"I'm glad you got here before he did," Braeden said.

She went over and climbed back onto the bed. They lay in the darkness, listening to the sounds of the house—expecting running footsteps or a cry of terror in the night—but all they heard was the crackle of the fire and their own steady breathing as they drifted in and out of sleep.

Serafina woke the next morning to the sound of Braeden's aunt knocking urgently on his locked bedroom door.

"Braeden, it's time to get up," Mrs. Vanderbilt said. "Braeden?"

Serafina slipped off the bed and looked for a place to hide.

"Here . . ." Braeden whispered as he pulled back a decorative brass vent cover on the wall beneath his desk.

"Braeden, are you all right in there?" his aunt asked through the door. "Please open up, darling. You're worrying me."

Serafina crawled into the air passage, and Braeden replaced the cover behind her. She watched him through the grille as he shoved the dress under his bed then glanced around the room to make sure there wasn't any other evidence that she'd been there. Gidean studied his master with interest, the dog's pointed ears raised upward and his head tilted to the side in inquiry.

"You don't say a word," Braeden warned him, and Gidean lowered his ears.

Finally, Braeden walked over to the door and opened it. "I'm here. I'm all right."

His aunt swept into the room, wrapped her arms around him, and held him. That's when Serafina realized that Mrs. Vanderbilt really did love Braeden. She could see it just in the way she clutched him.

"What's happened?" Braeden asked his aunt uncertainly.

"The pastor's son disappeared during the night."

When she heard the news of another victim, Serafina felt a terrible knot in her stomach. That made three children in three nights now. It was like something was driving the attacker anew, pushing him harder and harder. She'd been so relieved that she and Braeden had been able to escape the Man in the Black Cloak by hiding in Braeden's locked room, but now she realized all that meant was that he got someone else. Another child was gone. She had eluded the demon, but she had not *stopped* him.

Knowing that she had to find some way out other than through Braeden's room, she crawled down the passage to see where it would lead. She came to an intersection of two other passages. She took the one on the right, where she came to another split. There appeared to be a whole network of secret passages running through the house. *So this is where the rats have been hiding all these years.*

She crawled past vents that led into the various private rooms of the house—sitting rooms, hallways, bedrooms, even bathrooms. She saw maids making beds, and guests getting dressed for the day. Everyone was whispering in worry and confusion. No one understood what was happening. They were talking about shades and murderers. Biltmore had become a haunted place where children disappeared.

She saw the footman, Mr. Pratt, walking hurriedly down a corridor with Miss Whitney. "No, no, Miss Whitney, this is no normal killer," Mr. Pratt was saying as they went by.

"That's an awful thing to say!" Miss Whitney protested. "How do you know they're dead?"

"Oh, they're dead, believe me. This is a creature of the night, something straight from hell."

The phrase shocked Serafina. *Creature of the night,* he'd said. But *she* was a creature of the night. She'd used the phrase herself. Were creatures of the night evil? Did that mean *she* was evil? It horrified her to think that she was in some way associated with or like the Man in the Black Cloak.

"Well, what are we going to do about it? That's what I want to know," a man shouted.

She crawled a few feet through the passage in the direction of the man's voice and looked down through a metal grate into the Gun Room. From her vantage point, she could see a dozen gentlemen standing and talking about what was going on.

"There is nothing we can do," Mr. Vanderbilt said. "We have to let the detectives do their job."

Mr. Vanderbilt knew all the ins and outs of Biltmore better than anybody. He designed the place. Why all the hidden staircases and secret doors? And he was rich, so he had the money and power to do whatever he wanted. And he was a Vanderbilt, so no one would ever suspect him. Was this why he'd built a mansion in the middle of a dark forest?

So now here Mr. Vanderbilt was, telling everyone that there was nothing they could do but wait for the detectives to do their work. He was undoubtedly the person *paying* the private detectives, so they'd come up with whatever answer he wanted them to.

The other gentlemen shook their heads in frustration.

"Perhaps we should bring in one of the well-known detective agencies from New York," Mr. Bendel suggested. "These local chaps are asking everybody a lot of prying questions, but they don't seem to be getting the job done."

"Or perhaps we should organize another search party," Mr. Thorne suggested.

"I agree," Mr. Brahms said. "The detectives seem to think that one of the servants is taking the children, but I don't think we should rule out that it could be anyone in the house. Even one of us."

"Maybe it's you, Brahms," Mr. Bendel snarled, clearly not appreciating his implication.

"Don't be ridiculous," Mr. Vanderbilt said, getting between them. "It's not one of us. Just calm down."

"The womenfolk are terrified," said a gentleman she didn't recognize. "Every night, another child disappears. We've got to do something!"

"Do we even know if the attacker is an outsider or some-one inside Biltmore?" someone else asked. "Maybe it's a total stranger. Or one of our own men—Mr. Boseman or Mr. Crankshod."

"We don't even know if there *is* an attacker," Mr. Bendel said. "We haven't found any proof that these are kidnappings. For all we know, these children just ran away!"

"Of course there's an attacker," Mr. Brahms argued, becoming more and more upset. "Someone's taking our children! My Clara would never run away! Mr. Thorne is right. We need to organize another search."

Mr. Rostonov said something in a mix of Russian and English, but no one seemed to pay him any mind.

"Perhaps the children are falling into some kind of hole in the basement or something," Mr. Bendel suggested.

"There aren't any holes in the basement," Mr. Vanderbilt said firmly, offended by the suggestion that Biltmore itself might be a dangerous place.

"Or maybe there's an uncovered well somewhere on the grounds . . ." Mr. Bendel pressed on.

"The main thing is that we need to protect the remaining children," Mr. Thorne said. "I'm especially concerned for the young master. What can we do to make sure he stays safe?"

"Don't worry," Mr. Vanderbilt said. "We'll keep Braeden safe."

"That's all well and good, but we have to organize another search party," Mr. Brahms said again. "I have to find my Clara!"

"I'm sorry, Mr. Brahms, but I just don't think that's going to do any good," Mr. Vanderbilt said. "We've searched the house and grounds several times already. There's got to be something else we can do, something more effective. There has to be answer to this terrible puzzle. . . ."

Mr. Rostonov turned to Mr. Thorne and touched his arm for assistance. *"Nekotorye ubivayut detyey,"* he said to him.

"Otets, vse v poryadke. My organizuem novyi poisk, Batya," Mr. Thorne said in reply.

Serafina remembered that Mr. Bendel had mentioned that Mr. Thorne spoke Russian, but it still surprised her to hear it. Mr. Thorne went on to translate what was going on for Mr. Rostonov and tried to reassure him.

She thought it was kind of Mr. Thorne to help Mr. Rostonov, but suddenly Mr. Rostonov became very upset and looked at Mr. Thorne in extreme confusion. *"Otets?"* he asked him. *"Batya?"*

Mr. Thorne blanched, as if he realized that he'd made a dreadful mistake in his Russian. He tried to apologize, but as he did so, Mr. Rostonov became even more upset. Everything Mr. Thorne said to him made him more and more agitated.

Serafina watched all of this in fascination. What had Mr. Thorne said to Mr. Rostonov that caused him such anguish?

"Gentlemen, please," Mr. Vanderbilt said, frustrated with the arguing. "All right, all right, we'll do it. If that's what you think should be done, then we'll organize another search effort, but this time we'll search slowly and systematically from one room to the next, and we'll post guard positions in each room that we've completed."

The other men heartily agreed with Mr. Vanderbilt's plan. They were clearly relieved that some sort of agreement had been reached and there was something they could do. The feeling of uselessness was unbearable. It was a feeling Serafina had in common with them.

The men streamed out of the room to organize the search— all but poor Mr. Rostonov, who remained behind, red-faced and upset.

She frowned. Something wasn't right.

She had planned to use the air vents to find a way to get down to the first floor and then make her way to the basement to rejoin her pa, but now she had a different idea.

She turned around and crawled quickly back to Braeden's room. She stopped at the vent cover and listened. When she didn't hear Mrs. Vanderbilt's voice, she slowly cracked open the vent and peeked inside. Gidean stuck his nose into the crack and growled. Surprised, she recoiled, her back arching like a witch's best friend as she hissed at him. "It's me, you stupid dog! I'm on the good side, remember?" *At least I think I am,* she thought, remembering Mr. Pratt's comment about the evil nature of creatures of the night.

Gidean stopped growling and stepped back, his face happy with relief and his little tail nub wagging.

"Serafina!" Braeden said excitedly as he pulled her out of the vent. "Where did you go? You were supposed to wait for me in there, not crawl away! You'll get lost in all those passages! They're endless!"

"I wasn't going to get lost," she said. "I liked it in there."

"You have to be careful. Didn't you hear my aunt say that another boy's gone missing?"

"Your uncle is organizing a search party."

"How do you know that?"

"Do you know what the Russian word *otets* means?" she asked abruptly, ignoring his question.

"What?"

"*Otets*. Or the word *batya*. What do those words mean?"

"I don't know. What are you talking about?"

"Do you know anyone who speaks Russian?"

"Mr. Rostonov."

"Besides him."

"Mr. Thorne."

"Definitely besides him. Anyone else?"

"No, but we do have a library."

"The library . . ." she said. That was a good idea. "Can we go?"

"You want to go to the library *now*? What for?"

"We need to look something up. I think it's important."

She and Braeden crawled rapidly, one behind the other, through the secret passages of the house. For all his talent in befriending animals and his other good qualities, Braeden sounded like a herd of wild boars trampling through the passage.

"Shh," she whispered. "Quietly . . ."

"All right, Little Miss Softpaws," Braeden retorted, and urged her forward with a push of his head. "Just keep moving."

For the next few yards through the passage, Braeden made every effort to move more quietly, but he was still too loud.

"I'm going to get in big trouble if my uncle catches us doing this," Braeden said as they passed another vent.

"He can't even fit in here," she said happily.

They crawled past the second-floor living hall and then down the length of the Tapestry Gallery until they reached the south wing of the house.

"There it is," Braeden said finally.

She peered down through the metal grate into the Biltmore Library Room, with its ornate brass lamps, oak-paneled walls, and plush furniture. The shelves were lined with thousands of books.

"Come on," she said, and pushed through the grate.

Thirty feet above the floor, Serafina balanced on the high ledge of the hand-carved crown molding that supported the vaulted ceiling, with its famous Italian painting of sunlit clouds and winged angels. She climbed down the upper shelves like they were the rungs of an easy ladder. From there, she scampered like a tightrope artist along a decorative wrought-iron railing. Darting quickly over to the high mantel of the massive black marble fireplace, she leapt lightly onto the soft Persian rugs on the floor and landed on her feet.

"That was fun," she said with satisfaction.

"Speak for yourself," said Braeden, who was still thirty feet up in the air, clinging desperately to the highest bookshelf, looking scared out of his wits.

"What are you doing up there, Braeden?" she whispered up to him in confusion. "Quit fooling around. Come on!"

"I'm not fooling around," Braeden said.

She could see now that he was truly terrified. "Put your left foot on the shelf right below you and go from there," she said.

She watched as he slowly, clumsily climbed down. He did pretty well at first, but then lost his grip on the last bit, fell a short distance, and landed on his bottom with a relieved sigh.

"You made it," she said cheerfully, touching his shoulder in congratulations.

He smiled. "Let's just use the normal door next time, all right?"

She smiled and nodded. She liked how he was already thinking there was going to be a next time.

She gazed around at all the books lining the shelves. She'd never been here in the light of day. She thought back to all the books her pa had brought her, and how she would spend hours poring over the pages under his guidance, sounding out the letters until they became words and sentences and thoughts in her mind. Always wanting more, she would keep reading long after he'd gone to sleep. Over the years, she'd read hundreds of books, each one opening a whole new world to her. She marveled at how this one room contained the thoughts and voices of thousands of writers, people who had lived in different countries and different times, people who had told stories of the heart and of the mind, people who had studied ancient civilizations, the species of plants, and the flow of rivers. Her pa had told her that Mr. Vanderbilt had many keen interests and studied the books in his library; he was considered one of the most well-read men in America. As she looked around the room at all the leather-bound tomes, the intricate knickknacks on the tables, and the inviting soft furniture, it felt like she could spend hours here just exploring and reading and taking afternoon naps.

"That's Napoleon Bonaparte's personal chess set," Braeden said when he noticed her looking at the ornately carved pieces arranged in perfect rows on a delicate rectangular table. She didn't know who Napoleon Bonaparte was, but she thought it would be great fun pushing the beautiful pieces off the edge of the table and watching them fall to the floor.

"What's that?" she asked, pointing to a small, dark oil painting in a wooden frame sitting on one of the tables among a collection of other items. The painting was so faded and worn that it was difficult to make out, but it appeared to depict a mountain lion stalking through the undergrowth of a forest.

"I think it's supposed to be a catamount," Braeden said, looking over her shoulder.

"What's that?"

"My uncle said that years ago the local people used to use the phrase *cat of the mountains*, but over time it was shortened to *cat-a-the-mountains*, and eventually it became *catamount*."

As Braeden spoke, she leaned close to the painting and tried to make out the details. It was difficult to tell, but the shadow of the cat looked weird and all ajumble in the bushes behind it. It almost seemed like the lion was casting the shadow of a human being. She vaguely remembered the remnants of an old folktale that she'd heard years before.

"Are catamounts changers of some sort?" she asked.

"I don't know. My uncle bought the painting in a local shop. My aunt thinks it's ugly and wants to get rid of it," Braeden said, then pulled her away. "Come on. You wanted to know the meaning of a Russian word. Let's look it up." He led her to the corner behind the huge brass globe. "The foreign languages are over here." He scanned the titles of the books, saying each one as if he enjoyed the sound of the words. "*Arabic, Bulgarian, Cherokee, Deutsch, Español.*" It was clear that Braeden's uncle, who was fluent in eight languages, had taught him a few things. Now that they were in the world of words and books rather than scaling the precipitous heights, Braeden was back in his element. "*French, Greek, Hindi, Italiano, Japanese, Kurdish, Latin, Manx—*"

"I like the sound of that one," Serafina interjected.

"Some sort of old Celtic language, I think," Braeden said before continuing. "*Norman, Ojibwa, Polish, Quechua, Romanian.* Got it. Here it is. *Russian!*"

"Great. Look up the word *otets.*"

"How do you spell it?"

"I'm not sure."

"We'll have to go by the sound of it . . ." he said as he flipped through the pages until he came to the spot he wanted. "Nope, that's not it." He tried another guess. "Nope, that's not it, either. Oh, here it is. *Otets.*"

"That's it!" she said, grasping his arm. "That's what Mr. Thorne called Mr. Rostonov that upset him so badly. Is it some kind of terrible insult or accusation? Is it a sharp-fanged demon or something?"

"Umm . . ." Braeden said, frowning as he read the entry. "Not exactly."

"Well, what's it mean?"

"Father."

"What?"

"*Otets* means 'father' in Russian," Braeden said, shaking his head. "I don't understand. Maybe you misunderstood what Mr. Thorne said. Why would he call Mr. Rostonov 'Father'?"

She had no idea, but she pushed closer to get a better view of the entry in the book.

"I can't imagine Mr. Thorne making a mistake like that," Braeden said. "He's very smart. You should see him play chess. He even beats my uncle, and *nobody* beats my uncle."

"He seems to be amazing at nearly everything," she scoffed.

"Well, you don't have to be mean about it. He's a good man."

She took the book from Braeden and kept reading. It explained that *otets* was the formal way a child would address a parent in public. But the more intimate way, used only within the family, was the word *batya*, which translated roughly to "daddy" or "papa."

She frowned in confusion.

They were the same age and completely unrelated. Why in the world would Mr. Thorne repeatedly address Mr. Rostonov as his papa?

As Serafina and Braeden crawled back into the ventilation system, she asked, "Do you know all the gentlemen who are currently guests at Biltmore?"

"I've met most of them," Braeden said as he closed up the vent cover behind them, "but not all of them."

"Do you know which rooms they're staying in?" she asked as they made their way on their hands and knees along the shaft back toward his bedroom.

"The guests are on the third floor. Servants live on the fourth."

"But do you know the specific rooms?"

"I know some of them. My aunt put Mr. Bendel in the Raphael Room. The Brahmses are in the Earlom Room and Mr. Rostonov is in the Morland Room. It goes on and on. Why?"

"I have an idea. If the Man in the Black Cloak is one of the gentlemen at Biltmore, then he needs to store his cloak someplace when he's not using it. I've checked the closets and coatrooms on the first floor, but I want to check the bedrooms, too."

"You want to sneak into people's private bedrooms?" Braeden asked hesitantly.

"They won't know," Serafina pointed out. "As long as we're careful, they won't catch us."

"But we'll be looking through their private belongings. . . ."

"Yes, but we need to help Clara and the others. And we need to stop the Man in the Black Cloak from doing this again."

Braeden pursed his lips. He didn't like this idea. "Isn't there some other way?"

"We just need to look," she said.

Finally, he nodded his head.

Serafina followed Braeden along the shaft. Mr. Vanderbilt had called in private detectives, who now stood guard at various points in the corridors of the house. As long as they stayed in the ventilation system they were safe, but moving through the other parts of the house unseen was going to be far more difficult than before.

Serafina could tell that all the searches and the presence of the detectives weren't bringing solace to Biltmore's anxious inhabitants. She sensed that both the guests and the servants were losing hope. From what she overheard people saying to one another, there was an increasing sense that the children weren't just missing but dead. She had to defend her own heart from the same terrible conclusion. She'd seen them vanish, but her pa had told her that everyone had to be someplace. Even dead bodies had to be someplace. *We've got to keep looking,* she kept telling herself. *We can't give up. We've got to help them.* But when the members of the various search parties began to return without any sign of the children, people were more disheartened than ever.

Serafina and Braeden snuck into the Raphael Room and looked through Mr. Bendel's belongings.

"Mr. Bendel is always so cheerful," Braeden said. "I don't see how he could have hurt anyone."

"Just keep looking," she whispered, determined to stay focused.

She found all sorts of expensive clothing in Mr. Bendel's finely decorated traveling chests, including many stylish gloves and a long, dark gray cloak, but it wasn't the Black Cloak.

Next, they checked the Van Dyck Room, with its finely detailed terra-cotta-colored wallpaper, its dark mahogany furniture, and many paintings hanging by wires on the walls. "Mr. Thorne has always been very kind to me," Braeden said. "I don't see how it could possibly be him."

Ignoring him, Serafina searched the room as thoroughly as

she could, digging through all of the old chests that he'd left unlocked. She found no trace of the cloak.

"You like him too much," she said as she searched under the mahogany bed.

"I do not," Braeden protested.

"We'll see."

"He saved Gidean's life when Mr. Crankshod was going to kill him with an ax," Braeden said.

Serafina frowned. In Braeden's mind, the man who saved his dog could do no wrong. When they heard someone coming, they darted back into the ventilation shaft as quickly as they could.

"I don't think it's any of the gentlemen at Biltmore," Braeden said as they made their way to the next room. "It must be some kind of demon from the forest like we were talking about before, or maybe it's a stranger from the city who isn't known to us."

Serafina agreed that the lack of clues was discouraging, but there were still at least a dozen more rooms to check. They moved on to the Sheraton Room and the Old English Room.

When they searched the Morland Room, she looked into each of Mr. Rostonov's beautiful, hand-painted traveling cases. Her heart filled with sadness when she found a chest filled with lovely Russian dresses. They were such amazing gowns, with deep frills and exotic patterns.

"It doesn't feel right to be here," Braeden said uncomfortably.

As they were crawling through a shaft to the next room,

they heard several women talking in a hallway on the level below. They shinnied down a shaft to get a closer look.

"That's my aunt's room," Braeden said nervously.

"Let's stay quiet . . ." Serafina whispered, then peered through a grate to look into the room.

When Serafina looked down into Mrs. Vanderbilt's room, she beheld the glittering purple-and-gold French-style bedroom, with its elegant, curvy furniture and fancifully trimmed mirrors. She thought it was the most beautiful room she had ever seen. It wasn't rectangular in shape like a normal room, but oval. The gold silk walls, the bright windows, and even the delicately painted doors were curved along the lines of the oval. The bed coverings, draperies, and furniture upholstery were all finely cut purple velvet. The room positively glowed with sunlight, and she would have loved to curl up on Mrs. Vanderbilt's bed. She was just about to suggest to Braeden that they risk climbing into the room when Braeden grabbed her arm.

"Wait. There's my aunt," he said as Mrs. Vanderbilt came slowly into the room, followed by her lady's maid and her household assistant.

"These are such lonely and frightening times," Mrs. Vanderbilt said with sadness. "I would like to do something for the families, something to bring everyone together and strengthen our spirits. This evening, we'll gather in the Banquet Hall at seven o'clock. The electric lighting still isn't working, so stoke up the fires and bring in as many candles and oil lamps as you can. Arrange it with the kitchen so that we can provide everyone with something to eat. It won't be a formal sit-down dinner or any sort of party, mind you; it's just not the appropriate time for that, but we must do something."

"I'll go down to the kitchens and talk to the cook," her assistant said.

"I think it's important that we gain the comfort of spending some time together, whether we're frightened, grieving, or still holding on to hope," Mrs. Vanderbilt said.

"Yes, ma'am," her lady's maid said.

Serafina thought it was kind of Mrs. Vanderbilt to arrange the gathering.

It was well known at Biltmore that Mrs. Vanderbilt liked to learn the names and faces of all the children of both the guests and servants, and when Christmas came, she and her lady's maid would go shopping in Asheville and the surrounding villages and buy each one of the children a special gift. Sometimes, if she heard that a child wanted a particular present that wasn't available in the area, Mrs. Vanderbilt would send away to New York for it, and it would miraculously arrive a few days later on the train. On Christmas morning, she would invite all the families to gather around the Christmas tree, where she would hand each child his or her gift: a porcelain-faced doll, a soft toy bear, a pocketknife—it all depended on the child. Serafina remembered her own Christmas mornings, sitting in the basement, curled up on the stone floor at the bottom of the stairs, listening to the children laughing and playing with their toys above her.

Over the next few hours, the word spread, and the guests and servants began preparing for the upcoming gathering.

"My aunt and uncle are going to want me to be there, so I've got to go," Braeden said glumly. "I wish you could come with me. You must be as hungry as I am."

"I'm starving. It's going to be in the Banquet Hall, right? I'll be there in spirit. Just don't let anyone play the pipe organ," Serafina said.

"I'll sneak you some food," he said as they parted.

While Braeden went to his bedroom to dress for the gathering, Serafina snuck into position. She moved through the secret passages behind the upper levels of the organ that she'd learned about from Mr. Pratt and Miss Whitney. There she hid in the organ loft, among the seven hundred brass pipes, some reaching five, ten, twenty feet in height. From here she had a wonderful bird's-eye view of the room.

The Banquet Hall was the largest room she'd ever laid eyes on, with a barrel-vaulted ceiling high enough for a hawk to soar in. Rows of flags and pendants hung down from above, like the throne room of an ancient king. The stone walls were adorned with medieval armor, crossed spears, and rich tapestries that looked extremely old but well worth climbing someday. In the center of the room there was a massively long oak dining table ringed with hand-carved chairs intended for the Vanderbilts and sixty-four of their closest friends. But tonight, no one was sitting at the table. The servants had laid it out with a cornucopian buffet of food. In addition to the selection of roast beef, brook trout, chicken à l'orange, endless trays of vegetables, and rosemary potatoes au gratin, there were all sorts of chocolate desserts and fruit tarts. The pumpkin pie, like all pumpkin pie, looked like something a dog would eat, but the whipped Chantilly cream on top of it looked delicious.

She watched in silence as weary, saddened people streamed into the room, exchanged a few words with Mrs. Vanderbilt, and then joined the gathering. In what appeared to be a valiant effort to stay upbeat, Mr. and Mrs. Brahms came in and tried to eat some food and find some solace in the company of the others. Mr. Vanderbilt went over and spoke to them, and they seemed to find great comfort in his words and touch. He then went over to the pastor and his wife and consoled them about their lost son. He went next to Nolan's distraught mother and father. Nolan's father was the blacksmith, but he and his wife were welcome here. Mr. Vanderbilt spoke with them for a long time. The more she watched him, the more her feelings toward him softened. There seemed to be true and genuine caring in him, not just for his guests, but for the people who worked for him as well.

Braeden, following his uncle's example and looking particularly neat in his black jacket and vest, did his best to talk with a young red-haired girl in a blue dress. The young lady appeared to be more than a little frightened by everything that had been going on. There were other children there as well, looking scared and sullen. Mr. Boseman, the estate superintendent, was in attendance, along with Mr. Pratt and Miss Whitney and many other familiar faces. It seemed to her that the only person missing was poor old Mr. Rostonov. Serafina overheard one of the manservants come in and say that Mr. Rostonov had sent word that he was too heartsick to attend.

She glanced over at Mr. Thorne and Mr. Bendel, who were standing together near the fire. Mr. Thorne looked haggard and tired. When he started to cough a little, he covered his mouth and turned away from Mr. Bendel. It appeared Mr. Thorne might be feeling ill or coming down with a cold. Such a difference from the other times she'd seen him. Nobody was feeling good tonight.

When she saw that nearly everyone was present, Mrs. Vanderbilt turned to Mr. Thorne and put her hand on his shoulder. "Perhaps you would be kind enough to play something for us. . . ."

Mr. Thorne looked reluctant.

"Indeed," Mr. Bendel said encouragingly. "We could all use a bit of cheering up."

"Of course. I would be honored to oblige," Mr. Thorne said quietly, wiping his mouth with his handkerchief and gathering himself. It took several seconds, but he seemed to find a second wind. He glanced around the room as if looking for inspiration.

"Shall I send the footmen for your violin?" Mrs. Vanderbilt asked, trying to be helpful.

"No, no, thank you. I was thinking I would give that magnificent pipe organ a try . . ." Mr. Thorne said.

Serafina panicked. She had heard the pipe organ many times before from the basement. She couldn't even imagine how loud it would be when she was crouching among its pipes. It would break her eardrums for sure! She hurried to wiggle herself out of her hiding spot and escape.

At the same time, Braeden rushed forward and grabbed Mr. Thorne's arm. "Perhaps you could play the piano instead, Mr. Thorne. I do love the piano."

Surprised, Mr. Thorne paused and looked at his young friend. "Is that what you would prefer, Master Braeden?"

"Oh, yes, sir. I'd love to hear you play."

"Very well," Mr. Thorne said.

Much relieved, Serafina smiled at her ally's quick thinking and crawled back into her hiding spot.

Braeden risked a quick glance up toward her, his face momentarily betraying a self-satisfied grin. She couldn't help but smile in return.

Mr. Thorne walked over to the grand piano.

"I thought you played the violin," Mr. Bendel said.

"Lately, I've been tinkering a bit with the piano as well," Mr. Thorne said quietly.

He sat down in front of the piano slowly, almost shyly, as if he was uncertain. He sat there for several long seconds while everyone waited. And then, without taking off his satin gloves, he began to play. He played a soft and enchanting sonata with the grace of a virtuoso. The piece he had selected was not too sad, and not too happy, but was lovely in its own way, and it seemed to bring everyone together in mood and spirit. Serafina marveled at how music seemed to have an almost magical ability to unite the emotions of the people in a room. Everyone seemed to truly love and appreciate Mr. Thorne's playing except Mr. and Mrs. Brahms, who seemed to grow sadder with every note he played. Mrs. Brahms began to sob and pulled out her handkerchief, and then her apologetic husband had to take her away. The other guests continued to listen to Mr. Thorne's music as he finished the sonata.

"Thank you, Mr. Thorne," Mrs. Vanderbilt said, trying to stay positive. She looked around at everyone. "Why don't we all see if we can have a little bite to eat and something to drink?"

Braeden approached Mr. Thorne shyly. "You play wonderfully, sir."

"Thank you, Braeden," Mr. Thorne said with a small smile. "I appreciate it. I know you are a young man of discerning taste."

"A few weeks ago, when you first arrived at Biltmore, you told us a delightful story about the boy with three wishes."

"Yes?" Mr. Thorne looked at him.

"Do you have any others?" Braeden asked, looking around at the red-haired girl in the blue dress and the other children. "Could you tell us another story?"

Mr. Thorne paused and looked at Mrs. Vanderbilt, who nodded in agreement, looking proud of her nephew for his consideration of the others. "I think that would be wonderful if you could, Mr. Thorne. We'd all enjoy it."

"Then I shall endeavor to try," Mr. Thorne agreed, nodding. He slowly waved his arm to the children. "Let's all gather around the hearth."

As Braeden and the other children sat in the glowing light of the fire, Mr. Thorne lowered his voice into a dramatic tone and began to tell a story.

Watching and listening from the organ loft, Serafina could see that the children were leaning forward, following the story intently. Mr. Thorne's voice was soft at times, and then booming with force at other times. She found herself longing to gather around and listen with the other children. Her heart ached to be a part of the world he depicted—a place where all the boys and girls had mommas and papas and brothers and sisters. A place where the children played together in bright fields, and when they got tired, lay about in the shade of a giant tree on top of a hill. Serafina wanted to be in that world. She wanted to live that life. The story made her long to see her momma and hear her voice. And when the story was done, she thought Mr. Thorne must be one of the most magnificent storytellers she had ever heard.

Mrs. Vanderbilt watched Braeden sitting among the other children and looking up at Mr. Thorne. There was a contented look on her face. Braeden was finally making friends.

Serafina studied Mr. Thorne. There was no denying that he had warmed her heart. She'd loved his music and his story. And he had brought a sense of community and togetherness to the sad gathering for a little while. Braeden and Mr. Bendel were right—he was a man of many talents.

Afterward, as the gathering was breaking up, Mrs. Vanderbilt approached Mr. Thorne and gently embraced him. "Thank you, sir, for all you've been doing for us. I especially appreciate the way you've befriended Braeden. He thinks the world of you."

"I just wish I could do more," Mr. Thorne said. "These are such difficult times for everyone."

"You're a good man, Montgomery," said Mr. Vanderbilt as he walked up and shook Mr. Thorne's hand in gratitude. "Later this evening, I would like to invite you and Mr. Bendel to join me in the Billiard Room for cognac and cigars. Just us friends."

"Thank you very much, George," Mr. Thorne said, bowing slightly. "I'm honored. I look forward to it."

As Serafina watched the interaction, something didn't sit quite right with her. Mr. Thorne looked somber, as he should at a sorrowful gathering such as this, but she noticed something else, too. As Mr. Vanderbilt spoke with him, Mr. Thorne had the same look on his face that a possum gets when he's gnawing on a sweet tater he's grubbed out of the garden. He seemed pleased with himself—too pleased, and not just for his flawless playing and his wonderful story. He seemed delighted by the personal invitation to join George Vanderbilt's inner circle. Braeden had told her that his uncle and Mr. Thorne had only known each other for a few months, but now she could see there was a stronger connection developing between them, a growing personal bond. The Vanderbilts were one of the most famous, wealthy, and powerful families in all of America, and Mr. Thorne had just made himself a most valued friend.

She looked over at Braeden to see if he, too, sensed something was amiss, but he wasn't even looking at Mr. Thorne. As everyone was leaving the room, he was walking along the buffet table, discreetly stuffing pieces of breaded chicken into his pocket. Then he snatched a little jar of clotted cream from the scone tray. She couldn't help but feel her mouth watering at the sight of the glorious food. She'd forgotten how hungry she was, and Braeden seemed to know exactly what she liked.

As he followed his aunt and uncle out of the room, Braeden looked up at her.

She signaled for him to meet her outside. There was much to talk about.

She knew Mr. Thorne was well liked, but to her, he was too talented, too kind, too *something*. And she still couldn't figure out why he had called Mr. Rostonov "Papa."

She couldn't put it all together, but she smelled a rat.

17

Serafina met Braeden outside in the darkness at the base of the great house's rear foundation, where they hoped no one would see them. The forested valley of the French Broad River lay below them, and the black silhouette of the mountains layered into the distance. A mist was rising up from the canopy of the valley trees as if the entire forest was breathing.

"Did you see how well Mr. Thorne played the piano?" Serafina asked in disbelief. "Did you know he could do that?"

"No, but he can do a lot of things," Braeden said, pulling the bits of chicken out of his pocket and handing them over to her.

"You're right. He can," she said as she gobbled the chicken down. "We keep saying that, but how is it possible?"

"That's just the way he is," Braeden said as Serafina slurped up the clotted cream.

"But what do you know about Mr. Thorne?" she asked as she wiped her mouth. "I mean, what do you really *know* about him?"

"My uncle says that he should be an inspiration to us all."

"Yes, but how do you know you can trust him?"

"I told you. He saved Gidean. And he's been very helpful to my aunt and uncle. I don't understand why you dislike him so much."

"We've got to follow the clues," she said.

"He's a good man!" Braeden said, becoming increasingly upset. "You can't just go around accusing everyone. He's been nothing but nice to me!"

She nodded in understanding. Braeden was a loyal person. "But stop for a second. Who is he, Braeden?"

"He's a friend of Mr. Bendel and my uncle."

"Yes, but where does he come from?"

"Mr. Bendel told me that way back before the War Between the States, Mr. Thorne owned a large estate in South Carolina. It was burned and destroyed by the union troops. He'd been born and raised a rich man, a landowner, but he lost every penny and had to flee for his life."

"He doesn't seem poor now," she said, confused by the story.

"Mr. Bendel said that after the war, Mr. Thorne was so poor, he could barely survive. He had no house, no property, no money, and no food. He became a homeless drunk, wandering through the streets, swearing obscenities at any Northerner who happened to walk by."

Serafina frowned. "This is Montgomery Thorne you're talking about, the man who can do everything? Your description doesn't match with the Mr. Thorne I've seen."

"I know, I know," Braeden said in exasperation. "That's what I'm saying. He's had a hard life, a bad life, but he turned himself around. He's been nothing but kind to me. You have no cause to think ill of him."

"Just finish the story you were telling me. What else? What happened to him? How'd he get here?"

"Mr. Bendel told me that one night, after drinking too much in a pub in one of the local villages, Mr. Thorne was walking home, stumbled off the road, and got lost in the woods. He fell into an old well that no one used anymore and was badly hurt. I guess he was stuck down there for two days. He can't even remember who found him and helped him out of the well. But when he finally recovered from his injuries, he realized that he'd hit rock bottom in his life and would soon die if he didn't change his ways. So he decided to make a better man of himself."

"What does that mean?" she asked, thinking the whole story sounded like two buckets of hogwash, and that Mr. Bendel had been pulling Braeden's leg.

"Mr. Thorne got a job working in a factory in the city. He learned about the machines and got promoted to manager."

"The machines?" Serafina asked in surprise. "What kind of machines?"

"I don't know, factory machines. But after that, he became an attorney."

"What's that?" she asked. She couldn't believe all the stuff she didn't know.

"A lawyer, sort of an expert on laws and crime."

"How did he become an attorney when he was working in a factory?" The whole story was getting crookeder and crookeder.

"That's the thing," Braeden continued. "He worked and he applied himself and he made himself a better man. He traveled for a while, then he moved back here, bought a grand house in Asheville, and started buying land in the area."

"Come on . . ." Serafina said incredulously. "You're saying he went from a drunken, poverty-stricken wretch to a gentleman landowner?"

"I know the whole thing sounds impossible, but you've seen him. Mr. Thorne is a very smart man, he's very rich, and everyone loves him."

She shook her head in frustration. There was no denying any of that. But still, something wasn't right.

She looked out across the valley and the mist, just thinking. Nothing about Thorne's story made sense to her. It was like one of those tales that's filled with half-truths and deceptions, little twists in the telling. And she'd learned from hunting rats that where things were ajumble, that's where the rat had been.

"So where did your uncle meet him?" she asked.

"I think they were both being fitted for shoes at the custom shop downtown."

"Which explains why Mr. Vanderbilt's shoes sounded like his . . ."

"What?"

"Nothing. Why does Mr. Thorne always wear gloves?" she asked, seeing if she could pick up the scent on a different trail.

"I never noticed that he did."

"Is there something wrong with his hands? He plays the piano with his gloves on. Doesn't that seem very strange? And he was wearing leather gloves the morning the men found you in the carriage on the forest road, even though it wasn't that cold. And you said he was an expert at machines. . . . Do you think he could break a dynamo so that not even the smartest mechanic in the world could fix it?"

"What kind of question is that?" Braeden asked in confusion. "Why do you—"

"And how did a Southern plantation owner learn Russian?"

"I don't know," Braeden muttered, becoming increasingly defensive.

"And what did he say to Mr. Rostonov?"

Braeden shook his head, refusing to believe any of it. "I don't know! Nobody's perfect."

"You said he was extremely smart, could even beat your uncle at chess."

"Well, maybe I was wrong. Maybe he just made an honest mistake with Mr. Rostonov."

"Then why did poor old Mr. Rostonov get so upset? He was as nettled as a badger in a porcupine fight. But he wasn't just upset. He seemed scared."

"Scared? Of what?"

"Of Thorne!"

"Why?"

Serafina shook her head. She didn't know. Her thoughts were all discombobulated, but it felt like the clues to the mystery were swirling all around her. All she had to do was put them together. Where exactly was the rat hiding? That was the question.

"You told me that when your aunt met Clara Brahms she wanted you to be friends with her," Serafina said, trying yet another path.

"Yes."

"How did your aunt and uncle first meet the Brahms family?"

Braeden shrugged. "I don't know. My uncle knew them somehow."

"Your uncle . . ." Serafina said, sensing another connection there.

"Why do you say it like that?" Braeden asked defensively.

"My uncle doesn't have anything to do with any of this, Serafina. So just take it back!"

"Who told him about Clara being good at piano? How did he hear about her?"

"I don't know, but my uncle isn't responsible for any of this, I can tell you that much."

"Try to remember, Braeden," she said. "Who first told him about Clara Brahms?"

"Mr. Bendel and Mr. Thorne. They're always going to symphony concerts and things like that."

"And Clara was an exceptionally talented piano player . . ." she said, remembering the maid's words to the footman. She kept trying to think it through. She was getting the same tingling feeling she felt when she was closing in on one of her four-legged enemies.

"Yes, I heard her play the first night she came to the house," Braeden said, nodding. "She was extremely good."

"And you've heard Thorne play. . . ."

"Yes, you heard him. He's an excellent player."

And then Braeden paused. He frowned and looked at her in surprise. "You don't think . . ."

She just stared at him, seeing if he would come to the same conclusion she had.

"Many people know how to play the piano, Serafina," he said firmly.

"Not me," she countered.

"Well, no, me neither, not like that, but I mean a lot of people *do* know how to play the piano really well."

"And speak Russian and play the violin, too?"

"Well, sure. There's Tchaikovsky and—"

"I don't know who that is, Mr. Know-it-all, but is he also a chess expert?"

"Well, probably not, but—"

"And can he turn a team of horses and a full-size carriage around on a narrow mountain road?"

"You've gone crazy!" Braeden exclaimed, looking at her in bewilderment. "What are you talking about now?"

"I'm not sure exactly," she admitted, "but think about it . . ."

"I *am* thinking about it."

"And what do you see?"

"It's just a big mishmash as far as I can tell. Nothing means anything!"

"No. Everything means something. Think about the Black Cloak . . . You've seen it . . . It seems to allow the wearer to wrap people up and murder them, or at least capture them in some way . . ."

"It's horrible!" He shuddered.

"Maybe it doesn't just murder them . . ."

"I don't understand."

"Maybe it *absorbs* them."

"That's disgusting. What do you mean?"

"Maybe that's why Thorne accidentally addressed Mr. Rostonov as 'Father' and 'Papa.' Because Thorne had absorbed his knowledge of the Russian language from Anastasia."

"Are you saying that he consumed Anastasia's soul?"

She grabbed Braeden's arm so fast that it startled him and he jumped. "Think about it," she said. "The owner of the cloak absorbs his victims—their knowledge, their talents, their skills. Think about what that would mean, what that would be like. . . . If he absorbed enough people, he'd gain many skills and talents. He'd become the most accomplished man in society. He'd be smart. He'd be rich. And everyone would love him. Just like you said."

"I refuse to believe Mr. Thorne would do that," Braeden said. "It's just not possible." His whole body seemed to be tightening against her.

"It makes sense, Braeden. The whole thing. He's stealing souls. And he's coming for you next."

"No, Serafina," Braeden said, shaking his head. "It can't be. That's crazy. He's a good man."

At that moment, she heard a door from the main house creak open and the sound of someone approaching.

18

Serafina whirled around, ready to fight.

"Braeden, darling, what are you doing out here? It's time to come in now," Mrs. Vanderbilt called as she walked toward him.

Serafina breathed a sigh of relief, then darted into the bushes, leaving Braeden standing there alone.

"Who were you talking to just now?" Mrs. Vanderbilt asked.

"No one," he said, moving toward his aunt to block her view. "Just talking to myself."

"It's not safe for you out here," Mrs. Vanderbilt said. "You need to come in now and go to bed."

Serafina had never heard Mrs. Vanderbilt sound so tired and upset. The lady of the house clutched a long black coat around her waist to ward against the night's cold. It was clear that the disappearance of the children was taking a heavy toll on her.

Hesitating, Braeden glanced back into the bushes in Serafina's direction.

"Please come inside," Mrs. Vanderbilt said softly but firmly.

"All right," he said finally.

Serafina could tell that he didn't want to go, but he didn't want to upset his aunt any more than she already was.

Mrs. Vanderbilt put her arm around him, and they began walking back toward the house.

"Lock your door!" Serafina half coughed, half whispered to Braeden, covering her mouth with her hand to garble her words.

"Did you hear something?" Mrs. Vanderbilt said, stopping and looking out into the darkness.

"I think it was just a fox-call out in the woods," Braeden said casually, but Serafina could see him smile and was relieved he wasn't still cross with her for suspecting Mr. Thorne.

Stay safe tonight, Serafina thought as Braeden and his aunt continued toward the house.

"Listen, your uncle and I have been talking," Mrs. Vanderbilt said. "We're worried about you."

"I'm all right," Braeden said.

"Your uncle and I need to stay here with the guests, but we've decided that it would be best if you went away from Biltmore for a little while. We tried it before, but we think it's more important than ever now."

"I don't want to go away," Braeden said, and Serafina knew he was thinking of her.

"Just until things settle down and the detectives figure out what's going on," Mrs. Vanderbilt said, her voice getting progressively harder to hear as they went back into the house. "It'll be safer."

"All right," he said. "I understand."

"We've asked Mr. Thorne to take you with him in his carriage first thing tomorrow morning," she said. "Won't that be nice? You like Mr. Thorne, don't you? You'll get to see his house in Asheville."

As the door closed behind them, Serafina's heart filled with dread. Braeden trusted Mr. Thorne and would have no choice but to agree with his aunt and uncle's wishes.

The Man in the Black Cloak would finally get what he wanted.

I need a plan, Serafina thought as she went down the stairs into the basement. *And it has to be tonight.*

As she ate a late-night dinner with her pa in the workshop, she wanted to tell him everything and beg for his help to save Braeden, but there were no bodies, no weapons, no evidence of any kind to support what her pa would call her "imaginings" about the Vanderbilts' most trusted guest. Even her best friend didn't believe her! Her pa never would. But more than that, her pa looked so worn out. His hands were blackened and raw with the day's work on the Edison machine. He was under fierce pressure to get the lights back on. And rightly so. The darkness made the whole house the demon's domain.

But then she stopped in mid-thought and realized something. The darkness made it *her* domain as well.

"Are you all right?" her father asked as he scraped up the last of his potatoes with his spoon. "You haven't eaten anything."

She pulled herself out of her thoughts, looked at her pa, and nodded. "I'm all right."

"Listen, Sera," her pa said, "I want you to hunker down tonight. Keep to yourself, you hear?"

"I hear, Pa," she said obediently, but of course she wouldn't. She *couldn't*.

When they went to bed and her pa began to snore, she slipped out of the workshop and climbed the stairs that led outside to the estate grounds. Her mind was awhirl with thoughts and images and fears. She knew her pa wanted her to stay close to him, but for the first time in her life, she didn't feel safe in the basement. Staying in the basement tonight was death. It was doom. It would lead to a loneliness she could not bear. Over the last few days, she had felt increasingly constrained there. She didn't want to be inside anymore. She wanted the freedom of open space and true darkness.

As she walked outside, it was a beautiful moonlit night with a light snow gently falling on the grass and trees. She tried to think it all through. She knew what she had to do; she just didn't know how to do it. What stratagem could she devise to defeat the Man in the Black Cloak? If he were a rat, how would she catch him?

She walked to the edge of the forest and paused at the point her pa had told her she should never go beyond. Her first foray into the shadows of the forest two nights before had been difficult, terrifying.

But she kept going.

She pushed through the thick brush and walked into the trees. She delved into the forest using the moonlight and the starlight to illuminate her way. Despite all that had happened, she was still drawn here. This was where she wanted to be.

A glint of light caught her eye. She looked up and saw a falling star. Then another. Then ten dashing through the blackness. Then a hundred at once. A shower of falling stars streaked across the sky, filling the crystalline black heavens with blazing light. And then the shower was gone, leaving nothing but the stillness of the glistening stars and the glowing planets in the infinite space above her.

She heard tiny footsteps behind her, a small country mouse out foraging and now making his way back home to his family, warm beneath a hollowed log.

The forest was alive at night, filled with motion, sound, creatures, and light.

She felt comfortable here. *Connected*.

She walked a little farther, studying the lichen-covered rocks, the trees with their outstretched limbs, and the little rills of glistening water that ran beneath the ferns. Was this the forest her mother had come from?

Was this where she belonged?

She thought about why *she* could see that Mr. Thorne was the Man in the Black Cloak but no one else could. Not even Braeden. Why could *she* believe it but they could not? Because they were normal, mortal human beings, and she was not. She was closer to the Man in the Black Cloak than she wished to admit. Closer to being a demon.

She knew she couldn't fight the Man in the Black Cloak directly. He was far too strong. In their first encounters, she had barely escaped him with her life. A shiver ran down her spine just thinking about it. But she couldn't just keep running away and hiding from him, either. Somehow, she had to *stop* him. But he possessed an otherworldly power—if her theory about him was correct, then he had within him all the strength and capability of every person he'd ever absorbed into his cloak. And if she gave him another chance, he would surely absorb her as well.

No, she couldn't fight the Man in the Black Cloak head-on. Not alone.

She looked around her, and a dark idea formed in her mind. She asked herself the question again: If he were a rat, how would she catch him?

Suddenly, she knew the answer.

She'd bait him.

Fear rose up in her like bile from a half-digested meal. She wanted to turn away from the idea, to avoid it, but her mind kept going back to it as the only solution.

She thought of her pa's words once more: *Never go into the deep parts of the forest for there are many dangers there, both dark and bright. . . .*

You're right, Pa, she thought. *There are. And I'm one of them.*

Standing in the woods, she came to a conclusion about herself, something that she'd known deep down for a long time but that she had never wanted to come to grips with: She was not like her pa. She was not like Braeden. She was not human.

At least not entirely.

The thought of it brought a lump to her throat. She felt a terrible loneliness. She didn't know what it meant, she wasn't even sure she *wanted* to know what it meant, but she knew it was true. She was not like the people she loved. She'd been born in the forest, a forest as black as the Black Cloak and as haunted as the graveyard. She was one of them, a creature of the night.

She'd overheard Mr. Pratt say that the creatures of the night came straight from hell, that they were evil. She wondered about it again, her mind pushing through thorny brambles of conflict and confusion. Did evil creatures think of themselves as evil? Or did they think they were doing what was right? Was evil something that was in your heart or was it how people viewed you? She felt like she was good, but was she actually bad and just didn't know it? She lived underground. She slinked through the darkness without being seen or heard. She secretly listened to people's conversations. She pawed through their belongings when they weren't in their rooms. She killed animals. She battled. She lied. She stole. She hid. She watched children lose their souls. And yet she was still living—thriving, even—drawing energy and knowledge and awareness from each and every night that she prowled through the darkness and another child was taken.

She stood for a long time, thinking about why she was alive and the others weren't, and she asked herself again: Was she good or was she evil? She had been born in and lived in the world of darkness, but which side was she on? Darkness or light?

She looked up at the stars. She didn't know what she was or how she got that way, but she knew what she wanted to be. She wanted to be *good*. She wanted to save Braeden and the other children who were still alive. She wanted to protect Biltmore. She thought about the inscription on the base of the stone angel's pedestal: *Our character isn't defined by the battles we win or lose, but by the battles we dare to fight.* Standing in the forest at that moment, that's what she chose to believe. It was true that she was a creature of the night. But *she* would decide for herself what that meant.

She had two choices before her: to slink away and hide, or to dare to fight.

At that moment, she saw a plan in her mind and knew what she must do.

A part of her didn't want to do it. It would mean she could well die this very night. And her death would come at the moment in her life when she had finally crawled out of the basement and found a friend and begun to understand and connect to the world around her. She wanted to go home and sleep in front of Braeden's fireplace, and eat chicken and grits with her pa, and pretend like none of this was happening. She wanted to curl up in the basement behind the boiler and hide like she'd done all her life. But she couldn't. Thorne was going to keep coming. He was going to take Braeden's life. She had to stop him. She might die, but it meant that Braeden might live. He'd go on with Mr. and Mrs. Vanderbilt, and his horses, and with Gidean at his side. And that, she decided, more than anything, was what she wanted. She wanted Braeden to live.

She'd seen with her own eyes that the Man in the Black Cloak absorbed any child he encountered, but she knew that he wanted Braeden Vanderbilt next. She'd seen this when the Man in the Black Cloak attacked them in the forest. He hadn't come for Nolan, he had gone straight for Braeden. There was a talent in Braeden that Thorne craved: Braeden's expertise in horsemanship, but more than that, his almost telepathic connection to animals. She imagined what it would be like to be able to befriend all the animals around her, even to control them.

But she sensed there was something more as well, something that obsessed Mr. Thorne, that drove him even beyond Braeden. More and more, he had to take a child every night. Any child. And she'd use that need against him. She would meet him face-to-face on the most deadly battlefield she could think of. She would defeat him once and for all. Or she'd die trying.

She turned around and headed back toward the estate. As midnight approached, she went down the stairs toward the workshop.

It did not surprise her that her pa was asleep in his cot, snoring gently, exhausted from a long and difficult day. But then she saw something lying on her makeshift bed behind the boiler. As she stepped toward it, she realized it was the dress that Braeden had given her. Braeden must have come down and laid it there while she was gone. There was a note attached:

S,

A and U are determined. I'm leaving early in the morning with T. I'll see you in a few days. Please stay safe until I return.

—B.

Serafina stared at the note. She didn't want to believe it. He was really going to do what his aunt and uncle wanted.

But then she looked at the dress.

She was sure it wasn't Braeden's intention, but it was a perfect addition to her plan. Now she would look the part.

The time for sneaking and hiding was over.

She was going to make sure one man in particular saw her.

And tonight was the night.

The Chief Rat Catcher had a job to do.

20

Serafina put on the beautiful, dark maroon winter gown that Braeden had given her the night before.

The intricate black brocade corset felt tight around her chest and back, and she worried that when it came time to fight, it would restrict her. She twisted and turned to test her freedom of movement. The long skirt hung heavily around her legs, but even as unfamiliar as the girls' clothing felt, she couldn't help but be taken by it. It felt almost magical to be putting on a dress for the first time in her life. The material was fine and feminine and soft, like nothing she'd ever worn before. She felt like one of the girls in the books she read—like a *real* girl, with a real family, with brothers and sisters, and a mother and father, and friends.

She quickly scrubbed her face and brushed her hair and made herself as pretty as she could. It felt silly, but she needed to look the part. She tried to imagine that she was going to an extravagant dance, in a ballroom crowded with glittering ladies and gentlemen, and boys who would ask her to dance.

But she wasn't, and she knew it.

When she thought about the place she was going and the dark forces she'd meet there, it felt like she was jumping a chasm and she wasn't going to make it to the other side.

She tried to block it out of her mind and just kept lacing her dress up her back with shaky fingers, but she was having a terrible go of it. *Normal girls must have extremely long and bendy arms to do this every night,* she thought.

When she was finally done, she looked around at the workshop one last time. She couldn't tamp down the feeling that she wouldn't be coming back. She looked over to where her pa lay sleeping. She had seen how tired and overwhelmed he was. His struggles with the dynamo and searching for her these last few days had taken a toll on him. She wanted to curl up in the crook of his arm like she used to, but she knew she couldn't. *Sleep well, Pa,* she thought.

Finally, she gathered her courage and turned. She made her way through the basement, and then climbed the stairs to the first floor.

At the top, she paused. She took a deep breath, and then walked down the darkened corridor of the house.

She walked slowly, deliberately, not darting and hiding like she normally did, but walking down the center of the wide hallway like a proper young lady. She walked like the girls she had watched from the shadows so many times over the years. She did everything she could to take on the appearance of the helpless young daughter of one of the guests. She was no longer a predator; she was a vulnerable child.

The air was very still. Moonlight shone in through the windows, falling onto the marble floor. The grandfather clock in the Entrance Hall chimed off the twelve bells of midnight. The corridors of the house were mostly empty because it was so late, just a candle here and there to light the way for guests. But she sensed that there were a few people still awake.

As she made a slow promenade in her long, wide dress through the broad corridors of the house, it felt deeply strange not to be hunting, not to be the eyes of the predator but the prey that is seen. Her stomach churned. Her muscles flinched and twitched, begging her to dash away. She hated walking straight. And she hated walking slow. *You're a normal girl,* she told herself. *Just keep breathing, keep pulling air into your lungs. You're a normal girl.* It took every ounce of courage she had to just keep walking a straight line in the open.

She'd come up against the Man in the Black Cloak before, but she was determined to make this time different. Tonight, she was going to fight—fight on her own terms and in her own way, with tooth and claw.

She lingered near the Winter Garden, with its high glass ceiling, just outside the door into the Billiard Room, where she knew from what she'd learned at Mrs. Vanderbilt's gathering earlier that evening she had the best chance of setting her trap.

Suddenly, the door to the Billiard Room opened. Mr. Vanderbilt, Mr. Bendel, Mr. Thorne, and several other gentlemen were sitting together in the leather chairs and drinking out of odd-shaped glasses. The smell of cigar smoke wafted into the corridor. Mr. Pratt came out of the room with a large silver tray balanced on his hand and hurried down the hall.

Serafina stepped into a shadow behind a column to avoid being seen, and there she waited, lingering on the edge of darkness. She was a china doll, and she was a wraith, in and out of the shadows, a girl in between.

Finally, the fireside chat began to break up. Mr. Vanderbilt stood and said good night to each of his guests. Mr. Bendel shook everyone's hand, and then retired as well. In the end, only Mr. Thorne remained.

Serafina watched him through the open door, her heart pounding slow and heavy. He sat in the candlelit Billiard Room alone, sipping from his glass and smoking his cigar. *Come on out*, she thought. *We have business to attend to.* But he seemed to be enjoying a moment of personal triumph. She couldn't read his mind, but she tried to piece together what she knew about him and imagine what he was thinking at that moment.

After losing his plantation in the war and falling to the depths of ruin, here he was now, finally back to his rightful place again, a distinguished gentleman of the highest order, a personal friend of one of the richest men in America. All he had to do to get here was steal the souls and talents of a hundred lousy children, with their small, frail bodies and their pliable spirits.

But she wondered. Why didn't he absorb adults as well? Were they more difficult? And now that he had achieved his position in society, why did he continue with the attacks and risk discovery? If he'd been doing this for a long time, then why the sudden greed for young souls? What was driving him to absorb a child night after night? It had to be more than just the pursuit of talents. It had to be a need greater than anything that had come before.

She watched Mr. Thorne as he sat on the sofa, puffing on his cigar and sipping his cognac. There was something different about him tonight. His face looked gray. The skin under his eyes was wrinkled and flaking. His hair seemed less shiny and perfect than it did the morning in the Tapestry Gallery when she saw him for the first time, or when he arrived with the rescue party to take Braeden back to Biltmore.

Mr. Thorne set his empty glass on the end table and stood. Serafina's muscles tensed. The time had come.

Like the other gentlemen, he wore a formal black jacket and tie, and she could hear the movement of his patent-leather shoes on the Billiard Room's hardwood floor. But when she saw what he was carrying draped over his arm, her breath caught in her throat. It was the Black Cloak. Satin and shimmering and clean—the cloak was as much in disguise as she was. To any one else, it was but a fashionable covering. To anyone else, it might have appeared that the handsomely attired gentleman intended to take a quiet stroll on the grounds before he retired for the evening, but she knew the truth: it wasn't just a cloak, it was the Black Cloak, which meant he was bent on malevolent purpose. Here was her enemy. Here was the fight she'd come for. But she could feel her whole body quaking in her gown. She was scared to death. *At least I'm going to die in a pretty dress,* she thought.

He walked out of the room and into the corridor where Serafina was hidden in the shadows. She stayed perfectly still, but then he stopped just outside the Billiard Room door. He could not see her, but he could sense her there. He stood just a few feet away from her. Her heartbeat pounded. She had trouble controlling her breathing. He was right in front of her. All her well-laid plans seemed foolish now. She wanted to cower away, to flee, to slink, to hide, to scream.

But she steadied herself. She forced herself quiet. And she did what for her was the most terrifying thing to do in the world: she stepped out into the open.

21

Serafina stood in her dress in the candlelight of the corridor, where Mr. Thorne could see her.

His hair wasn't as dark as she recalled, but far more silvery now, and his eyes were a striking ice-blue. He looked much older than she remembered, but he was a startlingly handsome man, a gentleman of distinguished character, and for a moment, she was taken aback by it.

Her plan had been to pass herself off as a helpless little rich girl, a child guest of the Vanderbilts for him to prey on. Appearing to be easy prey was going to be part of her trick, the rat bait.

It was a perfect plan. But she realized now that it wasn't going to work.

As they looked at each other face-to-face, she could tell by his expression that, despite the beautiful gown she wore and her unusually well-combed hair, he knew exactly who she was. And it filled her with a wave of terrible dread.

She was the girl who had escaped his clutches the night he absorbed Clara Brahms. She was the girl who attacked him in the forest the night he took the stable boy. She was the girl who skulked through the darkness without need of a lantern, the one who could run and hide and jump and seemed to have impossibly fast reflexes. She was a girl with many talents. . . .

And now here she was, standing right in front of him. A prize for the taking.

It was too late to run.

When Mr. Thorne smiled, she flinched. But she stood her ground.

She was so scared that it hurt to breathe. Her corset felt like Satan's bony hand gripping her around her chest and squeezing her tight. Her limbs were hot with the burning drive to flee.

But she didn't. She mustn't. She had to stay.

She took in a long, slow, deep breath. Then she turned her back to him and slowly walked away.

She walked at what felt like a snail's pace down the corridor, pretending as though she had no idea who he was or that her life was in danger.

Her back was to him now, so she could not see him anymore, but she could hear Mr. Thorne's footsteps following her, getting closer and closer behind her, so close that the hairs on the back of her neck stood on end. Unable to control her fear, her arms and hands began to tremble. His footsteps behind her pounded in her temples.

There was no doubt in her mind that they were not the footsteps of a mortal man, but of the Man in the Black Cloak. This was the Soul Stealer. This was the fiend who had taken Anastasia Rostonova, Clara Brahms, Nolan, the pastor's son, and countless others.

And he was right behind her.

She looked down the corridor at the small side door ahead of her.

Just a few more steps, she thought, and she kept walking.

Three more steps . . .

Slowly walking.

Two more steps . . .

Finally, she slipped out the door in one quick movement and went out into the cold darkness of the night.

Mr. Thorne followed her outside, pulling his billowing black cloak and hood up around his head and shoulders as he entered the night.

As the snow fell gently down from the moonlit sky, she ran across the grass and ducked into the Rambles. The maze of twisting paths was a bewildering convolution of bushes and hedges with dark shadows, blind corners, and dead ends—a place where the Man in the Black Cloak had killed before. But she knew this place, too. She knew it better than anyone.

She moved swiftly through the maze. She imagined she'd

see the ghost of Anastasia Rostonova searching the paths for her little white dog.

The Man in the Black Cloak followed her down one pathway after another.

"Why are you running away from me, child?" he asked in a hideous, raspy voice.

Too frightened to answer, she just kept moving. When she looked over her shoulder to see how much of a lead she'd gained, she saw him coming up behind her. In the long, flowing black cloak, he flew a foot off the ground, standing erect, his arms stretched out like a wraith, his huge bloodstained hands reaching to grab her.

Her breath caught in her throat so severely that she couldn't even scream. Terrified, she sprinted forward with a burst of speed.

To stop was to die, and it was far too early to die.

Seeing a hole in the bushes, she dove through it. She left the manicured paths of the Rambles behind her and ran into the wild forest.

Tearing through the underbrush, she made quick time. She ducked behind trees. She scurried into and through thickets. She delved into the deepest shadows of the forest. She ran, and ran, and ran, deep into the darkest night, her nemesis close on her tail.

The thickness of the forest made it difficult for her pursuer. The trees grew so close together that an adult could barely squeeze between them. The spiny thickets were so bristling with thorns that they were nearly impenetrable. But with her smaller size and her agility, she could move easily, darting betwixt and between, scrambling below and leaping above. She moved as swift as a weasel through the brush. The forest was her ally.

She was terrified that he'd catch her and kill her, but she didn't want to lose him completely, either. When he fell behind or lost her trail in the snow, she slowed down to let him catch up. Deep into the woods she led him. She had studied the way and formed a map in her mind. But even with the shortcut she planned to take, they still had miles to go.

As she ran, she kept thinking about Braeden, her pa, and the Vanderbilts. She kept thinking about what had happened to Clara, Anastasia, and Nolan. She had to defeat Mr. Thorne. She had to *kill* him. Her only chance lay ahead of her.

She was out of breath and desperately tired. Her legs ached, and her lungs felt like she was breathing through steel wool. She wasn't sure how much farther she could run. But then she finally saw what she'd been running for.

Gravestones.

There were hundreds of them standing in the silver light of the moon beneath the bare branches of the gnarled old winter trees.

This was the place that terrified her, but she knew she must come.

She ran through the old cemetery. An eerie fog was rising among the twisted branches of the ancient trees and the decaying monuments of the dead.

She looked behind her. The Man in the Black Cloak flew toward her out of the mist, his bloody hands reaching for her.

Serafina ran with all her heart.

She dashed past Cloven Smith, the murdered man.

She leapt over the two sisters lying side by side.

She raced through the sixty-six Confederate soldiers.

She arrived, finally, panting and exhausted, at the small glade with the statue of the winged angel.

Serafina could hear the Man in the Black Cloak crashing through the brush behind her. She had only seconds before he arrived.

Fear flooded through her veins. She became sickeningly aware that she was bringing two great forces together and she was between them. From one direction or another, there was a good chance that death would soon be upon her.

She ran to the edge of the moonlit glade where the old willow lay with its upturned roots. The thick trunk and heavy branches of the fallen master of the forest swirled with ghostly mist. Its delicate leaves, somehow still growing bright green in the winter, glistened with the starlight.

Praying that the great yellow-eyed prowler of the night was out hunting, Serafina found the hole in the ground beneath the roots. She dropped down onto her hands and knees and crawled into the mountain lion's den.

She came face-to-face with the two spotted cubs, who stared at her with large, frightened eyes as she moved toward them.

"Where's your momma?" she asked them.

When the cubs saw that it was her, they jumped up in relief. They moved toward her, smelling her and rubbing themselves on her body.

She crawled past the two cubs and curled into a little ball in the earthen den.

Now the trap was laid.

Just as she had done when she crawled inside the machine in Biltmore's basement, she made herself very still and very quiet.

She steadied her lungs and her heart. She shut her eyes and concentrated, extending her senses outward into the forest.

I know you're out there someplace, hunting your domain. Where are you? Your cubs are in danger. . . .

Serafina could feel it. Out there in the darkness of the woods beyond the graveyard, the mother lion paused in her hunting. She tilted her head at the sound of two intruders in the forest. *Her* forest. Her cubs were in danger. She turned and charged back toward her den with all her speed.

The Man in the Black Cloak came into the angel's glade and looked around him. "Where have you led me, dear child?" he said, trying to figure out which direction Serafina had gone. He circled the stone pedestal of the moss-covered angel. "Do you think you can hide from me, little rabbit?" he asked.

I'm not a rabbit, Serafina thought fiercely. For a brief moment, she felt a sensation of triumph because it seemed like her plan was going to work. The Man in the Black Cloak would be left standing haplessly in the angel's glade. He would have no idea where she'd gone. She had disappeared. She had escaped him.

But then she remembered the snow. She had not accounted for the snow. Her tracks led straight to her hiding place. The tracks would betray her.

"Ah . . ." the Man in the Black Cloak said when he saw the tracks. "There you are. . . ."

He walked over to the den, got down on his hands and knees, and looked inside. "I know you're in there. Come on out, my dear child, before I become angry with you."

Serafina tried not to breathe. The Man in the Black Cloak reached deep inside the den, his bloody hand searching in the darkness. She could smell his horrible, rotting stench. The folds of his slithering cloak twisted and turned as it snaked its way through the opening, rattling in anticipation of the coming meal.

Holding the cubs against her chest in terror, Serafina pulled back as far as she could go. She knew that if that man's hand or the folds of his cloak grabbed her, he'd drag her out of the den and her life would end in the most hideous way.

"I'm not going to hurt you, child . . ." he rasped as he reached for her.

At that moment, all the power and ferocity of clawed motherhood came ripping out of the woods. Enraged by the intruder at the mouth of her den, the lioness pounced upon his back. The terrific momentum of her attack rolled him to the ground. She struck her front claws into his back and chest even as she sunk her teeth into his neck and head.

The Man in the Black Cloak shouted out in a shock of pain. He fought hard to defend himself from the powerful cat. He drew his dagger, but the lioness slashed his hand. Hissing and growling in fury, the lioness bit and clawed him repeatedly, mercilessly.

The Man in the Black Cloak punched and kicked and tried to get to his feet, but the furious lioness was too fast and too strong. He didn't have time to find the fallen dagger. He tried to slam her with a large branch, but she swatted him so hard with her razor-clawed paw that it ripped open his flesh and knocked him to the ground. Then she lunged at him and bit down on his neck, forcing him to the ground with her weight the way she would kill a deer. She held her powerful jaws clenched on his throat until he slowly stopped struggling and finally became still.

The Man in the Black Cloak went limp.

The lioness dropped him into a bloody black heap like the carcass of a dead animal.

The trap had sprung. A rush of joy and relief poured through Serafina. Her plan had worked! She'd finally defeated the Man in the Black Cloak. *She'd done it!* She'd saved Braeden. She'd saved Biltmore. *She'd really done it!* Her skin tingled with excitement. She wished she could somehow magically communicate with Braeden from a distance and tell him what had happened. It almost felt like she could turn herself into a bird and fly away. She'd fly up into the sky like a whip-poor-will and do loopty loops in the clouds until she was too dizzy to fly anymore.

Ecstatic, she began to crawl toward the entrance of the den so that she could run home, but it was too late.

Death was upon her.

The lioness, still fiercely angry, entered the den to kill the second intruder.

Her.

22

There was only one way in and out of the den, and the lioness was going to tear Serafina to shreds. The lioness would kill her the same way she had killed the first intruder. To the lioness, there was no difference between them.

With a surge of panic, Serafina scrambled to the back of the den, trying desperately to get out of the lioness's reach. She sucked air in and out of her lungs. Her legs were kicking and thrashing like the hooves of a panicked horse, but she had no place to go.

The lioness came straight in. Her muscles bulged and rolled beneath her tan coat. Her eyes blazed. She held her mouth partly open. Her massive, sharp teeth gleamed. Her breaths froze in the frosty air as her sides heaved in and out. Steam rose off her body. As she pushed her way in toward Serafina, the lioness growled a low and menacing growl, fiercely determined to kill the creature that had invaded her den.

Serafina cowered behind the cubs with her back against the earthen wall. She tried to brace herself, to stay strong, but she shook uncontrollably. Unable to escape, she pulled her legs up against her chest, ready to defend herself, ready to kick. She tightened her hands to scratch and claw. She snapped her teeth and snarled.

Just as the lioness was about to lunge toward her and snap her neck, Serafina looked straight into the lioness's face and screamed as loudly and violently as she could, her teeth bared and threatening, like a cornered bobcat. She wanted to let this lion know that she might be small, but she wasn't going to die easy.

Undeterred by Serafina's defense, the mountain lion stared her down with her huge, penetrating yellow eyes. Serafina gasped. The cat's eyes were the exact same color as her own.

She looked into the cat's face. And then, in the next second, she saw what appeared to be a flicker of recognition in the lioness's eyes.

The lioness hesitated, stopping just a few inches in front of her.

She could see in the animal's expression that the lioness was thinking the same thing she was: their eyes were the same.

They weren't predator and prey.

They weren't protector and intruder.

They were connected.

She looked into the lioness's eyes, and the lioness looked into hers. There were no words between them. There could not be. But in that moment, there was *understanding*. There was a bond between them. They were the same. They were hunters. They were prowlers of the night.

But even more than all that, they were *kin*.

23

With her back crammed up against the rear wall of the den and her knees pulled up to her chest, Serafina stared at the mountain lion in amazement. Her heart pounded. Her body was folded up so tightly that she could only take short, shallow breaths.

The lioness gazed at her with the most mesmerizing amber-gold eyes she had ever seen. How was it possible that they looked just like hers? Images and ideas flashed through her mind in a swirling confusion, but none of it made sense.

The lioness took another step toward her.

Serafina remained perfectly still, trying to breathe as steady as she could. She made no sudden movements.

She saw an intelligence and awareness in the lioness's eyes. They were filled with a gentleness and understanding far beyond that of a wild animal. She knew she could not speak to the lioness in words, but she yearned to.

The lioness pushed her nose against Serafina's shoulder and smelled her. The lioness's breath was loud in her ears, her lungs sounding like a bellows, the air rushing in and out. The moisture around the lioness's partially open mouth glistened, and her teeth shone. Her deep scent was both foreign and familiar to Serafina. She'd never smelled a lion in her life, but it smelled exactly the way she expected it would.

As she looked at the lioness, she wished more than anything in the world that she could somehow communicate with her. She felt a deep longing to know what she was thinking and feeling in that moment.

Serafina exhaled gently and then took in a breath and held it as she slowly raised her trembling hand and touched the side of the lioness's head. She caressed the lioness's fur.

The lioness stared at her, her eyes locked on her, but the lioness did not move, she did not growl or bite, and Serafina began to breathe again.

She stroked the side of the lioness's head and then down her neck. The lioness rubbed her shoulder against Serafina's body, and Serafina felt the power and weight of the animal against her, so much weight that it prevented her from breathing for several seconds and she almost panicked, but then the lioness moved again and she could breathe once more. When Serafina relaxed her folded knees, the lioness put her head against Serafina's chest. Serafina touched the back of her neck and her ears. Then the lioness slowly leaned down and lay down beside her, with her cubs around her, and swished her long tail.

Serafina held the fuzzy little mewing cubs in her arms and hugged them. She felt her chest swelling and her limbs tingling. She was filled with pride and happiness. The little lions were welcoming her—*they loved her*—and for a moment she was swept up with the feeling that she had finally come home.

She thought about how she was different from other people, the seeing in the dark, the moving quietly, the hunting at night. She looked at the palm of her hand and opened her fingers, and then examined her fingertips one by one. Were they fingernails or were they claws? What was her connection to the lioness? Why did she feel like she belonged here?

But the more she thought about it, the more ludicrous it became in her mind. She was a person. She was wearing clothes. She lived in a house full of human beings. And that's where she wanted to be. She had to get back to Braeden and her pa and the world she knew, the world she loved.

Clenching her teeth and shaking her head, she crawled out of the lioness's den. She stumbled into the open glade and stood beneath the stars in utter confusion.

She looked over at where the battle had taken place. The Black Cloak lay in a heap on the ground. Thorne's bloody body lay beside it. His other clothing had been shredded by the lioness's claws. Blood stained his white shirt. A large open wound bled at his side. His head and face were badly bitten and clawed. She could see his blood glistening, and she knew from watching rats die that glistening blood meant he wasn't completely dead yet. But he soon would be. Sometimes you killed a dying rat, but other times you just let it die.

Standing in the angel's glade, she looked up at the sky and the trees, and all around her. She had won! She had defeated the Man in the Black Cloak! It felt like every muscle in her body was alive and moving. There was a part of her that felt elated, almost euphoric, like she was floating on air. But another part of her was deeply confused. She had solved one mystery only to be confronted with another. Why did she feel this way inside? And why hadn't the lioness attacked her?

"What does it all mean?" she asked aloud in frustration. She took a few steps, kicking her feet roughly through the snow. She was so sick of not knowing anything, not having the answers. "Tell me what it all means!" she shouted to the heavens.

Put me on . . . came a raspy voice.

Serafina looked around her.

Put me on . . .

She felt the words in their ancient, raspy voice more than she heard them, and she knew exactly where they were coming from. She looked at the Black Cloak, lying there on the ground beside Thorne's body. The cloak lay crumpled in the snow by itself, torn from him by the force of the attack.

Imagine knowing all things . . .

"Shut up," she told the cloak, her words spitting out of her like she was reprimanding an uppity rat she'd captured.

Imagine being able to do anything you wanted to do . . .

She gritted her teeth and snarled at it. "You're dead! Now hush up!"

There's nothing to fear. . . .

Serafina felt the trembling agitation of pure fear growing deep within her. Every muscle in her body was telling her to flee, but she was too angry to go. She clenched her teeth. She wanted to fight. She wanted to win.

Put me on . . . the raspy voice came again.

She looked at the cloak. It was the cloak of power, the cloak of *knowing.* She felt an overwhelming desire to touch it. She wanted to hold it in her hands. She could feel it using its power to draw her in, and she didn't care. She wanted the power.

Imagine understanding and controlling everything around you. . . .

She took a step toward the cloak.

Put me on. . . .

She reached down and picked up the Black Cloak. The satin material reflected the sheen of the moonlight as she turned it over in her hands. Despite the running through the thickets, the flying through the forest, and the battle with the mountain lion, the cloak wasn't torn or dirtied in any way.

She examined the cloak carefully, looking for any sign or symbol of the power that it contained. As she moved the material through her hands, it didn't feel like a normal piece of clothing, but like a living, pulsing thing, like holding a giant snake.

Put me on . . . the cloak said again in its low, raspy voice.

She looked at the cloak's silver clasp, which was engraved with an intricate design: a tight bundle of twisting vines and thorns. When she held the clasp in the moonlight in just the right way, she could see the image of tiny faces behind the thorns.

She didn't know what it meant. It felt like she didn't know what anything meant anymore. A black and terrible loneliness welled up inside her, an anguish stronger than anything she had ever felt before. But what did the cloak do? How did it work? Did it really give its master the blessing of profound knowledge? Could it answer the questions that stormed through her mind?

You will become all-knowing, all-powerful . . . the cloak whispered.

Her head spun in confusion. Cloudiness closed in on her mind. She was unable to control herself. Her fingers grasped, her arms moved, and she began pulling the cloak around her. Drawn in by its powerful spell, she draped the Black Cloak over her back and shoulders just for a brief moment to see what would happen. She only wanted to wear it for a few seconds, just long enough to see how it felt.

As she pulled on the cloak, it spoke to her once more.

Welcome, Serafina. I'm not going to hurt you, child. . . .

25

As soon as Serafina put the cloak on, her world changed. The weight of the cloak on her shoulders felt strangely satisfying. The cloak gave off no stench or foul smell. There was no blood or fear while she was wearing the cloak. It made no rattling sound. Everything about it felt fine and good.

She used her fingers to clasp the cloak at her throat. Although it had been a full-length cloak on the much taller Mr. Thorne, it fit her body perfectly. She held out her arms and pivoted and looked at the cloak on her body. She thought she looked very sophisticated and aristocratic wearing it. Then she walked a few paces back and forth, testing how it draped and flowed. It felt like she was dancing with every movement she made.

"I look good in this," she said. Her voice sounded strong and confident.

She didn't feel nearly as confused, tired, and discouraged as she had just a moment before. No, she wasn't tired at all anymore. She felt rested, capable. Optimistic. She felt *powerful*. Wearing the cloak, she felt as if she could do almost anything, solve any puzzle, accomplish any task, play any instrument, speak another language, and if she tried, maybe even *fly*. It was a wonderful, glorious feeling, and she spun around the angel's glade kicking up the snow.

The power is within us . . . the cloak whispered.

She tried to imagine it. She'd be famous and popular, and everyone would love her. She'd have many friends and a huge family of people who adored her. She'd travel all over the world. She'd know more than everyone else. No one could defeat her.

We will work together. . . .

She'd be the most powerful girl in the entire world.

We will be a great force. . . .

With the fabric of the cloak wrapped around her, she began to understand things about it that she could not before. She could see its history, like a dark dream in her mind. The cloak had been conjured by a sorcerer who had lived in a nearby village. He'd intended to use it to gain talents and understanding, to learn languages and skills, and to become a great, unifying leader in society, but his creation went terribly awry. He hadn't just created a concentrator of knowledge: he'd created an enslaver of souls. When he realized what he had done, he tried to hurl the cloak into the village's deepest well. He fought with the cloak, tearing and pulling and throwing, but the cloak grasped at him and twisted around him and would not let go until, finally, the sorcerer threw himself and the cloak together down the well, thinking that he would destroy them both. As the years passed, the sorcerer's body rotted in the well, putrefied, but the cloak remained, perfect and unharmed, until years later when it was found by the drunken and desperate Mr. Thorne. The cloak had the power to acquire knowledge and capability, to concentrate the talents of a hundred people into a single person. She had seen what Mr. Thorne did with that capability. She imagined what she could do with it. She'd be able to do anything she wanted. She could go anywhere. She'd know *everything*. She'd finally find all the answers.

She ran her fingers down the fabric of the cloak and felt its potency coursing through her. It contained such tremendous capability, she thought. She tried to imagine what great things she could do with it, what good and beneficial deeds she could accomplish in the world. It seemed like it would be such a shame to waste that power. Someone had to use the cloak; it might as well be her.

Lift the hood of the cloak. . . .

She felt good and hopeful and buoyant.

Put on the hood. . . .

She reached up and gathered the cloak's hood in her fingers and pulled it onto her head.

Then she screamed in horror at the shock of what she saw.

The edges of her sight blurred into a dark and vibrating tunnel. She could still see the physical world directly in front of her, but the hood pressed in on her peripheral vision with a crush of dead children and adults pushing their faces up against hers. The faces of the dead children surrounded her.

A little blond girl cried as she pressed her cold dead face against Serafina's, touching her pleadingly with her grasping fingers. "I can't find my mother! Can you help me?"

"*Pozhaluysta, skazhite gde moi otets?*" a girl with long, curly black hair said, pressing her face against Serafina's.

"Please help me!" wailed a woman, only to be pushed out of the way by two more faces. The visages of terrified children and adults were crowded inside the cloak.

"The horses are trapped!" a boy shouted, pressing his face in among the others. "Watch out!"

Serafina screamed and ripped the hood from her head. She gazed around the empty glade, shaking and gasping for breath.

The souls of the dead people were imprisoned in the black folds of the cloak. This was the cloak's power: to enslave people's talents and hold their souls prisoner in a ghastly cage.

Come, little creature. . . . We shall be together. . . .

She shook her head, trying desperately to resist the cloak's powerful spell.

We shall control the world. . . .

255

"No," she said, gritting her teeth.

Everyone shall love us. . . .

"No!" she shouted. "I won't do it!"

She unclasped the cloak from her neck and tore it away. The act of ripping it from her body struck her such a blow that she fell onto her hands and knees, suddenly debilitated by extreme fatigue and despair. But, filled with determination, she got back up onto her feet. She tried to hurl the cloak to the ground, but the slithering creature tangled itself in her arms and wouldn't let go. She couldn't free herself from it.

Alone you are a weak little creature, but together we are strong. . . .

"No!" she shouted.

She knew that she had to get rid of the cloak. She had to *destroy* it. As the cloak roiled and twisted like black snakes in her hands, she tried to tear the material in her fingers, but they weren't strong enough to rend it. The cloak, seething and hissing, wrapped around her arms and her legs, clinging to her.

A bloody hand reached up from the ground and gripped her ankle.

26

Serafina screamed.

"Don't hurt the cloak, you stupid child!" Thorne snarled. Wounded and crazed, he yanked her to the ground, knocked the wind out of her, and held her down. "If you destroy it, then we'll lose everything!"

She struggled to escape him, but he clenched her by the arms and she couldn't get free.

"We'll work together," he rasped. "You with your abilities and me with mine. Don't you see? We're the same. We're on the same side."

Something was happening to him. Thorne's face was gray and deteriorating, his skin flaking off around his cheeks and eyes. His hair had turned gray and wiry. His mouth dripped with blood.

A wave of revulsion poured through her. She tried to kick him and bite his hands and pull herself free, but she couldn't wrest herself from his grip.

He held her to the ground with all his weight, pushing the air painfully from her lungs. She could feel her ribs bending, starting to crack. Despite his wounds and his decomposing condition, Thorne seemed to be getting stronger and stronger, driven by his greed for the cloak.

"I'll never give in to you!" she snarled into his face. "Never!"

"Then you're going to die, little mouser. . . ."

Pressing her down, he crushed into her. She couldn't breathe. Without air flowing through her lungs, she couldn't move, couldn't think. Even as she fought to get away, she felt her life draining from her, her arms and legs falling limp, her mind clouding with the white light of death.

She thought there was supposed to be a sense of peace when death finally came. But she didn't feel it. There was still too much to do in her life, still too many questions to answer, too many mysteries to solve, and it was the mysteries, the unfinished business, the *want*, that kept her going. She didn't want to die, especially not this way. But she could feel herself drifting now, the life ebbing out of her, her soul slipping away.

But she kept seeing a vision of her pa in her mind. She could hear his voice. *Eat your grits, girl,* he demanded.

I'm not gonna eat my grits! she shouted back at him.

Her pa gazed at her dying on the ground beneath her enemy's weight and he shook his head. *The rat don't kill the cat, girl,* he said. *That just ain't right.*

The rat don't kill the cat, she thought as she pulled her wayward soul back into her body with fierce determination. *The rat don't kill the cat,* she thought again as she felt a burst of new strength. She began to fight anew, pulling her arm free from her captor.

At that moment, a large black shape lunged out of the mist with a ferocious snarl and a flash of white teeth. At first she thought it must be some kind of black wolf. But it wasn't a wolf. It was a dog. A Doberman.

It was Gidean!

Gidean bit into Thorne's side and pulled him to the ground, then plunged in for another attack, biting and snapping. Thorne grabbed his fallen dagger from the ground and slashed Gidean in the side. Gidean yelped in pain and pulled back. Then the mountain lion charged out of her den and dove into the battle. She attacked Thorne with rapid swats of her clawed paws, her teeth snarling and her ears pressed back against her head, as if she was mightily perturbed that he hadn't stayed dead. Plunging back into the fight, the wounded Gidean chomped Thorne's arm, forcing him to drop the dagger, then tore into his shoulder and dragged him viciously across the ground, shaking him.

Serafina spotted the Black Cloak lying on the ground. She darted into the battle and snatched up the dagger that had fallen from Thorne's hand. Then she attacked the cloak with the blade. She was sure this was the answer. She cut and stabbed, trying to slice through the material, but the cloak fought against her, twisting and turning and rattling. Becoming a black seething coil in her hands, the cloak clutched at her and wrapped itself around her arms and then her body, and began to crush her. No matter how hard she tried, she could not cut the snaking cloth.

As the folds of the Black Cloak slithered around her neck and began to tighten, she tried to scream for help, but the cloak choked her breath short. Nothing but horrible gagging noises escaped from her clasped throat. Gasping for breath and clutching at her neck, she struggled to get up onto her feet. She stumbled toward the statue of the angel in the middle of the glade. *It had sliced my finger with the slightest touch.* In one swift motion, she hurled herself onto the point of the angel's gleaming sword. The sword slashed the side of her neck with searing pain as its tip pierced into the folds of the Black Cloak. The cloak screamed and hissed as the razor-sharp edges cut into it. Serafina grabbed at her neck and tore the cloak away, then clenched the material in her fists and slammed the cloak onto the sword point. She pierced it again and again. The cloak slithered and screeched, coiling like a tortured serpent. It writhed in her hands as she tore the cloth, but she did not relent. When she was finally done, there was nothing left of the Black Cloak but shreds lying at the angel's feet.

Serafina fell away, panting and exhausted, pressing her hand to the wound at her neck to staunch the bleeding. She looked over and saw Thorne pinned to the ground beneath her allies. Thorne was strong, but without the Black Cloak he was no match for the speed, power, and jaws of both Gidean and the lioness.

Serafina felt a wave of triumph pass through her. They'd done it. It was all over. It had to be.

But as Gidean and the lioness struck the final, killing bites into Thorne, his body emitted a frightening sizzling sound, like meat burning on a fire. His carcass vibrated as his skin burned and peeled down into blood and bones. A thick cloud of smoke emanated from his body as it rapidly disintegrated, as if enkindled by the air itself.

Gidean stepped back and tilted his head in confusion. The lioness retreated into the den to protect her cubs.

The stinking black effluence poured forth until the roiling smoke filled the entire glade. The whole area became a great, choking cloud. Serafina coughed, waved her arms, and tried to escape from the smoke.

"Come on, Gidean," she called, and pulled him back as she gagged on the horrible taste of the smoke in her throat.

Overwhelmed by the fumes and unable to see, she tripped over something and fell face-first to the ground. Whatever she tripped over was hard, like a branch. But when she looked, she realized it wasn't a branch. It was a human leg. She whimpered in horror and scrambled away from it. The body of a little girl lay on the ground, her arms and legs tangled and bent at crooked angles.

27

Serafina crawled several yards across the angel's glade, then got up onto her feet, her whole body shaking with fear. She looked again at the body of the girl lying on the ground. It had blond hair and wore a yellow dress. A yellow dress! How was that possible?

The body was facedown. Serafina couldn't see the face, just the hair, the sickly pale legs, and the crumpled fingers of the hands.

Just as she took a small, tentative step toward the body to get a closer look, one of the fingers twitched.

Serafina leapt back, grabbing Gidean for protection. Gidean barked and snarled at the body, his teeth white and gleaming.

The hand bent. Then the body's arm moved, then a leg. It was like a carcass crawling its way out of a grave.

Serafina's instinct was to run, but she forced herself to stay.

The body slowly got up onto its hands and knees, the hair falling around the face and covering it.

Serafina was horrified to think what the face was going to look like, imagining it to be the face of a carcass, bloody and rotted.

The thing stood erect on two feet.

Serafina watched in a paralyzed state of horror. Gidean lunged and snapped repeatedly, warding off the zombie's attack.

But then the head slowly turned and the hair parted and Serafina looked into the face. It wasn't a rotting monster, but the perfect features and lucid, pale blue eyes of Clara Brahms. Clara opened her mouth and spoke in a desperately sweet voice, "Please, can you help me?"

Serafina froze, astounded. Clara was alive! She stood before her in her yellow dress as bright and bold as a Sunday morning. Her body and her soul had been freed.

"I remember you," Clara said to Serafina. She reached out and clutched Serafina's hand. Serafina flinched back reflexively, but the hand that grasped her was warm and full of life. "I saw you," Clara said. "I called out to you. I *knew* you'd help me. I just knew it!"

Too shocked to speak or respond to Clara in any way, Serafina turned and looked across the glade. As the smoke cleared, it revealed the bodies of many children and adults lying on the ground.

The victims of the cloak woke up slowly, as if from a long, nightmarish sleep. Some of them sat on the ground in confusion for a long time. Others stood and looked around them.

A tall girl with long, curly black hair came up to Serafina and started speaking to her in Russian. She seemed very sweet, but scared and anxious to reunite with her father and her dog.

And there was a young man, as well, who didn't understand what was happening. "Have you seen my violin?" he asked repeatedly. "I seem to have lost it. . . ."

A small boy with a mop of curly brown hair, wearing an oversize coachman's jacket, touched Serafina's arm. "Pardon me, Miss Serafina, but have you seen the young master? I've got to get home. My father is going to be worried about me, and the horses need to be fed their grain. Do you know the way to Biltmore?"

"Nolan! It's you! You're alive!" Serafina grabbed the little boy and hugged him. "I'm so glad to see you. Don't worry. I'll take you home."

"You're bleeding, miss," he said, gesturing toward her neck.

She touched the wound. It hurt a bit, but the bleeding had stopped. "I'm all right," she said. The truth was, she'd suffered multiple cuts and bruises, but she didn't care about that. She was just so happy to be alive.

She looked at all the children, took a long, deep breath, and smiled. She felt a tremendous sense of relief, a sense of exultation. They were alive. They were safe. She had saved them.

Then Serafina saw among the cloak's victims a woman with long golden-brown hair, lying on the ground. She looked weak and confused, but she was alive.

Serafina went over to her. She got down on her knees and comforted the woman. As Serafina took her arm and helped her stand, she noticed how lean and muscular the woman was, but she seemed even more disoriented than the others.

"Where are my babies?" the woman muttered in slurred, hard-to-understand words.

When Nolan came over and covered the shivering woman with his jacket, she pawed it slowly and awkwardly around herself with her open hands, as if her fingers were stiff and didn't bend.

"You're safe now," Serafina assured her. "You're going to be all right."

The woman just stared at the ground, her hair hanging loose around her head. When Serafina slowly brushed back the woman's hair from her face, what she saw startled her. The woman had the loveliest face Serafina had ever seen. She had a perfect, pale complexion; high, protruding cheekbones; and long, angled cheeks. But her most striking feature was her amber-yellow eyes.

Serafina frowned. She looked at the woman in confusion and disbelief. The woman looked so familiar to her, and yet Serafina was sure she had never seen her before.

It was at that moment that she realized that it felt like she was looking into a mirror.

Serafina opened her mouth to speak, but her voice was trembling so badly she could barely get the words out.

"Who are you?"

28

The woman did not answer the question. She rubbed her eyes and face with the backs of her hands, then she looked around, glassy-eyed, taking in the forest and the angel's glade as if she did not understand what she was seeing or how she came to be there. The woman stumbled toward the opening of the lion's den beneath the roots of the willow tree.

"Where are my babies?" she asked frantically.

Seemingly ignorant of the severe danger of entering a lion's den, the woman went to the mouth of the den and looked in. She appeared to think her babies were in there. Serafina felt so sorry for her. The poor creature must have lost her mind in the imprisonment of the cloak. Worried that the lioness would attack the woman, Serafina reached to pull her out of harm's way. But then the woman made a series of sharp, guttural hissing noises, and the lion cubs came trundling out of the den in response to her call. Laughing, the woman dropped down onto her knees and encircled the cubs in her arms as they rubbed their shoulders against her, purring.

Serafina cringed, expecting the mountain lion to come charging out of the den at any second. But when she checked the den, there was no sign of the mother lion. Serafina scanned the trees nervously.

The woman, still on her knees with the cubs, lifted her hands and looked at her palms, as if they were things of amazement, opening and closing her fingers repeatedly, and she smiled. She rubbed her arms and her head and brushed back her hair like a person who had woken up from a terrible nightmare and had to reassure herself that she was still in one piece. She stood and looked up at the night sky and took a long, deep breath. Then she turned rapidly around, holding Nolan's jacket to her body. She laughed. She tilted her head back and shouted up at the stars. "I'm free!"

Still smiling, the woman looked around at her surroundings with a new brightness in her eyes. She looked at the graveyard, the stone angel, and the other victims. Then she looked at Serafina. The woman froze. She stopped smiling. She stopped moving. She just stared at Serafina.

Serafina's heart began pounding in her chest, a slow, steady rhythm. "Why are you looking at me like that?"

Suddenly, the woman lunged at her with a startling burst of speed. Serafina leapt back to defend herself, but the woman caught her with ease and held her by the shoulders, looking into her face.

"You're her!" the woman said in astonishment. "You're really her! I can't believe it! Look at you!"

"I—I . . . I don't understand . . ." Serafina stammered, trying to pull away.

"What's your name, child?" the woman asked. "Tell me your name!"

"Serafina," she mumbled, staring wide-eyed at the woman.

"Let me look at you!" the woman said, turning her first one way and then another, as if to take her measure in every way. "Just look at you! You're so big! How wonderful you are. You're amazing!"

Serafina reeled with dizziness as a new wave of confusion swept through her. What in heaven's name was this woman doing?

"Who are you?" Serafina asked again.

The woman paused and looked at her with compassion. "I'm sorry," she said gently. "I forgot that you don't know me. My name is Leandra."

The name meant nothing to Serafina, but the woman's eyes, her voice, her face—everything about her mesmerized her.

Serafina felt like sparks of a crackling fire were popping in her mind.

"But who *are* you?" Serafina asked again, clenching her fists in frustration.

"You know who I am," Leandra said, studying her.

"No, I don't!" Serafina shouted, stomping her foot.

"I'm your mother, Serafina," the woman said softly, reaching out and touching Serafina's face for the first time.

Serafina went quiet and still. She frowned in confusion. How could this be possible? She studied the woman's face, trying to make sense of its configuration, trying to understand if she should believe what she was seeing in front of her. Her mouth felt terribly dry. She licked her lips and then clenched them together, breathing through her nose. She tried to steady her breathing as she looked at the woman's hair, her hands, her sinewy body. But it was her eyes more than anything, her yellow eyes, that told her that it was true. This was her mother.

Serafina felt her face flash with heat. Suddenly, the image of her mother blurred as the tears welled in her eyes and brimmed over. She released a sigh that turned into a sob, then heaving sobs that she couldn't control, and her mother reached for her and pulled her into her arms.

"Oh, kitten, it's all right," her mother said, as her own sobs rolled against Serafina.

When Serafina finally spoke, her voice was so weak with emotion that she could only manage one frail and breathless word.

"How?" she asked.

29

The children and adults who had been freed from the cloak began to wander through the graveyard. Some of them spoke to each other, trying to understand where they were and what had happened to them, but their minds were beset by confusion. Many were too bewildered to speak at all. Nolan and Clara, along with the other children, stayed nearby; for they recognized Serafina, and they huddled together; but many of the adults wandered off, trying to remember their lives and their families. One man stood staring at a gravestone.

"That's me," he said, in shock. "That's my name. My wife and children must have thought I died. . . ."

Serafina understood now why some of the graves in the

graveyard had no bodies, but she still didn't understand how the woman standing before her could be her mother.

"What happened to you?" she asked.

The stars glistened in her mother's mesmerizing eyes. "I am a catamount, Serafina," she said, her breath filling the icy air as she spoke. "My soul has two halves."

Serafina breathed slowly in and out, trying to comprehend what her mother was saying, but it made no sense.

"Come," Leandra said gently, touching her arm. "Sit here with me for a moment." They sat on the ground beside the pedestal of the stone angel, facing each other. "I once lived in a village near here. I was a normal human woman, but I could also change shape into a mountain lion whenever I wished to."

As Serafina listened to her mother's story, everything else fell away. The cold air, the gravestones, the other victims of the cloak . . . Everything disappeared except the quiet, soothing tone of her mother's voice.

"I was married to a man who I loved dearly, and we were going to start a family. I was pregnant. He, too, was a catamount, and we spent much of our time together out here in the forest, running and hunting."

As her mother spoke, she gently wiped away the snow that was falling onto Serafina's hair. "But those were difficult times for all of us. The forest in this area was dying, twisted and withered by an evil force. . . ."

Serafina looked over at the remnants of the Black Cloak and the scorch marks on the ground.

"One day," Leandra continued, "I was walking down a path in human form, and I was attacked by an unimaginable darkness. . . ."

"The Man in the Black Cloak," Serafina whispered.

"During the battle, he wrapped his cloak around me. I fought for my life, but he was far too strong. My husband heard me screaming and came running. He, too, began to fight, but we were losing. I saw the Man in the Black Cloak strike your father down. In a matter of seconds, I was going to be overcome in the cloak's black folds. I was terrified. I feared for the lives of the babies inside me. I tried to change into a mountain lion to fight him with tooth and claw, but in that instant, the cloak sucked in the human part of my soul. I kept fighting, as fierce as any mother lion has ever fought, and I finally escaped and fled, but the cloak had torn me asunder."

"I don't understand," Serafina cried. "What do you mean? What is *asunder*?"

"The Black Cloak tore me apart, Serafina. It absorbed the human part of my soul, for that was its purpose, but it had never encountered a catamount before."

"So you were stuck in your lion form . . ." Serafina said in amazement.

"Yes," Leandra said, her voice ragged. "I became sick with grief. I couldn't find your father and feared that he was dead. My soul, my body, my love—they had all been torn apart, shredded to pieces. I did not want to live."

Her mother's voice faltered from a whisper to nothing at all, but Serafina moved closer to her. "But you were pregnant . . ." she said, urging her to continue.

"That's right," her mother said, lifting her head. "I was pregnant. It was the only thing that kept me going. I gave birth a few months later, but it was not as it should have been. You were the only one of my four children to survive, and I did not know if you would make it through the night. And what was I to do from there? You were human, and I was not! How could I care for a human baby?"

"What happened next?" Serafina pleaded.

"That same night, I heard the steps of a man walking through the forest," her mother said. "Thinking him an enemy, I almost killed him. I circled the stranger in the darkness and watched him for a long time, trying to look into his heart. Was he a good man? Was there strength in him or weakness? Would he defend his den with tooth and claw? This was not your true father, but he was a human being, and he was the only choice I had. I made the decision to let him take my baby. I prayed that he would carry you into the human world and make sure that someone took care of you, for though it broke my heart, I knew that I could not."

"That was my pa!" Serafina cried out.

Leandra smiled and nodded. "That was your pa. You were curled into a ball and so covered in blood that I barely got a good look at you that night. I honestly didn't know whether you would even survive, Serafina, and if you did, I worried that you would be terribly deformed. I had no idea whether you would come out normal."

Serafina went very quiet, and then she lifted her eyes and looked at her mother. In the frailest of voices, she asked, "Did I?"

Her mother's face burst with joy, and she threw her arms around her and laughed. "Of course you did, Serafina! You're beautiful. You're perfect. Look at you! My God, I've never seen a girl so lovely and perfect in all my life! That night when you were born, I thought that man might take one look at you and drown you in a bucket like an unwanted goat. I had so many crazy, dreadful worries. But here you are. You're alive! And you're perfect in every way."

When Serafina looked up at the sky, the stars were all glimmering and splotchy as she wiped her tears from her eyes. It felt like her heart was overflowing. She reached out her arms and hugged her mother. She wrapped her arms tightly around her, feeling her warmth and her strength and her joy and her happiness. And her mother held her close, almost purring, and tears fell from their cheeks, and the little cubs, Serafina's half brother and half sister, tumbled around their feet, joining in the family reunion.

"I can see that your pa raised you well, Serafina," her mother said, separating them a little bit and looking into her face. "When I saw you the first time here in the cemetery, I thought you were an intruder, and I attacked out of pure instinct. After twelve years, I was far more animal than I was anything else. It wasn't until tonight when I saw your eyes up close that I slowly began to realize who you were. And now here you are! And you freed me, Serafina. After twelve years, you have healed my soul. Do you realize that? I am whole again because of you. I have arms, I have hands, I can laugh, and I can kiss you! You saved me. And just look at you! You are the most perfect kitten I could have ever hoped for: you're fierce of heart, and sharp of claw, and fast and beautiful."

Serafina's cheeks burned with heat, and her heart filled with pride, but then she looked at the children waiting for her.

"It was the Black Cloak that did all this," she said.

"Yes." Her mother looked around at their confused and frightened faces as they huddled together among the graves. "They don't seem to know what happened to them."

"But you do . . ." Serafina said, looking at her mother.

She nodded. "Only half of my soul was in the Black Cloak."

"That must have been awful," Serafina said, trying to imagine it. "But why were all of his most recent victims children?"

"Mr. Thorne lived in this area for many years, avoiding detection by only capturing a soul every so often when he spotted a particular talent he wanted," her mother said. "But then something happened. The cloak began to take its toll on him. His body was aging severely every day. He was dying."

"The skin in the glove . . ." Serafina gasped.

"He started stealing the souls of children, not just because they had the talents he wanted, but because they had the one thing he most desperately needed."

"They were young . . ." Serafina said. "But how did you learn all this?"

Her mother stood, and brought Serafina to her feet with her. "There is much for us to talk about, Serafina," she said. "But we need to get these children home to their parents."

"But . . ." Serafina said. She wanted to keep talking, wanted to know more, and she was terribly scared that something would take her mother away from her again.

"Don't worry," her mother said, touching Serafina's face gently with her hand. "This isn't a fleeting run. I'm here now, and I'm whole again. In the days ahead, I will begin to teach you all that I can, just as a mother should. And you will tell me all about your life, too, to help me come back into the human world that I've been absent from for so long. We are together now, Serafina. We are family and kin, and nothing shall ever break that bond between us again." Tears streamed down her mother's cheeks. "More than anything right now, I just want you to know how much I love you. I love you, Serafina. I have always loved you."

"I love you, too, Momma," she said, her voice cracking as she wrapped her arms around her and wept in her mother's arms.

30

Serafina stood in the cover of the trees at the edge of the forest and looked toward Biltmore Estate. The sun was just rising in a clear blue sky, casting a golden light on the front walls of the mansion.

A large group of men and women on foot and on horseback were gathering together. There were ladies and gentlemen, servants and workmen, and there was an urgency in their movements.

They're organizing a search, Serafina thought.

Mr. and Mrs. Vanderbilt stood among them, their faces troubled with the news of yet another missing child. Mrs. Brahms stood with her husband, who was dressed in rugged clothing and ready to trek into the forest. Mr. Rostonov was there as well, holding his daughter's dog in his arms. Even the young maid and the footman, Miss Whitney and Mr. Pratt, had come out to help, along with the chief cook, the butler and his assistant boy, and many of the other household servants and men from the stables.

"If we're going to find her, we have to move quickly," Braeden shouted as he mounted his horse in one swift, confident movement.

Serafina's heart swelled when she saw him. That's when she realized what she was seeing. *Braeden* had organized the search. They were going out into the forest to search for *her*.

"Everyone, please gather around," Braeden called from atop his horse. She had never seen him so bold, so filled with leadership and determination. Rich or poor, guest or servant, he had brought them all together. It sent a wave of warmth through her cold, tired body.

Then she saw her pa. He must have woken up in the morning and discovered she was gone. Overcoming his fear of discovery, he went to the Vanderbilts for help, even though he knew it would expose her existence and betray the fact that they were living in the basement.

Braeden turned and gestured to the dog handlers. "Give them this," he said as he tossed a piece of clothing to the lead handler. It was her old shirt-dress. The four brindled Plott hounds bayed like it was a coon hunt.

"I looked for Mr. Thorne so that he could join us in the

search," Mr. Bendel said from atop his thoroughbred. "But I couldn't find him anywhere."

And you're not going to, Serafina thought with satisfaction as she watched the search party gather. *Ever.*

"Mr. Bendel, if you would, please take that group there and go east," Braeden said. "Uncle, perhaps you could take your footmen and go west." Braeden turned to the dog handlers. "When I put Gidean on Serafina's scent, he ran straight north, so that's where we'll try to pick up her trail. . . ." Braeden turned in his saddle and pointed in that direction.

And there he stopped.

At that moment, when Serafina knew Braeden would see her, she stepped out of the woods.

Unsure of what he was seeing at first, Braeden lifted his reins, pivoted his horse, and looked out across the lawn toward the trees. His eyes found her, and a smile spread across his face. She could see his relief and happiness.

"Who is that?" Mr. Vanderbilt asked in confusion.

"Is that the girl we're looking for?" Mrs. Vanderbilt asked.

Everyone turned toward Serafina and looked at her as she stood at the edge of the forest in her torn gown. Today, she wasn't hiding. For the first time in her life, she was being truly seen, seen by *everyone*. She stood there and just waited for them to understand what they were seeing. There was amazement in their expressions, not just from the presence of a lone girl standing at the edge of the woods, but also because of what stood beside her—a large, full-grown mountain lion. Serafina's bare hand lay on the lioness's neck, touching the animal, holding her. The mountain lion wasn't just there, but *with* her, strong and silent at her side.

On her other side stood a black Doberman. Gidean. The dog's shoulder was gashed and red with blood, but he stood strong and proud with the knowledge that he had fought his battle and won.

Braeden smiled. "I knew you'd find her, boy," he said under his breath.

When a young lad in a coachman's jacket stepped out of the woods and stood beside Serafina, expressions of surprise and disbelief and happiness spread across the faces of the search party. Then a young blond girl came out. Then several more children. Soon, a whole group of children stood with her and her two animal companions at the edge of the forest.

For a long moment, no one moved or said a word. No one could believe what they were seeing.

Then the little white dog leapt out of Mr. Rostonov's arms and ran as fast as its legs would take it. Everyone watched in stunned silence as the dog ran barking across the lawn and leapt joyfully into the arms of a raven-haired girl who laughed and hugged and kissed the little dog with abandon.

"Anastasia!" Mr. Rostonov cried out.

Anastasia Rostonova ran to her papa. They kissed each other on both cheeks, then she threw her arms around him and cried in desperate happiness. The sight of Mr. Rostonov finally reuniting with his long-lost daughter made Serafina want to cheer.

"There's my boy!" Nolan's father shouted and pointed. "Come on," he told the others. "It's the children! They're safe! They're all safe!"

Nolan embraced his father as the other stablemen patted the boy on his back, congratulating him on his safe return, and Serafina could see how pleased Braeden was that Nolan was all right.

Clara Brahms ran to her mother and father and swept her arms around them.

"Oh dear, oh dear, you're finally here," Mrs. Brahms cried as she held her little girl. "We've been looking for you everywhere."

As the lost children and their parents came together in joyful embrace, Serafina remained standing at the edge of the forest with the lioness. Her mother had been living in the forest for many years, and she was not yet ready to rejoin the world of humans, especially with a den full of new young cubs to care for. *My brothers and sisters,* Serafina thought, with a smile. She saw her mother staring at the great house, studying the crowd of people and dogs and horses gathered in front of it. Then her mother turned and looked at her. Serafina looked back at her, and she understood what she was thinking. As the lioness nuzzled her, Serafina hugged her, and kissed her, and ran her hands across her powerful shoulders. "I'll see you soon, Momma," she said. "I'll come to the den." Then the lioness turned to the trees and disappeared into the underbrush.

When Serafina looked toward the estate again, Braeden was riding toward her, and she couldn't help but take a breath when she saw him coming. He dismounted and dropped the reins. He stood in front of her and looked at her, and for what seemed like a long time, he did not say a word. She knew that her long hair was full of leaves and twigs, and that her face and neck were scratched and bleeding. The lovely dress he'd given her was stained with dirt and blood and torn in many places. But she could tell by the beaming expression on Braeden's face in the warm light of the rising sun that he didn't care about any of that; he was just immensely glad to see her.

"I like what you've done with the dress," he said.

"I think this is going to be the new style this year," she said.

Then they laughed and stepped toward each other and hugged. "Welcome home," he said.

"I'm so glad I'm back," she said. Braeden felt so warm and strong and loyal in her arms. This is what she'd dreamed of, to have a friend, to have someone to talk to, someone who knew her secrets. She didn't know what the future would bring, but she was just glad that she'd have Braeden with her when it came.

After a few seconds, her thoughts turned to what had happened during the night. The next time they were alone she'd tell him everything, but she didn't bother with that now.

"It's over," she said.

"Was it really Thorne?" he asked.

She nodded. "The cloak's destroyed, and the rat's dead."

Braeden looked at her. "You're amazing, Serafina. I'm sorry I didn't believe you."

Feeling left out of the homecoming, Gidean barked. Braeden knelt down and hugged his happy, wiggling dog. "You did good, boy," he said, rubbing his head.

"Thank you for sending him," Serafina said, kneeling down with him.

"I knew he'd find you."

"He found me, all right, just in time, and he fought like a champion," she said, remembering Gidean's heroic leap. Then she looked at Braeden again. "*We did it*, Braeden," she said. "You and Gidean and I, we found the Man in the Black Cloak and we defeated him."

"We make a pretty good team," Braeden agreed.

As she was speaking to Braeden, she saw her pa standing on his own at a distance. He was looking at her in amazement, relief, and uncertainty all at once. It was obvious from his shocked expression that he couldn't believe his eyes. Serafina could only imagine what he was thinking as he looked at her. His daughter, the girl he'd been hiding and protecting her entire life, was standing in broad daylight for all to see. She'd gone into the forest, deep into the wild. She'd stood with a lion. And now she'd come back home to him. She had led the lost children out from the forest, and now she was talking with the young master Vanderbilt like they were best friends.

She looked at her pa and thought about everything he'd done for her, all the risks he'd taken, all the things he'd taught her, and she loved him more than she ever had.

"It's just like you told me, Pa," she said as she approached him. "There are many mysteries in the world, both dark and bright."

As she put her arms around him, he pulled her into his huge chest and embraced her. Then he swung her around in a great circle while she laughed and cheered and cried.

When he finally put her down again, he looked at her and held her hands. "You're a sight for sore eyes, girl. I've been worried sick about ya, but ya done good, real good."

"I love you, Pa."

"I love you, too, Sera," he said, looking into her eyes. He turned and gazed around at all the people and commotion and then turned back to her. "Not that it matters none, but I finally got the dynamo workin' again," he said happily. "And I put a good strong lock on the electrical room's door."

"It *does* matter, Pa. It matters a lot," she said, smiling, thinking about how Mr. Thorne had sabotaged the dynamo to plunge Biltmore into darkness each night.

"I'm sorry, sir, I need to borrow your daughter," Braeden said to her pa as he grabbed her hand and yanked her away.

"Where are you taking me?" she asked nervously as he pulled her through the crowd of people gathered in front of the estate.

"Aunt, Uncle, this is the girl I told you about," he said, dragging her in front of Mr. and Mrs. Vanderbilt. "This is Serafina. She's been living secretly in our basement."

Serafina couldn't believe it. He had just blurted it all out, her name, where she lived, everything!

She slowly lifted her eyes and looked at Mr. Vanderbilt, expecting the worst.

"I'm very pleased to meet you, Serafina," Mr. Vanderbilt said, smiling and cheerful, and he shook her hand. "I must say, young lady, that you are my great hero today for what you've done. You are my Diana, goddess of the Wood, goddess of the Hunt. In fact, I shall erect a statue in your honor on top of the tallest hill in sight of the house. You have done what I could not. The police couldn't do it, and the private detectives couldn't do it. You brought all the children home. It's simply wonderful, Serafina! Bravo!"

"Thank you, sir," she said, blushing. She'd never seen him so full of praise. She couldn't help but laugh at herself for thinking that fancy shoes were the root of all evil. It seemed ridiculous now that she had been so suspicious of him.

"So, tell me what happened, Serafina," Mr. Vanderbilt said. "How did you find the children?"

She wanted to tell him, tell him everything, like a proud, four-legged mouser that lays her nightly kill on her master's doorstep. But then she remembered everything that had happened: the cloak, the cemetery. They were adults, and they were human. The last thing they wanted to hear were the grisly details of the rats she'd killed.

"The children were in the forest, sir," she said. "We just had to find them."

"But where?" he asked. "I thought we looked everywhere."

"They were in the old cemetery," she said.

Mr. Vanderbilt's brows furrowed. "But how did they get there? Why didn't they come back?"

"The old graveyard is heavily overgrown, like a maze now. Once you wander in, even by accident, it's a very dark and difficult place to escape."

"But *you* did, Serafina," he said, tilting his head.

"I'm good in the dark."

"But you were injured," he said, gesturing toward her neck and her other wounds. "You look like you battled the devil himself."

"No, no, nothing like that, sir," she said, covering her crusty neck wound self-consciously. "I just had a run-in with a nasty thorn. It'll mend. But the children were hungry and scared when I found them, sir, very confused, filled with nightmarish stories of ghosts and ghouls. They were terrified."

"It sounds like you all went through an extremely harrowing experience . . ." Mr. Vanderbilt said, his voice filled with both sympathy and respect.

"Yes, sir. I think we should try to make sure that none of our future guests go in that direction again," she said, thinking of her momma's den with her brother and sister. "I think the old cemetery is best left alone."

"Yes, that's sensible," he agreed. "We'll be sure to tell visitors to avoid that area. Far too dangerous."

"Yes, sir."

"Well," he said finally, sighing in relief and looking at

ROBERT BEATTY

Serafina. "I can't say I understand everything that happened, but I do know a hero when I see one."

"You mean a *heroine*," Mrs. Vanderbilt said. She put her hand out to Serafina in the fashion of fancy ladies. Serafina quickly tried to remember what she'd seen young ladies do in these situations, and did her best to approximate the motion of shaking her hand. Mrs. Vanderbilt's hand felt so soft and pillowy and clean compared to her own, and so different from the sinewy tautness of her mother's hands.

"It is very good to finally meet you, young lady," Mrs. Vanderbilt said, smiling. "I knew there must be someone new in Braeden's life. I just couldn't decipher who in the world it was."

"I am pleased to meet you as well, Mrs. Vanderbilt," Serafina said, trying to sound as dignified and grown-up as she could.

"Braeden said that you live in our basement. Is that really true?" Mrs. Vanderbilt asked kindly.

Serafina nodded, terrified at what she was going to say next.

"Do you have a job in the basement, Serafina?" Mrs. Vanderbilt asked.

"Yes," Serafina replied, feeling a smidgen of pride shining through her. "I'm the C.R.C."

"I'm so sorry, darling. I'm afraid I don't know what that means."

"I'm Biltmore Estate's Chief Rat Catcher."

"Oh my," Mrs. Vanderbilt said in surprise, looking over at

her husband and then back at Serafina. "I must admit, I didn't even know we had one of those!"

"Yes, you've had one for a long time," she said. "Pretty much since I was six or seven."

"It seems to me that it must be an extremely important job," Mr. Vanderbilt said.

"Well, yes, I take it quite seriously," Serafina said.

"You can say that again," said Braeden.

Serafina poked him in the side with her elbow and tried to keep from smiling.

"Well, in any case, thank you, Miss Serafina," Mrs. Vanderbilt said warmly. "We all appreciate what you've done. And you're such a little thing. I really don't understand how you did all this, but you brought the children home, that's the important thing. Thanks to you, we'll hear laughter again at Biltmore. It brings great happiness to my heart."

"Amen," Mr. Vanderbilt said, nodding. Then he turned and stepped toward her pa. "And you, sir. Where have you been hiding this daughter of yours all these years?"

"She's a good girl, sir," her pa said, both proudly and protectively as he came forward. Serafina could see the worry in his eyes about how Mr. Vanderbilt was going to react.

"I'm sure she is," Mr. Vanderbilt said, laughing. "And it's to her father's credit, I say."

"Thank you, sir," her pa said, taken aback by Mr. Vanderbilt's generous words as Mr. Vanderbilt shook her pa's hand. She could see the relief in her father's expression as he looked over at her.

Then Mr. Vanderbilt looked at his nephew. "And you, sir, where have *you* been hiding this new friend of yours?"

"Here and there," Braeden said with a grin. "Believe me, sir, she's easy to hide."

"Well, I can say this much, Braeden," he said as he put his arm warmly around him. "You know how to pick good friends, and there are few skills more important in the world than that. Well done, I say, well done."

She loved the smile that flooded across Braeden's face when his uncle congratulated him.

Mrs. Vanderbilt reached out and led Serafina by the hand. "Come with me into the house, little darling."

As she walked toward the house with Braeden and her pa, and several others, Serafina thought about what a wondrous thing it was. She had lived in the basement of Biltmore all her life, but this was the first time that she had ever walked in through the front door, and it made her feel like she was walking on a cloud. She felt like a real person.

"Now, let's us girls talk, shall we?" Mrs. Vanderbilt said as she put her arm around her. "Tell me, do you and your pa like it down in the basement?"

"Yes, ma'am, we do, but don't you mind that we're living there?"

"Well, I can't say it's the norm, and I can't imagine it being very comfortable down there for you. Do you even have proper linens?"

"No, ma'am," she said sheepishly. "I sleep behind the boiler."

"Ah, I see," Mrs. Vanderbilt said, horrified. "I think we can do better than that. I'll send down a couple of proper beds with nice, soft, down-filled mattresses; a full set of sheets and blankets; and, of course, some pillows. How does that sound?"

"It sounds wonderful, ma'am," Serafina said, glowing with anticipation. She just hoped she'd do it soon, because after all that had happened, she wanted to get under those covers and sleep for a week.

"Good, it's settled, then," Mrs. Vanderbilt said, pleased, as she looked at her husband.

"Sounds like a perfect plan," Mr. Vanderbilt agreed. "It's important that we take good care of the estate's C.R.C., especially with the kind of rats that we have around here."

Serafina smiled. Mr. V. didn't know the half of it.

As they went into the house, she turned and looked out across the forested mountains.

She knew now that there were darker forces in the world than she had ever imagined, and brighter ones, too. She didn't know exactly where she fit into it all, or what role she would play, but she knew now that she was part of it, part of the world, not just watching it. And she knew that her fate wasn't set by how or where she was born, but the decisions she made and the battles she fought. It didn't matter if she had eight toes or ten, amber eyes or blue. What mattered was what she set out to do.

She wondered with excitement what her mother would teach her in the days ahead, what new skills she'd learn, and what new things she'd see, walking through the day and prowling through the night.

She looked at the statues of the stone lions just outside the mansion's front doors. She wasn't just the Chief Rat Catcher anymore, but the defender against intruders and evil spirits. She was the protector of Biltmore Estate.

She was the hunter, the *Guardian*.

And her name was Serafina.

Acknowledgments

I would like to thank the staff and management of Biltmore Estate for their support of *Serafina and the Black Cloak* and their commitment to preserving an important part of America's history for the public to enjoy. Biltmore Estate is a wonderful place to visit and see where Serafina prowled, including the basement, the Banquet Hall, the Winter Garden, Mr. Vanderbilt's library, the hidden door in the Billiard Room, and so much more.

I would like to thank my wonderful editors at Disney•Hyperion, Emily Meehan and Laura Schreiber, and my excellent agent, Bill Contardi, for their belief in Serafina, their insightfulness in improving the manuscript, and their dedication to bringing her story to the world in the best possible way.

I would also like to acknowledge my wife, Jennifer, and my daughters, Camille and Genevieve, who played an important role in the creation and refinement of the Serafina story. My name may be on the cover, but this has been a grand labor of love for our whole family. I would also like to thank my two brothers, Paul and Chris, who have been with me from the beginning.

Finally, I would like to acknowledge the people who helped me to become a better writer over the years, including Tom Jenks and Carol Edgarian at *Narrative* magazine for their friendship and writing mentorship, Alan Rinzler for his editing and guidance, Allison Itterly for her work on the early version of *Serafina*, and all the other editors and readers who provided feedback on my writing over the years. If I have any ability to write at all, it's because I've been listening carefully to all of you.